# Her Spell That Cursed Me

*Her Spell Trilogy - Book Two*

Luna Oblonsky

## Content Warnings

- Suicidal ideation and Depression
- Eating disorders
- Gore
- Violence
- Child abuse/death
- Animal abuse
- Torture
- Human sacrifice

# Contents

# PART ONE

## PILGRIMAGE

# 1 - *Ariadne*

Ariadne's fingers dance across the keys of the pianoforte in a vain effort to obscure the incessant whispers of the surrounding crowd. She plays a frilly piece by Mozart, as opposed to the adagios and requiems she tends to favor.

When she glances up from beneath her dark lashes, the onlookers immediately avert their eyes, pretending to rearrange their jewels or straighten their collars. Stifling her wry grin, she returns her gaze to her hands.

Despite the music, she overhears the hushed conversation of two unfamiliar young witches nearby.

"Is that…?"

"I thought she was locked away in Greece."

"Did you see her eyes?"

"A familial trait."

"She does not seem particularly frightening."

Ariadne scoffs softly.

"You wouldn't dare say so if you were at the other end of her wand."

"I suppose not. Though I've heard speculation that her magic is impotent since… Well, you know."

Her jaw clenches.

"Only a fool would underestimate a Zerynthos witch."

Then the two witches wander farther away until they are out of earshot. Ariadne takes a deep, steadying breath and begins a new song, one of Scarlatti's sonatas in F minor. It isn't the most appropriate piece to perform at a party, but the melancholic melody is a comfort amid the loathsome scrutiny.

"Ariadne Zerynthos," a man's voice drawls.

She frowns, glancing up to a pair of imperious gray eyes.

"Lucas Van Hove," she says, mocking his formal cadence.

"A pleasure as always," he smirks.

A short spindly man, his clothes never seeming to be properly tailored, despite his supposed magical ability. He's as skilled in spell work as he is in conversation, his lavish lifestyle never requiring him to lift a finger, or a wand. He's the sort of warlock Ariadne particularly despises, indolent and vain, a man of leisure with nothing to show for his freedoms. All his magic squandered, as is so often the case for these aristocratic lollers.

When he goes to scratch his cheek, he makes a show of exhibiting his witch's mark on the index finger of his right hand, a red rooster. She cannot recall its significance, whether it be specific to the Van Hove family or a symbol of Belgium, his home country.

He wastes no time in leering at her mark, a bright orange flame evinced right over her heart. His covetous gaze lingers until Ariadne clears her throat in annoyance, and he remembers himself.

"I do relish your little excursions into society, though I must admit my concern," he says, leaning against the pianoforte far too close for her liking.

"Whatever concerns you have are of no interest to me," she mutters.

"You are a fawn amongst wolves, Ariadne." His voice drips with condescension. "Look at them all circling you."

Despite herself, she peeks around the ballroom again and sure enough, the witches and warlocks are all watching her with trepidation, scorn, or curiosity. She decides she does not feel like a fawn. More like an insect pinned to a board and encased in glass, unable to move or flee.

"I would be honored to accompany you on your visits, as an escort," Lucas says. "To keep the wolves at bay."

"As I've told you countless times before, I am not interested," she says, her voice hard.

"There are those with the capacity for attraction to both sexes..." he trails off.

"I am not one of them," she says firmly.

"Are you absolutely certain?" he asks in an infuriatingly patronizing tone. "I am sure I could convince you otherwise-"

"If there were ever such a man who could compare to women in the slightest, I doubt he would be you," Ariadne scoffs. "Why do you insist on tormenting me?"

"I trust my persistence is indicative of my undying admiration for you," he says, though his confidence wanes.

"It is only indicative of your tiresome obstinance," Ariadne snaps. "Do you enjoy rejection? It must be so, or perhaps you've a defective memory. Which is it?"

His mouth falls open in indignation, then he glowers at her, all pretense of geniality gone.

"Such poor manners," he sniffs. "First your little display with

Euphemia, which was most undignified, and now this. Perhaps that is why your mother keeps you far from civilized people."

"Oh yes, she means to protect you from my barbaric sensibilities. Best keep your distance," she snorts, grinning at the memory of her recent scheme.

Her friend, Euphemia Drakenström, the hostess of the evening, had been nearly forced into an arranged marriage by her family, but when Ariadne learned of their intentions, she did not hesitate to intervene.

They'd caused quite a stir that night, when they'd been 'discovered' in an amorous embrace while in the midst of a particularly wild party. It was an entirely contrived, strategic performance with not even a single kiss shared between them, but the subsequent whisperings and conflations would have one believe they were practically naked, rutting against one another, and scrambling to cover themselves when their liaison was unduly interrupted.

The exaggerated rumors of their tryst have given them both what they want. Any engagement the Drakenströms attempt to orchestrate is met with resounding declinations, allowing Euphemia to find a husband in her own time, if she so chooses. One who truly deserves her.

Ariadne is afforded a respite from the incessant badgering of ambitious bachelors, who've promptly redirected their attentions to more eligible, decorous, willing women. Though it seems Lucas is particularly thick headed, the final man vying for her affections.

"What would your dear mother say… if she knew what you were up to?" Lucas muses.

Her spine stiffens, her fingers halting on the keys so she may give him her undivided attention. He shrinks beneath her gaze.

"I beg your pardon?" she asks.

"I…" Lucas swallows hard. "I only meant-"

"If you mean to threaten me, do it properly," she challenges.

"I would never…" he stutters. "I could never…"

"No, you couldn't," she agrees. "To threaten a Zerynthos witch would go far beyond obstinance. It would border on insanity."

She glares at the man, knowing full well the effect her red eyes have on the weak. Lucas crumbles in seconds.

"My deepest apologies. I didn't intend… I would never dream of…" His forehead glistens with sweat.

"Of course," she says. "It was an unfortunate

misunderstanding."

"Yes! That's it. A misunderstanding." His shoulders slump with relief.

"Let us put it behind us," she says with a saccharine smile.

"Yes," he steps away. "Thank you."

"You're welcome," she says.

Lucas nearly jumps out of his skin when she slams her fingers on the keys and begins a new song. Then he skitters off in fright.

She fights to keep her expression neutral while her own fear simmers beneath the surface. She should have known that she could not keep her travels a secret forever. She's only bought herself more time.

"Ariadne!"

Reluctantly, she looks up. There at the other end of the ballroom, Euphemia smiles brilliantly and beckons her over. She hesitates, not wishing to leave the relative safety of the piano bench.

"Ari!" Euphemia calls again, this time with a trace of impatience.

She stands and smooths out the skirts of her vermillion dress as she approaches Euphemia and her companions where they sit on tufted chaises. She recognizes Gisela Holm, the neckline of her emerald green gown cut scandalously low. Her ostentatious diamond tiara glitters in the candlelight.

Nenet Nassry sits beside her in a bright yellow dress, with amethyst beads braided into her dark hair. Gisela whispers something in her ear and they dissolve into giggles, Nenet just barely managing to grasp Gisela's glass before its contents spill across the oak parquet floor.

On the other end of the chaise, as far from the two giggling witches as she can manage, sits Ksenia Ulanova in a far more practical black velvet gown. She swirls the champagne in her crystal glass with barely concealed boredom, until she notices Ariadne approaching.

Avoiding Ksenia's penetrating gaze, Ariadne chooses instead to admire the delicate petals of the blue daisies she'd gifted Euphemia, the exact shade of her mischievous eyes. She'd helped pin the flowers within the expanse of golden hair that shines as bright as the diamonds in Gisela's ridiculous tiara.

"Come sit with us." Euphemia pats the space beside her on the chaise she's perched on.

"You play exquisitely," Gisela gushes.

"Thank you." Ariadne forces a polite smile as she sits.

"Are you self-taught?" Nenet asks.

"Yes, mostly," Ariadne says, shifting in her seat. "My father plays a bit."

"I suppose music would be a great comfort," Gisela says, "Sequestered in the Thessalian mountains all these years… It must be awfully lonely up there."

"On the contrary, I prefer the solitude," Ariadne lies. "My studies keep me well occupied."

"Is that why you only manage to abscond in the night?" Nenet asks with an inquisitive stare.

"Parties tend to be held after sundown, if you hadn't noticed," Ariadne bristles.

Euphemia takes her hand and holds it tightly in her lap. "Where is Crescentia?"

"Flirting with Erik Virtanen," Gisela grins.

"Be a dear and go fetch her," Euphemia says.

Gisela's eyes narrow nearly imperceptibly at the command, but she does as she's told. Following her departure, Euphemia leans in close and puts her fan over her mouth to muffle her whisper.

"How bold of Gisela to judge Crescentia's flirtations whilst exalting you in the same breath," Euphemia giggles.

Ariadne smirks and tries to ignore the pleasant warmth of Euphemia's breath against her ear.

"Do you return her affections?" she asks, her sapphire eyes sparkling with curiosity.

Ariadne shrugs noncommittally. Gisela is pretty enough, and her family is fairly distinguished. There is nothing much wrong with her, apart from her obvious lust for power.

"I suppose you are far too preoccupied with a certain Valkyrie to concern yourself with other beauties," Euphemia teases.

Ariadne flushes and looks away. Before she can protest the claim, Euphemia straightens and snaps her fan closed. Ksenia glances between them, but still does not speak, so often a mysterious observer, her thoughts hidden behind her icy gaze. Ariadne envies her that.

"Euphemia, my darling," Crescentia exclaims as she bursts into the ballroom and runs up to them.

Euphemia laughs when Crescentia throws her arms around her neck and kisses her on both cheeks in greeting.

"I am in love," Crescentia declares as she finds a seat.

"Already? But you've not courted the fellow for very long," Euphemia says.

"I know it to be true in my heart," Crescentia insists. "He is exactly the sort of man I hope to marry."

"If that be so, I wish you every happiness," Euphemia beams.

"Then pray tell, why did you bid me to part with him?" she whines.

They discuss Napoleon's recent coup in France, which had not required a single casualty. Apparently, Crescentia's father had been overjoyed by the event, but Crescentia remains uncertain. She expresses her relief that the revolution is over, but she's unsure if the bloodshed is at a permanent end.

Ariadne swiftly loses interest as her eyes drift up to the painted ceiling depicting a menagerie of Norse water spirits, trolls, and fairies. It makes her think of her ballroom at home, which reminds her that the hour has grown late. She should leave before her father might notice her absence. Fortunately, her mother is away on one of her journeys and is not due to return for another week, or otherwise Ariadne would not have dared to sneak away, no matter how effective her invisibility spells have become.

"And just when I thought the night was lost to monotony," a sultry voice whispers in Ariadne's ear.

A sudden flush makes her skin hot when she sets her eyes upon Rebekka Magnúsdóttir, ravishing in her black suit that hints at her broad shoulders that Ariadne had once clung to while Rebekka kissed her senseless in the gardens just outside. She cannot recall how many months it's been since that day, her memory becoming muddled while those sea green eyes are trained on her.

Rebekka straightens to her full, impressive height, her gaze wandering down the column of Ariadne's neck to where her witch's mark is prominently displayed on her chest. It's as if the flame depicted there spreads across her skin, making her burn.

"Good evening, Ari," Rebekka says, stealing her hand to press a soft kiss against her knuckles, her lips lingering far longer than they need to.

"Good evening, Rebekka," Ariadne's voice trembles only slightly and she clears her throat.

"It seems even a lifetime of friendship is nothing compared to Ariadne's beauty," Euphemia teases. "I am eclipsed."

"You are nothing of the sort," Rebekka says. "There is enough of me for the both of you."

She winks before making her way round the chaise to kiss Euphemia's hand. Ariadne's cheeks still burn as she observes

Rebekka's confident charm, when she notices Gisela looking between her and Rebekka with a morose expression. Then Nenet catches her eye, takes a drink of her champagne, and lets her tongue drag along her top lip. Ariadne looks away, only to spy Lucas standing alone in the corner, still glowering in her direction. The feeling of so many eyes on her makes her skin crawl.

Then her stomach drops when she notices someone she doesn't expect. Tatiana Nicolo stares at her with striking blue eyes, a distinctive feature she shares with her younger sister, Vivien.

They haven't seen one another since that fateful day when Tatiana had cried over her sister's lifeless body and begged Ariadne to bring her back. Now Tatiana's expression is unreadable, neither condemning nor repentant. Ariadne abruptly stands.

"Pardon me," she mumbles, then turns to leave the ballroom.

"Ariadne?" Euphemia calls.

Passing by the line of dancing couples, she hastens down a dark corridor to steal away inside a sitting room where none of the candles are lit. Then she closes her eyes and wills herself to calm.

She admonishes herself, knowing that she must acclimatize herself to the faces that haunt her nightmares. She mustn't allow them to hinder her. Zerynthos witches are not permitted to show fear or remorse. She instantly regrets running away. It was foolish and will only draw more attention.

"Why did you run?"

Ariadne whirls around to find Rebekka leaning casually against the fireplace.

"How did you…?" Ariadne trails off. She did not hear anyone enter the room.

Rebekka only smirks as she pulls out her wand, made of perfectly clear Icelandic spar, and points it at the fireplace.

"Pyrkagiá," Rebekka incants, and the logs burst into flame, illuminating the playful glint in her eyes as she takes slow, deliberate steps across the room.

"Why did you follow me?" Ariadne asks, hugging her stomach.

"You know, they call you the Zerynthos ghost," Rebekka says, ignoring Ariadne's question. "Suddenly appearing at Euphemia's parties and disappearing without a trace."

"Her gatherings must be quite dull if the guests are so

preoccupied with my brief attendance," Ariadne murmurs.

"If only you were plain. Then you could come and go as you please without anyone taking notice," Rebekka jokes. "A flawless beauty like you should accustom herself to scrutiny."

A thrill goes through her at Rebekka's compliment that is as aggravating as it is disarming.

"That is not what compels their stares," she argues.

Rebekka takes one of Ariadne's dark curls between her fingers and twirls it round and round. "That is what compels mine."

They stare deeply into each other's eyes for a moment, until Ariadne looks away first, her cheeks burning.

"Why do you say such things?" Ariadne asks, swatting her hand away.

"What things?" Rebekka asks, tilting her head.

"You are flirting with me…" She intends it as a statement, but it sounds more like a question.

"Yes, I am." Rebekka grins with implacable confidence.

"But why?" Ariadne asks. "On account of my name? What is it that you hope to gain?"

She spares a glance down the dark hallway, wondering if she should rejoin her friends, or return to Thessaly.

"Look at me," Rebekka orders.

Resenting the command but seemingly unable to resist, Ariadne reluctantly meets her gaze and finds that her sea green eyes have softened.

"You can trust me," Rebekka says.

"Can I?" Ariadne asks.

Rebekka raises an eyebrow.

"I cannot trust anyone," Ariadne says, in a tone that implies the obvious nature of that simple fact.

"Allow me to be clear then, here and now, that I need nothing from you," Rebekka says. "I have more than enough magic, I am quite content with my position, and I do not seek a wife."

She takes another step closer and presses the tip of her wand beneath Ariadne's chin, coaxing her to hold her smoldering gaze as a slow, sensual smile curves the corners of her mouth.

"I want you. I do not need you," Rebekka clarifies. "At present, I want to kiss you until you cannot even remember your own name."

Heat spreads through Ariadne at the prospect. She remembers it so clearly, surrendering to passion for the sake of it, without theatrics or ulterior motives. Rebekka's kiss still lingers on her lips, her mouth occupying Ariadne's daydreams for weeks on end, and judging by Rebekka's smug expression, she is well aware of it.

Ariadne's back touches the wooden panel of the wall behind her, though she had not realized she'd moved. Rebekka has backed her into a dark corner of the room, away from prying eyes. She pockets her wand away in her suit jacket, then braces her forearm on the wall by Ariadne's head and leans in closer, making her every move deliberately and cautiously, as if she's worried that Ariadne might bolt.

"So… you suggest," Ariadne swallows hard when Rebekka leans in and presses a gentle, lingering kiss upon her neck, "that because you do not need me, I can trust you? That is a complicated argument."

"Consider it." Rebekka takes each of her wrists. "The scroungers are the ones you must be cautious of. They will use you for your name, their avaricious greed impossible to satisfy."

She places Ariadne's arms around her neck and leans in even closer, but not enough for their torsos to touch.

"I would not expect a scrounger to admit they were one," Ariadne says breathlessly.

Rebekka chuckles and the sound makes goosebumps trickle down Ariadne's spine.

"One kiss. That is all I want," Rebekka whispers against her mouth.

Ariadne's lips part, but she hesitates. They linger there, breathing in each other's air and luxuriating in the warmth of their proximity. Rebekka waits patiently while Ariadne's desire wreaks havoc inside her, at war with her doubts and insecurities.

"Do not hurt me," Ariadne says, more of a plea than a demand.

Rebekka pulls away, her eyes widening in surprise, and Ariadne stares up at her, all of her fear and longing laid bare in a fleeting moment of vulnerability.

"Never," Rebekka whispers. "Of that I swear."

Ariadne goes on her tiptoes and brushes her lips against Rebekka's. It is even sweeter than she remembers, the feeling of soft lips moving together. Such a simple, pure, sensational thing.

Rebekka's strong arms envelop her, drawing her in close, caressing her curves with rapt appreciation, making her feel small and delicate, then leaves Ariadne's mouth to drag her teeth across her jaw and bury her face into her neck. She gasps when Rebekka sucks on the sensitive skin there, and clings to her shoulders as she's pressed up against the wall, an unfamiliar, gnawing heat building in her stomach, making her squirm.

"Have either of you seen Ariadne?" Crescentia's voice echoes down the long corridor, and Ariadne tenses with displeasure.

"No," a vaguely familiar voice answers.

She recognizes it as one of the two witches who had been gossiping near the pianoforte.

"Last we saw, she was brooding over her music," the other witch says.

"Euphemia sent me to find her," Crescentia says with an air of self-importance. "If you see her, please inform me at once."

"Good luck. She has likely disappeared again."

"If she despises people so much, why does she bother attending parties?"

The two witches giggle amongst themselves and, to Ariadne's further irritation, Crescentia laughs with them.

"Ignore them," Rebekka murmurs, then licks up the column of her throat, making her suck in a shuddering breath.

"I cannot imagine what Euphemia sees in her."

"She sees the heir apparent of the Zerynthos Coven."

"Surely not," Crescentia scoffs. "If she can hardly manage polite conversation at a ball, how could she possibly lead a coven?"

Ariadne's skin burns with her indignation and lust. She tries to ignore them while Rebekka attempts to distract her with her mouth, but Crescentia's words cut through her desire.

"One of her cousins could assume the role in her stead."

"Not without the pendant. If Ariadne claims it..."

"She will still possess the same flaws," Crescentia says callously. "Should such a volatile witch have that sort of power at her fingertips?"

"Her grandmother did."

"Katrin Zerynthos was shrewd in her conquests," Crescentia argues. "Who can say how Ariadne would fare in her place... She could shatter the mind of anyone who would dare oppose her, as she did to Vivien Nicolo."

At that, Rebekka ceases her kisses to glance incredulously in the direction of the echoing voices.

"If that is how she treats her friends, imagine how she'd treat her enemies," Crescentia says.

Ariadne presses both her palms against Rebekka's shoulders

until she steps away.

"Ariadne," she whispers, taking another wary step backward.

Forcing her away around Rebekka, Ariadne storms out of the sitting room, and into the hall.

"You insidious hag!" she screeches as she turns the corner.

Crescentia's eyebrows nearly disappear beneath the curls framing her face. The other two witches, whose names Ariadne cannot bother recollecting, are equally terrified to behold her fury.

"Ariadne, I did not..." Crescentia loses her words.

"How dare you whisper such insults! You insolent, worthless miscreant!" Ariadne yells, all of her pent-up anxiety from the night expelling from her with every syllable.

"Forgive me, I did not-"

"I should wring your neck!"

Rebekka puts a hand on Ariadne's arm, but she wrenches it away and steps closer to Crescentia until their noses almost touch.

"You shall regret your slander." Ariadne reaches for her wand.

"Ari!"

Her fingers wrap her wand, but she does not draw it, because Samaira approaches them with an air of practiced calm.

"Ari, come." Samaira takes her arm and pulls her away.

"She should not have-"

"I know," Samaira says. "Come."

Ariadne lets out an angry grunt but allows Samaira to guide her to the other end of the corridor.

"Do you want your mother to hear of this?" she asks.

Her words immediately smother any aggression in Ariadne's countenance and replace it with reluctant caution.

"You should not make a spectacle of yourself," Samaira says.

"But did you not hear what she said?" Ariadne protests.

"No, tell me," she says.

Muffled wails make them stop dead in their tracks to look back where they'd come. Sharing a confused glance, they run back to where the three witches are trying and failing to speak around their tongues, which have swollen up to three times their size.

Rebekka is doubled over in hysterical laughter, while Ksenia stands tall and stern, still pointing her white marble wand in the gossipers' direction. She places it back into her skirt pocket, then approaches Crescentia, who chokes and sputters on her saliva.

"If I ever hear you speak of her in such a way again, I will make your entire body swell until you pop like the pustule you are," Ksenia says, menace dripping from every word.

Crescentia tries to respond but cannot manage more than a pitiful, unintelligible moan. The other two witches cover their mouths with their hands and flee, with Crescentia running close behind. Without tongues to reverse the incantation, or the skill to reverse the hex with only their minds, they will need to beg for another witch to intervene. The echo of laughter emanates from the ballroom and Ariadne bites back a smile. Perhaps next time they will think twice before speaking ill of their betters.

Rebekka snorts and slaps Ksenia on the back before she approaches Ariadne and says, "Until next time, Ari."

Rebekka kisses her softly on the cheek before taking her leave. She regrets that they could not finish what they'd started but knows she is far too incensed to enjoy herself now. There will surely be other parties.

"Was that entirely necessary?" Samaira asks, but even she struggles to maintain a straight face.

"It was the highlight of my entire evening," Ksenia shrugs.

She meets Ariadne's gaze and something passes between them, a newfound respect they did not previously share.

"It is nearly two in the morning, Ari," Samaira says, pulling at her arm again. "I shall accompany you."

"Fine," Ariadne sighs, then looks to Ksenia again. "Thank you."

She bows her head before walking down the corridor that leads to the ballroom, and calling over her shoulder, "I shall relay your farewells to Euphemia."

Ariadne burrows in closer to Samaira as she shivers in the cutting wind. They traverse the dark garden just outside Euphemia's manor and enter the forest beyond it. Samaira conjures a piece of light and holds it up for them both to see, casting shifting shadows of tree limbs across the barren earth.

"I hate them all!"

"No, you do not."

"They all hate me..."

"No, you exaggerate."

Huffing with frustration, Ariadne flinches when a powerful gust of wind cuts straight through her gown and makes her black cloak billow around her.

"They do not know you. I'd hoped these visits would remedy

that and I still believe it to be possible," Samaira says.

Ariadne looks up at the sky and is disappointed to find that the moon is not there.

"You will need to collaborate with them all someday," Samaira says. "You must make friends."

"I have friends," Ariadne mumbles.

"Euphemia, Rebekka, and I," Samaira says, counting on her fingers for emphasis. "Let us try for one more."

Ariadne grimaces, then recollects her exchange with Ksenia Ulanova after her unexpected hex on Crescentia. She could be a valuable ally, and one that Ariadne's mother would approve of for once. She is admittedly impressed by Ksenia's cool, calculated demeanor, everything she certainly is not. Perhaps by association, she can learn how to command respect with effortless grace, when so often she's only capable of cowering or exploding.

"I hope you enjoyed the rest of the party, at least," Samaira says.

"Tatiana saw me," Ariadne says.

Samaira tenses. "She is here? Did you speak with her?"

"No, of course not," Ariadne scoffs. "What would I possibly say?"

Samaira's silence speaks volumes.

"I doubt she wishes to speak with me anyhow," Ariadne mutters bitterly.

Samaira squeezes her arm, "You were only a child."

"So was she," Ariadne says, Vivien's screams echoing in her mind.

They reach a small meadow with an iced over pond. There, between two birch trees, is a portal back to Thessaly. Ariadne had happened upon the other entrance two years ago whilst on a clandestine stroll. It was a rare discovery and she'd prayed to Hecate in thanks for the tiny piece of freedom she'd been given. As usual, there was no answer.

When she had first stepped through, she'd crossed paths with a blonde girl in a pink nightgown on a midnight stroll in her family's woods. Euphemia managed to steal Ariadne's wand and capture her in a glass cage, demanding she confess her identity.

Ariadne had thrown every bit of venom in her arsenal to try to coerce her captor into freeing her, but Euphemia had seen straight through her vitriol, treating her like a stray animal caught in a trap, so accustomed to fighting for survival. It was

Euphemia's kindness that convinced Ariadne to speak the truth, and after learning the extent of her confinement, Euphemia had decided to make it her mission to provide a safe haven on the rare occasion that Ariadne could sneak away. Slowly, inevitably, they became devoted friends.

Euphemia has taken to throwing these parties with an exclusive, handpicked guest list and employs her considerable influence to keep Ariadne's visits a well-guarded secret. None would dare to cross her, or Ariadne for that matter, as none would be so foolish as to betray the heir apparent of the Zerynthos coven.

Though discretion remains a concern, it is a risk Ariadne has been willing to take, deciding to trust in Euphemia's ability to keep her safe, though considering the gossip Ariadne overheard today, and Lucas' insolence earlier, she does not know how much longer the ruse can continue.

"Shall I come and visit you on Saturday?" Samaira asks.

"Perhaps, if my father will allow it," Ariadne says. "I shall endeavor to keep him in good spirits."

"Do not trouble yourself. I shall see you when fate allows."

When Samaira embraces her, a sense of calm befalls her for the first time that night. While Euphemia tends to be Ariadne's abettor in mischief, the one to encourage her impulsive nature and enable her independent spirit, Samaira is her solace. She cannot imagine anyone who could make her feel safe as Samaira does. Such companionship is as rare as diamonds.

"Now go before you're caught," Samaira says as she pulls away from the embrace.

"You worry far too much," Ariadne grins for her benefit.

"I care for your peace more than you do, that is for certain." She rolls her eyes.

Waving goodbye, Ariadne steps through the portal to Thessaly and welcomes a respite from the frigid cold. Towering monoliths of stone cast shadows on the vast forest of black pine trees. Upon one of those mountains, her family's manor is silhouetted in the faint starlight. The windows remain dark, which gives her hope that she has not stayed away too long. She withdraws her wand, intending to conjure wings to fly up to her balcony and slip into bed.

"You look beautiful, fiore."

She chokes on her gasp and frantically searches the darkness until she spots a figure waiting within the trees. Her eyes adjust and she beholds the disapproving expression on her father's face.

He emerges and regards his daughter with bemused disdain, wearing his usual black suit with an undying aconite flower pinned to his lapel.

"Do not tell Mother," Ariadne implores in vain.

"You know I cannot keep anything from her," her father says.

"Please, I shall never use the portal again. I swear it," she lies.

He studies her, his umber eyes tired and resigned. Then he approaches the portal and peers inside but does not step through.

He rubs his forehead in frustration. "What a mess you have made."

"Perhaps if you did not keep me here against my will, I would not need to steal away in the night," she says. "I am nearly eight and ten. I'm not a child."

"There is no age you could reach that would absolve you from obedience. You know there are rules, Ariadne," he chastises. "They are put in place to protect you."

"Protect me? Or hide me away?" she asks.

He sighs and runs a hand through his dark hair, his gaze drifting toward the manor, likely wondering what his wife would do if she were not away. Ariadne's stomach twists with regret at realizing her mother will likely return from her travels early when she learns what has happened.

"You need not tell her," Ariadne says. "You need not do everything she says."

"She is my wife," he says.

"If that is what it means to be wed, I hope such an affliction never befalls me," she says, clenching her fists.

He scoffs and averts his eyes. She regrets her words, regrets any time she causes him pain, but she also hates how weak he is. A blindly acquiescent fool bonded eternally to a woman who only sees him as a mere extension of herself.

"You are very important," he says softly. "You cannot simply come and go as you please without an escort."

"I can take care of myself," she retorts.

"We thought you could until…" he trails off.

She squeezes her eyes shut and turns away.

"Brace yourself," he says.

It is the only warning she receives before a hand grips her hair and pulls her backwards so violently that her neck cracks. Ariadne cries out in pain and reaches up to try and pry her mother's fingers from her hair.

"I hope it was worth it," her mother growls in her ear.

She shoves Ariadne away so that she stumbles and falls into a pile of dead leaves. She quickly rights herself to face her mother's wrath.

"It seems we may need to chain you to your bed at night," she says.

Ariadne clenches her fists to keep her hands from trembling, the strain distracting from her dread. She glimpses her father's sympathetic expression, and it only serves to further infuriate her. He never does anything to help her. Never says anything to stop her mother. He only watches in disapproving silence.

"Did you or did you not engage in improper intimacies with Euphemia Drakenström?" her mother asks.

Ariadne's blood turns to ice as she looks between her parents. Her fears, it seems, were justified. She thought she'd have more time and silently curses whoever of Euphemia's friends had been traitorous enough to betray them. Euphemia will swiftly root them out, whoever they are, but it is too late.

"That is no concern of yours," Ariadne says, with her best show of indignance.

"Perhaps a truth spell will loosen your lips," her mother seethes, withdrawing her wand.

"No!" Ariadne screams, the force of her cry making her father flinch.

"Then speak," her mother orders.

Ariadne's breath quickens in her panic, but she sees no recourse. "I did, but-"

Her mother throws up her hands in frustration. "And you wonder why we do not allow you to run wild without supervision! I only hope your reputation is not ruined beyond repair or finding a suitable match for you will prove a harsher challenge than I'd anticipated."

This takes Ariadne entirely off guard. Her mouth falls open as she stutters, "A match? But I have not... Is that entirely... I am still in my youth."

"Oh, now you claim your youth when you find it convenient to do so?" her mother smirks. "Those days are nearly over. You'd best learn new excuses, though none will sway my judgement."

Ariadne looks to her father who smiles encouragingly at her, and it turns her stomach. "I shan't do it."

Her mother sighs with exasperation.

"I shall not be bonded to a stranger," Ariadne insists.

"Bonded?" her mother asks. "I never mentioned blood bonds. You needn't concern yourself with that."

Though she is relieved to hear it, Ariadne's confusion persists. "Then what exactly are you proposing?"

"You shall enter into a strategic alliance, as is proper for a witch of your breeding, to ensure your virtue is not stained further," her mother says.

"My virtue?" Ariadne scoffs, "I do not need-"

"We shan't allow you to leave home again without iron clad assurances that you won't ruin your own reputation or that of the family," her mother says. "Your name may compensate for many of your flaws, but a whore by any name is still a disgrace."

The insult makes its mark, but Ariadne fights to hide her mortification, though her furious blush gives her away.

"You shall accept the match we choose without complaint. I'd been vetting men, but I suppose a woman will do just as well," her mother says, with a slight wrinkle of her nose. "They will accompany you to afternoon teas, parties, all social engagements of any kind without exception."

"A lurker to spy for you," Ariadne says bitterly.

"A chaperone," her father says. "One who you may yet come to love, with time and-"

"Not likely," Ariadne mutters, just as her mother says, "Let us not concern ourselves with such trivialities."

He purses his lips and goes silent again.

"Eventually you will be expected to make appearances in society or there will be talk," her mother says.

"There is talk already," Ariadne says.

Her mother's eyes narrow, "Of what sort?"

Ariadne hesitates, then says, "There were witches who commented that…"

"Spit it out," her mother snaps.

"They said… if I am incapable of making conversation at a ball, how could I be expected to lead our coven someday," Ariadne says, unable to mask her shame at the insult.

Her parents exchange a worried glance as words pass between them through their bond. The seconds tick by agonizingly.

"It seems my concern was not unwarranted," her father says aloud.

"Yes… yes," her mother murmurs, then looks to Ariadne and says, "We shall ensure no one voices such indignities again."

"That shall take much convincing," Ariadne says.

"Do not worry your little head about it," her mother says. "Simply do as you're told, for once."

Her mother studies her, then reaches for her. Ariadne flinches out of habit, but her mother only takes a small dead leaf stuck in her curls and tosses it away. Flushing, Ariadne lowers her gaze.

"Now, if you are so full of excess energy to be out at all hours of the night, I'd say your schedule has been far too... lenient," her mother says. "Your studies shall commence at five in the morning from now on."

"What?" Ariadne's stomach sinks.

"On nights when you are not otherwise engaged, lessons shall extend to eight in the evening," her mother decides. "You could do with the extra practice."

"You cannot do that!" Ariadne shakes her head in dismay.

Her precious time alone, any moments she has to find joy in her music and books, would all be taken from her.

"Perhaps then you will finally be prepared to attend Lysander College in two years," her mother says.

"I am due to attend in one year," Ariadne corrects her.

"No, you will attend the following year," her mother says. "You've sealed that fate tonight with your abhorrent behavior. Not only is your magic not nearly disciplined enough, but you evidently are not to be trusted alone. Another year and you might be capable of succeeding in Morgan's trials, and you will learn your place."

"But you said..." Her shock turns to misery.

"I am always capable of changing my mind when it proves necessary," her mother interrupts.

"Wait, no, I apologize," she relents. "I shan't disobey you again."

"No, you won't," her mother says, the ghost of a smile reaching her lips. "I'm glad we are agreed."

Ariadne glares at her, tears pooling in her eyes at the thought of enduring this drudgery for yet another year. She is just as skilled in magic as her cousins' had been at her age, if not more so. This is a punishment, pure and simple.

"We shall discuss it further in the morning," her mother says, then extends her hand.

Ariadne looks down at it, then up into her mother's expectant red eyes. Reluctantly, she reaches into her pocket, retrieves her wand, and places the thin piece of obsidian into her mother's outstretched hand.

She hasn't time even to flinch when her mother's other hand strikes her across the cheek so hard, she stumbles away, cowering for fear of another blow, but it doesn't come.

"As you find your way back, I hope you shall take the opportunity to meditate on your place in this world." Her mother says calmly as she conjures herself a pair of black wings without the need of a wand. Ariadne observes the feat with envy. "You are the cause of your own suffering. If you would simply behave, your troubles would cease. I do not see why you cannot understand that."

She extends a hand toward the portal and whispers an incantation. With visible effort on her part, the doorway shrinks smaller and smaller until it disappears. The glimpse of Sweden fades away until it is but a memory.

And with that, her mother propels herself into the air and glides with effortless grace towards her manor. Then her father conjures his own set of silver wings, still refusing to look at her.

"How can you let her treat me so?" She asks, her tears flowing freely now, the stinging pain of her cheek lingering, making her wince.

He glances at her for only a moment, then turns his back.

"You shall not endure this forever," he says softly, then flies away behind his wife, leaving Ariadne to navigate the dark wilderness alone.

Her dancing shoes are not crafted to handle the uneven ground of the forest, causing her to trip and fall often. Soon the silk and gauze of her once beautiful red gown are tattered and torn beyond recognition.

She is nearly halfway home when the sun begins to rise. She will be expected to practice her enchantments the moment she returns, so she is in no particular hurry. It's doubtful whether her mother will permit her to brew a potion to renew her energy, despite the dangers of practicing magic without proper sleep. Her feet drag through the dirt as fatigue takes hold.

She crosses a meadow filled with purple aster flowers, persistent blooms surviving in defiance of Autumn's chill, where a break in the trees reveals a rocky cliff. From there, the Pineiós river is a distant blue serpent cutting through the landscape, the same river where Vivien had attacked years ago. She immediately averts her eyes, until she finds herself looking out and admiring the view despite the bleak emotions the sight evokes.

As the first rays of sunlight touch the edge of the cliff face, she has a fleeting thought. The sort she normally ignores and buries deep inside herself. A dangerous, terrible, all-consuming thought that compels her feet to move, bringing her closer to the precipice to peer over the edge and judge the distance to the ground.

She screams when the fabric of her gown's tattered train is ripped backwards, jerking her farther and farther away from the cliff's edge until she falls onto her back in the dirt amid the purple flowers. A massive gray wolf prowls around her, snarling angrily with trenchant white fangs.

Frozen in place, she is entirely unsure of what to do when faced with a wolf in the wild. Should she run? Or would that only entice the animal to chase her down? The wolf comes to stand between her and the precipice, and lets loose a thunderous roar, his bright yellow eyes flaring.

Then the wolf's demeanor abruptly shifts. He sits back on his hind legs and looks down at her with his head tilted to one side, panting with his tongue hanging out and his lips slightly upturned in a sort of smile.

She stares at the beast, unwilling to move just yet, so he stands and approaches her instead. She flinches when he sniffs at her cheek, then plops himself on top of her legs and rests his head in her lap. She still does not move or make a sound, until the wolf looks up at her and whines.

Hesitantly, she reaches out and runs her hand over the wolf's head and finds his fur to be much softer than she anticipated as she scratches behind his ears. He closes his eyes and sighs contentedly. It's then she feels their connection, as if he is a part of her that she never noticed was missing.

"Where have you been?" Ariadne sniffles. "You should have found me sooner."

Her wolf stands and licks the tears away. She pets him with trembling hands, then buries her face into her familiar's fur as her body is wracked with violent sobs. She prays for an end to her torment, that there be more to her life than this endless disappointment and judgement and cruelty. It is her final prayer to a Goddess that has never once deigned to respond and for the very first time, the silence emboldens her.

In that moment, she decides that her mother shall not break her. No matter what she must do, or who she may hurt, she will prevail. She will become the most powerful, formidable witch this world has yet seen. She will earn Morgan Le Fay's pendant and make herself impossible to tame.

# 2 - Iona

### June 1802 - One Month After Lysander College

"Ariadne," Iona whispers.

She jerks, whatever reverie she'd been dwelling on receding in an instant. Iona lifts herself up on her elbow to better observe her deft attempt at nonchalance.

Sighing and rubbing at her eyes, Ariadne says, "You may sleep longer. The sun has only just risen."

"My darling." Iona coaxes her hands away so she might press soft kisses on her flushed cheeks, her forehead, and upon each eyelid, before ghosting her lips against Ariadne's mouth. "How long have you been awake?"

"Not long," she says.

"Did you have another nightmare?"

"No, they've gone. All is well, I swear."

Aster jumps onto the bed and plops atop her, making her grunt from the weight. Ariadne scratches behind her familiar's ears to placate him, but he still whines and licks at her chin, which only fuels Iona's worries. Ariadne wriggles away from the wolf's kisses and climbs out of bed, combing her fingers through her unruly dark curls, wiping the sweat from her brow.

"Would you like to speak on it?" Iona asks, still unconvinced.

"No," Ariadne says quickly. "No, I'm well. Truly."

Iona sits up and hugs her knees to her chest as Ariadne crosses the room to fetch a cup from the cabinet in their small kitchen.

"Neró," she incants, and the cup fills with fresh water.

There is a slight tremble of her hand when she brings the cup to her lips before quickly setting it down on the countertop.

"Your worry is giving me a headache," she grumbles.

"Sorry," Iona says softly.

Ariadne takes a deep breath, gulps down the rest of her water, then turns to address Iona with a tired smile, her emotions buried within herself as if they'd never existed.

"Perhaps you should wear the dream talisman again," Iona suggests.

Ariadne's smile fades and she averts her eyes.

"It worked before," Iona says.

"I do not wish to burden your nights with my meaningless dreams. The nightmares are gone, so there is no need to wear it any longer," Ariadne says in a dismissive tone.

"You could never burden me," Iona reminds her.

They stare at each other for a moment, then Ariadne's expression turns wistful. "There you are worrying again."

"I cannot help it," Iona mutters.

"Shall I distract you?" Ariadne offers, raising her ebony eyebrows suggestively.

Iona's cheeks turn pink despite herself. "We cannot spare the time."

"I can be quick," Ariadne says as she bounds across the room and jumps onto the bed.

"You always make such claims and then we end up in bed for hours on end." Iona giggles as Ariadne crawls on all fours towards her and straddles her hips.

"You say that as if it were a bad thing," Ariadne says with a roguish grin.

"We must search more of the city today," Iona insists.

Ariadne groans and lets her weight fall just as Aster had done to her moments ago. Iona tries to pull herself out from under Ariadne's limp body, but she hasn't the strength.

"Do you aim to smother me?" she asks.

"I am not that heavy," Ariadne protests. "You are just frail."

Iona shoves at her shoulder until she rolls over.

"Another day of fruitless searching," Ariadne sighs.

"We shall find them today." Iona rises from their bed and stretches her arms over her head. "We must."

Approaching the standing mirror in the corner, she ponders a moment, then conjures a new chemise, cotton stays that lace snugly over her torso, and a simple linen dress with puffed sleeves and delicate white lace bordering the collar, which provides ample cover for her rather conspicuous pendant, a large opal stone bordered by two wings of onyx hung on a golden chain. It is undoubtedly beautiful, worthy of the abundant magic locked within, but it tends to glow whenever Iona casts a spell. At least while they coexist with humans, she finds it's best to keep it hidden.

The sea foam green shade of her dress perfectly complements her amethyst ring, which she now wears indefinitely on her left middle finger. Ariadne had conjured it for her based off the memory of her late father's ring and imbued it with a powerful communication charm, so they needn't bother with necklaces any longer and Iona can have a piece of her father with her every day. Ariadne made a bloodstone ring for herself with the same charm. She hasn't quite learned English yet, her sixth language, but she studies it diligently, as is her nature.

Once satisfied with her apparel, Iona conjures a brown bristled hairbrush and hands it to Ariadne, who takes it and pats the space in front of her on the bed. The act of care has become a sort of morning ritual that has a calming effect on them both. The moment the bristles make their first pass through Iona's long tresses; she closes her eyes and meditates on the day ahead.

She once again reminds herself that they are on holiday. It would be a crime not to enjoy themselves, and they can always return to Brazil sometime after their travels through Europe, perhaps in Autumn. However, she has a strong, persistent feeling that she should find her elusive family now, not later.

"We can always send a letter to postpone our trip to France," Ariadne suggests in answer to Iona's thoughts.

"Crescentia would be devastated if we miss her birthday next week," Iona reminds her.

Ariadne scoffs lightly. "I never understood the preoccupation with such things. It seems rather egotistical to make such a fuss over one's birth."

"It's important to her that we attend." Iona's brow furrows, but her eyes remain closed.

"It's far more important for you to meet your mother's family," Ariadne argues. "Once we've found them, it would be rude to leave in haste, would you not agree?"

"Wait." Iona's frown deepens. "When is your birthday?"

The brush goes still in her hair, and she can feel Ariadne's grimace through their bond even before she whirls around to pin her with an accusatory look.

"The 21st of… March." Ariadne braces herself.

Iona's mouth falls open in dismay. "Why did you not say anything? I should have asked…"

She faintly remembers Ariadne mentioning her zodiac was Aries during an evening class under the stars, but it had slipped her mind entirely. To be fair, she had been quite distracted by Morgan's trials and the malefician's relentless attacks.

"We were preoccupied with other matters at the time," Ariadne echoes Iona's thoughts. "You needn't fret over it. It means nothing to me."

"But…" Iona sighs with disappointment. "We should have

celebrated. Even if it was only a small affair."

"We did, in a way," Ariadne says, unable to meet her gaze. "It can at times fall on the Spring equinox. We spent a lovely afternoon together, and apart from my mother's impromptu visit-"

"But I would have done so much more if I'd known." Iona sighs with frustration. "I should have thought to ask Samaira. You never tell me anything of your own volition."

Ariadne shrugs, fidgeting with the hairbrush in her lap. "If it pleases you, we can throw an extravagant party next year."

"It is not the same," Iona insists.

"Then do your praephora trick and remedy it!" Ariadne throws up her hands in frustration. "Otherwise, I do not know what you want me to say."

Iona glares at her, and Ariadne pretends not to notice as she climbs out of bed and takes her staff where it rests against the wall. She is well aware that Iona knows practically nothing about her ability to travel into her own past, a rarity amongst witches. She's only experienced it once entirely by accident, and she has avoided moonstone since that day in class until she is of the mind to experiment with the mysterious skill.

Ariadne dons an ivory silk dress decorated with frills on the hem and sleeves, then pins a conjured flower into her dark hair, being careful of its delicate petals. She tends to wear a different bloom each day depending on her mood. Iona glimpses into her mind to learn that today's flower is a cattleya orchid, representing beauty and strength.

"Then we shan't celebrate my birthday this year either," Iona decides.

This has the desired effect. Ariadne's face falls and she is about to protest, but Iona puts up her finger.

"It is only fair," she says.

"You don't have the same aversion that I do," Ariadne protests.

"Neither am I egotistical. I can survive one year without celebrating." Iona shrugs, smirking with glee at her petty victory.

Ariadne makes an annoyed grunting sound, turns on her heels, and walks out the front door with Aster close behind with his nose turned upwards.

"What shall I do with her?" Iona asks Wisp where she sits curled up at the foot of the bed. The gentle fox lifts her head to peer up at her with intelligent orange eyes.

Gathering her hair to weave it into a braid, her mind returns to their vain attempts at locating the Evora family. Her mother's painting, which she'd found during her final visit to the cottage where she'd been raised, had proved misleading in the end. They'd arrived on a beach depicted in the painting, but it was far from the heart of the city, taking them nearly a full day's flight to reach it, which had cost them precious time. Having little knowledge of Brazil or her family's history there, the search is proving much more difficult to conduct than she'd anticipated. She'd hoped, perhaps foolishly, that her newly attuned clairvoyance would lead her in the right direction.

They've limited their use of magic in an effort to maintain discretion until they know what covens might reign in the area, but have quickly learned they needn't have worried, as they haven't encountered a single witch or warlock thus far. It is not entirely surprising, magic folk are not as populous as humans, but Iona would have thought to have encountered at least one.

She wonders if perhaps the Evoras have dispersed, moved on to a new city, or returned to Portugal. In the end, a search that was only meant to take a week at most has turned into a two, almost three weeklong endeavor. The summer solstice is fast approaching, a fact that Iona refuses to acknowledge just yet.

She'd considered sending a letter to her uncle and inquire as to what he might know, but she is hesitant to bother him while he mourns the disgrace of his only daughter, Elise. Samuel deserves time to heal with his wife undisturbed.

Iona gasps when a shimmering portal appears directly in front of her with Ariadne on the other side.

"Are we searching the city, or aren't we?" she asks.

"My, we are temperamental this morning," Iona says sardonically.

Ariadne leans against her staff and broods from beneath her long dark lashes.

"Very well. Let's go," Iona says.

They've made their home in a bungalow not unlike the one they inhabited during their Yule holiday the year before, deciding to conjure it at the edge of the city on the bank of the Rio Tamanduateí. They've taken to spending their days wandering the streets to observe the locals for any sign of magic or glimpse of a notable aura. As they pass by a partially built cathedral, Ariadne remains noticeably mute.

*I must say, your most attractive quality is your temper,* Iona thinks, her sarcasm enough to make Ariadne's lips twitch.

*I thought my hands held your highest appreciation,* Ariadne thinks.

Iona's cheeks heat. *Do you intend to sulk for the entire morning?*

*Or perhaps my eyes? You seem quite taken with those.* Ariadne ignores her.

*At present, your beauty pales in comparison to your impudence.* Iona meets her gaze, only to find herself lost in those very eyes that never fail to disarm her.

*You wound me,* Ariadne thinks. *However shall I cope without your steadfast admiration? I've grown quite accustomed to it.*

*Your own vanity shall sustain you, I'm sure,* Iona retorts.

Ariadne chuckles and Iona welcomes the sound. She takes Ariadne's arm and goes to lean her head on her shoulder, but Ariadne pulls away.

*Wait.* Her alarm makes Iona pause.

She searches for whatever has caused it. At the other end of the plaza stands an elderly couple with white hair and weathered skin, who observe them with shrewd disdain.

*You mustn't forget yourself here,* Ariadne warns.

The elderly woman makes the sign of the cross and kisses her fingers.

Iona averts her eyes. *I do not think it is our proximity that disturbs them.*

There are a rare few humans with an awareness of magic in the world. Iona's mother taught her from a young age to keep away from any person who stares too long or asks too many questions. One human alone is harmless but fear often causes them to swarm.

*Still, we cannot be too careful.* Ariadne's eyes narrow slightly.

*Can you not shroud us within an illusion so I may touch you whenever I please?* Iona asks.

Ariadne glances sideways at her with mock disapproval. *Are you requesting the use of an ancient artifact to make your morning stroll more pleasant?*

The labradorite stone on Ariadne's staff glows as she crafts a new illusion and sustains it with ease.

"Come here." Ariadne drapes an arm across her shoulders and presses her lips to Iona's cheek, lingering there with soft, gentle kisses, and grinning against Iona's skin when she incites the blush she'd hoped for.

Wisp and Aster follow on either side of their witches. Ariadne has already obscured them from view to prevent any panic from the humans and turned her irises from red to brown to avoid any odd looks. She can keep the illusions steady for hours on end without needing rest.

Though the staff gives Ariadne a wealth of magic, often more than she can hope to expend within a day, Iona's pendant possesses even greater power. Her spells can at times be overzealous while she grows accustomed to her new threshold of ability. She hopes to learn just how vast her magical ability has become once their holiday is through. Ariadne advised her never to take the pendant off under any circumstances.

*Do you sense anything?* Ariadne asks.

*No… nothing yet,* Iona says, letting her gaze drift across the bustling plaza.

Not a single aura is of any interest. She wonders if perhaps their search is entirely pointless, when Wisp's ears perk up and she runs ahead of them.

"Wisp," Iona hisses.

Aster runs after the fox before Ariadne can grab him.

*Where are they going?* Iona asks.

Ariadne shrugs and chases after the two animals with Iona close behind. They make their way across the busy square and down a back alley until they come across a wooden wagon painted the color of a ripened tangerine with two yoked oxen tied to it. The air smells distinctly of annatto and other fresh herbs.

"You will do as I ask, bruxa," a demanding male voice echoes off the stone buildings.

"I know not of what you speak," a gravelly woman's voice responds.

Iona and Ariadne make careful, silent steps around the wagon. There they find Wisp and Aster sitting near an old, wizened woman with wavy gray hair that reaches her upper thighs. Her dress is stark white against her tanned skin, and her posture is hunched.

A middle-aged man stands tall and threatening before the woman, though she does not seem intimidated by him in the least.

"Find another way to settle the score with your enemy," the woman says. "You lot do well enough with fists and muskets. You do not need help destroying each other."

The man spits at the woman's feet. Iona steps forward to help, but Ariadne grasps her skirt to hold her back.

*He is only a human,* Iona protests.

*She is not.* Ariadne doesn't let go.

"You will regret denying me my vengeance," he vows.

"You will have many more regrets than I when you leave this world," the woman presages.

His face, once red with anger, turns deathly pale as he storms off in a rage.

"Many blessings to you both," the woman says.

She turns and regards them with a discerning gaze and a reserved smile. When she steps closer to Wisp and Aster and pats them affectionately on their heads, Iona finds the old woman to be far more sprightly than she would have expected.

"Many blessings, senhora," Iona says, "Are you quite well?"

The old woman gestures behind herself with a smirk. "Men like him are far more frightened of me than I am of them."

Ariadne keeps hold of Iona's skirt, and she glances back at her questioningly.

The old woman curtsies. "I am called Jacira. What is your name, pendant bearer?"

Iona curtsies in turn. "My name is Iona Evora Lysander, and this is Ariadne-"

"A Zerynthos witch so far from home," Jacira says, her eyes resting on Ariadne's witch's mark.

Ariadne stiffens slightly, her mouth forming a thin line.

"Save your fear for what is to come, pequeñina. Do not waste it on me," Jacira says.

Ariadne narrows her eyes and is about to respond when they hear footsteps approaching. At first Iona worries that the man has returned but instead, a young woman turns the corner.

"Please!" the woman begs as she runs towards them. "Please help me!"

A weak cough and wheezing breath comes from a bundle clutched to the woman's chest. Jacira extends her arms and the woman immediately hands over her sickly child.

"She cannot breathe," the woman cries.

"She will," Jacira says with absolute certainty.

Before Iona can offer to heal the baby herself, Jacira takes the bundle with her inside the orange wagon and leaves the door ajar. A heady fragrance of herbs strengthens in the air. Ariadne's eyes are locked on the young woman, who paces back and forth in agitation.

*I do not sense danger here.* Iona glances at her. *You need not be so suspicious.*

*You've always been far more trusting than I.* Ariadne takes her wrist and gently pulls her closer.

A rattling of vials from within the wagon makes them all hold their breath.

*Why are you so convinced of her duplicity?* Iona asks.

*She likely sensed your power the moment we stepped through the portal. Do you not wonder why she chose to summon us now and not days ago? Or why she chose to conceal her own power from us?* Ariadne asks. *Crones like her are often so deftly attuned to their environment that they needn't ask questions at all. She intuited our names before she even beheld our faces. Such is the potency of age.*

A strong, healthy cry breaks the silence. The young woman sobs with relief as Jacira emerges from the wagon, the baby squirming and wailing.

"There, there," Jacira says as she returns the baby to her mother and presses her hand against the child's forehead and murmurs an indiscernible spell.

"Thank you," the young woman says to Jacira, though her eyes are only on her beloved daughter as her distress subsides.

"She'll be a handful," Jacira smiles wryly. "Keep a very close eye on her."

The woman thanks Jacira profusely and offers her money, which she refuses to accept.

*We are a world away from the troubles of home, and we have magic enough to protect us from unseen harm,* Iona thinks. *Can we not afford to be cordial?*

Ariadne's expression remains guarded, but she is partially appeased by Jacira's show of compassion. When the woman and her baby have gone, Jacira takes a seat within the wagon's doorway and produces a white rag to wipe sweat off her brow.

"Now," Jacira says. "We haven't much time before our visitor arrives-"

"Visitor? What visitor?" Iona asks.

"Please," Jacira says. "Allow me to explain."

"No, allow me."

The sound of wood scrapping against stone creates a faint echo against the surrounding buildings. As the sun disappears behind a cloud, an old man in a black suit and top hat emerges from the alley to their left, a mawkish smile fixed on his wrinkled face. His wood cane taps against the cobblestones with every step he takes. Ariadne gently pulls Iona behind her, which causes the man to stop in his tracks.

"There is no need for alarm." The man puts up his hands. "You've traveled so far to meet me, after all."

"Leave us in peace, Gonçalo," Jacira says. "Your cause will not appeal to her."

"And why shouldn't it? She is a Lysander, too, is she not?" Gonçalo asks, his voice tinged with menace.

"It seems you have us at a disadvantage, sir," Ariadne says.

"Of course, my apologies." He removes his hat and bows. "Gonçalo Evora, at your service. It seems you've already met my sister."

To hear the name spoken after so many days of searching should have filled her with joy, but it makes the hairs on the back of Iona's neck stand on end.

"Only just," Jacira says, "but we've much more to discuss, if you'd kindly be on your way."

Iona studies the man with growing suspicion and marks his persistent covetous stare lingering on her pendant.

"You are the spitting image of your dear mother," Gonçalo murmurs.

"You knew her?" Iona takes two compulsory steps towards him, but Wisp comes to stand in her way.

"Leona was my youngest daughter," Gonçalo says. "My pride and joy."

Jacira scoffs and Iona glances back at her with uncertainty before asking the man, "You are my grandfather?"

"Yes," his smile widens. "All these years… I wondered if we might meet someday on Samhain, if at all. How fortunate to see you now while I still have life left in me."

He opens his arms to embrace her, but when Iona glances at her familiar, Wisp's eyes plead for her to stay back. After a moment's hesitation, she peers into Gonçalo's aura and though he is disciplined enough to obscure it, the pendant's magic allows her to perceive fleeting images of flowing waters and a woman's mournful face. Her dark hair billows around her, the wind of a blustering gale casting rain upon her, mixing with her streaming silver tears. His burning hatred for this woman is undeniable, in stark contrast to his blithe demeanor.

Then his thoughts shift to the pendant again, and the rapacity she'd seen in his eyes is revealed to its fullest extent, compelling her to take a step away from him. His face falls as he lets his arms hang at his sides.

"You think you can fool a pendant bearer with empty sentiments?" Jacira asks. "You would need much more than that to deceive her."

"Please, I am so confused," Iona admits. "What is it that you want from me?"

"Want from you?" Gonçalo lets out a stilted laugh. "Only to be reunited, to introduce you to the rest of your family, so that we may be whole again."

"He wants retribution," Jacira warns.

"I am not a patient woman," Ariadne says through gritted teeth, her anxiety at their situation making Iona's skin itch. "Please won't someone speak plainly of their intentions?"

*No need.* Iona places a comforting hand on her arm to soothe her. "Good day, Grandfather. I hope when next we meet you shall be more forthcoming."

His smile fades. "What… Whatever do you mean? I have no-"

Iona turns her back to him and instead approaches Jacira. "What is it you wish to show me?"

Jacira's answering smile is radiant and filled with pride. "Come."

"You will regret this," Gonçalo says.

"Go back to Portugal." Jacira shoos him away and beckons them to step into her wagon.

Ariadne climbs after Jacira and holds out her hand to help Iona step inside. She marvels at the walls that are covered with plants, some dried and bundled together, and others growing from pots on shelves. Wooden cabinets are filled with countless vials containing potions of all colors and consistencies.

"She will never find peace!" Gonçalo calls after them. "You would have her suffer forever."

"And you would forsake her for your own gain," Jacira says. "Begone from this place. It is your home no longer."

Iona reaches down to help Wisp onto the wagon, while Aster makes the jump with ease. She spares a final glance at her grandfather, who glares at her without pretense, his countenance now devoid of warmth.

"Just like your mother," Gonçalo snarls.

"Yes, sir. I most certainly am," Iona says.

With a heavy sigh, he places his hat upon his head and takes his leave.

# 3 - Iona

She waits until he is far enough away that she can no longer hear his cane scrapping against the ground. Only then does she shut the wagon door with finality. It lurches without warning; the momentum causing her to stumble and accidentally bump into Ariadne.

"I thought I told you to watch where you step," Ariadne says, humor dancing behind her narrowed eyes.

Iona grins shyly and looks down at her feet to steady herself, still uneasy after the unexpected confrontation. Ariadne snakes an arm around her waist and sneaks a kiss on her cheek before helping her find a seat at the other end of the wagon. The potion vials rattle with the turning of the wagon's wheels.

"Where are we going?" Ariadne asks. *Are you alright?*

*Yes,* Iona assures her. *Are you?*

Ariadne gives her a short nod as she sits beside her and takes her hand again.

"The Rio Paraná," Jacira says.

Unfurling a map of Brazil they'd acquired at a store in town, Ariadne squints to find the river, pointing it out to Iona when she finds it.

"A week's travel, I'd say," Iona says.

"A week?" Jacira scowls. "What caliber of witch would I be if it took days to travel there? It will take an hour at most."

Iona stares at her in confusion, then remembers how swift the journey to Lysander College had been on Samuel's hot air balloon. The wagon must be enchanted in the same manner.

"Apologies, I…" Iona stutters.

"You're still thinking like a human," Ariadne says, not unkindly, but Iona admonishes herself all the same.

Jacira's demeanor softens when Aster sets his head on her lap. With slight hesitance, she pets the wolf and when he proves docile, she scratches the top of his head.

"Now then, I shall divulge my story in exchange for yours," Jacira says. "Tell me, how did an Evora come to claim the pendant of Morgan Le Fay?"

Iona tells the tale in great detail, starting with her mother and father's scandalous elopement, describing her solitary childhood in Cornwall, her time at college, and her success in the trials. She also gives a brief account of her cousin Elise, who had foolishly resorted to the use of dark magic in her attempt at stealing the pendant away, but the maleficium corrupted her beyond redemption. It was during their duel with Elise when Ariadne claimed the staff of Merlin, which was once thought to be lost to time within Lysander Forest.

"I've had spats with maleficians in my time," Jacira says. "It is good you defeated her while she was only a novice. Any longer and… Well, it is good that she is dead now."

"She isn't dead," Iona clarifies, taken aback by how flippantly she spoke of it. "Elise's leeching curse was deflected by Ariadne's magic. By her own hand, her magic was stolen away."

"She is still alive?" Jacira's jaw drops, "Que coisa…"

Iona doesn't know how to respond, and looks to Ariadne, whose expression has turned to stone.

Jacira's keen eyes flit between them. "An odd pairing, if you don't mind my saying so."

"Oddly perfect," Iona quickly says, before Ariadne might take offense.

She bristles anyway. "Is that why you took so long to introduce yourself?"

"Partially. When I recognized Morgan's pendant…" Jacira shakes her head with incredulity. "I couldn't quite believe it. I thought it prudent to keep my distance for a time until I knew it was safe. The last woman to wield it was no friend to me."

"Katrin?" Iona's heart sinks at the mention of Ariadne's grandmother.

"Her empire stretched across the Atlantic," Jacira says. "She made her fortune farther north, but every witch in Brazil knew her name, and that of her progeny. It seems you've taken a different path than she."

"Very much so," Iona nods. "As has Ariadne."

Jacira regards her with enduring skepticism but doesn't argue. "Anyhow, I am glad you did not acquiesce to my brother's suppliance. He is not to be trusted."

"Why?" Iona asks. "Within his aura, I saw a weeping woman. Do you know her?"

The wagon makes a sudden stop just as Jacira's expression darkens. "Come, and I shall explain."

They step out onto the bank of a new, vast river bordered by dense tropical forest. In the distance, a raging waterfall turns the water white as it rushes away from the jagged rocks and rapids, where farther out the surface of the flowing river is peppered with tiny droplets.

Iona conjures a white parasol and holds out her hand to feel the haze of mist against her palm. Within the warm air, she can also sense abundant magic lingering around them, invisible to the naked eye.

"What did your mother tell you of this place?" Jacira asks.

"Nothing at all," Iona says. "She was… quite reticent about matters of her past in an effort to protect me from harsh truths."

Jacira's brow furrows as she says, "Then I shall start at the very beginning."

She looks out at the water and takes a deep cleansing breath, a small smile reaching her lips as peace seems to fill her. Then she clears her throat.

"More than a century ago, the Evoras made the journey from Portugal to São Paulo in search of new strains of magic, since most of Europe had already been claimed by sempiterna families," Jacira explains.

"Many did so in those days," Ariadne interjects. "As new worlds were discovered, there were opportunities for conquest. Some families found greater success than others… There are formidable indigenous magic users who do not take kindly to interlopers."

"Indeed. In Brazil alone there are countless tribes, many of whom have deep ties to the magic of their land. They do not welcome outsiders, and I can hardly blame them," Jacira says.

"We may not meet them, then?" Iona asks.

"The Evoras are not particularly welcome. They know what our family attempted," Jacira says.

"But Iona is not her family," Ariadne argues.

"You of all people should know the irrelevance of such a sentiment." Jacira raises an eyebrow.

Ariadne's face colors with indignation, but Jacira returns her attention to Iona and continues on with her story.

"I trust your professors taught lessons on rituals, how they are practiced on sacred days?" Jacira asks, and when Iona nods, she says, "Another method of harvesting magic is through rituals performed in proximity to sacred sites, places in nature that are teeming with life and vitality, like this river. The magic lingers once it's been evoked, leaving its remnants within the earth, the water, the air."

Iona admires the beauty of the river, the pristine water and thriving greenery. She's reminded of Lysander Forest, the abundant magic thriving there, entirely self-sufficient and eternal. It would stand to reason that there would be other places exhibiting the same magic.

"The Evoras set their sights on this river." Jacira's gaze flickers to Ariadne. "To exploit the land and prevent those who were born to it from harvesting magic for themselves and their families."

"To what end?" Iona asks.

"To become sempiterna," Ariadne says, her voice clipped.

Jacira nods. "They hoped to take what they could manage to steal, then return to Portugal when one of them, or their children, gained a new witch's mark. In this endeavor, witches often leave the land bereft of life, uncaring of the devastation they leave behind."

"Like the wildwood in England," Iona murmurs, remembering her mother's tales of its ancient beauty before it was all destroyed by humans and witches alike, "And how did the Evoras fail to destroy this place?"

"Your great grandfather decided to romance a native woman in the hopes that the children they bore would possess the ability to more easily exploit the magic of this land to his own selfish ends. To him, it was merely a strategic alliance, all of his pretty words and romantic gestures a deceptive beguilement. He used her until it no longer suited him to placate her," Jacira says, "When your great grandmother learned of his ulterior motives, she was heartbroken. She attempted an escape with her children, but he threatened to kill her, forcing her to flee into the forest and leave her children behind. Then he spoke ill of her so viciously to the children, that whenever she tried to call them back to her, they ignored her pleas."

A gust of wind rustles the leaves and sends ripples across the surface of the river, and Iona can swear it carries the faintest echo of a desolate wail, but it's so slight a sound that she can't be sure she didn't imagine it.

"That's horrible," Iona says softly.

"Whatever became of her?" Ariadne asks.

"She died in the wilderness, lost to her unendurable grief," Jacira says.

Iona's eyes prick with tears. She cannot imagine the torment of watching your own children live on without you. It is a sickening thought.

"What do you know of restless spirits?" Jacira asks.

Iona thinks for a moment but cannot recall a lesson on the subject from Pari or any of her other professors.

"Restless spirits?" Ariadne asks, then her eyes go wide with recognition. "Did her soul not pass on?"

Jacira shakes her head. "She haunts the river still. Any Evora who attempts to perform a ritual in the surrounding forest, or to swim within its waters, will find many a misfortune befalling them. Lightning storms, floods, swarms of flesh-eating insects, rabid animals, snakes, poison, anything she might use to deter those who attempt to harm the river."

Iona stiffens, then scans the trees for any sign of a ghost watching them, or any of the terrifying deterrents Jacira had listed.

"I am the only one she seems to favor, and that is not from a lack of effort. In my presence, you are safe, but do not attempt to venture here alone," Jacira warns.

"You speak with her?" Iona asks.

"Yes, on occasion when she is not… inconsolable," Jacira says, her gaze distant. "She is… was my mother. I was too late in realizing the wickedness of my father and by then, she was already dead. I hope to help her find peace someday, if that is possible, and safeguard the river in her stead until my dying day."

She wipes a tear as it falls, then takes steps closer to the river's edge, dipping her hands into the fresh water to splash it on her face. Then she stands and lets out a shuddering, mournful sigh.

"Might I meet her someday?" Iona asks.

Jacira sniffles, then nods. "I will ask her."

Aster goes to Jacira and nuzzles his nose into her hand until she pets him and regards him with a melancholy smile.

"I wonder… how do the Lysanders fit into all of this?" Iona asks.

"Ah, yes. That is my brother's doing. Gonçalo was aggrieved by our mother's curse. The river became his obsession, as was our father's hope. Father refused to accept defeat and spent his final days trying to circumvent our mother's magic to no avail," Jacira says. "Gonçalo inherited this vendetta and knew he could not overcome the curse alone, so he decided to return to Europe in search of a powerful benefactor. The Lysanders agreed to consider his petition in return for his allegiance and faithful service for a number of years. They had their own coven, you see. A small but formidable group lead by your paternal grandmother."

Samuel had once told Iona of the Evoras' time serving the Lysander family. That had been how he and his brother, Victor, had befriended Leona Evora all those years ago. She recollects this with new insight now knowing why the Evoras had entered into such an agreement in the first place.

"With the Lysanders' help, Gonçalo intended to cast our mother out of this realm and into the next, then claim the river for his own," Jacira says.

"But… if she was sent to the other side, would that not end her suffering?" Iona asks.

"Restless spirits cannot find peace that way, as he very well knows," Jacira says. "Some part of my mother wishes to stay in this world, so much so that she's anchored herself here until the day comes when she should pass on completely. If she were forced out, her soul would be lost, trapped in purgatory, roaming endlessly without hope of resolution or reprieve of her sorrow."

"A fate worse than death," Ariadne murmurs.

"He would do such a thing to his own mother?" Iona asks incredulously.

"Quite easily. He sees the river as a mere commodity and our mother as an obstacle standing in the way of his self-proclaimed inheritance," Jacira says. "His efforts were in vain, in the end, but I knew he would come looking for you soon enough, when word of your victory reached him. His appeal would have been a carefully crafted manipulation, so you might think you were helping rather than hurting. Today was that day, as yesterday's stars predicted, and so I approached you before he could."

"Is that why you remained in Brazil? To fight against him should he ever try to return in force?" Ariadne asks.

"I would stay regardless. It is my home, my haven. I will never leave it behind," Jacira says. "With the magic I garner here, I travel across the continent healing those who would otherwise perish. It is my chosen penance."

"How did you save the baby?" Iona asks. "I too wish to become a healer, and the pendant is a powerful tool in that endeavor, but there is a great deal I still have yet to learn."

Jacira regards her with burgeoning pride that brightens her brown eyes. "I would be glad to teach you."

They spend the remainder of the afternoon discussing healing magic. Ariadne and Iona had been taught how to heal basic cuts and wounds at college, but Jacira knows how to regenerate entire organs with her magic.

"Entorpecida," Jacira murmurs, with a hand firmly pressed to her heart.

Then, in a rather unsettling demonstration, Jacira cuts a line down her torso to open her chest and removes her ribs to show them what each organ looks like, where they are located, and what services they perform for the body.

"Could we not dissect an animal instead?" Ariadne winces, her face turning a sickly shade of green.

"Unless you intend to become an animal healer, this is a more accurate representation," Jacira says in a casual tone. "If you mean to heal serious wounds, you must know what it is you are healing and why."

"So long as you are in no pain…" Iona forces herself to look.

"Yes, yes, not to worry," Jacira says. "This is the heart, these two darker parts are my lungs, this is the liver, the stomach, the intestines down there, and that is the uterus."

Ariadne heaves, putting a hand over her mouth. "Pardon me."

"You'd best accustom yourself to this if you mean to heal the sick," Jacira warns. "Blood and viscera are commonplace."

"What are those two?" Iona asks, pointing them out.

"The kidneys," Jacira says. "They purify your blood."

Once she's reattached her ribs and healed her chest, a feat that leaves Iona entirely in awe of the woman's casual mastery, Jacira takes them to her wagon to explain the many uses of her medicinal herbs. In that, Ariadne is already well versed and even manages to teach Jacira a thing or two.

"My father is exceedingly skilled in phytology," Ariadne explains. "He was my sole instructor on the subject."

"I would very much like to be acquainted with him so we might trade in secrets and skills," Jacira says. "One is never too old to learn."

Ariadne smiles. "I'll extend the invitation. Or…"

Her smile fades as she lowers her head, then clears her throat and walks away, leaving Jacira perplexed. She glances at Iona with a question in her gaze.

"Her mother exiled her when she did not claim the pendant," Iona whispers.

"Oh…" Jacira says. "Another family broken by greed. Will we never learn?"

Iona doesn't know how to respond, so she goes after Ariadne, finding her at the edge of the river.

"Ari," Iona says.

"Shh!" Ariadne hushes her, motioning for her to duck down.

Iona does so, going tense with fear as she takes careful steps to Ariadne's side. *What is it?*

*Look.* Ariadne points downriver where a majestic wild cat with orange fur and black spots laps water from the river.

*Beautiful,* Iona marvels.

"Ah, you've met Bea," Jacira says. "Magnificent, is she not?"

"Yes," Iona whispers, in complete awe of the creature. "What sort of animal is she?"

"A jaguar," Jacira says. "I see her cubs have left her."

"Oh," Iona sighs with disappointment. "I would have loved to see them."

Jacira hastens back to her wagon and rifles around inside until she returns holding a rolled-up piece of canvas and hands it to Iona. She unfurls it, revealing a painting of Bea with three cubs, two with orange fur and one with black fur.

"How lovely," Iona smiles.

A crack of thunder startles them and sends Bea scurrying back under the cover of the trees.

"It is nearly sunset," Jacira observes. "Come, I shall take you back. We mustn't be here after dark."

Iona is reluctant to leave, but when the rain becomes a torrential downpour, she is glad for the shelter of the wagon. Jacira entertains them with stories of her travels through Brazil, Paraguay, and Argentina, until the wagon comes to a stop all too soon.

"How long do you intend to stay in Brazil?" Jacira asks.

"Only for a few days more," Iona says. "We have prior engagements in France and Nepal."

"My, what a journey," Jacira says.

When they exit the wagon, they are only a few paces away from the bungalow. The rain is worse here, compelling them to run along the side wall towards the entrance.

"You are more than welcome to-" Jacira screams, a sudden and terrifying sound that has Ariadne wrenching Iona against her and using her staff to form a protective shield around them.

"What..." Iona gasps when they turn the corner where Gonçalo lays prone within a circle of acicular runes that burn her eyes to behold. "No... Oh no..."

His eyes open and unseeing, Gonçalo's chest is ripped open, his throat slit, his blood pooling in the mud. A truly gruesome sight. Jacira falls to her knees, her body racked with violent sobs, and Iona goes to embrace her, but Ariadne holds her back.

"The malefician could still be near," Ariadne hisses.

Iona searches for any movement in the surrounding trees. Though visibility is terrible in the darkness and rain, and though her eyes could deceive her, she imagines the malefician must have fled the moment their ritual was complete.

When Jacira cries out another anguished sob, Iona takes her arm back, giving Ariadne a reassuring look, before going to Jacira's side and embracing her, attempting to console her as best as she can. Ariadne approaches the circle and drags her foot over the symbols to wipe them away.

Jacira crawls to her brother's side, gingerly moving him so he's flat on his back. Upon further inspection, she gasps. "His heart... it is missing."

Iona meets Ariadne's gaze, reminded of the horse and the bear that Elise had mutilated. She'd only ever slaughtered animals but if she'd been left to cultivate her power, there is no knowing what horrors she could have committed, like the one they see before them now.

Conflicted emotions leave Iona entirely at a loss, unable to shed tears, though she is unspeakably aggrieved. She'd only just met the man, had turned him away when she learned of his mercenary schemes, and now he is gone.

"Why did the stars not warn of this?" Jacira relents, a thousand conflicting emotions at war in her expression, too. "Oh... I cannot... How could this happen..."

Iona only holds her, needing no explanation for her sorrow. She knows well the conflict of such feelings after what Elise had done to her and cannot imagine how much worse it would be to lose an estranged brother in such a violent manner. Thunder cracks overhead as the cold rain cleanses the earth of darkness and washes the blood away.

"Do not let the water touch your skin," Jacira warns, her throat raw from sobbing.

Iona and Ariadne take caution as they help her gently place Gonçalo's body into the Rio Paraná. Jacira trudges through the water with him, pulling the corpse farther into the dark abyss until it sinks beneath the surface.

"Descanse em paz," Jacira whispers.

A dreadful wail reverberates through the dark as the wind picks up into a vicious gale. Jacira is almost swept up in it, but she manages to crawl out of the water before the current pulls her under.

"It is Mother!" Jacira yells over the wind. "We must leave now!"

Ariadne crafts a portal with haste, pulling Iona through and holding out her hand for Jacira to take. They leave so quickly that Iona hasn't the chance to see much of anything except the faint outline of a womanly figure hovering over the water, obscured by wind, rain, and fluttering leaves.

Ariadne closes the portal, and at once the noise of the wind abates, leaving them in eerie silence.

"I wasn't sure if she'd…" Jacira says. "He is still her son. I thought it right to give him back to nature. Perhaps I was wrong."

"No," Iona says, "I do not interpret it as anger, but rather grief."

Jacira nods absentmindedly, letting the rain pelt her until her gray hair is dripping with it. They lead her back to the bungalow and give her a cup of tea to calm her nerves. It's only when Ariadne hands her a cup as well that Iona notices her hands are trembling.

"I must…" Jacira swallows hard. "I should send word to the family."

Iona and Ariadne simultaneously conjure a pen and ink before they realize what the other is doing.

"Thank you." Jacira takes the pen and ink from Iona and nods at Ariadne, who sets hers aside.

"Where will you send it?" Iona asks.

Jacira writes her note and sends it off, the letter disappearing with a small pop. "Lisbon. They live near to the Castle of Alcáçova. Did I not say?"

"No." Iona shakes her head.

"You may wish to visit them," Jacira says. "You should. They are still your family. They are not all like… Gonçalo."

Iona considers it but isn't sure if the timing is quite right. Perhaps someday she will venture to Lisbon, but she does not wish to impede on the Evoras in a time of great mourning, to divert the attention away from Gonçalo's passing, and risk enduring other attempted manipulations. She'd wished to learn of her history, and she has done so.

"What of the malefician?" Ariadne asks with impatience. "We should confer with any witches and warlocks nearby to see if they've noticed-"

"I shall convene with them in time." Jacira holds up her hand.

"You needn't concern yourself."

Ariadne blinks, then says, "My staff is capable of shielding against dark magic. I could help in the search and pursuit of the malefician."

Jacira's eyes widen at that, but still, she shakes her head. "We shall protect Brazil as we always have. It would be best if you rest tonight and depart in the morning."

"But why?" Iona asks.

"You are strangers to this land and will almost certainly be the first whom they suspect of treachery. That is very likely why the malefician left Gonçalo's body at your doorstep, to divert attention from the true culprit," Jacira says. "You would only distract from the search, which would lead to further bloodshed in the interim. You've dealt with a malefician before. You know how pivotal it is to find them before their magic grows too strong. You must leave at once and if we have need of your assistance, I shall send a letter."

"If you're sure." Iona exchanges a glance with Ariadne.

Jacira studies their forlorn expressions and her eyes soften. "Darkness shall always have a presence on this Earth. That we can never change. Grieve my brother's soul, then move on to brighter days. We are still alive.

# 4 - *Ariadne*

Silence once tormented Ariadne to distraction with endless anxieties, but with an open window into Iona's thoughts, she doesn't feel the need to impose upon her with words. She discerns the culmination of Iona's grief mixed with conflicted, complicated emotions over the death of her grandfather. She'd only just met him, and he'd died mere hours later. He was her blood, but she had no real connection to him beyond that, and she does not approve of his fervid desire for conquest.

Ariadne holds her close and sings to her late into the night, until finally Iona falls into a fitful sleep. It takes her much longer to drift off, her relentless musings impossible to stifle. She would admittedly prefer to stay and help Jacira find the malefician, but she's quite sure Iona couldn't endure another confrontation. Not so soon after defeating Elise. Ariadne is still reeling from it herself.

There is a persisting thought that Ariadne cannot shake. It was very odd that Gonçalo's body was left at their doorstep, of all places. If Jacira's theory is true, that the malefician hoped to frame them for the offense, it still concerns her that the malefician knew of their presence in Brazil at all. Perhaps it is only a coincidence… Perhaps Gonçalo had only happened to be near the bungalow when he died. He could have been waiting for them to return home so he might speak with them privately, without Jacira's interference.

Deep in her gut, Ariadne isn't so sure of anything, but if Jacira insists that she can handle this herself, they must respect it. She and Iona deserve a proper holiday with friends, a true respite from all this misery and brutality. By the morning, Ariadne is determined to make it so, for Iona's sake at least.

When they've packed up their bungalow, Ariadne crafts a portal that leads to a cobblestone street. Once they've stepped through to France, they trade lush greenery for quaint buildings and a grand cathedral with pointed spires. An unexpected wave of apprehension befalls her at the sight of such familiar surroundings. Iona senses it and looks at her in question.

"This way," Ariadne says, offering her arm.

Iona takes it and says, "You've been here before?"

"Briefly. I became acquainted with Crescentia through a

mutual friend, Euphemia. I told you of her, did I not?"

Iona looks away as she says, "Yes, you've mentioned her."

Ariadne hides her grin. She'd told Iona of her fictitious rendezvous with Euphemia. It seems she is not keen on the subject.

"I first met Crescentia when she snuck into one of Euphemia's parties uninvited," Ariadne says, in an effort to divert Iona's attention.

"That sounds like her," she says, a small smile reaching her lips.

"She danced with every warlock in the room, twice. It was quite the spectacle," Ariadne says wryly. "The other witches did not take kindly to being overlooked. They tried to force Crescentia out but luckily for her, Euphemia enjoys taking in strays."

"What do you mean by that?" Iona asks.

"She prides herself in her eccentric social circle," Ariadne says.

Iona ponders this with a furrowed brow, and she feels compelled to elaborate.

"Euphemia cares not where you are from or whose family you belong to. She revels in disrupting the order of things and wields the power of her name to uplift those around her," Ariadne says, her fervent admiration evident in her tone.

"When will I have the pleasure of meeting her?" Iona asks.

"I expect she will attend Crescentia's party," Ariadne says. "And if not, she will certainly attend the summer solstice ritual. Everyone will be there."

Ariadne winces when Iona's stomach flips at the prospect. It will be her first time leading a ritual for a large crowd. They'd intended to hold Iona's first ritual at college amongst friends, under the blood moon, but Elise had made that quite impossible.

"The solstice is still a week away," Ariadne says, draping a comforting arm around her. "Do not fret over it now."

She is about to say more when a sudden screech peels out from down the lane.

"Iona!" Crescentia calls as she sprints towards them, her honey blonde curls bouncing with every step. Iona runs to meet her, and they collide into an embrace.

"It has been an eternity of loneliness," Crescentia cries.

"I've only been gone a month," Iona laughs.

"Do not minimize my suffering," she sniffs.

"I wouldn't dream of it," Iona giggles. "I've missed you terribly."

Crescentia's smile widens and she takes Iona's hand. "Come, everyone is inside."

It is only then that Crescentia glances at Ariadne and smiles politely. "Good day, Ariadne."

"Good day," Ariadne says, forcing a smile.

Crescentia nearly pulls Iona's arm from its socket. "My family is here, and Erik as well. I simply must introduce you!"

"Of course," Iona says, letting Crescentia whisk her away.

They enter a modest half-timbered house that Ariadne faintly recognizes. She'd never been inside, had only seen it through the window of Euphemia's carriage on the way to some party or other. Crescentia throws open the front door and pulls Iona inside.

"She's here!" Crescentia yells.

Ariadne closes the door behind them and sets their suitcase down against the wall. There is the bustling of animated conversations and tinkling of teacups against saucers coming from the adjoining sitting room. All goes quiet when the three of them enter.

"May I present Iona Lysander," Crescentia says, barely able to contain her excitement.

"Evora," Ariadne reminds her. Iona gives her a grateful look.

"Oh, of course! Iona *Evora* Lysander," Crescentia corrects herself, but by then, everyone had already begun speaking over each other.

Ariadne leans against the door frame and watches as Iona is introduced to Crescentia's entire family in short succession. She can see each moment a new name appears in Iona's mind only to disintegrate as Iona unintentionally forgets it. Crescentia has five brothers and sisters, a vociferous mother, a stoic father, a jovial uncle who never frowns, and Erik, whose frown is permanently affixed to his handsome face.

Ariadne never much liked Erik Virtanen, a Finnish warlock of decent birth. He holds himself like royalty, his nose upturned and his brief smiles insincere. His family obtained their marks only a generation ago, a deer's antler outlined in amber brown that stems from his neck, branches up by his ear, and along his left cheek.

Crescentia prattles on about all the sights they will visit and food they will sample, but Erik is only half listening. He runs a hand through his straw blonde hair, his eyes wandering about the room. Then he notices Ariadne's stare. He clears his throat and refocuses on the conversation.

"You shall stay with Erik and me. Our humble abode is but a short walk from here," Crescentia says. "We've so much to do! Lyon is central to many cities of France, so all the best artisanal goods are made available to us. The finest wine you will ever taste!"

"Could we not conjure such things?" Iona asks.

"I suppose, but exploring the city is far more enjoyable," Crescentia says. "Allow me to expand your lexicon of cuisine. You will never want to conjure anything else ever again, I assure you."

She speaks in excessive detail of a piece of Saint-Marcellin cheese that she swears made her knees buckle. Ariadne fights the urge to yawn.

"We could visit the heart of the city tomorrow, if you'd like," Crescentia decides.

"We'd be delighted," Iona says. "Will you join us, Erik?"

"Of course," he says. "Though I might not stay out the entire day. There is much to prepare for Crescentia's party."

"Oh, how you dote on me," Crescentia grins. "He has worked tirelessly to plan a banquet in my honor."

"It shall be well worth the effort," Erik says with a small smile.

"How I hate waiting," Crescentia sighs, then shrugs. "I shall need many a distraction to help pass the time."

She grins devilishly up at Erik, whose cheeks go red. He clears his throat.

"How are you, Ariadne?" he asks. "It has been too long."

"Has it?" she asks, then quickly says, "I am well, thank you."

"Euphemia sends her love," Crescentia says. "She is most anxious to see you. Tales of your triumph at college have spread far and wide, as you can imagine."

"That is no surprise," Ariadne mutters.

"Witches who barely deigned to converse with me before now are begging for an invitation to my banquet," Crescentia says to Iona. "Simply because you will be there."

"Truly?" Iona asks, her eyes widening at the prospect.

"I turned them all away. Well, most of them. It would not do to have them gawking at you all night long," Crescentia says.

"Perhaps my attendance will prove too much of a diversion," Iona says.

"Nonsense. Of course, you must be there," Crescentia says,

then jokes, "Ariadne will scare them off."

Iona gives her a disapproving look and Crescentia chastens. "I only meant that no one would dare to impose upon you with Ariadne on your arm."

"We all knew what you meant, Crescentia," Ariadne says, narrowing her eyes.

Her amber eyes narrow in turn. "If I meant more than I said-"

"Then I'd be sure to hear it on the wind while my back was turned," Ariadne snaps.

"I…" Crescentia sighs and does not continue.

"There is no need for incivility," Erik says.

Iona looks between them, at a loss. Ariadne bites back her retort as her outrage brews within her from the old wounds that still fester despite the years that have passed. She could either stay and spar with Crescentia or take her leave to calm down. For Iona's sake, she chooses the latter.

"Please, excuse me," Ariadne says, bowing her head slightly and walking away.

*You are in desperate need of better friends*, Ariadne thinks.

*I shall not dignify that with a response*, Iona retorts, her thoughts immediately going to Ksenia.

Ariadne grimaces and reluctantly accepts that she has no room to criticize. She's glad when Iona does not follow her onto the street, but her relief is short-lived when she hears the sound of footsteps behind her. Glancing over her shoulder, she grunts angrily when Crescentia runs to catch up to her. She quickens her pace until they reach a small square with a tiered fountain at its center.

"Ariadne, wait!" Crescentia calls.

"You need not apologize for your idiotic comment."

"I did not come to apologize."

"What then?" Ariadne snaps as she whirls around to face her.

Crescentia looks down at her hands, hesitating as she gathers her thoughts.

"Cat got your tongue?" Ariadne asks, unable to stop herself.

Crescentia scowls. "Clever."

"Thank you," Ariadne smirks.

"Can I expect snide remarks like those throughout your visit?"

"I tend to express my discontent to a person's face, if that is what you are asking."

"Oh, come off it." Crescentia rolls her eyes. "As if I were the first witch to speak ill of the Zerynthos family."

"You did not speak of my family. You spoke of *my* character and *my* supposed propensity for violence," Ariadne reminds her.

"Shall we be at odds forever as a result?"

At first the question is accusatory but as the seconds tick by, Crescentia's expression grows increasingly contrite.

"Forgive me," she says softly. "I deeply misjudged you. After what you did for Iona, and for me..."

Crescentia runs her fingers over her new witch's mark. The laurel is starkly green against the pale skin of her wrist. "I owe you my life."

Ariadne is not unaffected by her apology but finds it quite convenient. She had years to say this before and chose to do so now that Ariadne is bonded to her new, powerful friend.

"I thought you were not apologizing," Ariadne says.

"Not for what I said in there," Crescentia says, gesturing behind her.

"And why is that?"

"I meant it. Iona has much less to fear with you at her side. Your name and reputation far precede you."

"As a damaged, impetuous rake?" Ariadne scoffs. "I am sure her association with me will only prove to be a hindrance."

She squeezes her eyes shut as regret fills her. She'd not meant to speak so candidly, and now Crescentia will run off and repeat it to Iona.

"You are Iona's protector," Crescentia says. "Fated. Or so she tells me."

"She trusts you far more than you deserve," Ariadne says.

"I would rather die than betray her confidence," Crescentia says with such fervency that her face goes red with passion. "I've learned from my mistakes. As have you, I presume."

Ariadne hates the accusation in her words, and the flush that creeps up her neck at the mention of her feud with Iona.

Crescentia's expression softens. "Allow me to help-"

"I do not require your help in protecting my woman," Ariadne says.

"Your temper still runs hot," she observes. "You cannot run the moment a conversation turns ugly or stay to rage at whoever provokes you."

Ariadne frowns at the far too accurate description of her impulsivity, and mutters, "This is perhaps the finest apology I've ever witnessed."

"I know how to play this game far better than you do,"

Crescentia says. "I know how to win the covens' affection, gain their trust, without possessing a drop of sempiterna blood."

Ariadne examines her expression and finds nothing to indicate duplicity. Crescentia takes a step closer.

"I should not be the only witch to benefit from Iona's generosity. I will stand with her," she says. "Will you let me?"

Ariadne sighs and pushes stray hairs from her eyes. "Iona does not require my permission to ally herself with you. I am not her keeper. I am her partner."

"I am not implying otherwise," Crescentia says. "However, if you are against me, it will make matters much more complicated. Needlessly so."

She stares into Crescentia's expectant amber eyes and decides that she does respect her decision to speak plainly with her, without pretense, or so it would seem.

Ariadne had once thought of Crescentia first when the malefician's identity was still unknown, but in that she had made her own misjudgment. Perhaps this quarrel is as impractical as it is counterproductive.

"Navigating high society will not be Iona's only obstacle," Ariadne says.

"What do you mean?" Crescentia asks.

Ariadne hesitates. She and Iona hadn't discussed what they should say about Gonçalo's murder. She does not wish to cause a panic, or to spread rumors at the expense of Iona's grieving family, but word will inevitably spread as it always does. Perhaps this could be a preliminary test of Crescentia's supposed loyalty.

"I shall tell you, but you must promise not to tell a soul," Ariadne says.

"I swear," Crescentia says, and upon seeing Ariadne's persisting hesitance, she says again, "I swear on my life."

Ariadne tells her of the maleficium ritual site, of Gonçalo's heart being stolen from his chest.

Crescentia's face goes pale with fear. "But… we've only just narrowly survived Elise. Is this what we should come to expect from now on? Are we to be overrun…"

"It is either horrid luck, or something far more sinister," Ariadne says. "It is too soon to tell."

Crescentia worries at her bottom lip as she becomes lost in thought. "What would you have me do?"

"There is nothing you can do. You are not a champion," Ariadne says. "Or a soldier for that matter."

"Neither is Iona," Crescentia points out. "Champion or no, she is peaceful by nature, unless provoked."

"She has no need to fight. I have protected her before and if I must, I shall do so again." Ariadne leans against her staff, studying Crescentia for a moment more, before making her decision. "Iona is more than capable of choosing her friends and allies. If she accepts you, I will respect that."

Crescentia nods, relief evident in her expression. "Thank you."

Then Ariadne takes a step forward, closing the distance between them, and glares down at her.

"But if you give me reason to doubt, if I see any sign of duplicity or self-serving behavior, I will..." Ariadne thinks for a moment, her eyes resting on the laurel mark. "I will take back what was given to you."

Crescentia takes a step back, "But... you cannot do that."

"Can't I?" Ariadne asks, raising an eyebrow. "Do not tempt me to give it a try."

Crescentia gulps and puts her hand over her mark, as if doing so would protect it.

"I already told you that I would never hurt her," Crescentia says, her voice trembling.

"Perfect. Then we have nothing to fear from one another," Ariadne says. "Let us return before we should be missed."

Crescentia nods quickly and turns to walk back to her family's home.

"And Crescentia?"

Crescentia looks back and regards her with caution.

"I accept your apology," Ariadne says. "You have always been a true friend to Iona and for that I thank you. My judgement of you at college proved just as erroneous, and I am glad to have been wrong."

Crescentia's expression softens again, and she opens her arms for an embrace.

"No, no." Ariadne cringes and holds out a hand to stop her. "None of that."

Crescentia rolls her eyes and snorts. "I know not how Iona can stand your mercurial nature. You're mad as an adder."

"I am perfectly sane, thank you," Ariadne says with indignance.

Crescentia's chuckles persist as they walk in stride with each other.

"If I did not know better, I'd say your patron goddess was

Lyssa, not Hecate," Crescentia jokes.

"Do not jest about that," Ariadne snaps, looking around nervously.

Crescentia's smile fades as she follows Ariadne's gaze. They wait in tense silence, but nothing happens. After waiting a moment longer, Ariadne motions for Crescentia to continue on and soon they can see the house from around the corner.

"You should know better than to provoke a Goddess," Ariadne whispers.

"I meant nothing by it," Crescentia says, peering at her with morbid curiosity. "What have you told Iona of your family's dealings with Hecate?"

"I have mentioned it… just not in detail," Ariadne says. "And it shall remain so until I decide to discuss it."

"And when will that be?" Crescentia asks.

"Soon," Ariadne says, noncommittally.

"How precisely does that work? I thought a blood bond left your memories and thoughts exposed. Certainly, Iona should have seen every one of your secrets by now," Crescentia says.

"She would need to willfully attune to my mind to discover specific memories. Our perception of feelings can at times be involuntary but only when they are at the forefront, too strong a thought to ignore. Beyond those flashes of compulsory insight, our minds are our own," Ariadne says, lifting her chin a fraction. "Besides, my mind is far too vast for her to find anything without first knowing what she searches for."

Crescentia snorts. "Humility still escapes you, I see?"

"My intelligence is renowned," Ariadne says.

"Embellished," Crescentia corrects her. "Anyhow, I'd search my lover's brain back to front within a day. I couldn't resist the temptation."

"And that is precisely why you shall never convince a respectable man to bond with you," Ariadne retorts.

"Perhaps she has already surveyed your tumescent mind and is too polite to inquire on what she found," Crescentia says.

The prospect horrifies Ariadne to her core, but she shakes her head. "Not so. I would have noticed if she had. She would have… Her countenance would have changed when addressing me."

"But she could look if she desired it?" Crescentia asks.

"She wouldn't," Ariadne insists. "This is Iona we are speaking of. She would never."

"I know," Crescentia agrees.

"Then why are you harping on it?" Ariadne snaps.

"Whether Iona sees it in your mind or not, she will learn of your past," Crescentia warns. "Better to address it now before another meddling witch alludes to it first, and Iona has reason to search."

"A meddling witch like you?"

"Or Ksenia."

Ariadne's mood darkens at the mention of her former friend.

"She lurks at parties," Crescentia murmurs. "She's always been a quiet observer when she wished to be but... I must admit her stares are disconcerting of late."

"She will not interfere with me again," Ariadne says.

"Or you could trust Iona with the truth," Crescentia says. "If she hasn't left you yet, I doubt much would deter her."

Ariadne glowers at her but she only giggles and playfully bumps their shoulders together. Ariadne fails to hide her reluctant smile, but she does heed Crescentia's words. She will explain everything to Iona... eventually.

Crescentia provides a detailed tour of Lyon's sights with seemingly endless walks to admire the buildings painted with warm colors and browse the merchants' carts assembled in the Place du Change. The week passes by swiftly and not unpleasantly, to Ariadne's great relief.

The city is rich with culture, food, and historical landmarks from a time gone by. It was once the ancient city of Lugdunum, established by the Romans, but when they left, Crescentia's ancestors felt compelled to stay on Fourvière Hill and remain there still.

As they stroll down a narrow cobblestoned street, Crescentia explains, "My ancestors coexisted with the Celts and practiced humble magic for many generations until one day, thirty years ago, a meteor fell from the sky just beyond the city limits. My mother had been walking alone that night to meditate under the full moon when she came upon the crater and found the celestial rock inside."

Crescentia lowers her voice, so the passersby are not alarmed by their talk of magic. "She performed a ritual and absorbed it, taking in all the energy accumulated over centuries of travel through the cosmos. With very few methods to harvest magic, it was extraordinarily fortunate that she happened upon it before anyone else could."

"What prevented her from harvesting in other ways?" Iona

asks.

"Katrin Zerynthos," Erik says bluntly, uncaring of Ariadne's apparent discomfort at the mention of her late grandmother. "She expressly forbade those not of sempiterna blood from attending her rituals or conducting their own in places where magic is plentiful."

Iona's brow furrows, and when Ariadne glimpses inside her mind, she sees fleeting images of the Rio Paraná in Brazil, and the blue comet ritual they'd taken part in at college. Iona's hand compulsively reaches up to brush her fingertips over the opal stone of her pendant.

"Anyhow," Crescentia says, with slightly forced enthusiasm. "The meteor gave my mother and her offspring considerably more magic and thus, I became part of the first generation of ennobled Léandre witches."

"Nearly ennobled," Erik corrects her, and Crescentia's smile falters.

"Until now, at least." Iona takes her hand and makes a show of admiring the laurel mark.

Her smile returns in full force. "My family's future has never looked brighter. We may yet become part of a coven soon, if my father has his way."

"Which coven?" Ariadne asks warily.

"Not yours," Crescentia rolls her eyes.

"Why not?" Iona asks.

Suppressing a sigh, Ariadne keeps her mind clear as best she can and gives Crescentia a stern look for encouraging this topic of conversation.

Crescentia chastens and with great care, she says, "The Zerynthos Coven is what would be considered one of the few remaining covens distinguished as a cult of mysteries with secret rituals only ever revealed to the devotees within their ranks. It's said that Hecate herself chooses her devotees, and-"

"The Leandrés would be quite out of place," Erik chuckles.

"No more than you would be, Virtanen," Ariadne retorts.

Erik sniffs indignantly but does not object. Crescentia and Iona both look at her as if she's grown a second head. Then she realizes she'd just defended Crescentia. She clears her throat, feigning nonchalance, but she can feel Iona's smile.

"What others are there?" Iona asks.

"There are covens for Freyja, Baba Yaga, Lilith, the Yama-Uba, Isis, The Morrigan, Nicnevin, Ishtar, Heka, Kali, Sekhmet, Circe, Erichtho," Crescentia counts on her fingers.

"A great many to choose from," Erik says.

"Not all are as... selective as Hecate, who has only seen fit to show favor to the Zerynthos line," Crescentia explains. "Oftentimes witches and warlocks who wish to further their interests for future generations will join another sempiterna family's coven in the hope that their magic will grow."

"That is what my family did, before we were marked," Erik says. "We served the Magnus Coven for five generations-"

"Five?" Iona's jaw drops.

"As faithful devotees of Freyja. I now benefit from their labors." Erik drifts his fingers over the mark on his cheek.

"And what precisely would be expected from a devotee?" Iona asks.

"It is entirely dependent upon who you worship," Crescentia shrugs, as if it were merely a trifle. "Most covens have ceremonial rites for their patrons, but none still boast direct contact as the Zerynthos family claims to have with Hecate. My father hasn't yet decided who we may appeal to, or perhaps we may abstain, like Euphemia."

"She is wise to do so," Ariadne says. "Covens come with far too many obligations."

"You only say that because-" Crescentia begins to say, but Ariadne silences her with a glare.

"Are covens only headed by Goddesses and the like?" Iona asks.

"Not always," Crescentia says. "Nostradamus had his own coven. He once lived in this very city when he advised Queen Catherine de' Medici."

Iona is successfully diverted by that tidbit of history as Crescentia coaxes her farther down the street, regaling her with stories of old prophecies Nostradamus had only deigned to share with fellow witches and warlocks.

They explore the rest of the square, then visit the Cathédrale Saint-Jean before taking a long walk along the Rhône and ending their day with dinner at Café du Soleil. During that time, Crescentia takes every available opportunity to proudly display the mark on her wrist. In the café, when encountering a witch friend of hers, she is sure to angle her arm just so to make the laurel impossible to overlook.

*Perhaps her mark should have been a peacock,* Ariadne thinks.

*You seem to wear yours proudly enough.* Iona's gaze lingers on her flame.

Ariadne presses a finger beneath her chin to guide her eyes

upward. *Careful, nymph. You wouldn't want the whole of France to whisper of your lack of decorum.*

*I could not be blamed for my captivation.* Iona's cheeks turn pink as she grins.

"We should go to the brasserie for a drink," Erik says.

Crescentia doesn't appear enthused by the suggestion, so he takes her hand.

"Don't you want your guests to have a thorough experience of Lyon?" Erik asks.

"I am sure they're quite exhausted after exploring town all day," Crescentia says, glancing at Iona for confirmation. "Admittedly so am I."

"Don't be such a bore," Erik says. "It is not that far a walk to Marcel's."

"…Very well," Crescentia relents. "If Iona and Ariadne are agreeable, we may have *one* drink."

She puts up a finger for emphasis and Erik smiles in triumph. They finish their dinner and make their way down the dark cobblestoned streets to a new part of town until they arrive at a seedy pub, the patrons varying in rank and stature.

Ariadne quickly wishes she'd worn a different dress with a higher neckline when a group of warlocks stare brazenly at her witch's mark the moment she enters, glaring at her with unabashed scorn. She tightens her grip on the staff and a deep growl rumbles from Aster.

Iona comes to stand beside her, and the men's eyes widen when they recognize the pendant. They turn away and whisper amongst themselves.

"Pay them no mind," Iona whispers, taking her hand.

She guides Ariadne to the bar where Crescentia speaks to a young man with a white apron tied round his waist. He looks to be no older than thirty years of age with shoulder length brown hair and warm brown eyes.

"May I introduce Marcel Beaumont," Crescentia says. "These are my friends, Iona Evora Lysander and Ariadne Zerynthos."

"Good evening," Marcel says, bowing his head as Iona and Ariadne curtsy. "It's not every day a pendant bearer enters my humble establishment."

Iona surveys the bustling tavern with a look of confusion. Ariadne does too, and notices Erik speaking to the same group of leering men at the front.

"This is your brasserie?" Iona asks.

"Yes, indeed it is," Marcel says.

"But…" Iona hesitates, "You are a warlock."

"Yes," Marcel says, tilting his head in question.

"Forgive me but… why would a warlock own a bar when we can conjure our own food and drink whenever we please?" Iona asks.

Ariadne grimaces as Marcel lowers his eyes to the pint glass in his hands.

"Have I spoken out of turn?" Iona flushes with regret. "I… I did not intend to denigrate your means of employment."

Marcel throws his rag over his shoulder and sets down the glass he'd been cleaning. "Allow me to amaze you with my powers of conjuration."

He pulls out his wand, made of a paler wood than Iona's, and waves it over the palm of his other hand, behind the surface of the bar.

He incants, "La plume."

After incanting five times more, a fluffy white feather gradually appears, one thin vane at a time at a terribly slow pace. He hands it to Iona with a small smile.

"My powers are known far and wide," he says dryly.

"Oh… I see," Iona says with a nervous smile.

Ariadne scrutinizes the feather. She is aware of those with less magic than they but hasn't met anyone with quite so little. Neither, it seems, has Iona.

"Do not tease her," Crescentia admonishes.

Marcel's smirk fades when he observes Iona's discomfort. He leans forward and his voice softens as he explains, "Not all of us are gifted to inherit the wells of magic you all possess. I have magic enough to practice simple spells, but my power is often overextended by midday if I am not attentive enough to reserve it."

Iona spins the feather between her fingers, testing its weight in her hand. They would barely need to think at all to conjure something so flimsy.

"I earn an honest living with what little magic I have to my name," he says. "I can conjure francs, which helps a great deal when business is slow. I can make decent healing potions should I ever fall ill, conjure wine or champagne when we have need of it. Otherwise, my life is quite mundane, I'm afraid."

Ariadne looks out at the crowd again and perceives the mixture of auras, some with the distinctive glow of magic and others without.

"And no one suspects you are a warlock?" Iona whispers.

He shrugs. "I am a fixture of the community, and the time of witch trials has ended, for the most part. So long as I am discreet, I am left alone."

Iona places the feather down upon the wooden surface of the bar.

"I suppose it must appear rather quaint to a sempiterna witch but alas, this is how most magic folk make their way in the world," he says, with slight condescension.

Ariadne narrows her eyes, but Iona does not appear vexed by his caviling tone. She remains introspective.

"When I once lived with my mother in Cornwall, we sold conjured pearls for our money," Iona says.

Taken aback, he asks, "Did you?"

"We would sell to merchants in far off towns and not so often that it would arouse suspicion," Iona says. "I was unaware of my own power then and did not know very many spells. I am still growing accustomed to my magic in all honesty, but I have not forgotten those days."

Marcel leans his arms against the bar. "Then you are not like our dear Crescentia, born with a silver spoon?"

"Mine was platinum," Crescentia says before taking a dainty sip of champagne.

"Mine was pewter," Iona grins.

Marcel's smile is small but warm. "Finally, a woman with perspective."

"I have perspective," Crescentia argues.

"A lady of your breeding could never understand the lives of peasants," Erik says as he approaches them.

"I suppose not," Crescentia acquiesces and tries to hide her discomfort at being belittled in the presence of her friends.

Ariadne clenches her jaw but resists her desire to tell Erik what a hypocritical sycophant he really is. Noticing her ire, Crescentia gives her a warning look and a subtle shake of her head.

Iona clears her throat and asks, "Sir, would you consider attending my ritual on the summer solstice?"

Crescentia and Erik gawk at her in utter disbelief, but Ariadne had seen the question ruminating in her mind and is impressed that she finally mustered the courage to ask it.

"I would like to formally invite you and any witch or warlock who wishes to attend. You are the perfect gentleman to spread the word," Iona says, gesturing to his many patrons.

Marcel scratches his cheek as he struggles to form a reply. "I appreciate the gesture, Miss Lysander, truly, but we are not the sort to attend such grand rites. They are reserved for sempiterna families."

"I care not for such useless exclusivity. All are welcome to attend my rituals," Iona insists.

"What a fascinating prospect."

Ariadne nearly jumps out of her skin at the voice. She'd almost forgotten its vile tone but the moment it touches her ears, every muscle in her body goes rigid. An unwelcome hand grips her shoulder and squeezes far too tightly, making her squirm away from Moira's unyielding grasp.

# 5 - Ariadne

Moira Zerynthos stands nearly as tall as Ariadne with the same voluminous black curls and cavernous ruby red eyes. Her smile is undercut by the bold hauteur in her gaze, that with which Ariadne is quite familiar.

"Good evening, Ariadne," Moira says.

"What are you doing here?" Ariadne asks.

Moira's eyes narrow nearly imperceptibly. "Still not the flower of courtesy, I see."

"Does your mother know you're here?" Ariadne asks.

"I go where I please." Moira trains her eyes on Iona. "And at present it pleases me to visit my dear cousin and her newfound sweetheart."

"To what end?" Ariadne asks.

Moira rolls her eyes. "Your paranoia is as unnecessary as it is vexing."

Ariadne gives her a withering look that has no effect whatsoever.

"You must be Iona," Moira says, looking her up and down before curtsying low.

Iona does the same, her doe eyes betraying her unease. "How do you do?"

"Very well, thank you," Moira says, her gaze lowering to admire the pendant.

It is only then that Moira bothers to acknowledge the others observing their exchange.

"Erik, how lovely to see you," she says, extending her hand to him.

"Moira," Erik smiles, leaning down to press his lips against the silk of her glove.

"Crescentia, you are looking well," Moira says, kissing both her cheeks in greeting.

While in close proximity, Moira takes Crescentia's wrist and holds it up to the candlelight to inspect the laurel mark.

"It is true then," Moira murmurs.

"You may have a better look at my party tomorrow," Crescentia says, pulling her wrist free of her grip. "My mark is prettiest in the sunlight."

"I meant to send a letter, dearest. I'm afraid I shall be

indisposed," Moira says.

"Pity," Crescentia says.

"Quite," Moira says.

Their counterfeit smiles are nearly identical. Moira turns her attention back to Iona.

"Come, let us sit. It's high time we become properly acquainted," Moira says, motioning to Marcel to bring her a drink.

"We were just leaving," Ariadne says.

"Do not be rude. It is unbecoming," Moira admonishes.

She picks a wooden table in the corner and takes a seat. The other patrons fall silent as they peer over at her, though she hardly seems to notice. Gingerly, she tugs off her gloves finger by finger and tosses them on the table in front of her. There in the center of her palm is her witch's mark. The air in the room seems to shift the moment that red flame is unveiled.

Then it seems the patrons collectively decide that two Zerynthos witches in one place is one too many. Before long, they are all trickling out and onto the street. Even the humans leave, though they likely do not understand why they feel compelled to do so.

*She is up to something,* Iona observes.

*The obvious hasn't escaped me, nymph.* Ariadne watches her face.

*I want to know what it is.* Iona glances at her.

*At what cost?* Ariadne asks.

Her heartbeat quickens when Iona approaches the table and sits down beside Moira.

*This is not a good idea,* Ariadne warns.

*Why would she travel all this way?* Iona asks. *Do you not wonder at her intentions?*

*No.* Ariadne clenches her fists.

*Are you frightened of her?* Iona asks.

*No.* Ariadne's indignance nearly obscures her lie.

*She cannot harm us.* Iona gives her a reassuring look. *Not here in such a public place.*

Ariadne glances around the now empty establishment. All that remain are their friends and Marcel behind the bar.

She does not want to stay, but neither does she want to appear weak. She wonders why she ever expected to find rest on her holiday as she reluctantly crosses the room to sit beside Iona and across from Moira. Erik and Crescentia follow suit, sitting beside each other across from Iona.

"There now, was that so difficult?" Moira asks.

Ariadne looks down at the table, unable to bear the sight of Moira's ruby eyes dissecting her. Moira will undoubtedly report every insignificant detail of her countenance to their mothers. She only hopes that Moira will also tell of the staff that rests against her chair, though she had not bothered to ask about it once. It is that seemingly inconsequential to her.

"Your father sends his love," Moira says.

Ariadne's eyes lift up to meet Moira's knowing gaze. She shifts in her chair to appear casual but knows she's said a thousand words with one look.

"Send my love back to him, will you?" Ariadne asks.

"I shall," Moira says, but her tone betrays her indifference. She may tell him, or she may not.

Ariadne crosses her arms and schools her features as Moira finally acknowledges the now empty room.

"We seem to have lost our audience," she chuckles. "It is just as well."

With a lazy wave of her hand, a harp is conjured by the hearth and begins to play. Ariadne recognizes one of Mozart's concertos.

"Much better," Moira says with a contented sigh, taking a moment to enjoy the music before saying, "I remember the very first time I heard this piece in concert. I was with my sister and-"

Moira abruptly stops and gives Crescentia such an impressive glare that it makes all of them stiffen in alarm.

"Do not try that again," Moira says, each syllable a threat.

Crescentia's cheeks turn bright red, and she nods once before looking down at her hands in her lap. Ariadne nearly rolls her eyes when she realizes what happened. Crescentia had tried to read Moira's aura. The foolishness of such an act is beyond her comprehension.

"As I was saying," Moira says, then stops again.

She taps her long nails against the wood of the table, then smiles.

"Crescentia, you've given me a marvelous idea," Moira declares.

"Have I?" she asks, cringing with regret.

"Yes, I know the perfect way for all of us to become better acquainted," Moira says as she pulls out her wand, a cylindrical piece of black hematite, and conjures a crystal glass of amber liquid for each of them, then incants, "Verità."

There is a collective gasp as everyone at the table feels the truth spell take hold.

"We shall play a game of truth and spirits." Moira pockets her wand, then explains to Iona, "We are each given the chance to ask a question of anyone at the table. They must answer truthfully or take a drink and forfeit their turn."

"I do not trust you enough to play this game," Iona says, then flushes at her candor.

"All the more reason to play," Moira says.

"The hour grows late. Perhaps we should retire," Erik suggests.

"Perhaps not," Moira says sharply, then smiles. "Come now, we are all friends. There is nothing to fear." She scrutinizes their faces and raises an eyebrow. "Unless you have something to hide."

They go silent and still as statues.

"I shall ask first," Moira says. "Iona, how do you believe Elise Lysander should be punished for her use of maleficium?"

Iona's face drains of all color, while Ariadne's blood boils with outrage.

"How dare you ask her that!" Ariadne snaps.

"She must have considered it," Moira says. "I am curious to learn of Iona's views on justice. Should Elise be killed?"

"No!" Iona says, appalled.

"Imprisoned?" Moira asks.

"...Perhaps," Iona says.

"For how long?" Moira asks.

"I... I know not," Iona says. "I am not the one to decide such matters."

"Aren't you?" Moira asks, her gaze lowering to the pendant.

"No." Iona narrows her eyes. "And that was more than one question."

"Quite right, my apologies," Moira says. "Ask away."

"Why did you wish to meet me?" Iona asks.

"I am curious about you," Moira says. "I wondered who could possibly defeat our own Ariadne at a test she'd trained for her entire life. And to win her heart as well... that woman must be quite extraordinary."

Though unsatisfied with the answer, Iona keeps her composure as she holds Moira's gaze. Ariadne goes next.

"Did our family send you here?" Ariadne asks.

"No, as I said before. However, they are concerned about you," Moira says, and when Ariadne scoffs, she sighs. "Even with a truth spell, you refuse to believe me?"

"Is a mind as warped as yours even capable of telling the

truth?" Ariadne asks.

"That is another question," Moira tsks. "But yes, I am. I have no reason to lie."

Ariadne clenches her jaw. "So you say."

A moment passes, then Crescentia asks Moira, "Do you truly have a prior engagement tomorrow?"

Moira smirks. "No, dearest. I was trying to be polite."

"I thought so," Crescentia says.

"You are not offended, I hope," Moira says.

"No, our indifference is mutual," Crescentia says. "However, I must wonder at your desire to meet us here, now, rather than simply waiting one day. Were you so impatient to make Iona's acquaintance? Or perhaps there is a pressing matter of a delicate nature that you wish to discuss in a more private venue."

Moira's smile persists, but her eyes harden, "I always did prefer intimate gatherings to discuss all matters, delicate or otherwise. I am not quite the reveler you are."

"Do not sell yourself short." Crescentia takes a sip of her drink with impeccable poise.

Then everyone looks to Erik, who appears the most disturbed by this predicament.

He hesitates, then asks Iona, "Now that you knowingly possess the ability to bestow a witch's mark, will you do so for others?"

Ariadne had not been expecting that question in the least and neither it seems had Iona. Crescentia narrows her eyes at him, then looks to Iona with thinly veiled curiosity.

"I have considered it," Iona admits. "I hope to lessen the disparity between sempiterna bloodlines and others, but I do not yet know the best method to reform the order we currently find ourselves in."

"To give marks away to any who ask would be unwise," Erik says, his fingers drifting along his cheek where his antler mark lies.

"Why do you say that?" Crescentia asks.

"Look how it's affected you," Erik says, then grimaces at his own words.

Crescentia's face falls. "What do you mean by-"

"Well now," Moira says, "let us not forget the rules of the game entirely. We are meant to ask one question each turn."

Crescentia scowls but nods her assent, and Erik is visibly relieved when Moira takes her turn.

"Are you willing to kill to protect the innocent?" Moira asks

Iona.

Ariadne's mouth falls open in horror. "I will not sit here and bear witness to this vindictive interrogation!"

"You may leave if you wish," Moira says with nary a glance in her direction.

Ariadne slams her hand against the table, forcibly drawing Moira's attention to her. "Do not presume to tell me what I may or may not do."

"Or what? You'll transport me across town?" Moira chuckles.

Ariadne flushes with indignation. "I am capable of more than that even without the staff."

Moira shrugs. "And so am I. What is your point, whelp?"

When Ariadne has no answer, Moira's smile returns, gleaming and self-satisfied. She raises her eyebrows at Iona, still expecting an answer.

"I..." Iona is beside herself with ambivalent distress, "I do not know."

"You do not know?" Moira asks incredulously.

"I could not advocate for violence in a supposed effort to prevent harm," Iona says.

"I see," Moira says.

"I believe life is precious and should be preserved," Iona says.

"Even Elise's?" Moira asks.

"Yes," Iona says, with reluctance.

"She must not have afflicted you that terribly if you are so quick to forgive her," Moira says callously.

"I have not forgiven her. I shall hate her until my dying breath," Iona says, her words like aberrant venom spewing from her lips. "She will pay dearly for what she did. For what she attempted to do. Life can be its own punishment if it is lived in suffering."

The ghost of a smile reaches Moira's lips. "In that, we can agree."

Ariadne is so stunned by Iona's answer that she nearly forgets to ask her own question.

"What do you possibly hope to gain from these inane questions?" Ariadne asks, unable to think of a better question.

"Insight," Moira says.

Ariadne waits for more, but Moira does not continue.

"Is that all you will say?" Ariadne asks.

"Yes," Moira smiles.

Ariadne slumps back in her chair. *We should have left.*

*Patience,* Iona implores her.

*Do you know me at all?* Ariadne asks.

A giggle slips past Iona's lips, and she puts her hand over her mouth in embarrassment. Moira looks between them with an inquisitive stare.

"What did you mean when you said, 'Look how it's affected you?'" Crescentia asks Erik, her frown deepening when she observes his rigid posture.

Erik takes a drink rather than answering, setting the glass down against the table with a grimace.

"Ah," Moira says. "A coward's move."

Erik glares at her and does not speak. If he tries, the spell might compel his true feelings to burst forth. He clutches the arms of his chair as he fights against the spell. Another question would release him from its compulsion, but Moira is uninterested in relieving his discomfort.

"Do you intend to continue your education in magic?" Moira asks Iona.

Ariadne's jaw tightens, despising Moira's enduring interest in only Iona. The others may as well not be here. She senses Iona's nerves at Moira's intense, probing stare.

"Perhaps someday, but I have no immediate plans to enroll in other colleges," Iona says. "Why do you ask?"

"When I heard the story of Elise's defeat, I must admit I was shocked by your inability to properly engage in battle," Moira says. "Ariadne did most of the fighting for you. Is that not so?"

"Yes, she is a natural warrior," Iona says.

"No, she isn't," Moira laughs. "Or at least, she was not always. She had years of training."

"Are you implying that I should train as well?" Iona asks.

"Perhaps you could do with a lesson or two in combative magic, unless you are content in your helplessness," Moira says.

Iona flushes. "I am not helpless. I am simply not a violent person."

"Why would you claim an instrument of war if you have no intention of using it?" Moira asks.

"It is not only useful in war," Iona argues. "It grants me power, which I shall use as I see fit."

"That pendant may as well be ornamental without the proper skill to wield it." Moira points to the staff where it rests against Ariadne's chair. "If that long lost artifact had not appeared when it did, you would be a wraith. Ariadne would be an eternal slave of Elise, doomed to forever adore and service her. All would have been lost. You do understand that don't you?"

Clenching her fists, Ariadne tries and fails to push away the memory of Elise's unhinged smile as she'd described what she planned to do to her. Iona's face creases with shame in reaction to Ariadne's thoughts, and she regrets the recollection immediately, choosing to stifle it deep down inside herself again.

"I am not so willing to leave such things to chance. Are you?" Moira asks.

"No," Iona whispers.

"I should hope not," Moira says.

"Why do you suddenly care what happens to me?" Ariadne asks.

"I have always cared what happens to you," Moira says.

"That's a lie," Ariadne snaps.

Moira raises an eyebrow and Ariadne's anger shifts to doubt.

"You never showed your care to me before," she says, crossing her arms.

"I may have the chance to remedy that soon," Moira says.

Ariadne is about to ask what she means but Moira puts up a finger and gestures to Crescentia. Then Ariadne remembers Erik, who is still fighting the truth spell and seems close to losing. His face is nearly purple from his exertion.

"What did you mean when you said, 'Look how it's affected you?'" Crescentia asks again, emphasizing every syllable.

Erik sighs and finally says, "Do you know how many years of harvesting it took for my family to earn our marks? Generations of rituals, too many to count. To simply give the marks away… it removes any value they possess."

"I did break my spine for it. Is that not price enough?" she snaps.

He flinches. "Of course, that was a terrible plight that you should have been spared from."

"And yet you still somehow believe I do not deserve my mark?" Crescentia asks incredulously. "What did you do to earn yours? Simply be descended from a 'highborn' family?"

"Yes," he says.

"That is a requirement of an entirely arbitrary nature," she argues.

"It is not," he protests with a petulant frown. "I know how to properly conduct myself in high society. You brandish your mark to everyone you meet! Your family uses you to climb above their station in life. It is most untoward. Those of higher birth are better suited to the regality of such a distinction."

Ariadne shifts impatiently in her chair. Crescentia's drama is not enough to distract from Moira's scheming.

"She is just as deserving as anyone!" Iona cries. "Can you not see that of your own beloved?"

"She is not my beloved," Erik says, then grimaces.

"What?" Crescentia asks.

"There it is," Moira says.

"Be quiet!" Crescentia yells, and Moira chuckles, putting up her hands in a gesture of deference.

"This farce is at its end," Erik stammers as he reaches for his wand within his suit jacket. However, he seems unable to locate it. He searches every pocket to no avail.

"You told me you loved me," Crescentia says with a trembling voice. "Was it a lie?"

"No, not then," Erik says, then groans with frustration.

He jumps out of his chair and rips his jacket from his shoulders, frantically looking in every pocket but still unable to locate his wand. Out of the corner of her eye, Ariadne catches Moira putting a hand over her mouth to hide her smile.

"You do not love me anymore?" Crescentia asks as she stands and approaches him.

Erik ignores her as best he can, but she snatches the suit jacket away and holds it out of his reach.

"Answer me!" Crescentia screams.

"I cannot wed you now!" Erik bellows. "There is no precedent for your situation. Would our children be born with your mark or mine? My family's legacy shall not be forgotten in favor of a nameless, insignificant bloodline. If I had known you would bear a mark of your own, I never would have…"

His shoulders slump as his innermost thoughts are brought to light irreparably. Crescentia lets his suit jacket fall to the floor, and only then does his elusive wand slip out of its pocket and roll across the stone floor. He quickly takes it and recants the truth spell.

"Crescentia…" Erik says. "I…"

Her lip trembles but she stands tall. "Go. I never wish to see you again."

He hesitates, then accepts that there is no taking back what he'd said. Angrily, he wrenches his suit jacket on and leaves, slamming the door behind him.

"Crescentia," Iona says, attempting to stand and go to her.

"No," she sniffles. "I should… I should like to be alone."

She practically runs out onto the street with tears streaming down her face.

"You knew that would happen," Ariadne accuses Moira.

"No, I did not know precisely what transpired between them," Moira says. "However, I can smell a lie from leagues away. I need no truth spell for that."

Ariadne frowns. It is a maddeningly inconvenient trait that Moira shares with Ksenia. Perhaps all the most wretched people possess such a skill.

"I suppose it is my turn," Moira says.

"This 'game' is over," Iona says, her voice hard.

Her pendant glows and Ariadne breathes a sigh of relief when the binding grip of the truth spell slips away.

"So be it." Moira shrugs and takes a drink.

"That was a horrid thing you did to Crescentia," Iona says.

"I did nothing to her," Moira shrugs. "She deserves the truth as much as anyone."

"If you believe truth is deserved, then you should follow your own advice," Iona says.

"Not one single lie has left my lips this night," Moira says in utter exasperation. "I must say, you both struggle with the concept of a truth spell."

"You have not been forthcoming of your intentions," Iona clarifies. "And so, this is an entirely futile, one-sided exchange."

"I concur," Ariadne says, relieved that she is finally seeing reason.

"I must see to my friend," Iona says.

"She expressed her wish to be alone," Moira says. "Best not to ignore her."

"I've no desire to play foolish games with you," Iona says. "Either speak plainly of your purpose here or leave us be."

Entirely at a loss, Ariadne racks her brain for any explanation for Moira's apparent obsession with Iona. Is it simply the pendant that interests her? That does not seem to be the entire truth. Ariadne observes Moira's face and like a haze of smoke receding, a stark realization dawns on her.

"No..." Ariadne says, not meaning to speak aloud.

Moira narrows her eyes when she senses her air of mystery may be lost.

"You *were* sent here," Ariadne says.

"I told you I-" Moira tries to speak, but Ariadne interrupts.

"We are leaving." Ariadne motions for Iona to stand.

She blinks in surprise, "But-"

"Now, Iona," Ariadne raises her voice.

Iona frowns and tries to search her mind.

*No,* Ariadne's thought reverberates through both their minds, making Iona flinch and ask, "Why are you upset?"

"There's no need for hysterics," Moira says.

"Iona, please," Ariadne says, taking her staff and creating a portal back to Crescentia's home.

"Will someone please tell me what is wrong?" Iona asks, and when Ariadne does not answer, she looks to Moira.

"Regrettably, I am not permitted to explain. I wish I could," Moira says. "Ariadne, however, is under no such restriction."

Moira smiles with glee at Ariadne's burgeoning panic. She trembles with fear that turns to anger, then to overwhelming dread. She is moments away from throwing Iona over her shoulder and fleeing the room, as undignified as that might be.

"Why couldn't you… Why could you not just let me go? I failed! I am worthless to you without the pendant. My mother's words exactly. And Iona is not a Zerynthos," Ariadne argues.

"Isn't she?" Moira asks. "She is bonded to you. Zerynthos blood runs through her veins."

"But that doesn't-" Ariadne stutters. "She cannot have her."

Moira laughs, a full bellied, ominous cackle that raises the hair on the back of Ariadne's neck.

"And you would presume to tell our Goddess who she can or cannot have?" Moira asks. "Impudent as ever."

Iona's jaw drops. "Hecate sent you?"

Moira sighs but does not appear all that put out.

"I still maintain that this was a social visit," she says. "But can you blame the Goddess for her interest in you?"

Moira reaches out and lets her fingers drift just barely over the pendant's opal. She recoils only slightly at the burning sensation of the magic locked within.

"The last woman who bore this was a reckoning upon this earth. She was Hecate's chosen…" Moira trails off.

"Chosen what?" Iona asks.

"I regret I cannot say more. Only those within the coven may know its inner workings," Moira says.

Iona frowns. "Then… Ariadne would know."

Ariadne clings to her staff as the room begins to spin. She closes her eyes and wishes everything would just stop. She needs to think, needs to find a way to get Iona away from here, short of dragging her by her arm. She never meant for the truth to come out this way.

Then she notices that no one has spoken. She opens her eyes.

"She hasn't told you?" Moira asks, unconvincingly. She knew. She must have sensed it, the way she always does with her well-tuned clairvoyance. That is doubtless why she was chosen to perform this disingenuous interrogation, though Ariadne still cannot fathom why Hecate would be concerned with the questions Moira had asked.

"Told me what?" Iona asks.

"Ariadne has yet to be inducted," Moira says, with that infuriating glint in her eye.

"But I had always assumed...I thought you inherited a place in Hecate's coven," Iona says to Ariadne.

"That is not how it works," Moira says.

"I can explain it," Ariadne interrupts, and to her shock, Moira falls silent and lets her speak.

Iona shifts to face her, her expression wary but not angered.

"Only those chosen by Hecate may have a place in her coven. Once inducted, they become her devotee, vowing to practice magic in Hecate's name so long as they may draw breath. Theoretically, any witch or warlock could find a place at her side if she found them worthy of it, but for countless centuries, she has exclusively chosen those from within our bloodline," Ariadne says, nervously smoothing out the skirt of her dress with her hand. "Despite that, she has not seen fit to show me her favor. I am the first in generations of Zerynthos witches to be... excluded."

There is a tense, brooding silence. When Ariadne peeks into Iona's mind, she finds a barrage of questions scattered across the recesses of her consciousness. Most prominent of all, why Ariadne chose not to confide in her, even after all they've endured. Ariadne grimaces and leaves her mind in peace.

"And you, my dear, are the first witch outside of the Zerynthos line who has interested her," Moira says to Iona. "It is quite an honor."

"But, what of Ariadne?" Iona asks.

Moira shrugs, "I cannot say. She was not strong enough before but perhaps now she may be worthy of my Goddess' favor."

At the mention of newfound strength, Ariadne glances at her staff, but Moira shakes her head.

"You weren't strong enough in here." Moira lightly taps her forehead with her index finger. "Not after your little spat with Vivien Nicolo."

Ariadne's rage turns into a chilling calm. "Then I'd say she greatly underestimated me. Just as you all have."

"Perhaps." Moira's expression betrays nothing. "That is for the Goddess to decide, but I regret it is not all that important now. You've made it quite clear in your rebellion, your petulance, your... disobedience, that you are not the sort of witch best suited for a coven. It's best you are left alone to your own devices, beholden to no one and responsible for nothing. That is what you wanted, is it not?"

Ariadne blinks and looks away, altogether unsure of how to respond to such an accusation when indeed she did defy the coven. She'd chosen Iona over them, and she'd been very sure of that choice until now.

She looks to Iona, who watches her with cautious eyes, and Ariadne is taken aback by a swell of unexpected and unwelcome envy at knowing Hecate would prevail upon Iona instead of her, after years of fervent prayer met with perfunctory silence.

"Why the need for all this secrecy?" Iona finally asks.

"It is not our place to question divinity," Moira says with a sharpness to her voice that makes Iona frown.

"Cryptic remarks will not convince me of anything," Iona says. "You may ask all the questions you wish, but I have yet to decide if your Goddess is worth following, especially if she failed to recognize Ariadne's value. Now I must bid you goodnight."

Moira grasps Iona's wrist. "Take care in how you speak."

"Or what? You will smite me?" Iona asks sardonically, trying to pull her wrist free.

"Not I," Moira says.

Ariadne shivers when a chill goes down Iona's spine the moment she comprehends what Moira implies. It's why Ariadne is so unwilling to have this conversation at all. A Goddess like Hecate could be anywhere, unseen and undetectable, and the Gods are not known for their equanimity.

Moira stands and takes a step closer until her face is far too close to Iona's. Ariadne's grip on the staff tightens, but Moira merely releases Iona's wrist and smiles down at her.

"There's so much you do not yet know," Moira says, running the back of her knuckle against Iona's cheek until she flinches and takes a step back. "I only hope I'm there to see the look on that pretty face of yours when you learn the truth."

"What truth?" Iona asks, her exasperation only making Moira's smile grow wider.

"Thank you for a most diverting evening. I'm sure I shall see you both very, very soon," Moira says as she saunters away.

She does not even glance at Ariadne or Marcel, who has been silently watching their confrontation from behind the bar. The moment Moira is gone, Iona goes to apologize, but Marcel puts up a hand to stop her.

"Do not spare a single worry on me, chère," Marcel says.

Taking a moment, Iona sucks in a few deep breaths before standing to approach him. She extends her hand, which he gladly takes and presses a kiss to her knuckles.

"Please, sir, I beseech you to attend the solstice ritual," Iona says. "Promise me that you will at least consider it."

Conflicted feelings war in Marcel's kind eyes, but he nods. "I shall consider it and spread the word of your invitation."

Iona gives him a grateful nod and barely glances at Ariadne when she says, "Let's go."

She takes Wisp into her arms, holding her close for comfort, and steps through the shimmering portal to Crescentia's home. Ariadne follows with Aster pushing his nose against her hand. She pets him thoughtlessly, her focus remaining on Iona's back as they silently enter the house.

For a moment she fears an awkward encounter with Erik, who may have returned to the house to retrieve his belongings, or Crescentia wailing over her loss, but the candles are all snuffed out and the house is silent as the grave. It isn't until they are safely inside the spare room that Iona pins her with an accusatory look.

"I meant to tell you eventually," Ariadne says. "I just…"

"Why would you keep something like that from me?" Iona asks. "I rely on you for more than just protection. You are also my guide in this confusing world. These covens and rules and histories are foreign to me. I do not ever wish to be so unprepared again."

Ariadne's ears burn at the reprimand, but she knows Iona is right. She finds herself at a loss for words.

"How have I not seen this in your thoughts?" Iona murmurs, more to herself than to Ariadne.

"I do not often ruminate on it," she says, wringing her hands. "I… was not ready for you to know. Please forgive me."

Iona fiddles with her pendant, lost in thought. "If Hecate offered you a place in her coven, would you accept?"

Averting her gaze, Ariadne considers how best to answer such an impossible question. If Moira is wandering about France, Hecate could be near as well. She could be in this very room with them right now. A paralyzing thought.

"Have you not read stories of the Greek pantheon? To deny a Goddess' decree would be a very poor decision," Ariadne says, and while under Iona's penetrating gaze, she finds herself rambling. "Hecate is one of the most powerful sorceresses of all with dominion over every witch since the beginning of time. Her magic is beyond what any of us could comprehend and my family's affinity to her is what has separated us from all the others-"

"But then... you would follow her for the rest of your life?" Iona asks. "What precisely does that entail?"

Ariadne shrugs. "I know not. I've tried convincing my cousins to tell me, but they are sworn to secrecy, as you've just seen."

She hangs her head as treacherous emotion fills her despite her best efforts.

"And this is why you were so determined to claim the pendant," Iona murmurs. "It was not only to appease your family's ambitions. Or rather... this was your family's ambition for you all along."

"Yes. In the end, I decided that if Hecate wanted me, she would have summoned me by now. I thought it was over. Done with," Ariadne says, unable to hide how much the Goddess' indifference pains her. "I prayed to her, but she has never once responded. Since I was a girl, I dreamt of meeting her when I came of age, learning from her, discovering my true strength, but it seems I am not worthy in her eyes."

Iona frowns. "She is a fool to-"

"Don't." Ariadne speaks louder than she intended, startling Iona into silence. "Please just... don't. I've accepted my fate. I should like to put it behind me."

Iona looks down at her pendant and surmises what Ariadne will not say. If she had claimed it, then perhaps Hecate may have welcomed her with open arms. She would have been the leader of her coven, as had always been expected of her.

"You sacrificed more than I initially thought when you gave this to me," Iona says, running her thumb over the pendant's stone.

"It was no sacrifice," Ariadne insists. "I did not want it. You needed it. That is all."

Iona stares at her for a moment, the slightest trace of suspicion in her eyes, and Ariadne's heart beats loudly in her ears as her anxiety flares within her.

"It seems she cares more for the artifact itself than the person who bears it, if what Moira says is true," Iona muses. "Has anyone ever dared refuse Hecate's invitation?"

Ariadne shakes her head no. Iona sits on the bed and holds Wisp closer, scratching behind her ears.

"Perhaps she will not want you," Ariadne says in an effort to comfort her.

"Why wouldn't she?" Iona asks, a trace of hurt in her voice.

"Consider what Moira asked of you. You are far too... honorable to hold her interest, or that of my family," Ariadne says.

"You are not like them either," Iona says.

Ariadne does not know if that's entirely true. If Moira had asked her the same questions, without any context given to sway her answers, she would have responded differently than Iona. She does not believe all life is inherently precious. If Elise is judged and sentenced to death for her crimes, Ariadne will not mourn her.

Iona's eyes soften when she senses Ariadne's heightened nerves. She sets Wisp on the bed and Ariadne nearly bursts into tears when Iona pulls her into an embrace.

"We are safe," Iona says softly. "No one may harm us."

Ariadne sinks into her warmth and tries to shake the unnerving feeling of being watched.

# 6 - Iona

Crescentia doesn't return home until the early hours of the morning, walking straight past the sitting room where they were awaiting her return. In a fit of inconsolable tears, she calls off her birthday celebration before locking herself away in her room and refusing to open her door for anyone. By the afternoon, when they still find themselves without anything to do, Ariadne suggests they practice combative magic and Iona reluctantly agrees.

Using one of her portals, Ariadne takes them to a wide-open field of green grass within a sun-drenched valley of purple mountains. Wisp and Aster gallop at full speed across the lush meadow to chase the dragonflies that flit across the tall grass. Iona is tempted to call Wisp back to her so she might hold her close to quell her disquietude.

"Don't fret," Ariadne says. "This is only our first lesson."

"I know," Iona says quickly.

Ariadne casts a spell on the earth to level a rectangular piece of land for their use. Iona worries at her bottom lip and considers her options, then wonders if she might be able to convince Ariadne to postpone. Deciding it can't hurt to miss just one day of practice, Iona approaches and embraces her.

Ariadne is perplexed at first, having kept her distance since their argument the night before, but eventually she holds her and presses a kiss on the crown of her head. Though it is unseasonably warm, Iona luxuriates in the heat radiating off her, breathing in her intoxicating scent of gardenias and cloves. She dares to rise up onto her tip toes and press a sensual kiss to the hollow of Ariadne's throat.

She inhales sharply then twines fingers in Iona's hair to pull her head back. Iona closes her eyes when their lips meet, and the world around them blurs into utter insignificance. She drags her tongue along Ariadne's bottom lip, delving inside her mouth and stroking her tongue just as she would between her legs. Ariadne lets slip a soft moan, then she pulls back and shakes her head to clear it.

"Iona, we cannot," Ariadne says.

"Why?" Iona pouts.

"We must practice for an hour at least." Ariadne takes a few more unsteady steps away.

"But could we not enjoy ourselves for only a moment?" Iona asks.

"You are trouble." Ariadne chuckles darkly, studying her expression.

Then she uses her staff to conjure a pair of tan trousers, a white shirt, and black boots for the both of them. A pair of stays encapsulate Iona's chest enough to support, but not so tight that she loses mobility.

"Trousers?" Iona raises an eyebrow.

"You cannot fight in a dress. Not easily, anyhow," Ariadne says.

Iona frowns and looks away.

"I knew it. You were stalling," Ariadne accuses, leaning on her staff and putting a hand on her hip.

"I am not thrilled by the prospect of fighting you," Iona admits. "What if I hurt you?"

Ariadne smirks, all arrogance and self-assured dominance. "You couldn't hurt anyone, nymph. That is the point."

"I can," Iona argues, gesturing to the pendant.

"You possess a great deal of power, but none of the necessary skill or motivation to cut down enemies," Ariadne says. "It is a matter of will, not might."

"I could..." Iona looks around and points, "reduce that mountain to rubble and bury you alive."

She grimaces at the prospect and Ariadne laughs. "I'm trembling with fear."

"I could put you to sleep," Iona says. "Or restrain you and take away your staff."

Ariadne's eyes flare at the threat, her fingers clenching only slightly around her staff.

Iona chastens. "In practice, I mean. I would never dream of-"

"There may be hope for you yet," Ariadne grins. "Regardless, you may be called upon to fight the new malefician, should they reappear. You must prepare yourself for that eventuality."

The mention of maleficians is sobering, but even so she shakes her head. "I refuse to fight you even in practice."

Ariadne sighs dramatically, then agrees, "Illusions then. No one can be hurt that way."

Partially appeased, Iona's apprehension remains despite her best efforts. Ariadne comes to stand in front of her and leans forward so they are eye to eye.

"You mustn't hesitate in the face of danger, Iona. Never again," Ariadne says solemnly. "I will protect you to my dying breath if it comes to that, but what will you do if you're ever alone? You cannot rely on others to fight every battle you face."

"I know… I do not want to be helpless," Iona says, her jaw clenching at the memory of Moira's insults. "What do you suggest?"

"We practice until you exhibit control over your new power," Ariadne says. "I'll teach you all I know."

She conjures a red ball and tosses it to Aster, who catches it between his sharp teeth and runs across the field with Wisp on his heels, a streak of orange and black fur.

"No looking through the bond. That would defeat the purpose of training," she says.

She reaches behind Iona's neck and unclasps the pendant.

She clutches the opal in her fist. "What are you doing?"

"You should practice with your wand for the time being," Ariadne says.

"But why would I not use the pendant? Is that not the point of these lessons?" Iona asks.

"You should learn to walk before you run, do you not agree?" Ariadne asks.

She doesn't agree at all, but Ariadne's mind is made up. She reluctantly tosses her pendant in the grass and withdraws her oak wand from her trousers pocket.

"Ready?" Ariadne asks.

Iona nods, then blinks and suddenly there are three identical tall, muscular men standing in a line before her. Their expressions are blank, their features generic, and each of them holds a wooden wand in their dominant hand. She takes an involuntary step back.

"Wrong way," Ariadne says.

Flushing with embarrassment, Iona stands her ground with her wand raised.

"Could I not start with someone smaller?" she asks.

"Their size intimidates you?" Ariadne asks. "You are a witch, not a boxer. Overpower them like you would any other."

Iona huffs, then yelps when one of the men runs directly at her.

"Halat!" Iona yells.

Ropes materialize around the man's wrists and ankles, forcing him to drop his wand and fall to his knees.

"Good!" Ariadne says.

The second man draws his wand and incants a spell in a language Iona does not recognize and she attempts to block it but isn't fast enough. The spell lifts her off the ground and she floats away into the sky, screeching as her limbs flail about. The momentum causes her to spin uncontrollably, and she almost drops her wand in her confusion.

"Don't panic!" Ariadne yells. "Think!"

But she is far too distracted by the ground getting farther and farther away. All she wants is to stop floating upwards.

"Kuelea," Iona casts on herself to stop her ascent.

She screams as she plummets back to the earth from far too high.

"Iona…" Ariadne throws up her hands in exasperation.

"Sciatháin!" Iona screams.

A pair of white wings burst from her back, ripping through the fabric of her shirt, and just as they are fully formed, she unfurls them. The force of the air strains against her shoulders but she manages to slow her descent moments before she hits the ground, her knees buckling as she collapses into the dirt. Ariadne sprints over to her and frantically checks for any injuries. Only when she is confident that Iona is unharmed does she scowl.

"Next time, you should cast those spells in reverse order," Ariadne says with abounding judgement in her narrowed eyes.

"You would have just let me fall?" Iona asks, silently admonishing her lapse in judgement.

"Perhaps that is what you need," Ariadne says. "That was pathetic."

Iona shrinks at the menace in her tone. Ariadne never speaks to her that way anymore. Not since Samhain.

"I do not respond to insults," Iona says. "If this is how I can expect these lessons to be, then perhaps I should train with someone else."

Ariadne's scorn turns to remorse, though her frustration remains. Iona wonders then if this was how she had been taught, every failure paid with mockery and derision. She dares to peer at Ariadne's foremost thoughts and just as she'd suspected, there are glimpses of her time learning magic in Thessaly, of her mother looming over her and scrutinizing her every move.

Ariadne flinches only slightly and Iona leaves her mind, neither of them acknowledging what they'd both seen.

Regardless of how Ariadne had learned, Iona will not stand for this sort of treatment in her own lessons. Her confidence is feeble enough without such ridicule.

Ariadne stands and holds out her hand. "Let's try again."

Iona takes her hand and hauls her down onto the ground beside her. Ariadne falls hard on her back with a startled yelp and while she's stunned, Iona climbs on top of her and pins her hands above her head. Then she fans out her wings like a feathered canopy, ensuring that Ariadne has nowhere to look but at her.

"Be nice," Iona says, glaring down at her.

She glares back and shakes her head. "No."

Iona sulks as she sits back on her heels, and Ariadne props herself up against her elbows.

"No, Iona, if I am meant to keep you alive, then I cannot be nice. I will be discerning, and I will expect improvement."

"Fine, but if you cannot be nice… please do not be cruel. I am trying, truly I am," Iona says.

Ariadne's expression softens and she reaches up to cup her cheek. "I know you are. I…"

"Swear it," Iona says. "Or we shall not continue."

"I promise to be… fair and even tempered."

"Even tempered?" Iona cannot repress her skepticism.

Ariadne sighs, her frustration creeping back. "What should I promise then?"

Iona considers it, then says, "To teach me as you wish you'd been taught."

Ariadne's eyes widen slightly at that, and she goes silent for a moment. Then she nods. "Alright. I promise."

Iona pulls in her wings and stands, offering her hand to Ariadne.

"Perhaps I advanced too quickly," she admits when she stands. "Let us start slower at first."

"I'd like that very much," Iona says.

"And perhaps," Ariadne trails off.

"What?" Iona prompts.

Ariadne chuckles to herself, then looks at Iona with an odd expression she cannot decipher.

"What is it?" Iona asks again warily.

"This needn't be a serious undertaking. Not between us," Ariadne decides. "I shall always be there to protect you, given my general fondness for your company and our bond connecting us for whatever brief interludes we spend apart. If you were ever in danger, I would know and use a portal to find you within seconds. There is also that dragon who came to your defense on the blood moon. If you were ever in peril again, he may reappear as well. So, all of this is an overabundance of caution, in my view."

"I suppose," Iona says.

"You will have many years to hone your power," Ariadne says, and it's a great comfort for Iona to hear it. "If the malefician does reemerge in Brazil, I will go and lend my magic-"

"But you should not go alone," Iona protests.

"My artifact is better suited to the job anyhow," Ariadne points out. "Your pendant cannot shield against maleficium, so far as I'm aware." She takes Iona's hand and gives her a reassuring look. "Moira was only attempting to sow doubt in you, as she so often does. She delights in toying with others' emotions."

"I'd gathered that," Iona says. "But what is it you are trying to say, really?"

Ariadne's eyes sparkle with mischief. "I propose a sort of competition to lighten our spirits and make this all a bit more... entertaining."

"Oh," Iona smirks. "For what are we competing?"

Ariadne deliberates for a moment, then levels her with a look that has her heartbeat quickening.

"I offer myself as a suitable reward for your efforts," Ariadne grins devilishly. "If you perform well, you may do whatever you wish to me for... let's say one hour."

Iona's flush spreads down her neck and Ariadne's smile widens.

"I suspected that would get your attention."

"And if I should fall short?" Iona asks.

"Then I shall have leave to do whatever I wish to you for an equal amount of time," Ariadne says. "Fair compensation for my expertise, I find."

Her doubts creep up, but she tries to feign indifference. "You have an unfair advantage."

"Yes, I do, don't I?" Ariadne's eyes sparkle. "I shall enjoy it while I can."

"And how will my performance be measured? Simply by your opinion?" Iona raises an eyebrow.

"Yes, nymph. Impress me, if you can," Ariadne goads her.

Iona looks down at her hands, unsure if she could ever strike fear in anyone's heart.

"Doubt yourself at your own peril. I will only benefit from your hesitance." Ariadne shrugs as she backs away.

"You are hoping for me to fail?" Iona asks incredulously.

"I only hope your lust for me shall prove an effective motivator." Ariadne waggles her eyebrows. "And my hunger for you will ensure I shan't make it easy for you."

Iona rolls her eyes, though her stomach flutters with anticipation. "Fine, but when I win, I shall take full advantage."

"I look forward to it," Ariadne says, her eyes flaring with curiosity. "For now, let's focus on the task at hand. You must overpower thirty men by day's end, or I shall claim victory."

"Thirty?" Iona's jaw drops. "But…"

"Or you may give in now," Ariadne shrugs. "It is all the same to me."

Narrowing her eyes, Iona steels herself. "Very well."

Ariadne recreates her illusory men but rather than observing from afar, she keeps close and blocks any spell that Iona misses to teach her how best to react, though each time she fails is a point against her.

She preaches the importance of swift thinking, being two or three steps ahead of an attacker at all times. They run the length of the field again and again as they evade the illusions and conceive of new ways to overpower them.

Even with Ariadne beside her and even knowing that this is all meant to be recreational in nature, Iona cannot smother her fear of pain. She remembers the burning acid of Elise's touch and the crunch of bone when Ariadne's nose had shattered. When Elise had floated above her, casting her spell to turn her into a wraith, Iona had been paralyzed, unable to escape the searing agony of Elise's will ripping her soul to pieces, before Ariadne saved her. She never wishes to experience anything like it again.

Flinching when an illusory man lunges at her with a spiked club, she throws a torrent of water to push him away, but he jumps back up and charges at her once more.

"You cannot avoid confrontation forever," Ariadne warns.

"I've already," Iona gasps. "I've already defeated twenty…"

"Two and twenty," Ariadne says. "Eight more."

Iona groans, her muscles protesting, but she holds her ground, incanting, "Fau fale!"

A blue house with white shutters materializes over the illusion and crushes him under its weight.

Not a second after his demise, another illusion appears, running at her with full speed. Her shoulders slump in defeat.

"Enough, please," Iona gasps. "I need a respite."

"You yield?" Ariadne asks.

"Yes, I yield!" Iona says.

Her heart sinks as the illusory man lifts his wand, but he disappears before his spell can manifest. Ariadne cranes her neck to observe the sun's position in the sky.

"I suppose we should cease for the day," she says. "Continue again tomorrow."

"Tomorrow?" Iona asks.

"Yes," she says, as if that were obvious.

Iona fails to hide her disappointment.

"I practiced combative magic for four hours," Ariadne says.

"Four hours?" Iona exclaims.

"Every day until my schooling finally ended," Ariadne says, grimacing at the memories. "Often with my mother, when she was not away."

Leaning against her knees to catch her breath, Iona tries to imagine such a grueling existence. She doesn't know if she can withstand these lessons every day and cannot fathom doing so for hours at a time.

Crossing the field, she retrieves her pendant where she'd discarded it. The moment the opal rests against her chest again, her limbs feel lighter, and her fatigue is lessened.

"How would you say you fared?" Ariadne asks.

Iona grimaces. "I did not defeat thirty men..."

"Still, you fared better than I expected," Ariadne says, as if that were any consolation. She is comparatively immaculate, without a hair out of place or a drop of sweat on her brow.

Iona yelps as she's pulled through the air and into Ariadne's waiting arms.

"Now about my prize," she grins.

She ducks her head into Iona's neck and sucks on her skin until her knees go weak.

"You will always declare yourself the winner. I am doomed to fail," Iona says breathlessly.

"Not so," Ariadne murmurs. "I shall gladly accept defeat if you earn it. In fact, I very much look forward to it."

It's then Iona realizes what deal she has entered into. "But if we are practicing every day..."

Ariadne chuckles darkly. "You had best learn quickly, nymph."

From through her closed eyelids, a flash of blue light makes her tense, then gasp when her shirt and stays slip off her body, the threads holding the panels of fabric together disappearing in an instant. Instinctively, she reaches up to cover herself, but Ariadne shakes her head slowly with a wicked grin, and it's all Iona can do to keep from shuddering when she allows the fabric to fall away until her torso is bare.

Ariadne's gaze drifts down to admire her, her hooded red eyes roving over the expanse of bare skin with great appreciation.

"I love your freckles," she murmurs, reaching out to run a finger over the tawny dots along Iona's collarbone.

"I do not," Iona mumbles.

"Really? Why?" she asks.

Iona opens her mouth to answer, then inhales sharply when Ariadne cups both breasts in her hands and ever so gently rubs the pads of her thumbs over her hardened pink nipples in small circles, over and over again. Iona's eyelashes flutter as the acute sensations awaken her desire.

"I asked you a question, nymph," Ariadne says.

She swallows hard. "They are like blemishes. Imperfections."

Her breath hitches in her throat when Ariadne leans in to press a gentle kiss to the swell of her breast.

"I vehemently disagree." She peppers soft kisses upon the splattering of freckles on Iona's chest, expressing her adoration of every single one.

"That is only because you do not have them," Iona breathes.

Her hands come to rest on Ariadne's upper arms, and she grips tighter when Ariadne pinches her nipples, rolling them with increased pressure.

"I especially love the freckles here." She kneads one of Iona's breasts in her palm. "And here." She reaches down to run a finger along Iona's inner thigh over her trousers, higher and higher.

She lets out a disappointed sigh when Ariadne's hand falls away without touching her where her desire grows, and she grins against Iona's skin, then resumes her onslaught of soft, barely there kisses.

"Please," Iona whimpers.

Ariadne chuckles, "Need I remind you that this time is for my pleasure, not yours."

"Then use me for your pleasure," she says, almost whining. "You needn't tease me-"

She sucks in a breath when Ariadne lifts her breast up toward her mouth and wraps her lips around the hardened peak, pulling lightly and swirling her tongue around the areola, then flicking back and forth over the sensitive bud.

"Ari," Iona sighs.

She suckles so gently, not nearly enough, and Iona leans into her. She tries grinding against Ariadne's thigh to relieve the ache building in her core, but Ariadne won't let her, wrapping an arm round her waist to hold her firmly in place.

"I need… more."

Ariadne ignores her, moving from one breast to the other. That nipple is even more sensitive than the first and Iona moans at the tantalizing sensation of Ariadne's persistent tongue, flicking and laving with increased pressure.

"I have spoiled you, haven't I?" Ariadne asks against her breast.

"No," Iona says.

Ariadne takes the nipple between her teeth, and she gasps.

"Alright, fine," Iona admits. "I suppose…"

"Your cunt sings for me," Ariadne grins against her skin.

Iona blushes so violently that her chest heats and turns pink beneath Ariadne's lips.

"But how will you learn if I so easily acquiesce the moment you ask?" Ariadne whispers.

She pulls Iona's nipple so deep into her mouth that she cries out, then whimpers when Ariadne soothes the hurt with her tongue, drawing a shuddering breath from her constricting lungs.

"You're torturing me," she whines.

"Fight harder tomorrow and earn your reward," Ariadne says. "Though by the looks of it, it would be just as much mine as yours."

Ariadne gives her nipple one final kiss, then pulls away. She stares at Iona's breasts and sighs contentedly.

"Perfect," she says.

Despite her chagrin, Iona cannot withhold her shy smile at the praise, then in an effort to move things along, she reaches for the buttons of her trousers and shoves them down her legs and kicks off her boots, until she stands there naked and ready.

"What shall I do with you?" Ariadne murmurs.

Iona hugs her chest and attempts an air of indifference, but the light breeze against her bare skin, and the heat in Ariadne's stare, makes it difficult not to squirm.

"Hmmm…" Ariadne taps her chin.

"Do not pretend to think," Iona gripes. "You knew what you wished to do to me before even suggesting-"

"Such impatience." Ariadne's grin widens. "I have a great many wishes in mind. I am merely choosing which I'd like to try first."

Iona sighs and puts her hands on her hips, glaring at her while she waits, and resisting the temptation to look through the bond. Entirely unfazed, Ariadne leans against her staff, drawing this out as long as she can, knowing the anticipation will only stoke Iona's lust.

When she holds out her hand, Iona eyes it, then reaches out to take it. She lets Ariadne coax her down onto her knees, where she sits on her feet and looks up expectantly, but Ariadne does not join her. Instead, she circles Iona where she sits, her eyes roving over her from every angle.

Iona's cheeks burn. "What are you-"

"Hush," Ariadne says. "Don't look. Or better yet, close your eyes."

There's a playful, carnal challenge in her gaze. She's waiting for Iona to decide whether she'll play along or beg to be touched. If she does ask for it in earnest, Ariadne will surely acquiesce, but she'll tease her viciously all the while, and Iona doesn't wish to give her the satisfaction.

She can easily turn the tables, have Ariadne splayed out in front of her instead, competition be damned. The pendant is still clasped around her neck and even if it weren't, it would take one word, one thought from her to end this now…

Iona bites her lip, faces forward, and closes her eyes.

"Good," Ariadne praises.

She keeps very still, her breath quickening as she waits for Ariadne to touch her, but she doesn't approach, instead continuing her path through the grass until she stands directly behind her. Then she waits impatiently for Ariadne to speak, but the silence drags on, and on, and on…

She cannot fathom what is taking Ariadne so long. It must be part of her game. If that be so, then Iona can play along, too. She goes onto her hands and knees, arching her back, and putting on display what she knows will tempt Ariadne to distraction.

"Spread your legs more," Ariadne rasps, and when Iona hesitates, she says, "Don't be shy. I've memorized every part of you by now."

Flushing even deeper, Iona obeys, dragging her knees against the grass to spread herself for her lover's appreciation. Then she waits again, her breath stuttering in her lungs. Ariadne continues her languid steps around and around. Sweat coats Iona's skin as she bakes beneath the powerful rays of the summer sun. It will undoubtedly turn her a shade or two darker, to Ariadne's delight.

The silence drags on, briefly interrupted by the sweet breeze rustling through the wild grass that tickles Iona's arms and legs. Ariadne makes no move to touch her, but Iona is acutely aware of her gaze, knowing how much of her is exposed. Her mind wanders, wondering what Ariadne means to do to her, knowing how marvelous it will feel when she does. She arches her spine even more as a silent invitation.

Ariadne chuckles darkly, her voice coming from the right this time, and Iona shivers at the sound, and wonders why she waits so long. Does she mean to drive her mad with want? Or perhaps Ariadne has no intention of touching her, and this is all just an amusement for her at Iona's expense.

Finally, she delves into Ariadne's mind, no longer willing to wait for her to reveal her intentions. There she finds a vacillating discordance of cravings nearly enough to finish her without a single touch.

At first there are thoughts of rapt admiration for the curve of her bottom, the fullness of her spread thighs, the sway of her breasts when she shifts her weight, the honeyed tan of her skin, and the particular pink color of her sex that glistens with her arousal, though her folds darken more to red with every passing second as her blood rushes there, swollen and throbbing in time with her quickening pulse. Iona blushes furiously at the image of herself through Ariadne's eyes, knowing if their roles were reversed, she would not have the restraint to wait this long before reaching out to touch, or lick, or...

Ariadne's musings shift to lecherous possessiveness that has Iona biting the inside of her cheek to keep from moaning. Ariadne revels in knowing that no one else will have her, touch her, taste her. She wants to brand her handprints on Iona's hips, her breasts, the planes of her back, marking her any way she can so everyone will know who she belongs to, and for Iona to do the very same to her.

Then her thoughts turn to fierce desire, with a sudden need to bury her face in Iona's cunt and drink every drop of her arousal until she drowns in it. She wants to delve her fingers so deep, that Iona's eyes roll back into her skull as her cries echo through the valley. A small whimper slips from Iona's lips unbidden.

"You'd like that, wouldn't you?" Ariadne teases.

Her thoughts turn mocking as she wonders if maybe this woman of hers has it far, far too easy. Spoiled rotten. That won't do. She should draw out Iona's pleasure, make her mad with desire, pleading for release, reminding her that she is the only one who can give her exactly what she wants, what she so desperately needs. Ariadne will never tire of that sound, the frenzied rasp of Iona's voice as she surrenders and begs for her pleasure despite her pride, like the good little nymph she is.

Iona pants heavily as she leaves Ariadne's mind, deciding that she doesn't care what Ariadne decides, so long as she does it now. She wants it, needs it so badly that she may combust. Her fingernails dig into the dirt beneath her, her every muscle clenching with anticipation, her core constricting with insatiable need.

A single finger traces a gentle line down her neck, making her flinch in surprise, then sigh with frustration when Ariadne withdraws her touch again. Even so, she doesn't dare open her eyes.

"Having trouble, nymph?" Ariadne asks.

"No…" she whispers.

Iona hadn't heard her approach, perhaps because her blood is rushing in her ears. She tries to listen intently, to gauge their proximity by attuning to their magnetism, their mysterious fated tether.

"It is exhilarating, is it not? The strength of your mind… The ability it has to drive you mad with endless possibilities," Ariadne muses, her voice coming from a different direction now, but still close.

"I suppose," Iona's voice trembles.

"Without a single touch, your cunt already weeps for me." Ariadne's voice reflects her exulting grin. "It seems I needn't exert myself as I have been, if this is all it takes."

"Ari…" It's a question, a plea, imploring her to end this now.

She startles again when Ariadne ghosts a finger along the curve of her spine, over her backside, before her fingertip slips through her wetness where it's pooled between her legs, tracing her entrance, circling the swollen nub at the top with not nearly enough pressure. Iona lets out a strangled moan.

"Do you see just how powerful your thoughts are?" Ariadne asks in a moment of solemnity. "Your fear is just as potent, just as effecting. If you let it, you will be reduced to nothing but a quivering, pitiful creature." Ariadne slips a finger into her and slowly, tantalizingly runs it along her inner wall. "Let's only allow your desire to accomplish that, shall we?"

"Ariadne," Iona says, this time with exasperation.

"Yes, love?" Ariadne asks.

"How much longer do you intend to torment me?" She cannot keep the impatient whine from her voice. Surely, she won't subject her to this for the entire hour. The thought simultaneously horrifies and excites her.

Ariadne chuckles almost adoringly, but there is still the teasing lilt that gives Iona pause. "I suppose you've waited long enough. Though next time, I swear, I shan't be so obliging. This is my prize, after all. You're only lucky I enjoy pleasing you so very much."

But instead of stroking her in earnest as she hopes, Ariadne removes her finger, and Iona whimpers with disappointment. She almost doesn't hear Ariadne's whispered spell and cannot quite decipher it.

"We've never tried this before," she says. "If you need to stop, you must tell me."

Iona's muscles tense in anticipation. "I understand."

"Relax," Ariadne instructs, and Iona obeys, willing her inner muscles to retract just as Ariadne inserts a foreign, smooth, slightly curved object inside of her. It slips right in without any resistance; such is the abundance of her arousal.

"What is that?" Iona asks as she adjusts to its size.

"Only a crystal," Ariadne says. "I thought quartz would be best."

Iona waits for elaboration, but Ariadne provides none.

"But why…" Iona's words are caught in her throat when Ariadne runs a thumb down her cheek, then along her bottom lip.

"Frémir," Ariadne whispers.

Iona cries out when the crystal pulsates inside of her, an unfamiliar vibration pressing relentlessly against her most sensitive spot inside, where Ariadne's magic fixes it in place.

"Oh!" Iona's arms and legs give out at the delicious rush of pleasure.

"Up you get," Ariadne says.

With great effort, Iona pushes herself back up onto her hands and knees. Her limbs tremble as she accustoms herself to the luxuriant sensations that are almost too potent to bear, while Ariadne cradles her chin in her outstretched hand, holding up

her face so she might admire her euphoric expression. Iona
squints her eyes to keep them shut.

"Do you like it?" Ariadne asks.

"I- Mmmm...." Iona loses the ability to speak when a sudden
jolt of pleasure stuns her. "Yes.... I.... I like it."

"Good," Ariadne says, releasing her jaw and stepping away
to admire her again from afar.

Iona's arms begin to ache from keeping her torso aloft, a
much more difficult task now that the stone wreaks its havoc
deep within her constricting channel. She thinks she must be
close, with how perfectly the vibrations stimulate her in ways
she hadn't thought possible, but she cannot quite reach her
precipice. Her hips roll of their own accord, trying to reposition
herself to find a better angle.

"You look positively sinful with your back arched like that,"
Ariadne says, and Iona's blush deepens at the praise. "I think..."

Iona waits for her to finish, then goes tense when she doesn't.
Her eyes still closed, she listens as Ariadne steps closer.

"Open your eyes," she says softly.

When Iona does, she finds Ariadne sitting cross-legged in
front of her, their noses nearly touching. She leans in further, as
if she means to take a kiss, but she only hovers her mouth so
close to Iona's that their breaths mingle together. Iona tries to
close the distance, but Ariadne pulls away just enough to evade
her.

"You beast," she groans.

"Quite clever indeed to insult the only one who can give you
what you want most." Ariadne peppers her cheeks and neck
with soft, unhurried kisses.

"Quite unwise to torment one with the power to unleash this
upon you tenfold," Iona threatens.

"Oh, darling," Ariadne grins. "Do not make empty promises."

But before Iona can make good on her threat, the crystal's
vibrations are doubly amplified, and her every muscle goes
rigid.

"Oh!" Iona cries out. "Oh... Ari, please!"

"Shhh..." Ariadne pulls her onto her lap.

Iona silences her with a ravenous kiss, wrapping her arms
round her neck so she cannot pull away. Ariadne kneads the
swell of her bottom, caressing the heated skin of her back, then
lacing fingers into her hair to pull her head back so she might
lick a path up her neck to nibble at the tender place just behind
her ear.

A devastating wave of pleasure has Iona crying out, her inner walls constricting around the steadily vibrating crystal, and Ariadne shivers from the residual pleasure seeping through their bond.

She grasps Ariadne's wrist and shoves her hand between her trembling thighs. Ariadne doesn't deny her, stroking and circling her swollen flesh with insistent fingers. It takes only seconds before she's crying out in ecstasy, grinding against Ariadne's hand as one climax blends into another.

"Mmm..." Iona squirms as the vibrations become suddenly painful.

But Ariadne is already pulling the stone out and Iona slumps against her with relief.

"Damn," Ariadne murmurs, marveling at how saturated the crystal has become, the wetness nearly causing it to slip from her grip.

"Did you..." Iona asks, panting.

Ariadne shakes her head. "I was too distracted by your-"

She hasn't even finished her sentence before Iona pushes her onto her back and rips her trousers down her legs.

"You needn't..." Ariadne starts to say but her words trail off when Iona snatches the crystal.

She puts it in her mouth to suck it clean, and Ariadne's eyes glaze over at the sight, so she takes her time drawing it from her mouth. Then she slips the crystal into Ariadne's cunt, her arousal rivaling Iona's own, and she incants the same spell to make it vibrate.

Ariadne's thighs tense at the sudden onslaught, trying to press them closed, but Iona shoves them apart to lie between them, laving and suckling at her pulsing bud until Ariadne lets out something between a moan and a laugh, and says, "I think I rather enjoy teaching."

# 7 - Iona

They return to Lyon with matching giddy smiles, after sharing a very long, very intimate bath to wash away the sweat of their training and subsequent lovemaking, but Iona's contentment is swiftly forgotten when they find that Crescentia's door is still shut. Iona considers knocking again, then thinks better of it. Crescentia will come out when she is ready. She instead goes down the stairs in search of the dining room for dinner. Ariadne follows close behind.

"Erik is a swine," Iona mutters when they reach the foyer. "If he wanted a weak woman, he should not have courted Crescentia and wasted her precious time."

"She was weak when he met her," Ariadne says, and when Iona frowns, she clarifies, "Her magic was. Now that she has her own mark, her circumstances are vastly different."

"But she is still the same person," Iona argues.

"In character, maybe, but not in rank," Ariadne says, her fingers brushing along Iona's spine where her crescent mark lies beneath the fabric of her dress. "These marks are more than decorative. They set us apart from all others."

"Yes, but if you lost all your magic tomorrow, my devotion to you would not change in the slightest," Iona says.

Ariadne's red eyes betray a swell of emotion. "And that is why I love you."

Iona cannot think when Ariadne looks at her that way, without pretense or mischief to undercut her sincerity. She sighs contentedly when Ariadne reaches for her, cupping her cheeks within her warm hands, and tilts her head back to kiss her tenderly, reverently, so starkly different from the ravenous, bruising kisses they'd shared moments ago.

"Good evening. Where is Crescentia?"

At the sound of the unfamiliar voice, Iona startles and pulls away from the kiss. By the front door stands a statuesque, immaculately dressed woman with bold blue eyes and cascading hair that is indeed like spun gold.

"Euphemia!" Ariadne exclaims, a radiant smile spreading across her face as she rushes over to her.

"It is lovely to see you again," Euphemia says, her voice warm and gracious.

Ariadne curtsies for hardly a second, then pulls her into an embrace. Her blue eyes go wide but she does not pull away. It is Ariadne who does, wringing her hands nervously as she remembers herself. They stare at each other for a moment, then Euphemia slowly, carefully wraps her arms around Ariadne's neck and begins to cry silent tears. Iona stands there watching, feeling as if she were intruding upon a private moment.

"I missed you terribly," Euphemia sniffles.

"I... I did not know we were expecting you," Ariadne says, her voice raw.

Euphemia steps back and conjures a handkerchief to wipe at her cheeks.

"I came as soon as I heard," Euphemia says, fussing with her hair. "Now please introduce me for propriety's sake."

"Oh! Of course," Ariadne clears her throat and extends her hand. "Iona, may I introduce Euphemia Drakenström."

Iona takes her hand, then curtsies briefly. "How do you do?"

"Quite well," Euphemia says, then leans closer to Ariadne. "And here I thought you exaggerated her beauty in your letters, but I now see your lengthy accolades were quite restrained."

Ariadne nearly blushes as deeply as Iona, and Euphemia giggles. "Oh, this shall be great fun indeed."

"Euphemia," Ariadne says in a warning tone.

"Where is Crescentia?" she asks again.

Iona's smile falls at the reminder of her friend. "She has locked herself away in her room and refuses to speak to anyone. We've afforded her time alone, but I am beginning to worry."

"That won't do at all." Euphemia frowns and approaches the stairs.

When they reach Crescentia's bedroom door, Euphemia raps her knuckles against the wood.

"Go away!" Crescentia calls.

"Open the door, please," Euphemia says.

There's a rustling from inside the room and a moment later, Crescentia throws open the door and practically leaps into Euphemia's arms. Her eyes are still swollen and red from her prolonged weeping and her honey blonde curls are a snarled mess of tangles.

"My darling girl, what has become of you?" Euphemia asks.

"Erik is a lousy, impotent, abominable, feckless bastard!" Crescentia spits.

She recounts the story in a barrage of half-sentences and dramatic flourishes while Euphemia listens intently, only seeming to be surprised by Moira's involvement. Then she pacifies Crescentia with an air of maternal calm.

"Did you not receive my letter? The party has been canceled," Crescentia says, then scoffs. "If there even was any plan for it... He'd have hardly made any effort at all and made me do it all myself."

"I received your letter, but I decided to ignore it," Euphemia says. "No friend of mine shall spend her birthday alone and distraught."

Crescentia eyes her warily. "I have no desire to throw a banquet. I do not have anything prepared, nor could I muster the energy to conjure, and the day is nearly over..."

Euphemia shakes her head. "I have other plans. Let's go."

"Go? Go where?" Ariadne asks.

Euphemia's blue eyes sparkle as she takes out her wand made of silver that shimmers in the twilight, and incants, "Kläda."

Crescentia's rumpled chemise transforms into a mauve gown with a brocade overlay on the skirt. She admires the craftsmanship, her sorrows momentarily forgotten.

"Now you two," Euphemia says, tapping her wand against her chin.

"I can make my own clothes," Ariadne protests, but Euphemia has already cast her spell.

Ariadne's dress turns from white to red with tiny roses embroidered on the golden trim.

"Roses?" Ariadne raises an eyebrow.

"Do not mock my favorite flower," Euphemia says. "They may be unremarkable to a horticulturist like you, but I adore them."

Ariadne reluctantly replaces the spring crocus in her hair for a perfect pink Juliet rose. A single petal falls while she adjusts it in her bun, but she conjures it away before it hits the floor.

"Will you humor me?" Euphemia asks Iona.

When she gives a shy nod of her head, Euphemia casts another spell with a flourish of her wand. Iona's light pink day dress darkens to a midnight blue evening gown with sapphirine crystals scattered across the skirt in geometrical patterns. The silk is so smooth, she cannot help brushing her fingers lightly across her puffed sleeve in wonder, then reaches up to gently touch the matching blue crystals affixed to her hair.

"Do you like it?" Euphemia asks.

"Yes," Iona says in amazement. "It's exquisite."

"You certainly are," Ariadne says, giving her an appreciative once over before handing her a blue rose.

Then, as if she were a princess from a fairytale, Euphemia holds out her hand and a white dove glides down the hall to perch on her finger. She gently pets her familiar as she leads the way downstairs and out onto the street where the dove takes flight again and watches them from the skies.

"My carriage is just there," Euphemia says.

"I could make a portal," Ariadne suggests, gesturing to her staff.

"That would ruin the surprise."

"But-"

"Come along," she says with a twinkle in her eye. "I have everything well in hand."

They approach a wooden carriage painted white and led by two dapple gray horses. Once they've all found their seats, Iona's stomach flips when the carriage lurches forwards. She glances out the window as the buildings blur into streaks of color, while Euphemia and Crescentia become engrossed in conversation about the state of Napoleon's new government.

"He is a bully," Euphemia insists.

"Yes, yes, he is awful," Crescentia says. "And yet there has been peace of late with the treaty signed. Perhaps the worst is truly over."

"Don't be so naive. His peace is precarious at best. He will likely break it himself. It's always a never-ending overture of coups and uprisings," Ariadne says. "His occupation of Rome will be short lived, that I can assure you."

"You would prefer Habsburg rule?" Crescentia asks.

"I would prefer Roman independence from all this madness," Ariadne says. "We've ruled over ourselves and others quite successfully, if you can recall."

"Until the end," Crescentia says.

"Whatever may happen, I only hope it does not reach Sweden," Euphemia murmurs. "Hugo should not see war at so young an age."

"How old is young Hugo?" Iona asks.

"Only six months," Euphemia beams. "He's at such a precious age, my darling cupid."

"Did he enjoy the gifts I sent?" Ariadne asks.

"Oh, he adores them! So unique, those little automatons," Euphemia smiles. "I keep them on his shelf beside his storybooks."

"You sent him your conjuration assignment?" Iona asks, remembering the intricate metal wind-up toys in the shape of a bird, a mouse, a snake, a spider, and a tree frog.

"I spent hours on those trinkets and did not wish for them to go to waste," Ariadne shrugs.

"I was rather impressed by your diligence in your schoolwork. I would not have expected you to make such an effort so early in the year," Euphemia says.

"She was showing off," Crescentia says.

"Why?" Euphemia asks.

"I was not," Ariadne protests.

Crescentia's grin widens. "They were at each other's throats once. A rivalry for the ages. It was quite entertaining to watch."

"Goodness, what did you do?" Euphemia raises an eyebrow at Ariadne.

"I did nothing! Or… well…" she stutters.

"How did you describe it, love? You simply overreacted?" Iona says sweetly.

Ariadne has the good sense to look embarrassed. "There is no need to revive such distant memories."

"Distant indeed," Iona says wryly.

"You committed your fair share of offenses, too," Ariadne says.

"Only after I attempted to pacify you," Iona reminds her. "By then, I felt I was well justified."

Ariadne rolls her eyes but does not dispute her.

"You neglected to mention the most entertaining details in your letters, as usual," Euphemia says.

"It is none of your concern," Ariadne grumbles.

"I do hope she was not too unpleasant towards you," Euphemia says to Iona.

"It was nothing I could not handle," Iona grins, "She is quite a gentle soul beneath it all."

"A Libra," Euphemia points a gloved finger at her.

"Why, yes, I am," Iona says, bewildered, and Euphemia gasps with great excitement.

"Twin flames!" She looks between them. "Oh, how romantic! How divine!"

"What are you on about?" Ariadne asks, still peevish.

"Aries and Libra often engage in a karmic relationship, given that you are absolute opposites," Euphemia explains. "You will help each other grow and evolve into your very best selves. I must refer to my almanac-"

"It's all nonsense," Ariadne says.

"Oh, hush," Euphemia scolds, rapping Ariadne's knee with her fan, then continues. "Twin flames are known to be drawn to one another with an almost magnetic pull."

At that, Ariadne and Iona exchange a meaningful look.

Then Euphemia says to Iona, "I can already perceive the change you've made in her. I commend you."

"So do I," Crescentia says, purposefully provoking Ariadne's agitation.

"You are all exceedingly rude to speak of me as if I were not here," Ariadne says, crossing her arms.

"On the topic of rude behavior," Euphemia levels her with a disapproving look, "now that I have been introduced to your beloved, it is high time you met mine."

"I shall," Ariadne agrees, abruptly chastened. "Bring him to the solstice ritual."

"Of course, I shan't miss it," Euphemia says.

Iona's brow furrows in confusion. "How is it that you have yet to meet her husband?"

Ariadne scratches her cheek. "Well…"

"She was far too preoccupied to attend the wedding," Crescentia says, seeming more like herself with every passing second. "She neglected to respond to any letters for nearly nine months, from what I've heard."

"You are getting on my nerves," Ariadne warns.

"Nine months? What happened to…" Iona asks, then identifies the reason in Ariadne's thoughts.

"That is an exaggeration," she says, unconvincingly. "There was a brief time after Elise ended our courtship-"

"From January until September of last year," Crescentia clarifies.

Ariadne glares at her. "When I was slightly… rebellious."

"A reputation was earned." Crescentia says haughtily. "Even I considered offering myself to her for a night after the stories I heard, for how could the adulations of so many women be hyperbolic. Some claim to have needed a week's rest after she was through with-"

"For the love of all that's sacred!" Ariadne groans, covering her face with her hands.

Iona chuckles wryly, giving Crescentia a warning look before consoling Ariadne in her mortification. "You told me of this already."

"Yes, but I would rather not recount every insignificant detail," Ariadne sighs with exasperation. "It was a time in my life that is now over."

"You may have difficulty avoiding the subject where we're headed," Euphemia says, her smile turning sheepish, and there is something else lingering behind her eyes that Iona cannot quite place.

Just then the carriage halts and when Iona steps out, she is struck by the stark change of scenery. All around them are rolling hills covered in the greenest grass she has ever set eyes upon. The verdant landscape contrasts greatly with the overcast sky, and there isn't a single tree to be seen in any direction. The air is humid and chilled, so Iona conjures a shawl to warm her bare arms.

"Oh…" Ariadne says when she beholds the manor made of dark granite stone built in the center of the secluded valley.

With three stories and many windows filled with candlelight, muted sounds of a raucous party can be heard through the walls. There are no other houses in sight, though it is too dark to see very far.

"Where are we?" Iona asks.

"Iceland," Euphemia says.

"I am in no mood for this sort of revelry," Crescentia sighs.

"I will be sure to remind you of that once Rebekka is through with you," Euphemia says, taking Crescentia's hand and pulling her along.

"Who is Rebekka?" Iona asks.

Euphemia glances at Ariadne. "You did not tell her of Rebekka?"

"No," Ariadne says shortly.

Euphemia's chagrined expression puts Iona on edge, and she is about to silently inquire about it to Ariadne, when Crescentia's eyes flit between them as she perks up.

"On second thought, I'm feeling much better," Crescentia says as she takes Iona's arm and leads her towards her house.

"Rebekka was an old flame," she whispers. "As I understand it, she was Ariadne's very first conquest. Ariadne wished to court her formally, before she was stuck with Elise, but Rebekka rejected her."

Iona's eyebrows raise. "Is she mad?"

Crescentia giggles. "No, she… Well, you shall see for yourself."

The moment the front door opens, they are met with a heady

scent of smoke and sweat. Euphemia leads them through the house as if she lives there, while Crescentia takes a goblet from a floating silver tray and downs its contents in one gulp. The halls and lavish rooms are filled to the brim with party guests, all in varied states of dress or undress.

As they enter a grand ballroom lit by crystal chandeliers, Iona tries not to gawk, though many of the guests stare brazenly at her with interest. A circle of couples weave to and fro in the center of the room, their laughter infectious as they make drunken efforts at dancing a cotillion.

"Where the blazes is Rebekka?" Euphemia mutters. She beckons them out of the ballroom and down another candlelit corridor.

Iona is nearly toppled over by two warlocks entangled an amorous embrace. Neither of them apologizes as one pulls the other into a room and slams the door. She puts a hand over her mouth to hide her bemused grin.

*Did Euphemia take us to an orgy?* Iona asks.

Ariadne's tight smile betrays her unease. *Rebekka's parties often devolve into some manner of bacchanalia.*

She takes two glasses of wine and hands one to Iona, before Euphemia grasps her arm and pulls her further into the crowd. Iona hastens to catch up with them when they reenter the ballroom and pass by a lively string quintet. The pining gazes of many a woman linger on Ariadne, though she seems keen on ignoring them.

One of the women, a petite brunette with green eyes, glares at Iona with brazen resentment and envy. Sensing her discomfort through the bond, Ariadne turns to glare back at the brunette, whose face pales as she looks down at her feet and scurries away.

"We may leave if you wish," Ariadne suggests, though it sounds more like she is asking in earnest.

"But you've only just arrived!" Euphemia protests.

"If I knew where you planned to take us, I never would have agreed to come," Ariadne hisses.

Euphemia's face falls. "But... I only wished to surprise you and cheer Crescentia up from her gloom. Why are you in such a horrid disposition?"

"You know well how I hate surprises," Ariadne says, glancing around at the witches pretending not to stare at them.

"If I may," Euphemia says in a placating tone. "I think this to be the perfect opportunity to clear the air before the solstice.

There have been abundant rumors floating about and your presence here will effectively quell them. Iona should make appearances in society anyhow. It's expected."

"A lovely list of sentiments that could have been expressed to us in France," Ariadne mumbles.

*We need not stay.* Iona takes a stray curl and tucks it behind Ariadne's ear.

She sighs heavily, but she's become conflicted.

Euphemia marks her indecision and continues with a hopeful smile. "You are no longer a piece of meat for them to quarrel over, now that you are bonded."

"It seems their yearning has been supplanted by bitterness," Ariadne remarks.

"Have you always been this fearful of them?" Euphemia asks.

Ariadne's nostrils flare. "I am nothing of the sort!"

Iona bites back a smile at her conflated outrage, and Euphemia shares a knowing look with her.

"I shall protect you," Iona teases.

*I am not afraid*, Ariadne insists, but her apprehension floats within her consciousness like a stagnant cloud.

*You must protect me then, for I find them all quite intimidating,* Iona admits.

*You possess greater power than anyone else in this room,* Ariadne points out.

*As do you.* Iona glances at the staff, and notices Ariadne's viselike grip around the smooth wood. *It seems we are irrational fools, the pair of us.*

A grin curves Ariadne's mouth. *Was that ever in question?*

She lifts Iona's hand to her lips, which elicits a thrum of whispers from their observers. Ariadne tenses when she hears it, and Euphemia laughs.

"You needn't flaunt her, Ari," Euphemia says in mock admonishment.

"I am doing nothing of the sort," Ariadne protests, her ears turning as pink as the rose in her hair.

*You can if you'd like,* Iona grins, and Ariadne fails to suppress her smile.

"Alright, alright. I suppose we may stay a while," she acquiesces, "but no more surprises."

"I swear it," Euphemia says, unconvincingly. "Now come along, my friends. We must find Rebekka, if she hasn't disappeared upstairs. I dare not interrupt her there."

"That would be unwise," Ariadne chuckles.

"What does she look like?" Iona asks. "So I might help look."

"Oh! Of course." Euphemia takes her hand and leads her to a wall of paintings just outside the ballroom.

There hanging on the wall is a floor to ceiling portrait of a tall woman with short flaxen hair and a roguish smile that is as disarming as it is cavalier. She wears an immaculately tailored black suit, and though Iona is mildly surprised to see a woman dressed in a masculine fashion, she finds it complements the woman perfectly.

"This is our Rebekka," Euphemia says with great affection. "My dear friend of nearly twenty years."

"Why, you are more like siblings then," Iona observes.

"She vexes me often enough, as a little sister would," Euphemia says wistfully, then her eyes brighten. "On second thought, perhaps we should divide our search. If one of you finds her, you could use the bond to summon the other. Is that not correct?"

Ariadne hesitates, "Yes, but-"

"We'll be swift as anything," Euphemia takes her arm. "Call to us if you find her!"

Iona nods, noting the apologetic look from Ariadne when she's pulled away. Iona smiles encouragingly, then turns her gaze back to the painting to examine it a moment longer.

She admires the particularly vibrant shade of Rebekka's green irises, like the sea in the midst of a storm. The whites of her eyes lie slightly below her irises, making her stare effortlessly seductive even in painted form. Almost hypnotic. Iona can see why Ariadne was once so smitten with her, and an unexpected swell of jealousy bubbles in her stomach. She frowns.

"It's a crude likeness, I find."

The unfamiliar voice is a sultry rasp far too close to her ear. Jolting, Iona looks up to see who had spoken and blinks in surprise to find the subject of the painting standing right there, her chiseled form draped in similar garb, with a purple lupine flower pinned to her lapel.

"I'd much prefer a portrait of you on this wall," Rebekka says with a charming smile. "Your hair would bring some much-needed color to the room. No one would be able to take their eyes off you."

"Um…" Iona takes a step away. "You are Rebekka, are you not?"

Her eyebrows lift slightly, her interest piqued. "Why yes, I am."

"We were looking for you," Iona stutters.

Rebekka takes a small step closer. "You found me. Now what shall we do?"

Iona's cheeks heat. *I found Rebekka.*

Faster than she thought possible, a portal bursts into existence right beside them and Ariadne leaps through, almost tripping on the hem of her skirt in the process.

"Ariadne?" Rebekka's eyes go wide at both the display of magic and the unexpected interruption.

"Iona." Ariadne takes her hand. "May I introduce Rebekka Magnúsdóttir."

She would have spoken, but the very moment Ariadne's hand touches hers, an unexpected wave of frisson spreads across her skin, making goosebumps rise and heat cascade over her until she can hardly think straight. It's all she can do to keep from pulling her hand from Ariadne's grip. When she looks up at her, Ariadne seems altogether unaffected and unaware of it. Blinking rapidly, she forces her features into neutrality.

"*You* are Iona Lysander?" Rebekka's shock turns to sheepish resignation and barely concealed disappointment.

"Yes, she is," Ariadne says in a pointed tone.

"Oh," Rebekka chuckles.

"You did not notice the pendant?" Ariadne asks.

"I am not one to notice a woman's jewelry," Rebekka says defensively, then becomes momentarily distracted when a witch with chestnut hair passes by.

Iona takes a deep breath, the luxuriant sensations waning at last as Ariadne's disposition seems to calm.

"Won't someone help me, please?" Euphemia asks, eyeing the portal warily. "I'm unaccustomed to this sort of travel."

Rebekka immediately extends her hand to help her step through. Iona cannot help grinning at the astonished expressions of the party guests watching on the other side, before Ariadne closes the doorway.

"You'd have thought there was a fire," Euphemia murmurs to Ariadne, who pretends not to hear it.

"Your presence has been sorely missed, Ari," Rebekka says. "I kept the beds of Europe warm in your absence."

Ariadne's grin is mordant. "You needn't have troubled yourself."

"Oh, it was certainly no trouble," Rebekka winks at her.

Iona watches in disbelief as Ariadne blushes and looks away with something close to shyness. In fact, she's never seen

Ariadne in such a state of constant bashfulness, and she finds it both adorable and insightful.

Neither Rebekka, Euphemia, or Crescentia show much fear of Ariadne at all, in great contrast to how most others treat her, and she seems to appreciate it despite her pretense of annoyance.

"Well now, we're all acquainted." Euphemia looks between them. "Would anyone care to dance?"

Crescentia passes by with a new cup tilted upwards, gulping down wine as if she had just traversed a desert for days on end. They watch her as she goes.

"What's the matter with her?" Rebekka asks.

"She ended her courtship with Virtanen," Ariadne says.

"I must offer her my congratulations," she says.

"Do so at your own peril," Ariadne grins. "And quickly, if you'd like her to remember it."

"Leave her be," Euphemia chastises.

Rebekka shrugs, unbothered. "Very well, I shall rejoice in secret. Our company is all the better without him, and doubly so with the addition of Iona."

"I heartily agree," Euphemia says.

Iona smiles shyly. "You are too kind."

The string quintet begins a new song, and Rebekka offers her hand to Euphemia. "You mentioned a dance?"

"That I did!" Euphemia lets Rebekka guide her to the dance floor and beckons them to follow.

When Ariadne pulls Iona along to join the line of couples in the center of the ballroom, she puts aside her disoriented thoughts. She is still daunted by the art of dance, but Ariadne knows every step from memory and points with her eyes where Iona must step.

*Wait,* Ariadne cautions, just before Iona bumps into the woman standing beside her. *One step left, then come forward.*

Iona nods and tries not to show her discomfort at being the only dancer out of step, while Ariadne moves with practiced grace, as if it were second nature to her. Out of curiosity, Iona peers into her mind to see the recollection of many a lesson in dance that her mother had once conducted. She had charmed Ariadne's feet to send a shock across her soles if she ever made a false move.

"Pardon me, miss," A gentleman says with a short bow of his head, and Iona realizes she had been so distracted by her horror at Ariadne's memory, that she'd missed her cue to cross to the other line.

"Apologies, sir." Iona curtsies clumsily, then shuffles across, her cheeks burning with embarrassment.

A moment later the song ends, and a waltz begins. Ariadne takes her hand and pulls her close, pressing her other hand against Iona's lower back as she guides her across the floor.

She seems much more at ease in her movements, reminding Iona of their first dance together, and when she glimpses into Ariadne's mind again, she finds the memory of Ariadne's father teaching her the steps without the use of pain inducing spells.

*You did well,* Ariadne encourages. *It is not an easy dance to learn.*

*Everyone saw,* Iona relents.

She lets out a muffled squeak of surprise when, without warning, Ariadne grasps her chin and presses a soft, luxuriant kiss to her mouth, until Iona remembers herself and pulls away, breathless.

*There.* Ariadne grins at her stunned expression. *Now that is all they shall bother to remember.*

*They shall think me a doxy.* Iona giggles despite herself.

Ariadne scoffs. *Surely not. I would need to kiss you far lower to earn you that moniker.*

When Iona's cheeks bloom at the prospect, Ariadne chuckles and coaxes her back into the rhythm. The blunder is indeed forgotten once they've danced with the highest of spirits and indulged in rich wine that has Iona swaying on her feet.

Before long they grow tired of dancing and Rebekka guides them to a quieter corner where they watch the remaining couples engage in a quadrille. Ariadne becomes noticeably more at ease in spite of the intrusive gazes of the other witches and warlocks, in part due to Rebekka riling her with teasing barbs that has Iona laughing so hard her stomach aches.

"If you spoke of that blasted pendant one more time…" Rebekka sighs in exasperation.

"You were under no obligation to listen." Ariadne turns up her nose.

"On the contrary, as your friend I found I must, or you would bore the women with your ramblings and repel them into the arms of others," Rebekka says.

"Into your arms, you mean?" Ariadne asks drolly.

Rebekka shrugs. "It is no fault of mine if you still could not manage to charm them, despite my teachings."

"Teachings?" Iona asks.

Rebekka grins and before Ariadne can interrupt, she says, "I taught her how to flirt."

Ariadne glowers. "You did not *teach* me-"

"Taught her many a skill in fact." Rebekka bumps her elbow into Iona's. "You're welcome."

Ariadne turns beet red, then looks to Euphemia with a pleading expression.

"Now, now." She gives Rebekka a reproachful look. "Iona is not yet accustomed to your crude attempts at humor. Do not scare her away."

"I meant no offense." Rebekka puts up her hands, appearing anything but repentant. "You are not so easily scandalized, are you, Iona?"

"Surely not," Iona grins shyly.

"Good," she smiles back.

Ariadne wraps a possessive arm across Iona's shoulders. Yet again, a rush of sensation travels over Iona's skin like a stiflingly warm breeze, and she lets out a shuddering breath, gripping her glass so tightly the stem almost snaps.

Rebekka glances at her in slight confusion, and Iona pulls away from Ariadne for fear of swooning in full view of everyone. She conjures a fan and unfurls it, fluttering it over herself for want of air. Ariadne's brow furrows and she appears almost hurt, but Iona cannot yet speak to explain or reassure her.

"More wine?" Euphemia asks, in an effort to distract from the awkward moment.

"No," Rebekka says with a grimace. "I am still recovering from last night."

"My, my. Do you aim to surpass the profligacy of last summer?" Euphemia asks, her humor returning.

"I doubted if I could until I found myself in a rather vulnerable state." Rebekka's cheeks turn pink. "I awoke in a Tuscan alleyway with a splitting headache and no memory of the previous night's events. Half my clothes were gone."

"You were robbed?" Ariadne asks incredulously.

"If I was, I'm sure the thief was most disappointed by my lack of coin." Rebekka smirks, "but more likely I paid some fair maiden a visit and left my jacket, shoes, and hat behind. I couldn't tell you when or where…"

"You must be more careful," Euphemia admonishes.

"Yes, yes. I'm sure if you had your way I would be embroidering cushions with you by the fire." Rebekka bats her eyelashes.

"Or settling down, as Ariadne has," Euphemia says.

"What would be the fun in that?" Rebekka asks.

They go on like that for a while, their voices blending into the cacophony of other conversations surrounding them. Iona takes a sip of her wine, and soon she is laughing along with the others, her discomfort forgotten, until she is overcome by the distinct feeling of being watched.

She looks over her shoulder to find Ksenia at the other end of the room dressed in a black velvet gown with ringlets of her pale blonde hair framing her face, staring intently at them. The prominent dark circles beneath her ice blue eyes make Iona wonder if she's slept a wink in the month since college ended. She is almost compelled to cross the room and speak to her, but Ksenia's gaze shifts to over Iona's shoulder.

"Good evening," Samaira says as she approaches wearing a sunset orange gown with a deep red sash thrown over her shoulder.

"Samaira!" Iona's spirits soar. "How good it is to see you!"

"And you, my friends," Samaira says, then opens her arms for Ariadne to embrace her fiercely. "I've missed you so! How have your travels treated you thus far?"

"They have been… rather eventful," Ariadne says when she pulls away. "We shall speak of it later."

Iona embraces Samaira, too, and when she looks over her shoulder again, Ksenia is gone. It's just as well. Iona has no real interest in speaking with her now or perhaps ever again.

Despite their surprisingly cordial exchange when parting ways in May, she cannot forget the many ways Ksenia had been cruel to both her and Ariadne when she'd thought she might have a chance at claiming the pendant for herself.

While Ariadne speaks animatedly with Samaira, regaling her with stories of Brazil's great beauty, there is a distinctive difference in Samaira's countenance, a gloom in her aspect that gives Iona pause. Then she glances down at Samaira's hands clasped tightly in front of her.

"Where is your ring?" Iona asks.

Samaira's smile fades as she tries to move her hands behind her back, but Ariadne is too quick, grasping Samaira's wrist and lifting it up to the candlelight. There is only a faint mark of lighter skin on her left ring finger, but no sapphire in sight. It's quite odd, since Samaira has never been without the ring since Iona first met her. Ariadne had told her of the ring's secret power to give Samaira visions of the future.

"I took it off," she says, gently freeing her wrist from Ariadne's grip.

"Why?" Ariadne asks.

"Is something wrong?" Iona asks.

"No! No, no, everything is… fine," Samaira says. "I merely needed a respite. That is all. There is no need for alarm."

"A respite from what exactly?" Ariadne asks.

Samaira sighs and looks over her shoulder, then leans forward and whispers, "Follow me."

She leads them away from the ballroom and down a long hall where she cracks open a door, then beckons them to enter what looks to be a well-used study. Dusty books are strewn everywhere, cluttering a collection of wooden shelves, and piled on every chair and table.

"We should not be disturbed here," Samaira says.

"Good," Ariadne says, looking at her expectantly.

"First I must ask, what did you find in Brazil?" Samaira asks.

Ariadne's responding sigh of frustration is ignored by them both as Iona conjures chairs and motions for Samaira to sit.

"There is another malefician," Iona says. "We found the remnants of their ritual and… my grandfather's body."

"Your grandfather?" Samaira's eyes go wide. "Oh, Iona, I am so terribly sorry."

She lowers her head. "I'd only just met him… My sorrow lies with his family, those who really knew him. It must have been a terrible shock for them, and to know he died so violently… He was slaughtered like an animal."

Tears threaten to spill from Iona's eyes, but her grief is overshadowed by confusion when Samaira does not seem entirely surprised to hear such awful news.

"You knew?" Iona asks, but Samaira quickly shakes her head.

"No, but… the darkness I've felt for months did not subside when Elise was defeated. On the contrary, it has only grown," Samaira says, fiddling with her lace fan in her lap. "I thought I was merely fatigued from a long year of study and perhaps there was residual maleficium still lingering from Elise's spells. When I left Austria, I thought all would return to normal. I wished it would… I'd hoped…"

"Samaira, please," Ariadne says. "Tell us what is ailing you."

She looks between them, and, to Iona's dismay, she begins to weep. It is disconcerting to see one so calm and composed as Samaira be so overcome with desolation, and Iona goes to kneel before her and grasp her hands tightly.

"Don't despair. Please…" Iona says. "Whatever it is, we shall face it with you."

Ariadne conjures a handkerchief and hands it to Samaira, who takes it gratefully and tries to compose herself.

"When I returned to Nepal, I felt sick. Not in body, but in mind," Samaira says softly. "I decided to abscond into the mountains to meditate and heal. My family has a small dwelling there, overlooking the valley. I stayed for three nights. On the fourth day, I had a ghastly… all-consuming vision."

"Of what?" Ariadne prompts.

Iona cuts her a look. *For pity's sake, let her speak in her own time.*

Ariadne clenches her jaw, her anxiety running rampant and putting Iona on edge as well, but she gives one short nod of assent. Iona's attention returns to Samaira, who leans in closer.

"All I see is darkness," Samaira mouths, so quietly that Iona strains to hear it, "and all I hear are screams."

"Whose screams?" Iona whispers, the hairs on the back of her neck standing on end.

"I could not say… When one is overcome with terror and agony, there is nothing recognizable in their voice," Samaira says.

Ariadne's eyes glaze over in remembrance. When Iona looks through the bond, she hears the memory of Vivien's screams. On that fateful night at the river, her former friend's voice was unfamiliar to her though they had been acquainted for many years. The sound was wild, unhinged. Iona shivers and leaves Ariadne's mind.

"Man or woman?" Ariadne asks.

"Woman, I think," Samaira says. "I had the same vision every day, time and again. Once it starts, I cannot not escape it. I am forced to listen, trapped in darkness, until it is over. Until whoever it is… dies. It is unendurable. When the vision reoccurred a third time, I took off the ring and have not dared to touch it since. That was one week ago."

There is a prolonged silence, wherein Iona cannot look away from Ariadne's face. She wants to reenter her mind but is frightened of what she might find there.

"If I had not been such a coward, perhaps your grandfather may have lived." Samaira wipes away another tear.

"You mustn't torment yourself with such hypotheticals," Iona says. "Who is to say if you would have seen it? You've no control over the visions you receive, is that not so? And you would not have recognized his face anyhow."

Iona looks to Ariadne for support, but she appears conflicted.

"Ari?" Samaira asks softly.

"I cannot imagine the torment you face. I cannot begin to understand… but this artifact is in your possession, and it is useless without someone to wield it," Ariadne says. "We shall never know what visions you may have missed since you decided to take the ring off. Perhaps you were not meant to prevent Gonçalo Evora's death, but there may be others."

"Ariadne," Iona protests, but Samaira shakes her head.

"No… she is right," Samaira says. "It was selfish of me."

"I disagree strongly," Iona says. "Why must you suffer needlessly?"

"It would not be needless if I may provide invaluable insight," Samaira says.

Iona shakes her head obstinately. "If our fate is sealed and predetermined, then nothing you see could change it."

"By choosing not to wear the ring, I do my part in sealing fate," Samaira insists. "If I wear it, we may have a chance to intervene."

"But… you could say that of anything at all. You are not solely responsible for preventing every tragedy from now until your death," Iona argues.

As another silence lingers, she reconsiders the magnitude of her words. In a sense, that is exactly what all three of them are now responsible for. Iona, as a pendant bearer, Ariadne, with her staff, and Samaira, with her ring, are all capable of saving innocent lives. Could they ever in good conscience decide to turn a blind eye?

"We must prepare ourselves for the days ahead," Samaira says. "I fear our troubles are far from over."

The door to the study opens and Euphemia steps inside with her dove perched on her shoulder. "What are you all doing hidden away in here?"

"Nothing," Ariadne says. "In fact, we were just leaving."

She offers her hand to Samaira, who takes it and stands, wiping the final remnants of her tears as she regains her composure and smiles.

"Good evening, Euphemia," she says.

"My dear, you look to be in need of a strong drink," Euphemia observes.

"If Crescentia hasn't drunk it all," Samaira's laugh is stilted as she follows Euphemia out of the room.

Iona wants to stand but finds herself frozen in place. Ariadne watches her with an unreadable expression.

*We should enjoy the party, while we can,* Ariadne thinks.

*I do not feel like celebrating.* Iona avoids her gaze.

"Wallowing in anguish will not bring him back to life," Ariadne says.

Iona's eyebrows raise incredulously. "What a horrid thing to say."

"We cannot change his fate now, nor anyone else's. Death is a terrible but unavoidable part of life," Ariadne says. "Did you forget what Jacira said?"

"Yes, we are still alive, but we should not be calloused to others' suffering whenever it suits us," Iona says.

"So says the woman who suggested Samaira abandon her artifact to avoid its negative side effects," Ariadne says.

"She should not be riddled with guilt for avoiding such terrible visions," Iona argues. "You should understand her aversion to a recurring nightmare, perhaps better than anyone."

Ariadne blinks and looks away. "My nightmares are a weakness. I would gladly welcome any benefit to be had from them."

"Ari," Iona sighs, but does not know what to say. She regrets mentioning Vivien at all, while the memory of her screams still ring in their ears.

Ariadne nearly leaves the room without another word but hesitates in the doorway. "The best way to honor the dead is by remaining vigilant and preserving life however we can. We shall require Samaira's help in that endeavor, and for that she needs her ring. Meanwhile, I shall have a drink with my friends. You are welcome to join us when you are ready."

Ariadne leaves the door open when she steps out into the hall. The echoes of the raucous party are grating on Iona's agitated nerves, but as the seconds turn to minutes, she cannot bring herself to walk the short distance to the door and close it.

She supposes she should go out there and find it in herself to be cordial, acquaint herself with new witches, craft new alliances, and set aside her worries for the moment. That is what she should do, but in truth, she hasn't the energy or the inclination. She cannot focus on such trivialities when a new threat still lurks out there somewhere, lying in wait.

Her spirits sink into despair upon the realization that perhaps this is how it shall be from now on. Defeating Elise had nearly killed her and Ariadne both. She does not know if she can muster the courage to face a malefician again, and yet more after, but it seems she must. Darkness will always exist.

"Iona? What troubles you?"

She startles and looks up to find Rebekka standing in the doorway and regarding her with concern.

# 8 - Iona

Iona quickly stands and smooths out her skirts. "I was… I should rejoin the party. Ariadne will be wondering where I am."

"She is not far," Rebekka assures her. "Why did she leave you here alone?"

Iona looks away, failing to think of a suitable explanation, while Rebekka closes the door and steps closer.

"Crescentia is out there drinking her weight in wine. Samaira is barely speaking and looks to be on the verge of tears. Ariadne is sulking at the piano like she used to when we were children," Rebekka counts on her fingers, "and now, you are upset as well."

Iona grimaces. "I apologize for our conduct. We did not intend to cast a pall on your festivities."

"I care little about that," she says.

While she finds Rebekka's concern endearing, she does not feel comfortable confiding in her when they've only just met. Instead, she puts on her best attempt at a smile and approaches the door.

"I should like to rejoin the others now. You can regale me with tales of your years of friendship with Ari," she says.

Rebekka chuckles wryly. "Are you sure you'd like to hear of them?"

Iona hesitates. "Do I?"

She slowly shakes her head, the mirth in her gaze making Iona avert her eyes.

"Fair enough," Iona says.

Rebekka shrugs off her blazer and sets it on the back of a chair, then unbuttons her cuff to fold her shirt sleeve up to her elbow.

"Did she ever mention me?" Rebekka asks, tilting her head slightly.

"Not by name," Iona admits. "But she told me of a time when she indulged in revelry of this sort to distract from her discontentment."

"Is that how she described it?" Rebekka raises her eyebrows.

"Well… not exactly," Iona stutters. "She does not often speak of those days."

Rebekka finishes folding her sleeves and Iona notices a geometric red mark on her forearm, just below the crease of her elbow.

"It is the Fehu rune, for Freya," Rebekka explains, having noticed her stare.

"I see. What does it evoke?"

"Abundance, growth, and magic. It is also a warning against greed, one I often ignore, to my father's great disappointment." A crooked grin forms on Rebekka's lips. "Ariadne once said that abundance suits me fine, seeing how I often delight in life's pleasures."

"Do you disagree?" Iona asks, returning her smile.

"I am a self-proclaimed libertine, it is true," Rebekka jokes with a shrug. "As was Ariadne, but I suppose for some those times must fade away. I am glad of any comfort our exploits may have given her. She is a tortured soul, indeed. Or at least, she once was. I find her to be much changed. Her anger... it is still present but does not seem to rule her any longer. I suppose we have you to thank for that."

"I could not take credit for her healing," Iona says. "Has word spread of Vivien's recovery?"

"Indeed, it has." Rebekka nods contemplatively. "In a thousand years, I never would have predicted such a redemptive turn of events."

"I hope everyone hears of it," Iona says, and when Rebekka gives her a questioning look, she says, "I wish for all to learn of Ariadne's compassion so they may know her true nature."

"You do love her," Rebekka says softly.

"Yes, of course," Iona says. "With all my heart."

"Forgive my doubt. It is simply the swiftness of your courtship that made me wonder," Rebekka says.

Iona flushes and fiddles with a gem embroidered into her skirt. "I cannot fault you for that. It has been a whirlwind."

"I would expect nothing less from Ariadne. She is the most impulsive woman I have ever encountered," Rebekka chuckles.

Iona tries not to take her words as an insult, but Rebekka must have seen the shift in her expression.

"Forgive me, I did not mean to imply that one would need to be thoughtless to bond with you." Rebekka's smile turns carnal as her appreciative gaze drifts over Iona's body. "It is no mystery why she became so hopelessly entranced. She is only fortunate to have gotten to you first."

Iona blinks in surprise. It's then she notices their proximity. Moments ago, their exchange had been entirely benign but following Rebekka's comment, she feels the need to put distance between them. Then the door to the study opens, and Iona hastily steps away.

"Iona?" Ariadne says. "Why haven't you-"

She stops short in the doorway, her posture rigid as her eyes flit between them.

"Ah, there you are," Rebekka says.

"Here I am." Ariadne's smile is tight, her eyes betraying her displeasure.

Rebekka beckons her closer. "Won't you join us? We were just discussing-"

Without another word, Ariadne simply leaves the room. Dumbstruck, Iona stares at the empty doorway, then runs after her.

"Please pardon us," Iona calls over her shoulder.

"Not to worry. Enjoy the party," Rebekka calls after her, an enduring levity in her tone.

Iona cannot leave the room fast enough, but even in her haste she struggles to keep up with Ariadne's long strides.

*It was nothing,* Iona thinks.

*I can read your mind,* Ariadne says.

Iona's brow furrows. *Yes, I know.*

Ariadne whips around and Iona nearly collides into her. *You are attracted to her. I see your lust clear as day.*

Iona's cheeks burn with mortified indignation as she grasps Ariadne's arm and drags her into a nearby bedroom. Relieved to find it unoccupied, Iona waves her hand to light the fireplace, then stands in front of the door with her arms crossed.

"You lust after her," Ariadne says again, in an infuriatingly accusatory tone. "Do not insult me by denying it."

Iona's flush deepens. "I cannot regulate my every thought or… involuntary reaction."

"Do not deny you wouldn't-"

"Your hypocrisy is staggering," Iona says, and when Ariadne stares at her in confusion, she continues, "Do not pretend to be unaffected by her. I can't recall ever seeing you quite so… meek and bashful."

"I was not," Ariadne fumes, but cannot hide her embarrassment at the accusation. "Nor was I alone in a room with her."

"If my thoughts prove indecipherable to you, then I should

hope you at least know my heart by now," Iona says. "Mere… attraction is nothing. I find women in paintings attractive. I found Professor Salvador attractive." At that Ariadne glowers, and it only angers Iona more. "That does not signify a real intention of pursuing those desires. Look through the bond and see for yourself."

Worrying at her bottom lip, Ariadne eventually nods as she enters Iona's mind to behold the full account of her conversation with Rebekka. A moment later, Ariadne's expression betrays her regret.

"It was one comment. That is all," Iona says, stepping closer to her. "She flirts with any woman in her path, it seems."

"I just… I know how convincing Rebekka can be when she sets her sights on someone," Ariadne says.

"Yes, I'm sure you are quite familiar with her techniques," Iona says sardonically.

Ariadne crimsons. "Don't jest."

"I wasn't," Iona stares her down, taking unexpected pleasure in how flustered she has become.

"Then why did you withdraw from my touch in the ballroom?" Ariadne asks. "You pulled away from me when… It will only encourage her if you imply a distance between us that-"

Iona clasps her fingers around Ariadne's wrist. The very moment their skin touches, Ariadne goes rigid, inhaling sharply, her eyes squeezing shut. Iona centers all their energy, all the frisson of their magnetism, until Ariadne sinks to her knees before her, the pretty moan escaping her lips nearly enough to break Iona's resolve.

"I pulled away because you were accosting me with our magic until I could hardly think straight!" Iona cries. "You're such a jealous fool, you did not even notice!"

She leans in closer, so their noses nearly touch and watches Ariadne as she gasps for air.

"Now tell me, why would I want her, or anyone else, when I can do this to you?" Iona asks, her voice mockingly sweet.

"Iona," Ariadne whimpers.

"Why? When I have already given you my heart, soul, and body?" Iona asks. "What more must I do to prove my undying devotion?"

Ariadne trembles as need courses through her, nearly unbearable for them both, but Iona's obstinance keeps her mind clear.

"Apologize for dishonoring me with your baseless insinuations," Iona demands.

"I apologize," Ariadne's voice cracks.

"Do you mean it?" Iona asks.

Ariadne can only nod, but when she tries to pull her in for a desperate kiss, Iona releases her wrist and steps away. Ariadne's hands smack against the stone floor, her chest heaving.

"I suppose I can forgive your impudence," Iona says.

Ariadne looks up at her with such a vulnerable, incredulous expression, that Iona cannot help the haughty chuckle that slips past her lips. Then Ariadne uses her staff to push herself up on shaky legs.

"Now, with that settled, shall we return to the party, darling?" Iona asks.

Before she can reach the door, Ariadne captures her lips in a possessive, all-consuming kiss, coaxing her mouth open to slip her tongue inside and draw out a moan. Before she can give into the temptation, Iona laces her fingers in Ariadne's curls and tugs just enough for her to pull away. Iona peeks into her mind and shivers at what she finds there.

"Control yourself," she whispers. "What do you mean to do? Pin me down and ravage me, make me scream loud enough for Rebekka to hear and know who I belong to?"

Ariadne groans low in her throat. That is precisely what she wants, the image of it at the very forefront of her salacious thoughts.

"How positively primeval," Iona rasps. "Perhaps if you had not made such hurtful assumptions, I might have indulged you. But now? I think not."

A thrill goes through her at knowing the power she holds, that they both hold over each other.

"I cannot go back out there," Ariadne says, and it is simultaneously a wanton plea and a doleful one.

Iona searches her gaze, then backs her against the closest wall, pressing up against her to keep her in place, leaning in to kiss her neck until Ariadne sighs contentedly.

"I shouldn't have…" Ariadne stops when Iona nips at her throat to silence her.

She caresses Ariadne's curves, tracing the seams and boning of her corset beneath the silk of her gown, marking every sharp intake of breath.

"Lift up your skirts," Iona demands, pulling away only slightly so she can hold Ariadne's gaze.

She considers it, her eyes darkening to a deep, transfixing red, until she reaches down to pull up the fabric to her waist, revealing her white stockings, red garters, the soft olive skin of her thighs, and the patch of black curls between her legs.

Iona squints, then reaches down to pull at the bow of one of the garters, slipping it off and bringing it up to her eyes. Her and Ariadne's initials are embroidered into the strip of silk, with delicate white flowers surrounding the filigreed letters.

"Surely Euphemia did not…" Iona looks up at her, recalling that Euphemia had been the one to dress Ariadne in her gown for the evening.

"No, of course not," Ariadne says, flushing at the thought. "I… conjured them later."

"Was it for Rebekka's benefit or mine?" Iona raises an eyebrow.

"Yours, of course!" Ariadne becomes so flustered that Iona has to fight to keep a straight face. "I've… I'm surprised you've not noticed those earlier. It's not the first time I've worn them."

Iona wraps the silk garter around the palm of her left hand, and Ariadne follows the movement, transfixed.

"I'm often distracted by the time I get to your stockings," Iona admits. "I truly admire your penchant for thoughtful details. Ever the aesthete."

She holds out her hand, which Ariadne takes to help her keep balance as she goes down onto her knees. From that vantage point, flanked by each of Ariadne's long legs, her glistening sex is bared to Iona's gaze. Her mouth waters.

"Someone may walk in," Ariadne says half-heartedly, regarding her with hungry, pleading eyes.

"Then kindly tell them to leave," Iona says. "My mouth will be otherwise occupied."

With that she lifts herself up to meet Ariadne's pink cunt and wraps her lips around her pulsing flesh, feeling the slight patter of a quickening pulse against her tongue, and eliciting a fevered moan.

Ariadne gasps when she suckles in earnest, the sound getting caught in her throat when she tries so hard to stifle it and fails. Lapping at her, tracing her lightly with her tongue, Iona revels in her abandon.

The smallest reactions are what Iona craves, a moan or squirm to betray her beloved's unending lust. Ariadne isn't one to beg whilst in the throes of passion, but her sounds, the little sighs and sharp inhales made despite her attempts to stifle them, the sudden tension of her muscles beneath her silken skin, are more than enough to fill Iona with unparalleled satisfaction.

Ariadne keeps one hand bunched in her skirts to keep them raised and laces the fingers of her other hand into Iona's hair to keep her in place, her fingers clenching ever so slightly when Iona sucks with increasing force, until Ariadne's knees threaten to buckle.

In the back of her mind, Iona decides she wouldn't mind if Rebekka happened to pass by the door and recognize Ariadne's strangled moans, her wanton gasps, as she draws Ariadne's pleasure higher and higher with every stroke of her tongue. Let Rebekka be overcome with burning regret and envy at knowing she will never touch Ariadne again, will never touch Iona even once, and she is all the poorer for it.

"Nymph," Ariadne grits out, and while her mouth remains open, Iona slides two fingers inside her and crooks them, stimulating that spot inside that drives her wild.

Ariadne cries out, louder than she usually allows herself, and Iona's cheeks heat at the wonderful sound. Wanting to hear it again, she removes her fingers and slips her tongue inside, licking languidly, teasing the textured knot of nerves-

"Iona," Ariadne moans again, her hips undulating of their own accord as she loses herself.

She comes undone with a rush of wetness that drips down Iona's chin, her legs trembling as she struggles to keep from collapsing. Iona doesn't let up until Ariadne pushes at her shoulders to stop, and she looks up to find Ariadne's mouth agape, her eyes shut tight, the prettiest of pink flushes on her cheeks.

Iona pushes herself back to her feet and waits a moment, giving Ariadne time to recover. When she does, she remembers herself and quickly releases her hold on her skirts, her iron grip on them leaving wrinkles that she attempts to smooth out with trembling hands.

Iona wipes the wetness from her chin with the back of her hand and takes slow steps towards her.

"I would never betray you." Iona grasps her chin and forces her to lock eyes. "I love you. Only you. Did you forget?"

"No," Ariadne says immediately. "I… I am sorry. I don't know what came over me."

Iona caresses her cheek and searches her gaze for insight. "You haven't been yourself since we arrived in France. What is weighing on you?"

"I hate these parties," Ariadne says with sudden fiery vehemence. "I can feel them all watching me. It makes my skin crawl. I once drowned myself in wine to dull the perception of their stares."

Taken aback, Iona asks, "Why ever would you attend these gatherings at all if you hate them so?"

"I never had the choice," she says. "Or... for a time I did frequent Euphemia's balls, but in those days, she protected me and made them almost enjoyable, controlled, safe. Later, when I courted... Elise," she frowns, "I was told where to go and with whom. Samaira and Euphemia attempted to safeguard me, but Moira was always there to keep watch, and Elise followed my every step like a stray dog begging for scraps."

Ariadne winces, fearing she might have spoken out of turn, but Iona schools her features, not wanting her to stop when she so rarely speaks of her past.

"It was difficult to evade her, though Rebekka often found ways to steal me away." At that, a small smile curves her mouth, but it fades all too soon.

Her lip quivers before she manages to stifle her emotions again, hiding them away where only Iona can glimpse shadows of them within the vast confines of her troubled mind.

"We may leave if you wish," Iona says, glancing at the staff where it rests leaning against the wall. "We always could have, if you truly wanted to."

Ariadne considers it, then reluctantly shakes her head no.

"Euphemia asked after you," Ariadne says. "We should stay a while longer, or she might take offense."

"I very much doubt she would scorn us for retiring early. Her earlier protests were not made in earnest," Iona says, but when Ariadne doesn't respond, she sighs, "Alright, but after I speak with her, I think it's best we depart."

Ariadne's shoulders visibly relax. "Agreed."

Satisfied that she'd both made her point and quelled Ariadne's anxieties, she takes the garter still wrapped around her palm, and unravels it, and hands it back to Ariadne. Then she pulls up her own skirt, and Ariadne's eyes glaze over. Pulling at the ribbon holding her blue garter in place, it disappears the moment it's unfastened. Then she looks at Ariadne expectantly.

A small smile tugs at Ariadne's mouth when she wraps her garter around Iona's thigh, tying it with a tight bow. Her fingers linger there, then try to sneak up higher along her inner thigh, but Iona grasps her wrist and guides it away, letting her skirts fall.

"We shouldn't be gone too long, or there will be talk," Iona says, and Ariadne sighs with disappointment.

"Are you still angry with me?" she asks in a small voice.

"No, I am annoyed at Rebekka for her lack of decorum," Iona says. "You are in desperate need of better friends."

Ariadne's smile is humorless. "Yes, but… are you still cross about Samaira and the ring?"

"No, I never was," Iona says, scrutinizing her face. "Did you think that I was?"

Ariadne shrugs and keeps her eyes down, and Iona sighs. Even with their joined minds, it seems they are not beyond miscomprehension. She cups Ariadne's face in her hands, gently running her thumbs over her cheeks, still warm from taking the pleasure Iona had given her.

"We shall have disagreements. That is only natural," Iona says. "For us especially."

Ariadne chuckles darkly, "Yes, I suppose you're right."

"We will trust each other. We will protect each other. We will be loyal," Iona says.

Ariadne smiles at the memory of their vows to each other while in the hot springs on Samhain. She leans in and takes a tender, gentle kiss.

"You are mine," Ariadne says against her mouth.

"For all eternity," Iona agrees. "Act accordingly, or I shall see fit to remind you."

Ariadne takes residence at the pianoforte while Iona lounges nearby with Euphemia and Samaira. She learns that Euphemia's dove is named Frida and she'd found her in the forest just outside her family's manor. The beautiful bird sings joyful tunes and harmonizes with Ariadne's melodies.

Crescentia is nowhere to be found, and when Iona asks after her, Euphemia whispers that she'd found a handsome gentleman and disappeared upstairs. They dissolve into a fit of giggles.

Rebekka seems entirely oblivious to the turmoil she'd nearly caused. She's redirected her attentions to a strikingly beautiful woman with coal black skin and dimples. As they laugh together in the corner, so enraptured by each other's beauty, Iona cannot help glancing at them in annoyance.

Rebekka's comment had been pointed but not necessarily

vulgar. Perhaps it had only been meant as a clumsy compliment, or she is only capable of speaking in flirtatious quips that have no real meaning behind them. Iona doesn't know for certain, but as she watches Rebekka enamor her new target, it appears that such empty flirtations are just that. Even so, Iona is permanently wary of the woman. She decides to keep her distance, for the sake of Ariadne's nerves as well as her own.

With a yawn and arching stretch, Wisp curls up against an already sleeping Aster and lays down her head against the tufted chaise they've commandeered. Iona yawns, too, and searches for a clock, knowing that it must be quite late, but the party is still in full swing. She does not want to keep Ariadne waiting much longer, though she appears quite patient where she sits, bathed in candlelight.

"What is it that you wished to discuss with me?" Iona asks.

"Hmm?" Euphemia frowns, then her eyes widen in remembrance. "Oh! I had hoped to discuss your plans for the impending solstice, namely the reception."

"Reception?" Iona asks.

"Yes." Euphemia furrows her brow. "Did Ariadne not tell you? For such grand rites as these, there is always a ball held thereafter."

"Oh…" Iona grimaces. "I hadn't thought of it. I wasn't aware-"

"Oh, but you must arrange a ball! It's expected," Euphemia says.

"I… We have no manor to hold a grand party," Iona stutters.

"Leave it to me," Euphemia says.

Taken aback, Iona shakes her head. "I would not wish to impose upon you and-"

"Nonsense! I absolutely adore parties," Euphemia says with a wide grin. "Hosting is one of my talents, and I've long been searching for an excuse to unveil my new ballroom. I've taken residence in my family's old estate, and we've recently finished our renovations. My Leonid has indulged my every wish, and I am quite proud of his handiwork. And after all, us Swedes are quite prolific at Midsummer festivities. We have a rich history of it. You concern yourself with your ritual, and I shall handle the rest."

"Alright… If you're sure," Iona says, unable to keep from smiling at her enthusiasm.

"Quite sure. Consider it my first gift to you in what I truly hope will be a long friendship," Euphemia says. "Tomorrow I shall draw up the invitations, have them sent by noon, and begin the decorations, and… Oh, I have so much to do!"

"Of course, I shall assist however I can," Iona assures her.

"You are too kind," Euphemia says, as if it is Iona extending the favor and not the other way round. "And it is the perfect occasion for you and Ariadne to meet my Leonid, of whom I may never have had the good fortune to court without Ariadne's intervention."

Euphemia chuckles and takes another swig of wine. Iona glances at the pianoforte, but Ariadne's eyes are cast down as she concentrates on her playing, oblivious to their conversation.

"She truly did not speak to you for nine months?" Iona asks in a low voice.

Euphemia's smile falters and she glances at the piano as well, then scrutinizes Iona's face before responding. "Longer than that. She did not attend my wedding. She did not visit me after Hugo was born. For a time, she did not even respond to my letters, though I still sent them anyhow."

"But why?" Iona asks.

Euphemia shrugs and attempts nonchalance. "Ari is a troubled soul. I try not to take such things personally."

Frida nestles against Euphemia's neck, and she smiles, running her finger against the dove's feathered cheek.

"But you are one of her closest friends," Iona says, her brow furrowing in confusion.

She cannot fathom why anyone would avoid such a kind, gentle soul. Though she's only known Euphemia for a day, she feels as if she could trust her implicitly.

"And I will always be a friend to her if she needs me, but I will not make a nuisance of myself. I watched over her from afar and waited," Euphemia says. "She still spoke to Samaira on occasion, and to Ksenia often, and they assured me of her wellbeing when I asked."

"Ksenia was a spy for Ariadne's mother," Iona says with great bitterness.

"I am not surprised to hear it," Euphemia's sapphire eyes darken. "I was not pleased when I learned of her snaking her way into Ariadne's good graces but knew it would only last for a time. It's just as it has been between The Ulanova and Zerynthos families for generations. If they were not allies, they would certainly be enemies. Ksenia and I were only acquaintances of convenience, her being Leonid's cousin and all."

"But why would she trust Ksenia in the first place, when she had you?" Iona asks, her insistence wearing down Euphemia's discretion.

"You may know Ariadne's thoughts better than I, being bonded with her." Unfurling her fan, Euphemia leans in close to whisper in her ear. "I suspect she was preparing herself for the days ahead. She was trapped by her family's expectations, and though I tried as I might to provide her the illusion of liberation, it was never enough. As she withdrew from me, she grew closer to Ksenia. Samaira would not let her go, even when she embraced cruelty. I credit Samaira for it. I could not stand to be around Ari when she became the shadow of herself."

Iona's heart constricts as she remembers how Ariadne was then. Overcome with anger and lacking any capacity for patience. Filled with impulsive aggression and no tenderness. All symptoms of her innermost pain.

"Her Goddess' silence... it tormented her, though she would never admit it. She hardly ever spoke of it and never in detail. If any of us ever dared to raise the subject, she would immediately withdraw into herself and vanish," Euphemia says. "When we left in search of Rebekka earlier, Ariadne told me of Moira's terrible game. She did not finish her full account of the ambush before she hurled herself through that portal." Euphemia lets out a wry chuckle. "But I can only imagine how upsetting that must have been for you."

"It was an awful way for the truth to come out," Iona says. "I wish Ariadne had seen fit to tell me of her own volition."

Pursing her lips, Euphemia glances yet again at Ariadne where she plays in the corner.

"May I make an observation?" Euphemia asks, and when Iona nods, she takes a moment to gather her thoughts before saying, "Ariadne has never been trusting with anyone, except perhaps Samaira. She craves affection with such intensity, but she is also terrified of it. I am frankly shocked she bonded with you at all, and it shows immense growth on her part, but she cannot be expected to transform overnight. She may always have a fear of vulnerability, one that she must shed away. In the interim, I beg you be patient with her."

"Of course," Iona says, and Euphemia takes her hand.

"I only wish for her happiness," she says. "Her mother... That insufferable hag."

Iona grits her teeth, a bought of anger making her skin hot. "Quite the understatement."

"Indeed. When I first found Ariadne in my woods, when we were children, she was a heart-stricken, skinny wretch. She had clearly been…" Euphemia averts her gaze, and to Iona's dismay, she appears to be holding back tears. "She had been harmed in some way. She cowered when I reached for her, as if she thought…"

Taking her lace fan, Euphemia snaps it open and flutters it beneath her chin in agitation.

"When one endures unimaginable cruelty, it leaves scars, both physical and mental," she says. "Magic can take the physical away, but there's naught to be done for the mental ones except to heal however one can, and that takes time."

"I understand," Iona says.

"Do you?" Euphemia asks with a penetrating stare. "I truly hope so."

"Iona Evora?"

They look up to address a red-haired man wearing a simple black suit. Looking to be no older than forty years of age, his smile is far too tense to reflect sincerity.

"I am she," Iona says.

The man bows low and says, "Good evening. I am very pleased to make your acquaintance."

Glancing sideways at Euphemia, Iona stands, curtsies, and offers her hand.

"Silvano Evora," he says, taking her offered hand and kissing it.

"Evora?" Iona's eyes widen.

"Oh, how lovely! Were you not in search of your kin, Iona?" Euphemia asks.

"Yes…" Iona says, trying to gauge the man's intentions, but he only smiles.

"Please sit!" Euphemia offers, pointing to an empty chair with her fan.

"If I may," he looks to Iona for approval, and she reluctantly nods, suddenly wishing Ariadne were sitting beside her, but not wanting her to scare the man off before she can manage to discover his true purpose here.

"My condolences for your loss, sir," Iona says.

Silvano lowers his head a moment, then says, "It was an awful shock. The funeral will be held next week if you… if you'd like to attend."

"I would be honored," Iona says, though she isn't sure if Gonçalo Evora would have welcomed her to his funeral, given the unfortunate nature of their first meeting. A twinge of discomfort makes her grimace at the thought of him visiting on Samhain to hear yet another plea for her intervention on his family's behalf. She hopes he will know such a meeting would be futile.

"He would have wanted you there," he says, reading the uncertainty in her expression.

"I'm not so sure of that. We did not become acquainted under the best of circumstances," Iona says honestly. "However, Jacira held a service for him-"

"Jacira did?" His tone is clipped with distaste.

"Yes..." Iona says, giving Euphemia a furtive glance.

She deftly intervenes. "I've only ever visited Brazil once on holiday, and I must say it is the most beautiful of places. The landscape alone is breathtaking and-"

"You've allied yourself with the likes of her?" Silvano interrupts, pinning Iona with an accusatory stare.

"I've not..." Iona sighs. "I do not wish to insert myself into generational grievances. Jacira has been most kind to me, and has explained the history of-"

"I highly doubt she told you everything, or you would have come home with Father when he called on you," he says, his restrained bitterness slipping into his tone. "Perhaps if you had, he would not have been left alone to be ruthlessly slain."

Iona's jaw drops, and Euphemia takes her hand, grasping it tightly.

"If you only came here to hurl insults at my friend, you may take your leave, sir," Euphemia says, an uncharacteristic coldness in her voice.

"You would turn your back on your own family?" Silvano asks.

"I've done nothing of the sort!" Iona protests.

"By withholding your power, you effectively have," he sets his jaw and stands. "My sister's impertinence seems to have been passed down to you."

"I will not take part in conquest on anyone's behalf, family or no," Iona says firmly. "Please take your leave, sir, or I shall call upon my partner to ensure your swift departure."

Silvano's eyes reflect a trace of fear at the mention of Ariadne, but not enough to deter him. If anything, it only incites his anger as he sheds what's left of his polite facade.

"I shan't be dismissed by the likes of you," he stands taller, peering down at her with an imperious air.

"I beg your pardon," Euphemia stands before Iona can hold her back. "But you could find no woman more worth your respect in this room, and you shall treat her as such."

"Euphemia," Iona tries to placate her.

"Her mother was a scourge upon our family! She was a whore and a coward," Silvano's voice grows louder. "The Lysanders cast us out into the street once Leona stole away their heir! They were appalled and rightly so."

Iona schools her features, though inside she is reeling at finally know the true reason the Lysanders did not aid their grandfather in his conquest. She had suspected it, but now she knows for certain.

"They were in love," Iona says.

"And look where that got them," he scoffs. "The Evoras should have their place in the ranks of sempiterna families, but because of my wretched sister, we have only a fraction of the magic we may have claimed. That which we are owed by birth. We may never recover the loss, not for generations."

Iona's brow furrows as she scrutinizes her uncle, the jewels on his fingers and the fine silk of his suit.

"You are hardly living in squalor," Iona observes, earning light chuckles from their observers.

Silvano turns red with anger and embarrassment. "We… That is not the point! That land is ours by right."

"My grandfather's obsession was shameful. To cast his own mother into purgatory… all for the sake of rapacious greed," Iona says. "You had best abandon this vendetta or you too shall find yourself equally disappointed by a life wasted in discontent."

"Do you presume to tell us where we should or should not be?" Silvano asks. "You are just another tyrant deciding on a whim who will rise and who will fall. No different than Katrin Zerynthos."

"I am nothing like her," Iona protests, the comparison frightening her.

Silvano turns to address the crowd, who have all gone silent to watch the spectacle of their argument. "Are we now meant to blindly abide the illicit offspring of a fallen witch and disgraced warlock? All because of a trinket hanging from her neck?"

"Yes," Moira says, a simple syllable spoken with calm authority.

Silvano pauses in his rant, confusion and outrage at war in his expression, as Moira saunters over to them, lazy and unbothered, her red silk dress draped on her like a second skin. She holds a gold rimmed wine glass in one hand and her wand in the other.

"You would defend the woman who stole your family's inheritance?" Silvano asks incredulously.

"Indeed, I shall," Moira says.

She's tall enough to meet Silvano's height, but to his credit, he does not stand down.

"Iona is chosen by Morgan herself. Who are you to question her judgement?" Moira asks.

"I will not accept-"

Moira flings her glass against the closest wall. It crashes into a burst of shards, spilling red wine everywhere, and earning gasps from their audience. Silvano does not dare to finish his sentence.

"Iona is Morgan's champion," Moira repeats. "She is only entitled to your respect. Apologize."

Silvano's mouth falls open in indignation. He goes to argue, but Moira puts up a finger to stop him.

"I am having quite a lovely evening. Do not ruin it for us both," Moira says, the threat lingering between them. "Apologize."

"That is not necessary," Iona says in a small voice.

"Iona." Moira shakes her head with disapproval.

She hugs her chest and holds her tongue as the silence drags on. Silvano holds Moira's unwavering stare, but not without effort. Moira's lips twitch as she taps her wand against her chin while she waits. A snake rattling its tail.

Iona jumps at the feeling of Ariadne's hand slipping into hers and is instantly comforted by her proximity. When Iona looks up at her, she appears just as surprised by Moira's presence and her intervention.

"I apologize for my outburst," Silvano says through gritted teeth.

Moira looks to Iona expectantly.

"I... I accept your apology," Iona says, her eyes flitting between them.

"There now," Moira says, pocketing her wand. "No harm done."

Silvano storms out of the room. There is the distant echo of his heavy footfalls, then the slam of a door as he leaves.

"Oh dear..." Euphemia says softly.

"It would not be a party without a quarrel or two," Rebekka

says with a nervous laugh. "Carry on, everyone."

The other party goers whisper amongst themselves as Rebekka approaches them.

"Are you alright?" she asks.

Iona blinks up at her, then says, "Yes."

Rebekka's eyes narrow imperceptibly. "Are you certain? I can-"

"She said she is fine," Ariadne says cooly.

Before Rebekka can respond, Ariadne ushers Iona away to where Moira sips from a new wine glass.

"Good evening, lovelies," Moira says.

"What are you doing here?" Ariadne asks.

"Defending Iona in your stead," Moira says.

"I did not need defending," Iona says.

"If you say so," Moira shrugs.

"It was not for you to insert yourself into my family's affairs." Iona sighs. "I doubt he will ever deign to speak with me again."

"Good riddance, I say," Moira says.

Iona huffs angrily. Of course she agrees, but it is not for Moira to decide. Jacira had claimed that others in their family were not so inclined to engage in conquest, but now, after being so publicly humiliated, she imagines Silvano will denigrate her to any of them who will listen.

"I know you were not invited here," Ariadne says. "Are you following us?"

Moira reaches out to pinch Ariadne's cheek. "Look at how observant you've become. I remember when your eyes were once permanently glued to the floor."

Ariadne squirms away from her and Iona's patience runs out.

"You're a damned hypocrite to preach the supposed respect I deserve while treating us with such insolent disregard," Iona says.

"My respect for Hecate surpasses all others. You have yet to earn mine." Moira gestures to the whispering crowd behind them. "Or theirs."

Iona glares at her, and Moira's infuriating smile returns.

"Anyhow, I do have a message to impart," Moira says. "I've come to invite you both to dine with us in Rome."

"Us?" Ariadne asks.

"All of us," Moira says. "The Zerynthos coven. Tomorrow at your father's villa."

Iona watches Ariadne's face, which has turned to stone. Part of her wishes Ariadne will rage at Moira for even suggesting such a thing, but another part is overwhelmingly curious as to why such an invitation came to be. Whatever Moira might claim, there is nothing spontaneous about any of this. There is something more.

"But... I am not welcome," Ariadne says. "Mother said as much when she visited me at college. If I didn't claim the pendant-"

"Do not worry about your mother," Moira reassures her. "My mother spoke with her."

Ariadne's skepticism is palpable. Moira rolls her eyes.

"Must you always be so gloomy?" Moira asks. "Do not forget who leads the Zerynthos coven. It is not Cintia Zerynthos, nor will it ever be."

"She won't take kindly to being undermined," Ariadne says.

"Oh, you should have heard her screams. It was quite an impressive tantrum." Moira chuckles. "Like mother, like daughter."

"And what of Grandmother's wish to exile me?" Ariadne asks, ignoring the barb.

At that, Moira's eyes darken, and she does not immediately respond. "My mother spoke with her also. The family agrees that exile would be rash. Fate did not intend for our family to keep the pendant, and we must accept that reality with grace."

"And I suppose this has nothing at all to do with Hecate?" Ariadne asks.

"I do not know if she consumes food beyond ambrosia and nectar." Moira's brow furrows as she pretends to consider it. "Nevertheless, she will not be dining with us, if that is what you're asking."

"I wasn't-" Ariadne sighs heavily. "Why then have we been invited?"

Moira's gaze flickers to Iona, then back to Ariadne. "Why not ask my mother yourself tomorrow? I am sure she would be happy to answer all your many inane questions."

And with that, Moira turns and walks away.

"Wait!" Ariadne calls after her. "We did not say we would accept."

"A dinner will be served regardless," Moira calls over her shoulder. "I hope to see you there. It shall be great fun indeed."

# 9 - Ariadne

Devising another lesson in combative magic is a most welcome distraction, but even that is not enough to quell her worrisome thoughts. She doesn't wish to consider the dinner invitation yet, or really at all. She'd prefer to pretend it was never extended, that it was all an awful dream, and her family still hates her, as she'd expected them to.

*You were conceived for one singular purpose: to serve your bloodline and its interests. Without that purpose, you are worthless.* Her mother's words repeat endlessly within her fretful mind.

"Ari!" Iona protests when she's accosted by yet another wave of faceless assailants, their attacks becoming more aggressive in reaction to Ariadne's tumultuous thoughts.

"Fight harder!" Ariadne calls from the stands of the gladiatorial arena she's crafted in the center of the secluded valley.

Iona huffs and makes her best effort at defeating each attacker, but her spells are almost always defensive. She often hesitates, as if she's afraid of harming the men, despite knowing they aren't real, and she avoids their attacks out of fear, not survival.

Ariadne sighs and takes her water goblet, beckoning Aster to follow her down the stairs to the arena of clay and sand. Iona is covered in it, her black trousers and white shirt stained red from falling down countless times.

"Can I not rest a moment?" Iona asks, then yelps when an illusory man charges at her.

"I am not sure how to teach you," Ariadne admits.

"Whatever do you mean?" Iona asks, trying to study her face, but she's distracted by another attacker wielding a sword. She opens up the ground and lets it swallow the attacker whole.

"Your first impulse when threatened is to panic and cower," Ariadne observes. "You do not fight on instinct."

Taking pity on her, Ariadne ceases her barrage of illusory men and allows Iona a moment to rest.

"Of course not," she pants. "I am not like you."

Ariadne turns away, trying not to take her words as an insult.

She is ever the brute, the violent aggressor with no capacity for restraint.

"No, that is not what I meant," Iona protests.

"What then did you mean?" Ariadne snaps, resenting her thoughts being read.

"I am not... strong in that way. I never was. Not like you are," Iona says.

"You must be," Ariadne says.

When Iona doesn't respond, Ariadne turns to behold her dejected expression.

She hesitates, than says, "I cannot change my nature. I will fight when I must, but there are many other ways to prevail in times of trouble."

"Not with maleficians," Ariadne says.

Iona has no answer to that and absentmindedly kicks a loose stone with her foot.

"You've fought with me before, and with Ksenia and Elise," Ariadne points out.

"I was blinded by rage," Iona says, wringing her hands. "I wasn't in my right mind when I did those things. Especially with Elise."

"Then I need you angry," Ariadne muses.

"That is not an invitation to provoke my worst impulses," she warns.

"And why ever not?" Ariadne cocks her head playfully. "I've quite a talent for it."

Iona eyes her warily, but a smile tugs at her lips. "I shan't be baited into quarreling with you."

"I suspect you avoid dueling with me because you know you would certainly lose," Ariadne says.

Iona frowns. "That's not so certain."

"Isn't it?" Ariadne raises an eyebrow. "I suppose we shall never know."

"And I suspect you are so set on dueling me so you might flaunt your spell work and stoke your ego at my expense," Iona retorts.

"Then you admit, I would easily best you?"

"I admit nothing! I am merely saying-"

"You needn't worry. I know how delicate you are and wouldn't wish to discourage you too terribly."

Iona scoffs in annoyance and Ariadne widens her stance, daring her to cast a spell.

"Have you forgotten that I can read your mind?" Iona asks. "I know what you aim to do, and it shan't work."

"Then I suppose we can instead determine my lust for you outweighs yours for me." Ariadne shrugs, feigning offense. "For if our roles were reversed, I would brave a hellscape of trials just for one taste of you."

Iona's cheeks bloom. "Honestly, why must you provoke me so?"

"Why must you be such a bore?" Ariadne sighs melodramatically and turns to walk away. "If I-"

She screams when a cascade of ice-cold water falls from above and drenches her to the bone. When she turns back to protest, Iona has her arms crossed and glares with indignation.

"You bore me with your incessant nagging," Iona retorts.

Wiping water from her eyes, Ariadne shivers. "That was freezing!"

"Who is delicate now?" Iona goads her. "A bit of cold and you fall to pieces."

But Ariadne notices the water spreading across the dirt, collecting at Iona's feet, so she turns it to ice. Iona slips within seconds and falls on her bottom before Ariadne can catch her, and to Iona's further irritation, she cannot help laughing.

It's to her own detriment though, because in her distraction, Iona casts another spell that shrinks her down to the size of a cat before she can bring up her shield.

"No shrinking spells!" Ariadne protests, holding up her shirt as it becomes a dress pooling around her shrunken form.

"A bit late to set rules," Iona says. "But if we are, I say your shield is cheating."

Ariadne manages to recover her natural height and readjusts her clothing before glowering at Iona, who by that time has rid the ground of ice and stands on her feet again, waiting expectantly.

"Fine, no shield," Ariadne acquiesces, letting it fall away.

Less than a second later, the ground within the confines of the arena trembles, then explodes with the growth of hundreds of trees stretching up towards the sky, their branches snapping and trunks groaning as they climb, the thick canopy of leaves blocking out the sun.

Aster cowers, barking in distress until the growth ceases and all at once, there is silence. Ariadne gapes at the show of power, her heart racing in her chest, when she notices that Iona has disappeared.

At first, she considers it all could be illusion magic, but when she reaches out to touch the bark of a nearby tree, she winces when she gives herself a splinter. Pulling the thin shard of wood from her forefinger, the tiny wound produces a single drop of blood. It's then she knows it must be real, for Iona would never give her even the illusion of pain.

"Iona?" she calls, trudging through the new forest. "Who is flaunting their power now?"

A distant giggle makes her whirl about, but there is nothing but green leaves and hanging vines.

"Find her," Ariadne whispers to Aster, who puts his nose to the ground, sniffing furiously to seek out Iona's scent.

She follows behind her familiar, ready to cast a spell at a moment's notice, but the lush greenery is too impressive to ignore. It's yet another reminder of the disparity between their artifacts. The staff could perhaps evoke half of the trees needed to cover the arena, but never this many. If only Iona could channel this power into defeating her enemies, it would ensure that no one could ever harm her.

"Iona?" Ariadne calls out again, wondering if she might be sitting in one of the many arena seats and laughing as she watches Ariadne wandering about aimlessly.

"Yes?" Iona whispers in her ear, and Ariadne cries out in surprise, but when she turns to look, no one is there.

"This isn't exactly a duel if you refuse to face me!" Ariadne calls, and Iona's responding giggle echoes in yet another direction, making Ariadne turn in a circle, searching for any footprints or disturbance in the leaves that might indicate where the invisible Iona has gone.

She considers how best to proceed. She could start cutting down trees to clear the area, but she fears one of them might fall onto Iona. She considers using fire but would risk the same issue. She looks up at the thick branches, wondering if she could break through them with conjured wings, but she could never spot Iona from up there.

A length of vines descends upon her, swirling around her torso, her arms, her legs, hoisting her aloft and lacing its tendrils around the staff to pull it from her grip before she can react.

"Hey!" Ariadne protests, trying to wrench her wrists free, but she's well and truly bound.

"My, my, what's this?" Iona reveals herself and grins up at her. "I've caught a Zerynthos witch unawares. Whatever shall I do with her now?"

Ariadne's struggles and writhes but the vines won't budge,

and the staff hangs high above, out of her reach. She grunts with frustration.

"Admit defeat," Iona demands.

"I can still…" Ariadne kicks her legs in vain, the faintest of ideas emerging.

But when Iona's gaze locks on hers, her attempts at escape become halfhearted. Those hazel eyes transfix her, entrance her, the flecks of gold glittering with mischief and awakened desire.

"Will this insatiable lust never cease?" Iona whispers. "Every spare moment when my mind is allowed to wander, all I can think of is you…"

Ariadne chuckles, her core warming. "Then let me down, and I shall-"

"Of what I wish to do to you," Iona corrects her, then goes on her tiptoes to position her mouth so close, her warm breath caresses Ariadne's parted lips. "How I wish to kneel before you and let you use my mouth until you collapse."

All the breath leaves Ariadne's lungs at the promise in Iona's eyes, that she will do as she says if given the chance. She so often prioritizes Iona's pleasure, which is as much a pleasure to her, especially given their bond, but it seems to have only delayed Iona's hunger for her, which has turned ravenous indeed.

"Were you counting the men I defeated?" Iona asks, her eyes sparkle with glee.

"Um…" Ariadne inhales sharply when Iona presses a soft kiss just beneath her jaw.

"Five and thirty, by my count," she says. "And you, my dear, I count as three."

"Only three?" Ariadne asks, slightly offended.

"Five then," she giggles. "All the better, for I have surpassed your quota, and bested you, all in one day."

Ariadne bites her lip, realizing what this means.

"I've won my reward," Iona whispers against the skin of her neck.

It's all Ariadne can do to keep from surrendering, from letting Iona have her way with her. She curses her relentless competitiveness when her hint of an idea takes form. She may not have her staff, but her wand is tucked away in her boot, and she can still cast small spells with only her mind, though it won't be easy.

"You haven't defeated me," Ariadne says, and with great concentration, she incites the growth of a thin vine that sprouts from Iona's preexisting stalk. She wills it to grow longer, and longer, using her ankle as a trellis.

Iona pulls away to glare up at her. "You are strung up and helpless! How could you claim otherwise?"

"If an enemy had you in this position, would you just keel over and let them kill you?" Ariadne tilts her head, the vine crawling at a snail's pace up the leather of her boot.

"No..." Iona pouts and crosses her arms. "But you are only delaying the inevitable. Hang there for the entire afternoon if you must. I shan't release you until you've admitted I've bested you."

Ariadne shrugs as best she can with her arms stretched out wide by the vines, and Iona rolls her eyes.

"Fine, cling to your pride if you must," Iona says. "But I shan't be deprived of my spoils."

Ariadne's next words are silenced by Iona's kiss, a kiss clearly meant to disarm. Iona sucks on her bottom lip, tugging it between her teeth only to release it, then lick at her top lip. When Ariadne opens her mouth, Iona slips her tongue inside, sliding it against Ariadne's with slow, calculated strokes, until her brain empties.

The vine she'd been coaxing up her ankle goes limp, falling back to the ground, and she admonishes herself for all her effort lost. She tries splitting her attention in two, unable to resist Iona's fervent kisses, but unwilling to abandon her attempts at retrieving her wand.

Iona only makes it worse by reaching up to cup Ariadne's cheeks, her featherlight touch drifting along her neck, to her breasts, her hips, until she slips a hand inside Ariadne's trousers. She moans despite herself, her vine withering away again after making it halfway up her calf.

"Your capacity for stubbornness can be admirable, but is this silly contest truly worth your deprivation?" Iona asks, sliding her fingers back and forth with agonizing slowness. "Or do you believe you are the only one of us capable of driving the other mad with want?"

Ariadne's inner muscles constrict at the threat in her words, wondering how long she could possibly last when Iona knows her body so well. She'd been fool enough to teach her and now suffers luxuriantly as Iona watches on with a gloating smile.

"I-" Ariadne clenches her jaw when Iona slips a finger inside her. "I shan't surrender."

"Are you certain?" Iona's grin widens as she pulses her

fingers, marking the unmistakable constriction of Ariadne's inner muscles as she fights against the sensation.

"I am not in so vulnerable a state as you insinuate," Ariadne protests, her vine finding its way up to her knee, mere moments from slipping inside her boot and twirling itself around her wand.

Iona raises an eyebrow, withdrawing her hand from Ariadne's trousers, and she tries to keep the disappointment from showing in her expression.

In a disorienting shift of equilibrium, the vines haul Ariadne to the ground of dry leaves and dense soil. Four vines keep a tight hold on her wrists and ankles, while the others proceed to rip her clothes to shreds until she is left in a very vulnerable position indeed.

"Iona," Ariadne chuckles with nervous anticipation. "I've yet to yield. You have no victory yet."

"Like hell I don't!" And she stomps her foot in frustration, which only makes Ariadne chuckle adoringly at her, stoking Iona's irritation. "I was most acquiescent to your whims when you declared yourself the winner."

"Well, submission is in your nature, love. Not mine," Ariadne retorts.

"Oh, spare me." Iona laughs and puts a hand on her hip.

Ariadne glowers at her. "My view of you is often from above, if you can recall. I would be more than happy to remind you."

Iona opens her mouth to respond, then seems to think better of it.

"What?" Ariadne prompts.

Iona takes her quite off guard when she says, "Are you honestly implying that Rebekka… "

Flushing with mortification, Ariadne strains her neck to give her an incredulous look. "Are you truly speaking of Rebekka while you have me-"

"I am only skeptical of your claim that-"

"Upon my word, I cannot believe-"

"In the library, I would not say Gisela and Nenet were simpering beneath you. They had you eating out of their hands," Iona continues. "Not that it matters much at all, except in principle."

Letting her head fall back, Ariadne huffs, her cheeks burning.

"Am I meant to assume you only refuse to submit to me?" Iona asks. "I would find that most unfair."

"You… have never wanted that before," Ariadne says.

143

"I want that now." Iona's pendant glows as her clothes fade away into nothing. She holds Ariadne's gaze unflinchingly. "And considering I have *earned* my victory-"

"Only when I yield," Ariadne says firmly.

A flash of something dangerous crosses Iona's eyes. "Is that so?"

Lamenting her choice of words, Ariadne holds her stare but does not respond.

Iona's wicked grin has her blood rushing south, watching intently as Iona comes to kneel between her spread legs. She sighs with frustration when Iona reaches for her boot and pulls it off. Her wand, her final instrument of escape, slides out and falls to the ground by Iona's knees.

"Ah," Iona grins. "I see now why you delayed."

She gathers her hair in her hands and twists the lustrous strands into a messy bun at the crown of her head, then takes the wand and weaves it through, securing her hair in place.

"Now, will you yield?" Iona asks.

"No," Ariadne shakes her head.

"Very well." Iona pulls off the other boot and tosses it to the side, the vines at Ariadne's ankles tightening and slithering so they wrap all the way up to her knees.

Her hands clench into fists when Iona reaches out to stroke her again where her wetness has gathered, a treacherous indication of her arousal despite her attempts at concentration. Then Iona crawls up her body, leaning in close so her breasts dangle only a breath away, her hardened nipples so close to Ariadne's mouth, but when she lifts her head to try and capture one between her lips, Iona pulls away with a haughty grin.

Her heartbeat quickens when Iona comes to straddle her, pressing their cunts together and grinding against her, causing ripples of pleasure with every swirl of her hips.

"Otvoren," Iona incants.

It's a spell Ariadne does not immediately recognize, but she quickly learns what it does when her mouth opens and can no longer close. No matter how she strains her jaw, her lips cannot meet and to her chagrin, her every reactionary sound is left unmuffled.

Iona pulls her hips away, and when she draws back down, it's one of those perfect, overwhelming strokes that has Ariadne squeezing her eyes shut, but when normally she could bite the inside of her cheek to keep from crying out, her moan is obscenely loud, making her blush with embarrassment.

Iona giggles breathily, her eyes flaring. "Do that again."

Ariadne tries to speak, but none of her words can take proper shape in her mouth before another moan is drawn from her, even louder than the first.

*That's… That's not fair.* Ariadne gasps, wanting her to go faster.

"I never agreed to play fair," Iona says. "Only to win, which *I have.*"

Ariadne grunts with indignation. She's unable to move, unable to thrust up from beneath as she tends to do, setting the pace, spurring Iona on until she loses control.

Willing herself to relax, she reminds herself that her objective remains the same, except now her wand will be slightly more difficult to acquire in its new position. She wonders if Iona's hair will unravel on its own, but she's made an impressive knot that withstands her undulations.

Iona is deftly composed as she gauges Ariadne's every reaction, employing an impressive amount of patience and attentiveness that proves lethal. Though Ariadne tries to keep her expression neutral, to hold back her vulgar moans, every time her muscles tense, her breath hitching compulsively, her legs pulling at the vines in an attempt to clench her thighs shut, Iona misses nothing.

She grips one of Ariadne's thighs as leverage while her other hand reaches up to caress Ariadne's breasts, pulling at one nipple, then the other, until she can't help but squirm, her sneaking vine going limp yet again before it can pull the wand from Iona's hair.

Ariadne sighs with frustration, which Iona mistakes for passion, her eyes blazing with desire. Her hips begin to piston almost aggressively, keeping a vigorous pace that has Ariadne crying out in a most undignified manner, betraying just how glorious it feels, until she's so close to falling apart that her thigh trembles beneath Iona's hand.

But before she can reach the precipice of her pleasure, Iona slows her hips, rolling them in smooth, gentle circles, and Ariadne lets out a heavy, shuddering breath. When she opens her eyes, Iona stares down at her, the sight making her stomach flip. Then the spell on her mouth fades, allowing her to speak.

"Yield," Iona says, her short pants undercutting her command.

"No," Ariadne says, but her voice breaks embarrassingly.

Trying again, she wills her vine to lift off the ground like the head of a python, reaching for the wand where it pokes out from Iona's bun.

"This will be a very long hour," Iona mutters, as much to herself as Ariadne, for she is just as desperate for release, if not more so.

The vine withers the moment Iona's hips move again in earnest, reducing her to a constrained mess of conflicting desires. She is so sensitive now, her heartbeat pulsing between her legs. She tries breathing through her nose, but it quickly proves impossible when Iona abruptly slows her movements yet again, ruining both of their pleasure mere moments before they can reach it.

"Iona," Ariadne grits out.

"Yield!"

"I will not-" She moans when Iona presses into her again, mercilessly, until she can no longer hide her state of exquisite torment. Gasping and pulling against her bindings, a sheen of sweat beads on her chest, her forehead, as she scrunches her eyes shut.

On a lark, she slips into Iona's thoughts, finding a mixture of enthusiastic fascination and acute frustration at the forefront, along with the hazy recollection of Ariadne whimpering on her knees at Rebekka's party. Seeing how she'd looked through Iona's eyes makes her cheeks heat, hating how helpless she'd been, but some small part of her loves it, too.

Iona knows well that she is the only one who can relieve the burning ache inside, can draw this out for hours and leave Ariadne wanting in the end. If Iona weren't so desperate herself, her little moans growing increasingly wanton, Ariadne may have feared that outcome. She leaves Iona's mind and puts on a provoking grin.

"Not so easy, depriving yourself, is it, nymph?" Ariadne asks. "Insatiable thing that you are."

Iona whimpers, her hips swiveling wildly, until she groans as she forces herself to slow yet again. "I can... I won't stop until you yield."

"I suspect you shall before I do," Ariadne mocks her, making her voice low and sensual.

Iona shakes her head stubbornly. Even Ariadne has never waited this long without letting her have her pleasure. When next Iona forces herself to draw back, she pants heavily, her cheeks flushed, then slumps her shoulders, and stops.

For a fleeting moment, Ariadne thinks she may have gotten to her, but Iona lifts her hips and flips herself around. Iona's cunt, glistening with her unmet desire, hovers above Ariadne's head, bared to her avaricious gaze.

She cries out at the first drag of Iona's tongue against her core, her inner muscles clenching deliciously, but a new sort of tantalization begins when she realizes that Iona has no intention of lowering her pelvis down, electing to keep her bottom raised high in the air, so that Ariadne can see her, but cannot touch or lick her.

"For fuck's sake," Ariadne mutters, painfully aware of how near she is to her breaking point.

*You taste divine.* Iona moans against her.

Ariadne strains against the vines, momentarily distracted when she realizes that they haven't withered one single time, while her meager vine is brown and shriveled on the forest floor.

Iona suckles and licks at her without recourse, her hardened nipples almost tickling as they drag against Ariadne's lower stomach. She looks down the length of Iona's freckled body, trying to avoid looking up, but when Ariadne does hazard a glance, her mouth goes dry.

Iona's arousal seeps from within her, a drop of it slipping from her folds and dripping down her inner thigh, leaving a glistening trail of wetness in its wake. Transfixed, Ariadne's eyes follow the droplet, overcome with the need to lick it up, just as Iona sucks her pulsing flesh deep into her mouth.

"I... I..." Ariadne gasps, so close it will take her seconds before she...

Iona withdraws, teasing her with soft kisses and tender licks, and Ariadne's exhalation is closer to a sob.

In a final, desperate attempt at pulling the wand free from Iona's hair, Ariadne's head begins to ache from the exertion, but no matter how hard she tries, she cannot position the vine at the right angle to latch on and pull the wand free. It's like threading a needle, but she is too far gone, beside herself with want, her concentration like a bowstring ready to snap.

"Ari," Iona whimpers, pleading for a respite despite already having the power to do anything she wants, but she can still feel Ariadne's pleasure through the bond, is only capable of depriving herself for so long, and Ariadne cannot deny her.

"Fine!" she says through gritted teeth, letting her furtive vine fall as she accepts defeat. "I yield! I surrender!"

Iona moans, a wild, exultant sound, as she eats Ariadne with abandon, and her own vines go slack. Ariadne wrenches her wrists free of them, reaching up to grip Iona's hips and pull them down to her waiting mouth, as she's so longed to do.

She can feel Iona trying to keep her pelvis suspended slightly, not willing to press her full weight down, but Ariadne will have none of it. She buries her face in Iona's flood of desire, uncaring if Iona might smother her, for it would be a glorious death indeed.

She feasts, drinking deeply of her essence, and Iona cries out her pleasure, a few strokes of her tongue setting her off like a powder keg, taking Ariadne with her, and they let loose their passionate cries of utter relief as overwhelming sensations wash over them at last, leaving them boneless and sated.

With great effort, Iona lifts herself up just long enough to right herself and collapse against Ariadne's chest. She trembles, burrowing in close as Ariadne wraps her arms around her, until their breathing slows and the only sound is the rustle of leaves in the gentle breeze.

"I suppose... that was worth the effort," Iona pants, her voice small but triumphant.

Ariadne lets out an exasperated sigh. "I've been a horrid influence on you."

Iona giggles, and soon Ariadne cannot help but join her, their laughter peeling out into the lush forest. Curled up in a twisted pile of limbs, Iona presses her head to Ariadne's chest to listen to her heart, which still beats slightly faster than normal, her limbs too heavy to lift just yet.

Silence lingers, and Ariadne's muscles grow tense with displeasure, her bliss fading away far too soon. She waits for Iona to speak, knowing what she will ask.

"Shall we discuss the invitation? Or are we still avoiding the subject?" Iona asks, hesitant.

"No," Ariadne says.

"No, we are not avoiding the subject or-"

"I do not wish to speak of it."

The branches above them thin to show the position of the sun low in the sky.

"It is nearly nightfall," Iona says softly.

"I'm aware of that," Ariadne says.

Lifting herself onto her elbow, Iona says, "Look at me."

But she cannot bear to, instead keeping her eyes on the sky and the clouds slowly moving overhead.

"We could ignore it," Iona says with uncertainty. "Or invent some excuse to postpone. We could claim that I needed to prepare for the solstice tomorrow and could not spare the time."

"That would be unwise," Ariadne says.

"Why?" Iona asks. "I do not wish to set the precedent that we are at their beck and call."

A smile threatens to form on Ariadne's lips. "It is a dinner invitation, not a summons."

Iona slumps on top of her. "It is more than that, and you know it."

Pressing her lips against her fire touched hair, she holds Iona close, running fingertips along the ridges of her spine.

"This is an opportunity for you to foster a strategic alliance with a powerful sempiterna family," Ariadne says, resenting how formal she sounds, but knowing well the truth of her words.

"I am not convinced that I should want them as allies," Iona says.

"You do not want them as enemies," Ariadne says solemnly. "You should not offend them."

"I thought they were already offended by your refusal of the pendant," Iona says.

"They aren't aware that I refused it," Ariadne reminds her. "They only know that I did not manage to claim it. I should like to keep it that way."

"What difference does it make?" Iona asks.

"If they know that I willingly gave the pendant away, it will add insult to injury. If they only think you were stronger than I am, it would be better for both our reputations," Ariadne says.

"Then we are attending the dinner?" Iona asks.

"Yes," Ariadne says. "We must."

"Very well," Iona says. "I should like to bathe before we leave."

"I think that would be best," Ariadne says, pulling a twig from Iona's tangled hair, then chuckles when she shoves her shoulder, and stands on shaky legs.

In the hall of Crescentia's home, they find her just getting out of bed, her door opening just a crack as she pokes her head outside.

"Crescentia," Iona says.

"Oh!" she jumps, pressing a hand to her heart, then immediately brings it to her head and winces. "There is no need to shout."

"Where did you disappear to last night?" Iona asks.

"Nowhere," she says with something akin to guilt crossing her face, though Ariadne cannot imagine why.

"Euphemia mentioned a handsome man," Iona waggles her eyebrows. "You must tell me everything later."

"Yes, later," Crescentia agrees, waving them off.

"He's still here, isn't he?" Ariadne asks, smirking when Crescentia blushes crimson.

"Oh," Iona laughs. "Why did you not say? We shan't keep you. Or would you prefer us to leave? It is your home after all, and I would not wish to overstay our welcome-"

"No, no. Stay as long as you wish. I am glad for the company," Crescentia says, cutting a glance at Ariadne.

"We will be gone for supper soon anyhow. At Moira's invitation, we are to dine with Ariadne's family in Rome," Iona informs her.

"Oh..." Crescentia sobers instantly. "How curious."

"Isn't it?" Ariadne shares a knowing look with her, which escapes Iona's notice.

"Shall I... Would it be helpful if I came with you?" Crescentia asks, more to Ariadne than Iona.

Ariadne quickly says, "That won't be necessary."

"Alright," Crescentia says, averting her eyes. "Well, um... Have a pleasant time, I suppose."

"Likewise." Ariadne winks at her, and grins when Crescentia's blush returns and she escapes inside her room.

"Do not tease her," Iona whispers.

"Why?" Ariadne asks.

"She's just been through a terrible ordeal, if you can recall. You mustn't quarrel," Iona insists.

"I would never," Ariadne says.

Ignoring Iona's suspicious look, she conjures a bath of steaming water with a layer of white gardenia petals floating across the surface. A long soak does wonders for both their muscles, though it does little to quell their dithery nerves. Across their bond, their anxieties feed on each other as they consider every possibility of what might go wrong.

Running a brush through Iona's hair is a small comfort, the soft strands like unwoven silk against her fingers, but contrary to other times, they do so in silence. Iona then conjures a lavender gown of diaphanous satin, reminiscent of her Samhain dress. Without much thought, Ariadne conjures a purple hydrangea and hands it to Iona for her hair. She smiles and takes it gingerly, pinning it in place.

Ariadne tries as she might but cannot find herself comfortable in anything but red, her family's color. She tells herself the color suits her best and that is why she wears it, but she can hear her mother's nagging voice in her head telling her that she must wear the color at all official gatherings. She doesn't wish to invite any undue criticisms tonight.

The silk dress she conjures is simple but elegant, with a drapery fastened to her right shoulder by a golden brooch embezzled with diamonds, and a demi-train that swishes behind her whenever she walks. She clasps her favorite ruby necklace around her neck and when she catches a glimpse of herself in the mirror, she feels transported a year into the past, before her life had been altered irrevocably.

"You are a vision of beauty," Iona says with adoring eyes.

Ariadne forces a smile, for she is not like Iona, who flushes with pleasure at every bit of praise. In fact, she tends to recoil against compliments, even when they're well intentioned, for they only serve to make her feel ornamental.

"And of strength, as well," Iona continues. "Regal as ever."

She meets Iona's gaze and is taken aback by her expression of dauntless conviction.

"I wish to make one thing clear, here and now," Iona says. "I have no interest in joining their coven. Not in the slightest. So long as your mother is among their ranks, I shall not be. What she did to you is shameful. You may one day choose to forgive her, but I certainly never shall."

Ariadne's heart swells in her chest, filling with gratitude in the face of Iona's loyalty. "I never thought as much, but I am glad to hear you say it all the same."

Iona reaches for her hand and pulls her close.

"I am not attending this dinner to placate your family," Iona says. "I only wish to learn why they need me so badly."

The Villa Mitriora sits two stories high on Aventine Hill in Rome. Named for Ariadne's father's family, the Palladian style villa has been passed down through generations, ever since their ancestors left Triora during the witch trials of the 16th century. For the Zerynthos family, it acts as a second home during the warmer months of the year. It is not so much a prison as the manor in Thessaly but is not a welcome sight either.

*Who is that?* Iona asks.

A young woman with long dark curls, wearing a garnet red

gown, sits alone on the front steps looking up at the sky. A flame mark lies just above her right collarbone.

"Marina," Ariadne calls.

Marina does not respond or deign to tear her gaze away from the sky.

*Moira's sister,* Ariadne explains.

*Is she well?* Iona asks.

*I couldn't say,* Ariadne sighs, then steps closer. "Marina?"

Marina startles, then looks at her and blinks.

"Ariadne?" she asks, "Oh... I thought... Or well I suppose you would... But..."

She trails off, then looks back up at the sky.

"Good evening." Iona curtsies. "I am pleased to meet you, my name is-"

"The stars are in odd places," Marina murmurs.

"Pardon?" Iona asks, then looks up.

Ariadne does too, but the azure sky has not darkened enough to reveal the heavens.

"But the stars are not yet visible," Iona says.

Marina squints, "Are they not?"

Iona shakes her head slowly.

*Ignore her,* Ariadne suggests. "We shall see you at dinner."

She takes Iona's hand and guides her up the steps.

"Your scales are unbalanced," Marina says softly.

Iona glances back at her once more. *She is... strange.*

*Marina is relatively harmless.* Ariadne grimaces. *Though I warn you, she has a tendency to impart the wisdom of the stars, and her insight is not always pleasant.*

When they reach the threshold, the door opens of its own accord. Iona searches for who had opened it, but there is no one in sight. She goes tense with unease.

"Frightened of a house, nymph?" Ariadne teases.

"Is it alive?" she asks.

"No, only enchanted to remove the necessity for servants," Ariadne says. "All the grand houses have charms like these."

She offers her arm and leads them both through the threshold. It creaks closed behind them as they go past the entrance hall and into the atrium, a centralized room with a deep pool of crystal-clear water in the center of the floor. Red and white geometric mosaics decorate the walls.

Just beyond the pool on the far wall is the lararium, an altar to Hecate. Carved in stone, it depicts her holding a torch in one hand and key in the other, with a snake slithering at her feet.

Incense burns on a shelf just beneath it, smelling distinctly of frankincense and mugwort. Ariadne surveys the room, but there is no one in sight.

"Moira did not say where we should go," she murmurs. "Perhaps the drawing room or the solarium… Or perhaps we should see if my father is in his study."

"Is there no one here to greet us?" Iona asks. "Or was Marina meant to with her cryptic remarks?"

"I regret that my daughters are not the most welcoming."

From a hall to their left, Aunt Xiomara emerges in a gown of violaceous red. She wears her dark curls loose down her back and has a jeweled ring on nearly every finger, with a massive ruby displayed favorably over all the others. Her flame mark is small but prominent, right beside her left eye.

Ariadne remains frozen with uncertainty, until her aunt extends her arms wide, and she runs to her. Aunt Xiomara laughs and squeezes her tightly.

"Let me look at you," Aunt Xiomara says, pulling away to scrutinize her. "All in one piece, I see?"

Her gaze rests on the staff, her eyes widen in wonder.

"And the first not to return from Lysander College empty-handed," Aunt Xiomara says. "It is a triumph, my dear."

Taken aback, Ariadne asks. "Then… you are not angered?"

"Not at all," Aunt Xiomara says. "I am quite intrigued by this turn of events."

Her gaze shifts to Iona, so Ariadne steps aside, allowing her to approach.

"And it is not for us to question fate's design," Aunt Xiomara says with a curtsy.

Iona curtsies low and when she rises, there is more than a trace of confusion in her hazel eyes.

"Good evening, and welcome to the Villa Mitriora. I am Xiomara Zerynthos," she says with a warm smile. "You must be Iona."

"Good evening," Iona says in turn. "I am pleased to meet you."

"You have my congratulations." Aunt Xiomara gestures to the pendant. "It suits you."

"Thank you," Iona smiles shyly.

"Shall we join the others? I'm famished," Aunt Xiomara says.

"Yes, lets." Ariadne takes Iona's arm again.

Aunt Xiomara leads them out into the peristylum, an open courtyard with a garden of well-manicured rosemary bushes and cypress trees. Then they ascend the stairs and make their way down a long corridor lit by burning candle sconces. Paintings adorn the walls, most of them depicting witches with the same curled dark hair and red eyes.

*I thought you hated your family.* Iona gives her a questioning look.

*I hate my mother.* Ariadne clarifies. *There are a few of the others whose company I moderately enjoy.*

*Oh… which of them do you favor?* Iona asks.

*My Aunt Xiomara, Uncle Raul, my father, my cousin and grandmother on my father's side, and I can stomach Marina in brief intervals.*

*The rest are like your mother?* Iona asks.

*There are none so terrible as her.* Ariadne clenches her jaw.

They reach the end of the hall and Aunt Xiomara opens a door that leads to the solarium, a large sitting room with a collection of chaises and klines scattered about. Two of the walls and the ceiling are made of immaculately clean glass, similar to her own bedroom in Thessaly. Except instead of plants obscuring the windows, the sprawling view of Rome is unobstructed. The final traces of sunlight paint the clouds pink and makes the rooftops glow orange.

It is one of her favorite rooms in the villa, most of all because of the grand pianoforte that sits in the corner. In the shape of a wing, it's much larger than the one she'd practiced with in Thessaly and made of dark ebony wood. She might have played a song or two before dinner, if it weren't for the people awaiting their arrival.

Moira sits prim and perfect in her scarlet dress and when she sees them enter, her eyes brighten. "Ariadne! I knew you'd come."

She bounds over to them and envelops Ariadne in a stifling embrace until she squirms away. It is never a good sign for Moira to be in such a fine mood.

Her other cousin, Sebastian, sits slumped in a most ungentlemanly fashion, his unfocused eyes reflecting his boredom. When Aunt Xiomara introduces him to Iona, he doesn't see fit to look at them or even to bow his head in greeting. Her Uncle Raul, a devilishly handsome man with tanned skin and dark hair, is the exact opposite.

"Bona nit, Ms. Lysander," Uncle Raul says, pressing his lips upon Iona's hand, and giving Ariadne a mirthful look. "It is a pleasure to meet the woman Ariadne risked exile for."

Iona's flush is immediate, and Ariadne smiles wryly.

"Do not make fun," Ariadne says.

"But of course. Wouldn't want Cintia to hear. She would have our guts for garters," Uncle Raul pretends to grimace with fear until his wife smacks him on the arm.

"Did I not describe them perfectly?" Moira asks, coming to stand beside her father. "They are an exquisite pair, like out of a fairy book."

"Yes, my darling. Well done," Uncle Raul says, kissing her forehead.

"Where is Zephyra?" Aunt Xiomara asks.

"Late as ever," Moira shrugs.

"And Cintia?" Aunt Xiomara asks.

"We should be fortunate if she attends at all." Moira brushes past Ariadne and whispers. "Or rather, unfortunate."

"We shall all dine as a family," Aunt Xiomara says firmly.

"I am here!" Aunt Zephyra bursts into the room.

She wears a linen dress that is also red, but lighter in shade than the others, and her curls are pinned in haphazard clusters that cascade from the crown of her head. The constant dishevelment of her appearance somehow always manages to be effortlessly avant-garde. When she turns her head, the hint of her flame mark can be seen just beneath her ear. Flustered, she greets Iona with a curious gaze, giving her a thorough once over.

"Sebastian!" Aunt Zephyra snaps her fingers at him. "Come and greet our guests, you slothful thing."

He takes his time standing and approaching them with his hands buried in his pockets.

"Good evening," he says in a monotone voice.

"Stand up straight and fix your shirt," Aunt Zephyra hisses at him. "Your father, rest his soul, would be appalled by your lack of decorum."

"Zephyra," Aunt Xiomara says in a placating tone. "Have you seen Cintia?"

"She won't arrive at dinner until the third course," Marina answers for her as she enters the room like a phantom, almost floating across the floor with barely a sound.

Aunt Xiomara sighs. "She cannot be convinced to attend the entire meal?"

Marina shakes her head no, then looks out at the night sky through the towering windows, offended by the translucent barrier between her and the stars.

"I suppose that is to be expected." Aunt Xiomara sighs, then smiles at Iona. "I apologize for my sister. She does not adapt well to changed plans."

"She shan't be missed," Iona says.

Ariadne's eyes widen at her boldness, but to her relief, Aunt Xiomara lets out a hearty laugh.

"Come, let us convene in the dining hall," Aunt Xiomara beckons the family to follow her, then murmurs in Ariadne's ear. "I like her."

# 10 - Ariadne

The dining room is bathed in the light of innumerable candles burning brightly on the crystal chandeliers and the sconces hanging from the walls. Yet more candelabra illuminate the mahogany banquet table, which has been laid out with ten settings of fine China painted with pomegranates, apples, and red roses.

Ariadne pulls a chair back and gestures for Iona to sit, observing the others as she pushes in Iona's chair and walks round the table to sit across from her. She is relieved when Marina and Uncle Raul sit on either side of Iona and resigns herself to be seated between Moira and Sebastian. Aunt Zephyra sits beside her son, and Aunt Xiomara takes the seat at the head of the table, leaving two chairs empty, one for each of Ariadne's parents, who have yet to arrive.

"Where is Father?" she asks.

"Lost in his study again, no doubt," Moira says.

"Did no one bother to fetch him?" Ariadne sets her napkin on the table so she might go and find him herself.

"Calm yourself, Ariadne," Aunt Xiomara says, motioning for her to remain seated. "He will be along any moment."

Reluctantly, she sits and takes back her napkin. When she looks up again, there is a boiled egg covered in herb sauce sitting before her in a bronze egg cup. She reaches for her glass goblet filled with red wine and takes a substantial sip.

"Buon appetito," Aunt Xiomara says.

There is the clinking of spoons as they begin to eat their eggs. The silence is unsettling and Ariadne fidgets with her spare hand beneath the table.

"Would this be your first visit to Rome, Iona?" Aunt Xiomara asks.

"Yes, it is," Iona says.

"You should explore the city. You must enjoy the warmth after your years sequestered in Cornwall," Aunt Xiomara says.

"Indeed." Iona glances at Ariadne. *Gossip is swift amongst witches.*

*You've no idea,* she smirks.

"I imagine it was challenging to be confined in one place for so long," Aunt Xiomara says.

"It was not so bad…" Iona says, but she is entirely unconvincing.

"A necessary sacrifice, I suppose. Your grandmother searched quite vigorously for you three. One mistake and you could have been discovered," Aunt Zephyra says, then looks around the table. "Do you not recall how consumed by it she was?"

"Like a madwoman," Uncle Raul agrees.

"You knew her?" Iona asks Aunt Zephyra.

"Not well, but I did speak with her on occasion," Aunt Zephyra says. "It is a shame you were never given the opportunity to meet her. Such a fuss over the elopement… It was quite the scandal in its time. All of society was buzzing over it for many years."

"Oh…" Iona's mortification at the prospect renders her speechless.

Aunt Zephyra continues on, undeterred. "Do you find it very difficult to assimilate into civilization again after being so long a recluse?"

"Um… No, not particularly," Iona says. "I have… Or rather, I was acquainted with humans while I lived in Cornwall."

"How dreadful," Aunt Zephyra says. "If only I'd known how charming you were, I would have spoken on your behalf to your grandmother so she would leave your family be."

The surety in which Aunt Zephyra spoke of it, as if no one could refuse her, has Iona's brow furrowing, but she does not respond.

"I imagine old Caitriona Lysander regrets her choices, seeing how you are triumphant where her chosen heir has failed," Aunt Xiomara says.

"Yes, well… I doubt she could have predicted how events would unfold," Iona says pragmatically, her grip tightening around her spoon.

"Was she not a talented soothsayer?" Aunt Xiomara asks her sister.

"'Talented' is a favorable description. I suspect whatever her bones told her was a prediction of Iona's success, not Elise's. Those methods are not the most forthright," Aunt Zephyra shrugs.

Iona lifts her spoon to her lips. *How many courses do you expect they'll serve?*

*At least five.* Ariadne stifles a grimace.

Iona lets out a small sigh. The next course is a warm bowl of stracciatella soup.

"Zephyra, I meant to ask. Whatever happened with the lycanthropes in Moldavia? Has the population been tempered?" Aunt Xiomara asks before taking a dainty spoonful of soup.

"As best as we can expect…" Aunt Zephyra says. "Such a pesky disease."

*Lycanthropes?* Iona asks.

*Werewolves,* Ariadne clarifies.

*Oh…* Iona gulps. "How do you hope to temper the population? Is there a cure?"

"Goodness, no! No, we must hunt them before the disease spreads too far. It's not all bad, I suppose. I do love a good hunt." Aunt Zephyra's eyes sparkle at the thought. "Do you hunt, dear?"

"No," Iona shakes her head vigorously.

"Ah, you must try it, but perhaps another time. Their war with the Russians creates such chaos that there is little to be done to stop it spreading, even with our intervention," Aunt Zephyra sighs.

"They had best resolve their differences swiftly before Napoleon catches his second wind," Aunt Xiomara says.

"But is there not a treaty in place?" Iona asks.

"Those are easily broken," Aunt Xiomara says with a wave of her hand.

"The Treaty of Amiens shall last one year," Marina says. Everyone looks to her and she sits up straighter in her chair. "The stars told me there will be a war between France and most of Europe lasting nearly two decades."

"Goodness," Iona says softly.

"Many will die," Marina says in a matter-of-fact tone. "The complacency of peace breeds the most insidious darkness."

"Don't fret," Aunt Xiomara says. "The humans will sort out their differences in their barbaric manner as they always have. We have our own conflicts to contend with."

"Is there nothing to be done to prevent it?" Iona asks.

"Prevent it?" Aunt Zephyra asks. "Why ever would you want to concern yourself with that?"

Iona stares at her, unable to comprehend her confusion.

"If it is so important to you, appeal to your King," Moira suggests. "Follow in old Merlin's footsteps as it were."

Iona blanches. "I could never gain an audience with the King of England."

"And why not?" Moira asks. "His guards couldn't stand against a witch of your caliber, surely. He would have no choice."

"And after I cut down his guards and corner him in his throne room, what then? Why would he listen to me?" Iona asks, her frustration growing.

"If you cannot convince a human king to take your advice, why should any of us give you a second thought?" Moira asks.

Color reaches Iona's cheeks as she looks down at her soup.

Ariadne elbows Moira in the ribs and she has the audacity to say. "Ow! What was that for?"

"Moira." Aunt Xiomara gives her a warning look. "You shall be cordial, or you may leave."

"Yes, mother," Moira grumbles.

"She has no real experience in war or diplomacy anyhow. Not enough to properly advise anyone, human or witch," Aunt Zephyra says. "It takes great humility to know when you are out of your depth. You are wise to acknowledge that, Iona."

"I am not…" Iona sighs with rising irritation. "It does not take a lifetime of experience to know that wars are pointless and only result in the needless deaths of young men and boys. It should be avoided at all costs."

"You are welcome to try, but fate is not so easily swayed," Aunt Xiomara says.

"Why are witches so indifferent to the suffering of humans?" Iona asks, baffled by their apathy.

"Did you forget the witch trials? What they did to us? To their own people?" Aunt Xiomara asks, then realization fills her eyes. "Or perhaps you did not learn of our histories."

When Iona has no answer, Aunt Xiomara cuts Ariadne a disapproving look, then sets her spoon down and steeples her fingers.

"Humans are intolerant creatures. They spurn us, wish us ill, and claim their gods tell them we are evil devil worshipers who prey on children and make unholy unions with animals." Aunt Xiomara wrinkles her nose in disgust. "Some witches and warlocks deign to involve themselves in human affairs, but I find the practice futile. If they do not want our magic, I am more than willing to oblige them. If they choose to burn us for our mere existence, then they have earned our apathy. We have enough problems of our own. Best to concern yourself with your own kind."

"The king is mad anyhow," Sebastian mutters before taking a

large gulp of wine.

Iona opens her mouth to protest, but the sound of the door stops her. Ariadne's father enters, straightening his collar with a sheepish smile.

"Ah, Petro. Impeccable timing," Aunt Xiomara says with a smile.

"Apologies for my tardiness. My cereus flowers are nearly ready to bloom. I hate to part with them," Petro says.

Ariadne stands, forgetting her napkin as it falls to the floor beneath the table, and smiles as her father envelops her in a warm embrace.

"Welcome back, fiore," he says. "I've missed you."

"Cereus flowers?" Ariadne raises an eyebrow.

"They flower only one night a year," he says, his eyes alight with excitement. "I hope you may see them while you are visiting."

"A fine enough excuse, I suppose," Ariadne smirks.

"Come, come. Sit, Petro before your soup goes cold," Aunt Xiomara says, though she mirrors their smiles.

On the way to his chair, he approaches Iona where she sits. She wipes her mouth and looks up at him, then offers her hand.

"It is a great pleasure to meet you, Ms. Lysander," he says, then bows and kisses her hand. "I will be forever grateful to you for your heroism in protecting my daughter from dark magic."

"On the contrary, sir. She protected me," Iona says.

"Oh, I am sure she did," he says. "But all the same, I am glad to know that she was not alone in her toil."

"You helped me immensely," Ariadne interjects. "Do not diminish your bravery."

Iona smiles shyly, unwilling to accept the praise.

"You may yet learn humility by association." Her father winks at her, then finds his seat beside Marina, and Ariadne's apprehension subsides for the first time that night.

"I propose a toast," Aunt Xiomara says, raising her goblet. "To Iona and Ariadne. As you begin your lives together, we wish you every happiness. May your marriage be a blissful dream that never ends, from now and into eternity."

"Marriage?" Ariadne nearly drops her goblet in surprise.

Aunt Xiomara reaches for Uncle Raul's hand, her ruby ring glittering in the candlelight. He gazes at her with rapt admiration.

"I must admit, when I heard rumor of your bond, I was a tad disappointed at your choice to elope, but I remember all too well how passion can incite spontaneity," Aunt Xiomara says. "The ring you chose is quite beautiful. Very unique."

Iona places a hand over her amethyst ring to hide it from view. Wincing, Ariadne looks down at the bloodstone ring on her own hand. It is on the wrong finger, but she can see how her aunt may have gotten confused.

"No, no," Ariadne laughs nervously. "We are not wed."

"Not wed?" Aunt Zephyra asks, appalled.

"But you are bonded." Marina's brow furrows.

"Yes, we are," Ariadne says.

"You will be together for all eternity," Marina says, raising her eyebrows expectantly.

"Yes, but we are not wed," Ariadne stresses, unable to look Iona in the eye.

"Engaged then?" Aunt Xiomara asks, and when Ariadne doesn't respond, she frowns.

"We have not discussed it," Iona says in a small voice.

"That is…" Ariadne sighs, hating to discuss such a private matter without speaking with Iona first. "I imagine we shall be someday, but we are in no particular hurry."

"Oh… I see," Aunt Xiomara says. "And the rings?"

"Communication rings," Ariadne explains.

Moira laughs into her napkin and Ariadne glares at her, which only makes her laugh harder.

"A thousand apologies. I should not have assumed," Aunt Xiomara says.

Iona reaches for her goblet and takes a long drink.

"But… you must marry before you bear children," Aunt Zephyra says.

Iona nearly chokes on her wine, quickly setting her glass upon the table to keep from spilling it down her front.

"Zephyra…" Aunt Xiomara rubs her forehead in frustration.

"You do want children, don't you?" Aunt Zephyra asks, ignoring her sister.

Iona coughs into her napkin, unable to respond.

"Yes, we do," Ariadne replies for her. "But worry not. Our intimacies do not result in unintended offspring, no matter how hard we may try."

"Ariadne!" Iona sputters, her face going bright red.

She grins at Iona's embarrassment, deciding if they must endure this, she may as well join in the fun. Aunt Zephyra bursts into raucous laughter, placing a hand over her chest and leaning back in her chair. Moira and Marina let a few giggles slip but they attempt to compose themselves when their mother gives them a warning look. Even Sebastian cracks a smile.

"Wicked thing." Aunt Zephyra points at Ariadne with her spoon.

"They needn't marry in haste if they do not desire it," Ariadne's father says when the laughter dies down. "It would merely be a formality now, would you not say? After bonding as you have, there is nothing more committed than that."

"Yes, I should say so," Iona agrees, letting out a stress-filled breath.

"In any case, when you do decide to hold a ceremony, I should like to offer the villa as a possible venue," Aunt Xiomara says to Ariadne. "Or your grandfather's manor. Constantinople is a vision in springtime, and I know you favor natural blossoms."

"Perhaps we should discuss it at a more appropriate time," Ariadne says with a pleading look.

"Fair enough," Aunt Xiomara chuckles. "All the same, I do wish you both every happiness."

When they have finished their soup, there is a main course of roast lamb, fresh bread, roman cabbage, glazed mushrooms, artichokes, seasoned mussels, and Lucanian sausages. In time, the conversation turns light and easy, much to Iona's evident relief.

Uncle Raul tells the story of when he was a teenager and accidentally turned himself into a mouse. He was stuck in that state for more than a week and was nearly eaten alive by a stray cat before his mother found him in their garden. Then Aunt Zephyra tells tales of her recent travels through Persia, Siam, and Morocco. All the while, Aunt Xiomara watches on with a smile, her focus being primarily on Iona. It does not escape Ariadne's notice.

The door to the dining room slams open, making everyone at the table flinch, and Ariadne squeezes her eyes shut. The ever-recognizable sound of her mother's footsteps against the stone makes her cringe. A chair at the other end of the table scrapes backwards. When Ariadne opens her eyes again, her mother stares back at her, goblet in hand.

"Cintia," Aunt Xiomara says, her voice even. "How good of you to join us."

Cintia peers at the food laid out on the table and scrunches her nose, then conjures a plate of greens and a small bowl of broth.

"Good evening, child," she says.

"Good evening, Mother," Ariadne says with as much indifference as she can muster.

"That is the gown you chose?" Cintia asks with a look of distaste.

Ariadne glances down at herself. "What is wrong with my gown?"

Her mother huffs and takes a bite of her food, not caring to elaborate. Every eye at the table is drawn to Ariadne, making her shift uneasily in her chair. All her worrying over her dress was in vain it seems. She could have woven the fabric and sewn it by hand. It would make no difference.

Without thinking, Ariadne reaches for a serving fork to place another slice of lamb on her plate, but her mother makes an obnoxious noise from deep in her throat. Ariadne pauses and makes the mistake of looking in her mother's direction to behold her expression of judgement and utter disdain. It is enough to make Ariadne pull her arm back and put both her hands in her lap, her appetite diminishing.

*Ignore her,* Iona encourages.

Ariadne glances at her, then away, reaching for her wine instead.

*I'm fine,* Ariadne assures her.

She blinks in surprise at finding the piece of lamb she'd wanted sitting on her plate, steaming as if plucked straight from a roasting spit, though it was not there before. When she looks up again, the pendant still has a faint glow from the conjuration spell Iona cast. Their stare lingers a moment, the surrounding conversations fading into the background, and Iona's gaze softens to reveal her concern.

Ariadne isn't used to anyone watching her so closely, unless it is in an effort to surveil her, suppress her, control her, never out of love, but there's no doubt of Iona's motivation. It's written all over her face, at the very forefront of her mind, entirely unmistakable.

So, Ariadne lifts her fork and knife, cuts a piece of lamb, and puts it in her mouth, only then remembering how famished she is. Her nerves had kept her from eating all day long, a horrid habit she's not succumbed to in months. As she thinks of it now, she's not done so since courting Iona.

Ariadne can feel her mother's eyes boring into her, but before she can speak, Aunt Xiomara interjects. "How were your travels?"

"Fine," Cintia says.

"Spain is quite lovely in summer, as I recall," Aunt Xiomara says. "Though I imagine the covens did not give you much chance to enjoy it."

"No, they did not," Cintia snaps. "Which is why you sent me there in your stead, I assume. They are at each other's throats."

"I found it quite odd that you were sent at all," Aunt Zephyra murmurs. "You aren't known for your skills at diplomacy."

Ariadne snorts before she can stop herself, and it makes a slight echo in the silence. She braces herself for her mother's rage, but instead she turns on Iona.

"Have you met with the other great covens yet? Or are we the first?" Cintia asks.

Iona's mouth is full, and she hastens to swallow her food down. "Yours is the first, but I imagine-"

"Have you been studying then? Which other colleges do you plan to attend?" Cintia asks.

"I haven't... I..." Iona stutters.

"Surely you require additional schooling, without a mother or father to properly train you in magic," Cintia says, glancing at Ariadne. "You once scorned me for my strict instruction but now do you see how incompetent you'd be if I'd not done so?"

"I am not incompetent," Iona says, before Ariadne can say as much.

"Is that so?" Cintia raises an eyebrow. "Then do you hope to be of service now? There is the lycanthrope situation that has grown quite unmanageable. Have you yet been to Moldavia?"

"I've only just heard of-" Iona tries to say.

"What of the vampires in Romania? Or the growing hostilities in Spain?" Cintia asks, her voice increasingly sharp and impatient. "Or are we meant to deal with all these many disturbances alone?"

Iona goes silent and Ariadne admonishes herself for not preparing her for this sort of questioning.

"What exactly have you been doing all this time?" Cintia narrows her eyes. "Your ignorance is appalling. You must be aware of these matters as a supposed leader of your people. Or do you aim to waste your time on frivolity? Bedding my daughter in every country?"

Iona blushes furiously. "No, of course not! I've only just claimed the pendant-"

"Leave her be," Ariadne snaps.

*Do not let her provoke you,* Iona cautions. *It is alright.*

"No, it is not. She cannot expect you to solve all the world's problems in mere weeks!" Ariadne argues, realizing too late that she's mistakenly responded aloud.

Her mother's eyes flare, a humorless smile reaching her lips. "Ah, that's right. You are of two minds of late. I suppose I should have expected my daughter's laziness to be catching."

"Must we have all this unpleasantness?" Aunt Xiomara tries to interject.

Cintia leans forward, staring daggers at Ariadne, and says, "I remember when you once told me you'd rather die a thousand deaths than bond yourself to another."

Ariadne's heart stutters in her chest as she shrinks beneath her mother's glare, while her father clears his throat.

"Is that true?" Iona asks, and the hurt in her voice turns Ariadne's anger to contrition.

"I… I am capable of forming new opinions," she says.

"Your every firmly held belief seemed so easily discarded in the face of such beauty." Cintia gestures irreverently at Iona. "I suppose I can hardly blame you for your weakness."

"I am not weak," Ariadne grits out.

"Thoughtless… Impulsive… You never learn," Cintia sighs.

"I did not bond with her on an impulse," Ariadne insists.

"How long did you court her before joining your souls?" Cintia asks.

Ariadne hesitates as she struggles to find some way of embellishing the truth.

"Well now, let's not forget," Aunt Zephyra interjects. "You and Petro courted for a mere three months before you were engaged."

"Engagement is not the same as a blood bond," Cintia sniffs, then points her finger at Ariadne. "How could you, who thinks in seconds rather than years, possibly comprehend the true breadth and permanence of eternity? And to enter into such a bond without consulting me, your mother. Or Xiomara, the leader of your coven."

"I am not part of this coven. Or have you forgotten?" Ariadne seethes.

Cintia's jaw ticks. "I remember your every failure, of which there are many."

Ariadne's fist clenches around her fork, the metal digging into her palm.

"She bonded with me to counteract a blood magic spell," Iona interjects. "Elise attempted to use me to murder her and nearly succeeded."

Aunt Zephyra gasps with ample melodrama. "I never liked her."

Cintia only studies Iona's face, then takes a long drink from her goblet. Judging from her slight grimace, whatever she has in her cup is much stronger than wine.

"It was not done thoughtlessly, nor solely out of love. She's saved my life many times over. She is the bravest woman I know," Iona says.

"You do not know many people," Cintia scoffs with a dismissive wave of her hand. "I am uninterested in your opinion of my own daughter. You who manipulated her into abandoning her duty. An inherited trait, it seems. Your mother did the same to your father and had she not, perhaps he might still be alive."

"Take care in how you speak of my mother," Iona says, but the intended venom is overshadowed by the pain in her voice at such a horrible accusation.

"If you were a danger to Ariadne, then you should have remedied it yourself," Cintia continues. "Not used her soul to save your own."

"Do not speak to her that way." Ariadne has to fight to keep from shouting.

"I shall do as I please in my own home!" Cintia yells.

Ariadne slams her hands on the table, rattling the plates and silverware, as she leaps to her feet. "You shall not disrespect Iona in my presence!"

Aster snarls from where he sits behind Ariadne, but Cintia hardly notices. She stands as well and points a sharp nail in Iona's direction.

"She stole your inheritance! Distracted you from your studies and turned you against your own Goddess! You are a fool to let her outwit you, overpower you, turn you into a loyal lapdog. After all I did to prepare you for the trials, all those years of tireless instruction, all for nothing!" Cintia screeches. "Because of her, the little thief!"

"She did not steal anything!" Ariadne yells. "It was my choice to give it away and-"

"Ariadne..." Iona winces, but it is too late.

Cintia's mouth falls open in horror. "Give it away?"

Ariadne's anger turns to regret in an instant. "Or rather... I didn't..."

"You gave the pendant away?" Cintia asks, her voice an

incredulous whisper. "You must be joking..."

Ariadne slumps into her chair and rubs her face with her hands.

"How is that possible?" Aunt Zephyra asks.

"Morgan allowed this?" Aunt Xiomara asks.

"You are in so much trouble," Moira whispers with glee.

"Skáse!" Ariadne incants as she pulls her hands away to glare at her vexing cousin.

Moira's mouth melds shut, her scream of outrage muffled by the newly conjured skin where her lips once were. Ariadne takes great pleasure in watching her cousin struggle to reverse it.

"Ariadne Zerynthos! You know better," Aunt Xiomara scolds.

"As does she," Ariadne says.

To her disappointment, Moira manages to reverse the spell without needing to speak it aloud. She rips the skin apart and her lips reform.

"Scoundrel," Moira spits at her.

"Demon," Ariadne retorts.

"We must all calm down," Aunt Xiomara says, though even her patience wanes.

"I deserve an explanation, mongrel." Cintia's voice is chilling.

"I did not want it," Ariadne says. "There is nothing more to discuss."

"And what of my wants?" Cintia asks. "What of the needs of your family?"

"I did what was best for me," Ariadne says.

"And for her," Cintia says, gesturing to Iona.

"Yes, for her as well," Ariadne says.

"She is an imposter, then. Not a true champion," Cintia says.

"No!" Ariadne yells, then with effort she lowers her voice. "Iona prevailed in the trials just as I did. Morgan left it to us to decide who should claim it. I chose to give it to her. She *is* Morgan's champion, as much as Grandmother or any other witch who wielded it."

"Fascinating," Aunt Xiomara muses.

"Who else knows of this?" Cintia asks.

"No one," Ariadne says. "And it shall remain so."

Cintia studies her, her gaze flickering to Aunt Xiomara, before saying, "Indeed. It shall never leave this room."

"There now," Aunt Xiomara says, relieved. "With that settled, may we please continue our meal without all this ruckus?"

"I always did enjoy a show with my dinner," Moira says under her breath.

"Your grandmother will be appalled when she hears about this." Cintia rubs her temples.

"I do not concern myself with the opinions of the dead," Ariadne says.

"Yes, you've made that abundantly clear," Cintia sneers. "And that is precisely why Hecate cannot be bothered with the sorry likes of you."

Her words may as well have been a physical blow, stealing all the air from Ariadne's lungs, but she refuses to let it show.

"Please let us eat in peace," Aunt Xiomara pleads.

Glaring at her food, Ariadne is entirely uninterested in finishing it now. Instead, she admires the red hue cast upon her fingers from the candlelight shining through the wine in her glass. She swirls it around, then brings the goblet to her lips, drinking deeply, finding it bitter.

She pleads inwardly that her mother will just let it lie. They will never agree. She will never be enough for her, or Hecate apparently. There is nothing more to be said.

"I cannot fathom why you thought that hideous dress would be appropriate," Cintia mutters.

"I could eat naked instead," Ariadne retorts, which earns her a chuckle from Moira.

Withdrawing her wand in a practiced, fluid motion, Cintia casts a silent spell before Ariadne can react, and she sucks in a pained gasp as her stays constrict so tightly around her chest and stomach that they will doubtless leave awful marks.

"At least lace yourself properly," Cintia says. "Your posture is slipping."

Ariadne tries to protest but she cannot breathe. Her fork clatters against the table as she places a hand over her chest, each inhale shorter than the last.

"Stop!" Iona exclaims.

She extends her hand out in front of her in the direction of Cintia, who is thrown backwards out of her chair and flung across the room where she slams violently against the far wall and crumples to the floor in a heap. Iona screams in fright, then looks down at her hand in dismay.

"Good heavens!" Aunt Xiomara cries, jumping from her chair, unable to decide between running to Ariadne's aid or Cintia's.

There are shocked gasps and exclamations from one end of the table to the other. Ariadne breathes a sigh of relief when her laces slacken enough for her to inhale fully, her breasts and ribs aching from the smothering constriction. As she sucks air into her lungs, her head spinning and hands trembling, Iona rushes to her side.

"Are you alright?" Iona asks, frantically inspecting her.

"I'm fine," Ariadne pants.

"I thought... But I did not intend..." Iona puts her hand on her cheek as they both look to where Cintia is splayed across the floor.

Ariadne's father, Aunt Xiomara, and Aunt Zephyra all gather round her mother to try and help her back to her feet.

"Get off me!" Her mother shoves them away and tries to stand, then cries out in pain.

"What is it?" Her father searches frantically for the injury.

"My ankle." She winces and pulls up the edge of her skirt to reveal the bone jutting out of her skin.

"I shall fetch a potion," Her father says.

"No need," Aunt Xiomara says, pulling out her wand. "Philisa."

Cintia cries out as the bones snap back into place. She rubs the newly healed skin and sighs when the pain dissipates.

"Go," Aunt Xiomara says.

Cintia's eyes almost glow. "I beg your pardon?"

Aunt Xiomara only stares at her, showing a rare menace that makes all others in the room go still and silent. Cintia's breathing is ragged as she staggers to her feet and glares at Iona with barely contained rage.

A low growl draws Cintia's attention downward as Wisp shifts only partially, her fur bristling as she grows twice her size and bares her sharp white teeth in warning. She takes a wary step back, then huffs with enduring outrage.

"I shall not soon forget this," Cintia spits, then storms out of the room with her husband at her heels.

Aunt Xiomara, Uncle Raul, and Aunt Zephyra follow after them, whether to speak in private or ensure her mother's departure, Ariadne cannot tell. Sebastian had already slipped out of the room at some point, unbeknownst to anyone else.

"Welcome to the family." Moira smirks at Iona, then gently takes Marina's hand and leads her down the hall.

Once they're alone, Ariadne stands, wincing in pain at the bruises forming across her torso from the boning of her stays digging into her skin. Iona wrings her hands, her nerves and guilt more than apparent in her expression and impossible to misinterpret through their bond.

"I think you've made an excellent impression," Ariadne says, laughing nervously.

Then she finds that she is unable to stop, her laughter becoming almost painful as she gasps for air and braces an elbow against the back of her chair.

"Ari," Iona says with a worried look.

"Did you see how high she flew?" Ariadne dissolves into hysterics.

Iona hesitantly reaches for her. "I am so terribly sorry."

Ariadne's laughter is unhinged even to her own ears, but she cannot stop.

Iona keeps hold of her even when she tries to pull away. "Please, you are frightening me."

"No... No, it's funny. You should have seen the looks on their faces when," Ariadne gasps. "When they... When they-"

She bursts into tears and Iona seems almost relieved to see it as she holds her gingerly, not wanting to aggravate her bruises, but Ariadne doesn't care. She clings to Iona, and weeps into her shoulder as lividity and shame take their toll.

# 11 - Iona

"What is it?" Ariadne asks.

"A Cornish pasty," Iona says.

Ariadne inspects the golden-brown pastry with curiosity, while Iona conjures one of her own, filled with beef, potatoes, turnips, and onions. Having been unable to finish their dinner after the chaos that ensued, and now that Ariadne has wept all her tears, a Cornish pasty is as good a meal as any to eat on the front steps of the villa, not requiring the use of plates or silverware. Ariadne tries at first to refuse it, but the grumbling of her stomach is impossible to hide, and Iona is unwilling to let her starve.

She's always noticed the small, persistent ways Ariadne avoids eating. It was worse when they'd met. At every meal she'd conjured a bowl of thin soup and a cup of clove tea, time and time again. She was much thinner in those days, her bones sharp against her skin and her height only emphasizing her gaunt appearance.

Though Iona had been often unsure of how to nurture her, she's never brought attention to her observations when she knows well how defensive Ariadne can sometimes be. Instead, she found ways of naturally encouraging Ariadne to eat her fill during their feast at Yule or their weeks of holiday in Brazil. She's found that it's not a matter of hunger for Ariadne, more of a compulsion to avoid 'overindulgence' as her mother calls it. Day by day, meal by meal, she's witnessed Ariadne shedding those harmful impulses away as she allows herself to live unhindered by them.

All these months later, Ariadne is healthy and radiant. She has always been a transcendental beauty but is now even more so. At times, Iona finds it difficult to look at her without blushing as she admires the strength of her limbs, the swells of her curves, and the contentment in her eyes.

Whether it is due to Iona's encouragement, Ariadne's own inner healing, or a mixture of both, she cannot be sure. Ariadne's thoughts never dwell on such things. She prefers to bury her torments deep within herself, but now it seems they've all been brought to the surface at once. Iona doesn't wish for her progress to be ruined in one horrid evening.

"I would often bake these with my mother when we lived in Cornwall, but only when we had the ingredients to make them. At times there were riots over food… If only I'd been able to conjure then. I could have solved everything quite easily," Iona muses, then takes a bite of her pasty. She waits for Ariadne to follow suit, but she hesitates.

"I am not hungry," Ariadne says again.

"Yes, you are." Iona raises an eyebrow at her, and her cheeks turn pink at being caught in a lie.

"I can wait until breakfast," Ariadne says. Her nose is still red from crying but her hunched posture makes it abundantly clear that she doesn't wish to speak of what occurred in the dining room.

"Allow me to put it this way," Iona says, in a foolhardy attempt at humor. "If you wish to eat me later, you'd best finish the entire pasty."

Ariadne lets out an incredulous snort. "Is that a threat?"

Iona takes another bite of her own pasty, a mischievous grin threatening to form on her lips as she chews.

"You drive a hard bargain, nymph." Sighing dramatically, Ariadne takes a small bite of her pasty and hums her approval before taking another larger bite. She says around her mouthful, "I would riot if someone dared to take this from me."

Iona chuckles and shuffles closer to rest her head against Ariadne's shoulder. As silence falls between them, a wave of fatigue washes over her until she finds it difficult to keep her eyes open.

"What a palaver," Iona murmurs.

"Quite," Ariadne says.

"I am sorry for breaking your mother's ankle," Iona whispers.

Ariadne snorts again. "She deserved it."

"Do not say such things," Iona scolds.

"I would have done it myself if given the chance," Ariadne says.

"No, you would not," Iona says.

Ariadne sighs. "No… I suppose not. But you needn't fret over it. It was only broken for a minute or two."

"I still… I do not want your family to think me a violent person," Iona says. "I did not realize it would happen. It was an accident."

"They surely know that," Ariadne says. "Nothing about you

would ever make one think you are violent."

"I must be more careful," Iona murmurs, more to herself.

"On the contrary, that sort of power is what I've been trying to draw from you during our lessons," Ariadne says. "You should embrace it so you might learn to control it."

Iona mulls it over in her head as she chews, consumed by a litany of thoughts. She had been enraged, disgusted, to witness a mother committing such an awful act upon her own daughter. Humiliating her, causing her pain in full view of her entire family. It is beyond anything Iona can fathom. But there is another, nagging thought that she cannot stifle.

"If you wish to break the blood bond, I will not take offense," Iona says.

"What?" Ariadne stiffens. "Why would I want that?"

"But... was it true? What your mother said about you never wanting to bond with another woman?"

Ariadne does not respond immediately. "Yes, but... that was before I met you."

"Why did you say it?" She lifts her head from Ariadne's shoulder to study her expression, which is riddled with conflict.

"I'd only ever witnessed my parents' bond, and it often disturbed me," Ariadne says softly. "It seemed like a cruel imprisonment for my father. I often pitied him, though perhaps I shouldn't have. He chose it, after all. To lose one's autonomy so entirely, and so permanently... I could not imagine desiring such an affliction."

"Then why did you agree to bond with me?" Iona asks.

"I love you," Ariadne says simply.

Iona's heart swells at the words she will never tire of hearing.

"I would not let Elise take you from me," Ariadne says. "I would not let you die. It would have destroyed me along with you. I... I wouldn't survive it..."

A sudden rise of fear takes Iona off guard, so clearly conveyed through the bond that if she'd been in another room, she'd have wondered if a terrible monster had appeared before Ariadne, its teeth bared and claws sharp.

She takes Ariadne's hand, and it trembles beneath her palm. "I owe you a great debt of gratitude for-"

"You owe me nothing," Ariadne says.

"Ari." Iona caresses her cheek. "Listen."

Ariadne lowers her gaze, then presses a kiss to Iona's palm and waits for her to speak.

"I will be forever grateful to you for your bravery and

devotion," Iona says. "However, Elise is without power now. She cannot hurt me anymore. Merlin spoke of a way to reverse the bond, though it is difficult and he did not explain how."

"I do not want that," Ariadne says. "Please believe me."

Iona searches her gaze, then her mind, for any trace of doubt and finds none. Her stomach flutters when Ariadne leans in to steal a gentle, lingering kiss.

"If you're sure," Iona breathes.

"I am," Ariadne says. "My soul is yours forever, and you are mine."

At the sound of a throat clearing behind them, they pull away from each other and find Xiomara standing by the door with a hesitant smile.

"Might I have a word?" she asks.

Xiomara guides them through the villa's winding halls, and Iona struggles to keep up with her and Ariadne's long strides. When they make their fourth turn only to find another seemingly endless corridor, Iona looks about in confusion.

*Do not try to make sense of it.* Ariadne takes her hand and coaxes her forward.

*How can a hall be there if we already turned...* Iona looks over her shoulder, losing her bearings entirely.

*The villa is enchanted.* Ariadne reminds her.

*Then how do you know where you are going?* Iona asks.

When Ariadne shrugs, Iona steps closer to her, not wanting to lose track of them and find herself lost in a never-ending hallway with no apparent end.

Eventually, Xiomara stops at a tall door with a wyvern carved into the wood. They step into a vast library with three stories of shelves filled with thousands of grimoires, scrolls, and tomes of all sorts. Breathing in the comforting scent of old paper, Iona runs her hands along the spines, then picks up a well-worn book on the Conjuration of Living Creatures and leafs through it.

"Your father beseeched me to give this to you," Xiomara says, offering Ariadne a flask. "A healing potion."

"I have no need of it," Ariadne says.

"It is not brave to linger in pain for the sake of it," Xiomara says. "Or to subject Iona to it on account of your own stubbornness."

Ariadne lowers her eyes and wordlessly takes the flask. She drinks and rubs at her ribs, at the bruises that will disappear before Iona can lay eyes on them, but the memory of them will never fade, nor the disgust for the one who caused them.

When Ariadne and Xiomara sit at a small table in the corner, Iona returns the grimoire to its place on the shelf and approaches them.

"Perhaps a family dinner was not my finest idea," Xiomara grimaces.

"What possessed you to think it would be if my mother was in attendance?" Ariadne asks.

"She is…" Xiomara rubs her temples. "I shall never comprehend the voracity of her discontentment."

"Neither shall I," Ariadne mumbles.

"I'm appalled by her behavior," Iona says, then winces. "Even so, I did not intend to physically harm her. I do apologize."

"Do not think on it for even a second, Iona," Xiomara says. "Anyone could see it was an accident. You do not yet know your full strength. And frankly, she deserved it."

"I said the same," Ariadne says.

"No one deserves pain," Iona argues.

"When violence is dealt, one cannot be surprised when it is reciprocated. I was seconds away from intervening myself, and she would not have enjoyed that much more," Xiomara mutters gravely. "Though I do appreciate your apology. I shall convey it to Cintia. She has decided to return to Thessaly alone. Perhaps it is for the best."

"Father is still here?" Ariadne asks, genuine shock in her voice.

"Yes, he elected to stay," Xiomara says, sharing in her surprise.

"But why… Ah. The cereus flowers," Ariadne says, a small smile reaching her lips. "He will not wish to part with them before they bloom."

"That explains it," Xiomara smirks. "I suppose it is just as well. We shall be traveling tomorrow anyhow, for the solstice."

"Where will you travel to?" Iona asks.

"There is a place in the Sibylline Mountains," Xiomara says. "In fact, that is what I wished to discuss with you."

"Yes?" Iona sits up taller in her seat, lacing her hands together on the tabletop.

"What precisely are your plans for the solstice?" Xiomara asks.

"Well… I'd intended to hold the ritual in Lyon," Iona says. "With the reception to be held at the Drakenström's manor in Sweden."

"Lyon?" Xiomara arches an eyebrow.

"Yes, Crescentia Léandre resides there and has been kind enough to host us for the summer," Iona says.

"Is that the only reason you chose it? Because it happened to be where you were at the time?" Xiomara asks.

Iona flushes. "Is that not appropriate? It would be like any other ritual, like the ones we had at college."

When Iona glances at Ariadne, she appears equally confused.

"There are certain customs that would be expected," Xiomara says. "For instance, the location. Generally, it would be someplace elevated so we might be closer to the sun's light and warmth."

"During the day?" Iona asks.

"Yes, of course. When the sun reaches its highest point," Xiomara says.

She studies Iona's face, perceiving her uncertainty.

"Is Samuel Lysander still withdrawn from society?" she asks. "I'd hoped he'd at least send a letter to guide you in these formalities, to better prepare you for your introduction to the covens."

"I am more than capable of advising her in these matters," Ariadne says, with a trace of indignance.

"You've attended one sabbath ritual of this size before, to my knowledge," Xiomara says. "Do you truly believe that is enough to know what is customary? What time the ritual should begin, which directions to face, what words to incant, how to prepare beforehand? What do you know of such things?"

Iona observes the warring emotions of Ariadne's expression, until finally she frowns and looks down at her hands.

"Not all magic is learned in books, my dear, and Iona is already at a disadvantage with only one year of study. If she should flounder, the covens will remember," Xiomara says, not unkindly. "Admittedly, a great deal of it will be theater, a show of power and grace. Us witches are known for our dramatics, but traditions shouldn't be ignored."

Xiomara addresses Iona directly, her gaze filled with concern.

"The great covens will not be the only ones observing you," she warns. "Any maleficians lurking in the darkest places of our world shall watch for any sign of weakness in you, and for any trace of dissension amongst our ranks. It is during these times of transition that they often strike in bolder ways, stealing as much magic as they can before disappearing for another decade or two. There have already been three attacks this month alone.

Leeching spells."

At that, Iona and Ariadne share a worrisome glance, remembering their brush with leeching spells in Lysander Forest, when Elise stole magic from Iona's very soul to enrich herself. The pain had been unparalleled, that which Iona hopes never again to endure.

"Haven't you heard?" Xiomara asks. "The youngest victim is but three and ten... she will never cast another spell. We are only fortunate no one was killed, but I suspect the worst is not yet over."

Iona's blood runs cold. "How do you know of this?"

"The council has been monitoring the situation for some time," Xiomara says.

"Council?" Iona asks.

"The heads of all the prominent sempiterna covens form a council to convene in times of trouble and represent our interests in a fair and equal forum," Xiomara explains. "I represent the Zerynthos Coven."

Iona looks to Ariadne for reassurance, and she gives a shallow nod.

"Has word reached you of the attack in Brazil?" Iona asks.

"What attack?" Xiomara asks, her spine straightening. "Tell me."

Iona recounts her grandfather's gruesome murder and Xiomara's face drains of color.

"Four attacks," she muses. "This cannot be."

She stands and paces the floor, her hand over her mouth and her eyes distant.

"Aunt Xiomara?" Ariadne asks.

"We need this ritual now more than ever," Xiomara says.

The crushing magnitude of responsibility weighs on Iona's shoulders. "I... I shall try my very best..."

"If I may," Xiomara says. "And perhaps you will not accept my assistance, but I must offer it."

"What sort of assistance?" Ariadne asks.

"A mentorship, if you will," Xiomara says to Iona. "You wouldn't have been taught this sort of thing at college. Most witches aren't called upon to conduct rituals like these at such a young age, if at all. I'd always intended to instruct Ariadne when the time came, when we thought she would be the one... Well, that time has passed now. You will be expected to perform flawlessly or otherwise cast doubt on Morgan's decision."

Xiomara comes to sit before Iona again and takes both her hands.

"Please stay here with us so tomorrow morning we might prepare," she implores. "Take my place at the ritual in the mountains. Many of the covens already plan to attend, and more still might come when they hear of your involvement. I can take you there at dawn."

"Oh…" Iona looks to Ariadne, entirely unsure of what to say.

"Even if only for the solstice, I feel it is imperative that your strength be deemed undeniable. Your reputation must be spotless," Xiomara says.

"It *is* spotless," Ariadne says.

Xiomara lets out a frustrated sigh, as if there was more, she wishes to say, but can't. Iona's intuition flares, and she takes her hands back.

"If we are discussing reputations," Iona says, "your mother is still feared years after her passing and forgive me, but I do not know if I should be so closely associated with her coven on such a pivotal debut, if I am to avoid comparisons."

Xiomara narrows her eyes. "Then why did you bond with her granddaughter?"

Iona opens her mouth, then closes it. She looks to Ariadne, resenting her prolonged silence, her expression still unreadable.

"You are already associated with us, Iona, and just as you are not your grandmother or your disgraced cousin, I should hope you would not assume anything of me, or Ariadne for that matter," Xiomara says.

"Of course, I only meant…" Iona trails off, unsure of how to voice her concerns without offending her further.

"What do you gain from Iona's success?" Ariadne asks.

"Marriage notwithstanding, given your bond of blood, she is a part of this family now and we take care of our own," Xiomara says. "I only wish to help."

"Does Cintia agree with that sentiment?" Iona asks.

"She is not the head of this coven," Xiomara says. "I am."

Iona sits up straighter as she bolsters her resolve. "If we are family as you claim, then please be honest here and now. Why was Moira sent to question us? What does Hecate want with us? With me?"

Xiomara's expression becomes guarded as she weaves her fingers in her lap. "I am afraid I cannot say."

"Why?" Ariadne asks.

"On Hecate's command, I cannot say," Xiomara repeats.

"Forgive me."

"Why should we trust you if you keep secrets from us?" Iona asks.

"I made a vow to serve my Goddess. If I broke that promise, would that not also make me untrustworthy?" Xiomara raises a brow.

Iona sees no indication of deception, but she has been fooled once before. She crosses her arms and looks pointedly at Ariadne, who studies her aunt's face.

"If you are so opposed to accepting my help, and Samuel cannot advise either, then I implore you to find someone else to counsel you in this matter," Xiomara says. "Though I am unaware of anyone with the insight I could provide, considering I've attended many of my mother's rituals and conducted countless of my own besides."

*Say something,* Iona demands.

*It is ultimately your decision.* Ariadne's eyes flit to hers. *It's your ritual, not mine.*

*Do you trust her?* Iona asks.

Ariadne hesitates. *Yes.*

*Are you certain?* Iona asks.

*She has never hurt me. And she is right. Perception is everything to these people. Shows of strength are crucial to gaining respect and becoming a proper leader. Isn't that what you wish for?* Ariadne asks.

*It could be a ploy... to gain our trust and deliver us to Hecate,* Iona muses.

*Undoubtedly it is,* Ariadne agrees. *However, if you meant to avoid such things, we never should have come here to begin with.*

Iona cannot argue that. She'd come to determine why Hecate is so interested in her. If she could spend time with Xiomara, earn her trust in turn, perhaps she could achieve two goals in one.

*I wish I could speak with Samuel,* she relents.

*What do you think he would say if you could ask him?* Ariadne asks.

Iona considers it for a moment. *That wisdom can take many forms. That we are not our families. And that there is more than one way to solve a problem.*

"I did have one other matter to discuss," Xiomara says. "In regard to Elise's imminent trial."

Ariadne grimaces, shifting uneasily in her chair, and Xiomara gives her a sympathetic look.

"I imagine it is a very difficult subject. I regret the need to discuss it with you at all," she says.

"You will preside over the trial with the council," Iona realizes, suddenly understanding why Moira was so fixated on it before. Her own mother will take part in deciding Elise's sentencing.

"Yes, with a heavy heart I shall," Xiomara says. "When the trial commences, you may be called upon as witnesses to her crimes. We will also be requesting Crescentia Léandre's attendance."

"Is there not enough evidence to convict her?" Ariadne asks. "I may be a witness in her trial, but Iona need not do it. She is-"

"I will do it," Iona decides.

Ariadne looks at her in surprise. "Are you certain?"

"Yes," Iona says. *I must, or I could never forgive myself.*

"You have my gratitude. I shall relay your answers to the council tomorrow," Xiomara says. "It is good for us witches to stand united against maleficians. We should not allow dark magic to reemerge as it once was in the old days. It would be ruinous for us all."

Perceiving nothing but sincerity in Xiomara's countenance, Iona finds it truly baffling how different this woman is from her sisters, from her own daughter. It strikes her then that Xiomara reminds her a bit of Samuel in that way. Trapped in the midst of those she would otherwise avoid, forced to coexist with them. She is the voice of reason in her volatile family. A peacemaker.

A clock on a nearby shelf chimes ten and Xiomara's eyes go wide. "My, is that the time?"

"We should return to Lyon," Ariadne says, reaching for her staff to make a portal.

"Wait," Iona says.

She is reminded of the fear etched into her grandfather's face when they'd found his corpse, reflecting the terrible pain he endured in his final moments. If one ritual, performed well enough, could in any way prevent such a travesty from occurring again, instilling fear in those who deal in violence and terror, then perhaps she should put her misgivings aside. She cannot afford to turn away allies, not now. Maybe fate brought her to Xiomara at this moment for a reason.

"The hour has grown late," Iona says. "Perhaps we could stay and if you have any advice for tomorrow's ritual, I would be grateful for it."

"Splendid!" Xiomara says with a radiant smile. "I shall have a room made up for you. We will serve breakfast at sunrise, which should allow us ample time to prepare before noon."

She continues on animatedly, telling them of the importance of sleep the night before a ritual of this size. Then she sends them off to bed, assuring them that they will discuss it all at length tomorrow.

## 12 - Iona

She would have thought she'd be accustomed to sleeping in a strange bed by now, but no matter how hard she tries, she can only manage to drift off for short intermittent periods before waking again to the dark, unfamiliar room. Her worries about the solstice, Ariadne's family, Elise's trial, all simmer within her until she cannot bear it a moment longer.

She flips onto her back and sighs in frustration, her eyes wandering about the darkness. This room belonged to Ariadne during many a summer when her family took residence in Rome. There are traces of her strewn about; a collection of plants by the window, a shelf full of grimoires against the wall, a collection of Sappho's poetry left open on her bedside table, but it's clear Ariadne hadn't resided here long enough to truly make her mark on it.

Iona sits up in bed when she notices the space beside her is empty.

"Ariadne," Iona whispers.

There is no answer.

*Ariadne,* Iona calls, and waits.

*Yes?* Ariadne asks.

Iona sighs with relief. *Where did you go?*

*The solarium. I couldn't sleep.*

Iona yawns but knows that she doesn't have much chance of sleep either. She crawls out of bed, cracks open the door, and peers out into the dark hallway. Conjuring a ball of light, she holds it out in front of her, then realizes she hasn't a clue which way to go.

*You should go back to bed,* Ariadne says. *Remember Aunt Xiomara's advice.*

*I am just as restless as you,* Iona admits. *How do I get to the solarium from here?*

*Aster will show you.*

A brush of fur against her leg makes her jump, and she presses a hand over her mouth to muffle her yelp.

"Aster." Iona lets out a shaky laugh. "I did not see you."

183

He sits in the middle of the hall and lets his tongue hang out, his mouth upturned as if he's laughing at her. Wisp rubs up against him and nips at his chin.

"Would you show me the way?" she asks.

Aster nods and canters away, undeterred by the veritable darkness of the winding halls. Wisp trots ahead with him and sniffs at every door, her black tail wagging as it often does when she's allowed to explore.

Iona follows, but when she turns a corner, only the tails of the wolf and fox are visible to her. She moves as fast as she can without making noise enough to rouse the entire house, but the animals elude her more and more.

"Slow down!" Iona hisses.

She turns another corner and goes still. Before her is a hallway adorned with golden sconces, the white candles still lit and dripping wax onto the floor. At the other end is a wooden door painted deep purple with a golden doorknob that glitters in the flickering candlelight.

Blood rushes in her ears as she is overcome with an odd sense of foreboding, and yet she cannot help feeling drawn to whatever is on the other side of the door. She takes a step forward, then another, and another, until she is nearly halfway down the hall. Her heartbeat quickens as she hastens her steps.

With a violent lurch, she's tugged backwards so roughly that she falls onto her back on the floor. She looks around herself in a panic for whoever had done it, but no one is there. Wisp barks from the other end of the hall, back where she'd come, but the fox does not seem to know what had accosted her either, which only fuels Iona's dread.

She pushes herself onto her feet and runs away, uncaring of any noise she might make. As fast as her legs can carry her, she makes it all the way down the hall, which leads to another, and another, until she thinks she might be running in endless circles.

A growling bark startles her, and she lets loose a terrified scream as Aster jumps on her, scratching at her arms with his paws.

"Oh, Aster!" Iona exclaims. "Why did you leave me?"

He whines, then scratches at a nearby door that looks familiar. Iona wrenches it open and lets out a heavy sigh when she finally finds the solarium lit by a blazing fire in the hearth and a crowd of stars shining through the tall windows.

There at the other end of the room, Ariadne sits at the pianoforte in only her chemise, her feet bare and her dark curls loose and wild across her back. She is in the midst of a song when she hears Iona enter and stops to give her a dubious look.

"Did you run here?" Ariadne asks.

"I…" Iona tries to catch her breath. "I do not like this villa very much at all."

Ariadne chuckles. "Neither do I."

"I saw a purple door," Iona says. "I… I fell."

"A purple door?" Ariadne asks, then shakes her head. "There are no purple doors."

"But…" Iona shakes her head. "Perhaps it was a trick of the light… Or I was still dreaming…"

Rubbing her forehead in confusion, she approaches the pianoforte and comes to sit on the bench beside Ariadne as she resumes her song. Iona recognizes it immediately, *Les Barricades Mystérieuses*. Ariadne had once played it in the student's parlor at college.

"Why did you not wake me?" Iona asks.

"You looked so tranquil. I did not wish to disturb you," Ariadne says.

Iona puts her hand in Ariadne's lap and rests her head against her shoulder.

"Are you alright?" Iona risks asking.

"Yes," Ariadne says.

Iona hesitates, then says, "I have so many doubts of late. I resent all this uncertainty… All these secrets…"

"As do I," Ariadne says.

Iona looks up at her and places a hand against her cheek.

"You need only say the word and we shall leave this place and never return," Iona says.

Ariadne stops playing to regard her with a vulnerable expression. "You are asking me to make that choice for you?"

"No, I only meant… if being here causes you pain, then it's not worth the trouble. No one should treat you as your mother and Moira do, as if you are beneath them. I despise it."

The rising vitriol in Iona's tone makes Ariadne's eyes go wide, until she hides her vulnerability away again, and lets her fingers rest lightly over the keys.

"I'm accustomed to it by now," Ariadne says. "It matters little to me."

She begins a new song with a slower tempo. Iona watches her face, and senses Ariadne's tempestuous emotions ranging from outrage to humiliation to melancholy.

"It matters very much to me," Iona says.

"I'm not so fragile, Iona," Ariadne says. "Do not worry over me, please."

Sighing, she decides to let the matter rest for now. "Very well."

She watches Ariadne in silence, admiring the way her slender fingers slide over the ivory. No matter how many times she may witness it, she finds Ariadne's musicality remarkable and unspeakably attractive.

She glances at the sheet music and reads that it is a piano sonata called Parthia. It has a rather cheerful melody that contrasts greatly with Ariadne's brooding expression.

"How do you read this?" Iona asks, squinting at the black dots and lines scattered across the sheet music, then leans back when the page flips on its own.

"It is quite easy with practice," Ariadne shrugs. "You should see the new Beethoven piece I'm learning. There are twice as many notes in half as many pages."

"But you're not even looking," Iona notices.

"I memorized this sonata years ago. The sheets are there in case I forget a note or two."

"But how long is it?"

"Approximately five and twenty minutes."

Iona scrutinizes the pages again. "You know all of those notes by heart?"

"You do not believe me?" Ariadne asks.

Iona smirks and places a hand over her eyes. "Prove it."

"You are still unconvinced of the boundless potential of my superior brain?" Ariadne asks slyly.

"I am more than convinced of your arrogance," Iona retorts.

Ariadne's fingers do not miss a beat as she continues playing. In truth, Iona cannot tell if the sonata is performed correctly or not. She's never heard it before and cannot read the music to confirm accuracy. However, the smile threatening to form on Ariadne's lips is motivation enough to continue teasing her.

"You are peeking," Iona says.

"My eyes are closed," Ariadne mutters, deep in concentration.

Iona conjures a strip of silken black cloth and ties it over Ariadne's eyes, making a bow at the back of her head. Her hands continue to roam over the keys unhindered.

"You are using magic somehow," Iona accuses.

"Where is my staff, nymph?" Ariadne asks with exasperation.

Iona glances at the staff where it rests against the pianoforte. Then an idea emerges, and her grin widens.

"I remain highly skeptical." She lifts the hem of her skirt up to her thighs to throw her leg over Ariadne's lap. She sucks in a breath and pulls back her hands to let Iona straddle her.

"What are you doing?" Ariadne asks, her voice dropping an octave.

"Keep playing," Iona commands, guiding Ariadne's hands around her torso.

Her fingers find the keys and after a moment's hesitation, she continues the song. Iona leans in and peppers soft kisses upon her long neck, then licks a path up to her ear. Ariadne shivers and accidentally plays a discordant note, only to continue in ignited defiance of Iona's distractions, just as she'd predicted. Ariadne's vanity would never allow her to turn down a challenge.

"Am I meant to lose this game?" Ariadne asks, feigning indifference.

Iona slowly, tantalizingly tugs at the drawstring of Ariadne's chemise until the bow comes undone and the white cotton fabric falls open, exposing her olive skin to Iona's appreciative gaze. She slips a hand inside to cup Ariadne's breast in her palm, squeezing gently, and running a thumb over her peaked nipple. Ariadne inhales sharply and plays another foul note despite her best efforts.

"Was it not you who told me that you always win?" Iona asks innocently.

Ariadne shakes with quiet laughter and Iona kisses the edge of her smiling mouth. While trying her best to reach the correct notes with Iona's body in the way, Ariadne does quite a fine job at pretending she isn't there, though the thrumming pulse on her neck would suggest otherwise. Iona traces the vein with her tongue.

One part of the sonata ends and another begins. Ariadne breathlessly explains there are five sections of the piece in all. Each interpretation is meant to explore the theme of the song in a new way. The second part has more notes than the first, and a slightly faster tempo.

Even when Iona repositions herself to suckle at Ariadne's nipple, while running her thumb in steady circles around the other, Ariadne manages to maintain an air of elegant implacability. That is, until Iona tugs up the skirt of her chemise.

"Iona," Ariadne chuckles darkly, her fingers faltering.

"Did I say that you could stop?" Iona asks.

Ariadne sighs, but her cheeks turn a pretty shade of pink as she continues playing even as Iona reaches between their bodies to stroke her ever so softly. Ariadne's breathing deepens, her full red lips parting, her breasts rising and falling heavily.

Her hands slam against the keys when Iona rubs her in relentless circles without warning.

"Have you forgotten the rest?" Iona taunts.

"You're deliberately sabotaging me," Ariadne growls through gritted teeth.

"And you have exaggerated your musical prowess," Iona goads her.

She groans as she attempts to carry on with her performance. The tempo becomes haphazard, her notes not nearly as precise. Iona slows her fingers, leaning in to suck on Ariadne's neck again, but this time with the intention of leaving marks behind.

"What brought this on?" Ariadne asks, her voice shaking.

Iona pulls away to give her a dubious look that she cannot see through the black silk of her blindfold. "I shall never require a reason to touch you."

Ariadne grins. "Yes, but... someone could hear or walk in. I haven't locked the door or cast an enchantment on the room to-"

When Iona sinks two fingers deep inside of her, she lets out a strangled moan, her hands pausing on the keys as she loses herself in the sensation of Iona's fingers delving in, stretching her, stroking languidly.

Her fingers go still and Ariadne whimpers.

"Did I say," Iona grazes her jaw with her teeth, "that you could stop playing?"

"No..."

"Then why is there silence?"

Ariadne continues and nips at Iona's shoulder, making her squirm away. As she presses the heel of her hand against Ariadne's apex, she curls her fingers inside and pulses them in time with the music, teasing her mercilessly.

"Iona..." Ariadne says her name like a prayer.

"Not too distracting, I hope," Iona teases.

"Not at all." Ariadne's hips shift restlessly against the bench.

Iona grins as she conjures a stone like the one Ariadne had used on her in the valley. She makes it only slightly bigger than a shilling, and curved inwards at the center like a tiny bowl. She positions it where she wants, directly atop Ariadne's swollen nub.

"Frémir" Iona incants.

Ariadne nearly jumps up from her seat, when the small piece

of stone sends a vibratory jolt of pleasure through her. The pendant glows as Iona's magic keeps the stone in place, so even when Ariadne's squirms, she cannot escape the sensations.

"Oh," Ariadne pants. "Do you mean to ruin me?"

"Never," Iona cups her chin. "Where is my music?"

Ariadne chuckles darkly. "Oh, I am going to make you-"

Iona silences her with a passionate kiss, welcoming Ariadne's tongue as it pushes past her lips, sucking on it precisely the way she likes to between Ariadne's legs, which elicits a distinctive shudder from her as she continues her song in earnest.

Iona shifts in Ariadne's lap as her own pleasure builds through their bond, making it so much more difficult to tease, but not impossible. She slips her hand between Ariadne's thighs again and pushes two fingers inside, only to leave them there, barely moving, even when Ariadne tries to grind her hips against her.

Ariadne's own hands become frantic against the keys, desperate to finish the sonata so she can finally have her release. Frowning, Iona laces her fingers in Ariadne's soft curls and pulls her head away to break the kiss.

"Slower," Iona demands.

"No," Ariadne growls.

Iona withdraws her fingers and steals away the stone. Ariadne's responding sigh of frustration is nearly enough for Iona to demand she start the sonata over from the beginning.

"Don't you dare," Ariadne growls.

While her mouth is open, Iona slips her fingers inside, momentarily startling Ariadne before she dutifully sucks on them, swirling her tongue around them, until they're clean. Iona's core throbs but she holds fast, waiting for Ariadne to obey. When she continues playing, it's at a slower tempo. Iona grins.

"Much better, darling," Iona says, as she reattaches the stone and slides two fingers back inside Ariadne's slick core, marveling at how wet she's become.

The fifth and final section of the sonata begins, and Iona makes the most of her remaining minutes to tease Ariadne within an inch of her life.

"The song is almost over," she warns, panting heavily.

"So soon?" Iona asks.

Ariadne huffs. "Not soon enough."

"Awe," Iona coos. "Are you so desperate for me, my love?"

Ariadne's cheeks turn bright red and Iona kisses one of them softly.

"Say it," Iona demands.

"Yes," Ariadne's voice trembles.

"Yes what?" Iona asks, as Ariadne so often does to her.

"Yes, I am desperate for you," she whispers between panting breaths.

Iona raises an eyebrow. "Then why are you so quiet?"

Ariadne swallows convulsively. "Everyone will hear."

"No. Only I will, I swear it."

Ariadne lets out a fevered, desperate moan and Iona's heartbeat stutters at the sound.

"This whole time?" she asks incredulously.

"You are not the only one with magic," Iona grins. "I would not leave you so exposed."

Ariadne leans in to kiss her and Iona allows it, for a moment. Then she pulls away, leaving her wanting. Now assured that no one can hear or interrupt them, Ariadne's wanton sighs and moans accompany the music, like a prima donna's obscene aria sung in harmony with the sonata.

Iona keeps her on the edge, drawing out their exquisite torture with featherlight kisses and calculated strokes, until finally Ariadne plays one final low note. Her shoulders slump as the sonata ends at long last, then she rips her blindfold off to reveal red eyes mad with desire.

"Very good," Iona grins.

"If you stop, I will tie you down and make you cry from desperation," Ariadne threatens as she spreads her legs wider and digs her fingers into Iona's hips.

As delicious as that sounds, Iona wouldn't dare stop, not when they are both so close. She strokes faster and harder as Ariadne kisses her with abandon, losing herself in her pleasure, having never looked so beautiful, so uninhibited. To see her laid bare this way, beyond reason or modesty, is addictive. Iona never wants it to end.

With a violent tremor, Ariadne falls apart, her inner muscles spasming around Iona's fingers. She moans Iona's name, her voice cracking from the force of her cry, and Iona falls with her, trembling from the intensity of their pleasure, but never looking away from Ariadne's convulsing form, the look of purest ecstasy on her perfect face, as a rush of warm wetness coats Iona's palm.

They take a moment to catch their breath. Ariadne winces slightly as Iona removes her fingers and they stare at each other for a moment, both of them unable to believe what has just transpired. Then Ariadne laughs, a joyous, incredulous laugh that makes Iona's spirits soar.

"I suppose you do know the song," Iona concedes, and Ariadne rolls her eyes before pulling her in close.

"Such depravity." Ariadne's voice is a low rasp. "I did not think you would be so brazen in my family's home. You are far too… respectable."

"You've had a horrid influence on me," Iona giggles.

Her fingers drift over Iona's cheek, then she leans in to kiss her so tenderly that Iona thinks she might just float away.

"Now what did you say earlier?" Ariadne asks.

Without warning, she detaches the music rack, tossing it aside and scattering sheet music across the marble floor. Then she lifts Iona up and on top of the pianoforte's lid and looms over her until she lays flat on her back against the smooth wood. She's forced to rest her feet on the piano keys, creating dissonant chords that contrast greatly to the sonata.

"Take it off before I rip it off," Ariadne growls.

Eagerly, Iona gathers the fabric of her chemise and lifts her hips so she can pull it over her head and toss it onto the floor, her streak of dominance dissipating while under Ariadne's seductive glare.

She hooks Iona's legs over her shoulders but does not immediately sink her mouth onto her. Instead, she presses soft kisses upon Iona's inner thigh, lightly running her teeth over the sensitive skin, though Iona is already dripping with arousal. A part of her wonders if Ariadne aims to torment her in turn, as she surely deserves.

"Ari," Iona whimpers.

Ariadne looks up at her from between her legs, and Iona instantly knows what she wants.

"Please," Iona begs. "Please, I need you. Only you."

Then she remembers Ariadne's earlier threat and her core clenches hungrily. She wants to forget everything, to lose the mental capacity to worry about the solstice or maleficium or anything else. She glares down from beneath her lashes, and Ariadne's eyes glint as she awaits her command.

"Lick me until I cannot bear it any longer."

"Again?" Ariadne grins against her tender skin. "Well, if you insist."

She chokes on air at the first stroke of Ariadne's tongue. She doesn't tease, doesn't hold back, does not even let her breathe. Iona is slightly embarrassed by how little time it takes for her to climax once, but she does not endure it for long because Ariadne doesn't let up for even a moment. If anything, she doubles her efforts.

Her entire body seizes as Ariadne sinks one, then two fingers into her, thrusting hard and deep, while flicking her tongue rapidly against her swollen flesh, until she squeezes her thighs against Ariadne's ears as she reaches another peak and falls apart a second time. Ariadne continues on as if she hadn't noticed.

Iona winces when she becomes too sensitive, nearing the point of pain. Ariadne hesitates, almost pulling away, but Iona entwines her fingers into Ariadne's curls and holds her head in place.

*Harder.*

Ariadne moans against her, making her shiver. She sucks Iona's flesh deep into her mouth, curling her fingers simultaneously, and Iona cries out as she fists Ariadne's hair hard enough to pull strands from her scalp. She climaxes a third time, and a fourth, a fifth, until she loses all control and becomes a writhing, pitiful mess of whimpers and unintelligible sighs.

Ariadne's ministrations are feverish as she nears her own limit, having ridden through Iona's pleasure along with her. Hardly possessing strength left to raise her head, Iona peers down the length of her body, now covered in a glistening sheen of sweat, with Ariadne's left hand reaching up to grope at her breast. She can barely make out Ariadne's face through the hot tears pooling in her eyes, streaking down her flushed cheeks, obscuring her vision.

*Are those tears, nymph?* Ariadne taunts. *It's a wonder you've any water left in you.*

She replaces her fingers with her tongue, thrusting deep inside, while circling Iona's nub with her thumb. Iona screams, her back arching towards the ceiling as pleasure explodes from her, until she's quite sure her heart will give out.

"Stop!" Iona squirms away.

Ariadne pulls back with a self-satisfied grin as she licks Iona's desire from her lips, a drop falling her from chin before she can catch it. "You lasted longer that time."

Iona can hardly comprehend her words when she slumps against the pianoforte, her chest heaving as the room spins.

"Breathe, love," Ariadne says, though she is panting heavily, too.

Iona nods weakly and focuses on inhaling and exhaling, her

thighs trembling uncontrollably beneath Ariadne's hands.

"Don't faint, now," she jests.

"I… won't… you…" Iona struggles to think of a word. "…cretin."

"Sharp words indeed," Ariadne chuckles.

She gathers Iona up in her lap, stroking her hair and whispering soothing words.

"How kind of you to distract me from my troubled thoughts," Ariadne murmurs into her hair. "Your cunt is far more diverting than my piano, I must admit, and the sounds you make are far prettier than that of any instrument."

Iona giggles and in doing so expels what little remains of her energy. She's moments away from drifting off to sleep in Ariadne's warm embrace.

"The sun is rising," Ariadne murmurs. "The long day."

Iona cannot even lift her eyelids to look. "Hmm…"

"Come, let's go to bed." Ariadne presses a kiss to her forehead. "We may yet have an hour before we are expected at breakfast."

Iona whines but she needn't have worried. Ariadne stands with her cradled in her arms.

"Perhaps you have caught my laziness," she chuckles.

Iona makes an unintelligible noise in protest and Ariadne laughs again. She somehow manages to take her staff from where it rests against the pianoforte and create a portal back to her bedroom.

Iona doesn't let go, even when Ariadne tries to set her down onto the bed and pull away. Sighing, Ariadne climbs into bed beside her, her staff still in hand. Iona drifts off to sleep with her head cushioned by Ariadne's chest, her strong, steady heartbeat like a somnolent lullaby.

## 13 - *Iona*

She startles awake when she notices how rested she feels.

"Ari," Iona shakes her shoulder.

"What? What is it?" Ariadne's eyes pop open in surprise, and a protective shield encapsulates them. When she sees there is no danger, she slumps against the pillow and her grip on her staff goes slack.

"We slept too long." Iona yawns and stretches her deliciously sore muscles.

Then she freezes in place when she marks the sun's position through the window. It is still rising, just as it had been when they fell asleep.

"But…" Iona says.

Ariadne stretches and groans. She puts her arms behind her head and gazes at her with appreciation, then bolts upright. "Your chemise."

Iona glances down at her nakedness, then up at Ariadne who has both her hands over her mouth, her eyes wide.

"It's still in the solarium?" Iona squeaks.

Ariadne laughs through her fingers and Iona shoves her shoulder.

"We must find it before someone else does!" She leaps out of bed and quickly conjures on clothes.

"Don't fret," Ariadne says through her laughter. "They'll convene in the dining room for breakfast. We can go and fetch it before anyone should notice."

There's a knock on the door and Moira calls, "Happy Solstice! Cease whatever lurid act you're in the midst of and get dressed."

"Leave us be, Moira." Ariadne throws a pillow at the door.

"Do not go back to sleep or Mother will be cross," Moira says. "We are all gathering in the solarium for coffee and cakes."

Iona smacks her hand against her forehead, and Ariadne snorts with laughter.

"Your grandmother and cousin arrived unannounced this morning," Moira says, in a less enthused tone.

Ariadne stops laughing abruptly, then jumps out of bed and runs to the door, pulling it open to say, "Nonna and Frankie are here?"

"Yes, so look alive! It's rude to keep them waiting," Moira says, appearing regal as ever in her coral pink dress. She turns on her heels and saunters down the hall without another word.

"Nonna and Frankie, your father's mother and nephew?" Iona says, trying to keep track.

"Wear blue," Ariadne suggests. "It is Nonna's favorite color. And leave your hair down. Or... No, pin it up that way you do."

Iona racks her brain, then conjures pins and fixes her hair in place so a few stray pieces frame her face, then changes her dress from white to sky blue.

"Yes, perfect," Ariadne smiles, then pecks her on the cheek before rushing to the looking glass hung on her wall.

"Should I be nervous?" Iona asks.

"No! Or... Um..." Ariadne deliberates. "Nonna can be quite discerning, but I do not know anyone worthwhile who hasn't adored you."

Iona flushes with pleasure and smiles wide. "That is very sweet of you to say."

"Oh..." Ariadne wipes her hands down her face. "That blasted chemise. We cannot let them see it. Perhaps they won't..."

Iona worries at her bottom lip. "We shall find some way to hide it. Or if I can see it, I might be able to make it disappear before anyone should notice."

"Good day," Marina says as she passes by their open door.

"Good day," Iona and Ariadne say far too loudly to be casual.

Marina doesn't seem to notice as she hums to herself and glides away.

*We mustn't look so guilty.* Ariadne fusses with her hair and conjures a midnight blue dress, pinning a delphinium into her braided bun.

*The longer we wait, the more difficult it will be to-* Iona begins, but Ariadne takes her hand and pulls her out the door and down the hall.

They burst into the solarium where they find Moira, Marina, Petro, and two newcomers all sitting by the windows drinking coffee and admiring the sunrise. They are not far from the pianoforte, but when Iona quickly scans the floor for any sign of the chemise, she cannot see even the slightest hint of the white fabric anywhere.

She gasps when Aster collides into the back of her legs and nearly topples her over in his haste to get around her.

"Aster," Ariadne chides.

The wolf bounds over to a very old woman with white hair and weathered skin. She waves a leg of mutton in the air in front of her, and there on her forearm is a witch's mark of a wolf that looks remarkably like Aster. He sits obediently and waits for his treat.

"Good dog." The old woman rewards him with the treat and scratches behind his ears.

Wisp approaches with her ears slightly pulled back in hesitance until the old woman notices.

"Bellissima." The old woman smiles, conjuring a leg of rabbit and offering it to the gentle fox.

Wisp takes it within her jowl and skitters away to sit and eat beside Aster.

"Why do you linger there in the threshold?" The old woman eyes them with disapproval.

"Nonna," Ariadne smiles as she approaches and leans down to embrace her where she sits. "I wasn't aware you would be visiting-"

"This is my family's estate. I need not announce my comings and goings to anyone," Nonna says.

"Of course," Ariadne clears her throat.

"Have you finally learned to eat?" Nonna asks, looking her up and down.

"Uh…" Ariadne's smile falls.

"Good," Nonna says, "I was beginning to worry."

Iona quickly interjects. "How do you do? My name is-"

"I know who you are," Nonna says. "I have eyes, girl. You needn't introduce yourself when Morgan Le Fay's pendant hangs from your neck."

"Oh." Iona looks down at the pendant. "I suppose you're right."

"Of course, I am," Nonna says brusquely, but there is a twinkle in her umber eyes. "I hear it is you I should thank for the absence of my infernal daughter-in-law."

Iona lowers her eyes shyly, but her blush doesn't fully manifest until she hears what the old woman says next.

"Well done, my dear. With spirit like that and a bosom like yours, I shan't be astounded by my granddaughter's sudden undying devotion to you."

"Nonna!" Ariadne protests.

"Mother, please," Petro sighs.

"Oh hush, I'm only joking," Nonna grins. "Sit."

She pats the space beside her on the chaise, and they quickly do as they're told. Ariadne conjures a cup of clove tea and takes a nervous sip.

*Please tell me you see it.* Ariadne cuts her an imploring look. *I do not know if I'd survive Nonna's scathing remarks should she discover it before we do.*

*Neither could I.* Iona struggles to keep a straight face. *But I cannot see it anywhere.*

*Where did you throw it?* Ariadne's impatience is palpable.

*Against the wall by the pianoforte.* Iona cranes her neck to try and get a better look.

The sound of a throat clearing makes her refocus on the group of witches and warlocks who are all staring at her expectantly.

"Pardon?" Iona asks.

"What are you looking at?" Nonna asks.

"Apologies, I… I thought I saw a lark through the window," Iona says.

"If you are quite done admiring the morning's splendor," Nonna says dryly. "Please allow me to introduce my grandson, Francesco Mitriora."

She gestures to a young man sitting on an adjacent chaise.

"Please, call me Frankie," he says with an exceedingly kind smile that puts Iona at ease. He has short, dark curls that bounce with his every movement, and the same umber eyes as his grandmother.

"Now tell me, how does this oddity work?" Nonna asks, gesturing to the staff.

As Ariadne explains the staff's capabilities, it is clear how proud of it she is, and it's quite endearing. Everyone is so often preoccupied with the pendant, but the staff is just as much of a marvel, especially given how mysteriously it had presented itself.

However, as Ariadne tells the story of how she'd found the staff, and how time had stopped all around her as she'd claimed it, Iona fiddles with her amethyst ring absentmindedly. She already knows the story well and the mention of Elise always dampens her spirits. On a sudden impulse, she covertly slides off her ring. Ariadne's words morph until her speech turns from English to Italian, and Iona schools her features as she finds herself enraptured.

To hear such a beautiful language spoken by the voice she

loves most in the world is a distinct pleasure. It matters not that she can only decipher a word or two. Otherwise, mundane expressions sound like poetry to her ears. It reminds her that she should continue her study of the language when next she has a spare moment, so she might hear Ariadne speak to her this way all the time.

Then Ariadne says something, and looks to her in question, so she quickly slides the ring back on.

"Pardon?" Iona asks.

Ariadne glances down at her hands as she secures her ring back into place, a small smile reaching her lips. "Did you see another bird, nymph?"

Iona smiles shyly at the tease and the endearment. "I was merely swept away by your talent at storytelling."

"Ah," Ariadne says, mirroring her smile. "I asked if Merlin alluded to the location of the staff when you spoke with him on his island."

"No. He only explained how a blood bond could counteract Elise's blood magic," Iona says.

Nonna spits on the floor in disgust and Petro grimaces.

"It was Merlin's suggestion to bond with one another?" Moira asks.

"Yes, though Samuel later told me he suspected it was the only option, but did not wish to encourage it," Iona says.

"I can understand his hesitance," Petro says. "To bond so quickly..."

"We needn't discuss this again," Ariadne says sharply.

Petro nods in reluctant acquiescence and does not continue. There is a brief moment of awkward silence.

Then Frankie sets his coffee down. "Ariadne, I have a sudden desire for music. Would you be so kind?"

Her eyebrows raise slightly at the request, but she sets her tea down on a nearby table and stands. "Certainly."

As Ariadne makes her way to the pianoforte, Iona's anxiety subsides. Perhaps she can find the chemise and discard of it so they might continue their breakfast in peace.

"Iona." Frankie stands and offers his hand to her.

Surprised, Iona takes it, and he guides her toward the pianoforte. Ariadne begins playing a lively sonata and glances at them briefly before looking back down at her hands.

"I feel as if I know you already," he says.

"Is that so?" Iona asks.

When they reach the pianoforte, she cannot help blushing at

the sight of the wood she'd lain across mere hours ago.

"Yes, from Ariadne's many letters," Frankie says, "and this."

With an impish grin, he reaches into his blazer to slowly pull out the missing chemise, though it seems impossible for it to fit within such a small pocket.

"Which of you harlots left this here?" He looks between them with mocking contempt.

Ariadne's hands slow as she sighs heavily with a mixture of relief and chagrin. Frankie makes the chemise disappear before anyone else can see and leans in close.

"Do not stop playing, or they will grow suspicious," he whispers urgently.

Iona snorts out a laugh and Frankie looks to her in confusion.

"Yes, Ariadne, did we say you could stop?" Iona whispers, tilting her head.

"Do not… Just be quiet," Ariadne says with a bashful smile as she continues her song.

"I thought your wild days were behind you," Frankie whispers, then gives Iona an apologetic look. "Forgive me for jesting. I know we've only just met, but I couldn't resist."

"This is your fault." Ariadne glares at Iona from beneath her dark lashes.

"It wasn't my idea to-"

"I did not hear you protesting-"

"Now, now," Frankie says. "No need to quarrel. I shall only make jokes for a year, two at most. No real harm has been done."

Ariadne sighs heavily, and Frankie giggles with delight.

"I'm mortified," Iona admits, but she giggles along with him.

"No, no! Do not be," Frankie assures her. "I was in a much worst predicament just yesterday in fact. Was nearly thrown out a rare beauty's window in her haste. Fortunately, she allowed me to use the stairs."

Ariadne laughs. "So, nothing has changed with you then?"

"On the contrary, everything has irrevocably changed," Frankie says. "My heart has been stolen."

"By whom?" Ariadne asks.

"I was hoping you would enlighten me as to your prior acquaintance with her," he says.

"Oh… Does she know me?" Ariadne asks.

"Unfortunately, yes," he says, an accusatory frown reaching his lips. "I shared a glorious night with her, but when we awoke the next morning, she saw my mark." He brushes a hand over his left shoulder where beneath his shirt and jacket, Iona wagers a wolf mark is displayed. "And the woman whispered 'Ariadne will kill me' with such dread it gave me a chill on her behalf. Then she threw me out onto the street before I could manage to button my trousers!"

Ariadne's eyes widen at that, and she glances sideways at Iona.

"She never told me her name, and in the flurry of the morning I was not permitted to ask. She was beautiful though. Long blonde hair… big brown eyes… and wild," Frankie waggles his eyebrows.

Iona grins, until a thought emerges. It couldn't be…

"I met her at Rebekka Magnúsdóttir's soiree," Frankie says. "I heard you were there, somewhere, though I did not see you. I suppose I wouldn't have had much chance, being otherwise occupied and quite foxed, truth be told."

Ariadne locks eyes with Iona and her mouth falls open in horror.

"Did she have a mark in the shape of a laurel on her wrist?" Iona asks.

"Yes, in fact she did. I've never heard of such a mark before. Have you?" Frankie asks.

Ariadne leans her elbows against the piano keys to put her head in her hands. "No, no, no, no…"

"What is it?" Frankie asks over the discordant notes ringing from the piano.

Meanwhile, Iona cannot form words through her incredulous laughter.

"It is not funny, Iona!" Ariadne protests.

"Do you know her?" Frankie asks in earnest. "If you do, please tell me. I should like to see her again."

"No, you do not," Ariadne says firmly.

"And why is that?" He narrows his eyes.

"She is-" Ariadne begins to say.

"Careful," Iona says, as her laughter subsides.

Ariadne cuts her a withering look, then says, "She recently ended a long courtship with Erik Virtanen. She is likely not of a mind to-"

"Do not assume her thoughts," Iona says. "Her name is Crescentia Léandre, and she is a dear friend of mine."

"How fortuitous!" Frankie exclaims.

Ariadne grumbles unintelligibly, but Iona ignores her. "She means to attend my ritual today, and the reception afterward.

You are most welcome to attend, and I would be glad to introduce you to her more formally there. That is, if she is agreeable, of course. I would need to ask her."

"I would be eternally grateful to you if you did," Frankie says.

*Why would you offer such a thing?* Ariadne protests.

*Calm yourself.* Iona glares at her. *They will not be wed in a day. You are being foolish.*

*You do not know Crescentia or Frankie as I do. They may well be wed within a fortnight.* Ariadne glowers. "She did this on purpose to annoy me."

"Why would she?" Iona scoffs. "I doubt she thought of you at all."

"If she did, then it was certainly a sweet revenge," Frankie sighs dreamily.

Ariadne deliberates, then her annoyance subsides. "On second thought, perhaps you're right."

"Oh…" He chuckles wryly. "Yes, there is that."

"What?" Iona asks.

"I shan't say it," Ariadne says, looking to Frankie.

"I suppose if you are family now, you may as well know," he says. "I was not always as you see me now. I became my proper self almost a year ago."

"Oh," Iona says, though she doesn't understand.

Ariadne looks again to Frankie for approval, and he nods his assent.

*He was born a girl,* Ariadne explains. *He never was one in mind or soul, so when he gained enough magic, he used spells to transform into his true self. He need only cast them once every month to maintain his transformation.*

"I've never heard of such a thing," Iona says, marveling at the possibilities of what magic can accomplish. "Is it secret?"

"Some are more vocal about such things than others," Frankie shrugs. "I've nothing to hide, but nor did I inform the town crier, so to speak, and I do not often run in the same circles as Ariadne."

"Crescentia must not have heard, or she may have avoided you," Ariadne says.

"Oh…" Frankie's face falls.

"For being my cousin," she clarifies. "She avoids Sebastian like the plague, despite her fortune seeking."

"They would be a disastrous match," Iona mumbles, recalling his permanent frown and vacant eyes.

Frankie's frown reappears. "You do not think she will refuse to see me again, do you? You would not keep us apart."

Ariadne glowers and looks away, until Iona shoves her shoulder.

"She wouldn't dream of it," Iona says, a warning in her tone.

"What are you all whispering about?" Nonna asks.

"Nothing," they all say in unison.

When they've returned to their seats and reclaimed their cups, Petro says, "Have you yet heard Beethoven's latest sonata? It is quite a triumph. One of his best, I'd say. I have the pages in my study-"

"Euphemia sent them to me months ago," Ariadne says. "I've nearly learned it, but the third movement is quite complex."

"Ah." Petro's face falls slightly. "Good. I doubt it will present much of a challenge to such a prolific player."

"She is only so skilled for having nothing else to do in that dreary place you call home," Nonna says with impressive bitterness.

"Mother," Petro tries to say.

"I rejoice at knowing I no longer need to threaten abduction to see my own grandchild while you kept her under lock and key. It is a miracle she did not turn out like this one." Nonna points to Marina. "All weird and unsettling."

"A pleasure as always." Moira narrows her eyes. She takes her sister's hand, but Marina had been gazing up at the sky and did not seem to hear the harsh remark.

"I expect frequent visits," Nonna says to Ariadne. "Or I shall be very cross with you."

"Of course," Ariadne says, sitting up straighter.

"And you," Nonna says to Iona. "If you are so fond of nature, you will much prefer Triora to Rome."

"Triora?" Iona asks.

"Yes, do you know it?" Nonna asks.

In fact, she does. It was where she'd traveled to through one of the moonstone arches in Morgan's trails and met Lucretia before she was killed by the townsfolk.

"There were witch trials held there, were there not?" Iona asks.

"Indeed." Nonna's eyes darken. "Our family was nearly swept up in them before they departed for Rome. I now reside in our family's former estate, which had been left abandoned."

"Why would you return to a city that once attempted to kill your ancestors?" Iona asks.

"Rome is no better," Nonna sniffs. "Far too many human

zealots walk these streets."

"If only they knew of the witches residing right under their noses," Xiomara says as she steps gracefully into the room.

"They would waste no time in lighting their torches," Nonna says wryly.

She rises to her feet with noticeable effort. Frankie stands and offers his hand, which she promptly swats away.

"You are most welcome, Lavinia," Xiomara says. "How long shall we have the pleasure of your company?"

"Only for the solstice, I'm afraid," Nonna says. "I find myself less interested in travel. An old woman needs the comforts of home."

"Of course. I regret I cannot stay, but we must speak later." Xiomara smiles warmly at her, then her eyes rest on Iona. "If you are finished with breakfast, there is much to be done before noon."

Iona and Ariadne quickly gulp down their tea and follow Xiomara outside where a carriage waits to take them to the Sibylline Mountains. The coach bumps and jerks as the horses haul them uphill with supernatural speed. There hidden in a narrow valley of stone is a small lake of dark blue water. Xiomara leads them to the shore and takes a deep breath of the thin mountain air.

"This is the Lake of the Sibyl, named for The Apennine Sibyl, an ancient prophetess who lived in a cave nearby and often came here to meditate and commune with nature. The lake is fed by snow and rain," Xiomara says. "Places like these are perfect for rituals. Can you sense it?"

Iona closes her eyes and when she concentrates, she can feel a very faint prickling across her skin and down the column of her spine. "Yes. There is abundant magic here."

Xiomara leads them to the shore of the lake, then turns to address them.

"A witch's sabbath is practiced far and wide in some form or other," Xiomara says. "There is no singular method of harvesting magic. I know the Greek rituals, your uncle can teach you the druidic way someday, and there are many countless cultures with their own customs, of course. As you grow older and travel, you will learn what suits you best."

Iona nods, grateful for her guidance. She feels like a student again after weeks of lounging aimlessly. While she's truly enjoyed her holiday, it is high time for her to be of use, as Morgan intended.

"Come," Xiomara says, offering her hands.

Iona takes them and Xiomara grasps tightly. She takes deep breaths in and out, and Iona follows suit, closing her eyes.

"I can sense your apprehension," Xiomara says.

Iona's eyes pop open and she goes to apologize, but Xiomara squeezes her hands.

"No apologies. No shame. No regret," Xiomara instructs. "You must let all negativity fall away."

Iona nods and lowers her head, breathing deeply in and out again. Doubt is a heavy weight on her consciousness. She worries about her place in this society of highborn witches, the formality of a ritual she is meant to perform for the first time for a great crowd of strangers, and, most of all, she harbors a deep concern about the covens' reaction to her invitation to witches and warlocks without a coven.

She hadn't told Xiomara of this, and it seems Moira has neglected to mention it, to Iona's surprise. Perhaps Moira did so to sabotage her, because she knows it will be received poorly by their peers. She dreads that Marcel and others will come only to be ostracized, but if she announces her intentions, the sempiterna covens might not see fit to attend.

Or, worst of all, there is always the chance that Marcel was unable to convince any in his acquaintance to attend. Then she might need to find some other way to convince them, on an individual basis if need be.

Her pendant is one of the best conduits for magic to be imbued upon others. If she can help anyone in that endeavor so they may be able to conjure more than just feathers, it would mean more to her than any approval given by the covens. If she can somehow manage to appease both at once, it will be her greatest triumph.

Following a peaceful interlude of silent mediation, Xiomara has her wash her face in the waters of the lake, before having her strip down to her chemise to anoint her with oil that smells distinctly of apples and cypress. Xiomara dips fingers into her bowl and presses runic symbols upon Iona's forehead, wrists, ankles, and knees, then has Iona lower her chemise to her waist to draw symbols over her heart, her womb, at the base of her neck, and along the curve of her spine.

Her knees buckle as she feels suddenly very lightheaded and nearly collapses into the dirt.

"Iona?" Ariadne catches her and holds her up.

"Not to worry," Xiomara says calmly, pressing a gentle hand

against Iona's forehead.

Her eyelids droop as she nearly faints, her limbs heavy with an unpleasant prickling sensation that makes her itch.

"Deep breaths," Xiomara reminds her.

Iona leans her head against Ariadne's chest and listens to her steady heartbeat, until the sickening feeling finally subsides.

"There now," Xiomara says. "All better."

Ariadne helps her back onto her feet, keeping hold of her even when she's steadied. "What happened?"

"I am exposing her soul to the magic around her, removing the barrier. It can be disorienting at first," Xiomara says.

When they are certain Iona will not faint again, Ariadne braids her hair into a single plait down her back and conjures a pink mallow flower, fixing it to the end with a ribbon, then presses a kiss to Iona's shoulder and steps away.

"There," Xiomara says, setting her bowl aside and rubbing the excess oil into her hands.

Iona discreetly pulls her chemise back up to cover herself. "What will I wear?"

"That is entirely your decision," Xiomara says. "It can be beneficial to remove every barrier, but if you would not be comfortable…"

"In front of all those people?" Iona's cheeks burn. "I would not prefer that at all."

"I thought so," Xiomara chuckles. "Then I suggest this."

She conjures an airy robe of white silk that drapes itself over Iona's body. The gossamer fabric is thin enough to see only the slightest hint of her tawny freckles beneath but provides suitable cover for her chest and legs. Most of her back, however, is left exposed, nearly to the base of her spine. Iona cranes her neck to try and look behind herself and see just how much of her is bare.

"You should not cover your mark," Xiomara explains. "You must wear it proudly."

Xiomara takes Iona's braid and pulls it forward, so it rests against her front, the pink petals of Ariadne's flower stark against the white of the robe.

"Now, I will demonstrate the ritual and then you will meditate for the remainder of the morning," Xiomara says.

"Is that necessary?" Ariadne asks, glancing at the sun's low position in the sky.

"A clear mind will foster greater results," Xiomara says.

"We were able to perform the rituals at college without all this fuss," Ariadne says with slight skepticism.

"And what were you able to manifest? A few streams of magic at most?" Xiomara asks. "Allow me to show you what a sabbath ritual can produce."

A constant wind blusters through the secluded vale, causing stray hairs to come loose from Iona's braid to tickle her bare back. The sun's rays provide luxuriant warmth as the minutes tick by at an agonizingly slow pace.

Xiomara swims in the lake, undeterred by the cold, and Iona listens for the distant splashes. Ariadne sits beside her, though she doesn't bother with silent meditation, opting instead to read a book while she waits. Iona cannot help harboring a bit of jealousy but reminds herself that she must be diligent.

After hours of silence, Iona is quite sure she has considered every possible way the ritual could fail. She could trip on her robe and fall on her face. She could pronounce the incantation incorrectly or forget it altogether, standing there in dumb silence while the covens mock and scorn her. She cannot stand the thought of disappointing her friends or proving to her enemies that they were right to doubt her.

Perhaps she will not evoke the abundant magic that everyone expects. The previous pendant bearer had been more than a century old and far more adept in all manner of arcane knowledge. Iona has only studied for one solitary year, much of it preoccupied by Elise's infernal attacks. How could she ever compare?

*Stop.* Ariadne's thought is an unyielding force. *The ritual will be perfect as you are. Word will spread of your strength and grace until every person with even a trace of magic knows your name. Come autumn, you will preside over a legion of witches and warlocks alike, all vying for your favor. Mark my words.*

Ariadne stands and offers her hand, pulling Iona to her feet, then jerking her forward roughly so they are flush against each other. Ariadne's warmth seeps through the thin fabric of her dress, raising goosebumps across her skin.

"I would not give my heart to a weak woman." Ariadne stares her down in that way that always makes her heartbeat stutter. "Are you weak?"

Iona holds her intense gaze and slowly shakes her head. "No."

"No. You most certainly are not." Ariadne glances up to the sky. *Now show them what I know to be true.*

Iona looks over her shoulder. A line of carriages making their way up the mountain at otherworldly speeds, making streaks of black against the grey rock. The bright sky is littered with witches and warlocks flying on brooms or gliding through the air on conjured wings.

Ariadne steps away but keeps hold of her hand. *Show them why Morgan chose you.*

# PART TWO

## INCURSION

# 14 - Iona

When all are gathered, there are more than twenty covens accounted for, conversing amongst themselves in hushed tones and shifting with restless anticipation. They'd only just been informed of Xiomara's decision to step aside in favor of Iona when letters had been sent far and wide the previous night. Their expressions range from dubiety to outright scorn, but fortunately none of them saw fit to abstain.

Within the crowd of strangers, Iona spies a few familiar faces. Crescentia, of course, is there with her family. She waves and motions for Iona to stand taller and not look down at her feet.

Phoebe Kimball, Crescentia's friend from America, stands close by with a very old woman leaning against her arm and brandishing her wand as she speaks, making those around her visibly nervous.

At the other end of the crowd, Kokuro Sato wears a kimono as black as her lustrous hair and delicately embroidered with red flowers, the petals so thin they look almost like sea urchins. Her family stands silently around her, observing the crowd with keen eyes. One of the men has a thin angular sword strapped to his waist with his hand resting on the hilt.

Professor Pari, Professor Yun, and Professor Salum are there with their families. Iona half hoped to see Samuel and his wife Violet in the crowd, too, but thinks better of it. He is still in mourning. She wonders where Elise is now, if she is locked away in a cell, or lying in bed unable to see past an illusion keeping her docile.

She shakes the thought from her mind, then notices Rebekka standing tall above the rest of the crowd with her family, who are also quite intimidating in size and stature. She gives Iona an encouraging smile when they catch each other's eye. Iona quickly looks away and finds Euphemia on the arm of a rather handsome gentleman with red hair and familiar ice blue eyes.

*Leonid Morozova.* Ariadne comes to stand beside her.

Within Ariadne's mind, an image flashes like the glint of a mirror in the sun, showing Leonid as a boy with a dimpled smile. When they were children, on one of Ariadne's mother's trips to Russia, she had fallen on a patch of ice. Leonid had helped her back to standing, while the other children only laughed and kept playing. Beyond that, they have hardly spoken, but she never forgot it.

*Does Euphemia know of your prior acquaintance?* Iona asks.

*I do not think so. She means to introduce me today.* Ariadne gives Leonid a shallow nod, which he returns.

*Why did you not tell her?* Iona asks.

Ariadne shrugs. *I never would have stood by and let her marry an unkind man. I was contented when I learned it would be him.*

Then she is distracted by someone else in the crowd. Iona looks in the direction of her gaze and finds Ksenia drifting aimlessly through the mass of people. The circles beneath her eyes have darkened even more, making her appear almost skeletal. She pointedly avoids looking their way.

*She is not well,* Ariadne muses. *Odd. I do not see the other Ulanovas anywhere.*

*You could... If you wanted to speak with her...* Iona trails off.

*She's not my problem any longer.* Ariadne scans the crowd again and visibly relaxes. *Samaira is here.*

It's a great comfort to both of them. Samaira smiles warmly, the sapphire ring glittering on her right hand. If some catastrophic disaster were to befall them, she surely would have warned them of it by now.

Movement brings Iona's eyes back up towards the sky, where a group of about twenty witches and warlocks descend on brooms, and her spirits soar when she recognizes Marcel's face among the newcomers. The other families notice them too, but seem far less eager for them to arrive, many of them scowling and whispering in earnest. Marcel lands first and glances about nervously, then sees Iona and smiles politely.

She goes to him, cutting through the crowd, and curtsies low in greeting.

"Good day, Ms. Lysander." Marcel bows his head respectfully.

"You are most welcome," Iona says, as the others gather around him.

They eye her warily and seem ready to jump on their brooms and fly away at any moment.

"Please, come." Iona beckons them forward.

She ignores the whispers and disapproving looks of the other covens as she guides the group to the very front of the assembly.

"Are you certain this won't cause trouble?" Marcel whispers, but Iona puts up a hand.

"I've never been so sure of anything," Iona says. "Thank you for placing your trust in me."

His eyes soften and he bows his head. "I am most grateful for the invitation."

She returns to the wooden platform and looks out at the crowd with a renewed sense of purpose.

"It is nearly time," Xiomara says, shooing Ariadne away. "Go and stand with the family."

Ariadne glances at Iona with a trace of reluctance, then gives her hand a kiss and goes to stand beside Marina. Without Ariadne's grounding presence, Iona's anxieties bubble back up to the surface. So many eyes are on her, expecting her to fail, or expecting absolute perfection.

"I wish your mother could have been here to witness this joyous occasion," Xiomara says softly.

Iona blinks in surprise, overcome with a swell of emotion at the thought of her mother standing at the front of the crowd, smiling with pride.

"In her stead, and as a mother myself, I would like to offer my blessings on this sacred day," she says. "May your magic shine bright and true."

Xiomara embraces her the way only a mother can, with gentle warmth and enduring strength. A wave of peace washes over her until all her worries seem trivial. She is meant to do this. She is meant to be here.

"Thank you," Iona says, quickly wiping at her cheek when a tear falls.

Xiomara only smiles, then goes to stand with her two daughters.

"Blessed be," Iona says, her voice echoing against the mountainside.

"Blessed be," the crowd responds.

She conjures four pyres at each corner of the space, for the North, South, East, and West. Breathing in the smoke, she raises her arms toward the sky.

"Veneficae et venefici exaudi orationem meam," Iona recites. "Patria est. Caelum nostrum est. Est aqua nostra. Ignis cum dicimus urit."

At the final statement, the pyres burn ever brighter, the pleasant heat a welcome respite from the cool wind.

"Prima nox iterum irruit in nos, ut sciamus gloriam. Ostende nobis viam," Iona says. "Essentia magicae lava in nobis."

"Essentia magicae lava in nobis," the crowd repeats, their litany ringing out again and again.

The pendant glows in response and slowly, like a rising sun, light materializes around them until the air is permeated by it. Iona squints as the magic consolidates into tendrils of brilliant golden auroras. It gathers, moving closer and closer to where she stands, until it collects within the pendant's stone.

The opal grows hot against her skin, close to burning her, until the magic explodes outwards, beams of light shining from Iona's chest, the force of it making the crowd stumble backwards. The magic reaches so high that it touches the clouds and makes them glow in brilliant yellows and oranges and pinks. Brighter even than the sun blazing above them, it nearly blinds Iona with its brilliance.

"Magicae messis," Iona incants. "Magicae messis… Magicae messis…"

She whispers it to herself, her chants drowned out by the laughter and exclamations of the crowd. The magic constellates closer until it's confined inside the boundaries of the four pyres, all within reach of the crowd so not a trace of it will be lost.

The covens dance wildly, twirling and twisting about as their souls feed on the vestal magic, and they become drunk with power. Circling the pyres, they rejoice in the abundance.

Iona falls to her knees with a sudden rush of euphoria, her heartbeat thrumming almost painfully fast, the magic setting her soul alight. She laughs and laughs until her cheeks hurt, while Wisp jumps and bounds around her, trilling and barking with unfettered glee.

It lasts for nearly an hour, until Iona can hardly stand it. There is more magic than the crowd could ever hope to claim in a year's worth of rituals. Eventually it fades, returning to the earth and air.

When Iona is able to think clearly again, she locks eyes with Ariadne. Her cheeks are flushed with excitement, her red eyes filled with pride, and her skin shimmering with the magic her body can hardly contain. Iona looks down at herself and sure enough, she is shimmering, too. Tiny tendrils of light illuminate her veins.

With effort she pushes herself back onto her feet, right before Ariadne can manage to run to her and offer her hand. Iona waves her off, but Ariadne loops an arm round her waist to lift her from the pedestal and onto the rocky ground.

"I told you," Ariadne whispers in her ear.

Iona smiles and takes her hand, then goes to Marcel to make sure he is well.

"I've never…" He shakes his head in utter astonishment, unable to speak.

"Calice," Iona incants, and a golden goblet appears in her hand in an instant. She motions for Marcel to do the same.

He pulls out his wand and incants, "Calice."

A goblet appears in his hand, too, not quite as quickly, but much faster than his previous conjuration of the feather. He holds the chalice gingerly, as if it were a fleeting apparition. Then his friends withdraw their wands to cast various spells and marvel at the swiftness of their magic, a new power that will change their lives irrevocably. The covens watch on with expressions ranging from bemusement to outright contempt, but Iona pays them no mind.

"Thank you," Marcel says, his voice thick with emotion. He reaches for her hand, kissing it and bowing low. His friends bow and curtsy as well.

"Please spread the word," Iona says. "All are welcome."

Once the excitement has died down, Iona keeps a tight hold on Ariadne's hand as she traverses the crowd, unsure of who to introduce herself to first. Ariadne leads her to a group of eleven blonde witches, all draped in blues and whites, with spaces made on their clothes to show their marks of pink flowers, each with two blooms connected to each other by a stem. Iona scrutinizes the mark on one of their shoulders.

*The twin flower, the mark of the Drakenströms,* Ariadne thinks. *They symbolize balance and harmony.*

"Good day," Iona curtsies, and they curtsy or bow in response.

"A beautiful display of magic, Ms. Lysander. You should be very proud," One woman says, then regards Ariadne with recognition. "I always knew you would rise above it all."

"Thank you, Mrs. Drakenström." Ariadne's smile is only slightly forced. *Euphemia's mother.*

*Ah,* Iona eyes her, then addresses the coven. "Many blessings."

They respond in kind, and do not seem nearly as dismayed by the presence of Marcel and his friends as the other covens. Iona supposes she should have expected such temperance from Euphemia's kin.

Then Euphemia herself approaches with her husband, Leonid,

and Ariadne stands taller in anticipation.

"You were an angel!" Euphemia embraces her tightly. "All that light in your hair, in your eyes… Oh, how lovely it was!"

Leonid clears his throat, a smile in his eyes, though his countenance is reserved.

"My love, be patient. I must ensure Iona knows how spectacular she is," Euphemia says to him. Frida coos on her shoulder in agreement.

Flushing at Euphemia's exuberance, Iona is quick to offer her hand to Leonid. "I am very pleased to meet you, sir."

"The honor is mine." He kisses her hand, then glances at Ariadne.

"We've met before," Ariadne says.

"Yes, a friend of Ksenia's," Leonid says.

"No longer," Ariadne says shortly.

A small smile reaches Leonid's lips, transforming his expression into something softer. "Splendid. Then I need not pretend to like her."

Ariadne chuckles at that and Iona relaxes. Euphemia then prattles on about the Midsummer celebration she has planned and of the many Swedish traditions and revelries to be had.

"Good day, friends," Crescentia approaches and takes Iona's arm. "If I may, I'd be happy to introduce you to the other covens. They are all anxious to meet you."

"Indeed, there are alliances to be made. We shall have plenty of time to speak at home," Euphemia says, taking her husband's arm. "Until then!"

Crescentia takes them to see Phoebe Kimball first, who introduces them to her grandmother, Eleanor Kimball, and her parents, William and Margaret Kimball.

"I knew the moment I set my eyes upon you on our first day at college. I just knew you were special. Your aura was positively breathtaking! All those blues and indigos…" Phoebe nudges Ariadne's arm. "Isn't it a divine spectrum?"

"Very." Ariadne grins at Iona's blush and lightly runs a knuckle over her cheek.

"I imagine it's beauty has tripled now that it has joined with another," Phoebe muses.

"Joined?" Iona asks.

"Yes," Phoebe says. "You are bonded, are you not? Your auras are now fused into one single entity, a mixture of both."

Phoebe squints, then her eyes widen. 'There! I can see them!"

"Come now, Phoebe. Don't be rude," William Kimball

chastises his daughter.

"But Father, you should see..." Phoebe peers at them with great interest. "Oh, Ariadne, there is far less black in your aura of late. A fortunate improvement indeed, for it once terrified me. I've never seen anything quite so bleak..."

Ariadne scowls. "Your readings are as unwelcome now as they were then."

"You are so red," Phoebe chuckles. "But between you, there is lavender. How lovely."

Ariadne goes to protest, but Crescentia deftly redirects them. "Apologies, but we must be off. Many people still to meet."

"Many blessings!" Phoebe calls, waving at them as they go.

"Was I always that irritating?" Crescentia mutters to Ariadne.

"Worse at times," Ariadne retorts.

"I am so sorry," she shudders.

Before Iona can inquire as to what Ariadne means, Crescentia swiftly introduces her to nearly every family in attendance, with covens from Peru, Siam, Tripoli, Morocco, Persia, and India. Crescentia knows them all by name and whispers any relevant gossip in Iona's ear.

She is most excited to be introduced to the Dayalu family, a reserved and soft-spoken coven adorned in vibrant robes of yellow, red, and blue, and ornamented in golden bangles, rings, and jantars. The women have their hair woven into long braids, some of which almost brush the floor.

Samaira is a most welcome presence after entertaining a barrage of strangers, and Iona takes her aside while Crescentia and Ariadne converse with Samaira's parents.

"How are you feeling?" Iona whispers, glancing down at Samaira's ring.

"Quite well," she says, but when Iona gives her a pointed look, she admits, "Slightly overwhelmed at present. There are..." She looks around herself, her eyes becoming unfocused. "There are so many threads. They are everywhere."

"Oh... I had forgotten about that," Iona says.

Samaira had divulged the secrets of her artifact to Ariadne at the very end of their year at Lysander College. The ring not only gives her fleeting glimpses of the future, but it also allows her to see the threads of fate that lead every soul down their predestined path.

"What do they look like? The threads?" Iona asks.

Samaira points with her finger and makes a line through the air, focusing on an apparition that Iona cannot perceive. "They are like thin, shimmering lines of light that emanate from us all. I must concentrate to see them, the odd pattern they make. All woven in some manner that I cannot interpret, but undeniably intentional."

"Perhaps in time you will learn how to interpret the weavings," Iona says.

"I certainly hope so, though I do not wish to be swept up in unavailing pareidolia," Samaira says. "For now, I haven't any dire warnings to impart and for that I'm grateful."

"But what of the visions of darkness?" Iona asks. "Are you still tormented by them?"

At that, Samaira averts her eyes. "I've... grown accustomed to them now."

Iona doesn't believe it for a second but when she tries to protest, Samaira silences her with a look.

"I know you to be the sort of person who takes it upon themselves to rid others of their pain," she says. "I do not need that from you, priya. Save your compassion for those who are lost."

"Iona?" Crescentia calls, beckoning her to continue on.

She doesn't wish to leave, not when a feeling of foreboding sinks deep in her stomach, but Samaira curtsies and backs away.

"Many blessings," she smiles warmly before rejoining her family.

Crescentia leads them to a new family with another familiar face, then whispers in Iona's ear, "The Nassrys, from Egypt."

"Many blessings, Nenet." Iona embraces her.

Dripping in golden jewelry, with beads of lapis lazuli braided into her dark hair, Nenet is as flawless as ever. Her family watches on with bemusement, appearing like gods chiseled in stone.

"You performed beautifully," Nenet whispers.

"Thank you," Iona says with a shy smile. She's endured far too much praise for one day.

A young girl with wild curls and big brown eyes hides behind Nenet's skirts and looks up at Iona with curiosity.

"And may I introduce my little sister, Sara," Nenet says, then frowns down at her. "Who should be waiting in the carriage with Teta, but she never did learn to obey."

"Good evening, Sara," Iona smiles at her. "How old might you be?"

"Two and ten," Sara says, in a soft voice. "I couldn't take part in the ritual, but Mother says I can attend the party."

"That's very generous of her," Iona says.

"You've no business attending a ritual yet," Nenet says. "You haven't even found your wand."

"I will!" Sara frowns with determination. "Sooner than you did."

"I doubt that." Nenet grins.

Then her mother calls to her, and Sara runs off.

Nenet lets out an exasperated sigh. "Her wand is all she speaks of lately. She's grown quite obsessed."

"She's darling," Iona says.

"She can be, I suppose," Nenet says, but her fondness for her sister is clearly evident in her smile.

"And where is your twin?" Ariadne asks and Nenet rolls her eyes.

"Gisela remains in Denmark with her family," she says. "The Holms did not see fit to attend."

"Oh…" Iona says.

"We look forward to greeting them at the equinox when they inevitably realize their misjudgment," Ariadne says dryly.

"I did advise her to convince her mother to reconsider, and I believe she tried but…" Nenet shrugs. "Anyhow, allow me to introduce my mother and father."

Iona extends her hand for Nenet's father to kiss and notices his mark; two snakes intertwined around his forefinger. It's beautiful, one of Iona's favorites. She then wonders idly where Nenet's mark is, as she'd never noticed it before.

Her vision is fragmentarily overtaken by an image in Ariadne's mind, a memory of Nenet, naked and writhing, her full lips parted, as Ariadne feasted on her. She had reached up to brush a thumb over Nenet's mark, the two serpents twisted together at an angle along the ridge of her hip bone.

Iona flinches and the image fades, there and gone in less than a second. Ariadne's face turns beet red with mortification.

"No… I…" Ariadne loses her words.

"Is everything alright?" Nenet asks, her brow furrowing in concern.

Iona stares at her with utter incredulity at having watched such an intimate moment that she was not meant to see.

"Um… Forgive me. I am still recovering from the ritual," Iona stutters, her cheeks heating.

"Should we find you a place to sit?" Nenet asks.

"No, no." Iona waves her hands. "Thank you, I must… Please excuse me."

She curtsies clumsily, then walks away, her stomach in knots.

*I do not know what happened... I...* Ariadne's thoughts are frantic. *You wondered where her mark was, and I thought... and then I realized-*

*It's alright,* Iona lies. *You didn't intend to.*

*I swear I didn't,* Ariadne insists.

*I know,* Iona says, but even knowing that she struggles to process what she'd seen. It is quite a shock to see Ariadne in that position with anyone other than her.

"Why did you leave so suddenly?" Crescentia approaches, then notices their discomfort. "Whatever is the matter?"

"Nothing," Iona says.

"Are you certain?" Crescentia asks.

"Everything is fine," Ariadne says with a pointed look.

"I merely... required a moment," Iona says.

Crescentia holds Ariadne's gaze. "I see."

Taking a steadying breath, Iona puts on her best smile.

"Please, do not fuss over me," she says. "Who should I speak with next?"

"There's no need to rush." Crescentia places a comforting hand on her shoulder.

But in truth Iona would be most grateful for the distraction. She doesn't need time to dwell on what she'd seen, not with a sea of witches and warlocks observing her every move.

The distress of the unwanted memory is still written all over Ariadne's face, her remorse and embarrassment so stifling that Iona finds it difficult to concentrate.

"Are you two twittering silently amongst yourselves while I stand here in silence?" Crescentia asks.

"No. Or... not at the moment." Iona glances sideways at Ariadne.

"It's horrid being so constantly excluded from your conversations," Crescentia grumbles.

"Less gossip for you to circulate." Ariadne rolls her eyes, making an effort to appear unfazed.

While in search of some distraction, Iona notices Frankie passing by, nervously readjusting his green cravat, and when he meets her gaze, his eyebrows raise in silent question.

"In a rare turn of events, I find I have a bit of news to share with you," Iona says, and Crescentia's penchant for intrigue is reawakened.

"Do tell!" She smiles in anticipation.

Iona leans in close. "I have recently become acquainted with a handsome gentleman by the name of Frankie Mitriora. Do you know of him?"

Crescentia shakes her head, confused.

"He bears a wolf mark on his arm," Iona says.

Crescentia's amber eyes widen. "The man from the party? How did you…"

Then she looks to Ariadne with pure dread.

"You needn't fear my wrath," Ariadne jokes, an edge to her tone.

"But… I was so certain you would hate me again," she says.

"I will if you dare to treat him poorly," Ariadne warns.

"I would never," Crescentia says, appalled at the suggestion. "I did not know of him. How is that possible? I learned the name and mark of every sempiterna witch and warlock the world over. Was he sequestered in his youth as you were?"

Ariadne frowns at that and looks away, so Iona whispers in Crescentia's ear. Her mouth falls open in shock.

"Oh, my stars… " Crescentia whispers. "I hadn't heard…"

"Do you fancy him?" Iona asks, already knowing the answer.

"I… Or rather, I could hardly… He was so…" Crescentia stutters, her cheeks going red as she recalls that night.

Iona laughs. "My goodness, you cannot even speak!"

"He is certainly more of a gentleman than Erik ever was," Crescentia grins, her blush deepening.

"Wild was the word he used to describe you," Iona says conspiratorially. "Hopelessly enraptured, he was."

"Admittedly, so was I." Crescentia's grins falters when she glances down at her laurel mark.

"None of that." Iona takes her hand.

"Why would he risk-"

"Any who would be threatened by your power simply does not deserve you."

"I do want children someday…"

"Then you shall have them, and they will only be stronger because of you. And anyhow, you've only just met him. You should enjoy his company, and anything else can be discussed later," Iona insists. "Frankie asked if I might introduce you formally tonight, if you are amenable to it. Begged me to in fact. It was quite endearing."

Crescentia's grin is exultant. "Then I suppose I may end his suffering, if he were to call on me."

"Why wait?" Iona asks, gesturing to where Frankie stands alone, looking rather dashing in his black suit, his dark curls slicked back and his umber eyes glimmering with hope, though he pointedly avoids looking their way.

Crescentia's own eyes brighten at the sight of him, then she hesitates. "I shall find him later."

Iona goes to protest, but Crescentia takes her arm and coaxes her along. "I must finish the introductions first."

"Don't wait on my account," Iona says.

"There is always the reception. This night is of paramount importance, and I shan't leave you," Crescentia says. "If he adores me as you claim, an hour or two of waiting will only make him all the more desperate for my attentions."

"Ever the wise strategist," Iona grins.

"However will he break your code?" Ariadne rolls her eyes.

"Perhaps I should dye his skin red instead," Crescentia retorts. "Or paralyze him with poison. Is that not how you prefer to make your attraction known?"

Ariadne flushes with indignation. "That is entirely-"

"No quarreling!" Iona exclaims, standing between them. "Honestly, the both of you."

Ariadne scowls and walks away in the direction of Frankie.

"Oh…" Crescentia says, dejected. "You do not think she will speak ill of me, do you?"

"She'd better not," Iona says sternly. *Or you will not be permitted to touch me for a month.*

*Do you think so little of me?* Ariadne glances back at her. *And do not make such unrealistic threats. You would not last a week.*

*Shall we test that theory?* Iona asks.

Ariadne only smirks, and when she reaches Frankie, she whispers in his ear, and his immediate smile is all they need to know that all is well. He fusses with his clothes, until Ariadne seems to quell his nerves with a comforting speech.

Amidst it all, the other covens whisper amongst themselves and glance at the members of the Zerynthos coven with trepidation. It is not exactly fear that populates the many expressions of the crowd, but rather a deeply rooted respect. Ariadne's family appears unaffected by the scrutiny, but not unaware of it.

Xiomara and Raul only have eyes for each other, and Moira seems to thrive off the attention and stares provokingly at anyone who looks at her too long. Marina is, as always, gazing up at the sky, and Sebastian is nowhere to be found, likely too bored to stay for any length of time.

Zephyra speaks with Petro, pontificating with wild gestures

while he listens with a genteel smile that betrays his disinterest. Upon further observance, Iona finds that Ariadne's physical features favor her mother almost entirely, but her mannerisms are very much like her father's.

She vaguely recalls Ariadne mentioning, with the brevity in which she often speaks of her childhood, that her mother had occasionally taken extended journeys with no word as to where she was going. Consequently, Ariadne spent considerably more time with her father, whenever she wasn't otherwise occupied by her vigorous studies, which would explain how very much like her father she was, seeming to have only inherited a fraction of her mother's effortless fury. It's then Iona notices Cintia's absence and wonders idly whether she's taken her leave early and hopes it is so.

"Do not ask me," Crescentia says, having noticed the subjects of Iona's stares.

She opens her mouth to speak, but Crescentia puts up a finger.

"Ariadne will strangle me for gossiping," she says, with slight sincerity. "Or tell Frankie I have syphilis or some awful thing."

"No, I would never allow it," Iona says, chuckling at the thought, then whispers. "Why do they all stare?"

Crescentia sighs heavily and relents to the temptation. "Katrin's legacy is a lasting one. Every coven was once affected by her conquest, and they haven't forgotten it."

"Katrin stole from them?" Iona asks.

"Not exactly," Crescentia hedges. "The covens have always ruled over territories, each with their own treasures. The river in Brazil you told me of is a fine example. Places like that, rich with magic, are coveted and must be guarded, or others will try to seize control of them, like the Evoras attempted to do. At present there are not very many conflicts, apart from one in Spain, a dispute over caves in Majorca, but when Katrin died…"

"They fought over what she left behind," Iona guesses.

"It was a bloodbath," Crescentia says under her breath. "Katrin had a presence in nearly every country, even held control of Lysander Forest for a time, and as the head of the council, she alone determined who could harvest magic and who could not. The covens swarmed when she was gone… You are fortunate to have been hidden away during that time of unrest."

Iona frowns. The irony of Silvano Evora's accusations is laughable after having learned this. He did not have any moral ground to stand on, accusing her of controlling fortunes like Katrin while trying to steal land away in the same breath. It is staggeringly hypocritical.

"Has the Zerynthos coven attempted any conquests since Katrin's death?" she asks.

"No," Crescentia says. "It was curious... Everyone thought they would try to keep hold of their empire, but when Xiomara became the new leader of the coven, she simply stepped aside. She's only maintained her mother's seat as the head of the council. All else was left for others to apportion."

"Really?" Iona eyes Xiomara, who now converses with Nonna, their laughter traveling to them on the air.

"I've heard it was Cintia who resisted and wished to fight to maintain their supremacy, even without the pendant to safeguard their interests, but Xiomara wouldn't allow it. There is a permanent rift between them as a result," Crescentia whispers.

Iona had seen it at dinner, the unspoken animosity between the two sisters. It is immensely fortunate that Xiomara happens to be the older of the two, or who could say what state the world would be in.

"Come." Crescentia beckons her to follow. "There is someone special I'd like you to meet."

Ariadne rejoins them, and they traverse the multitude of people towards a short, voluptuous woman with long dark hair and grey eyes. The woman's gaze rests on Iona, and she smiles.

"May I present Lady Monton," Crescentia says, with a curtsy.

Iona recognizes her name immediately. "You are an advisor to King George III."

"Yes, Ms. Lysander," Lady Monton says. "At least, I aim to be. The man is quite obstinate."

"Iona was raised in Cornwall, not far from Tintagel," Crescentia says.

"I'd heard. Lovely scenery in those parts," Lady Monton says. "I live in London myself, but I summer in Brighton."

"Oh, I adore Brighton! My mother and I traveled there on rare occasions when we sold pearls to a merchant in town," Iona says. "But it proved too far a distance to visit often."

Lady Monton grins and holds out her wrist. There lies a bracelet of perfect pearls on a golden chain.

"I never knew they were of your making," she says. "Only that they were surely conjured with magic, so perfectly round and lustrous. I saw this in the window one morning and knew I must have it. Imagine my surprise when I heard the story of your trade."

Iona gently takes her hand to examine the pearls more closely. "Goodness…"

"They are all the more precious to me now, knowing you and your mother crafted them," Lady Monton says.

"Were you acquainted with her?" Iona asks when she marks the familiarity in Monton's tone.

"Not closely, but her skill in conjuration was a credit to her. I saw her briefly at one of the Lysanders' balls. What a pretty thing she was. You're her spitting image." Lady Monton leans in. "And if I may be so bold, I did notice her sneaking off with your father at the end of the night, a triumphant smile on his face." Lady Monton giggles, until her expression turns wistful. "They deserved better."

Iona's smile falters. "Yes, they did."

Crescentia steers the conversation to other topics, much to Iona's gratitude. Lady Monton tells of the ordeal with the Americans and how she'd tried to convince the King of his shortsightedness in allowing the situation to escalate into war.

"Phoebe claims that it was inevitable. The Americans would have rebelled eventually," Crescentia says.

"Any witch can tell you the value of that land," Lady Monton sighs. "Anyhow, it's over with. I am far more concerned with his declining mental state."

"It is not just rumor?" Iona asks.

"I'm afraid not," Lady Monton says. "The stars warn of a war looming. If Napoleon continues with his interference in the West, and they fail to agree on the fate of Malta, they will inevitably clash again. It was always a precarious peace."

"Is it wise, allowing a madman to rule during a time of war?" Ariadne asks. "There have also been rumors of an impending regency. Perhaps that would be best."

"Sane, mad, what difference does it make?" Lady Monton asks with exasperation. "Men long for war. They think it makes them strong. Peace is much more difficult to maintain. I do what I can to preserve harmony and rebuild trust between us and the humans. We mustn't ever return to the darker days of witch trials." She shivers at the thought.

"That is why I thought to introduce you two," Crescentia says. "Iona would be very successful as a diplomat."

Taken aback, Iona shakes her head. "I do not know if I am prepared for such an immense responsibility."

"Not now, maybe, but in time you will," Crescentia says with absolute confidence.

"I would be delighted to discuss it with you. The world has no shortage of peacemakers," Lady Monton says.

Iona looks between them, unsure of what to say. Then a hand brushes lightly against her spine, gentle and nearly imperceptible. She turns to see who it is.

# 15 - Iona

"Anyhow I'd forgotten that I'd already put the hemlock in. Or at least, I'm fairly certain that's what caused it," Kokuro chuckles, her eyes crinkling sheepishly. "I was mute for an entire month."

"A month?" Ariadne laughs. "And there was no way to reverse it?"

"My parents tried everything," Kokuro says, then chuckles. "Perhaps they only claimed to. They surely enjoyed the silence."

"Do not tell my parents or they shall 'spill' a drop or two in my morning tea," Crescentia laughs with her.

"Perish the thought," Euphemia grins.

"Where is Lady Monton?" Iona asks.

They all stare at her in confusion.

"Lady Monton?" Ariadne asks. "She chose not to attend the reception."

Iona looks to the west, and the sun lies much lower in the sky than she would have expected.

"But… I was only just speaking to her," she says.

"Monopolized her, more like," Crescentia says.

"I'm sure she was flattered by your interest in her profession," Euphemia says.

"If I'd known you would have so many questions, I'd have waited to introduce you on a less eventful evening," Crescentia agrees.

Smoldering warmth radiates behind her, and she looks behind her to find a massive bonfire, many in fact, littering a vast open space, with a dense, dark forest beyond. Many of the guests from the ritual are gathered near the fires, conversing with lively excitement, some of them dancing with thin streams of magic manifesting around them.

In the distance, there is a manor of brown brick with many windows and a flourishing garden. Drakenström manor, she remembers vaguely. Euphemia's home with her husband and son.

Iona rubs at her temple, suddenly feeling lightheaded, as if the air has lost its vitality.

"I fear someone has indulged in too much mead," Crescentia says with a nervous chuckle, taking Iona's cup from her.

"No, I..."

"There you are," Xiomara says.

A vision in red damask silk, she approaches with a middle-aged woman and a girl who looks to be no older than three and ten, with the same blue eyes and forlorn expression as her mother.

"You're white as a ghost, dearest," Xiomara observes. "Are you well?"

"I'm fine." Iona clears her throat and, with effort, puts on a smile.

"Forgive the intrusion, but I did not think this could wait even a moment," Xiomara says. "May I present Regina Sullivan and her daughter, Harriett Sullivan, of Scotland."

The mother and daughter curtsy low, and Regina says, "It is an honor to meet you, Miss Lysander."

"Can you help me?" Harriett asks, her eyes ringed with red.

"Harriett," Regina gives her daughter a disapproving look.

"Help you?" Iona asks.

"The child is an unfortunate victim of a malefician's spell. The one I told you about," Xiomara explains in a low voice. "Her magic was leeched away."

"Oh..." Iona murmurs, realizing what they hope for her to do.

She glances at Crescentia, who mirrors her conflicted feelings. She still hasn't decided whether giving a mark is a virtuous gift or a hindrance, after all Erik Virtanen had said.

But when she regards the young girl, her eyes so filled with desperate hope, she cannot find it within herself to refuse. The girl is so young with so much life ahead of her, and to live without magic is too awful a subjugation to endure, especially considering the pain she'd suffered when her magic was stolen.

"Do you know what this might mean for her?" Iona asks Regina.

"Yes," Regina says. "Please... I only wish for her to be healed. Marcel Beaumont is a friend. He told me you might help."

Iona holds out her hand and Harriett takes it eagerly. Hesitating only once more, Iona closes her eyes and centers herself.

"Philisa," Iona incants, chanting the spell again and again.

Magic seeps from her to Harriett, the spell draining her, but not nearly as much as it had when she'd cast the spell on Crescentia. She supposes it might be because the girl is so young, her well of magic being much smaller. Across the girl's forehead, a crown of ivy appears with delicate green leaves and curling stems.

"Oh, my stars," Regina exclaims.

"What is it?" Harriett asks.

Regina conjures a mirror and holds it up to her daughter's face, which breaks into a jubilant smile when she marvels at her crown, touching it lightly with her fingers, unable to believe it's real. Her eyes brimming with tears and she wraps her arms round Iona's waist and clings to her.

"Now, now. Let's not overwhelm her," Regina says, but there are tears brimming in her eyes, too.

"Thank you," Harriet sniffles, pulling away.

"Use your magic wisely," Iona cautions with an encouraging smile.

"I shall. I swear it," she says.

"There were others," Regina says, reaching for Iona's hand. "Two others whose magic was stolen. Would you help them, too?"

She agrees without a second thought, and they arrange a time for her to visit the Sullivans' village within the next week. It is a comfort to know she might finally be of use.

"Well done, Iona," Xiomara says, before she ushers the mother and daughter away.

Once they've left her, Iona's happiness fades when she meets the probing stares of the surrounding crowd who had watched her heal the girl's magic and bestow a mark. She imagines the rumor of Crescentia's healing had spread as rumors so often do in these circles but seeing it before one's eyes is entirely different.

*They stare at me, not you,* Ariadne lies, putting a protective arm around her.

She traces the line of Ariadne's jaw with her finger. *Let them look.*

Drawing her down for a soft, sweet kiss, Iona's feeling of disorientation subsides, the pain in her head dissipating, until she cannot recall what had upset her in the first place. She wonders if perhaps it truly is the mead that's to blame for her confusion. She cannot imagine what else it could be and does not wish to ruin the evening.

"Would you like one?" Kokuro holds up two vials of green potion.

"What concoction have you brewed this time?" Ariadne asks warily.

"Merely a festive libation," Kokuro says, with a mischievous grin.

"The stars are so bright..." Crescentia drawls, spinning in erratic circles and laughing hysterically with Euphemia, whose pupils have blown so wide she looks like a startled cat.

"When last I sampled one of your 'libations', I awoke on the shore of the Holm family's pond in naught but my stockings." Ariadne grins at the memory but shakes her head. "I shan't risk that tonight."

"Awe... Do not let Iona domesticate you," Kokuro protests, then elbows Iona in the ribs. "Tell me, would you not wish to see her in such a state?"

"I would, actually," Iona grins.

Flushing, Ariadne raises an eyebrow. *Are you truly considering it?*

*Only if you are,* Iona admits. *I do not wish to try it alone.*

"These will not leave us mute, will they?" Ariadne takes the two vials.

"That was many years ago," Kokuro scoffs. "I am as accomplished in phytology as you, make no mistake of that."

Iona eyes her with persisting reservations. "How long will the effects last?"

Ariadne downs an entire vial in one gulp.

"Enjoy!" Kokuro frolics across the grass to where Crescentia and Euphemia are attempting a dance.

"This is new," Ariadne murmurs. "I taste belladonna."

"What?" Iona's stomach drops. "Is that not poisonous?"

"Ginger... Star anise... Liberty cap... and-" Ariadne's eyes widen in alarm. She calls to Kokuro, "Is there opium in this draught?"

"Only a drop or two!" Kokuro says.

"What else?" Ariadne asks.

"There are many, many, many ingredients. I cannot possibly remember them all," Kokuro laughs hysterically as Crescentia spins them around and around, almost falling into a bonfire, but Euphemia manages to pull them away just in time.

Ariadne grimaces. "Perhaps you should abstain."

"Why did you drink it?" Iona asks.

"You told me you wished to try it!" Ariadne exclaims. "How could I know you would suddenly change your mind? You are so indecisive-"

"I take time to think," Iona retorts. "A foreign concept to you, I know."

Ariadne purses her lips but fails to stifle a wheezing laugh that has Iona struggling to keep a straight face, the residual effects of the potion trickling through the bond, making her feel odd.

"Why are you laughing?" Iona asks, a rogue giggle escaping her lips.

Ariadne's smile fades abruptly, she blinks as if to clear her vision, then reaches out to take a piece of her red hair between her fingers, marveling at it.

"Kokuro has outdone herself," Ariadne mumbles. "Do you not feel it? I would have thought…"

"Only a little." Iona worries at her bottom lip. "Is it safe?"

"Probably," Ariadne mumbles. "I feel… amazing."

"Oh, I'm sure you do." Iona shakes her head incredulously.

"We are off to the woods," Euphemia declares as she runs up to them. "Come with us so we may-" she frowns, "Iona, won't you try the potion?"

"I… I am not sure," Iona admits, wondering if she should remain lucid in case Xiomara approaches her again, or any of the other remaining council members in attendance.

"But we must make merry!" Euphemia throws an arm around her neck and speaks with emphatic hand gestures. "No misfortune shall befall you so long as the light of oaken fire shrouds us and casts away the baneful shadows. Let us be like fae for a night and…" She's momentarily distracted by the flames, the sparks that crackle and burst in the air.

"Let us go!" Crescentia cries. "What is the delay?"

"Won't you come with us?" Euphemia implores. "Set aside your troubles and exalt in our good fortune."

Moved by her impassioned plea, and the whimsy in her sapphire eyes, Iona sighs. "Oh… alright."

"Splendid!" Euphemia kisses her on one cheek, then the other, and takes Crescentia's hand to gallop across the field in the direction of the woods.

"She is quite convincing when she…" Iona trails off when, to her displeasure, Ariadne's eyes are not on her but rather locked on Rebekka where she stands by a bonfire to the east, though she appears quite oblivious to Ariadne's glare.

"Ari," Iona says, but still, she doesn't respond, her full lips downturned, her posture tense.

So, she snaps her fingers directly in Ariadne's ear, making her recoil and scowl, a protest at the tip of her tongue, but Iona captures her chin in her hand and pulls Ariadne's face down to hers, not giving her a chance to speak.

"I would like to drink the potion," Iona says. "May I have it?"

Slightly disoriented, Ariadne blinks at her, until finally she finds her voice. "Do not snap at me."

"How else can I hope to gain your attention when you neglect me in favor of your absurd fixation?" Iona scowls, then releases her chin.

She reaches for the vial in Ariadne's hand, but she unstoppers it and drinks it all.

"Are you mad?! You will make yourself sick from-" But her protests are muted by Ariadne's kiss.

Coaxing her lips apart, the contents of the second vial spills from Ariadne's mouth into hers, tasting of sweet berries, with a bitter tanginess. A drop escapes through the seam of their melded lips, dripping down Iona's chin, and she pulls away, giggling.

"My every other thought is of you. How much more of my mind do you wish to inhabit?" Ariadne murmurs in her ear.

"All of it," Iona jests. "So that you might... not..."

The sparks from the fire cast iridescent rainbows shimmering in the smoke, and when she looks up at Ariadne to ask if she too can see them, she is swiftly lost in the beauty of Ariadne's eyes that glow a thousand shades of red all at once. When her gaze drifts lower to Ariadne's chest, her mark seems to sway back and forth, as if the flame is alive and burning. Iona reaches out to touch it, running the pads of her fingers along the swell of Ariadne's breast, and the soft skin is warm. Pleasantly so.

Chuckling darkly, Ariadne takes her hand and leads her deep into the forest, navigating the wilderness with a sense of familiarity. The leaves are like silken butterfly wings against Iona's arms, the ground like shifting sand beneath her feet, her limbs light as air as she frolics through the flowering ferns to another massive blazing fire that seems to lick at the clouds above. Many witches are already gathered there, shedding their gowns and unpinning their hair to dance without inhibition around the flickering flames.

Iona's every breath is expelled in laughter, endlessly, joyously, until her stomach aches from it. She joins in the songs and chants, drawing magic from the air to bask in its eternal glow, absorbing the raw energy emanating from the earth and sky. The streams of magic are not so plentiful as were in the earlier ritual but are more than enough to thrill the other witches, their cheerful exclamations like a balm to her battered nerves.

Ariadne's persistent caresses are constant and sensual, though not inherently lustful. The potion's influence on the senses is intoxicating beyond belief and they cannot seem to bear even a moment's separation. Iona feels as if their lungs are now joined, and every bit of air she inhales is from within Ariadne, seeped in the very essence of her, and every breath Iona expels is given to Ariadne, breathing life back into her in turn.

She tries not to fixate too hard on her breaths for fear of fainting and instead focuses on Ariadne's fingers drifting over the skin of her arm with a featherlight touch, her brow furrowed in concentration, and her lips moving with silent words.

"Are you counting my freckles?" Iona asks incredulously.

"You shall require an abacus to keep track," Crescentia giggles, taking her hand and pulling her around in circles until they are both dizzy and collapse onto the forest floor, convulsing with laughter.

"You made me lose count," Ariadne pouts.

Then Euphemia approaches, her golden hair billowing around her as she spins, and Frida flitting around her in her own sort of dance, as Euphemia recites, "I know a bank where the wild thyme blows, where oxlips and the nodding violet grows, quite over-canopied with luscious woodbine-"

"With sweet musk-roses and with eglantine," Iona finishes the verse.

"Well done!" Euphemia's smile widens, and she twirls about, unable to keep still in her inebriated state. "Are you a lover of Shakespeare?"

"My mother was," Iona says, "We often read his works together and-"

"Have you seen them performed?" Euphemia asks, and when Iona shakes her head, she exclaims. "Oh, but you must! I shall take you to Covent Garden where-" She looks up, her face going slack as she marks the position of the sun. "We must return to the party!"

"Why?" Ariadne asks.

"We must hurry, or we might miss the handfasting!" Euphemia says, gesturing for them to find their clothes, "I'd almost forgotten!"

"A handfasting?" Iona asks.

"Quickly! Or we shall miss it!" Euphemia runs, "The sun has almost set!"

Once they've all dressed, Euphemia, Crescentia, Iona, and Ariadne run through the trees, Wisp and Aster bucking and bounding ahead of them, leading the way back to the open field. The other witches choose to stay behind and continue their merriment.

By then, most of the potions effects have waned, and their minds are partially set to rights. Iona can only see the slightest sheen of rainbows in the flames, and she's finally stopped laughing, her stomach muscles cramping from her exertions.

When she looks up, confusion creeps into her consciousness when she finds the sun hovering over the horizon, casting purple light on the transitional sky. "How is it still day?"

"Here the sun sets much later in the summer," Euphemia explains. "It is only two hours to midnight, I'd say."

"Goodness," Iona murmurs, her fatigue beginning to catch up with her.

"We didn't miss it!" Euphemia points at a man and woman whose hands are joined with a rope wrapped around their wrists, binding them together. "A handfasting is a betrothal. It's customary to hold them on Midsummer's Day."

Another woman presides over the ceremony, her voice not quite carrying over to them, but Iona doesn't mind. The smiles on the couple's faces are brilliant as the bonfires burning around them, and when it's finished, they remove their hands from within the cord wrapped around them, and pull at each of the ends, tying the knot firmly into place. Then they come together for a kiss and the onlookers clap and cheer, celebrating their love.

"How romantic," Iona sighs, tears pricking at her eyes as she imagines performing the same ceremony someday.

"Would you like to dream of Ariadne tonight?" Crescentia breaks her reverie.

"Hmm?" Iona asks, giving her a confused look.

"Come, I'll show you," Crescentia takes her hand and takes her away from the bonfires, the grass only barely illuminated by the twilight, and gestures to the wildflowers sprouting at their feet. "Euphemia once told me that if you pick nine flowers and put them under your pillow tonight, you will dream of your one true love, and your future together."

They begin picking the most perfect blossoms they can find, including a few twinflowers, until Iona has a bundle of them in her fist.

"I hope to dream of Frankie," Crescentia says.

"I suspect you will not do much dreaming tonight," Iona grins, then turns to share a look with Ariadne, but she is not there.

Suddenly frantic, she searches the crowd, but Ariadne is nowhere in sight.

"Where is Ariadne?" Iona asks, spinning around in search of her.

"She excused herself a moment ago and said she would return shortly," Crescentia says.

"But…" Iona frowns, wondering why Ariadne would not see fit to tell her so.

"Must you be joined at the hip at all hours?" Crescentia asks.

Iona flushes with embarrassment. "Of course not."

"Then let us enjoy the party and she will return when it suits her," Crescentia says. "You mustn't cling to her, or she will only grow to resent it."

"I do not cling to her." Iona narrows her eyes.

"She may as well be chained to you," Crescentia mutters.

"Why are you so antagonistic towards each other?" Iona asks. Crescentia looks away, but Iona doesn't let her avoid it. "Tell me now or I shall ask her, and you know she won't deny me."

"It was nothing," Crescentia says, sheepish. "I said something… foolish. An ignorant comment about Vivien, speaking of things I knew nothing about. She was so angry… I regret it now."

"When was this?" Iona asks.

"Three years ago, at one of Euphemia's parties," Crescentia says. "I apologized to her in Lyon."

"Did she accept?"

"Yes."

"Then why are you still at each other's throats?"

"We are cordial enough…"

"You must be kind to her, even when she makes it…. difficult," Iona says. "She has been through hell."

"I know," Crescentia says. "Or rather, I've heard things."

"Then show her compassion, please," Iona says, then gently bumps her shoulder. "Or I shall only assume you mean to steal her away. I won her heart through discordant exchanges after all."

"I would rather my cunt shrivel up and fall off," Crescentia says, wrinkling her nose in mock disgust.

Iona dissolves into giggles as Crescentia continues to make faces for her amusement.

"Fear not," she says. "I mean to make Frankie fall madly in love with me by month's end, and if Ariadne detests me, that will prove rather difficult."

"You needn't court him in haste," Iona chuckles.

"My love is all or nothing," Crescentia shrugs.

As if sensing the topic of their conversation, Frankie emerges from behind a bonfire and lingers there, seemingly unsure if he should approach.

"Go to him," Iona says, and when Crescentia opens her mouth to protest, she insists. "Go now! Or the poor chap will die from waiting!"

"Oh… alright," Crescentia says. "If you're sure you have no further need of me."

Iona embraces her and says, "I am ever so grateful for your guidance. I would have been lost without you."

"That's for certain," Crescentia grins when she pulls away.

She skips toward Frankie, whose posture goes rigid when he sees her. He bows low, then takes her hand and kisses it reverently.

"Perhaps they will be wed in a month," Iona chuckles to herself.

Then she tries to find a suitable a vantage point to see as much of the crowd as possible, but there is no sign of Ariadne anywhere. She'd hoped to locate her, just for her own peace of mind, then perhaps find Euphemia to continue their frolicking.

When there is absolutely no trace of her, Iona finally reaches out for Ariadne's mind. There lies the image of Euphemia's face, her smile wide as she recounts a piece of idle gossip regarding Vadoma Lovell, their classmate from college. Behind her, there are walls covered with expensive floral wallpaper and wide windows, indicating that they must be somewhere inside Drakenström Manor.

Iona makes her way across the field and passes through the gardens, but as she gets closer, she isn't sure which door to enter. She doesn't wish to pass through the ballroom and risk being stopped by countless people along her way. She turns a corner but all she finds is an empty patch of grass and a line of glass doors. Unsure if she should risk getting lost, she lingers outside, debating whether to call out to Ariadne to come and find her instead.

"Good evening," Rebekka says.

Iona jumps nearly out of her skin as she whirls around to face her.

"Rebekka," Iona gasps.

Her grin widens, "Not who you expected to find?"

"No... I-" Iona shakes her head. "Have you seen Ariadne? I cannot find her anywhere."

"No, I can't say that I have," Rebekka says. "Did she leave you alone amidst that crowd of buzzards?"

Iona frowns, glancing over Rebekka's shoulder at the distant throng. "I would not call them that."

"You're meeting them at their best, vying for your favor," she says. "They all want you..."

Her gaze slowly wanders down. At first, Iona assumes she's admiring the pendant as many have done, but it becomes clear that Rebekka's focus lies a touch lower. Iona's skin heats, awareness making her tense with discomfort.

"...As an ally," Rebekka continues, an easy smile lifting her lips. "But do not let them fool you. Every single one of them has their own selfish motivations and-"

"Do you think me obtuse?" Iona asks.

Rebekka stops short, her blonde eyebrows raising in surprise.

"Do you think me witless? Simple?" Iona asks.

"No," Rebekka shakes her head slowly.

"Then why do you act as if I cannot see through your thinly veiled comments?" Iona asks. "Do you actually believe I would fall prey to your graceless flirtations?"

Rebekka lets out an incredulous laugh. "Graceless?"

"I am Ariadne's," Iona says firmly. "I am hers. Forever. You could never compare."

"I meant no offense." Rebekka puts up her hands in a gesture of deference. "Please forgive my impertinence."

"Relay your apologies to Ariadne," Iona says. "If you truly are her friend."

With that she turns and picks one of the glass doors at random, wrenches it open, and slams it behind her.

Still unsure of where she should go, she looks into Ariadne's mind again, and tenses with displeasure at seeing Nenet's face in place of Euphemia's. The glimpse of Ariadne's salacious memory repeats in Iona's mind over and over again and despite knowing it's foolish, her skin goes hot with indignant jealousy. She could just call out to Ariadne now, but she is not in a rational mood at present. She has a far more compelling way to draw Ariadne back to her.

# 16 - Ariadne

Tatiana Nicolo catches her eye from across the burning fires, her face distorted by the heat and smoke. Like every time before, Ariadne is paralyzed with fright that she tries her best to stifle, or otherwise Iona will sense it. Even knowing that Vivien is well again, she can't escape the searing sense of foreboding that creeps down her spine at the haunted look on Tatiana's face.

"Pardon me," Ariadne mumbles, nearly whispering.

"Where are you going?" Crescentia whispers back.

To Ariadne's relief, Iona remains entirely oblivious while she watches the handfasting.

"I need..." Ariadne stifles a gasp. "I'll return in a moment. I need..."

Crescentia searches for what frightens her, until she finds Tatiana across the way.

"Go," Crescentia tells her.

Ariadne hesitates, glancing at Iona.

"I'll keep watch over her," Crescentia says. "Go."

A rush of gratitude fills her, and she forces herself to walk, not run, through the mass of people, her claustrophobia flaring.

"No... no..." Ariadne forces her breath to slow, her thoughts reeling. Iona cannot know. She cannot bear it. Not now. Not ever. She looks over her shoulder to see if Tatiana is following.

"Ugh!"

She collides directly into Ksenia, almost knocking her to the ground. Cringing, she puts space between them and hugs her chest.

"Pull yourself together." Ksenia looks her up and down.

"Do not speak to me like that!" Ariadne snaps. "In fact, do not speak to me at all."

"Gladly." Ksenia brushes past her.

Ariadne resumes her path towards Euphemia's manor, passing by a pair of open French doors that lead to the ballroom filled with yet more people dancing in a more formal setting. It's there she overhears the familiar, irritating whispers of the two irksome witches who'd gossiped with Crescentia years ago.

"She doesn't seem like the sort-"

"If she bonded to Ariadne Zerynthos, I doubt she has any qualms. They will use her to reclaim everything. The obedient heir they've always wanted."

Ariadne's steps slow as she listens, despite her better judgment.

"Then why would she share magic if she only means to hoard it?"

"Katrin once dictated who could cultivate their power. Perhaps she'll do the same, favoring the common folk in place of us."

"I am not convinced…" The witch lowers her voice. "And we should be wary of discussing this here."

"Ksenia is no friend to Ariadne any longer, and rumor has it she does not much like Iona either. We need not fear another hex from her."

"Yes, but… Ariadne steals magic."

Ariadne's heart stops and she creeps closer to the opened doors to hear them more clearly.

"That hasn't been confirmed as truth… not yet anyhow. We must await the trial to know for certain."

"Everyone knows Elise Lysander is without magic. Ariadne took it all. She may as well be a malefician, or well on her way to becoming one."

"I'm not sure… but I must admit, I fail to see how such a spell could not have some sort of corrupting effect on her soul. A Zerynthos malefician… Could you imagine it?"

The witches go silent, their fear palpable. Ariadne forces her feet to move, considering whether to go inside one of the manor's many rooms and take a moment to calm down, but the thought only incites her claustrophobia again.

"You're flickering," Marina says.

Ariadne jumps. She hadn't noticed her cousin leaning against the wall, watching her with hazy red eyes.

"What are you on about?" Ariadne asks.

Marina's face scrunches with confusion as she scrutinizes the sky. "Your stars. They're flickering."

"And that means what exactly?" Ariadne asks.

"It is a terrible omen indeed," Marina says gravely.

Ariadne resists the urge to roll her eyes. "You see omens everywhere."

"They are everywhere," Marina says. "Why do you still run from her?"

Ariadne stiffens and forces her features into neutrality as best she can. "What do you mean?"

"Your fear is a tumor," Marina says. "It will only grow until you cut it out."

"I haven't the time for this," Ariadne scoffs, but Marina's words unnerve her, as they so often do.

She slips inside the manor, away from Marina, away from the incessant whispers and probing stares, until she reaches the front entrance. She takes her staff from where she'd left it by the coat stand, already feeling better with it in her grasp. Even while knowing no one could take it, the magic inside preventing them, she still prefers to keep it close.

She throws open the front door and goes down the steps to the front courtyard where rows of carriages lie waiting for their owners, the horses making soft whinnies and grunts. Nothing but sprawling countryside stretches out in either direction and the immensity is a strange comfort.

How had she not considered whether Elise's magic would have any lasting effect on her? She doesn't feel any different, but perhaps the maleficium is dormant, festering inside, lying in wait to overtake her. If there were any negative effects, it probably… potentially would have manifested by now. Iona could heal her regardless. She shouldn't worry about it, but now the awful possibilities pollute her every thought.

Her heart thrums dangerously fast in her chest, even as she tries taking deep breaths of fresh air, but that only succeeds in making her lightheaded. Or perhaps that is a residual effect of Kokuro's potion. She turns back, intending to seek out Iona wherever she is, to find comfort in her embrace, but she abruptly stops short and wishes she could disappear from that very spot.

"What are you doing sneaking about?" her mother asks. She leans against a white marble column at the top of the front steps, holding a cigarette in her right hand and flicking the ash to the wind.

"Nothing, I…" Ariadne loses her words.

"Leave me be." Her mother lifts the cigarette to her lips and turns away.

She should. She should go upstairs and lie down. She should find Iona and tell her why she flees from the very sight of Tatiana. She should use her staff to travel anywhere else in the entire world, or leave for another world entirely, until she feels well enough to return. But her mother's words are salt in her wounds.

"Why did you lie about our lineage?" Ariadne asks.

"What?" Cintia asks, smoking escaping from her mouth and

nose as she looks over her shoulder to glare down at her.

Ariadne climbs two steps. "You claimed we were descended from Hecate. That our eyes are hers. That we are children of gods. It was all lies. Morgan told me when Iona and I won her trials."

"Iona won," Cintia retorts. "You forfeited."

"You avoid the question still?" Ariadne asks. "Did you not know yourself?"

"I know everything," she seethes.

Ariadne scoffs. "How long can I expect the charm on my eyes to last? It will fade eventually, will it not? As all transformation spells inevitably do, without magic to restore it. How many times did you cast the spell on me while I was unaware? Why go to such lengths to perpetuate your charade?"

Cintia flicks away her cigarette and motions for her to ascend the remaining stairs.

"You want to speak of this now? So be it," she says, her tone conveying her boredom. "The eyes are nothing more than a tradition passed down by our ancestors. It's meant to mirror Hecate's beauty. It will fade within the next year or two, if you choose to let it. Nothing to get hysterical over."

"I am not hysterical-"

"Do you not recall the weeks after you shattered Vivien's mind?" Cintia asks.

Ariadne grits her teeth. "What of it?"

"I could never forget it myself. Your infirmity. You may as well have been dead," she says. "Forgive me for treading lightly, for I would not wish to incite another of your nervous collapses."

"Why must we speak of this again?" Ariadne had fled the party to avoid discussing this exact subject.

"Do you wish for me to answer your question, or don't you?" Cintia narrows her eyes, and when Ariadne does not object, she continues. "Your confidence was obliterated that day. I needed to motivate you somehow, or all would have been lost. The story I wove was an attempt at inspiring you to strive for more, reminiscent of a story our ancestors once perpetuated to maintain our status in society. It worked, did it not? You regained your tenacity when you thought power was owed to you. You believed it all too easily."

"I was terrified of being cast out of the family if I should fail," Ariadne argues. "It seems that threat was empty as well."

"I did and said what was necessary to fix you," Cintia says. "I shan't apologize for it, if that is what you hope for."

"I would never expect that of you," Ariadne says. "Your lies were in vain anyhow. Samaira was the one who nursed and restored me as best she could. You did nothing."

"Nothing?" Cintia yells. "I made you into the witch you are. You wouldn't have that stick," she regards the staff with disdain, "if it weren't for my toil.

"I did not succeed because of you! I did so in spite of you," Ariadne says.

Cintia throws up her hands. "Nothing I do is ever good enough."

"At long last you understand," Ariadne says sarcastically.

Cintia raises her hand, and Ariadne flinches, bracing for the sting, but before a blow is struck, Aster lets out a ferocious snarl, his fur rippling with the threat of transformation. Taking a wary step back, Ariadne silently admonishes herself. She could have blocked the blow with the staff's magic, but her instincts overpowered her logic.

"It is not a stick," Ariadne says, making her voice steady. "It is the staff of Merlin, a sacred artifact once thought to be lost forever-"

"A prize of consolation, nothing more." Cintia turns up her nose. "You wish for me to praise you for such a meager accomplishment?"

"It is more than Sebastian or Marina could manage, or your precious Moira," Ariadne says. "With it, I healed Vivien, and-"

"At my suggestion," Cintia reminds her. "Though I care not how you clean up your messes. I raised you not to make them in the first place."

"I can shield against maleficium," Ariadne says. "No other witch alive can say as much."

Cintia studies her with a shrewd gaze that never fails to make her feel entirely exposed, then conjures a new cigarette, bringing it to her lips and taking a long drag.

"Why did you not claim the pendant?" Cintia asks.

Ariadne sighs heavily. "I told you-"

"No." Cintia narrows her eyes. "What is the true reason you relinquished it?"

Ariadne only stares at her in confusion.

"I wondered this, while I spent time in Thessaly to recollect myself after your lover shattered my ankle," Cintia says with bitterness.

"Only after you attempted to smother me," Ariadne says.

"You exaggerate." Cintia rolls her eyes. "Why would you hold pure power in your hands and simply give it away? It is unfathomable."

"To you, maybe," Ariadne says.

"You claim that you 'did not want it' but have neglected to explain why," Cintia presses.

"It was never meant for me," Ariadne says.

"Nonsense. If that were true, Morgan wouldn't have given you both the ability to take it," Cintia says.

"Why then?" Ariadne asks. "What reason have you fabricated to comfort yourself in your failure to control me?"

Cintia's smirk is dangerous as she takes a step closer, flicking her cigarette so the ashes fall at her feet.

"You did not want the bane that comes with it," Cintia says. "You saw the toll it took on your grandmother, even if you did not fully understand it, though soon enough you will. You knew well the obligations you'd inherit at rituals such as these, the endless expectations of the great covens, for the rest of your unnatural life. You did not want the responsibility, so you gave it to Iona instead. You sealed her fate or rather imposed yours onto her."

"That... That is not true," Ariadne shakes her head.

"Do you realize the extent of the adversity you've inflicted upon her?" Cintia slowly circles her. "Do you love her at all?"

"Of course I do!" Ariadne exclaims.

"I was wrong in calling her your doll," Cintia says, taking slow deliberate steps. "In truth, she is the surrogate for a burden you alone were meant to bear. You shirked your duty, passed it along to another who is hopelessly unprepared to handle it."

"No, you're wrong," Ariadne flinches as her mother looms like a bird of prey spotting a mouse on the forest floor.

"Mere proximity to power could never satisfy me, but I suppose you are more like your father than I originally thought," she says. "All too happy to watch on with dutiful subservience."

Ariadne bristles at the comparison. Though she does love her father dearly, she would never wish to become like him, and her mother's knowing smile reflects her perception of those fears.

"I gave Iona the pendant to protect her from Elise," Ariadne insists. "She sought it of her own volition. I never imposed it on her!"

"She nearly died at Elise's hand, even with the pendant at her disposal," Cintia says. "It was not a lack of power that failed her.

It was her inexperience, that which you certainly do not lack. Why could you not have claimed the pendant instead and used it to its full potential?"

Ariadne's mouth falls open, but no sound comes out.

"A lifetime of instruction that I took great pains to provide you, all to be capable of wielding that specific artifact," Cintia says. "There is no one alive who could do so better than you. And yet, I am meant to believe you gave it away because... of what exactly?"

"It was the right decision," Ariadne's voice wavers. "You are twisting the truth."

"You 'did not want it'," Cintia scoffs with utter disdain. "How marvelous it must be to live life with such flagrant self-indulgence."

"Why are you so convinced I would be better suited to it?" Ariadne asks. "You think less of me than anyone, except perhaps Grandmother. You cannot profess my inferiority while also complaining of my supposed waste of potential."

"Your refusal to accept your fate is the source of my discontent." Cintia gestures in the direction of the party. "That parade of introductions orchestrated by that charlatan of a witch, Clementia-"

"Crescentia," Ariadne says.

"Whatever." Cintia rolls her eyes. "It wouldn't have been necessary for you. We ensured your place in high society was well established, with painstaking care, until you decided to besmirch your own reputation by bedding any fricatrice who would have you and-"

"None of them want me!" Ariadne yells. "They hate me! They always have, and the blame for that is yours as well as mine. Do you think the pendant would have erased their contempt for our family? For me?"

"Do you think those people 'liked' your grandmother?" Cintia laughs. "They needed her. They respected her. They tolerated her for their own gain, just as they will do for your vapid chit."

"Do not call her that," Ariadne snaps.

"Her egregious impropriety will disgrace her in due course," Cintia says. "The rabble she invited to tonight's ritual will surely tell everyone they know of her thoughtless charity, until we are overrun. Do you truly believe the sempiterna families will stand for such flagrant disregard of our traditions?"

"They haven't a choice," Ariadne says. "And I do not agree

with your assumptions. I am not Grandmother, nor will I ever be. The covens would never have treated me as they did her."

"Your staggering insecurity aside," she shakes her head incredulously. "To sacrifice your place in our Goddess' coven, to relinquish any claim you had to your birthright… That is what I shall never comprehend."

"If Hecate wanted my loyalty, she should have answered my prayers." Ariadne spits the words out. "She had many an opportunity to do so, and yet she never did."

"Vengeance then," Cintia muses. "I suppose in your mind, that would seem logical."

"What use does a Goddess have with a pendant, anyhow?" Ariadne asks. "If she wanted it so badly, she should have expressed that to Morgan. Or explained it to me herself."

She is treading on dangerous ground now, criticizing Hecate's choices, but she cannot stay silent in the face of these accusations.

"I've never seen the Goddess with my own eyes," Ariadne continues. "I've only your word that your description of her desires is true."

Cintia conjures a glass of wine and takes a long sip, her gaze never leaving Ariadne.

"Regardless of what Morgan may have hoped for, that pendant is a weapon," she finally says. "Has Iona begun training in combative magic yet, as Moira suggested? How is she faring thus far?"

Ariadne only glares at her.

"Not well, I gather?" Cintia asks with a smirk.

"She needn't be some hardened warrior." Ariadne looks away to hide her doubts. "She is… a benevolent healer who aims to rid the world of corruption."

"Is that what the world needs in times of imminent war? A prim, irenic saint incapable of protecting them?" Cintia asks.

"Morgan thought so," Ariadne says, starting to doubt it herself. "I will not let her come to harm."

"So that is your chosen profession then? A glorified watchdog?" Cintia asks. "I suppose with you defending her from every enemy she garners, she needn't ever raise her voice or cast a single spell. I merely thought your ambitions were far greater than that of a guardian."

"I did not ask for your opinion on the matter," Ariadne says as she turns and hastens toward the front door.

"Does she know of the illusions you gave Vivien?" Cintia

asks.

Ariadne stops dead in her tracks and squeezes her eyes shut.

"No? How curious. Moira informed me of Iona's shock when she learned of your failure to earn Hecate's favor. It seems you could not even trust her with that. I am no longer surprised that she accepts you, when she hardly knows you at all," Cintia says.

"She knows me better than anyone," Ariadne says, her voice breaking.

"What else have you concealed within the deepest recesses of your mind?" Cintia asks. "You can hide away your worst qualities for a time, but not forever. Blood bonds have a way of bringing them to light. Ironic, considering it was your desperate attempt at ensuring she can never leave you. You know as well as I that you will never deserve her. Better to trap her so she has no choice but to stay."

"Stop," Ariadne begs, her throat growing so thick, it hurts to speak.

"Am I wrong?" Cintia asks. "For your sake and hers, I truly hope so. To break a blood bond is to rip two souls apart and risk fracturing them in the process. Some never fully heal, never find companionship again for the rest of their miserable lives."

"We've no reason to break the bond. I have nothing to hide." Ariadne crosses her arms to hide her trembling hands. "She knows of my imperfections."

"She certainly will," Cintia says. "I pity the poor creature, to be bound to you for all eternity. I can think of nothing worse."

"She loves me." It is all Ariadne can think to say.

"For now." Her mother waves her off. "Run along. Enjoy defending your beloved from the peril you've subjected her to."

Then her mother laughs, as if it is the finest joke she's ever heard. Ariadne wrenches open the front door and slams it shut behind her, but her mother's cackle still echoes in her mind. She drops her staff and puts hands over her ears, but it does nothing to block out the taunting, mocking sound.

Putting as much distance between her and the insidious woman outside, Ariadne trips on her feet, nearly falling onto the checkered tile, and collides directly into Euphemia in her haste.

"Ari!" Euphemia grasps her arms to steady her, then frowns. "Whatever is wrong?"

"Nothing," Ariadne says, unconvincingly.

"Why are you weeping?" Euphemia reaches to wipe away the tears, but Ariadne cringes away.

"I'm not," she says firmly, swiping her hands across her

cheeks with unnecessary force.

Euphemia gives her a once over. "Should I find Iona?"

"No," Ariadne says quickly, then feigns nonchalance, "All is well. I must go."

"No, you should stay and keep me company instead," Euphemia says, grasping her wrist.

Ariadne's anger flares as she tries to wrench herself free. "Why do you always order me about? Am I some pet to you, too?"

"No," Euphemia says calmly.

"Just because I once thought you beautiful does not mean I am ever at your command," Ariadne says petulantly, "Your beauty could never compare to Iona's anyhow."

"Oh, undoubtedly," Euphemia agrees, her voice maddeningly even.

"And I did not need you asking after me last summer as if I were some errant child," Ariadne rambles. "Ksenia told me of your constant inquiries."

"I am sure she did," Euphemia says.

"I never asked for your meddlesome interference in my life," Ariadne rambles on. "I never needed you."

"I've gathered that," Euphemia says.

"Then please, just… return to the party and leave me be," Ariadne says with a dismissive wave of her hand.

"Oh, if I am not permitted to order you about, then likewise you have no power over me." Euphemia lifts her chin. "This is my house, and I shall do as I wish."

"Fine, then I shall go," Ariadne huffs and tries to leave, but Euphemia keeps hold of her arm.

"I must insist you stay with me a while," she says.

"Why? Why won't you just leave me be?" Ariadne asks, refusing to succumb to her emotions.

"You are in a right state… I couldn't very well unleash you on the covens and expect anything less than catastrophe. You will only regret your actions later. Nor should you isolate yourself to fixate on whatever is tormenting you," Euphemia says. "And lastly, despite your best efforts, I am quite fond of you, you foolish thing. I've not seen you in months and would very much enjoy your company."

Ariadne's shoulders slump with exhaustion and she rubs her face so hard it hurts. Her mother's words, her threats, her cruel precognitions are like haunting vermin buzzing in her ears, making her skin crawl. Euphemia takes a cautious, quiet step towards her, then carefully embraces her, whispering soothing words.

"Forgive me," Ariadne sniffles. "I did not mean what I said, I..."

Euphemia holds her until she weeps openly, unable to hold back her tears anymore, however embarrassed by her emotions she might be. She does not know how long they stand there before Ariadne finally pulls away, refusing to meet Euphemia's gaze.

"Who has made you so wretched?" she asks, appalled.

"I..." Ariadne hesitates.

"Tell me, Ariadne," Euphemia orders.

"It was only my mother," she says, in a pitiful attempt at nonchalance. "She intercepted me on the steps and-"

Euphemia scowls as she storms to the door and wrenches it open without a second thought.

"No, don't!" Ariadne cries, but to her great relief, her mother is not standing between the pillars, cigarette in hand, as she'd been moments ago. She must have wandered back to the party or returned home to Thessaly in her carriage.

Euphemia huffs with disappointment. "I certainly did not invite that harpy to my home. She had best avoid crossing my path, for I have many a word to-"

"Stay away from her," Ariadne says, perhaps too forcefully, because Euphemia's eyebrows raise in surprise. "I do not want you near her."

"Alright," Euphemia says softly, shepherding her back inside.

"Promise me," Ariadne insists.

"I promise," Euphemia says, then adds, "but I shan't promise to stand idle if I see you mistreated."

Ariadne tries to protest, but Euphemia puts up a finger to silence her.

"I knew it the moment I found you in my woods that day," she says. "That portal was meant to bring you to my doorstep. We were destined to be friends, and so we shall always be."

Ariadne's tormenting thoughts abate for a moment as she remembers that day when Euphemia had found her, shivering and feral, and snuck her into the nearby dining room to conjure her a feast of fish, fresh berries, soups, meat pies, cakes, more food than Ariadne could ever hope to eat. They'd gorged themselves until the sun rose and Ariadne resigned herself to leave, though she'd wished she could stay forever.

"I shall not suffer any harm committed to my friends,"

Euphemia says with fierce determination. "We are children no longer. Any affront to you shall be met in kind."

"You mustn't concern yourself," Ariadne says softly.

"Oh, but I shall," Euphemia says, without a trace of doubt. "Samaira and I may duel over who is your very best friend, but I shall leave that for another, less sacred day."

Ariadne grins despite herself. "And I've no say in the matter?"

"None whatsoever," Euphemia smiles back, and her eyes betray her relief. "Now come to the sitting room and gossip with me."

Ariadne scoffs with mock contempt. "You are worse than Crescentia."

"Perhaps, but I am the very best at gathering secrets." Euphemia waggles her eyebrows. "Crescentia only totes yesterday's news, most of which she gets from me."

"Amaze me then," she acquiesces, letting Euphemia pull her along. "What has everyone been up to while I've been away?"

They enter the sitting room, with a marble fireplace, Turkish rugs, decadent furniture, but there, by the bay windows, is a pianoforte painted carmine red.

"Play for me while I tell you?" Euphemia asks.

"Surely you didn't..." Ariadne looks to her, but she only smiles encouragingly and gestures for her to take a seat.

She does so, bewildered, unsure if she should thank Euphemia, or perhaps she shouldn't assume it's for her. She knows Euphemia doesn't know how to play, but perhaps Leonid does, and he also happens to favor red. But when she looks up at Euphemia, leaning with her head against her hand on the piano's lid, she knows without a doubt that the instrument is meant for her.

"Will you play the sonata I sent you?" Euphemia asks.

Ariadne pales. "Oh... Um... No, I..."

She giggles, "I shan't force you, silly. I only asked because I've heard it's quite beautiful."

"I require more time to practice," Ariadne says.

"Fair enough," Euphemia says, unbothered, just as Frida soars into the room and lands upon her shoulder.

Settling on Mozart's seventeenth piano sonata, Ariadne plays the joyful song while Euphemia prattles on about births, deaths, and scandals of all varieties. It's a familiar soliloquy that fills Ariadne with a rush of nostalgia for somewhat simpler times.

In those days, she and Euphemia would sit by the hearth in

her parents' ballroom, lounging on chaises and drowning themselves in expensive champagne, laughing at whatever drama their peers were embroiled in that particular week.

"Someone stole clippings of Vadoma's datura," Euphemia says conspiratorially. "She sent letters far and wide warning us against it, and she may very well hex the leaves next time, so take care which plants you cut clippings from."

"If she insists on cultivating her plants in forests rather than greenhouses, how can she possibly expect to maintain ownership?" Ariadne asks. "I've told her countless times, unless she deigns to raise up signs, or some such thing, no one would know they are property. They will think it wild."

"She claims greenhouses stunt the growth," Euphemia shrugs.

"Control the growth," Ariadne corrects her. "It could be deer eating the datura for all we know."

"Should we see any deer flying about, the mystery shall be solved." Euphemia giggles and Ariadne joins in.

When their laughter subsides, there is nothing but the song to fill the silence between them.

"I've missed our talks," Euphemia says softly.

Ariadne plays a false note, grimacing in annoyance, but she refuses to respond.

"I was admittedly distracted by the wedding, and my lying in," Euphemia admits, "but I never did forget you. I feel as if you wished I had."

"That's not so." Ariadne shakes her head.

"Why then?" Euphemia asks. "Why did you cast me aside as you did?"

"I did not cast you aside," Ariadne scoffs defensively, the sonata's tempo racing faster in her agitation.

"You did," Euphemia says. "Even Iona thinks so. She inquired about it quite persistently and I could not deny it."

"When?" Ariadne looks up, abruptly ending the song.

"While you were sitting at the pianoforte at Rebekka's party," Euphemia says.

Ariadne runs a nervous hand through her hair and mutters, "You did not…"

"I did not what?"

"I was angry. Not with you."

"I should hope not," Euphemia says with mild indignance.

Ariadne frowns as repressed emotions rise up again. "You did not protect me as you promised."

Euphemia's face falls. "I did try."

"I know."

"I tried to visit-"

"I know."

Euphemia sighs, at a loss. "Would you have bid me abduct you in the dead of night? Take you to the farthest ends of the Earth and live as hermits in some forgotten meadow, like the witches from fairytales?"

Though she means it as an outlandish jest, Ariadne imagines it with a sudden fervent longing. If only they had escaped together, hid themselves away, left marriages and pendants and duty behind. Led peaceful, simple lives.

"They would have certainly found us," Ariadne murmurs.

It is a pleasant fiction, one that she wishes were true, but only if she could still meet and love Iona. Otherwise, she would gladly live through all her misfortunes again than risk losing her.

"It was your idea to commit that lascivious farce in the first place. I know well the destruction of rumor. It spreads faster than disease, faster than fire, and impossible to reverse once spoken. Even I could not prevent that forever. I tried to warn you against it, but you were adamant it must be so," Euphemia says. standing and taking her hand, "You wouldn't listen to reason. You are too self-sacrificing."

"Your parents would have betrothed you to some awful man unworthy of your hand, and you would have been sent away! I couldn't allow it to happen. Scandal was the better alternative. Even if-" Ariadne stops abruptly, a rush of rage overwhelming her, and Euphemia observes her warily.

"What?" she asks.

"It was Ksenia who told them..." Ariadne says. "Of course, it was her."

Euphemia's expression darkens as she considers it. "Iona told me of her treachery. I suppose it is possible-"

"I am a year older than she, and if I'd attended college that year as planned, she would have been too young to compete," Ariadne says. "It was her. I know it."

Euphemia considers it, but to call it coincidence would be folly.

"That bitch," Ariadne spits.

"Indeed," Euphemia says softly. "I am ever so sorry. I never should have allowed her to attend my parties. I did not recognize her lust for ambition. She is so difficult to read, so quiet..."

Ariadne sighs as her anger subsides. It was so long ago now, and in the end, she has all she could ever want in Iona.

"It was worth the trouble," she decides.

"It certainly was for me," Euphemia agrees with a small smile at the thought of her beloved family.

"I am glad you were given a choice," Ariadne says. "That is all I wanted for you."

"All I wished for you was freedom, so it seems we are the both of us victorious. Iona is darling, and the way you look at her..." She grins at Ariadne's blush. "You are hopelessly besotted."

"Yes, yes," Ariadne waves her off.

"I am delighted to see you happy. It warms my heart," Euphemia says. "Do not allow anyone to take that away."

Ariadne's eyes meet hers, and for a moment she wonders if Euphemia had overheard her mother's words on the front steps, but she gives no indication. She only stares back with a trace of concern, and fathomless affection.

"See! They are playing with it!"

"Sara!" Nenet cries. "You mustn't run! This is not our..."

She stops in the doorway, then sighs when Sara runs straight up to the pianoforte.

"May I play?" she asks.

"Ariadne is already playing," Nenet gripes. "And she is far better than you-"

"I've been practicing!" Sara protests.

"I will tell Father of your disobedience," Nenet warns. "It is far past your bedtime, anyhow. The other children are in bed-"

"No, I am not tired!" Sara whines.

"She may play if she wishes to," Ariadne rises from the bench, gesturing for Sara to sit.

"I have permission," Sara says with a haughty smile.

"Ugh... Very well." Nenet rolls her eyes.

Eagerly, Sara jumps onto the bench, her short legs unable to reach the pedals, and begins playing random notes.

Euphemia smooths out her golden hair and says, "I'm afraid I must be off. Leonid will be wondering where I am."

"Of course," Ariadne says. "Many blessings."

Euphemia places a warm palm against her cheek, then goes down the hall toward the courtyard.

"She has grown a head taller than last I saw her," Ariadne observes as she approaches Nenet.

Sara, unaware of their conversation, slams her hands against the keys with far too much force, making Ariadne wince.

"When was that?" Nenet's brow furrows as she tries to remember.

"Last summer, I believe," Ariadne says.

"Yes, that's right." Nenet grins at the memory. "What fun we had."

Ariadne clears her throat, a flush creeping up her neck.

"I wasn't quite sure of the match between you and Iona, but I see now my doubts were foolish," Nenet says. "Apart from that awkward departure earlier, all seems very well between the two of you."

Ariadne's blush deepens, and she keeps her eyes cast down. "Apologies, she was… rather faint. The ritual took its toll."

"Hmm," Nenet hums, unconvinced, but Ariadne refuses to explain further.

Sara remains entirely oblivious to their conversation, but Nenet takes a step closer anyway, and speaks in hushed tones.

"I must admit…" Nenet starts, then thinks better of it. "Or rather I suppose you've always been capable of inhabiting either role, when you were with Gisela and I, but after all your rollicking with Rebekka, I always thought you'd pair with someone more… dominant."

"Iona is more assertive than you might think," Ariadne says, recalling their game with the vines, and at the pianoforte.

"I truly hope so," Nenet says, "or otherwise, the covens shall eat her alive."

"Everyone underestimates her," Ariadne says with sudden fiery conviction.

Nenet raises her eyebrows slightly. "I do not perceive her kindness as weakness, but others may."

"She is not always meek," Ariadne insists. "When provoked she can be quite… intimidating."

"Know that from experience, do you?" Nenet grins, then laughs at Ariadne's sheepish look. "I am glad she made you suffer before forgiving you."

"That she did," Ariadne chuckles.

*What did I do?* Iona asks.

Ariadne flinches in surprise, making Nenet's eyes widen with concern.

"Why are you so excitable today?" she asks.

"I… Everything is fine," Ariadne assures her. *I shouldn't have left you.*

*Do not apologize,* Iona thinks. *Just come here.*

*I shall, I just...* Ariadne pauses when she senses Iona's jealousy. *You've nothing to fear.*

*Rebekka propositioned me again.*

Ariadne's jaw clenches with outrage. *What did she say?*

*Look.*

Grateful for her transparency, Ariadne delves into her mind to recount the conversation. It sickens her, watching Rebekka so brazenly make her desire known, though it is no true surprise. At the sight of Iona walking away, with Rebekka rightfully admonished, Ariadne's anxiety would have disappeared entirely, if it weren't for Iona's tertiary thoughts on the very outskirts of her mind which cannot deny Rebekka's beauty, her stature, her bold allure. That which had once captivated Ariadne, too.

She is painfully aware of Rebekka's everlasting patience. Even when she had regretfully informed Rebekka of the newly arranged courtship with Elise and warned that she would never be free of her family, Rebekka had only smiled and had not been deterred in the least. If anything, the obstacle in their path had only seemed to peak her interest.

At every subsequent party, Rebekka had watched, waited, and meddled when she could, romancing Ariadne right under Elise's nose. It had never progressed very far, for Elise would always manage to find them too quickly wherever they could manage to hide, but Rebekka would only kiss her senseless in parting and leave her wanting more.

Rebekka had waited until Elise's time finally ended, stoked Ariadne's lust in the interim, until she thought it might burn her alive. Perhaps it was cruel of her, in fact she knows it was, but once Elise ended their odious courtship after Yule, she'd stolen away to Iceland within the hour, deciding she had nothing to lose anymore. Rebekka's patience had lasted only until Ariadne explained her presence there and told her in no uncertain terms that Elise was truly gone.

Rebekka had taken her right then in a spectacular display of ravenous hunger unleashed in a long night of insatiable passion. It had been her first time in bed with a woman, and Rebekka had taken great pleasure in that fact, something Ariadne would only understand later when she'd been the first to ravish Iona under the stars.

She'd never mistaken Rebekka's interest in her for love, but she had no need for it then. At the time, it had been exactly what

Ariadne craved; someone to hold her, to make her forget, to make her melt.

Rebekka will wait for Iona, if it suits her, even if it takes years.

Ariadne has little fear of infidelity, not from one so honorable as Iona. However, should she make one too many mistakes, should she ruin things as she so often does, and Iona decides that bonding with her was a mistake, then Rebekka will be waiting, ready to take Iona without remorse.

"Do not abuse the instrument like that!" Nenet scolds her sister, interrupting Ariadne's tormented musings.

*Did you see?* Iona asks, still waiting.

*Yes,* Ariadne responds, forcing her emotions down. *She is shameless in her pursuits, and you are the most beautiful woman present. I would think it odd if she did not at least try to seduce you.*

Iona's flush of pleasure is undercut by her enduring concern. *I made myself quite clear. She shan't bother me again.*

*And I shall reiterate those sentiments,* Ariadne assures her.

*What?* Iona asks.

"Gisela remains bitter, I'm afraid," Nenet says.

"Oh… Is she?" Ariadne asks, uninterested.

*You mustn't quarrel with Rebekka,* Iona warns. *She is a council member's daughter, and such a scandal would only-*

*It shan't come to blows, but I cannot let this go unanswered.* Ariadne clenches her fists.

"Gisela had her heart set on you," Nenet says.

"She never loved me," Ariadne scoffs. "She was only ever interested in my name."

"That is true enough," Nenet admits, "but her pride was hurt regardless."

"Forgive my apathy," Ariadne says dryly. "I never once promised her any commitment. I'm frankly relieved to be free of her infatuation."

*I do not think it wise to-*

*Iona, please, I cannot manage two conversations at once.*

"Do not pretend to be unfamiliar with the pain of unrequited affection," Nenet says. "We haven't forgotten your forlorn looks whenever Euphemia entered a room."

Ariadne's jaw ticks. "I do not know what you mean."

"You beseeched Gisela and I to distract you the night of Euphemia's wedding, and we rose to the occasion, but we both knew who you were trying to forget," Nenet says.

*I do not wish to hear any more,* Iona complains.

*You are not required to.* Ariadne hopes she will leave her mind.

She doesn't want Iona to hear this either.

"As I've told you before, my arrangement with Euphemia was entirely platonic," Ariadne says, a partial truth, truer now than it was then. "Do not dare to insinuate otherwise in Iona's presence, or Euphemia's for that matter. I will not have the past drudged up again."

*Won't you come to me now?* Iona asks.

*For heaven's sake!* Ariadne snaps. *Why? What is so pressing? Can't you see?*

Ariadne looks through Iona's eyes and, in an instant, her mind empties. Iona has stripped naked and positioned herself in front of a mirror, kneeling with her legs spread wide to give Ariadne a devastating view of her full reflection, every curve and freckle on display.

"I should find Iona," Ariadne says.

"Very well." Nenet's lips thin with displeasure.

Ariadne goes to leave, then hesitates.

"I never intended to cause Gisela any pain," she says for good measure. "I hope she will attend the equinox ritual so we might resolve our differences and move forward, but she owes Iona a sincere apology for the things she said in the student's parlor. Do not think I've forgotten it."

Nenet nods slowly, then waves her off. "Many blessings."

"Many blessings," Ariadne says then walks away. *Where are you?*

*The spare room. Second door on the left.*

The moment Ariadne is alone in the hallway, her knees grow weak as she bites back a moan. Luckily there is no one there to hear her.

*Iona,* Ariadne chuckles darkly.

*You took far too long.* Iona's finger slips through her folds as she plays with herself.

*At least let me climb the stairs before you-* Ariadne lets out a frustrated sigh as Iona strokes faster.

*Come,* Iona commands.

# 17 - Iona

Ariadne nearly breaks the door off its hinges when she bursts into the spare room, but her face falls when she finds Iona fully dressed and perched on the edge of the bed.

"There you are." She fights to keep a straight face when she observes the blatant disappointment on her beloved's face.

"But…" Ariadne looks between her and the cheval mirror in the corner that she had only just been kneeling in front of.

"Close the door and sit with me, won't you?" Iona pats the space beside her on the bed. "I wish to speak with you."

When Ariadne slumps onto the mattress, she leans her elbows on her knees and rubs her face in her hands.

"I am not confident I can survive another frank conversation this night," she says, her voice betraying just how exhausted she's become.

It's then that Iona identifies a variance between them. For Ariadne, social gatherings are an emotional labor that seems to drain the life from her, leaving her irritable and sluggish. Iona has found that she does not mind them. Perhaps it was her prolonged isolation early in life that made her unaware of this aspect of her personality, but she truly does enjoy dressing up in fine clothes, meeting new and interesting people, and though she has less experience in the art of conversation, she's not as daunted by it as she once was.

She never had so many people watching her, admiring her, revering her. She shan't let it get to her head, but she would be lying if she claimed she got no pleasure from it. For Ariadne, it seems such attention is torturous.

"We should remain here for the rest of the night," Iona decides.

Ariadne pulls her hands away to look at her in surprise. "Really? But… are you not needed for more introductions?"

"There will be other rituals," Iona shrugs. "I'd prefer to rest. It has been a very long day."

"Indeed, it has," Ariadne sighs.

A fraction of the rigidity in her posture fades, but Iona observes persisting agitation in her demeanor and decides more is needed to comfort her. Anything to keep her from seeking out

Rebekka, for that couldn't possibly end well.

"Lay on the bed," Iona says.

Ariadne's eyes brighten with renewed interest. "I thought you wished to speak."

"I do," Iona says. "Lay on the bed, please."

"As you wish," Ariadne grins, shuffling up the mattress to lay on her back.

"Turn round." Iona motions for her to flip onto her stomach.

Ariadne's brow furrows slightly, but she does as she's told. Iona climbs on top of her, straddles her hips, and makes their dresses and stays disappear. Slicing a line down the white cotton fabric of Ariadne's chemise, she pulls the tear apart to expose the smooth expanse of Ariadne's back.

Letting her fingers drift lightly over Ariadne's shoulder blades and along her spine, Iona delights in the slight shift of her muscles in response. She massages Ariadne's shoulders and finds a great deal of tension there. Tightening her grip, she kneads the muscles until they go soft and malleable.

"Mmm," Ariadne moans her approval.

She presses her thumbs along the curve of Ariadne's spine from her neck all the way down to the two dimples of Venus on her lower back. Then she lightly grazes with her nails as she moves her hands back up, making Ariadne shiver as she repeats the movement a few times, slow and gentle.

Goosebumps rise along Ariadne's shoulders, trickling down to her lower back, and Iona observes with fascination as they spread. She leans forward and licks the skin to feel the pebbled texture against her tongue and Ariadne sucks in a breath at the contact, tensing with anticipation.

Iona grins and leans back. "I've noticed something."

"Hmm?" Ariadne relaxes again.

"We've never spoken of what we found in the arches during Morgan's trials," Iona says, "What did you see?"

Ariadne folds her arms in front of her and rests her head against them. "I traveled far into the past the first time. The witch I spoke with did not know the year, but I surmise it must have been... the eleventh century or so judging by her clothing and speech."

Iona ghosts her fingers over the two dimples on Ariadne's lower back and idly wonders what causes the divots to occur, as she does not share this feature on her own back. Out of curiosity, she very lightly presses her thumbs into the dimples, slowly adding pressure until Ariadne sucks in an involuntary gasp.

"Um…" She squirms. "I… saved the witch from a mob of humans. They chased us through a marsh all through the night, could barely see a thing except when their torches were too close. Fortunately, we found a place to hide until dawn, and she told me of how the townsfolk had turned on her when their wells ran dry."

"What of the second arch?" Iona asks, conjuring a glass vial of lavender oil and pouring its contents generously.

Ariadne lets out a soft moan when Iona rubs the oil in, spreading it evenly, until her olive skin glistens prettily in the candlelight, so smooth that Iona's hands slide with hardly any resistance, sometimes pressing in with her palms or using just the pads of her fingertips to trace the subtle bumps of Ariadne's spine.

"Ari?" Iona asks when she catches Ariadne's eyelids drooping.

"Renaissance," she mumbles, "The witch brewed a love potion, but I convinced her to toss it into the dirt."

Iona's hands falter. Reaching for a pillow, Ariadne buries her face into the bundle of feathers, clearly not wishing to speak any more of it. So, Iona runs her nails along the nape of her neck, sinking her fingers into her thick, dark curls, and scratches her scalp. Ariadne makes an indiscernible noise of pleasure into the pillow and Iona closes her eyes as she feels the faint echo of the sensation through their bond.

Ariadne turns her head to the side to say, "I cannot concentrate when you-"

"And the third arch?" Iona prompts, lacing the fingers of her other hand in Ariadne's curls and making circular motions with her fingers.

"1969." Her eyelids flutter closed. "Three witches held a seance. Their minds were clearly altered by some manner of herbs or intoxicants. Their questions were difficult to interpret. I fear I was a disappointment to them."

Skimming her nails back and forth over the tender skin just behind Ariadne's ears, Iona asks, "What did they wish to know?"

"How…" Ariadne shudders. "Must you do that?"

"You do not like it?" Iona asks.

"…I do, but I may as well be Aster." Ariadne expels a shaky breath as another array of goosebumps trickle down her neck.

Iona elicits yet another soft sigh from her and grins. "Focus, love."

"They asked about… the nature of fate," Ariadne says.

"To what end?" Iona asks.

"They wished to alter predestined events they'd foreseen, and I told them it was impossible to do so," Ariadne says, "Or at least, I've never heard of a spell to accomplish it. They seemed confused by my answer. I explained to them that fate is woven by Gods, not meant to be altered by mortals on a whim."

"Did they tell you what they wished to change?" Iona asks.

"There was a war they wanted to prevent… or end," Ariadne says, arching into Iona's touch when her hands return to the smooth contours of her back, massaging in the final traces of fragrant oil. "Who did you see?"

Iona recounts her conversations with Delia and Vanessa, both of them strong young witches in times of personal strife. She leaves Lucretia for last.

"Triora?" Ariadne cranes her neck to look back at her. "I wonder if Nonna knew her."

"I believe it was before her time, but perhaps your Nonna's mother might have been acquainted with Lucretia before they fled the city."

"How dreadful, to know there was nothing you could do for her." Lying flat on her stomach again, Ariadne presses her cheek against the pillow.

"It was awful…" Iona whispers. "Whatever did she do to deserve such a terrible fate?"

Ariadne goes quiet for a moment, then says, "In my experience, the goodness of a person does not determine how their fate unfolds. There are many who suffer for no reason at all and there is no sense to be made of it."

"I suppose you're right," Iona says.

Lucretia had faced her death with bravery that Iona deeply admires. She still thinks of her often, and her plea to never be forgotten.

"I am sorry I left you," Ariadne whispers.

"Why did you?" Iona asks.

With her mouth partially covered by her hand, Ariadne's red eyes are distant as she stares out her window at the moon hung among the blue clouds.

"Are we allowed secrets from each other?" Ariadne asks.

Iona goes still. "What do you mean?"

"You could read my thoughts, sense each feeling, examine every single memory if you wanted, but you rarely ever delve that deeply," Ariadne says, her voice betraying her gratitude, "And yet, you were cross when I withheld the truth about Hecate and…"

"I am not owed your every thought and memory. Those are private, not secret. What are thoughts anyhow? Fleeting whispers, not absolute truth. Deeds are far more important," Iona says. "And I never needed a bond to know your feelings. You wear your emotions like a second skin." Ariadne hides her face away into the pillow, and Iona chuckles. "In fact, please do keep your thoughts well hidden if it will spare me glimpses of your past intimacies."

Ariadne groans with mortification, the sound muffled by her pillow. "That was purely accidental. It shall *never* happen again."

"See that it doesn't," Iona says, trying to keep her voice light, but there is an edge to her tone.

"It won't," Ariadne says again.

When another silence grows between them, Iona lightly runs her nails over Ariadne's back to calm her, until the renewed tension in her muscles subsides. She traces the very faint indent of Ariadne's ribs along her sides, the bones far less visible than they once were.

"The reason you left the field, is it a secret?" Iona asks.

Ariadne doesn't respond, and in so doing gives her answer.

"I trust you to tell me what I should know," Iona says. "I was only cross before because… I did not like how Moira used my ignorance against you."

That seems to surprise Ariadne in some way, but true to her word, Iona does not look into her mind to see why. Instead, she drapes herself across Ariadne's back, blanketing her in warmth and pressing an ear to her skin to listen to her steady heartbeat. Ariadne sighs contentedly, taking Iona's hand and pressing it to her lips.

"I trust you, too," Ariadne says softly. "I do."

And there it is. The slightest trace of deceit that Iona cannot ignore but is too frightened to confront. Ariadne's statement is more of a hope or a wish, but not the absolute truth, and the distinction is as alarming as it is hurtful. It lingers there, a haze of nocuous candor that neither of them can escape.

"I know," Iona says anyway, pressing a kiss to Ariadne's shoulder before pulling away and caressing her into a stupor.

She hadn't intended to sense the equivocation of Ariadne's words, but at times, the bond's insights are compulsory, the same as the unwanted images she'd seen of Nenet. She hopes that in time they will gain better control of the magic, of their own minds, so that such infringements will not occur, but for now, it has proved a recurring aggravation.

On Samhain, Ariadne had admitted it was difficult for her to trust. She'd claimed she would try, and Iona had accepted that, for the time being, but she struggles to comprehend why Ariadne still cannot trust her now, after everything they've endured together. Does Ariadne not know how everlasting her love is? What more must she do, or say, to convince her?

She reminds herself that their love is still new, still so fragile, despite their bond. Perhaps in time, this will resolve itself. She will prove her love with each passing day, until Ariadne's doubts are eradicated.

She is increasingly aware of how difficult life has been for Ariadne, understands now more than ever how hellacious her mother is. To live for years with someone like that... Of course it would have a lasting effect on a person. Of course, Ariadne will need time, and Iona will give her that, because she knows their love is true, even if it might not be perfect.

Before long, Ariadne's breathing grows heavy and slow. Iona peers around the mass of dark curls and just as she'd suspected, Ariadne's eyes are closed, her full red lips slightly parted. With exceedingly careful movements, Iona lays down without waking her and admires her beautiful face, which reflects serenity at last.

Stars flicker within an ink black sky. At first, they are like pinpricks of light, so small that she squints to make them out, until they glow brighter and brighter and brighter, their blinding glare shining like a thousand suns, making her eyes water, but try as she might, she cannot blink or look away. All at once the sky goes dark again, the outlines of light still scorched onto her vision as brumous spots of deep blue.

The spots morph into petals that drift on the wind, kissing her cheeks and filling her nostrils with a sickly-sweet scent of roses. She holds out a hand to catch petals in her palm and bring them up to her nose to breathe them in, drunk on the fragrance.

Her eyes close, then she flinches at the crash of broken glass shattering the silence and compelling her eyes to open in a sudden panic only to find herself in an endless field of flooded grass. When she looks down, she expects to see water and mud making her toes cold and wet but instead finds blood so red it's stark against the vivid green. The torrent flows between the stalks, staining her feet and ankles, and making her wretch. She runs from it, her footsteps splashing droplets of red onto the hem of her white skirts. She takes refuge within a dense, dark forest.

It's there the screaming starts, though from where she cannot decipher, and she cannot decide whether to go to it or run from it. She only runs aimlessly as silent tears stream down her cheeks, but her steps are meager and slow, despite her haste. No matter how she labors, she remains stuck in the same spot. Her neck is bare, her wand nowhere to be found, and when she calls for Ariadne, or Samuel, her mother, her father, no one comes.

After a while her steps slow, her panicked breaths heaving from her chest, until she is wracked with an awful cough as the air is poisoned with heavy smoke. She looks behind her to find the forest ablaze with waves of ravenous fire that rush towards her, angry and calamitous in its unrelenting destruction, but her feet will not move. Her cries are drowned out by the cracking of the branches and the roar of the searing flames that reach for her.

There, within the scintillant blaze stands a dark figure cloaked in black, her back hunched, her face indistinguishable, with a golden dagger strapped to her waist. The scabbard glistens tantalizingly by the light of the inferno, as if anticipating the moment the blade will be unsheathed and plunged into its next victim. A child's cry rings out above the clamor, forlorn and faint.

"Iona!"

With a jerk, she wakes to find her cheeks wet with tears and Ariadne hovering over her, her eyes wild and filled with concern.

"Iona," she says. "It was only a dream."

"She's coming," Iona chokes out. "She's watching me… She can see me even now."

"What?" Ariadne asks, her face going pale with dread. "Who? What did you see?"

A prickling sensation dances along her fingers and toes from too much air too fast, so she forces her breaths to slow. Disoriented, Iona almost forgets where they are, until she remembers the ritual, the spare room in Euphemia's manor, caressing Ariadne into slumber, only to be ravaged by such a terrible dream.

"Look," Iona says.

Ariadne delves into her mind and beholds the remnants of the dream before it slips from Iona's memory entirely, as dreams so often do. Even as she thinks on it then, she can only recall fleeting images and hazy details. With every passing second, Iona only remembers the terror, but not the cause.

"It was only a dream," Ariadne says, though she does not seem so sure of it herself.

They both know well that dreams are never *just* dreams, but rather omens. Perhaps not as clearly rendered as Samaira's insights, but still they should not be ignored.

So instead, Ariadne amends, "She only means to frighten you, whoever she is. I will never let anything happen to you. I swear it."

Iona nods, knowing that the pendant's magic will protect her, too, but even with that assurance, her face scrunches up as she fails to suppress her sobs.

"Come here." Ariadne embraces her. She listens to Ariadne's heart again, and it calms her enough that her trembling slowly subsides.

They yelp when a letter appears with a pop and lands on the bed in front of them.

"For goodness sake!" Ariadne snaps, taking the letter and tearing it open. Her frustration turns to stern resignation as she reads.

"What is it?" Iona asks.

Ariadne lets out a heavy sigh. "Samaira had another vision."

The vision was of sand that stretched out for leagues in every direction, but not much else. Samaira did not see any faces or hear any voices, but the vision remains a substantial glimpse of what's to come. They dispense letters to any witch or warlock they can think of who live near desert, sending a warning of a potential attack. Word of the recurring malefician attacks has already spread far and wide, sowing unease among their ranks.

Even if they cannot prevent the attack itself, perhaps less blood will be spilled if those in peril are cognizant of the danger, so long as they are not overtaken by panic. Children will be kept safely in their homes, and no one will wander after dark.

Euphemia insists that they stay with her while they await more news, claiming that she feels safer with them close by, but really Iona suspects it is for Ariadne's benefit, to provide her a place of peace and tranquility far from her family.

They take their tea in the garden with young Hugo, a

charming little boy with his mother's blue eyes, and in the afternoons, Ariadne plays piano while Iona and Euphemia read by the windows. It is a picturesque escape, but it does little to preoccupy the mind.

To pass the time, Iona is almost grateful to practice magic with Ariadne in the sunlit valley. There is nothing to be done while they wait except prepare. Samaira has returned to Nepal to meditate in isolation. She will send a letter the moment she gets another glimpse of the future or perceives any insight from the threads. Days pass with no news, and Iona's foreboding only grows.

"If we are called to fight, we shall be ready," Ariadne says in answer to Iona's anxiety ridden thoughts.

"You seem so sure we can protect them," she says.

"Indeed, we can, when you overcome your fear," Ariadne says.

Kicking a loose stone with her boot, Iona leaves her doubts unspoken.

"I thought you'd be in finer spirits," Ariadne says. "I let you wear the pendant this time."

"How generous," Iona mutters.

A burst of heat hits her backside, and she yelps, more from surprise than anything. She turns to glare at Ariadne who smirks and raises her eyebrows expectantly.

"We haven't finished," she says, gesturing to the line of targets laid out in the grass.

Iona conjures a ball of fire in her palm and hurls it at one of the targets. It nearly misses, hitting one of the outermost rings.

"Decent," Ariadne says.

Iona sighs. She'd done this once before at college when she first learned how to conjure fire, but Samuel had been kind enough to set the targets much closer. She has to aim well to hit her marks, and it turns out she has yet another weakness to add to her growing list of faults.

She conjures another fireball and hurls it, missing another target entirely. The ball bounces through the grass, leaving a trail of fire as it rolls away.

"These did nothing against Elise," Iona mumbles.

"If we'd burned the forest down around her, it might have made a difference," Ariadne says.

"Why didn't you?" Iona asks with slight sarcasm.

"Crescentia lay unconscious somewhere in the trees, and there were other students searching for the ritual site. A fire could have burned them, too," Ariadne says. "And most of all, you would have never forgiven me for killing your cousin."

Iona frowns. "If she hadn't been my cousin, would you have killed her?"

"Yes," Ariadne says, without hesitation.

Taken aback, Iona says, "You told me you weren't a killer."

"Defense of oneself or others is not murder," Ariadne argues. "There is a significant difference between the two."

Iona's mind races, so many questions threatening to burst past her lips, each of them too frightening to ask.

"Let's continue," Ariadne suggests, sensing her turmoil.

She conjures another ball of fire and hurls it. It strikes the side of another target but doesn't quite hit the center.

"You've given up," Ariadne accuses.

"No..." Iona says. "Can I not step closer?"

"Ten bullseyes," Ariadne says. "That is all you need. It is not that difficult."

Glowering at her, Iona makes all of the targets combust, the flames burning them up in seconds until they are reduced to piles of ash.

"You are the sorest loser," Ariadne chuckles.

"You've specifically chosen a skill I am horrible at so you can win again," Iona says.

"Would you prefer another flying lesson?" Ariadne asks.

"No," Iona says quickly, recalling their lesson the day before, when Ariadne had crafted an illusion of a manticore chasing her about the sky to practice evasive maneuvers. It had been a most unsettling lesson indeed.

"What should we do then?" Ariadne asks.

"Something useful that I am capable of mastering!" Iona slumps onto the ground and pulls a few blades of grass with her fist, fiddling with the pieces of green between her fingers.

Ariadne walks away and Iona stiffens, wondering if she'd angered her past the point of speaking, which is never a good sign.

But Ariadne returns with a handful of stones in her hand. She drops them to the ground and sits cross-legged in front of her.

"Moira taught me this trick." Ariadne plucks up one of the stones and holds it in the center of her palm. "Démolir."

Iona flinches, expecting an explosion, but there is none.

"Throw this," Ariadne says, then quickly clarifies, "Throw it far."

Standing and gingerly taking the stone from her, Iona throws it as far as she can and, just as she'd suspected, the stone explodes the moment it hits the ground, chunks of dirt flying up into the air from the force of the blast.

"Clever," Iona says.

"Try it," Ariadne says, motioning for her to sit again.

They spend a few minutes enchanting the stones until all are imbued with magic. The feat had once been a challenge for Iona at college, but with help from the pendant she finds it significantly easier.

"Now the fun part." Ariadne takes half of the stones for her own and steps forward.

They throw their explosive stones far, admiring the damage they create, riddling the earth with deep craters, nearly shattering their eardrums from the deafening bursts, until they've run out of ammunition.

"Those might be better for the likes of you," Ariadne says, conjuring water to clean the dirt from her hands. "No need to aim as accurately, so long as you throw them far enough."

"It is an adequate alternative," Iona admits.

"I suppose we can finish for the day," Ariadne says. "Unless you think you can hit six more targets."

Iona snorts, conjuring away her clothes to make it easier for the both of them.

"Suit yourself," Ariadne grins.

"I'm yours," Iona says with a mockingly coquettish smile. "What is your fantasy now?"

She inhales sharply when Ariadne sends a gust of air to shove her backwards. She puts out her arms to break her fall, but she lands on a soft plush cushion.

Ariadne conjures one of her own and sits gracefully atop it.

"But…" Iona marks the space between them.

"Do not be a sore loser here, too," Ariadne says. "I've won. Fair is fair."

"Yes, I know," Iona says. "But how am I meant to touch you from over here?"

"Who said anything about touching me?" Ariadne asks.

She stares at Ariadne with her brow furrowed, until realization dawns.

"You want me to…" Iona trails off.

"Touch yourself," Ariadne says.

"You could have me do anything you want," Iona says.

"I know," Ariadne says.

"And this is what you came up with?" Iona squeaks.

"Put on a show for me, nymph. I more than deserve it after your rather lackluster performance today," Ariadne mocks.

Her gaze is a caress as it travels down Iona's exposed skin, making her heartbeat thrum in her chest and between her legs. She remains frozen in place.

"Do not tell me you've forgotten how, since I've been responsible for all your pleasure for nearly a year," Ariadne taunts.

"If you want me to do this, you must be silent." Iona flushes.

Ariadne stands and approaches her. "On the contrary, love. I intend to be quite vocal."

She's aware of her every breath, every pulse of her blood, as Ariadne takes her left hand and slides off her amethyst ring, holding her gaze as she does it, then stands tall and removes her own bloodstone ring, placing both of them in her trousers pocket. Then Ariadne returns to her cushion and sits, leaning her head against her hand and waiting for Iona to decide if she'll obey.

"Non sono una donna paziente," Ariadne says.

Iona sucks in a breath at the sound of her unaltered voice. Ariadne's responding smile is infectious until they are both giggling. Out of curiosity, Iona peers into her mind and finds her thoughts unreadable too, a mixture of many languages jumbled together. All Iona can decipher with any clarity are feelings and images, which are always the easiest to perceive.

"Nýmfi?" Ariadne raises an expectant brow.

She lowers her gaze and feels suddenly very shy. Ariadne has seen her in countless vulnerable positions, but nothing quite like this. She will be entirely exposed and performing an act she's only ever performed in private.

"Oh, ne sois pas timide, mon amour. Nous sommes désormais bien au-delà de cela," Ariadne coos.

"Just… hush," Iona says, her flush deepening. "I know not what you say, but I'm certain it would only irritate me."

Ariadne's eyes flare as she grins, reveling in the effect her words wreak on Iona's nerves.

"For goodness sake," her voice trembles as she shifts so she is kneeling atop the cushion.

Ariadne's smile disappears the moment her legs are spread wide, utterly transfixed when Iona runs her hand from her neck to her breast, squeezing it gently, pinching her pink nipple between her thumb and forefinger. She lets her other hand drift past her ribs, over her stomach, to brush against her swollen flesh between her spread thighs and lets out a soft sigh.

"Koíta me," Ariadne demands.

Her lids flutter open as she meets Ariadne's gaze, the approval there telling her that she must have done something Ariadne wanted. Her eyes had been closed. Perhaps Ariadne wants them open.

Iona glares from beneath her lashes as she moves her middle and ring fingers in slow circles, her lips parting as her pleasure simmers. She relishes the thought that Ariadne can feel an echo of every stroke, though to her credit, Ariadne does not let on. She only stares back with hooded ruby eyes.

"Allora queste delizie potrebbero commuovermi la mente, per vivere con te ed essere il tuo amore," Ariadne murmurs.

Iona moans, her fingers moving faster as she palms her breast and squeezes firmly, the way Ariadne often does. She shudders as she slips one finger inside, then another, curling them into herself as she thrusts in and out.

"Amo modum quo tremis," Ariadne whispers. "Sa'amut min 'ajlik hubiy."

Whimpering softly, Iona pulses her fingers against her most sensitive spot until she trembles with need. Then Ariadne stands and takes leisurely steps through the grass. Iona feels her eyes roving over her, drinking her in, committing it all to her perfect memory.

"I need you," Iona begs, hoping the desperation in her tone will be indication enough of what she wants.

Ariadne climbs onto the cushion and has Iona lean against her so her full lips are in line with her ear. She whispers strings of beautiful words, a soliloquy of sweet nothings to spur her on as she loses herself. Despite the barrier of language, the reverence in Ariadne's voice needs no translation.

Snaking a hand around her torso, Ariadne whispers in her ear, "Are you so desperate for me, love?"

Iona startles, turning to look back at her in shock, but she only laughs and holds up her other hand to show that she's put her ring back on. Sighing with impatience, she allows Ariadne to slide her amethyst ring back into place where there is now a line of paler skin to indicate its constant presence on her finger. Ariadne peppers soft kisses down her neck to her shoulder, then back up again.

"Nymph." Ariadne's breath tickles her ear. "You know better."

"Yes," Iona breathes. "I am desperate for you."

Ariadne's long fingers replace hers, sliding through her wetness and making her squirm.

"I can tell." Ariadne grins against her cheek, her other hand slipping around her throat and holding her still.

Then she doesn't tease any longer, slipping two fingers inside and stroking her far better than she can to herself, reaching around with her other hand to fondle her aching breasts, and has her falling apart in no time at all. Ariadne clings to her as she finds her pleasure too, her cries muffled by Iona's hair.

"There aren't words enough in a thousand languages to express my love for you," Ariadne whispers in her ear.

Iona's chest heaves, Ariadne's words bringing tears to her eyes. "You needn't go to such lengths to beguile me. I am already yours."

Ariadne only tilts her chin to claim her mouth with a possessive kiss.

Upon their arrival in Scotland, Harriett Sullivan greets them with bouquets of white heather for luck before she and her mother guide them to their home in the lowlands near a city called Bearaig a Tuath. Following the witch trials of King James VI, the Sullivans, and any other families who had managed to escape, created a new village by the sea called the Loch nan Bana-bhuidsichean and hid it away with illusion magic. The spells are sustained by the entire village, each witch and warlock collectively shouldering the strain, so it is not so heavy a burden.

Some of the cottages are made with heavy grey stones and thatched roofs, while others are built in a more modern style, with shingled roofs and taller chimneys. The cool sea breeze is starkly familiar, reminding Iona so much of Cornwall. The scent of brine brings back memories of her walks to Tintagel, swimming in the ocean, and lounging on the beach beneath the cliffs where her mother's white cottage once stood.

When she observes the townsfolk gathered in the central square, she does see a few other witches with marks, one in particular having a green triskelion on their forearm, and it brings Iona comfort to know that Harriett will not be alone in having one. She will grow up to be like Crescentia, a witch who knows what life is like without a mark, who can hopefully provide a new perspective to her community, with the power to be heard.

The two women in need of healing are in a far worse state

than Harriett. One has three deep gashes across her face, one of them just barely missing her right eye. When Ariadne inquires about the injury, Regina explains that healers have already visited, but they've struggled to mend the wounds entirely, only managing to remedy them a little bit at a time, despite their proficiency.

It seems the maleficium prevents the healing magic from penetrating. However, with Ariadne's help, Iona manages to heal the woman's face and renew her magic. When it's done, there are three sprigs of thorns where the gashes once were. A new mark.

The other woman is badly burned on her left side, with open wounds on her shoulder and her arm. She's hardly able to lift her head from her pillow, her red hair plastered to her sweaty forehead. When she is healed, a ring of purple primrose flowers encircles her wrist, her forearm, all the way up to her shoulder.

The spells take their toll. Iona leans against Ariadne, fatigue nearly overtaking her, but she forces herself to keep awake long enough to say her goodbyes to Harriett and Regina.

Ariadne's arm tightens around her waist. "Are you-"

"I'm only… winded," Iona assures her.

Unconvinced, Ariadne crafts a portal to Drakenström Manor and helps her step through.

"You should rest," Ariadne says.

"I am well," Iona insists.

But when they pass through the threshold, Euphemia stands there waiting for them, grim-faced, with an unopened letter in her hand.

"It arrived only moments ago." She offers it to Ariadne. "I did not think it right for me to open-"

"It's in Samaira's hand." Ariadne frantically rips it open, pouring over the words, and her face pales.

"What does she write?" Iona asks, her stomach sinking.

"I see a skirmish amid rain and waves," Ariadne reads, her voice trembling. "Blood spilt amid a fruitful wasteland. Time will wait on account of one whose thread will be cut short… This is gibberish."

She flips the paper over, sighing with frustration at finding no other message.

"Perhaps you should journey to Nepal and speak with her," Euphemia suggests.

Iona takes the letter to read for herself, searching for any insight that may aid them, until she notices a blot of ink in the corner that forms a familiar shape.

"Ariadne," Iona grasps her arm, drawing her closer.

They squint at the paper, but sure enough the blot has undeniably formed the shape of a snake. They share a look of dismay, for whether Samaira meant it intentionally or not, it is an omen they cannot ignore.

"What is it?" Euphemia asks.

But Ariadne wastes no time crafting a portal and gripping Iona's hand as they cross over to Cairo, the late afternoon sun beating down upon them. They approach a great house surrounded by palm trees, the walls made of pale stone, with multiple domed roofs and mashrabiya windows.

Iona gets barely a glimpse inside at the small garden courtyard with marble floors and an ornate fountain at its center, when Nenet runs out to greet them.

"How did you know?" she asks.

"Samaira." Ariadne runs to her. "What's happened? Are you well?"

Nenet shakes her head, tears brimming in her eyes. "We've been searching ceaselessly for hours. Sara, she is missing."

# 18 - Iona

Panting heavily, Iona climbs to the top of a sand dune beneath a nearly full moon and a glittering expanse of bright stars. Despite the sweat coating her brow, she shivers from the unrelenting chill of the endless desert, a sea of sand stretching out in all directions. Nenet trudges ahead of them with frantic strides, her feet slipping through the shifting sand in her haste, with Ariadne close behind her.

"When did you last see her?" Ariadne asks.

"At midday. She went to her room after we'd shared meal and…" She doubles over, panting heavily from her exertions. "My mother went upstairs to read with her, but she was not there, or anywhere in the house."

"She can't have gotten very far," Iona says. "We will find her."

Nenet's face creases with worry. "We've sent letters everywhere we could think of, asking her to return home, but we've received no answer."

Iona wonders if they should bring Samaira here to use her ring. Surely in such a desolate place Sara's thread would be easily spotted.

*Samaira would only be a liability*, Ariadne thinks.

Iona frowns. *Why?*

*She does not fight. She is a pacifist*, Ariadne explains. *If this ends in a battle, we would be at a great disadvantage, dividing all our efforts to protect her.*

Iona's brow furrows. *Even so, her guidance would be exceedingly helpful.*

They cannot search the entire desert, even with the help of Nenet's parents and friends, who are searching in other areas. She can hear them calling Sara's name in the distance, when a thought emerges.

"Meydana çıkarmak," Iona incants.

A trail of black and blue maleficium emerges, floating through the air like smoke. She follows it down the slope of the dune, in the direction of the north star, then climbs up another dune, and stops short.

"What are you doing here?" Marina asks, her red eyes wide.

"I… What are you doing here?" Iona asks, dumbfounded.

"The stars led me here," Marina says, and she looks up, as if surprised she did not know this would happen.

"Marina?" Ariadne says. "How did-"

"The girl," Marina says. "Has she been found?"

"No," Nenet says when she joins them. "What business do you have in this desert?"

"The stars told me of tragedy this night," Marina says, her voice soft. "I came to see if I might be of use."

Tears pool in Nenet's eyes, but she blinks them away. "We cannot stop. We must keep looking for her. She must be... She must be so frightened."

Nenet runs ahead again, tripping over her feet and kicking up sand everywhere, as she follows the trail of maleficium still lingering in the air, unveiled by Iona's spell. They follow her in earnest, their panting breaths and the distant cries of Sara's name from the rest of the search party the only sounds in the great expanse. That the stars bothered to tell of Sara's disappearance only fuels their collective dread.

At the peak of yet another dune, Iona leans against her shaking knees, her muscles screaming at her to stop. She looks back at Marina, marking the concern on her face.

"Do you feel it?" Marina asks in a low voice.

"Feel... what?" Iona pants.

"Darkness," she says, her red eyes wide with fear.

Iona straightens and looks around, searching for any changes in the atmosphere. Straining her perception, she does sense the slightest trace of malignancy, that which she is now acutely familiar. It had once filled her up, burning through her veins and spreading across her skin, when Elise had attempted to turn her into a wraith.

"Be on your guard," Marina says when she reaches the top of the dune, then shakes her head with frustration. "You should not be here."

"Where would I be but here, aiding Nenet?" Iona asks.

Marina only sighs and continues on. Nenet and Ariadne are very far ahead of them now, mere dark specks on the horizon.

"Wait," Marina grasps her arm, holding her back. "Look."

From their high vantage point, they spot an oasis in the midst of the rolling dunes.

"The stars," Marina murmurs, points up, then down at the oasis. "We must hurry."

Ariadne and Nenet notice their diverted path and sprint towards them.

"Is she near?" Nenet asks. "That stupid girl! I told her not to search for her wand. I should have known she would sneak away. I should have watched her… I should have…"

"We will find her," Ariadne says.

"Does she not realize the danger she's in?" Marina asks.

"My parents thought it wise to withhold the truth from her, to shelter her," Nenet huffs angrily. "They did not want her to be afraid, but it would have prevented this."

They reach the peak of the second dune and on the other side, they approach the flourishing oasis. Palm trees and grass border a pool of clear water; the still surface littered with lotus flowers.

"I do not know of this place," Nenet says with an uneasy expression. She circles the pool of fresh water, searching for any sign of her sister.

"Lotus," Marina says softly, sharing a meaningful look with Ariadne.

"What is it?" Iona asks.

"It might not be…" Marina sighs. "Did you learn of floromancy at college?"

"A bit," Iona says. "But I thought lotus flowers represent purity."

"They can also be an omen of death." Ariadne's voice trembles.

Iona blanches. "But… that does not mean-"

A heart wrenching scream of misery pierces the air.

"No…" Ariadne sprints in the direction of the sound.

Iona's legs turn to lead, holding her in place, even as she longs to move. Across the oasis, beyond the pool of lotus flowers, Nenet weeps over her sister's lifeless body.

"We were too late," Marina relents, her gaze lifting to the stars, persistent confusion in her eyes.

Nenet's cries are heart wrenching, the sort of sounds one can never forget, that which become a permanent fixture of the mind's definition of suffering.

Just like the attack in Brazil, the poor girl's chest has been ripped open, the viscera of her organs spilling out onto the grass, her blood staining the sand.

Ariadne hesitantly puts an arm around Nenet's shoulders and holds her as she's wracked with sobs. She covertly inspects the corpse's chest, then looks to Iona, her red eyes brimming with tears not of sadness, but rage.

*The liver is missing.*

Iona sucks in a breath, realizing what this might imply. Could it be the same malefician? The weight of that prospect makes her even heavier, until she fears she might sink into the sand beneath her.

She cannot bear to look at the dead girl, her young face so full of promises now broken. She turns away, her breath coming in heavy gasps, her tears overflowing, until she goes rigid.

There, in the distance, a dark womanly figure stands motionless, draped in black with a hood obscuring their face, which is also wrapped with black strips of fabric. A golden dagger is strapped to their hip, the handle still dripping with blood. Iona stares at the hunched figure, who watches them in silence, so still that she might have been made of stone. Iona chokes on a scream stuck in her throat.

She blinks.

The cloaked figure stands before her, now only an arm's length away. Iona screams, and the sound breaks any hesitance the figure clung to. The malefician lunges for her, reaching for her throat.

"No!" Ariadne cries.

"Propulsar!" Marina casts, her black nephrite wand drawn.

The assailant is thrown backwards, tumbling over the sand like a stone skipping across water. Marina runs after them with a determined, clear gaze. The figure jumps to their feet, then hovers, dodging spells and throwing a few of their own that Marina deftly avoids.

Wisp's fur ripples as she shifts to her full size, a monstrous beast large as a bear, and curls herself around Iona.

"Run!" Ariadne calls from across the oasis, a protective shield already covering her, Aster, and Nenet.

Wisp nearly rips Iona's dress with her teeth as she throws her witch onto her back and gallops at full speed towards Ariadne. Clutching Wisp's fur for dear life, Iona looks behind her at the malefician, who ignores Marina's barrage of spells, darting through the air in Iona's direction instead.

"Neró," she screams, turning the small pond into a wave that hits the malefician with brutal force, knocking them off balance just long enough for her and Wisp to reach Ariadne.

Sliding off Wisp's back, Iona runs into Ariadne's outstretched arms and clings to her.

"Why is she not running?" Nenet points beyond the protective barrier.

Nimble and quick, Marina manages to hold her own against the malefician, narrowly avoiding the spells slung at her.

"Sastri!" Marina conjures a spike of solid iron that she hurls through the air.

Again and again, she throws the spikes until one impales the figure's shoulder, making them cry out in pain.

"You've made your kill! Now leave us be!" Marina screams.

The malefician's shoulders shake with silent laughter as she pulls the spike from her shoulder and tosses it to the ground. Holding her arms out wide, she throws back her head to gaze up at the sky.

First as a trickle, then as a steady stream, blazing fire rains down in clumps of red that turn the sand into molten glass wherever they fall.

Ariadne's shield protects them from the brunt of it, but Marina is left to evade the torrent of flaming meteors, blocking as many as she can until one strikes her in the chest, making her scream in pain as it sears her flesh.

"Marina!" Iona cries, not understanding why she won't run.

"Stay there!" Marina cries, cowering in the sand as the malefician slowly lowers themselves to the ground and stalks toward her.

Iona goes to run for her, but Ariadne grasps her arm.

"No!" Ariadne holds her back.

"We cannot leave her to die!" Iona cries.

"I'll go and-" Ariadne's eyes becomes so wide, that Iona whirls around, expecting the malefician to be directly behind her.

Instead, her mouth falls open in sheer amazement. The dire scene before them has gone still. The fire falling from the sky floats aloft, the malefician is frozen mid-stride, and Marina's look of terror is fixed on her face, unmoving.

All of time has stopped.

"I've seen this only once before," Ariadne whispers.

"How..." Iona gingerly turns to look, unsure if moving will disturb the magic.

The staff's gem pulses with light as it maintains the spell. Ariadne stares too, marveling at the scene before them with a mixture of horror and wonder.

Iona then remembers the morning of the solstice, when she'd been so sure they'd overslept. Ariadne had fallen asleep with the staff in her hand. She must have frozen time then, too. Perhaps she'd done it many times before without realizing it.

"I didn't..." Ariadne shakes her head. "I'd thought it was an isolated incident when the staff presented itself but..."

She flinches, her knees buckling as if struck by a heavy weight.

"What ails you?" Iona asks, searching frantically for signs of any injury.

"It's… heavy." Ariadne's every word is strained. "I cannot… I do not know how long I can keep it-"

With a terrible crash, time starts again. Marina screams, staring her death in the face.

"Make it stop!" Iona cries.

Eyes wide, Ariadne stares up at the labradorite stone, willing it to glow, willing the magic to work, but nothing happens.

"I cannot," Ariadne begrudgingly admits. "Protect Nenet!"

"Wait!"

But Ariadne has already sprouted wings and hurls herself into the air. She throws an explosive spell at the malefician while she's distracted by Marina, and she's thrown backwards, falling in a heap.

"Gíinos," Ariadne aims her staff at a mound of liquid glass and hurls it at the figure, but she narrowly dodges out of the way, extending a hand and cooling the glass so that it falls to the ground and shatters.

Ariadne flinches violently at the sound but manages to reach Marina where she lies.

The malefician sprints towards them with their hand outstretched, a spell nearly cast.

"Izrezati!" Ariadne slices through the figure's torso, a diagonal gash from shoulder to hip.

She roars in pain and falls to the sand on her hands and knees. Iona holds her breath, but the malefician doesn't stay down.

Through the many layers of black fabric, blood seeps from the gaping wound, until it heals before their very eyes, muscle and skin weaving together before a single drop of blood is spilled, and the fabric of her robe along with it, until it's as if Ariadne hadn't cast her spell at all.

Iona senses Ariadne's mind going blank just as hers does, both of them entirely at a loss of how to fight a being so impervious to their power.

The malefician reaches out a hand and an even deeper laceration slices across Marina's torso, making her scream in agony. Blood gushes from the wound, darkening the linen of her ruby dress, as she falls to her knees.

Ariadne goes to her, putting a protective arm around her

shoulders.

A whisper of a laugh comes from the malefician as she approaches, lifting her hand to cast another spell. Just before she strikes, Ariadne creates a shield around them, and the spell doesn't permeate.

The malefician goes still in confusion, then tries again, this time with vigor, but the spell has no effect. When she tries a third time, the spell rebounds from the shield and hits the malefician instead, making her spontaneously combust in an explosion of flames. She screams in outrage, running and extinguishing the flames, working to heal her self-inflicted burns.

"Philisa," Ariadne presses her hands against Marina's gaping wound.

She winces, hissing out a breath, then sighs in relief when the wound heals, the seconds ticking by agonizingly. When Ariadne pulls her shaking hands away, they are dripping with Marina's blood.

"Pyrkagia!" Nenet screams, redirecting any fire still raining down upon them, sending it all to the figure in an impressive feat of strength fueled by her unimaginable grief.

The malefician lifts themself up into the sky to avoid the onslaught. Marina whispers something to Ariadne, then stands and sprouts wings.

"What are you doing?" Ariadne yells, but Marina ignores her and catapults herself into the air to follow the malefician.

While the assailant is engaging with Marina, Iona runs to Ariadne's side with Aster and Wisp at her heels.

"We must retreat!" Iona cries. "We cannot fight her."

But Ariadne watches her cousin attacking the malefician with practiced skill and grace. Marina dives through the air and throws spells that nearly incapacitate, but the malefician is always faster.

"No," Ariadne says through gritted teeth. "I won't run."

Nenet leaves her sister's body and runs to them. "She's right. Our adversary is too strong."

A portal appears behind them as Ariadne unfurls her conjured wings. "Go. When she is dead, I shall follow."

She ascends into the sky even as they call after her and Aster barks in protest.

"She's going to get herself killed," Nenet says through her tears.

Before Iona can reply, an inhuman shriek punctures the air.

They collapse to their knees as their ears ring from the shrill screech of a language Iona recognizes as maleficium spell, an infernal anathema that incapacitates them, leaving them vulnerable.

Ariadne and Marina can hardly keep themselves in the air as they writhe in pain with their hands over their ears. They are unable to even hear their own screams over the paroxysmal clamor. Aster and Wisp run from the sound, bucking and cowering as they try to escape it, but they do not get far.

The sand shifts beneath them, roiling and churning. Nenet tries to reach her sister's body, but the grains quickly cover Sara's form, and she is lost forever. Iona reaches out for Nenet's hand as they begin to sink.

"No, no, no," she sobs, clinging to Iona for dear life.

"Halat!" Iona conjures a rope, binding their joined hands together tightly. "Sciatháin!"

Her wings form, feather by feather, and she tries as she might to keep her and Nenet above the surface so she can fly them both to safety, but behind them the dune becomes a rogue wave, crashing down upon them in a deluge of sand, burying them alive.

The pressure against every part of her makes it impossible to claw her way out of the darkness. Sand fills her ears, her mouth, her eyes, grating against her skin. She clutches Nenet's hand even as she sinks lower, lower, lower.

*Iona!* Ariadne's thought is a resounding scream.

The sand rips apart in a spectacular propulsive divide that frees them from the darkness, a new chasm forming with them its valley. They cough and sputter, their mouths filled with sand. Coarse grains scratch beneath Iona's eyelids, making it impossible for her to have more than a faint sliver of vision. She can barely see the glow of her pendant as her spell fades.

The deafening maleficium spell finally ceases, though the abrasive ringing still lingers in her ears. Blind and nearly deaf, she's vulnerable against any attacks, but holds her hand out anyway to withstand whatever terrible spell the malefician casts next.

"Démolir!" Marina incants from the sky, and an explosion shakes the ground.

"Iona!" Ariadne's cry is muffled.

"I cannot see!" She coughs, spitting out bits of mud from her dry mouth.

"She's gone." Marina lands a little way away, her voice

muted. "I tried to… but she made a portal and disappeared before I could follow."

"Neró," Ariadne tilts Iona's head back. "Blink,"

She flushes the sand from Iona's eyes with a gentle stream of water until most of the tiny grains wash away and she's able to open her lids without pain.

"Philisa," Ariadne presses her hands against Iona's ears until the ringing dissipates, and her hearing is renewed.

Then they both help Nenet, Iona with her ears and Ariadne with her eyes. To her horror, there is blood leaking from Nenet and Ariadne's ears and dripping down their necks. She reaches for her own ear and finds fresh blood on her fingertips.

Elise had never been able to do that, to incapacitate with only the words of the spell, let alone its effect, but Elise had been a novice. She'd only practiced maleficium for mere months.

*This malefician is much older,* Ariadne agrees.

"Is everyone alright?" Marina asks.

No one answers. Wisp and Aster return, having been saved from the sand by Iona's spell. The animals' heads hang low, and they remain silent. Iona does not know what to make of their abandonment or their subsequent shame.

She looks to Nenet, who is in such shock that she cannot even cry anymore.

"I must… find my family." Nenet shivers. "Tell them what has happened here."

Iona's heart breaks for her, at beholding the look of detachment on her face. It is too much for any of them to process, except Marina, who watches them with quiet compassion.

"Lethe," Marina incants, her wand pointed at Nenet's forehead.

Iona gasps. "What are you doing?!"

Ariadne takes Marina's arm, but she pulls away and continues her memory spell until she's satisfied.

"It had to be done," she says.

"But… What are you… What do you mean?" Iona asks, her head spinning.

"There is no excuse for taking another witch's memory!" Ariadne yells.

"I'm afraid there is," Marina says. "Forgive me, I cannot explain here. Please, come."

"Where?" Iona asks, just as Ariadne says, "We are not going anywhere with you until you explain."

Marina glances between them, her red eyes an abyss of untold mysteries. If there's any mind that Iona is curious to read, it would be hers, but when she tries, she finds Marina's aura impenetrable.

"I'm afraid your despair must wait for the morning, but your questions will be answered in due course. We must return to Rome immediately," Marina looks them up and down, "for a much-needed bath."

They leave the sleeping Nenet in the outskirts of her parent's land, where Marina assures them, she will wake with all her memories of the malefician's attack. She will only forget that they had been present with her, and how she'd gotten away. Any will assume that the malefician was the one who took her memory to protect their own identity.

Iona's senses are numb. She faintly perceives Ariadne's hand at the small of her back guiding her through the portal to Rome. They track sand everywhere, but Marina insists they wait in the solarium while she goes to fetch her mother.

Iona sits while Ariadne paces back and forth, back and forth, until she suddenly stops and glares.

"Don't," Ariadne scolds.

"Her death is on my hands," Iona says.

"She was dead long before we arrived."

"Exactly. I should have seen... something. I should have known..."

"Even Samaira couldn't predict the fatality with exact precision," Ariadne points out. "Had we not been there, Nenet, her parents, or any number of innocent people may have perished if they'd found the ritual site first."

"Then why did you refuse to escape when we had the chance?" Iona asks. "We should have retreated before anyone else was harmed."

"Marina and I could have defeated them, if I hadn't been..." Ariadne sighs, *distracted.*

Iona flinches, "Distracted?"

"I did not say that," Ariadne says.

"But you thought it." Iona narrows her eyes.

Ariadne scratches at her scalp to rid her hair of sand, refusing to meet Iona's gaze. "I should have known you could save yourself from the sand, but I wasn't... certain. I abandoned the fight to rescue you and-"

"We shouldn't have needed rescuing! Nenet and I nearly died

due to your obstinance," Iona insists. "How would you have found us buried that deep?"

"I would have…" Ariadne blinks, at a loss. "I would have thought of something. You should have left with Nenet when I made the portal."

"You know perfectly well that I never would have left you behind," Iona says.

An awful silence stretches between them and Iona's thoughts drift again, unable to stop depicting Sara's cherubic face as her corpse sunk beneath the sand.

"There is nothing you could have done to stop it," Ariadne insists.

"I know you mean to comfort me," Iona whispers, "but there is no excuse for my failure."

Ariadne clenches her jaw. Her guilt radiates through their bond, mixed with her fury that simmers beneath the surface. Iona closes her eyes and tries to ignore it, but Ariadne feels so deeply. Her emotions are like wildfire eviscerating everything in its wake.

"Such a tragedy," Xiomara says as she enters with Marina close behind her.

She rushes to Ariadne and embraces her, then Iona. With a heavy sigh, she goes to stand by the solarium window, cradling a wine glass and staring out at the view, though there is not much to see in the dark. Ariadne sits beside Iona, with Marina sitting across from them.

"I thought the solstice ritual would be enough to deter these devils… To remind them of our power. It seems I was wrong. I wish you had come to find me so I may have accompanied you to Egypt." Xiomara eyes her daughter with a trace of disapproval, but Marina holds her stare with the unwavering surety of a diviner.

"It wasn't meant to be," Marina declares. "Ariadne and I were nearly an even match for the fiend, I must say. She fought valiantly."

Ariadne sits up straighter in response to the praise, which is well earned. "I tried to see their face, but they kept evading me."

"It was the same malefician who attacked in Brazil," Iona says.

Xiomara's eyebrows raise. "How do you know?"

"A heart was stolen from my grandfather, and Sara…" Iona cannot continue, her stomach churning.

"Her liver was stolen," Ariadne says. "I saw it."

"Why would they do such a thing?" Iona asks.

"Spoils of their kills?" Ariadne surmises.

"No." Marina shakes her head. "They mean to use them as ingredients for a future ritual. To what end, I cannot imagine."

"Their rituals require mortal remains?" Iona asks, repulsed. "Is it not enough for them to steal others' magic? They must desecrate their bodies as well?"

Marina's distant gaze returns as she shifts closer and places her hands in her lap.

"There is intrinsic energy in all living things. In you." Marina gestures to Iona. "In her." She gestures to Wisp where she sleeps on the rug by the fire. "In me." She places a hand over her heart. "We would never dream of stealing that away for our own gain but to a malefician, it is merely a life force to consume. Many maleficians use animals in this endeavor, but older, more experienced sorcerers possess the skill to sacrifice other witches, humans, anything that lives. On occasion, they are known to harvest the organs of their sacrifices."

"How do you know all of this?" Iona asks.

Marina doesn't respond and looks to her mother. Xiomara purses her lips.

"She won't wish to be kept waiting," Marina prompts.

"I know well her desires." Xiomara's voice is firm.

"We are beyond secrets now, would you not say?" Ariadne asks. "It is Hecate you speak of, isn't it? What has she got to do with this?"

Xiomara regards Ariadne with conflict in her gaze. "I tried to shelter you from this for as long as I could... but it would not last forever."

"I am not asking for protection." Ariadne's eyes flare. "I want this pain, this gruesome death, to end. That is all that matters now."

"Why do you hesitate, Mother?" Marina asks. "You know as well as I that the time has come."

"Yes, yes..." Xiomara says. "Fetch Moira. Send her to me. Then prepare the sanctuary."

Marina stands and leaves the room without another word.

"What sanctuary?" Ariadne asks.

"In light of recent events, Hecate wishes to speak with the both of you, tonight," Xiomara says.

Iona's heart races in her chest as she takes Ariadne's hand, needing to feel her. "Could you not impart her message to us now?"

"If you wish to unveil the truth, you must speak to her directly," Xiomara says.

*Ari?* Iona calls to her.

*I must know.* Ariadne clutches her hand. *This mystery has plagued me my whole life. I cannot refuse her.*

Iona squeezes her hand back. *I am glad to hear you admit it, finally.*

Ariadne glances at her, her turmoil laid bare in her gaze. *I only denied it because I never thought this day would come. To be acknowledged… for the very first time.*

Then for her sake, and the sake of the dead, Iona will assent. She will face a Goddess because she has glimpsed Ariadne's memories, her sleepless nights praying to Hecate, begging her to answer, only to be ignored. If this is the closure she requires for those years of silence, Iona will not deny her, even if the prospect is terrifying.

The door to the solarium opens and Moira steps in. "Marina told me everything."

"We haven't much time." Xiomara stands and motions for them to follow her.

Along the way, she explains that normally they would perform this sort of ritual during a new moon, but Hecate made an exception due to the severity of their circumstances. First, they must be cleansed of any impurities before they may enter the sanctuary and present themselves.

They're led to the atrium where the shallow pool beneath Hecate's statue has been filled with lavender, eucalyptus, and fragrant oils. They bathe in the warm water until all the sand and blood is washed away, leaving the water a light shade of pink with a thin layer of grit beneath their soles.

Xiomara leaves them there to help Marina with the preparations, leaving them with Moira. Only when they are deemed pristine does she allow them to climb out of the pool to be anointed with oil, just as Xiomara had done to Iona in the Sibylline Mountains.

"What symbols are you drawing?" Iona asks as Moira presses an oiled finger against her spine.

"Oh, symbols of death, hatred, degeneracy," Moira says casually.

When she stiffens, Moira laughs.

"Must you joke at a time like this?" she asks.

"As opposed to the perfect days when no one dies or suffers anywhere in the world?" Moira asks. "Misery is everywhere.

You're only fortunate to have been sheltered from the brutality of life until recently."

Lowering her head, Iona asks, "What are the symbols then?"

"Protective runes. Runes to disenthrall your soul, to increase the potency of your magic," Moira says. "Nothing nefarious, I swear."

She finishes Iona's back, then steps around to face her again, inspecting her with a shrewd gaze.

"Ah, I almost forgot." Moira leans forward to trace a triangular symbol over Iona's womb.

Then she draws her wand and conjures a red robe that dwarfs Iona's form in billowing silk, so thin that she still feels exposed.

Moira then shifts her gaze to Ariadne and motions for her to approach. Hugging her chest, Iona observes Ariadne's air of implacable indifference that hides her lingering anxieties. Iona perceives them all, along with the sharp nail Ariadne presses into her palm to keep her hands from trembling.

"I'd wondered if I'd ever see this day," Moira muses, dipping a finger into her bowl of oil and marking a symbol on Ariadne's forehead. "If there's anything to be said of you, your tenacity is quite extraordinary."

Ariadne's eyes go wide before she recovers. "Do not go soft now."

Moira smirks at her. "Tenacious like... a weed. Impossible to be rid of."

"Much better." Ariadne's lips twitch, but she cannot manage a smile.

Moira patiently draws the symbols on Ariadne's wrists, knees, and ankles.

"When did you first meet Hecate?" Iona asks.

"We are inducted into the coven when we reach adulthood," Moira says. "Nearly five years later and still I haven't acclimated to the experience. My mother is the only one of us who seems at ease in the Goddess' presence, and Grandmother treated her like an old friend, though I doubt it began that way when she was young."

"What is she like?" Ariadne asks, her voice small.

Moira pauses in her drawing, reverent wonder filling her eyes. "I haven't the words to describe her... She has unparalleled beauty. She radiates power. And the moment she's gone, you miss her terribly. It's... life altering."

Ariadne's mask slips, betraying her fear as she takes a shuddering breath. Moira motions for her to turn around so she can draw symbols along her spine.

"Iona should be the one ridden with nerves, not you," Moira says. "You are a Zerynthos witch. This is the natural order of things."

Moira's words only shift the dread from Ariadne to Iona, her heartbeat quickening with her unease.

"Three years she's neglected to…" Ariadne bites her lip, not daring to finish.

"Years may as well be seconds to a Goddess," Moira reminds her. "Whatever you do, don't complain. Be grateful she's graced you with her presence at all. We are mere mortals, deserving of nothing."

"Are they ready?" Xiomara reenters the atrium wearing a similar red silk robe.

"Nearly," Moira murmurs, and while she finishes her work, Iona agonizes over her comments.

Would Hecate scorn a witch like her, sired under such unorthodox circumstances and laying claim to an artifact Ariadne had been bred to wield? She's wondered this for days, ever since she learned of the Goddess' looming presence over the Zerynthos family.

But even now, while Moira drapes Ariadne in red, and Xiomara consoles her with soothing words, their eyes keep drifting to Iona, filled with rueful doubt that only stokes her uncertainty. She's failed to save a second victim from a gruesome death. Hecate will know.

"Why are we the only ones anointed?" Ariadne asks when Moira puts the oil away.

"It is you our Goddess will speak with tonight," Moira says. "We are merely the summoners."

"Come along," Xiomara hastens them.

They rush down the hall, turning this way and that, until finally they reach the purple door, it's golden doorknob glittering in the candlelight.

Iona tugs on Ariadne's arm. *I found this door the night of the solstice.*

"Has this been here all the while?" Ariadne asks her aunt.

"You never noticed?" Moira smirks.

"This room is only accessible to those who commune with Hecate." Xiomara pulls open the door.

The small, pentagonal room is dimly lit with five black candles burning in a circle on the floor. A haze of smoke obscures the light even further, smelling of sweet floral incense.

Marina waits for them there, her eyes opening when they enter.

"Leave your staff by the door," Xiomara says.

"Why?" Ariadne asks, her grip tightening around the wood.

"You won't be needing it," Xiomara says.

For a moment, Iona thinks she might object but slowly, reluctantly, Ariadne sets her staff against the wall.

"Take your places," Xiomara instructs.

Marina and Moira kneel parallel to each other with their heads bowed, while Xiomara guides Iona and Ariadne to the circle of candles and has them kneel, too. Another inhale has Iona's vision blurring. Upon searching for the source of the sweet-smelling smoke, she cannot identify anything burning apart from the candles. Her limbs grow heavy, and her breathing slows.

Xiomara extends her arms wide and closes her eyes. She takes a heavy breath in, then exhales loudly, a smile reaching her lips.

"Vasílissa ton machón, tyligméni sti skiá, evlógisé me me tis mágisses pou se ypiretoún," Xiomara incants, and though Iona still wears her ring, the words remain foreign to her.

The lurking shadows in the corners of the room encroach upon them until the candles are specks of sombre light barely illuminating the dark. Prickles cover Iona's skin as her heartbeat wanes to a creeping pace, until she wonders if it will beat again each time it stops.

"Gynaíka tis nýchtas, ákouse tin prosefchí mas kai odígisé mas sto skotádi," Xiomara falls to her knees, genuflecting to a force unseen.

The candles blaze with a startling flare of fire, scalding Iona's skin as she cowers, leaning into Ariadne.

The shadows corporealize into a mass of darkness, plying and fusing into itself, until they form a statuesque womanly body, tall and rawboned. Gloom ripples away, revealing immaculate olive skin and glittering kohl lined ruby eyes that glow, casting vinaceous light upon her cheeks when she looks down upon them. She is draped in black with golden bands adorning each arm. Silver curls of voluminous hair fall loosely against her shoulders, her ageless beauty oppressive in its intensity.

"Iona Evora Lysander." Hecate says in a dulcet voice.

She stares up at the Goddess, her lips parting but unable to form words, until Ariadne elbows her in the ribs.

"Yes?" Iona whispers.

Hecate extends her hand with just the hint of a smile. Iona takes it and Hecate pulls her to her feet.

"Come along." She beckons them forward.

A shimmering portal appears but doesn't reflect what lies beyond, the way Ariadne's do. Hecate steps through, the gleaming doorway surging with raw power.

*Are you certain of this?* Iona asks, unable to look away from the portal.

Ariadne takes her hand. *It is a bit late for second thoughts, nymph.*

*I suppose you're right.* Iona steels herself as she crosses through to the other side.

# 19 - Ariadne

A sprawling field of pale white asphodel flowers spreads far and wide in every direction. Their sweet fragrance combines with a pungent scent of sulphur. There are no stars or moon in the darkness above them. There is no wind to make the flowers sway. The stalks stand upright in an eerie stillness as Ariadne roams with her hand outstretched, brushing her fingertips against the soft petals. The only light emanates from a golden torch in Hecate's upraised hand as she guides them across the Underworld.

"I have been most anxious to meet you," Hecate says to Iona.

"So I've heard," Iona says.

"Yes, I'm well aware of Moira's lapse in discretion," Hecate says with disapproval. "So over-exuberant in her work, but I must remind myself of her youth. She will learn."

"Given the current circumstances, I believe total candor to be the best course of action," Iona says.

"Agreed," Hecate says. "There is no time for anything else."

They reach the end of the flower fields as the ground turns from dirt to soft grass.

"Do sit down," Hecate gestures ahead of them.

Three chairs and a circular table materialize instantaneously; the swiftest display of conjuration Ariadne has ever before witnessed. The furnishings are gilded with gold trim, the surface of the table glossy and black. As they sit, Hecate sets her torch in the very center of the table where it hovers. Then she conjures herself a goblet of wine and an array of food, from clusters of grapes, epityrum, fresh bread, and sliced cheeses. Taking a grape, Hecate pops it into her mouth.

"I would offer you sustenance, but I trust you know why that would be unwise." She smiles apologetically.

"I couldn't eat anyhow," Iona says, her voice betraying her despair, but she swallows her tears and sits up straighter in her chair. "Please, impart your message."

"Of course," Hecate says, glancing at Ariadne for the briefest moment. "This may come as quite a shock."

Iona reaches below the table to take Ariadne's hand, gripping it tightly.

"As a Goddess of witches, I bless all who practice magic," Hecate says. "However, there is a reason I've favored the Zerynthos family for so many generations and made them my devotees on Earth, whose task is as monumental as it is essential; destroying maleficians."

Letting out a compulsory gasp, Ariadne's grip becomes a vice around Iona's fingers, until she worries that she might crush them. Hecate regards her with knowing eyes.

"But I've never heard of such a thing," Iona says. "I thought maleficians were too powerful to be confronted."

"For the average witch, certainly, but my coven stands apart. We do not have the luxury of avoidance, or otherwise the world would be overrun with darkness," Hecate says. "Maleficians are as rare as they are because my coven makes it so. We do not allow them to live, safeguarding those too weak to fight against them."

"Even Katrin?" Iona asks, with equal incredulity in her tone as Ariadne harbors within herself, that which has struck her mute despite her thousands of questions.

"Especially Katrin," Hecate says. "She was the bravest, most lionhearted of all, endured unknowable terrors, endless carnage, nightmares that would drive others mad."

"How is this possible?" Ariadne whispers.

Her every memory of Katrin is bleak. She was an angry, bitter woman who never said one kind word to her, even in death.

"You must understand, Katrin's burden was immense. Only a stalwart, resilient woman could withstand it," Hecate says. "You may not wish to hear it, but your grandmother was a hero of the highest order."

Her heart rejects the claim, but her mind reels from the revelation, recalling how her mother would abscond on trips at random intervals, leaving her alone with her father. She would rejoice in those times, wishing they'd last forever, but inevitably her mother would return, and her vigorous instruction would continue.

Her mother had claimed the trips were obligatory, like Aunt Zephyra's travels to Moldavia. Ariadne wonders now if there is a lycanthrope infestation at all or if it was a lie to conceal Aunt Zephyra's true activities in the area.

"But… how is it that no one knows of this?" Ariadne asks. "Surely if my family has been killing maleficians for centuries, they would be legends like Morgan."

"It is a rigorously guarded secret," Hecate says. "If

maleficians knew of whom to evade, it would make your family's endeavors infinitely more complicated. The devils would run the moment they saw a flame mark. Just as a maleficians's anonymity is their greatest asset, so do your family wisely keep their true intentions hidden, with no accolades or recognition of any kind."

Iona's face is gravely serious as she digests this news, while Ariadne is overcome with a profound emptiness. For this to be happening the entire time, right under her nose...

"Katrin disguised her interference as conquest," Hecate says. "Maleficians can be drawn to places of power the same as any witch, performing rituals to grow stronger. Under Katrin's watchful eye, the maleficians were left with very few options to harvest magic, all while the covens could still perform their own rituals as they saw fit."

"Her empire was a lie?" Iona asks.

"All in an effort to prevent further bloodshed," Hecate says. "With the pendant, Katrin could protect countless innocents from harm. And now, so must you."

Iona's eyes widen in horror. "Me? But... What of Xiomara? Is she not the leader of your coven?"

"Xiomara does not possess the pendant," Hecate says. "Nor any other artifact of great power. You must take on the role, continuing Katrin's work, or the attacks will only multiply with every passing day."

"Why are you not able to fix this yourself?" Ariadne asks, her accusation far more angered than she'd intended.

Hecate's glowing eyes flare, making Ariadne squint at the sudden flash of divine light.

"As it has always been between Gods and mortals, you must fight your own battles," Hecate's voice booms. "I may guide you in your hour of need, but I am not obligated to interfere in a way you deem acceptable. I owe mortals nothing, and you should be sure to remember that."

"We meant no offense," Iona says quickly.

Hecate regards her with softer eyes. "I can appreciate how difficult this night has been, with emotions running high."

"Yes," Iona says with relief. "We only wish to understand."

"You shouldn't have been put in this position to begin with," Hecate says, staring directly at Ariadne as she says it. "But there is no changing that now. I'm afraid this is not a request, but rather a commissioning of your magic. It is most imperative for you to ally with my coven in this time of great peril. This malefician cannot be suffered to live and she is too strong for ordinary witches to defeat. You must hunt her and end her, or who knows what havoc she will wreak."

"End her? But I've never-" Iona stutters.

Hecate takes Iona's other hand, pulling her closer. "There is a delicate balance in your world, between entropy and symmetry. It must be preserved at all costs."

Ariadne looks between Iona's disconsolate face and Hecate's obdurate one.

"You must not fail," Hecate says. "Or countless innocents will die."

Ariadne gasps awake, coughing violently when the smoke accosts her lungs and nearly chokes her. Iona wakes beside her, trembling uncontrollably.

"No…" Iona shakes her head. "No, I cannot endure this again. Not again…"

"Iona." Xiomara kneels beside her. "Breathe. It will be alright."

"Why is this happening?" Iona sobs.

"I know not, dearest." Xiomara pulls her into an embrace, stroking her hair to soothe her. "We will defeat her and set this all to rights."

"How?" Iona asks.

"Why didn't you warn me?" Ariadne's voice is foreign to her own ears, its somber, empty tone drawing all eyes in the room to her. "Why? Was it some sort of test?"

"If it was, you failed," Moira says, crossing her arms.

"Moira," Xiomara snaps. "Hold your tongue."

"If I'd known, I never would have…" Ariadne's breath comes in gasps as she claws at her chest.

Iona crawls across the floor to her, but Ariadne cannot bear to look at her, shame and regret turning her stomach. Even when Iona presses herself against her back, whispering consoling words in her ear, she cannot think beyond her panic and rage that roils within her, beyond her control.

"I did warn you. We should have sent Iona alone," Moira murmurs to her mother.

"Like hell you will!" Ariadne yells, jumping to her feet and charging toward her cousin. "She is not some pawn for you to sacrifice!"

"No, only you are allowed to treat her so," Moira smirks.

Holding out her hand, the staff flies through the air and into

Ariadne's grasp. "Dominari somnia!"

Moira goes limp, her head hitting the floor with a sickening crack when she falls. Ariadne crafts an illusion of sand, of Moira sinking beneath it just as Iona had, until she's submerged in abrasive darkness, unable to move or scream.

"Ariadne, you let her go right now!" Xiomara screams, falling to her knees beside her daughter to try and wake her.

"How could you trust *her* with this, and not me?" Ariadne yells. "Why do you always lie? You all lie..."

Iona presses a hand against Ariadne's forehead and incants, "Sove."

"Can you blame her?" Iona's voice is a faint echo.

"Of course I can," Moira says indignantly. "She hasn't a semblance of self-control, and yet she wonders why we never deigned to involve her."

"You lie to her for years on end, and yet you are amazed when she lashes out!" Iona snaps.

"Always the victim," Moira grumbles.

"You were the one lying prone at her feet," Iona says. "Your bitterness only betrays your shame at being so easily pacified."

Moira scoffs, "If I truly wished to, I could-"

"Please." The fatigue in Xiomara's voice is palpable. "I beg you, please stop bickering. I can take it no longer."

Ariadne stirs, fighting against the sleep that confines her. A warm hand cups her cheek.

"Wake up," Iona whispers.

Moaning softly, Ariadne tries to lift her eyelids, but they are too heavy. For a moment she wonders if sleep wouldn't be a comfort. She doesn't want to face her problems, to see Iona's face contorted by disappointment or fear.

"She will be livid with you, too, for quelling her," Moira warns.

"Perhaps, but I know she will forgive me," Iona says. "I, too, have given in to rage, and she forgave me for it."

"You?" Moira snorts. "I cannot imagine it."

"Continue speaking to me thus and you shan't need to imagine it," Iona seethes.

Moira only chuckles in a condescending manner. "You truly are a pair."

Ariadne stirs. Soft lips press against her forehead, so lightly she can hardly feel it.

"Come back to me," Iona whispers.

With a heavy sigh, Ariadne opens her eyes. Iona's smile is weak, her eyes tired, but to Ariadne's relief there is no anger.

*I didn't…* Ariadne doesn't know how to finish the thought. *I shouldn't have…*

A flash of memory overtakes her vision, of Iona hurling Cintia across the dining room, then of her attacking Ksenia during one of their lessons at college.

*I have no right to criticize.* Iona runs her thumb against Ariadne's cheekbone.

Though she isn't sure if their outbursts could ever be compared, Ariadne is grateful for any amnesty she can be afforded.

"The tormentor awakens," Moira says snidely.

"Must she be here?" Iona complains to Xiomara.

"No." Xiomara glares at her daughter, who puts up her hands and steps away in silence.

Ariadne stretches her aching limbs. They'd carried her back to the solarium and laid her across a chaise by the fire. The sun rises in the window, shedding light upon their weary faces.

"How do you feel?" Xiomara asks.

Humiliated, betrayed, ashamed. "Fine."

Iona helps her sit up and stays kneeling at her feet, clasping Ariadne's hand firmly between both of her own.

"Good," Xiomara says. "Now I shall only say this once. If you ever, ever use your magic against my family again, I will have Hecate drop you down a chasm so deep within the Underworld, that even Hades himself will struggle to find you. Do you understand?"

Iona goes to protest, but Ariadne squeezes her hand to stop her. It would be a grave mistake to anger Hecate, not when she is evidently watching them so closely, or to offend her family, if they are all that tempers the existence of dark magic in their world.

"I understand," Ariadne says, though she refuses to apologize. Thankfully, Aunt Xiomara does not ask it of her.

"The others have arrived," Marina says, making herself known where she's perched on the windowsill.

"You are a part of this crusade now, irrevocably," Xiomara says. "I expect loyalty above all else, or we shall never prevail against the darkness."

With that, she leaves to greet the rest of the coven in the atrium. Ariadne slumps in her seat, her fatigue nearly causing her to faint.

"Can we not sleep first?" Iona asks. "We've been awake all night."

"This sort of work does not follow a strict schedule," Moira says. "Best to acclimate yourself with exhaustion, as I have."

"Is that why you are ever a contemptuous bitch?" Iona asks. "If that be so, please find your rest if it might rid us of your insufferable excuse for a personality."

Ariadne's mouth falls open in utter disbelief, as does Moira's.

"Why I never…" Moira frowns, seemingly torn between taking offense or laughing.

"Iona, darling, you truly are wearied." Marina giggles by the window, earning a sideways glare from Moira.

"Though I do sympathize with your woeful incognizance of the true burden you so ignorantly accepted, do not unleash your discontent onto me. My patience does have limits," Moira says, a warning in her tone, in contrast with her well-practiced smile, until her eyes sparkle with renewed mischief. "You should have seen the look on your face when the Goddess appeared. Your eyes were like that of a frightened deer. It was well worth the wait."

Iona pouts and rests her head in Ariadne's lap, ignoring Moira's smug expression and Marina's enduring giggles.

*You never cease to surprise me with your outbursts.* Ariadne plays with her hair.

*Likewise.* Iona closes her eyes.

Ariadne's fingers go still within Iona's soft red locks, but she keeps her eyes shut, finding whatever rest she can before the family converges.

When they are all gathered, Marina recounts the events of the previous night, tells of the malefician's alarmingly powerful spell work, and of her piercing unintelligible screeches that incapacitated and nearly deafened them.

"It is like nothing I've ever seen," Marina says. "She must be very old… "

"Then we are certain it's not related to the smaller attacks of late?" Sebastian asks.

"I doubt it," Moira says. "I don't see why a malefician that strong would bother with leeching magic from children. Those are lesser witches, who shall be dealt with soon enough."

Ariadne is taken aback by her casual mention of defeating a malefician, lesser or otherwise. The others merely nod in agreement and carry on.

"How is it that you knew this attack would take place in the desert?" Aunt Xiomara asks.

"Samaira's artifact grants her prophetic visions," Ariadne says. "We sent a letter in warning, but the child snuck away anyhow."

"Such a shame…" Aunt Zephyra says with a heavy heart.

"It is good you have such a powerful ally," Aunt Xiomara says. "Of course, we ask that you do not disclose our secret to her, as it is imperative that we maintain anonymity. We tend to rely on Marina's insight to warn us of the future."

"I must admit my frustration," Iona says. "Samaira's vision was unclear, not as they have been in the past. She did not even see who would die. And forgive me, but Marina only saw Sara's death in the stars after it was already too late to rescue her."

"I'm surprised they saw anything at all," Aunt Zephyra says. "You must understand, just as we work tirelessly with our magic to anticipate the malefician's next move, so too will she use her power to shroud herself in darkness and make it near impossible to detect her. With both forces of magic in constant opposition-"

"One offsets the other," Ariadne murmurs.

"Exactly. We must use whatever shreds of insight we can acquire to the best of our ability. It will not be easy. It never is," Aunt Zephyra says. "We've also lost the element of surprise. If she sees your faces again, she'll know to run or attack on sight, but I suppose there is no remedying that now."

"There was no chance of defeating this one in a single attempt," Aunt Xiomara says. "What we are reckoning with is more than likely a Crone, a very old, sage malefician who has awakened from dormancy. They would be capable of the spells Marina described and will attack however many times as is necessary to gather ingredients for a grand rite, then go back into hiding again for another few decades or more. We must find them before they do."

"How old could she be?" Iona's eyes go wide.

"It may be impossible to know for certain, but I would wager a guess that her impending ritual is meant to keep her alive a while longer," Aunt Zephyra explains. "There is no spell that can make one immortal, but maleficians have long cultivated infernal necromantic spells to delay the aging process, most unnaturally, and it can have side effects. That is likely why she hides her face. Who can say what abomination she has become, a grotesquerie beyond imagining."

"When next Samaira does have a vision, I insist that at least one of us accompanies you to ensure your safety in battle," Aunt Xiomara says.

"Is that entirely necessary?" Ariadne asks.

"How many maleficians have you killed?" Cintia asks.

Staring her mother dead in the eye, Ariadne says, "I've defeated one."

"I've killed seven and fifty maleficians," Cintia says. "Moira, how many have you slain?"

"Five and twenty," Moira says, "thus far."

"Indeed, all of us here have defeated more than twenty, if I'm not mistaken." Cintia glances about the room. "And you've 'defeated' one, accidentally, and only due to the intervention of Merlin."

"If you hadn't kept this from me all this time, my accomplishments would rival yours," Ariadne says, straightening her spine.

"You, who is incapacitated by nightmares and intimidated by crowds?" Cintia tilts her head.

Ariadne's cheeks burn. "I did not cower when darkness came for me and Iona. You should not have doubted my strength."

Aunt Xiomara sighs, "Must we-"

"And when exactly should my doubts have been alleviated?" Cintia asks. "If your spat with Vivien was enough to nearly unravel you, then how could you be expected to duel a malefician, whose magic is capable of turning your mind inside out? The very idea is ludicrous. We wondered if even Morgan's trials would prove too difficult for you in the end."

Ariadne clenches her jaw, keeping her emotions buried deep, as her character is torn to shreds while her entire family watches on, stone-faced. She thinks back on every gathering, every holiday and ritual, and sees her memories with new eyes. They all knew. All except for her.

"At least the pendant, if you'd managed to claim it, would have fortified your power. We intended to explain everything then, and if you failed, never to tell you at all," Cintia says. "Never in our wildest imaginations did we predict Morgan allowing you the option to give it away. If you'd like someone to blame for this delay in your enlightenment, it would be her. I told you so... so many times how important it was for you to claim it. It is solely your fault that you failed to heed me and your grandmother."

Ariadne struggles to keep her voice steady. "Neither of you saw fit to explain-"

"A true Zerynthos witch puts duty above their own selfish whims. They follow orders and place loyalty to the coven above all else," Cintia says. "What, do you think Hecate explains her every intention to us in detail? If you cannot heed simple, plain instructions, how could you possibly be trusted?"

"If I may interject," Marina says, addressing Ariadne with clear eyes. "You were valorous in last night's duel. Your defeat of Elise Lysander should not be diminished either. In truth, we did worry if you were not suited for this sort of warfare, but it seems we are indeed forged from the same fire. If it weren't so, Hecate would not have taken you with her to the Underworld."

"Is that why she ignored my prayers?" Ariadne asks. "She once thought me too weak?"

"No," Aunt Zephyra says softly. "A Goddess of her caliber cannot possibly answer every prayer."

"What does it matter now?" Cintia asks. "We must focus on the task at hand. These petty concerns are of no consequence."

"Is that why you treat me so abominably? You deemed me too weak to kill for you?" Ariadne asks.

The air in the room thins. Cintia glares at her, clenching her jaw so tight, she may well break a tooth.

"That is in the past now," Aunt Xiomara says. "We must put aside our differences, our personal grievances, and be as one united force."

"There is to be no accountability?" Iona asks.

Cintia turns her glare on Iona, who doesn't flinch.

"You are the worst mother I've ever had the misfortune to encounter," Iona says. "I will not fight alongside you."

"I beg your pardon?" Cintia spits the words.

"Iona," Aunt Xiomara says.

"Never," Iona says, with that look in her eye. Ysolde Lysander's look, that which is carved into stone in the Lysander College courtyard.

Aunt Xiomara's eyebrows raise, glancing briefly at her sister's sullen expression, before nodding. "Very well. Another of us will accompany you when the time comes."

"You will take orders from her?" Cintia yells.

"A crone, Cintia. You know as well as I that we cannot hope to defeat one without Iona and the pendant. She has set her terms," Aunt Xiomara says, and she hesitates before saying. "Frankly, you needn't have tormented Ariadne in such a heinous manner. If I'd known the full extent of it, I would have intervened long ago. I cannot change that now, but neither can I claim ignorance of your indiscretions."

"Unbelievable." Cintia rises from her chair and storms out of the room, slamming the door behind her.

Flinching at the sound, Ariadne looks down at her hands and realizes she'd been unconsciously picking at her skin. She winces and pulls her hands apart, not wanting to cause Iona any discomfort.

"With that settled, I must rest, or I shall be of no help to anyone," Iona says, grasping Ariadne's hand and guiding her to the door.

"Yes, of course," Aunt Xiomara says. "Take all the time you require."

Iona steps into the hall first, and as Ariadne follows, she overhears a whisper from Moira.

"Ferocious little thing, isn't she? When she's impassioned enough."

# 20 - Ariadne

Draco is a curved line of luminous stars flying across the black abyss of night. Beneath her, sharp blades of cool grass tickle her arms and legs. She lays out flat, staring up at the stars whose secrets always seem to escape her.

Turning her head to the side, she waits for her eyes to adjust to the dim luminescence and recognizes the open field where the blue comet ritual had been held.

After a moment, she stands and tries to reorient herself, not remembering when or how she'd arrived in Lysander Forest. Then she remembers Iona, a smile curving her lips at the mere thought of her, and she traverses the clearing in search of her beloved.

The bordering branches catch on her hair and skirts as she pushes past them, but instead of her foot meeting dirt or stone, she enters a familiar hallway of Drakenström Manor, with tall, opened windows bordered with sky blue curtains that billow in the light summer breeze.

"Euphemia?" Ariadne calls, but there is no answer, only the faint echo of a string quartet in the distance.

She follows the sound, entering the ballroom, and fights to keep her expression neutral when she's pinned by a hundred stares. When normally the crowd would look away for propriety's sake, their stares linger, none of them blinking even once. She grows increasingly unsettled.

"Where is Euphemia?" Ariadne asks, "Or Iona, or…"

Silence. They stare unflinchingly at her, and it makes her skin crawl. Hesitantly, she steps through the mass of bodies to search for herself.

Rebekka barrels into her, her deep laugh piercing the quiet, making Ariadne yelp in surprise.

"She's so fast!" Rebekka leans against her knees to catch her breath. "Come, help me catch her!"

"Who?" Ariadne asks, when another giggle makes her whirl about just in time to spot the ends of Iona's red hair whipping through the air behind her as she runs past a distant doorway and out of sight.

"Iona!" Ariadne calls.

"You shan't capture a nymph that way." Rebekka grins,

shrugging off her white blazer and tossing it aside. "You must chase her."

Her confusion only fuels Rebekka's mirth, her peals of laughter devolving into hysterical wheezes.

"Suit yourself," she manages to say through her laughter before she runs after Iona with great speed.

"But... Why must we..." Ariadne grunts with frustration, then runs after Rebekka. "Wait!"

She makes it to the other end of the ballroom, turning the corner, and hesitates. Not a single candle is lit, the impervious darkness thick and uninviting. But Iona's raspy giggle drifts towards her like bonfire smoke, drawing her in.

She steels herself and runs into the dark, only to turn another corner and enter the hall of portraits in the Villa Mitriora. She doesn't falter, running with purpose when she overhears Rebekka's persisting laughter in the distance, and wrenches open a door, bursting into the Lysander College library.

She heaves in a breath and sneezes from the sheer volume of dust floating about, a layer of it covering the books, tables, and chairs. Mrs. Ainsley would never have allowed the library to fall into such disarray.

"Ari..." Iona's faint whisper comes from the far end of the room.

"Cease this foolish game!" Ariadne makes her way past the lines of wooden tables to the shelves on the other side. "Rebekka is searching for you."

Iona only laughs, the sound growing fainter still. Ariadne reaches the shelves, turns another corner and to her annoyance, she finds herself back within the forest. Fireflies dance in the tepid air, their lights flashing on and off.

"Iona!" Ariadne growls. "Why won't you-"

As she makes her way around another tree, she stops short. There leaning against a hawthorn tree is Iona. She is clad in a threadbare nightgown, its fabric more like gauze in how little it obscures her nakedness beneath.

"Here I am," Iona says, her coquettish grin widening in response to Ariadne's surprise.

"Why did you run from me?" she asks, quickly closing the distance between them to take Iona into her arms. Her skin is so warm beneath Ariadne's fingertips, as if she'd just been sunbathing.

"I wasn't running from *you*," she giggles.

Rebekka calls out Iona's name into the night, still searching in vain, and Ariadne tenses with displeasure.

"Oh, how desperately she wants me," Iona whispers.

"She cannot have you," Ariadne says fiercely, drawing her ever closer and pressing kisses to her neck until she sighs happily and shrugs off the straps of her nightgown. They slip from her shoulders to rest against the crooks of her elbows.

Ariadne drags her mouth down lower to worship Iona's breasts, pulling away for only a second to gaze upon the perfect swells. Instead, she stares at Iona's collarbone, at the freckles scattered there, and she frowns, murmuring, "Your freckles."

"What of them?" Iona asks, impatiently raising her chest up to Ariadne's mouth.

"They aren't right," Ariadne says.

Iona's smile fades, reflecting her hurt at the comment.

"They aren't in the right places," Ariadne clarifies, running fingers over the tawny dots.

Iona giggles. "What are you on about?"

"I could draw them from memory," Ariadne murmurs.

"Don't be silly," Iona says. "I have far too many for you to know them all by heart. Why are you so distracted?"

Ariadne's response catches in her throat when, before her very eyes, Iona's freckles begin to glow like stars speckling her honeyed skin.

"Don't stop," Iona whines, taking Ariadne's hand to try and guide it between her legs.

"You… Can you not see?" Ariadne asks, flinching when the light glares so brightly, it hurts to look at her.

Ariadne jerks awake, a gasp moments from escaping past her lips until she notices Iona's body draped over hers, her eyes closed in peaceful sleep.

Closing her eyes, Ariadne wills herself to calm. It was only a nightmare. She is only being paranoid, insecure, foolish…

Try as she might, her nerves leave her restless, but she cannot slip out of bed without waking Iona from her slumber. The weight of her soft body, usually a pleasant comfort, only fuels her creeping feeling of claustrophobia. She simply must leave this room and clear her mind.

"Iona," Ariadne whispers.

She whines, her arms wrapping around Ariadne's torso and squeezing her tight, unintentionally exacerbating her growing discomfort.

"Don't go." Iona's voice is barely a whisper.

Ariadne grins despite herself and whispers, "If I don't, you will be responsible for changing the bedding when I-"

"Ugh." Iona scrunches up her nose and flips over onto her back. "Go then... but come back."

Ariadne's discomfort lessens when she's been released, but it gives way to a bereft longing for Iona's warmth, which only serves to confuse her. She hesitates, wondering if she should stay, but in the end, she crawls out of bed. Aster stretches and yawns, jumping off the bed and cantering to her side. She scratches behind his ears and takes a deep cleansing breath.

Iona has already fallen back to sleep, her red hair cascading over the white pillow, her chest slowly rising and falling, with Wisp sleeping soundly at her feet. She is so beautiful... it hurts for Ariadne to look at her, as if she is still glowing like a second sun.

It turns her stomach in knots as her thoughts turn repetitive, incessant, maddening. She cannot lose her, could never live without her. She cannot lose her. She can't. She won't. She-

Sighing, she takes her staff and escapes into the hall, conjuring a warm red robe over top of her chemise. She must find solace somewhere, perhaps the library. Or she could dip her feet in the atrium pool. A bath sounds quite lovely to her in that moment. The oils she and Iona had bathed in to cleanse themselves for the ritual are still fragrant on her skin and hair, an inescapable reminder of their voyage to the Underworld.

But she passes by a door left partially ajar. Through it, the faint hum of her father's voice drifts to Ariadne's ears. She stops to listen, recognizing the aria, "Alma del core", from the Italian opera *La constanza in amor vince l'inganno,* one of her father's favorites.

Pushing open the door, she enters his study. Piles of books on agriculture, herbalism, and phytology litter the small room that extends out into an equally small alcove of windows where her father tends to his plants. A steaming cup of clove tea rests on the sill.

"Fiore." He smiles when he notices her in the doorway. "What a pleasant surprise."

"Good day," she says, until she notices the sunset through the windows. "Or rather, good evening."

"Should you not be in bed?" Her father's brow furrows. "I'd have slept for a week if I'd endured the misfortunes of last night."

Just the mention of sleep makes her eyelids droop, but she fights against it. Instead, she admires the flourishing plant life

her father has cultivated. His night-blooming cereus has yet to flower, the buds appearing as if they're moments away from opening. Perhaps tonight it will have its fleeting moment of beauty.

"You knew, as well, I suppose," Ariadne says, unable to withhold the resentment from her tone.

He frowns and turns his back to tend to his chrysanthemums. The delicate white petals glisten with water droplets.

"It was not for me to intervene," he says.

"Oh, perish the thought," Ariadne says.

"Why would I contest the decision to spare my only daughter from battling heinous foes?" he asks.

"I wouldn't have sired a daughter at all if I knew what Hecate would expect of her," she says.

A twinge of sadness fills her at the truth in that statement. Iona had once expressed her desire to have children someday, but how could they ever justify bringing a child into this mess, to raise them as Hecate's soldier.

"You are angry at me for your very existence?" he asks, incredulous.

"No," she says. "I am angry that you blatantly lied to me all this time."

His jaw clenches. "If you only came here to argue, I would ask that you please leave me in peace."

Sighing with frustration, she regards the cramped space with pity. The sorry excuse for a study is his only haven within his own family's villa. Perhaps it is inconsiderate of her to confront him here, when she knows well the value of solitude.

She nearly makes it to the door, but her father's gasp has her whirling about in alarm, mere moments from conjuring a shield.

"They are blooming!" He points to his cereus cactus, the first of the nocturnal flowers popping open before their very eyes. "I knew tonight would be the night!"

Their quarrel set aside, they huddle around the plant and watch intently as each bud bursts apart to reveal thin, spindly white petals, their fragrance like jasmine and vanilla. Ariadne lifts one to her nose and breathes deeply.

"Brilliant!" he exclaims, practically trembling in his excitement. "Such ephemeral beauty… You must bring Iona to see the blossoms before they wilt at sunrise."

She nods, hoping Iona will awaken in time, and asks, "In your travels, have you yet gone to Brazil?"

"I can't say that I have," he says.

"We journeyed there in search of Iona's kin, and explored part of the country together," she says. "The diversity of flora was astounding, many of the species unknown to me."

"Is that so?" His brow furrows in contemplation. "I must plan a trip and see them with my own eyes."

With his shears, he clips a sprig of lavender from a pot in the corner, handing it to her. She lifts it to her nose, breathing in the calming scent, and it reminds her of Iona, of Samhain, of their vows to each other.

"I quite like Iona," he says, as if reading her thoughts.

"Most do."

"Such a lovely young woman. You chose well."

"You are in the minority of that opinion." She picks at the calyx of the lavender, plucking them and letting them fall to the floor of the study.

"You put far too much importance on the thoughts of others," he says. "If you are content, then what does it matter?"

"Yes, when have negative opinions ever led to misfortune?" she asks sarcastically.

He doesn't respond, and she admonishes herself for the lapse in civility.

"Your approval means far more to me than their opposition," she says softly.

His smile is renewed. "I meant to tell you earlier, but I must express my admiration for your decision to heal the Nicolo girl. It was very good of you."

She meets his gaze and beholds the pride expressed there, mixed with an emotion she cannot quite place. He leans in to press a tender kiss to her forehead.

"You have an opportunity to right many more wrongs, as you did with Vivien, and I do hope you will rise to the challenge," he says. "With that staff of yours, you can protect those unable to protect themselves."

She lowers her gaze, her emotions too overpowering to conceal. "I shall try."

She lifts one of the cereus blooms to her nose and breathes deeply, committing its scent to memory.

"You look dreadful, fiore," her father says with concern. "Please, go to bed and rest."

"I cannot," Ariadne says.

"Why?" he asks.

She hesitates, then admits, "I am plagued by nightmares again. Not of the river. New ones."

"I see," her father says, then ducks his head to browse through his apothecary cabinet. He gives her a glass vial of a blue luminescent potion. "Take this when you return to bed. It will grant you a dreamless sleep, that I swear to you."

She holds the vial gingerly. "Many thanks."

He pulls her into an embrace. She stiffens initially, but as the seconds pass, she lets herself go slack as she is nearly overcome by her suppressed emotions. He kisses the crown of her head, then pulls away sooner than she would have wished.

"Now go," he says.

When she returns to her room, Iona has flipped onto her side, facing away from the window. Drinking the sleeping potion in one gulp, the mixture tasting of poppies, valerian root, and chamomile, Ariadne pulls back the covers and shuffles closer to Iona, pressing her torso against her back and breathing in her scent of crisp ocean air.

"Hmm…." Iona sighs contentedly, taking Ariadne's arm and cradling it against her.

Her final thought is of her hand pressed against Iona's chest and her fingertips brushing the pendant's opal, its surface smooth and cool.

Iona insists on training at dawn the following day, even when Ariadne suggests they rest a while longer. There is an adamance in Iona's disposition that compels her to acquiesce, though at first, she makes the practice easier, not wishing to cause Iona any undue distress.

"You're holding back," she accuses.

"We needn't work ourselves to the bone," Ariadne protests.

"I must make up for lost time," Iona says. "Who is to say when the malefician will strike next? They could attack tomorrow. Or right this very minute."

"Or it could be months from now."

"I cannot afford to assume as much. I must be prepared. I cannot sit idle, hoping for a reprieve. Not when others would be harmed due to my complacency."

They've been using illusions again to practice spell work, with the illusory men only casting simple charms. Ariadne measures Iona's expression, her determination, and sighs.

"You told me to be nice," Ariadne reminds her.

"Don't," Iona says. "Be ruthless."

They hold each other's gaze, until the labradorite stone glows. The pastoral valley melts away, becoming a desolate landscape of flat, featureless land.

An exact copy of the malefician appears between them, her billowing robe flowing in the gentle breeze.

"She won't announce her spells," Ariadne warns. "And when she strikes blows, it will hurt."

Iona widens her stance and glares at the illusory figure, undaunted. She conjures a ball of fire, hurling it at the illusion with a grunt. The figure steps out of the fire's path and casts a spell on the dirt beneath her, so it swallows her up until only her head peeks out.

Struggling, Iona closes her eyes and, with effort, breaks her arm out of the ground and claws her way back up.

The malefician circles her and slices a shallow cut across Iona's exposed back. She cries out in outrage, more so than pain, and turns to glare at the illusion, with her bottom half still stuck beneath the rock.

A bolt of lightning crashes so loudly, Ariadne screams and takes cover. It strikes the illusion directly, making it convulse in agony, until it collapses on her hands and knees. In that time, Iona manages to pull herself out of the ground and jump to her feet.

Healing the cut on her back, Iona casts her own cutting spell, slicing across the illusion's face, straight through the fabric wrapped over it. But when the black linen falls away, a featureless mask of bloody skin is all that is revealed. Iona grunts, then casts another spell, and another, until a rapport between her and the faceless illusion is established, a relentless push and pull.

Ariadne tries as she might to predict every one of Iona's spells, without looking through the bond, but she is indomitable in her every movement. Her methods are still, at times, unrefined. She has blind spots, hesitations, miscalculations.

Ariadne exploits every weakness, but she is not entirely without mercy. The illusion only strikes her just enough to sting in places that can withstand it, her back, her stomach, her shins, her shoulders, avoiding her face and stomach altogether. Every blow the illusion makes only incites Iona's tempest, the wealth of anger bourgeoning in the depths of her soul.

The only difference between their anger being that Iona's does not cause her to scream or lose herself to a frenzy. She goes deathly silent while she ascertains the most efficient way to retaliate three times over.

When the hour is nearly over, Iona is dripping with sweat and covered in dirt, her red hair loose and wild against her shoulders, her white shirt ripped and covered in stains. It is the hardest she'd ever fought, and Ariadne knows why, but she dares to take a look through the bond anyhow.

All Iona thinks of is Sara's face, and the face of her grandfather in Brazil, oscillating repeatedly between the two. Her guilt has transformed into vengeance, single-minded and fierce. The illusion disappears and Iona's expression reflects disappointment.

"That's enough for today," Ariadne says.

"I can continue," Iona protests.

"No," Ariadne says firmly.

Iona blinks and looks down at her hands.

"You did very well," Ariadne says, her voice betraying her veneration.

Iona does not meet her gaze, so she approaches and presses a finger beneath Iona's chin. She reluctantly looks up at her with boundless hazel eyes.

"I speak the truth," Ariadne insists.

The storm in her gaze recedes, until whatever had possessed her is gone. She cups Ariadne's face in both her hands, pulling her face down for a kiss. It's soft, lingering, tender. Then she wraps her arms around Ariadne's neck and holds her close, gently stroking the nape of Ariadne's neck with her nails.

Ariadne sinks into her warmth and closes her eyes, pleasant prickles running down her back from Iona's caresses. She waits to see what Iona might choose to do next, but she doesn't. They simply stand there holding each other in silence, an inescapable feeling of foreboding crossing between them.

"What would comfort you most while we await the fray?" Iona asks.

Ariadne goes to pull away, to read Iona's expression, but Iona tightens her hold, burrowing her face in Ariadne's neck. She rubs Iona's back to soothe her while she thinks for a moment, then whispers her answer in Iona's ear.

When Ariadne confesses that she cannot bear to spend one more day in that prison of a villa, Iona has their things packed within the hour. If the coven has need of them, they will conjure a portal and arrive in haste. Otherwise, Iona agrees there is no reason for them to stay. Xiomara wishes them well and promises to write if there is any sign of their enemy.

They travel to Triora, where Nonna welcomes them with

open arms. Frankie resides nearby with his parents, but decides to stay with them, too, to keep them company. Within a week, even while their solicitude does not wane, their spirits are moderately lifted.

July swelters even hotter than June, but Ariadne doesn't mind in the slightest. She spends her days in her Nonna's sprawling gardens, filled with produce and flowers of nearly every variety, and an orchard of Annurca apple trees. With green mountains in front of her, and the modest orange roofed house behind her, she feels as if she can breathe for the first time since they'd left Brazil.

"Are you certain of your relation to Frankie?" Crescentia asks.

Sighing heavily, Ariadne cracks open an eye to glare up at her from where she lays in the grass. The only annoyance she now endures are Crescentia's constant visits with Frankie. Today she wears an airy white linen dress, her golden hair loose against her shoulders and fair cheeks pink from long days spent in the sun.

"Quite certain," Ariadne says.

"He must have inherited all the charm in your family," Crescentia chuckles.

"Go bother him then, if you enjoy him so," Ariadne grumbles.

"Best not let Iona hear you speak to me in such a way."

"Likewise."

Crescentia smirks, and Ariadne pushes herself up onto her elbows.

"I like him very much," Crescentia says, observing her expression with caution. "Truly, sincerely, beyond his skills in-"

"He is my cousin," Ariadne says, scrunching up her nose in disgust.

"Poetry!" Crescentia finishes, then scoffs. "Your lewd assumptions are no fault of mine. Though you would not be wrong about-"

"What do you want, Crescentia?" Ariadne asks.

"Would you be very cross if I wed him?" she asks.

Ariadne balks at her. "Stars above, you've just met him!"

"Yes, but I should not grow attached if you'll skin me alive for accepting his proposal," Crescentia says.

"Why do you feel the need to ask my permission to irritate me?" Ariadne grumbles. "Do as you wish! I cannot stop you."

Crescentia's responding smile is so sweet and full of hope, that Ariadne fights to keep her frown intact.

"You are an entirely ridiculous person." Ariadne slumps onto her back and stares up at the slow-moving clouds.

"Crescentia!" Frankie calls from within the house. "Where have you gone?"

Ariadne expects her to run inside, but she lingers.

"We are visiting the quarry for a swim this afternoon," Crescentia says. "Might you join us?"

"No," Ariadne says. "No, thank you. I am fine here."

"I asked Iona, but…" Crescentia winces.

"Leave her be. She has much on her mind."

"I gathered that."

"Go." Ariadne waves her off. "Enjoy the summer."

"If you need anything… Someone to lend an ear…" Crescentia says.

"I don't," Ariadne says.

"Very well." Crescentia runs off toward the house. "I'm here, Frankie!"

Ariadne closes her eyes and tries to sleep while basking in the warm glow of the sun. She supposes Crescentia must think she spurns their coupling for shallow, inconsequential reasons. Of course, she does not relish the thought of tolerating Crescentia's presence at every family gathering for the rest of her life, but she is already stuck with her as Iona's friend.

In truth, she does not wish for Frankie to tell Crescentia anything about her, her upbringing, her family, her secrets. She hopes that Frankie will be discreet and know that she wishes for such things to be private, not whispered in every ear across Europe and beyond, as Crescentia tends to facilitate.

"Nipotina!" Nonna calls.

Sitting up, she searches for her grandmother, who waves at her from within the orchard.

"Come, help me with these," Nonna says.

Ariadne stands and brushes dirt from her maroon skirts, taking her staff from where it rests against the house, and conjures an apron as she walks. She helps her Nonna pick apples while Aster sits between them, panting heavily from the heat.

"Is it not too early to pick them?" Ariadne asks.

"Some are ripe enough," Nonna assures her. "Trust me, child. I know what I'm doing."

"Of course," Ariadne says quickly.

They pick apples in silence for a moment, with Nonna lightly smacking Ariadne's hand if she reaches for an apple she doesn't approve of.

"Where is Iona?" Nonna asks.

"Studying again," Ariadne says.

Before leaving Villa Mitriora, they'd gathered a selection of grimoires from the library so Iona can continue expanding her lexicon of spells. There will always be crossover from one spell book to another, but every fifty pages or so, a new incantation will emerge. She has poured over nearly half of the books they'd borrowed already.

"She will make herself sick," Nonna says.

"I already inquired if she wished to join me," Ariadne says, shrugging to mask her concern.

"You should not have given her the option," Nonna says.

"You wish to get me in trouble," Ariadne says, cutting her a wry look.

"Lover's quarrels are the spice of life." Nonna's eyes twinkle.

"Then I'd say my life with Iona is almost too spicy," Ariadne grimaces.

"Passion, jealousy, and drama are in your blood. You'd best embrace it," Nonna says. "That excitement is what attracted her to you in the first place, was it not?"

"It is also what she complains about the most," Ariadne protests.

"She knows the woman she loves," Nonna says. "I see how she has you wrapped around her finger, doting on her hand and foot."

"She does not!" Ariadne blushes scarlet.

"You'd best acquaint yourself to complaining, too. That's half of what a marriage is," Nonna says.

"We aren't wed," Ariadne reminds her.

"I should keep you in separate rooms, then?" Nonna raises an eyebrow.

"Uh…" Ariadne's heart sinks.

Nonna chuckles. "You wilt at the mere thought of a night's separation from her? My, my, you are hopelessly smitten."

Ariadne's flush deepens. "Nonna…"

"If you insist on taking your time to propose, then you must hold the wedding on Samhain so I might see your dress in the afterlife," Nonna says.

Shaking her head incredulously, Ariadne picks another apple, trying to hide her face within the branches. "I shall keep that in mind."

Nonna eyes her, then picks another apple and tosses it into a wicker basket behind her.

"I gave you a week," Nonna says.

"Pardon?" Ariadne asks.

"A week to tell me what is troubling you. I've lost my patience," she says, "Out with it."

"I… I don't know what you mean," Ariadne stutters.

Nonna puts her hands on her hips and, though the elderly woman is more than a head shorter than her, Ariadne gulps.

"I suppose I do have concerns…" Ariadne hedges.

"And what might they be?" Nonna asks.

It all comes out in a rush. Tatiana Nicolo's haunting presence at the solstice ball, her mother's vicious words on the front steps of the manor, the comments from the two witches in the ballroom, all of it spills from her lips until she cannot say another word without telling the coven's secrets or relenting her anxieties about Rebekka's enduring interest in Iona, which she could never explain to her own grandmother. Fortunately, what she does divulge proves enough to satisfy her grandmother's inquisition.

"My word," Nonna says. "That is… a great deal to consider."

Ariadne bites her lip and waits for her to organize her thoughts.

"Do you feel changed since consuming Elise's power?" Nonna asks.

"No…" Her skin itches with discomfort at the prospect. "I never considered there might be negative effects. Stupid of me, I suppose."

"Those are your mother's words," Nonna chastises. "This is an unprecedented situation. I don't see how you could have predicted its outcome."

She picks another apple and spins it in her hand to admire its red luster.

"You needn't panic over it," she decides. "Any ailments would have manifested by now. It was Elise's spell, not yours, that leeched her power away. Is that not so?"

Ariadne frowns. "But if maleficium was transferred to me-"

"I doubt the staff would poison you," Nonna says, "but I suppose if it unnerves you so, you should avoid leeching curses in future."

"That may prove difficult, with malefician attacks becoming frequent," Ariadne murmurs.

"Speak with Xiomara," Nonna suggests. "She might even ask Hecate on your behalf. A Goddess of magic will know if there is anything to fear."

She hadn't considered asking Hecate for guidance in this matter. Perhaps if she prays, this time Hecate will deign to respond. She is far more comfortable asking Aunt Xiomara but does not know how to do so without Iona overhearing, and she should not be burdened with this when she has more than enough to concern herself with.

"As for the pendant, I don't see why you should torment yourself over it now, no matter who's decision it was or wasn't," Nonna says. "Iona has it. It cannot be undone. She must live with that, and she has you to help her. Your mother may hate you for your choice, but how is that any different from before?"

Nonna waves her wand, made of copper, and the apple in her hand is sliced. She offers it to Ariadne, who picks the smallest piece. As she takes a bite and chews, appreciating its tart sweetness, she supposes Nonna is right.

"Do you regret giving her the pendant?" Nonna asks.

"No," Ariadne says on an impulse, but the more she considers it, the less certain she is of her choice.

"Then what is the problem? She did want it, after all," Nonna reminds her. "You must trust her to know what is good for her."

"I do," Ariadne says.

"No..." Nonna muses. "I don't think you do."

"I am telling you that-" Ariadne sighs. "Would I have bonded to her if I did not trust her?"

"On the contrary. I find that blood bonds can lead to the very absence of trust," Nonna says, her eyes darkening.

"I don't know if I agree," Ariadne says, contemplating her eternal vulnerability and Iona's in turn. It is an ever-constant crucible of verity between them.

"You call her nymph?" Nonna asks.

A small smile lifts Ariadne's lips. "Yes, at times I do."

"A water spirit with no real magic, only an ornamental woman of beauty. Is that truly what you think of her?" Nonna asks.

"No, of course not. It is only a pet name," Ariadne says, then admits. "I said it once as a slight, but it's since turned into an endearment. Without context you may judge it harshly, but it is said with love."

"That matters not. You should recognize her strength more than anyone," Nonna says. "Names have power. You shouldn't belittle her, even in jest."

Ariadne lowers her head, thinking back on the recent times she's said it, and hopes that Iona never felt disparaged. Nonna takes another bite of apple, her umber eyes dissecting her.

"As for Tatiana, it is quite simple," Nonna says. "You must confront her. When next you see her, take her aside and listen. Whatever it is she has to say, it cannot be any worse than your fear of the unknown. You've already healed her sister. She may wish to thank you for it."

Ariadne snorts, and Nonna narrows her eyes.

"You are so quick to assume the worst," she says. "Listen to her and move forward. Or let her presence repel you at every gathering you attend, until she decides to make a scene at the worst possible moment."

Offering Ariadne another piece of apple, Nonna gives the rest to Aster and tosses away the core. She casts a floating spell on the basket to bring it back to the house.

"I am not entirely ignorant of your family's secrets," she says.

Ariadne stiffens, but Nonna puts a hand on her shoulder.

"Do not tell me anything that would cause you harm," she says. "As my son has told me countless times, only those within the coven may know its inner workings. He only knows what Cintia deigns to tell him."

"How do you know?" Ariadne asks. "What have you heard?"

"My mother once told stories of the time before Katrin's ascent," Nonna says. "Maleficians were far more common in those days, capable of destroying entire cities. They are the reason for the horrid reputation of witches amongst humans, who were the most vulnerable in the attacks. It induced the plague of witch trials. So much death… primarily of common witches and warlocks, or unfortunate humans scapegoated by their community."

Being reminded of Iona's recollection of Lucretia's plight in this very city more than a century ago, Ariadne looks out at the city of Triora and wonders if Lucretia's grave was ever marked, so she might leave flowers for her.

"When Katrin claimed the pendant in her youth, and a new age began, the maleficians mysteriously withdrew from the world. A rather fortuitous coincidence, wouldn't you say?" Nonna asks.

Unsure whether she can confirm such a thing or not, Ariadne doesn't respond.

"No one ever speaks of such things, but many have observed Katrin's influence. It is why no one ever thought to oppose her in her conquest. The great covens sought her protection and were willing to give her anything in exchange," Nonna says. "If

Iona has been inducted into the Zerynthos coven, then I can understand your unease."

She sets the basket of apples on her kitchen table and takes a seat. "Do not let your fears cloud your judgement. Support her. Protect her. That is all you can do."

Ariadne nods solemnly, grateful for any advice when she feels so completely lost.

"In that spirit, is there anything you might do for her now?" Nonna asks. "If she carries on this way, she will work herself to death."

"I shall think of something," Ariadne says, pondering how to navigate Iona's prolonged isolation.

# 21 - Ariadne

She finds Iona hunched over a grimoire, sitting cross-legged on the bed in the spare room upstairs. The window is left partially ajar, letting in golden afternoon light and fresh air that smells faintly of ripened apples.

Iona smiles at her when she enters, but her hazel eyes behold the sort of exhaustion that cannot be quelled by sleep alone.

Ariadne approaches her, leaning down to press a gentle kiss to her forehead, then her cheek. "You've been confined to this room long enough."

Iona frowns slightly, her eyes returning to her grimoire in earnest. "I've more studying to do."

"You are allowed respites," Ariadne says.

"There isn't time," she mumbles.

Sighing, Ariadne studies her a moment, then looks to her staff and wonders if perhaps she could make the time.

She centers herself, a thrill going through her at the sight of the labradorite stone glowing. Steadily the sounds of birds grow silent, the breeze in Iona's hair goes still, and all of time stops.

She takes a moment to admire the feat and wonders about the scope of the magic. Is time frozen everywhere? Or does it only reach a certain area? For the sake of experimentation, she releases the staff and to her disappointment, the spell dwindles as time starts again.

"Your sulking shan't change my mind," Iona murmurs.

"Is that so?" Ariadne asks, and the mischievous tone of her voice must have given her away, because Iona tenses and peers up at her.

"What are you up to?" Iona asks, glancing at the staff where it stands on its own without toppling.

"Nothing." Ariadne reaches for it and with effort she concentrates again, making time stop at her will. The weight of time is a constant pressure against her mind, most uncomfortable but not unendurable.

Then she frowns, tapping a finger against her chin as she considers her next move. After a moment's deliberation, she takes the grimoire in Iona's lap and sets it aside on the comforter. Then, one handed, she puts her shoulder against

Iona's middle, wraps an arm around her waist, and with a bit of shuffling and finagling, she manages to lift Iona up and onto her shoulder, with her legs dangling in front and her arms hanging at Ariadne's back.

"Oh, she will be furious." Ariadne grins and carefully steps out of the room, goes down the stairs one careful step at a time, and slips out the front door.

But on her way down the path towards the garden, the weight of time becomes a crushing albatross revolting against her spell. The weight of it is too much to withstand, though she tries anyway, until she trips on a loose stone and her concentration breaks. The spell ceases at once and Iona gasps at her sudden shift in gravity.

"Ariadne Zerynthos, what have you done?" Iona kicks and squirms, trying to break free.

"We're almost there." She groans and giggles when Iona tries to wrestle for her freedom.

"Release me at once!" Iona protests and turns the ground beneath them into a deep pit of mud.

Ariadne yelps and nearly falls as she sinks down to her knees in the muck and Iona manages to wriggle out of her hold. Wisp comes bounding out of the house in search of Iona and runs over to them with a toothy grin, Aster at her heels.

"How on earth did you manage that?" Iona asks.

"I'm only practicing my spell work, same as you," Ariadne says.

"You are a constant nuisance," Iona huffs, her pendant glowing as the mud turns back into solid soil, leaving their hems stained brown.

"Since you are already outside, you may as well-"

"I must continue my studies," Iona insists even as Ariadne takes her hand to coax her farther down the path.

"The grimoires will still be there when you return," Ariadne says.

"But there is so much I have yet to master." Iona succeeds in pulling her arm away. "I'll study for one more hour, then I'll return."

Ariadne scowls when Iona walks away, then clicks her tongue at Aster. The wolf gallops over to Iona and tackles her to the ground, subduing her with a barrage of slobbering licks and kisses.

"Aster!" Iona sputters, but the wolf won't let her rise. "Make him stop!"

"You need rest."

"No, I must study!"

"I shan't let you waste away in that room."

"I'm not-" Iona lets out a giggle when Aster tickles her neck with his sniffing nose. "For goodness sake! Aster, get off!"

"He won't listen," Ariadne smirks. "Aster, lie down."

The wolf slumps his full weight on top of Iona, making her grunt.

"I'll tell your grandmother of this," Iona threatens, trying to wriggle herself free, but Aster won't budge and continues sniffing and licking at her face.

"This was Nonna's idea, actually," Ariadne grins.

"Surely not-" Iona squeals when Aster nuzzles his wet nose against her ear. "Ari!"

"Aster, come." Ariadne pats her leg, and he immediately jumps up and runs to her side. She scratches behind his ears, then conjures a bloody steak and tosses it into his mouth.

Iona wipes slobber from her face and gives Wisp a reproachful look. "A lot of help you were…"

Wisp tilts her head to the side, her tongue hanging out as she pants from the heat.

"Lay here with me," Ariadne implores. "Please?"

Iona sighs dramatically, then glares up at her from beneath her lashes. "I propose a compromise."

Iona lies with her grimoire propped against her bent legs and her mane of red hair spread out across Ariadne's lap, who gently strokes the lustrous strands, then sets to work making thin, delicate braids. Chicory flowers grow wild around them, and Ariadne weaves in the stems until Iona's hair is filled with tiny blue blossoms.

"May I practice a spell on you?" Iona asks.

"You may do whatever you wish to me," Ariadne says.

Iona rolls her eyes, but her blush is immediate. Ariadne bites back her grin.

"Nun-eul humchida," Iona incants.

In a fading gradient of color and light, Ariadne's vision slowly goes black.

"Can you see?" Iona asks.

"No," Ariadne says, swallowing down her discomfort.

But Iona senses her unease and quickly reverses the spell, then says, "That could be useful."

"Indeed," Ariadne says.

When Wisp tries to dig a hole in Nonna's vegetable garden, Iona reprimands her, so the fox goes to play with Aster in the orchard instead. Ariadne reaches out a hand and a ripened apple flies through the air and into her palm. Iona barely notices her conjuring a paring knife and cutting off a piece, until Ariadne presents the slice of fruit to her, pressing it against her mouth until Iona parts her lips and takes a bite. Ariadne eats the other half.

"Have you ever tried this spell?" Iona asks around her mouthful and lifts her grimoire up so Ariadne can see.

"Armatura," Ariadne reads. "Yes, on occasion. Though I am not partial to armor. It can be exceedingly heavy and restricts movement too much for my liking."

"But it can shield from attacks," Iona says.

"Only physical ones," Ariadne says.

"I would not be opposed to wearing it, if I could bear the weight. I wouldn't wish to be encumbered either," Iona says. "But here it says you can enchant the armor with protection spells. That is of great interest to me."

"You can make another ring to accomplish the very same." But when Iona gives her an annoyed look, Ariadne acquiesces. "It is a fine enough option. If it will provide you a greater sense of security than by all means, cover yourself in metal."

Iona's frown deepens and she turns to the next page. In truth, Ariadne resents the idea that she should feel the need to craft armor at all, but after Ariadne's failure to protect her in their last encounter with the Crone, she can hardly blame Iona for want of fortified defenses.

"How many enchantments could I cast upon the armor?" she asks.

"It depends," Ariadne says. "Objects can only house so much magic, or otherwise the power will destroy it to break free. Only those with a mastery of enchantment, like Morgan and Merlin, can house a great deal of magic without suffering those repercussions, thus making their artifacts so valuable. I would wager two, perhaps three spells would not cause you trouble."

"Even with the pendant?" Iona asks.

Ariadne considers it. "Perhaps four or five with the use of the pendant. You would need to test it and see."

"Hmmm…" Iona's brow furrows in concentration.

Ariadne offers her another piece of apple, but Iona shakes her head. She shuts the grimoire and tosses it aside, opting instead for a tome bound in black leather with no title embossed on the cover or spine. She hesitates before opening it and Ariadne leans in closer to read with her.

The book had been a gift from Aunt Xiomara upon their departure. She'd explained that it is a secret index of the family's many brushes with maleficians over the decades.

Katrin's own scrawl litters the first page and recounts an encounter with a malefician who had a particular obsession with corrupted necromancy. The witch poisoned the water supply of an entire city so that she could revive the townsfolk as wraiths to do her bidding and protect her from opposing forces. Iona leafs through the many pages filled with handwritten scribbles.

"Phobokenesis," Iona murmurs, running her finger lightly over the page as she reads aloud. "She exploited my fear, mining my worst terrors from my deepest memories. A moment longer and she would have defeated me, but I severed her head from her body while she thought me incapacitated."

Ariadne recalls running through the snow, Iona's screams echoing through the barren trees, the freezing water that had nearly drowned her, just like in her countless nightmares of Vivien. Elise had evidently attempted this sort of magic on her, though she hadn't known there was a name for it.

"Two maleficians dueled to the death and their battle left a scar upon the earth. Many humans were casualties as their-" Iona's eyes widen and she brings the book closer to her eyes to ensure she read correctly. "-their life force was siphoned to strengthen their spells, draining their vitality and leaving nothing behind but empty husks. Their bodies littered the countryside, a haunting necropolis." Iona lets out a pitying sigh. "At last, one witch overpowered the other and consumed her power for her own. I then set out to defeat her in turn."

"My mother once told me that maleficians can never form covens," Ariadne murmurs. "I suppose this is why. It would stand to reason that they are incapable of coexisting for any length of time. They would only tear each other apart."

Iona takes a steadying breath, flips to another page, and reads, "My dreams are not my own. I feel her burrowing into my psyche, whispering doubts and derisions…" She skims the words, then continues. "I nearly mistook the dream for prophecy, but all she tells are lies. I buried her in pieces."

Iona flips to another page, then another, until Ariadne reaches out to stop her. "That is my mother's handwriting."

"Oh," Iona frowns and reads. "She lives in shadow. I must keep candles lit in every corner and crevice of my room or she will emerge and slit my throat while I sleep." Iona's voice conveys her awe. "She controlled darkness itself? Perhaps another crone."

"How did my mother defeat her?" Ariadne asks.

She scans the page, then says, "She let darkness fall and when she felt the malefician's presence encroaching upon her, she set fire to the room, and the malefician with it. She nearly burned herself alive but managed to withstand the flames long enough to survive."

Her mother told her stories of these sorts of awful calamities that Iona describes, but Ariadne had never imagined they were memories. She'd assumed such tales were commonly told to children as a way to frighten them into obedience, and wonders what it may have been like if she'd known the truth, as Moira, Marina, and Sebastian did. A part of her envies their camaraderie, their shared experience of studying together, fighting together, while she was kept locked away.

"There you are," Crescentia says, running up to them, her blonde hair still wet from swimming.

Iona quickly snaps the book closed and puts it at the very bottom of a stack.

"I thought you'd never leave that awful room," Crescentia says, then gasps at the flowers adorning Iona's braided hair. "Oh, how lovely!"

Frankie comes up behind her with a permanent smile affixed to his amiable face. "Good day, Iona. Ariadne."

"Good day." Iona musters a smile in return. "I trust you had a pleasant swim."

"Indeed, the water was the perfect temperature," he says, his gaze lingering on Crescentia.

Ariadne suspects the water could have been frozen and he wouldn't have noticed the difference so long as the object of his affection were there with him.

"Iona, might you spare a moment to dance with me?" Crescentia asks.

"Dance?" Iona frowns.

"When next we attend a ball, you should be prepared," she explains. "I'll teach you."

"Oh… I am not sure." Iona bites her lip.

"Euphemia did the same for me when I entered high society," Crescentia says. "Knowing the steps will be great comfort to you."

Ariadne is taken aback when Iona reluctantly takes

Crescentia's offered hand and twirls them both round and round, until Iona lets out a small giggle.

Crescentia continues her rollicking as she says, "Which would you like to learn first? The quadrille, the polonaise, the cotillion, galopade, mazurka, scotch reel-"

"Goodness, are there truly that many?" Iona's smile fades.

"Perhaps a contredanse," Ariadne suggests, and when Iona looks to her, she explains. "We danced it at Rebekka's ball."

"I quite like that idea," Crescentia says, withdrawing her platinum wand to conjure a single fiddle that plays a cheerful song. "Frankie, Ariadne, on your feet."

She arranges them in two separate lines, Crescentia across from Iona and Frankie across from Ariadne. When the music starts, Crescentia calls out instructions and guides Iona by the hand.

"There, now skip," she demonstrates. "Step forward, then back. Now take my hand and spin round."

A few times, Iona accidentally steps in the wrong direction or loses her footing, prompting Crescentia to halt the dance for a moment and review the steps at a slower pace. Upon their third rehearsal, Crescentia also instructs Iona on the great covens by first reciting all their many attributes, then testing Iona's memory.

"The Ulanovas," Crescentia says, gesturing for Iona to step forward.

"Their mark is rye," she says. "Olesya Ulanova leads them."

"Correct," Crescentia says.

"The Kimballs," Frankie prompts.

"Their mark is a bat. Eleanor Kimball leads them," Iona says.

"And where do they hail from?" Crescentia asks.

"Massachusetts," Iona says.

"Very good, Iona!" Crescentia spins her around. "Next should be… the Nassrys."

Ariadne cringes. Iona's steps slow, until she stops entirely.

"Oh…" Crescentia winces. "Perhaps we shouldn't discuss them in their time of mourning. It is ever so awful…"

"I should like to retire to my room," Iona says, her voice bleak.

"Whatever is wrong?" Frankie asks.

"Nothing," Iona says, her breath catching in her throat. "I am tired."

Frankie looks up at the early evening sun in confusion.

"Alright," Crescentia says, suspicion brewing in her gaze.

"We can always continue tomorrow."

Iona shakes her head. "I cannot."

"But why? You are doing so well and-"

"Crescentia, please," Iona says forcefully, then in a softer voice continues. "I... I am sorry, my friend. I know you mean well."

"Are you ill?" Crescentia asks. "Perhaps Ariadne can brew a tonic for you."

*Don't withdraw again so soon,* Ariadne pleads. "Your prolonged seclusion could very well be what causes your infirmity."

"You are well aware of what troubles me." Iona frowns. *A child has died. I cannot go on as if nothing has changed.*

*No one is asking you to,* Ariadne insists.

"I must study," Iona gives her a pleading look, her thoughts returning to little Sara's mangled body sinking beneath the sand.

"You cannot hope to learn every spell in existence in mere weeks," Ariadne argues. *I can protect you, now that we know our enemy.*

"That is precisely the issue. I haven't time to waste on frivolous dancing," Iona relents. *And who shall protect them with you so preoccupied with my wellbeing?*

"You're keeping secrets from me again," Crescentia accuses.

Iona opens her mouth, then closes it, her expression betraying her guilt.

"You promised you wouldn't," Crescentia says, crestfallen.

"The secret is mine to tell," Ariadne lies. "Leave it alone, for she would never betray my confidence."

Crescentia meets her gaze, and she only hopes their new truce will be enough to placate her curiosity.

"Well now, if Ariadne does not want to speak of it, then we must respect her wishes," Frankie says. "Come, my treasure."

Crescentia scrutinizes Iona a moment longer, then sighs. "Very well."

"Good day to you both," Frankie says, with a polite bow of his head.

Crescentia takes his arm, and they whisper in hushed tones as they walk away toward a white carriage by the roadside. A surprising rush of envy compels Ariadne to frown as she watches them go. Their courtship is young but seemingly so effortless, uncomplicated, like breathing. For a fleeting moment, she wishes it could be so for her and Iona.

"She only wished to help you." Ariadne watches Iona's face

intently.

"And I only wish to save the next poor soul ensnared in the Crone's trap," Iona says in a low voice. "I can learn to dance another day. Any day. Not now."

With that she turns on her heels and makes her way back to the house. Ariadne does not dare intervene. Any goodwill she'd relied on is gone, and she fears there will be no comforting Iona for at least another day or two.

And yet that night, when Ariadne dares to interrupt Iona's reading again, gently closing her grimoire and blowing all the candles out, Iona reaches for her immediately, burrowing in close and sighing heavily, so exhausted that it radiates off of her and into Ariadne through their bond, until her own eyelids droop despite her leisurely activity that day.

But Iona does not sleep. She fights against it, shifting to gaze at Ariadne, her freckled face barely illuminated by the moonlight shining through the open window. Slowly, she lifts herself up to press a tender kiss to Ariadne's lips, lingering there a moment longer than she normally would, before pulling away with such reluctance.

So, Ariadne pulls her back, repositioning them so Iona lays on her back partially beneath her, their noses brushing softly as they kiss with unhurried affection, not seeking anything more than closeness and comfort.

Something wet touches Ariadne's fingertips where she cradles Iona's cheek, and she opens her eyes to find that Iona is silently weeping. She goes to speak but Iona opens her eyes, quickly shaking her head no, and bringing Ariadne back down to kiss her again.

And so, she does as Iona bids, reveling in their salutary embrace, until Iona's lips mold to hers less and less, soon going limp altogether when her breathing slows and sleep finally takes her. When Ariadne wakes the following morning, Iona still slumbers deeply with Wisp curled up against her, with her small head resting on Iona's shoulder.

When Ariadne's stomach grumbles, she carefully slips out of bed and goes downstairs to the kitchen for a spot of breakfast, intending to go right back upstairs, until she spots a letter sitting unopened on a table by the door.

A rush of conflicting emotions fills her when she takes the note, tearing it open to read Samaira's delicate script.

*I see Iona's melancholy. Perhaps I can help.*

Brass wind chimes make tinkling, pinging sounds as rain drops fall against them where they hang from the roof of the stone house carved into the side of a grey mountain, a structure undeniably constructed through the use of magic.

Ariadne knocks on the front door and glances at Iona, who admires the water dripping from the bells, her eyes not entirely focused on what she sees. Then a young girl with tanned skin and dark hair opens the door. She wears a bright yellow dress, and, in her arms, she holds a familiar orange tabby cat.

"Oh," Ariadne says, surprised.

"Namaskāra." The girl bows and smiles shyly.

"Good morning." Ariadne bows to her, motioning for Iona to do the same. "We've come to call on Samaira. Is she here?"

"Yes, she is at the peak." The girl sets the cat down and beckons them to follow her.

She leads them up a steep mountain path that twists around and around. Bracing against the wind and rain, Ariadne struggles to keep pace with the sprightly child. She hates the cold, despises rain even more, but this visit isn't for her.

When she cannot help glancing again at Iona, there is a renewed sense of calm in her expression, just as Ariadne hoped. The weather is somewhat similar to what Iona has grown accustomed to from her days living in Cornwall, much more so than the warm summer days in Triora.

They reach the summit where Samaira sits cross-legged on a rock. She is drenched with rain, her black hair loose against her back, and her expression reflecting perfect serenity.

"Samaira," the girl says. "Forgive the interruption. Your visitors have arrived."

Samaira opens her eyes and slowly returns to the present moment. She smiles and blinks away the raindrops that catch on her eyelashes.

"Thank you, Ehani," Samaira says, sliding off the rock and onto her feet.

Ehani bows again, then hastens back down the path, while Samaira embraces Ariadne and Iona in turn.

"You'll catch your death in this storm," Ariadne says.

"On the contrary, cleansing rain is exactly what I need," Samaira says.

"Is she your relation?" Iona asks, gesturing to Ehani.

"No, no, she lives in a monastery not far from here," Samaira says. "I am teaching her magic."

"She is a witch?" Iona asks. "How did you come to find her?"

Samaira leads them back down the mountain and Ariadne strains to hear her over the wind.

"Ehani's parents sold her into indentured servitude, so she ran away. She was skin and bones when I came across her climbing the mountain," she says. "I sensed magic in her and knew I must help however I could."

"She is not human?" Ariadne asks.

"There is a touch of magic in her ancestry somewhere," Samaira muses. "Even if she hadn't, I couldn't very well leave her there to starve."

"The poor dear," Iona says. "She seems very well now. Healthy, I mean."

"Once she'd found her wand, the very first spells I taught her were the conjuration of bread, water, meat, anything she might need. Her well of magic is quite shallow but with practice I hope it will grow," Samaira says.

She tells them of Ehani's progress as they descend the mountain path, explaining that she is particularly gifted in phytology. There is an outbreak of smallpox in the Kathmandu Valley, and Ehani often brews healing potions to help prevent infection. Under the cover of night, they fly down to heal as many humans as they can before the sun rises.

Shivers creep down Ariadne's back when they finally make it inside. She sheds her rain-soaked cloak and rubs her arms, clenching her jaw to keep her teeth from chattering.

"I've needed this time apart to recollect myself," Samaira says. "But I must say, I've missed you both an awful lot. Oh!"

Iona pulls her into another fierce embrace, which she returns wholeheartedly, before glancing over Iona's shoulder. In Samaira's brown eyes, Ariadne sees conveyed what she'd already noticed. Iona is not herself, as if her inner light has dimmed.

"What say you to a warm cup of green tea, perhaps dal bhat tarkari, and yomari?" Samaira pulls away and gently cups Iona's cheeks.

"Is that food?" Iona asks, her voice thick with emotion. "I would very much like to eat."

Samaira's responding smile is warm but brief. She goes rigid, her eyes rolling into the back of her head, and her terrible scream has Iona flinching away, but she catches Samaira before she can collapse onto the floor.

"Ari!" Iona looks at her in panic. "What is happening? What should I do?"

She rushes over and helps Iona slowly lower her to the floor.

"She is having a vision, I think," Ariadne says.

Samaira screams again, this time in agony, and Ariadne tries to take her hand, but the sapphire ring burns her, the stone glowing as the vision persists. Instead, Ariadne carefully repositions her hand to run a thumb back and forth across the black and red feathers of Samaira's witch's mark, depicting a crimson sunbird on the back of her hand.

"We're here," Iona whispers as she brushes hair from Samaira's eyes. "It's alright. You will be alright."

All at once, it's over. Samaira goes limp, groaning as her eyes roll back into place, and she presses a hand to her forehead.

"Oh," Samaira winces.

"You had a seizure." Iona's shoulders slump and she expels a shuddering breath.

"Yes," Samaira says. "Well… Not to worry."

Iona and Ariadne exchange a concerned look as Samaira stands and brushes dust off her skirt.

"I would also like to eat," Samaira says, with a tired smile.

"Does that happen every time you have a vision?" Ariadne asks.

"No." Samaira averts her eyes. "Only when I see the darkness. Only once per day."

*We cannot allow her to endure this a moment longer.* Iona smooths her trembling hands against her skirts.

*When last she removed her ring, the malefician made their first kill,* Ariadne reminds her.

*Yes, but they committed their second just as easily. It was Marina's reading of the stars that told us when the murder occurred, not Samaira's vision.* Iona pushes herself onto her feet.

Ariadne considers this, taking Iona's hand when it's offered. *I suppose, but just as before, we do not know what sort of visions might present themselves. Without the ring, we are all the more blind.*

Iona pulls her up, while Samaira rolls her shoulder and sighs at the ache in her strained muscles.

"Stop worrying over me," she says firmly. "Removing the ring is just what the malefician would want."

"Perhaps I was unfair to expect this of you," Ariadne says, but Samaira puts up her hand.

"I am strong," she says. "We must all make sacrifices."

She wavers on her feet, until Iona takes her arm and steadies her.

"I shall speak no more of this," she says. "Please, I must… I would like to sit down."

They usher her to the dining room where they sit and conjure the food that Samaira had suggested. Ariadne watches silently, ruminating over Samaira's plight. Her friend acts as if nothing had happened and had Ariadne not seen it with her own eyes, she never would have guessed that Samaira had been convulsing on the floor with a terrible vision only moments ago.

"Iona, I wondered if you might accompany me to the valley tonight to heal the sick," Samaira says.

Iona's mouth is full of rice, which she promptly forces down to say, "I would be very glad to. Is it quite safe?"

"We will keep our distance from the infected," Samaira assures her. "Ariadne and I had our own trips to the valley on occasion, when her family would visit."

"I often wonder… how was it that you two met?" Iona asks.

"Shall I tell it?" Samaira asks, and when Ariadne nods, she says, "My father hails from India and has a home near The Sundarbans mangrove forest. Within the swamp, there are ghost lights called Aleya that appear on the darkest of nights."

"Ghost lights?" Iona asks.

"In your culture, they are called will-o'-the-wisps," Samaira says, reaching down to scratch beneath Wisp's chin until she trills with contentment. "My father's family were stewards of that forest and its magic for generations."

"Until my grandmother intervened," Ariadne says, her voice hard.

"Katrin struck an alliance with my family to allow them continued access to the mangroves so long as they abided by Katrin's rule," Samaira says, unperturbed. "And so, one day, Ariadne was brought along by her mother to visit the forest when we were both… seven years old, I believe. A year before Katrin died. We hosted the Zerynthos family at our estate during the summer monsoon."

"It stormed day and night," Ariadne remembers, glancing out a nearby window at the mild rain pattering against the glass.

"One night, our parents were away performing their rituals," Samaira says.

"We were meant to be asleep," Ariadne says with a disapproving look.

"I was asleep," Samaira lifts her chin, "but an Aleya shown through my bedroom window and woke me. I was utterly transfixed by the most beautiful blue light I'd ever seen, rivaling the glow of magic itself. Wanting to see it closer, I snuck outside

329

to investigate."

Ariadne interjects, "It was lucky that I'd shared a room with her that summer or-"

"No, no!" Samaira protests. "You said I could tell it."

Smirking, Ariadne takes a bite of food and allows her to finish. Being drawn into the story, Iona leans against the table and rests her chin in her hand.

"The Aleya lured me deeper into the mangroves. I paddled a boat out onto the Arpangasia River, thinking the light might be leading me to my wand," Samaira says. "But I lost track of it in the midst of the storm, which only grew more treacherous. The wind knocked me right off my feet and into the water."

"Goodness!" Iona exclaims. "What did you do?"

"It is not what I did," Samaira says. "Now mind you, Ariadne was the most sullen, circumspect child I'd ever encountered. I was well terrified of her, was even scared to sleep near her some nights when she shared my room. It was her eyes... As a child, they unnerved me."

"You've never told me that," Ariadne mutters.

"I was quite sure she hated me. She never spoke a word to me unless forced," Samaira continues. "Imagine my surprise when the girl dove into the water, like a darter bird, and propelled us both from the river *with her mind.*"

"At seven years of age?" Iona's mouth falls open in awe, then her brow furrows as she glances at Ariadne. "But that was before you found your wand."

"Two years before," Ariadne nods.

"One moment I was sinking, the next she grabbed my wrist, and we were catapulted out and onto the riverbank!" Samaira exclaims.

"You are making it sound far too dramatic," Ariadne gripes.

"It surely was! I thought I'd died, and a demon was taking me to Patala as punishment for my disobedience," Samaira says.

"You've never told me that either," Ariadne chuckles.

Samaira chuckles with her. "Then she practically carried me through the wind and rain until we returned to the house."

"You were always heroic, then?" Iona asks, with reborn light in her eyes.

"I wasn't," Ariadne sighs.

"I almost certainly would have drowned," Samaira says.

"But how did you know where to find her?" Iona asks.

"I followed her when she left her bed," Ariadne says. "Tried calling after her, but the wind was too loud. I barely made it to her in time."

"We dried our dresses by the hearth and huddled together for warmth." Samaira smiles at the memory. "I thanked Ariadne for saving me and she told me, through chattering teeth, how stupid I was to be out there in the first place. We've been the best of friends ever since."

Iona snorts. "Heroic and insolent. You've not changed at all."

Ariadne's ears burn, but Iona caresses her, running a thumb softly over her cheekbone, until she looks up.

*For all your shows of arrogance, you never have learned to accept praise,* Iona observes.

"It was not heroic," Ariadne says again. "Anyone would have done it."

Iona only smiles and takes her hand; a tender gesture Ariadne has sorely missed. Finding Iona's hand much warmer than her own, Ariadne cradles it between both of hers and takes to tracing Iona's veins while she listens to Samaira's many tales of their unlikely friendship.

They exchange stories well into the early hours of the morning, until they don their cloaks and fly down the mountain to the valley below. In their arms, they carry bottles filled with yellow potion that Samaira had brewed with care. They disperse the potion in wells, fountains, every water source they can find.

"Will they not taste it?" Ariadne whispers, opening her bottle and sniffing the concoction. It smells of lemon and nettle.

"They have not seemed to notice. The water dilutes the potion," Samaira shrugs.

Then they trek to the outskirts of town where a collection of tents is scattered across the grass. Samaira explains that the infected people reside there until they either heal… or not. Iona goes straight towards the encampment.

"Wait." Samaira takes Iona's hand and holds her back.

"Why? I can help them."

"We must be cautious. What will the city think if every sick person became well again all at once? An act of god… or a far more sinister assumption."

"Why would they assume-"

Samaira silences Iona with a look.

"Do not forget the witch trials," Samaira says. "Innocent humans should not suffer on our account, nor any true witches who live here."

Iona looks out at the small collection of tents with a mixture of regret and sympathy.

"Is there nothing to be done for them, then?" she asks.

"If you only healed them partially, that would not be as suspicious," Samaira says. "That is what Ehani and I do for as many as we can."

Grateful for the suggestion, Iona approaches the camp, her pendant glowing as she becomes invisible. They wait for her reappearance, until a flash of light cuts through the darkness within one of the tents, then another, and another, washing the sickness away. Once each tent has been visited, Iona reappears.

"There," she says. "I took their pain away, and the rest will alleviate with time."

"Well done," Samaira says.

Iona beams, and in that moment all Ariadne can think of are her mother's words, meant as an insult, calling Iona an irenic saint. Despite all the darkness, all the disappointment and death, her light is never stifled for long. Truly she is as close to a saint as Ariadne had ever witnessed, and she has never felt less deserving of her.

They decide to take the scenic route back up the mountain. It isn't easy, the roads being steep and rocky, but it's worth it when they look out at the view as the sun begins to rise. With the rain gone for the moment, visibility across the valley is much clearer. There is an enormous mountain in the distance, it's peak covered with pristine white snow.

"Which mountain is that?" Iona asks, pointing at the marvel of rock and ice.

"That is Sagarmatha, the goddess of the sky," Samaira says.

They stop to admire the behemoth mountain in a tranquil moment of silence. The light of dawn crests over the ridges, turning the clouds bright orange, and reminding Ariadne of a particular flower. She conjures a marigold and hands it to Iona, who takes it with a smile.

*You do deserve me,* Iona reminds her.

She tries to avert her eyes, to withdraw into herself, but Iona presses soft, increasingly persistent kisses on her cold cheek until she elicits a smile.

# 22 - *Iona*

Waiting in Nepal is both a respite and a torture. The threat of an imminent attack poisons any serenity Iona may have found within the majestic mountains, along with horrible, indecipherable nightmares, and the ever-present suspiration of Ariadne's fear coalescing with hers.

She trains tirelessly with Ariadne every single day, honing her ability to react, to think quickly on her feet, learning how to meet every attack with an appropriate counter spell. Afterward, she often joins Samaira in silent meditation on the mountaintop, though she is not as successful at clearing her mind just yet. She spends the hours thinking, obsessing over her shortcomings and her incurable foreboding, until she is too exhausted to do anything but nestle in Ariadne's pacifying embrace, staving off sleep as long as she can despite her exhaustion.

The dreams are a deluge of abstract warnings and disturbing images that Iona cannot make sense of. She can never seem to wake from them on her own. Either the dreams release her at dawn, or Ariadne shakes her awake when she cries. She's taken to enduring them silently though, rather than worrying Ariadne with them, when she still struggles with her own recurring nightmares of her youth. Neither of them opts to wear a dream talisman out of pure stubbornness, as they refuse to subject the other to their suffering.

Iona tells every detail of her dreams to Samaira, or whatever she can manage to remember, and she is equally disturbed and confused by them. They pour over grimoires meant to help in the interpretation of dreams, but every insight is paired with a contradiction. Whether they be omens of the future, or another one of the Crone's deceptions, they cannot yet determine, but Iona is reluctant to trust them.

At times, she returns to Brazil and practices healing magic with Jacira and Ariadne, which proves a comforting diversion from her troubles. The inner workings of the body become less of a mystery the more she observes Jacira's mastery and, in time, attempts the spells herself.

Jacira explains how the magic encourages the body to heal at an accelerated pace, how knowing what ails her patient will allow her to pinpoint the best method of healing, whether it be a spell or potion. Some humans seek Jacira out, asking her to heal their burns, broken bones, ailing lungs, infected cuts.

Other times they go to human villages in the countryside where disease may manifest. Malignant croup, malaria, the bloody flux, and all manner of awful maladies plague the masses, but Jacira has cures for those willing to accept them. Some refuse, as is their right, but Iona pities them all the same. The only malaise they cannot deter is that of time. The older the patient, the more difficult it can be to coax the body into healing itself.

Iona suggests conjuring coins for the poor and though Jacira says it can be harmless in small, rare instances, if they should conjure an imperfect copy of a coin, or if a person known to be destitute suddenly becomes rich overnight, it could cause that person harm. They could be accused of counterfeiting, a capital offense in most countries.

Therefore, Jacira prefers to offer her services free of charge, and will cast spells on crops to help them grow. There never seems to be enough food, so Iona often leaves loaves of bread behind, especially in the homes of children. It takes such insignificant effort to conjure that it shames her, how much she has when others have so little.

It's not until the final day of July that Samaira notices their threads aiming away from Nepal to the west. Iona halfway hopes it is just an indication of another visit to Brazil, but she'd only just visited days ago. Though she knows their interlude in Nepal would not last forever, she resents the awareness of its inevitable end. Her decisions no longer feel like her own, more like a prescribed, elaborate illusion of which there is no escape.

"Tea?" Samaira asks, offering her a cup.

"Thank you," Iona says, taking it from her, and sipping the turmeric brew with appreciation. It warms her from the inside.

They sit together on the summit of Samaira's mountain to meditate at sunrise. Orange and pink clouds collect in the firmament and obscure the view of the valley below. It reminds Iona of the mountain where Morgan had presented the pendant to the three of them, but Samaira had abstained because she already had an artifact of her own.

"Where did your ring come from?" Iona asks.

"Ah." Samaira looks down at the glistening sapphire with both fondness and resignation. "I'm afraid that is a mystery lost to time. This artifact is so ancient, that the original owner is forgotten."

"There isn't a soul who remembers?" Iona asks incredulously.

"None that I've ever encountered. Perhaps someday that might be so for the pendant, too, when Morgan Le Fay's name is uttered no more," Samaira says.

Iona cannot imagine it, but she supposes enough centuries could make it so.

"All that is known is the place in which the ring manifests, and how to claim it," Samaira explains. "It was a test of stamina. When the previous bearer passed on, I and many of my peers climbed to a mountain peak much like this one and sat in silence, meditating on life and the universe, without sustenance or interruption."

"For how long?" Iona asks.

"However long it took," Samaira says. "Many relented in the first day or two, others lasted a week, the very last of us remained longer than a month."

"A month!" Iona's jaw drops. "But… how is that possible?"

"It rained nearly every day, so we could drink at least. Otherwise, we endeavored to separate ourselves from earthly desires. We fed on magic itself. It healed us, sustained us, so that we might endure another day. It was by far the most rewarding spiritual experience of my lifetime," Samaira smiles. "I lost track of the sunrises and sunsets… I left at the beginning of June and did not return until July. I was quite delirious by then and needed rest for a week or two to regain my strength."

"Goodness… How many did you outlast?"

"We never counted, nor does it matter much to me. It was not a competition. It was an enrichment." She sets down her teacup and spins her ring around her finger. "As the sun set on the horizon, I watched as the sapphire materialized at my feet. I didn't dare pick it up until darkness fell, and when I did, I saw the faintest light of my thread guiding me home."

"Please tell me you at least conjured food before climbing back down," Iona says.

"Yes, a bit of bread and cheese," Samaira assures her. "We do not need all that much, evidently. What I truly missed were my friends, Ariadne especially. I went to visit her in August, and she was… much changed. More like the woman you met when college began in September."

"I see," Iona says, taking another sip of her tea.

"She expels her anxiety through rage," Samaira observes. "And you seem to endure yours in silence."

In support of her statement, Iona doesn't respond, not

knowing what to say or how to say it.

"Holding onto pain and regret can be a terrible burden," Samaira says. "If you ever wish to speak-"

"Two souls are gone forever on my account," Iona says. "I fear the time for speaking is over. I must... I must be more. I must be stronger."

"You cannot save everyone," Samaira says.

"It seems I cannot save anyone," Iona mumbles.

"Not so," Samaira shakes her head. "Crescentia would not walk without your intervention."

"I would not have been capable of healing her if Ariadne hadn't saved me," Iona says.

"It will not do to compare heroism," Samaira says. "You and Ariadne will be in never-ending competition on that score."

Reluctantly, Iona does admit to herself that she'd saved Nenet in the desert, though she cannot speak of it and Nenet will never remember it.

"These battles are never simple," Samaira says. "You save who you can, and that's all you can do. All we can do."

"But will it be enough?" Iona whispers.

Samaira goes to answer, then goes rigid. Iona reaches for her, expecting her to go into convulsions as she does whenever the vision of darkness overtakes her, but she merely looks unseeingly into the distance, her lips parted and eyes wide.

"What do you see?" Iona asks.

"Phoebe Kimball," Samaira says. "Running... through a cemetery."

"When?" Iona asks.

Samaira's eyes focus again, and she looks to Iona. "This very night."

The Kimballs reside on the edge of a lush oak forest in a Massachusetts town called Ashland, a haven Phoebe's ancestors fled to during the witch trials in Salem and never deigned to leave. Iona and Ariadne travel straight there from Nepal after sending a letter to Rome in the hope that the Zerynthos Coven will join them soon.

Upon leaving Nepal, they trade sunrise for sunset. Ariadne sprints up the front steps and bangs loudly on the front door of the two-story colonial house, painted white with blue shutters.

"Phoebe?" Ariadne yells, cupping her hands around her eyes to peer through one of the windows.

"Where else could she be?" Iona asks.

The neighing of horses behind them has Ariadne running to Iona's side, until they recognize the carriage pulled by white horses, it's coach painted red, and the spokes of the wheels gilded with gold. When it stops in front of the house, Zephyra and Sebastian step out wearing dark shirts and trousers.

"We received your letter," Sebastian says.

"Where is Aunt Xiomara?" Ariadne asks.

"Council meeting," he says.

"There've been unrelenting attacks all week. Animal sacrifices littering the wilderness. It's madness," Zephyra says. "Her attendance will be expected, or it will draw unwanted attention."

Iona's stomach sinks. "Why did no one inform us? Should we return-"

"No," Sebastian says firmly. "You cannot be diverted by lesser threats. Let the others handle it."

"Your only concern is the Crone," Zephyra agrees.

"Iona?" Phoebe calls. "Ariadne?"

Renewed hope fills Iona when Phoebe emerges from the forest, surrounded by flickering fireflies that dance over the grass.

"She will not see us," Sebastian says.

Iona goes to ask why but Zephyra silences her with a firm shake of her head.

"No one can know," Zephyra reminds her. "We must conceal ourselves or we may lose the element of surprise. I recommend you do the same, but the choice is yours."

When Phoebe approaches, Sebastian and Zephyra step away in the direction of the carriage and converse amongst themselves in quiet whispers.

"You may warn her if you wish," Sebastian calls over his shoulder. "Make it quick, and do not trust your eyes."

As they walk away, Iona swears she can hear Sebastian murmuring to his mother. "Is she ready for this sort of confrontation? We'll need to keep an eye-"

"What a lovely surprise!" Phoebe pushes a strand of her chestnut hair behind her ear when she reaches them.

Forcing her insecurities down, Iona goes to curtsy, until she notices dark red stains on Phoebe's white apron, and her fingertips.

"Are you hurt?" Iona asks, reaching for her hands.

Phoebe looks down at them, momentarily alarmed, until she laughs. "Oh! No, I was only picking blackberries. I hardly made it back before nightfall. Would you like one?"

She lifts her small wicker basket, but her welcoming smile turns to a frown when she marks their grim expressions.

"Is anything the matter?" she asks.

"I regret not having seen you at the party," Iona says. "Did she tell you why it was cancelled?"

Phoebe gives her an odd look, than says, "Crescentia? Of course, she told me everything. Erik is a cad, but that's a surprise to no one but her."

Iona lets out a sigh of relief, then gestures to the house. "We must speak in private immediately. You may be in grave danger."

They convene in the drawing room and Iona takes it upon herself to explain everything, because Ariadne is nearly bursting at the seams with impatient agitation. The letter they'd sent still sits on a table in the foyer, unopened.

"Samaira's vision warned of an attack tonight. You must stay inside," Iona says. "Where is the rest of your family?"

"My mother and grandmother left for London today to attend the council meeting." Phoebe's face pales when she glances at a clock on the mantelpiece. "But Father went into town this morning. Come to think of it, he should have returned by now."

Before they can stop her, Phoebe runs to the foyer, takes her broom from its hook, and does not even close the front door behind her when she hurtles into the night sky in the direction of town.

"Phoebe, wait!" Iona conjures wings and takes to the sky after her.

Ariadne does the same, while Sebastian and Zephyra opt to take their carriage. Aster and Wisp jump in with them.

*Don't stop her.* Ariadne takes Iona's hand. *She will lead us to the malefician.*

*We cannot use her as bait!* Iona protests. "Phoebe, please! We must be cautious!"

"I cannot see him, I…" Phoebe's grip on her broom slackens, her torso slumping forward until she falls right off and plummets towards the ground.

Iona yelps, diving down to catch Phoebe before she falls, but a sudden comber of fatigue hits her, impossible to withstand.

"Iona?" Ariadne shakes her shoulder with one hand.

Jerking awake, she sits upright and looks around in a panic. "Phoebe-"

"I'm here," she says and though she looks frightened out of her wits, she is otherwise unharmed.

Ariadne's protective shield encapsulates them where they lay in the grass.

"Please, we must go," Phoebe begs. "I must find my father."

"Give her a moment," Ariadne snaps. In a softer voice, she asks, "Are you alright?"

"Yes… Yes, I'm fine." Iona rubs her forehead.

Ariadne helps her stand, keeping an arm around her waist to steady her.

"Keep close to me," Ariadne says, "or you'll fall asleep again."

Phoebe reluctantly obeys as they press on, but it's clear she wishes she could run at full speed into town. As they approach, the quiet is unsettling. All around them is deathly still. There are squirrels and birds littering the ground, but not dead. They are all fast asleep.

"Oh dear," Phoebe points ahead of them.

A girl and her mother lie side by side in the grass on what must have been a morning stroll before they'd collapsed in a heap.

"How long have they been there?" Ariadne murmurs.

They are soon given an indication when they reach Main Street and are accosted by a rancid smell that has them fighting not to gag. The dark street is littered with sleeping humans, all lying in their own waste. By the looks of them, they'd been like this for at least a day, more likely two or three.

"They will die of thirst," Iona whispers. "We must help them."

"We will," Ariadne says. "Phoebe, do you see your father among them?"

"No," Phoebe whispers, her apron pressed against her mouth and nose. "Have you ever heard of anything like this?"

"My grandmother told me powerful maleficians could do this sort of thing but… this is dreadful," Ariadne says. *Do you see Sebastian or Aunt Zephyra? They may be unable to enter town without my help.*

Iona shakes her head, then conjures globules of water and sends them floating through the air to the humans' mouths to keep them alive for a little while longer.

*She's leeching their life force.* Iona looks to Ariadne for confirmation, and she nods solemnly.

"Father!" Phoebe calls.

The ground quakes and Ariadne grabs Iona's arm to pull her closer. A few seconds later, the rumble fades until it is silent again.

"Be quiet!" Ariadne hisses. "Your father won't hear you if he's asleep."

"But how are we meant to find him?" Phoebe asks.

"If he only went into town this morning, it's possible he might be on the outskirts," Iona realizes. "He'd have fainted before he could get very close."

"Right," Phoebe says, a glimmer of hope in her eyes. "Let's go."

They run as fast as they can to the edge of town with Phoebe leading the way.

*The carriage.* Ariadne nearly points but catches herself.

In the distance, the Zerynthos' carriage sits idle, the horses' heads hanging low in sleep. As they approach, it becomes clear that Phoebe still cannot see it despite walking right by the carriage, nearly running straight into it.

"Wait," Ariadne says. "I need to catch my breath."

While in proximity of Ariadne's protective magic, Sebastian and Zephyra slowly awaken where they sit slumped on the bench.

"Oh, hang it all," Zephyra grumbles. "How long were we asleep?"

When Ariadne goes to answer, Sebastian puts up a hand.

"Don't speak," he says. "She still cannot see us, can she?"

"We mustn't linger," Phoebe says. "Please, we must keep going."

"Good," he says. "We will follow."

"He must be close." Iona takes Ariadne's hand again.

They run, with Zephyra and Sebastian following silently, until Iona gets a stitch in her side and starts to fall behind.

"Where is he?" Phoebe's lip trembles.

The ground quakes again, more violently this time, and they nearly fall to their knees.

"Ugh!" Ariadne cries out.

Iona looks about frantically, then cringes when thousands of worms, springtails, woodlice, centipedes, and all manner of burrowing insects burst up from the soil. They're everywhere, writhing and swarming until the grass has disappeared beneath them.

"Oh god," Phoebe wretches.

"Underground," Ariadne says, just as Iona considers the same possibility.

"Do you know of any tunnels beneath the city? Or perhaps caves?" Iona asks, then screeches and shakes her foot to dislodge a centipede trying to crawl up her leg.

"…Yes. Yes!" Phoebe says with sudden enthusiasm. "When they escaped Salem, my ancestors took shelter within caves in the woods until it was safe."

"Take us there," Ariadne says, then uses the staff to repel the insects with a gust of wind and creates a walkway bordered by thin lines of fire in the direction of the forest.

They sprint through the trees, the earth gently quaking all the while, until they reach the caves, which at first appear to be a meager pile of gray rocks. Upon further inspection, they find a newly made tunnel going deep within the earth. Ariadne hesitates.

"Come!" Phoebe yells, taking Ariadne's wrist and pulling her forward.

"Hey!" Iona yells.

Phoebe lets her go, her eyes widening at Iona's shout.

"Do not haul her about like that," Iona says, taking Ariadne's hand. "Are you-"

"We must press on." Ariadne's voice breaks at the sight of the cramped, dark tunnel.

"Keep hold of my hand," Iona whispers.

"You should leave Phoebe behind," Sebastian whispers.

Iona looks over her shoulder at him.

"She is too emotionally involved," he says. "She will only hinder us or give in to recklessness."

Iona slowly shakes her head no. Phoebe would never forgive them, especially if something awful happens to her father. They have no right to force her to stay behind. Sebastian frowns with disapproval but does not protest further.

Phoebe walks ahead as far as she dares without leaving the protective barrier of Ariadne's magic. The labradorite stone lights their way through the humid darkness that grows colder with every step.

"Phoebe!" a male voice calls.

Phoebe gasps as they all stop short and listen.

"Phoebe!" the voice screams.

"Father!" She bolts down the tunnel, no longer caring if she stays within the protective shield.

"Wait!" Iona calls.

They sprint after her, and Iona even tries to cast rope around her waist to pull her back, but she disappears into the darkness.

"It may be a trick!" Iona yells after her.

They reach a fork in the tunnel and strain their ears to listen for any footsteps splashing in the wet dirt, but there is naught but eerie silence. Iona conjures another ball of light, holding it up to further illuminate their path.

"What a bloody shambles," Iona mutters, then glances apologetically at Sebastian. "Perhaps we should have left her behind."

"That much is clear," Zephyra says. "You mustn't let your tender heart obscure your judgement, or-"

The tunnel quakes terribly, the unstable dirt shifting as it collapses. Ariadne screams, huddling closer to Iona.

"A cave in!" Sebastian yells. "Run!"

A barrage of dirt and stones tumble down behind them, getting closer and closer. They try casting spells to slow the collapse, but the earth doesn't listen to their pleas.

A boulder drops directly on top of Sebastian, hitting him hard on his back and knocking the wind from his lungs. He falls to his knees, crying out in pain.

"Gíinos!" Iona incants, and the earth just barely obeys, but the force of the malefician's spell is nearly incapacitating.

She holds fast as Ariadne runs back for Sebastian, dragging him up and pulling him along, screaming as dirt rains down upon them and nearly buries them alive. Then Zephyra goes to help too, each of them taking an arm and dragging Sebastian away, just as Iona's counter spell breaks and the deluge of earth continues its path towards them.

Ariadne is near to hyperventilating by the time the quaking ceases and they make it to yet another fork in the tunnel. Sebastian gathers himself while his mother fusses over him, searching for any wounds that she can heal.

"Shhh..." Iona rubs Ariadne's back and gives her space to breathe. "Think of the sun. Of the mountains in Nepal, and the cold air and wind against your face. Think of... the ocean at sunset, of swimming in the open water, of the sky, the clouds, the stars."

Ariadne lets out a shuddering sigh, her entire body trembling violently while she leans forward with her hands braced against her knees.

"No turning back now..." Sebastian mutters, kicking a rock in frustration, until a look of realization crosses his face. "We should have located Phoebe by now. The sleeping hex hasn't reached this place."

"That's one advantage, at least," Zephyra says.

The tunnel quakes again. Ariadne lets out a guttural scream unlike anything Iona has ever heard, as if she were stretched across a torturer's table while he flays skin from her bones.

"Go!" Zephyra grasps her son's arm and runs down the tunnel to their right.

They follow close behind, dodging rocks and debris, until they reach another fork. Zephyra hesitates, then goes left, and Sebastian follows, but mere seconds before Iona can enter, there is a distinct pull against her back that slows her down and the tunnel's entrance caves in.

"Ariadne!" Zephyra cries, her voice muffled by the dirt. "Iona!"

"We're alright!" Iona calls, then asks Ariadne. "Why did you pull me back?"

"What…" Ariadne shakes her head and cannot say anything more past her panicked gasps.

"We must break through!" Sebastian calls.

They try, placing hands against the dirt and whispering desperate incantations, but the earth does not obey their spells. Mere specks of soil and rock shift the smallest amount.

"It won't budge," Iona relents.

"Don't fret," Zephyra says. "We shall continue on in search for the Kimball girl. You should take the other tunnel and find an exit."

"Very well," Iona says. "Be careful!"

"Of course," Zephyra says. "Keep your wits about you, dear!"

"I cannot take this much longer," Ariadne admits, her entire body shaking.

"We shall survive this," Iona promises. "Take deep breaths."

Ariadne clutches her hand as they traverse the darkness until they reach another fork, and another, until Iona loses all sense of direction.

"Phoebe!" Iona calls.

The ground opens up. They scream at the sudden cold as they're submerged in sludge up to their waists. Ariadne clamors for her staff when it falls out of her hands and sinks into the muck, while Iona's ball of light floats on top.

"I cannot find it," Ariadne's breath comes in panicked pants as she reaches farther into the mud and grasps around blindly.

"Find what?" Iona asks.

"Find… We must find…" Ariadne says, until her brow

furrows.

Iona looks around, but they are alone. "Where are... Where are the others?"

"Who?" Ariadne asks.

"I could have sworn there were others," Iona mutters. "Where've they gone?"

"I don't know," Ariadne frowns, her brow creasing in concentration.

Iona glances about again until she feels suddenly lightheaded and she almost topples over, but the woman manages to catch her.

Iona steps away, touches her forehead, and says, "I feel so strange."

The woman stares, her expression reflecting the confusion Iona feels.

"Who are you?" the woman asks.

"Don't you know me?" Iona asks, unsure herself if she'd ever seen the other woman before.

The woman gazes at her with penetrating, appreciative eyes. "I would certainly remember meeting one so beautiful as you."

Iona flushes. "But you don't?"

"I'm afraid not," the woman says.

"Did you find what you searched for?" Iona asks.

"What do you mean?" the woman asks.

Iona bites her lip. "Um..."

"Not to worry," she says. "We'll make sense of this somehow."

Iona finds comfort in the woman's eyes, in the warmth of her voice, though she knows not why.

"We should find help," Iona decides.

"Should we?" the woman asks.

"If we're lost, perhaps we should."

"Oh... Are we lost?"

Iona thinks hard, then nods slowly. "We are."

"Oh," she says.

"Follow me," Iona says, turning around.

With great effort, she trudges forward in an attempt to reach the ledge and pull herself out of the pit, but she nearly trips over something lodged deep within the mud.

"Be careful," the other voice calls from behind her.

Iona frowns, reaching down in front of her and fishing out a long stick.

"What is this?" Iona asks.

The other woman approaches and reaches for the staff. "I've seen this before…"

They gasp as a burst of magic creates a nearly translucent barrier around them. A rush of awareness fills Iona, until she remembers everything at once.

"Ari," Iona reaches for her with trembling hands.

"That was very… very close," Ariadne says.

They embrace for only a moment, their stuttering, anxiety-ridden breaths filling the empty space, until Iona pulls away. "Phoebe."

"She must be wandering these tunnels with no memory of who she is," Ariadne murmurs.

"Help me," Iona says.

After a bit of struggle, Ariadne lifts her out of the pit, and she reaches down to pull Ariadne up.

"Sebastian and Zephyra may be stuck somewhere, too," Iona says.

"We'll find them," Ariadne assures her.

Keeping her arm round Iona's waist, Ariadne leads them down the tunnels, her breaths coming faster than normal as she fights to control her fear.

"Help!" cries a faint, fearful voice.

Phoebe huddles in the fetal position on the ground cradling the smallest piece of light Iona has ever seen, barely enough to cast a glow on her tear-streaked face.

"Phoebe," Iona sighs with relief. "You mustn't run like that again!"

"It was so dark," Phoebe cries. "But Father… I thought he was…"

Iona whispers soothing words and helps Phoebe onto her feet, brushing dirt from her skirts. But their relief is short-lived when tremors have them running from yet another barrage of dirt and stones until the way they'd come is blocked off. Ariadne sighs angrily.

*How are we meant to find Sebastian and Zephyra now?* Iona asks.

*They're on their own.* Ariadne gives Phoebe a withering glare. "Stay close to me, or I will put you to sleep and carry you over my shoulder."

"Ari," Iona says with disapproval.

"I… I won't stray," Phoebe stutters. "Forgive me."

Conjuring a string of rope, as she'd done with Nenet in the desert, Iona ties their hands together just in case they lose their wits again, or Phoebe gives way to desperation.

"Come," Iona pulls her along, holding onto Ariadne with her other hand.

The tunnel grows increasingly narrow until they are forced to walk in a line.

"I think there's a way out!" Ariadne says. "I see light."

Sure enough, ahead of them is a dead end marked by a thin rectangular outline in the dirt. When their earth spells still have no effect, Ariadne conjures a shovel and digs manically, though the dirt is dense and nearly impenetrable.

On the other side, there is a distinctive scratching sound, followed by a familiar bark.

"Aster!" Ariadne cries with great relief. "We're here! Dig!"

The seconds tick by agonizingly, but eventually, Aster and Wisp's paws break through. On the other side is a dark room with walls covered in names carved in the stone. Ariadne hands the staff to Iona so she can climb out first, offering a hand to Iona, then to Phoebe.

*A mausoleum.* Ariadne lights two lanterns by a set of stairs, their way out. *We are below a cemetery.*

*We cannot dwell on that now.* Iona peers back into the darkness they'd just escaped. *We must find Sebastian and Zephyra.*

Ariadne tenses with displeasure, taking her staff back. *I don't think I can stomach going back in there. It's a miracle we made it out at all.*

"My ancestors are buried here," Phoebe whispers, appalled. "I shan't allow this sacred place to be defiled by dark magic. I can think of nothing more terrible..."

Just like in the Sibylline Mountains, the abundance of magic is a pleasant trickle against Iona's skin, the magic of Salem witches saturating the earth, a bountiful resource to be tapped.

"Help me! Please!" a male voice calls.

"Father!" Phoebe calls back and tries to run.

"No!" Iona jerks her backwards before she can elude them.

"I warned you not to run!" Ariadne yells, her patience at its limit.

"We must help him!" Phoebe sobs. "Please! Please!"

To their collective dismay, she reaches out to try and pull the staff from Ariadne's grip, but the artifact's magic burns her palm, making her cry out in pain.

"But..." Phoebe holds her stinging hand against her chest and stares at Iona in confusion. "You were able to-"

"You had best hold your tongue, as my tolerance for your recklessness has long been spent," Iona snaps.

"Forgive me." Phoebe breaks down in tears, and Iona regrets her lapse of control, only slightly.

*I don't trust her not to do something daft.* Ariadne glances at her.

*We cannot leave her behind.* Iona bites her lip.

*We could. We should. She will only slow us down or be captured like her father,* Ariadne argues. "The longer we wait, the worse it will be."

Reluctantly, Iona nods and Ariadne's staff glows as she incants, "Sove."

Phoebe goes limp, and Ariadne catches her and scoops her up into her arms.

"We cannot save him with her in the way," Ariadne says, hastening her along. "We must focus."

Iona nods, but her guilt is a debilitating malaise. She takes Ariadne's staff for her before ascending the steps. At the entrance of the mausoleum, made of aged white marble with two columns on either side of the black wooden doors, they step out into a massive cemetery with row after row of grey headstones covered in bright green moss. A tenebrous sky hangs over them with thunder booming in the distance, but no rain falls.

Ariadne sets Phoebe down on the steps, careful of her head, but almost picks her right back up when a portion of the ground ahead of them implodes, a few gravestones tumbling down into a newly made pit. Sebastian crawls up from out of the ground with Zephyra not far behind him.

"That was ghastly," Zephyra says, then notices Phoebe. "Is that truly necessary?"

"Yes," Iona and Ariadne say in unison.

"The clouds," Sebastian points up.

Iona follows his gaze and squints.

"They're moving in a circle," she says, tracing the swirl of clouds with her finger.

"A cyclone," Sebastian says.

A flash of bright light makes them flinch, followed swiftly by the deafening crack of thunder. The lightning flashes three times more before the sky darkens again.

"I'd hazard a guess that she is there," Sebastian says.

"Your powers of deduction are a credit to you," Ariadne says sardonically.

"Let's not delay," Zephyra says, "or we will find nothing but the man's corpse."

Ariadne nods, her aunt's words having a sobering effect on

them all. She says, "Stay close to me and my shield will protect us."

"That shan't be possible at all times," Sebastian warns, "The battle will surely separate us."

Ariadne shrugs, pulling Iona closer to her and they begin their descent into the storm. They leave Phoebe in the mausoleum, deciding she will be much safer there and leave Wisp behind to watch over her. Though Iona feels lost without her quiet fox always following behind her, Aster is significantly larger and capable of ripping an enemy to shreds.

Deciding it can't hurt, Iona also conjures a piece of armor with the spell she'd read about in her grimoires. Opting for a breastplate of steel, sturdy enough to protect her but not so heavy that she cannot move, she imbues it with protective spells.

"That may be useful," Zephyra says, "but you should not rely on tangible barriers to protect you."

"What would you suggest then?" Iona asks.

"The best way I've found to kill a malefician is through the use of diversions," Zephyra advises. "While they're distracted, go up behind them and slit their throat, rip out their heart, slice them in half, what have you."

"Oh," Iona says, entirely unsure if she could do anything of the sort. It is one thing to practice with illusions. To cut through flesh and bone, ending a life by your own hand, is an entirely different matter.

"She will aim to distract us, too, until her ritual is complete, but you mustn't let her," Zephyra warns. "Even a second's hesitation could be your undoing. You must remain vigilant and resolute."

Iona nods, though Zephyra's every word only succeeds in tearing down her confidence, despite her good intentions. They venture deeper into the cemetery as humid air picks up and the clouds above them move faster still, until they have to fight against wind.

A wall of torrential rain advances towards them, the veil of impenetrable water overtaking them faster than Iona thought possible, drenching their clothes within seconds and obstructing their vision. The grass turns to mud beneath their feet until they reach floodwaters rushing swiftly across their boots.

A bloodcurdling screech fractures the silence, creating quakes so violent, they are brought to their knees in the shallow water. Ariadne's shield mutes the noise only partially and Iona covers her ears with her hands, cringing at the awful vibrations accosting her eardrums.

A firm hand grips her shoulder, and the clamor stops. When she looks, Sebastian motions with his other hand to calm herself, and Iona realizes then that he's removed her ability to hear, just as Ariadne had done in the siren pool.

Sebastian points to his eyes, then to their surroundings and Iona nods her understanding. No longer able to hear any threats that may arise, they will be considerably more vulnerable, but there's no recourse.

She scans the tombstones for any movement, until something catches her eye and makes her tense, but when she draws her eyes back, there's nothing but rows of stone partially submerged in black water.

Until she does spot something bobbing in the water, floating right past her, and she screams and clings to Ariadne's arm. A disembodied leg, the rotting skin grey and covered in maggots, drifts along a slow current that flows deeper into the rows of tombstones.

*That's revolting.* Ariadne puts a hand over her mouth.

Bubbles ripple over each grave as pieces of human flesh and bone float up to the surface. The pungent stench of putrefaction fills the blustering air.

Sebastian points to the accreting carnage, denoting the passage of the remains, and beckons them to follow him deeper into the water. Iona truly wishes to do the exact opposite, but she steels herself and holds her breath, stray strands of hair slipping out of her bun and whipping at her cheeks.

Sebastian sinks to his waist in a sudden drop off, then manages to climb back onto solid ground. Ahead of them, the disembodied limbs and bones sink into the abyss and do not resurface.

Iona looks to Zephyra, who doesn't seem sure of what to do next, so Iona looks to Ariadne instead.

*Should we-*

An explosion of turbid water erupts, propelling mud, grass, and rock everywhere. It's only Ariadne's arm around her waist that keeps Iona from tumbling through the air, while Aster bites the tail of Ariadne's coat, the fabric straining against his weight. The staff becomes an anchor in the earth that Ariadne clings to, while Iona reaches out a free hand to Sebastian and Zephyra, before they're swept away into the squall.

Within the newly made chasm, Iona can make out the

malefician hunched over a man. When she squints hard enough, she identifies Phoebe's father, William, chained to the ground but still alive. His face is contorted in pain as he screams, blood dripping from his ears, and his horror-stricken eyes searching everywhere for some means of escape.

The Crone gestures wildly, the wind following her every movement, as she conducts her ritual. Despite the blustering air, the symbols drawn in the dirt remain undisturbed and burn Iona's eyes, compelling her to look away.

For a moment she thinks of hurling a boulder or a massive slab of metal at the malefician, bringing down a lightning strike, or creating a wave to flood the chasm, but the risk of hurting William is too great.

Ariadne could make a portal, drop him right next to them, but then the malefician could slip through, too, and attack. She could conjure a blade, many blades, and send them flying through the air, but the Crone can heal so quickly that it might not make a difference. There is no element of surprise, no upper hand that Iona can determine. Their only way forward is to attack head-on. Iona's mind races, trying to think of every possible angle, spell, attack in her arsenal.

The Crone stops mid-gesture, her hooded face tilting up to stare directly at them. Faster than Iona thought possible, she launches an inferno of white fire their way. It doesn't penetrate the shield, but Ariadne flinches, her expression betraying her doubt in its continued integrity. Panicking, Iona searches for Sebastian and Zephyra for guidance, but they are no longer behind her.

They leap into the chasm, converging on the malefician at once. Zephyra attacks in front, dodging the malefician's spells, while Sebastian advances from behind and severs one of the malefician's arms clean off. Iona watches in horror as the malefician grows the arm back in mere seconds, staving off their attacks with ease and tossing Sebastian away as if she were waving off a fly. He hits the chasm's rocky wall and crumples in a heap, dazed but still alive.

Ariadne creates a portal down to the pit and steps through and holds out a hand for Iona to follow, but the malefician tackles her to the ground. Iona screams, and tries to jump across, but the portal closes too soon.

All at once, without Ariadne's magic to protect her, the wind and freezing rain pelts her, making her teeth chatter. Aster howls and gallops into the fray, transforming by the time he reaches the bottom, his teeth jagged and claws sharp.

Iona can just barely see Ariadne in the distance wrestling with the malefician, who makes a vigorous attempt at trying to take the staff away, but Zephyra pulls her off and pierces her ribs with a dagger, pulls it out and plunges it back in again, before the malefician bucks her off, only to be mauled by Aster, his teeth snapping and ripping at the Crone's arms, trying to get to her face.

Iona slides down into the pit and nearly falls on her face as she traverses the jagged rocks and uneven ground, finally making it to the bottom with a splash. The rain pools up to their calves, making it difficult to move swiftly.

The malefician slowly pulls the dagger from her side and buries it in Aster's chest, making him cower and convulse in terrible pain. Iona runs to his aid, casting a healing spell before he can lose too much blood.

Enraged, Ariadne jumps up and plunges a conjured steel sword directly into the Crone's stomach, twisting the blade and shifting it up towards the heart, but still the malefician won't succumb. Instead, she touches the sword and turns it to molten metal.

Ariadne cries out and pulls her hand away, just as the Crone strikes the back of her hand across Ariadne's cheek, throwing her backwards into the murky water, pervaded with disembodied pieces of rotting flesh.

Iona runs to her, reaching out to grasp her arm and heal her burns, but Ariadne throws out her unmarred hand, sending a gust of wind that tosses Iona back. Sebastian intervenes, throwing fire to keep the Crone at bay while he helps Ariadne to her feet again.

Iona hesitates, still wishing to help, but-

*Stay back!* Ariadne's thought is a resounding command that makes Iona flinch, both from the force of it, and the fear disseminating from Ariadne to her. Fear for her safety, her lack of training, her vulnerability.

It's enough to deter Iona entirely. She skirts around the fight, running instead to Phoebe's father where he lies prone. She kneels beside him to remove his chains and take him to safety while the malefician is preoccupied. He looks up at her with hope, struggling in earnest but unable to break free. He is completely covered in awful cuts and bruises, one of his eyes so very swollen he cannot possibly see with it.

She casts a spell to take his pain away, the same spell that

Jacira had cast on herself in Brazil, and Iona confirms its effectiveness by the pure relief on the man's face.

Then she attempts to cut through the metal, or make the chains disappear, but magic has no effect. Hesitantly, she grasps the fetters to see if she can carry him away, but the metal burns like acid and creates painful blisters on the skin of her palms.

Crying out, she wrenches her hands away and while the pain travels up her arms and into her chest, the malefician comes up behind her, grabs her by the hair, and pulls her flush against her chest.

Iona twists and turns, bucks and kicks, tries to conjure wings to fly away, but they're pinned down against her back.

The Crone wrenches Iona's head back and screams a spell directly in her ear, and though she cannot hear it, she can feel every decibel shredding through her brain, the vibrations radiating in her very bones, pulsing through her skull, until she goes limp.

Her only thought is a reckless one as she uses the remnants of her strength to cast a mirror spell on the Crone, so she might feel her pain with her.

The malefician cringes away, letting her fall as she endures her agony. Iona can barely lift her head, but a small, gloating smile reaches her lips. When she can no longer hold herself up, she sinks beneath the shallow water just barely high enough to submerge her.

Her mind loses its lucidity, her vision going black, her consciousness fading like a gentle wave slipping back into the sea. She just barely perceives being flung through the air and into someone's arms. The soft caress of fingers are unmistakably Ariadne's, pressing against her forehead, cupping her cheek, rocking them back and forth. Ever so slowly, the light of a fire spell fills her vision again, and a moment later she's able to comprehend what she sees.

Sebastian and Zephyra continue the fight, with Aster swiping his claws and snapping his teeth, but it's no use. The Crone is hunched over Phoebe's father, who is already dead and disemboweled.

She rips out his lungs, holding the dripping organs covetously against her chest, then dumps his body into the mud, as if it were comparatively worthless.

Iona sheds a tear as a portal emerges, there and gone in seconds as the Crone disappears without a trace, before Sebastian or Zephyra can pursue her.

Feeling comes back to Iona's limbs, which gives way to pain. She cries out and Ariadne holds her closer, stroking her cheek and keeping her still as she continues healing her. Then Ariadne must have renewed their sense of hearing because Iona is suddenly accosted by Ariadne's sobs and Sebastian's bellowing voice.

"We had her!" he yells. "We had her, and you let her go! You imbecile!"

"Sebastian, darling," Zephyra says in a placating tone.

"I will not fight alongside these amateurs again! I care not what Aunt Xiomara says. I won't do it!" Sebastian screams.

"Forgive me," Iona rasps.

"Why did you go for the father, when the malefician was right there! Did you not think... We could have ended this and now others will die!" Sebastian yells, pacing erratically through the sludge. "I cannot-"

"No!"

Phoebe's cry is a death knell that silences any venom Sebastian may have spewed.

"How..." Ariadne glances at her staff.

If it had not been her that freed Phoebe from sleep, it must have been the Crone. A final cruelty.

"Father," Phoebe whimpers as she jumps down into the pit.

"Don't touch the chains!" Iona warns.

Phoebe had been about to, but she holds back, hovering over her father's broken body as she's racked with the most awful sobs, pressing her hands to her broken heart.

"I did not..." Phoebe gasps. "I did not even get to say goodbye."

Zephyra's head hangs low as she approaches, placing a hand on Phoebe's shoulder, before pointing her wand and incanting "Lethe."

Ariadne weeps. "Must you-"

"She cannot know we were here," Zephyra reminds her. "All she will remember is the attack, wandering the tunnels, and waking to find her father's body."

Phoebe collapses and Zephyra props her head up above the floodwater, shedding tears of her own, which she wipes away as she fights to regain her composure.

"We nearly succeeded," Zephyra says, with a small sigh. "But we cannot afford to give into despair."

Sebastian's frown persists, but he does not continue his tirade. He only glares at Iona, hostility laid bare in his red eyes.

# 23 - Iona

"Iona goes nowhere without me." Ariadne's voice is a low, menacing, absolute promise.

She squares off with Sebastian in the atrium of the Villa Mitriora, just barely making it through the door before they are at each other's throats again.

"We had a fleeting window of opportunity, with the Crone distracted by Iona's pain, but you were too lost in hysterics!" Sebastian yells. "How are we meant to succeed when you so blatantly prioritize her over us?"

"She nearly died!" Ariadne yells back. "What was I meant to do?"

"Kill the Crone!" Sebastian screams, a vein in his forehead bulging from the force of his words. "For the greater good-"

"I would rather die a thousand deaths than to let you lot gallivant across the world using Iona as some sort of expendable weapon! It is out of the question!" Ariadne spits.

"Then perhaps you should fight alongside us instead, with that staff of yours," Zephyra suggests. "Though not equal to the pendant, it did prove surprisingly useful."

"Yes. Then Iona could stay here and... knit. Or garden with your father. Perhaps those tasks would better suit her prim sensibilities," Sebastian says acerbically.

Ariadne glances at Iona, a trace of doubt in her eyes, but she says, "Hecate entrusted this quest to Iona, not I."

"And due to her misjudgment, another innocent man is dead, and the Crone is one step closer to committing whatever horrors she plans to wreak on our world. There is a higher purpose at play here. More significant than you, or me, and certainly her." Sebastian gestures angrily at Iona.

"Sebastian!" Zephyra snaps. "Show some compassion for pity's sake! She was well intentioned."

"I..." Iona clears her throat, not bothering to wipe away her tears. "I thought I could save him. That's all I wanted..."

Sebastian tries to approach her, but Ariadne steps in his way. He glares at her, then peers over her shoulder.

"Our only goal," Sebastian says, slowing his speech to a condescending pace, "is to kill the malefician. All else is secondary. The longer that witch survives, the more lives she will take, and that blood shall be on your hands."

"You had best stand down now, Sebastian," Ariadne grits out, their foreheads almost touching as she takes a step closer and stares him down. Aster snarls at her side.

"Cease this foolishness!" Zephyra says. "We shall not resort to infighting. It won't bring that man back to life."

"Hecate wanted you, not her," Sebastian says to Ariadne. "These are the consequences of your cowardice."

Ariadne lunges for him, and Iona reaches out to hold her back, but instead catches her as she falters, fatigue near to overtaking her. She leans against Iona, blinking rapidly as she fights to maintain consciousness, while Sebastian watches on with something bordering on apathy. Ariadne's cheeks color with embarrassment.

"You should rest and replenish your magic," Aunt Zephyra advises. "It's a wonder you're still standing after healing Iona from the brink of death."

Shrugging Iona's hands away, Ariadne uses what remains of her strength to storm off, clenching and unclenching her fist as she goes. Iona follows after her, glad to put as much distance between her and Sebastian as possible. She dearly misses the time when the man hardly spoke.

"Ari," Iona says.

Ariadne's footsteps slow, until she stops altogether. "I do not know what to say to you, Iona. I need time…"

Silent tears drip down Iona's cheeks as she turns away, but Ariadne grabs her arm to hold her back. Confusion fills her as she regards Ariadne warily.

"I…" She trails off, her voice thick with anguish.

"Do you wish to be alone?" Iona asks.

She shakes her head. "I don't know."

Iona pulls her arm from Ariadne's grip and stands there, observing the conflicting emotions in her tormented gaze.

"I could feel you," Ariadne mouths. "I thought…"

Iona's heart sinks. "Oh… I am so dreadfully sorry, I-"

"I've felt it twice now. Twice within a year," Ariadne whispers.

Iona stares up at her, at a loss for words.

"Am I truly all that stands between you and Death?" Ariadne asks, her voice but a whisper.

Shame settles in Iona's gut, taking all her words, making them seem meaningless and hollow. Ariadne steps away, her head hung low, and Iona lets her go.

Any faith placed in her is broken, eradicated by one fatal lapse of judgement. She should have ignored Ariadne's attempt to keep her from the fray. She should have used all she's learned these past months and proven herself capable of wrath when the situation demands it of her.

The more she dwells on it, the more she decides it is not one lapse, but many. She's failed again and again to be strong the way others needed her to be. Her fear rules her, weakens her, and she doesn't know how to overcome it.

"Psst!"

She startles, whirling to face Moira where she leans against the wall, observing her with a small, humorless smile.

"Let us take a short trip," Moira whispers.

"A trip?" Iona wipes away her tears with the back of her hand.

"Some air would do you good, I'd wager." Moira looks her up and down.

"Ariadne will not wish to leave," Iona says.

"Good. I did not invite your guard dog." Moira brushes her dark hair over her shoulder.

"But where-"

Moira puts up a finger to silence her, then crooks it. Iona hesitates, glancing in the direction Ariadne had gone. Part of her wishes to reach out through the bond, but she can hardly stomach her own grief without opening her soul to another's. She looks down at Wisp, who reflects her doubt.

"Fine. Stay here and wallow in self-pity," Moira says, walking away.

"Wait!" Iona calls.

"I wait for no one, dearest," Moira says.

Sighing with frustration, Iona gathers Wisp in her arms and holds her close as she follows Moira outside where the red carriage awaits, drawn by pristine white horses.

"Have you yet been to Denmark?" Moira asks, once they've taken their seats and the carriage jerks forward.

"No," Iona says.

"Rold Forest is quite beautiful, though the trolls can prove irksome at times." Moira wrinkles her nose at the thought. "We could venture there upon our return, if you'd like. You go weak at the knees for forests, I hear."

Iona flushes. "I have an appreciation for nature."

"Hmm..." Moira hums with disinterest. "I'm partial to cities myself."

"I imagine one so fond of attention would gravitate towards populous regions," Iona murmurs.

Moira chuckles. "Do not pretend to be above such things. You lavished in the covens' sycophancy on the solstice, far better than I would have thought. I was admittedly impressed."

"If I thought so lowly of every person I met, I would be very often surprised by their achievements," Iona says bitterly.

"On the contrary, my expectations are permanently high," Moira says. "Your surpassing them is… a capricious feat."

Iona narrows her eyes. "Meaning?"

"You have much to learn," Moira says, her gift in condescension seeming to be a familial trait, "but when you allow yourself to thrive without contrition, you are indeed a wonder to behold."

With that, Moira swings open the carriage door and steps out. Iona follows and when the frigid ocean air fills her lungs, she nearly breaks down again from an overwhelming bout of melancholic nostalgia, but Moira does not give her much chance to take in the view off the cliffside. She walks with purpose towards a tiny village of only twenty houses.

"Why are we here?" Iona asks.

"There was an attack just this morning. Yet another leeching spell," Moira says, tapping the tip of her hematite wand against her chin.

"There is a malefician nearby?" Iona gapes at her. "Why on earth did you take me… I should not be here. I will only make matters worse."

"If you intend to pester me with your self-flagellation, you may wait in the carriage until I'm through." Moira cuts her a glare.

Iona opens her mouth, then shuts it and stews in her indignation.

"Don't fret," Moira says, "This one is only a baby."

"How do you know?" Iona asks.

"Meydana çıkarmak," Moira incants.

Traces of blue and black maleficium appear in the air around them, though only in thin, vaporous streams.

"There would be more if the malefician were stronger," Moira says. "My guess is they will celebrate tonight under the stars."

"Is that a common practice?" Iona asks.

"It may as well be a tradition for these wretches," Moira says. "The stolen magic elicits a sense of ecstasy, a sort of drunkenness, not unlike what we may experience when we harvest magic on ritual days, but significantly more potent. A malefician will give in to that sybaritic frenzy in isolation and perhaps slaughter an animal or two to bathe in their blood. The cover of darkness allows them the freedom to indulge in that sort of depraved hedonism."

"You know a great deal about this," Iona observes.

"The knowledge has been passed down through my family for generations," she says.

She walks away and Iona struggles to keep up with her long strides. They follow the trail of maleficium down the edge of the cliff to the beach.

"I do not wish to be rude," Moira says, "but allow me to handle this. You'd only get in my way, in your current state of mind."

She puts out her arm, forcing Iona to stop short, then continues on with her wand at the ready and goes past a massive grey boulder. Iona flinches at the sound of an explosion that propels sand and rock shards everywhere. There are continued sounds of a scuffle, screams of pain, then an awful gurgling sound that turns Iona's stomach.

"There," Moira says. "It is safe now! You may approach."

Iona remains frozen still, her breath stuttering in her lungs, until Moira pokes her head from around the edge of the boulder.

"Oh, for goodness sake," Moira chuckles. "All is well, I swear it."

Forcing her feet to move, Iona approaches her, noting a drop of blood on Moira's chin that she hadn't bothered to wipe away. Impatience has Moira reaching out to grasp her wrist and drag her forward through the shifting sand to where a small pyre has been erected. A middle-aged witch with mousy brown hair is chained to the ground, her hands bound behind her back, and her unseeing eyes blank.

"See? Only a novice. Not like the Crone... I don't envy you that fight," Moira says, then gestures at the woman. "Harmless as a lamb. I took her eyes, her wand, and her tongue."

Iona cringes when she spots the severed tongue discarded in the sand within a pool of dark blood, until a wave pulls it out to sea.

"Now," Moira says, "let's see about you gaining some much-needed confidence."

"What do you mean?" Iona asks, truly regretting following

Moira now.

"Kill her," she says.

"What?" Iona stumbles back.

The malefician hears this and struggles in earnest against her restraints, crying out in fear but unable to articulate much more than wails.

"Kill her," Moira points at the woman. "The first is always the most difficult, but I've made it so easy for you. With it over and done with, you shall find it easier in time until you don't think of it at all."

"No!" Iona exclaims. "Are you mad?"

"Iona…" Moira rubs her forehead in frustration. "This woman stole magic from her own mother, a decrepit old woman unable to care for herself, then slit her mother's throat and watched her drown in her own blood. She has nothing to offer this world but pain and suffering."

"I cannot do it," Iona insists.

"Take a moment to consider it."

"…No."

"Why?"

"It would violate my every closely held belief in…" Iona struggles to articulate all her mother once taught her, "compassion… decency… mercy…"

Moira stomps through the sand, leaning down until their faces are far too close. "If you are too weak even to do this, I doubt you will be much use to anyone. Or shall I go fetch Ariadne to do it for you?"

"Please take me home." Iona's lip trembles. "I want to go home."

"Where is that, exactly?" Moira asks.

Iona stares up at her, blinking away tears. "Is… Is there no way to reform her? Or imprison her? How much of it was her, or the poison of maleficium corrupting her mind?"

Moira rolls her eyes and steps away. "Oh, my word, Iona. You're making this far more complicated than it need be."

She approaches the malefician and snaps her fingers to get Iona's attention.

"Look," Moira says, then flicks the woman's ear.

A spike of ice goes clean through her skull, through one ear and out the other end. Blood drips off the tip of the spike as the woman goes rigid, her terror-filled eyes bugging out of her head. Iona screams, putting her hands over her mouth, and watches in horror as the woman spasms, then falls to the sand, dead.

"That's all it is," Moira says.

Iona trembles, then doubles over and vomits everything in her stomach, until there is nothing left, but her body still heaves.

"There, there…" Moira awkwardly rubs her back.

Iona flinches away, sputtering, "You're depraved."

Moira's red eyes are hard and unrepentant. "Imagine, if Ariadne hadn't been so obstinate, if she had sent a letter to her mother, or to mine, informing them of your troubles at college, Elise would have been dead within a day. Instead, you suffered for months, not knowing what to do or who to attack. It must have been torturous for you both. So unnecessary. That is what these townsfolk would suffer if left alone to fight a witch infinitely more powerful than they, and who would only grow more impossible to kill with every passing second. Just today, an entire town was nearly decimated, wasting away in a deathlike sleep, or so Sebastian tells me. If you'd have managed to kill the Crone in the desert, they would have been spared those unspeakable horrors. The memories of their plight were wiped away from those humans' minds, but even so, the trauma will still sit in their bodies for years to come. So, tell me, what is the greater mercy?"

"You mutilated her." Iona can barely speak the words aloud. "I see no mercy in this."

"Neither do I."

A myriad of conflicting emotions pass over her at the sight of Ariadne leaning against the side of the cliff. She wonders how long Ariadne had been there watching. She doesn't meet Iona's incredulous gaze, instead keeping her eyes trained on Moira, frowning with distaste.

"Then you are both fools," Moira shakes her head. "When either of you discovers a way to defeat darkness without bloodshed, I will be glad to hear of it. Until then, you must set aside your misgivings and accept the cost of peace."

She then goes to the base of the pyre were a knapsack is left discarded. Rifling through it, she pulls out a black book covered in symbols branded onto the leather binding, the runes overlapping in an illegible, hideous pattern. She tosses the book into the flames and shields her face when it explodes in a blaze of sparks.

"Reconcile yourself to the great wisdom of our Goddess," Moira says. "Or else these misfortunes will become commonplace. We are already burdened by the sheer multitude of maleficians born every day. If more like the Crone are awakened by our inefficacy, the darkest times of our histories shall be upon us once more. You cannot be weak. You cannot relent. You cannot fail."

Only when the maleficium grimoire turns to ash does Moira leave with her head held high, glancing only briefly at Iona before retracing her steps back up the trail to the waiting carriage. Once she's far enough away, Ariadne turns her eyes to Iona, her gaze softening only slightly.

"How did you know…" Iona swallows hard, her throat raw.

"I saw an image of the beach in your mind and read your thoughts to know it was Denmark." Ariadne glances at her staff and shrugs. "That seems to have been enough. I suppose…"

She trails off when Iona's eyes drift back to the dead woman. She's surprised she has any left to shed, but sure enough, hot tears drip down her cheeks, until her breath comes in ragged gasps.

"Do not look at her," Ariadne says softly.

Iona averts her gaze as strong arms envelop her, and she sinks into Ariadne, needing her warmth more than she ever has.

"Moira is right, you know," Hecate says.

Ariadne's arms tighten around her, but the gesture provides little comfort. Reluctantly, Iona leaves her embrace to find the Goddess draped in black, her golden earrings glinting in the moonlight.

"Perhaps I've misjudged you, Iona," she says as she stoops over the fallen malefician. "Do you not understand the magnitude of our current circumstances?"

"She is trying," Ariadne says, but Hecate silences her with a look.

"You need not be brutal, like Moira, if you do not wish to." Hecate stands and approaches them. "I merely ask that you do what must be done to protect the lives of innocents. How you accomplish that is your own to determine, but these subsequent failures will only cost us in the end. We do not have the luxury of time."

"I will prevail," Iona says. "I will… I must."

"Indeed, you must." Hecate's smile does not reach her red eyes. "And with that assurance, go and rest my daughters."

Her black skirts drift over the dead malefician's body and it disappears in the blink of an eye. The Goddess nearly disappears as well, but Ariadne takes bold steps towards her before Iona can think to hold her back.

"Why must all this fall on Iona's shoulders?" Ariadne asks. "Do you not possess the magic to intervene? Surely the Crone does not have greater power than that of a Goddess of magic."

Hecate's form shimmers in a partial state of incorporeality, but Ariadne's words stop short her exit. She gives Ariadne the oddest of looks that slowly turns to resignation.

"Follow me," Hecate finally says, and with a wave of her hand, a portal appears.

Hecate lifts her gilded torch to light the way through an abyss so dense with shadow, the blackness is almost tangible. Every step is more strenuous than the last, as if their weight is doubled within these hidden depths of the Underworld. Perhaps gravity works differently in this realm. Perhaps gravity does not exist here at all.

Iona thinks of Morgan's marsh, and of Merlin's secluded island. She wonders if their heavens are tucked away somewhere here or if they exist on another plane of reality entirely. And what of the many other powerful beings that Crescentia had listed who rule over their own covens?

She decides that the enormity of life, death, and divinity are far too vast for her to worry on then. Not with Ariadne's grip so tight on her arm that she loses circulation. Her short anxious breaths so loud in Iona's ear, she worries her beloved might faint.

"Ah, here we are," Hecate says when they reach the gaping mouth of a cave so massive, the light from her torch shed a scant glow against the outermost edges. "Take care not to fall. The rocks can be a touch slippery."

"What is in there?" Iona whispers.

"Nothing dangerous," Hecate says.

"Not another damned cave," Ariadne murmurs so quietly, Iona strains to hear it.

"It is safer for you in there than out here, I assure you," Hecate says, glancing over their heads with sharp eyes.

"Why?" Ariadne asks warily.

An ominous flapping sound comes from far in the distance. They tense with apprehension.

"There is a nest of harpies nearby," Hecate explains. "They may feel compelled to investigate the light and would not hesitate in flaying you alive for their supper."

Iona shudders at the terrifying image of a harpy in Ariadne's thoughts; half-woman half-bird, with a formidable power over wind.

"Where exactly have you taken us?" Ariadne asks.

"Tartarus," Hecate says, in such a casual tone, it takes Iona a moment to comprehend what she's said.

"As in… the pit of eternal suffering?" Iona asks incredulously.

"Some might agree with your description," Hecate says. "Now come along before your souls acclimate to this place, and you won't be permitted to leave."

That seems enough to inspire Ariadne forward, her grip on Iona's arm tightening even more when they enter the cave. The deeper they descend, the worse their anxiety grows.

"Is it very much farther?" Ariadne asks, her voice an octave higher than normal.

When Hecate gives Ariadne a distasteful look over her shoulder, Iona quickly says, "Forgive me, but was it truly necessary to bring us here?"

"Some things are better seen with one's own eyes," Hecate says.

When a subtle but distinctive gleam of light appears in the distance, Iona mistakes it for an exit and sighs with relief, until they approach the source of the glow. The thinnest of spindly threads are woven in a desultory pattern, without any perceivable rhyme or reason. Iona stops short when the threads become too densely woven to avoid, not wishing to become tangled up in them, but Hecate continues walking, her body going right through the threads as if they aren't there.

"What… is that?" Ariadne asks.

"Come and see," Hecate says, with slight amusement at their unease. "I have someone I'd like you to meet."

Steeling themselves, with barely enough courage between the two of them, they step through the web of threads and reach an immense cavern. The ceiling is nearly imperceptible from below; the walls made of black reflective stone and dripping with cool moisture. Iona identifies the stone as obsidian, the same as Ariadne's wand. The threads are everywhere, looping and twisting around themselves, some taut and others slack. A structured tangle.

"Allow me to introduce Arachne," Hecate says, pointing above her head. "The weaver of fate."

Iona gasps, putting a hand over her mouth, when she sees what Hecate points to. It is a bulbous black spider with long thin legs, not much bigger than a common spider on Earth. The numinous silk pulses with life as it's woven in a new, continuous pattern, Arachne's thin legs manipulating it as she sees fit. She never stops working even to acknowledge their presence.

"But... what of the Moirai?" Ariadne asks. When Iona looks to her in question, she says, "The fates, Clotho, Lachesis, and Atropos."

"They had their time, much of it in fact, but as the fabric of reality tends to do, it shifted into a new age. Immortals are not fixed in time, merely unhindered by it. After all, the Moirai were not always the conduits of fate, in the time before Nyx birthed them," Hecate says.

*I thought an immortal's power would be preserved eternally just as their souls are,* Iona thinks.

*The Titans once held dominium over our world before the Olympians overthrew them,* Ariadne thinks. *Gods are not so permanent as they would have you believe.*

Hecate glares, and Ariadne shrinks beneath her gaze.

"As a Titan myself, I can assure you of our vitality," she says. "The cosmos are not stagnant. On the contrary, even the most steadfast of axioms can change in an instant."

Ariadne stutters, "Apologies, I-"

Hecate ignores her. "Before we were 'overthrown' as you say, there were the primordial Gods and Goddesses, Nyx being among them. Her power persists to this day, regardless of who might reign in Olympus."

"Primordial?" Iona asks, hoping to regain Hecate's attention, finding her blatant animosity for Ariadne unnerving.

"The very first of our kind, the protogenoi. They are their elements personified. Nyx, for example, is not merely a Goddess of Night. She is night. Night is her. There is no separating the two," Hecate says, with a lilt of reverence in her tone. "Now tell me, Iona, do you know the story of Arachne?"

"Not well." Iona keeps her eyes locked on the spider, wary of it jumping on her without warning.

"Arachne was once a human woman. Her gift was weaving, and, in a lapse of judgement, she compared her talent to Athena, Goddess of Wisdom, the very last Olympian anyone should risk angering. Apart from Hera, I suppose." Hecate shrugs. "Athena disguised herself and challenged Arachne to a weaving competition. She wove a tapestry depicting the Gods' infidelities and follies, while Athena wove a tapestry of their triumphs. Arachne's tapestry was a flawless work of art, so perfect that even Athena could not deny it. In her anger, Athena destroyed the tapestry and transformed Arachne into a spider, vowing that Arachne's descendants would be cursed to weave for all eternity."

Iona gulps but has the smallest trace of sympathy knowing there is a soul trapped inside the creature, unable to escape her toil.

"For most, her story ends with her downfall but as you can clearly see, she was destined for more," Hecate says. "When Nyx heard of Arachne's punishment, she took an interest in her. You see, Athena was a tad overzealous in her use of power. She'd also imbued the spider with her wealth of wisdom, though Arachne had no outlet for such a gift on Earth. Rather than letting the spider waste away, Nyx gifted her with immortality and provided her a new eternal task of weaving fate, like the Moirai once did. As the world grows older, populations surge and destinies become increasingly more complex. Arachne uses her talent at weaving to make sense of the threads, that which lead us down our predestined paths, as no one else could. And so, here she is, ever diligent in her work."

Arachne halts, her many eyes regarding the thread upon which she perches, then opens her jaws and severs it with a single bite. She lands on a thread just beneath it, as the thread she cut withers away into dust, its light and life extinguished.

"Oh…" Iona relents the death of the stranger, and wonders idly who it may have been, and why the spider determined that their life was at its end.

Hecate squints, searching the web for a specific thread, then points up to her right. "That is your thread, Iona."

"It is?" She cranes her neck to admire the thin strip of glowing silk. "How strange…"

"It is tied to Ariadne's thread, there." Hecate points to a parallel thread, both of them knotted together. "You've noticed the unrelenting pull of fate connecting you by now, I expect?"

Iona flushes and nods her head. "Yes, we've noticed."

"Quite rare," Hecate says, "Not many find themselves in such an inevitable union arranged by fate. Who can say why she did it? Arachne's wisdom is her own to comprehend."

"I always thought the comet caused it," Iona murmurs, recalling the blue streak of light that graced the sky.

"A comet? Perhaps that was the catalyst. The exorbitant celestial magic would have been all Arachne needed to tie your souls together," Hecate says.

"This... is all that governs life and death, the rise and fall of empires, the thriving or suffering of countless millions of people?" Ariadne asks incredulously. "A spider?"

"As opposed to what?" Hecate tilts her head.

"Anything else!" Ariadne exclaims. "It's no wonder the world is so rife with misery and injustice if fate is dealt out this way."

Taken aback, Iona tries not to internalize Ariadne's description of fate's impact on reality, considering it was also what brought them together. She frowns when she accepts that it is also what perpetually tries to tear them apart and finds herself eyeing the spider with similar resentment.

Hecate shrugs, "The universe is hopelessly flawed, it is true. There were once many more heralds of fate, but all have fallen away over the millennia. Arachne is all that's left, all that's keeping the world in some sort of balance. But think, even if I myself took on the role, you would only lament any hardships you've faced and blame me for them. I suspect any answer you'd receive would only serve to disappoint you, whether Arachne was the weaver, or the Moirai, or any other entity imaginable."

Ariadne turns her eyes down to glower at the floor, overcome by a rush of memory that Iona resists the urge to view, deciding instead to take a step closer to Hecate.

"This is all truly enthralling," Iona says, fighting to keep her voice even, "but what has this got to do with the Crone?"

Hecate points to another thread, no different from any of the others, that intersects with her and Ariadne's own conjoined threads.

"This is the Crone's thread." Then she points to another thread set apart from theirs. "And this is mine. As you can see, our paths do not intersect." She traces the air to show the many intersections between the Crone's thread and theirs. "You two are fated to oppose this enemy, not I."

"And that alone is why you refuse to intervene?" Ariadne asks, appalled.

"Arachne's wisdom is unparalleled, and her determination of the future is inevitable," Hecate says. "Even if I wished to defy fate, it is simply impossible. All will unfold as it was meant to. I shall assist if I can, but I cannot promise anything more." Upon seeing Ariadne's frustration, Hecate's expression softens the smallest amount. "It can prove difficult to accept your total lack of control over your place in the cosmos, but such is the encumbrance of mortality. Even immortals are not exempt from it. If you take issue with that, you may air your grievances to Arachne herself."

Though the spider has eight tiny black eyes, not one even glance in their direction. For a fleeting moment, Iona tries to read Arachne's aura but finds none to detect. Her transformation may have altered her soul as well as her physical form, or perhaps the Goddess of Night was wise enough to shield the aura away to prevent witches like her from predicting fate too accurately.

She must tell Samaira of this revelation, as it greatly alters her understanding of the sapphire ring's power. She wonders if it is connected to Arachne somehow, or perhaps it once showed all manifestations of fate when there were others spinning their patterns too. Perhaps in time the artifact will give Samaira the wisdom to interpret the threads as the spider does, not only the ability to perceive their existence.

Iona grunts at a familiar pull against her back that brings her attention to the spider. Arachne had jumped and lands upon her thread, the weight of her tiny body pulling the line taut. They watch as her spindly legs pull again on their threads and to Iona's horror and fascination, there is another ghostly tug that has her taking a step backwards. Ariadne feels it too and clenches her fists as she watches the spider crawl away.

"I believe that is her way of saying hello," Hecate says with an endearing smile.

"H- Hello," Iona stammers, feeling rather foolish.

Ariadne's frown becomes more pronounced. "And this is your way of telling us we are alone in our quest?"

"I never claimed to be your savior," Hecate says sharply. "Use your power to defeat the evil that plagues you. You've an entire coven at your disposal, and magic enough to overcome this labor."

"Is there no way to divert our fate to better our chances?" Iona asks, then gasps when Arachne flinches, her long black legs flailing as she nearly falls from her perch on one of the higher threads.

Iona holds out her hand to catch her, but Arachne rights herself, shakes off her malady, and continues on as if nothing had happened.

"The Crone is of a similar mind as you, Iona," Hecate says gravely.

"That was her?" Iona's blood turns to ice in her veins, making her shiver.

"I've witnessed Arachne's frailty of late, and it deeply concerns me. Her seizures started after the first of the rituals, when your grandfather was slain. Though the Crone's plan may still be obscured, we can be certain of one thing," Hecate says. "If she manages to impose her will over Arachne, to rewrite fate to her own benefit, then the Crone's wrath shall indeed be an insurmountable reckoning. In this, Moira spoke true. If the Crone is not defeated soon, her power shall exceed your ability to oppose her. Then nothing shall stand in the way of whatever dastardly intent she has for your world, and mine."

# 24 - Iona

"Iona?" Euphemia asks.

"Hmm?" She looks up.

Ariadne, Leonid, and Euphemia all stare at her expectantly. Her eyes return to the cake she'd bitten into. It has strawberry filling, the red pouring out onto her plate like a pool of blood. She sets it down and clears her throat.

Euphemia glances at Ariadne before saying, "I asked how you enjoyed your time in Nepal. Those mountains are so majestic, are they not?"

"Oh, yes. It was… like a painting." Iona forces a smile.

Euphemia smiles back but it doesn't reach her eyes. "Might we take a turn about the gardens before we depart? The freesias are in full bloom."

"That's a splendid idea," Ariadne says, setting her teacup and saucer aside.

Euphemia reaches into an oakwood bassinet to cradle Hugo against her chest. He babbles and laughs, which in turn makes his mother laugh and press kisses upon his rosy cheek.

When they walk through the gardens, a butterfly with copper wings flutters near Hugo's face. He reaches for it, nearly grasping one of its wings, until Euphemia takes his hand and gently scolds him.

Though Iona wishes she could simply live in this moment, all she can think of is Phoebe. She's not sure how she could ever stand to be in the same room with Phoebe again, not after failing to save her father. She almost wishes Zephyra had taken her memory, too, but that would be the greatest cowardice of all. She will live with this guilt for the rest of her life and can only hope that the coming days will not add to its stifling weight on her heart.

"We shall join you in a moment," Ariadne says.

Iona blinks, and notices Euphemia, Leonid, and Hugo leaving the gardens.

Ariadne shifts from one foot to the other, then says, "Perhaps we should return to Nepal instead. We could always-"

"I would like to see the play," Iona says, straining to bring life to her voice.

Ariadne studies her. "You can hardly muster conversation."

"I doubt there will be much talking during the performance," Iona says. "Except by the actors, of course."

Ariadne rolls her eyes. "Alright then."

She walks away but Aster lingers a moment, a soft whine drawing both their eyes to him.

"Aster, come," Ariadne orders.

The wolf obeys, but his head hangs low, his tail tucked between his legs.

"I do not wish to be a nuisance," Iona whispers.

"Did I claim that you were?" Ariadne asks.

"No, but..."

Ariadne storms off, leaving her standing amidst the blossoming garden, her senses overwhelmed by the sickeningly sweet air. After a moment's hesitance, she scoops up Wisp and presses her face into the fox's fur, scratching her cheek as she goes back to the house.

Along the way, she passes by an opened door that leads to an ornate sitting room. A flash of memory overtakes her vision, of Rebekka's lips against Ariadne's neck, her hands roaming brazenly over her restless form, whispering sweet nothings in her ear. Iona cringes, trying to will the memory away, but it takes too long to fade.

Wisp's yelp is what breaks the reverie. In her panic, she'd dropped the poor fox onto the marble floor.

"Oh!" Iona reaches out and inspects her for injuries.

Wisp looks at her with distrust at first, not knowing what she's done to deserve the mistreatment. With her ears pressed down, she lets Iona pet her until she's pacified.

"I'm so terribly sorry!" She kisses Wisp's head.

"What happened?" Ariadne asks as she enters the foyer.

Iona glares up at her. "Why were you thinking of Rebekka?"

Ariadne regards her with confusion. "I was not-"

"Clearly you were." Iona points to the sitting room, the setting of the memory she'd unwillingly observed.

Ariadne opens her mouth, then closes it, her cheeks burning with mortification.

"Keep your sordid thoughts to yourself," Iona says, gently taking Wisp into her arms again and pressing apologetic kisses onto her cheek.

"I wasn't thinking of her," Ariadne insists.

"Perhaps not intentionally," Iona allows. "Regardless, I would prefer not to see that sort of thing, if you don't mind."

Ariadne crosses her arms defensively. "Was it not you who

said thoughts are fleeting whispers?"

"Yours are incessant. I'll go mad from them, I swear to you." Iona's voice breaks.

"Iona," Ariadne calls, but she ignores her and continues on her way to the foyer where Euphemia, Leonid, and Hugo are waiting.

Wordlessly, Ariadne follows and crafts a portal to a London alleyway far from the prying eyes of passersby. They then walk across town, giving Iona the opportunity to admire the city she's heard so much about but never had the opportunity to visit. The clopping of hooves drowns out the many conversations of the bustling crowd as the Londoners go about their business. There is a constant drizzle of rain as they navigate dirty puddles. Twilight falls and the lamplighters climb to the tops of the lanterns to illuminate the growing darkness.

Iona clings to her silence, while Ariadne makes half-hearted conversation with Euphemia about times gone by and old friends who have since wed and had new babies. Leonid is equally silent, but his quietude is altogether natural and intentional, reminding her a bit of Ksenia, when she once sat beside her in their classes day after day.

When they reach the Covent Garden Theatre, she admires its doric portico in front and the people gathered outside in their finest clothes. Euphemia, dressed in a suitably decadent Paris green gown, hurries them into the saloon. Iona welcomes the respite from the cold, putrid wetness of the city streets.

A grand staircase covered in red carpet leads to the theatre seats. Within the crowd populating the saloon, Iona recognizes some of the witches and warlocks she'd met during her ritual. They nod or curtsy at her as she passes, making her feel almost like royalty.

It is there they meet Crescentia and Frankie, who shall sit with them in their box above the auditorium. Frankie whisks Ariadne away to speak with a group of acquaintances across the saloon, while Crescentia takes Iona to a quiet corner to regale her with stories of her and Frankie's romantic exploits. Iona struggles to engage with her but does not wish to take out her frustrations on her friend as she had mistakenly done in Triora.

"Don't be cross if I sleep through the play." Crescentia yawns. "Frankie does not give me a moment's rest anymore."

"So long as you don't snore," Iona giggles.

"No... I talk in my sleep, actually." Crescentia leans her head against her shoulder.

"That's much worse," she grimaces.

"This theatre will burn to the ground..."

Iona startles at the sound of Marina's voice right beside her. When she finally notices Iona's look of dismay, she quickly says, "Not to worry. It shan't happen for six more years."

"Are you certain of this?" Iona asks, a deep melancholy filling her at knowing the theatre's beauty is only fleeting.

"The stars don't lie," Marina says. "They follow fate's design."

"Come, Marina. We mustn't dawdle." Moira comes and takes her sister's hand, then says to Iona, "Enjoy the performance."

She gently guides Marina toward the stairs where they join their parents. Raul takes his daughters upstairs while Xiomara lingers and meets Iona's gaze, giving her a respectful nod before following behind them.

"Shall we find our seats? The show will begin soon," Euphemia says as she approaches Leonid.

"Are you well?" Leonid asks.

Iona looks up at him, finding concern in his usually reserved expression.

"Yes, thank you," she says.

"Iona, you must be a saint to endure this woman's endless prattling on." Frankie sneaks an arm around her waist.

Ariadne shoves him away and takes her place by Iona's side. "I was merely explaining-"

"Ophelia explains the flowers herself in the monologue!" Frankie says with exasperation.

"Not in detail," Ariadne argues.

"I would like to hear," Iona says, an attempt at an olive branch, which does not escape Ariadne's notice. Her expression softens as she begins to speak.

"No, do not ruin the story!" Frankie tries to press a hand over Ariadne's mouth to silence her.

"I've read the play before." Iona giggles when Ariadne ducks away from Frankie's hand and glares at him indignantly.

"Oh," Frankie says. "I should've guessed you'd both be bookish women."

"Frankie can hardly read at all," Ariadne retorts.

"Not so!" Frankie protests. "I'm more partial to Twelfth Night, myself."

"Of course you are," Ariadne chuckles and Frankie tugs on one of her curls, making her cry out and attempt to slap him in the arm, but he only laughs and hides behind Crescentia.

"Come, come!" Euphemia claps her hands to silence them. "We truly must find our seats or we will miss the beginning."

They make their way to the box on the righthand side of the stage just as the two actors playing Bernardo and Francisco walk on to begin the performance of Hamlet. It is a stark, glorious enhancement to see the words brought to life, rather than reading them on the page. Iona had read every Shakespeare play with her mother many times over in their cottage by the sea, and though her imagination is fine-tuned, it could never compare to this.

She finds herself waiting impatiently for act three to see Ophelia's tragic monologue. The actress playing her is sensational, making the complexity of iambic pentameter sound as natural as common speech.

Ophelia runs onto the stage with her bouquet in hand, her hair mussed and dress in tatters, with a mad look in her eye and tears streaming down her flushed cheeks. She gives rosemary and pansies to her brother, for remembrance and thoughts. Fennel and columbines to the Queen.

*For flattery and infidelity*, Ariadne explains.

"There's rue for you," Ophelia says, offering a flower to the usurper King.

*For bitterness,* Ariadne thinks.

"And here's some for me," Ophelia continues. "We may call it herb of grace o' Sundays. You must wear your rue with a difference."

Ophelia holds up a single white flower delicately in her hand, as if it may break.

"There's a daisy. I would give you some violets, but they withered all when my father died." Ophelia weeps and falls to her knees.

*The daisy?* Iona asks.

*Innocence,* Ariadne thinks. *And the violets are faith.*

When the curtain closes, Iona is roused to her feet. She claps as loud as she can muster when Ophelia's actress takes to the stage for her bow.

"What a revelation!" Iona exclaims as they make their way back to the saloon.

"I take it you enjoy theatre, then?" Euphemia grins.

"I love it," Iona sighs dreamily. "Oh… When Hamlet said he loved Ophelia once, but no longer… What a fool he was!"

"Indeed," Leonid says.

"I shall take you to see all of Shakespeare's plays, and others if you'll permit me," Euphemia promises her. "Won't we, darling?"

Leonid smiles at his wife with limitless adoration in his eyes. "Of course."

"Thank you," Iona says. "Truly, I... I am glad for the diversion."

Euphemia's eyes soften as she takes her arm and says, "It is quite easy to fall into despair in dark times, but we mustn't let ourselves."

"There is a pub down the road," Crescentia says. "Might we extend the night there?"

"A splendid idea!" Frankie says.

When they are all in agreement, they roam the dark streets of London with Crescentia and Frankie speaking animatedly, while Euphemia and Leonid watch on in amusement. Set apart from the rest, Iona's elation subsides.

As they gather in the bustling pub and trade in stories, jokes, and barbs, Iona watches, content to listen and laugh. She finds herself filled with immense gratitude at the camaraderie she's found amongst these people, wishing her life could be just this. Simple, joyful, peaceful.

Her greatest comfort in her remote disposition are the soft, soothing circles Ariadne draws with her thumb on the back of her hand, never imposing upon her with thoughts or spoken words, though she is doubtless aware of Iona's insurmountable gloom. It's Ariadne's quiet consolation that fills her with great affection, compelling her to rest her head against Ariadne's shoulder.

When they return to Drakenström Manor late in the night, Euphemia and Leonid swiftly retiring to their room, Iona takes Ariadne's hand, hating the uncertainty she finds in Ariadne's red eyes, and is about to speak when she notices a letter sitting unopened on a table by the door.

A jolt of dread makes Iona gasp and has Ariadne tensing immediately to see what has upset her. They rush to the table, only to find that the letter isn't marked with Samaira's hurried scrawl, though the writing is still familiar. Iona opens it, reading her Uncle Samuel's message with cautious anticipation.

The Lysanders' estate lies hidden away in Döbling, nestled in the hills that border the Vienna Woods. Beyond a collection of lush, overgrown shrubs, the white house sits three stories high with a green roof and many clouded windows. Dragons are carved into the stone of a fountain in the center of the main courtyard, spewing streams of water from their mouths in place of fire.

Opening the wrought iron gate, Ariadne leads the way to the door with a familiarity that Iona can't help noticing. She must have been here countless times before to call on Elise. Iona cannot imagine how odd it must feel to return, nor does she glimpse at her thoughts to see.

Instead, she reaches for Ariadne's hand. They haven't spoken of the malefician attacks, of the unwanted memories, or what should be done about their grim circumstances. Iona fears that to speak of one would open the flood gates for all their disagreements to occur at once.

Last night, Iona had awoken to find herself alone in bed but heard Ariadne's piano through the bond without meaning to. It is becoming increasingly difficult not to slip through, as if they are growing more attuned to one another with time.

Ariadne had practiced her piano all through the night, consumed by learning the third movement of the Beethoven piece Euphemia had sent her. Every time she'd missed a note, she would slam her hands on the keys in frustration, then start again. It's a miracle she did not wake Hugo, but Iona suspects Euphemia cast a spell on his nursery to muffle the sound.

She had watched through Ariadne's eyes, marveling at how one song could have so many notes in such quick succession, until the sun rose and Ariadne had returned to the spare room. She'd seen that Iona was awake, too, but made no excuse for why she'd not slept. Yet another matter left unsaid.

Ariadne raps the bronze doorknocker three times, a thousand memories percolating within her. Iona reaches out to lightly brush her fingers over the dark circles beneath her forlorn eyes, until she closes them and pulls away.

Iona's arm drops to her side, just as Samuel opens the door. Haggard and gray, it's evident he hasn't shaved in days, and his clothes are rumpled. It's an altogether different image of her uncle than she's used to, until he smiles and she's reminded of the man she knew.

"Iona," Samuel smiles. "How glad I am to see you!"

"Samuel," Iona goes to him, throwing her arms around his neck and kissing him on his prickly cheek.

He laughs but it's as if he had forgotten how, the stilted sound making Iona pull away from the embrace and look him over with concern.

"Ariadne, you are most welcome," Samuel says, taking her hand.

"Prof... Mr. Lysander." Ariadne's smile is polite as she curtsies.

"Come, come," Samuel beckons them inside.

He takes them to the sitting room where he serves tea and asks them about their time in Brazil and Nepal. Iona tells him of meeting Jacira, and the peace she'd found in Nepal, then forms a haphazard string of half-truths to explain their presence in Rome. Ariadne deftly affirms each lie with a comment or two but otherwise allows Iona to speak on their behalf.

"Did you know of the Evoras' transgressions?" Iona asks.

"Leona did not often speak of it, but I did know of your grandfather's ambitions of conquest in the New World," Samuel says. "Your mother was always against it, as I'm sure you've guessed. She had no qualms about ruining her family's relationship with mine, only seeing it as a fortunate byproduct of her elopement."

"It seems they have yet to forgive her for it," Iona mutters.

"Oh?" Samuel rests his cup on a nearby table, reaching out to gently pet Wisp on the head where she sits beside him.

Iona recounts her confrontation with Silvano Evora. She hasn't seen or heard from her uncle since that night, not even at the solstice ritual, where she wondered if she might see more of her family, but none of them saw fit to attend. Perhaps they hadn't heard or thought they were unwelcome.

She tries not to take offense, but their continued silence stings each time she remembers it, though lately she hasn't had much time to ruminate on such matters. On second thought, she is relieved not to be inundated with yet more conflict when she has enough to worry about with Ariadne's family.

"Do not take it to heart," Samuel says. "They are the unfortunate ones to be estranged from one so kindhearted as you."

Iona forces a smile, though the compliment is grating when she has never thought less of herself than in the past couple of days. When she winces, bringing a hand to her forehead, he rushes to her side.

"I'm well," she assures him. "I've been having these fleeting aches in my head... But they always pass before long."

Samuel frowns. "Are you-"

"Who is here?" a female voice calls from upstairs.

Samuel grimaces and sets his cup and saucer down. "Pardon

me."

"Is that Mrs. Lysander?" Ariadne asks, her eyes brightening.

"Yes, but… Please wait here a moment," Samuel says before leaving the sitting room.

Ariadne's brow furrows. *She doesn't sound like herself.*

"Violet, darling, Iona and Ariadne are here to visit," Samuel calls up the stairs. "Won't you come down and-"

"Oh…" Violet mumbles.

"You needn't strain yourself," he says in a low voice.

"Nonsense," she says. "Of course, I must greet our guests."

Iona sits up straighter, then jumps to her feet when Samuel reenters the room with a woman on his arm who looks just as weary as he. Her long brown hair is unruly, and she wears a chemise with a blue velvet robe over top of it, as if she'd just gotten out of bed.

"Iona," Violet smiles, "How good it is to finally meet you."

Iona curtsies. "I am very pleased to meet you as well, Aunt Violet."

Samuel keeps hold of his wife's hand. "Would you like a cup of tea?"

"I can manage," she says, pulling out her wand, made of glass, but before she can conjure anything, she smiles, "Ariadne, you rascal. I thought we'd seen the last of you."

Ariadne chuckles nervously, standing and wiping her hands on her skirts. "Apparently not."

"Come here." Violet opens her arms for Ariadne to embrace her. "You may not believe it, stubborn thing that you are, but I am truly glad to see you again."

"Are you well, Mrs. Lysander?" Ariadne asks in a soft voice.

"No, my dear," she answers with a melancholy smile. "I do not see how I could be."

Ariadne's lip trembles. "I am-"

"No," Violet says with fiery conviction. "You will not apologize. Do not even speak the words."

Her eyes widen. "But I only meant-"

"It is my daughter who should repent for her atrocities," Violet says. "She never will, of course."

"Violet," Samuel says.

"It must be said," she insists. "She is my greatest shame."

Violet's eyes glisten as she looks to Iona.

"I should have gone with your mother and father. I was too… selfish. Foolish. It was my choice to stay behind, and now…" Her face creases with shame. "They offered to take us with them, and we should have gone, should have put an ocean between us and them, your grandparents. Then Elise may have been like you, not driven to such destruction for the sake of... vainglorious greed."

Violet angrily wipes away her tears before they fall, then reaches out to cup Ariadne's cheek. "Keep hold of your joy. It is so fleeting... in this cruel world."

The moment Violet steps out of the room, she unleashes her sobs and runs up the stairs, slamming a door behind her.

"I..." Samuel shakes his head, unsure of what to say.

Ariadne leaves the room, walking right out the door and into the street. Iona takes a step.

*Don't,* Ariadne begs. *Please, I... I need a moment.*

"Should we go after her?" Samuel asks.

Iona sighs heavily, then shakes her head. "No."

He gives a short nod, then clears his throat, searching for something to say.

"I heard your solstice ritual went exceptionally well," Samuel says.

Iona forces a small smile. "Yes, it did."

"I regret my absence but... I could not leave her here. Not like this," he says. "My sabbatical this semester may extend for the entire year at this rate. I haven't yet decided."

He takes heavy steps to the chaise and slumps down, putting his head in his hands. Iona sits beside him and puts a comforting hand on his shoulder.

"You needn't worry about me," Iona says. "I only wish there was something more I could do."

He pats her hand. "I've also heard Xiomara has taken you under her wing. I'm glad for it... That you were not left alone."

"She's become an unexpected ally," she says. "I find most Zerynthos witches to be misunderstood, flawed creatures, not the awful bedlams they are often made out to be."

"Most?" He raises an eyebrow.

"Moira and Cintia live up to their hostile reputations... And Sebastian has grown to hate me," she says. "Though perhaps I deserve it."

"Whatever could you have done to deserve that?" he asks.

"I..." Iona averts her eyes. "I made a mistake."

He regards her with concern. "What sort of mistake?"

"Nothing dire," she says, and though it pains her to lie, she feels it would be selfish to burden him with her troubles, even if she could be truthful, "We merely had... differing priorities and it led to a clash. It is nothing to worry about."

"I see," Samuel says. "I trust Xiomara will pacify him. I've always found her to be a decent, even-tempered woman. I am glad it's her who shall preside over Elise's trial."

Iona hesitates, then asks, "Where is Elise now?"

"The other council members have her," Samuel says. "They will not tell me where and a part of me is glad for it."

She wonders if Elise has been trapped in an illusion all this time, or if she's imprisoned somewhere deep in the earth, or locked up high in a tower. "Why are the proceedings so delayed?"

Samuel conjures a flask and pours a drop of whiskey into his tea. "Most maleficians are killed for their crimes, often by witches avenging their fallen loved ones, or by those deft enough to discover their identity and ambush them. In this case, the malefician is still alive, but powerless. She is a witch no longer, which is an entirely unprecedented turn of events. It will be the trial of the century."

Iona frowns. Surely Elise's crimes cannot go unpunished, but if she has no magic, there would be no use in taking her wand or restricting her power. To some she is considered a human now, entirely irrelevant.

"I imagine it's proved difficult to determine how to progress with all these malefician attacks ravaging the world..." Samuel muses. "It is not normal, this resurgence of darkness. Not since-"

"Before Katrin?" Iona asks.

Samuel glances at her, then nods, "Yes."

Iona gazes at her pendant, holding the opal gingerly in the palm of her hand.

"My only consolation is knowing how you thrive. Your benefaction of magic has caused quite a stir. Some are wondering if, due to your intervention, the disparity of power will not be so vastly divided as it has been." Samuel admires the opal with reverence. "Your father would be exceedingly proud of who you've become."

Something breaks inside of her, but she hasn't been able to cry since yesterday. Even when she thinks she might, no tears form. It seems she's finally run out. She swallows hard and schools her features.

"If there comes a time when you can spare an evening, might you attend one of my rituals?" Iona asks. "It would be a great comfort to me if you were there, but only if you are able-"

"Of course," Samuel promises. "Perhaps for Yule. I shall speak with Violet. If Ariadne would be so kind as to send a portal-"

The front door closes, and Ariadne reenters the sitting room with Aster. "I can send a portal."

"I would be most grateful," Samuel says. "Now if you would excuse me, I must see to my wife a moment."

"Of course." Ariadne's smile is tight, the tip of her nose slightly reddened.

Samuel leaves, and Iona slumps back in her chair. When she beckons Aster over to her, he jumps up on the chaise and rests his head in her lap. Wisp sniffs at him, then goes back to sleep.

*Are you well?* Iona asks. *You weren't gone long.*

*I was gone for nearly an hour,* Ariadne says, lifting her staff.

*An hour?* Iona gasps.

*I'm getting the knack of it, I think. The magic is a bit temperamental.* She admires the labradorite stone. *I tried to stop time again once it had started, but the staff wouldn't allow me. It seems to only work once or twice a day, but perhaps I only need practice for it to work at will, like with the portals.*

Iona becomes lost in the memory of their Yule holiday, and her wish that they could stay there forever and leave everything behind. Her heart aches for that time, when all was peaceful for just a moment. If only they'd had the staff with them then.

"I miss that time, too," Ariadne says softly.

Gently, Iona moves Aster's head from her lap and runs into Ariadne's arms, burrowing into her neck and breathing in her scent.

"I never planted the gardenia you gifted me on Yule," Iona realizes.

"Oh...." Ariadne says. "I suppose there's been nowhere to plant it, but someday... One day, I will grow you a luscious garden as far as the eye can see. You can plant it there, for you cannot relocate it once it's taken root, and its flowers will never wilt."

"Ever?" Iona pulls away just enough to look up into her red eyes.

When Ariadne nods solemnly, Iona is reminded of Moira's comment made the previous night that had resonated deeply with her. She has no home. Neither of them does. They've been nomads for months now, with no end to their peripatetic lifestyle in sight. She cannot imagine settling anywhere when so much is still uncertain.

# 25 - Iona

Days turn to weeks, and before long the autumnal equinox is upon them. Another ritual, another harvesting of magic amongst friends and adversaries. There are many more covens present the second time around, with the noted absence of Kokuro Sato and her family. There is also a diverse crowd of Marcel Beaumont's acquaintances who marvel at the spectacle and seem more at ease this time.

Xiomara suggests holding the ritual at a walnut tree in Benevento where witches have long gathered for sabbaths over the centuries. Iona does as instructed and the rush of power is just as rapturous as the solstice, an all too fleeting moment of perfect clarity and euphoria.

The reception is held at Villa Mitriora this time, mostly out of necessity, and Xiomara is insistent that she does not mind hosting. Given her bouts of fatigue and aches that prove increasingly difficult to withstand, Iona is grateful for the assistance.

Just as before, Crescentia takes her through the crowd to fraternize with the many covens, but there is a definite shift in the air, whispers percolating whenever her back is turned, and critical looks from witches peering at her from behind their lace fans.

Ariadne elects to stand with Frankie, who speaks with her excitedly, until she hushes him, and takes him inside to speak more privately. Iona watches her go and tries not to lament her absence too strongly.

"Oh…" Crescentia grimaces.

"What's wrong?" Iona asks.

"The Virtanens." Crescentia reluctantly slows her steps. "Or… would you prefer to meet them? I could introduce you…"

"I cannot possibly meet *every* family in attendance," Iona says, taking her arm, "They can wait until Yule. Or perhaps Spring."

"I adore you," Crescentia grins as she embraces her fiercely before leading her to a new family and making another round of introductions. She singles out every remaining council member in attendance, so that Iona is sure to meet them all.

Night falls by the time she is reunited with her college professors, Rayowa Salum, Corella Yun, Josephine Salvador, and Talulah Pari.

"Where is Ariadne?" Yun asks.

"She... I'm not quite sure to be honest." Iona scans the crowd again, but cannot find her or Frankie anywhere, so she sips her wine and searches for anything else to say. "She'll be along any moment. Are you enjoying the summer?"

"Yes, indeed," Yun says. "The sage in my garden flourished while I was away. My daughter tended to it painstakingly and I must say I am quite proud."

"How old is she?" Iona asks.

"Nearly four and ten. I can hardly believe it," Yun says with a wistful smile.

"And already she has quite the talent at phytology," Pari comments.

Yun beams with pride. Pari tells of her son, who is nearly six and can already see glimpses of the future. Iona cannot imagine having such insights at so young an age. Salum tells of her twenty grandchildren. She knows them all by name and disposition.

"And your family is well, I trust?" Iona asks Salvador.

There is a collective wince from the other professors, and Iona immediately regrets her inquiry.

"All is well with me. You are very kind to ask," Salvador says with a polite smile.

"Forgive me, I..." Iona is grateful when Crescentia approaches.

"Might I take her away for just a moment?" she asks.

"Of course," Salvador says. "It was lovely to see you, Iona."

Iona curtsies and lets Crescentia take her away again.

"Where to now?" Iona asks.

"Do not hate me," Crescentia begs.

"The Ulanovas then." Iona mirrors her expression. She'd been unsure what to make of their decision to attend this ritual, when they'd decided to abstain from her first.

"I shall ensure it is a brief exchange," Crescentia promises.

"Not brief enough," Iona mutters.

The Ulanovas congregate beyond the bustling crowd with an imperious and sullen air about them. Their necks and fingers glitter with jewels, and not one of them possesses a familiar. Iona lifts Wisp into her arms, finding comfort in her warm fur against her chest.

"Olesya Ulanova is their leader," Crescentia reminds her. "Ksenia's mother."

"Oh dear…" Iona schools her features.

She searches for any sign of Ksenia in their company, but she is nowhere to be found, which is curious but not all too surprising. She must have departed after the ritual or is keeping to herself somewhere on the outskirts of the party.

Olesya is a tall, intimidating figure with her daughter's blonde hair and icy blue eyes. Her husband, Nikolai, stands behind her with emerald eyes and spectacles that he adjusts to better appraise them. Crescentia makes the introductions, and they all bow and curtsy. Iona clears her throat.

"It is lovely to make your acquaintance, Mrs. Ulanova," Iona says.

"Quite," Olesya says, her voice thin and sharp. "Though you did take your time in making it."

Iona flushes. "My apologies, there are a great many covens to-"

"Yes, yes." Olesya waves a disinterested hand. "Now that you're here, we may discuss the rather alarming rise in malefician attacks."

At the very mention of maleficians, the ballroom goes quiet, just as the nearby string quartet finishes a song. For a few agonizing seconds, Iona's heartbeat thumps loudly in her chest, so loud she wonders if Olesya can hear it, too.

"Do you intend on aiding us in tempering these hostilities?" Olesya presses.

The quartet begins a new song, and the melody jolts Iona into speaking. "Yes, of course."

"The council will be relieved to hear it," Olesya says. "Though the Lysander seat has been regrettably empty of late."

"My uncle is convalescing-"

"Yes, I am well aware," Olesya sniffs. "The least you could have done for that man was give his daughter a quick death."

Iona flinches. "I beg your pardon?"

"He shall suffer indefinitely now," Olesya says. "A spectacle made of his misfortune… He and his wife should have been spared the humiliation, but it is too late now."

"I shan't deal in death and lawless castigation," Iona says. "Nor will Ariadne."

"She's had no issue with such things before." Olesya raises an eyebrow. "I suppose she's outgrown her ruthlessness."

Refusing to acknowledge the reference to Vivien, Iona says, "Ariadne's staff contains magic that can repel maleficium and-"

"Is that so?" Olesya glances at her husband.

"And I am studying combative magic to-"

"Studying it?" Olesya's eyes widen in dismay. "You mean to tell me you've no defensive training at all?"

"No, that isn't exactly-"

"Did your mother not teach you?" Nikolai echoes his wife's disbelief.

"She could not..." Iona stutters. "It is rather complicated."

"How on earth did you manage to claim the pendant with such deficient instruction?" Olesya asks. "And where is Ariadne? If she is the one with any chance of defeating a malefician, perhaps she should hear my appeal."

Olesya looks her over, entirely unimpressed by her silence. Iona does not wish to speak only to regret her words later, though it is becoming increasingly difficult to restrain herself, her frustration transmuting into barely restrained contempt, but she knows she mustn't cause a scene.

"Fetch Ariadne, won't you?" Iona whispers to Crescentia, who nods rapidly and wastes no time in slipping into the crowd, far away from the Ulanovas.

"You are the one Morgan chose?" Olesya asks. "She must have a sense of humor."

"She did not choose me for my talent at war," Iona says, flushing.

"That much is woefully apparent," she says. "Regardless our lands must be safeguarded, and you will be expected to join in our defensive-"

"Now, now," Xiomara says as she approaches, draped in a gown of Tyrian purple. "This is simply not the time, nor place for such inquiries."

"I'm not much concerned with formalities when darkness lurks at our doorstep," Olesya says, but her words have considerably less bite.

"And yet, I must insist you withhold your concerns for a more appropriate occasion," Xiomara says, her smile tight.

Olesya's eyes flit between them, then she chuckles darkly. "I must commend you for your cunning, Xiomara. What, did you advise Ariadne to seduce her competition in the event that she should fail? Supplying you with a pliant vassal queen to further your ambitions."

Iona's cheeks burn. "My union with Ariadne was not arranged, and I am of my own mind."

"Indeed. And if I may be so bold, it's Iona who has Ariadne entirely besotted," Xiomara grins, despite the tension between them all.

"That's not… I wouldn't say it quite like that." Iona bites her lip to hold back her nervous smile.

Olesya scowls but finally lets the matter rest. "Where is Cintia?"

"I'm afraid I've not seen her. You know how she can be at these sorts of gatherings," Xiomara shrugs. "She'll be hiding away somewhere."

Olesya gives them a brief curtsy before leaving with her husband following dutifully at her heels. Iona exhales with relief at her departure.

"Don't fret," Xiomara says in a low voice. "You handled that quite well."

"Did I?" Iona looks up at her with skepticism.

"Olesya is a chronic sniveler," Xiomara rolls her eyes. "When the maleficians are dealt with, and the Crone defeated, she will come to you with any number of complaints besides. She detests asking for help, as it's an admission that she hasn't the power to resolve her own problems, so she will punish you any way she can."

"I see," Iona says. "I shan't take her words to heart then."

"Good," Xiomara says, then appraises her fondly.

"What?" Iona asks.

"My usefulness shall only last for a brief interlude," Xiomara decides. "Soon enough I suspect you shall indeed become a queen amongst nobles, navigating our tempestuous natures with effortless grace."

Iona looks down at her hands. "That is a far too generous prediction."

"Nonsense," Xiomara says. "I see now what Morgan saw in you. A budding diplomat bringing with you a time of peace and unity. I welcome it."

"But…" Iona sighs, "Olesya is right to doubt me. I haven't mastered my spell work yet and-"

"Neither had my mother, when she first claimed the pendant," Xiomara shrugs.

That gives Iona pause. "Hadn't she?"

"No, not at all," Xiomara says with an encouraging smile. "Her expertise took years to amass even with the pendant's enhancements. She'd had a modest education in her childhood, not half what our Ariadne was afforded, and had only just graduated from college when she set out to forge her empire."

Iona averts her eyes at the mention of Katrin's conquest,

though Xiomara doesn't seem to notice.

"You mustn't compare yourself to her, even if others choose to," she says. "You are so vastly different in nature and in ambition, and there is more than one brand of strength."

"But the Crone... I cannot afford to be weak," Iona whispers, unable to keep her dejection from her voice.

"That does not fall on your shoulders alone," Xiomara reminds her. "Even when you reach your full strength, the Zerynthos coven shall always be at your disposal. As a fated leader of our people, as a Lysander witch, it's almost certain you will be a future council member. Though seats are not always inherited, I imagine when Samuel chooses to step down, you will be his successor. That day may come sooner than I'd anticipated... Then you shall have the support of all the great covens, and as the years pass it will likely be your old school mates presiding over the council with you. Thus is the way of things, the passing of the torch."

It's a great comfort, knowing there is a system in place to support her, but still Iona looks down at her pendant, and sighs.

"If not for Morgan's decree," Iona murmurs, "I would wonder if Ariadne should have kept the pendant after all."

When she looks up, Xiomara meets her gaze, a flurry of emotions glistening within her red orbs. "It does not do to question fate, Iona. Futile, in fact. And anyhow, I'm sure if Ariadne had claimed it in your stead, she would have troubles of a different sort." When Iona regards her questioningly, she continues, "Not all quandaries are best met with aggression and... impulsivity. How do you think she would have conducted herself in the face of Olesya's recent accusations?"

When Iona grimaces, Xiomara gives her a knowing look.

"I find that temperance is a rare skill of its own, far more valuable than militance," Xiomara says. "Worry not, dearest. All will resolve itself in due course."

Then Raul appears across the room and Xiomara's smile turns radiant.

"Now if you'll kindly excuse me, I think I may yet have a dance or two in my future," Xiomara says.

"Of course," Iona curtsies.

"Won't you join us?" Raul asks when he approaches and takes his wife's hand in his.

"Oh... I'm afraid my dance partner is indisposed," Iona says with an apologetic smile.

"Surely Ariadne wouldn't object," he says. "Allow me to find you someone suitable. There would be many a man or woman who would be honored to serve you."

"A splendid idea, darling," Xiomara says to him, then places a hand on Iona's shoulder and murmurs, "It does not do to dwell in sadness."

Iona lets out a small sigh, then acquiesces. "Very well, but only one dance."

Raul sets off into the crowd while Iona follows Xiomara to the dance floor. In hindsight, she is most grateful for Crescentia's tutelage, for she isn't as daunted by the prospect of dancing as she has been at every other party she's attended. She runs through the steps in her head, muttering the count to herself, when Xiomara excuses herself to find her husband.

Scanning the surrounding mass of people in search of Crescentia, Iona wonders what is taking her so long. It would be splendid timing if she returned now with Ariadne in tow. When the string quartet begins a new waltz, Iona stands there awkwardly, still without a partner, until someone comes up behind her, takes her hand and sweeps her away, twirling them about, making Iona dizzy, until she realizes the one holding her is Rebekka.

"Unhand me!" Iona wrenches herself away.

"Oh, come now. It is only a waltz," Rebekka grins, undeterred.

"You are precisely the last person on earth I would ever wish to dance with," Iona says, keeping her voice low for both their sakes. The other couples swirl round and round, seemingly unaware of their squabbling.

"It would be a terrible shame if, in all your life, you'd have only danced with one woman," Rebekka murmurs, mocking her whispering tone. There is a double meaning in her words that makes Iona's fists clench.

"If it were anyone but Ariadne, I might agree with you," she retorts. "Kindly find another woman to pester and spare me your company."

Iona turns to walk away and collides directly into Ariadne.

"Oh!" She cries out, relieved until she takes in Ariadne's enraged expression. " Oh… Ari-"

Just as it had in Iceland, their fated magnetism radiates within her, stealing the breath from her lungs and making her flush with heat, unable to resist it, until she releases her grip on Ariadne's arms and steps away.

"Have you no shame?" Ariadne seethes, barely noticing the

affect she has on Iona when she's glaring at Rebekka, who simply rolls her eyes and walks away. Ariadne tries to follow her.

"No, no. Wait," Iona hisses, reaching for her again. "Look at me."

She cups Ariadne's face in her hands, drawing her gaze back to her, and withstanding the intensity of their magic bearing down mercilessly, until her knees go weak.

"Do not let her rile you," Iona beseeches her. "She is nothing to me. You are everything."

But Ariadne's features have turned to stone, unyielding and unrelenting, her emotions broiling inside her.

"Come," Iona pleads, taking her hand. "Please? Please? For me?"

Ariadne lets out a shuddering breath, but she allows herself to be pulled away from the ballroom, past Crescentia, whose bewildered expression is nearly comical. They enter the hall, and Iona means to take Ariadne upstairs to her room, to console her until she's calmed down, and it's then she realizes she cannot recall how many days it's been since they've been intimate.

Her own anger bubbles beneath the surface, hating Rebekka for ruining what could have been a halfway decent evening. She would welcome a distraction from it just as much as Ariadne might. Longs for it, in fact, after their magic inadvertently awakened her desire and still tingles at her fingers where they're woven with Ariadne's.

She is moments away from suggesting they take their leave early when Ariadne pulls her into a dark alcove within an empty hall and pins her against the wall with such a possessive, desperate kiss that steals her breath and makes her moan.

"Quiet," Ariadne murmurs against her lips.

It takes every ounce of restraint within her to keep silent as Ariadne's hands rove over her, groping and caressing her like a woman possessed.

"We should-" Iona sucks in a breath when Ariadne burrows into her neck, kissing and nipping at her skin. "We should... not do this here. I cannot keep quiet if you do that."

"I need to feel you," Ariadne says, not bothering to whisper, and Iona tenses with alarm until she notices the total silence surrounding them.

Craning her neck to look down the hall, in the distance she can glimpse the foyer filled with people, all frozen in place.

Ariadne has taken her staff from where it had been haphazardly leaning against the wall, the stone glowing with a steady pulse of light, and with her other hand she pulls Iona back, lacing fingers into her hair to keep her in place as she kisses her with abandon.

Iona lets go entirely, uncaring when Ariadne's magic rips away her clothes, because seconds after Ariadne's hand moves from her hair to stroke her between her legs, circling her sensitive flesh, then thrusting into her without warning.

Iona gasps, squeezing her eyes shut as Ariadne ravishes her against the cold stone, pressing her hips into her again and again, her long fingers stimulating her deep inside until she can't breathe, can't think, can't do anything but whimper and grind her hips with equally ravenous hunger, starving for Ariadne's touch.

Until suddenly time slips back into its normal rhythm, and it takes everything within Iona not to scream in frustration. She looks up at Ariadne, silently pleading with her to stop time again. She certainly tries to, mirroring Iona's frustration, but time will not yield again.

"Useless," Ariadne hisses angrily.

Iona grins despite her disappointment as her pleasure fades and her breathing slows. She quickly conjures on clothes again before someone should see her, then says, "Make a portal to your room so we might-"

"...more preoccupied with the lives of common folk than us, but they run no risk of being slaughtered with hardly any magic worth leeching away," someone whispers.

Tensing with displeasure, Iona peers around the corner again to discern the source of the voice.

"How many of us need die before she deigns to intervene on our behalf?" the same witch whispers.

Struck by a wave of fury, Iona storms down the hall and confronts a blonde woman whose green eyes widen in surprise at being caught.

"What did you say?" Iona asks.

"Iona." Ariadne tries to coax her towards the stairs.

"No, if you hold grievances against me, I wish to hear them," she says, aware of the petulance in her tone but no longer caring to feign politeness. Not when her nerves are already rattled, everything within her wound so tightly.

"Uh..." the witch looks between them, with a trace of familiarity towards Ariadne, then glances at the witch beside her for help.

"You two never did learn to keep your mouths shut," Ariadne snaps, then in a gentler voice says to Iona. "Ignore them. They're imbeciles."

A flash of memory, of the two witches gossiping about Ariadne time and again, tearing down her self-worth as if it were sport. Iona glances at her, and she lowers her head, abashed.

"We were never in such constant peril under Katrin's rule," the other witch sneers. "She may have been a tyrant, but she, at least, had the good sense to prioritize the interests of sempiterna covens over those nameless scum."

"They have as much of a right to attend my rituals as any of you. I shall not stand for such blatant prejudice." Iona considers it, then narrows her eyes. "You are no longer welcome here."

The two witches raise their eyebrows in utter shock. One of them stutters, "But-"

"Conduct your own rituals elsewhere," Iona says. "I never wish to see your faces again."

"You cannot turn us away!" the blonde witch cries.

"Indeed, I can," Iona says. "Consider it a blessing. Maleficians will have far less interest in you without abundant magic, or so you claim. Your safety, and that of your ancestors, is permanently assured."

An incredulous chuckle escapes Ariadne's lips and the witches glare at her.

"Just as I suspected!" Silvano Evora approaches from where he'd been listening silently. "Your charity is only an act. We must do as you say or risk-"

Ariadne goes to stand between them, but Iona pushes past her to confront her enraged uncle.

"Oh, come off it," Iona scoffs. "You are only bitter that I won't conquer land for a family that scorns my very existence!"

Silvano's face turns red with indignation. "You mistake-"

"I am but a commodity for all you parasites!" Iona spits. "Merely a tool for your own selfish collusions!"

"Iona," Ariadne's voice is low, the disapproval in her tone only inciting Iona's anger until it reaches a boiling point.

"How in good conscience can you claim to deserve magic more than those who can barely cast two spells in one day!" Iona yells. "I will not apologize for-"

A hand brushes down her spine, and she cringes away from it.

"No," Iona whimpers.

"Pardon?" Gisela asks.

"I…" Iona rubs her face as memories fade into nothing.

"Iona?" Crescentia reaches for her hand.

She flinches away. "I wasn't finished, I…"

"Finished with what?" Gisela asks, raising an eyebrow.

A splitting headache radiates behind her eyes, and any time she attempts to recall anything past a few seconds ago, a blinding pain has her crying out and squeezing her eyes shut. Someone takes her arm and pulls her off to the side.

"Find Ariadne," Crescentia whispers to Gisela.

"I am not speaking to her," she says.

"That hardly matters!" Crescentia snaps.

An angry huff, and Gisela's footsteps clatter off into the dense crowd.

"What do you need?" Crescentia whispers. "Tell me."

"My head," Iona whimpers.

A gentle hand rubs her back in soothing circles. She struggles to lift her eyelids and look up into Crescentia's concerned amber eyes.

"Perhaps a cup of chamomile tea would help," Crescentia suggests. "My mother suffers from hemicrania from time to time, and she often drinks it."

"Please take me inside," Iona pleads. "I must lie down."

"Of course," Crescentia takes her arm. "Lean against me."

Her head lolls against Crescentia's shoulder as they slowly make their way along the outskirts of the party. Her eyelids droop again as fatigue nearly incapacitates her, until an image of Gisela overtakes her vision, her eyes alight with mischief and desire, shrugging her chemise off her shoulders to reveal her breasts to Ariadne's gaze.

Iona jolts, suddenly wide awake as she tries to shake the image from her head, but the memory is not fleeting as the others have been. It continues on, showing Gisela perched on a bed, beckoning Ariadne closer, until Nenet joins her and comes to lean against her friend's back, reaching around to cup Gisela's breasts in her hands, pressing soft kisses to her neck, all while looking directly at Ariadne, daring her to join them.

"No," Iona cringes, as the view of the two women grows closer, more detailed, when Ariadne had stepped out of her own clothes before climbing onto the bed, reaching out to touch…

"What's ailing her?" Salvador asks as she approaches, though Iona still cannot see.

"I… I'm not sure," Crescentia says.

"Iona, can you hear me?" Salvador asks.

"Yes," Iona murmurs, the memory finally fading, but she deeply dreads its return.

"Let me help you," Salvador says, taking her other arm.

She and Crescentia guide her to the villa and set her down in a chair against the wall of the atrium.

"I'll find Ariadne," Crescentia says. "Gisela will not know where to bring her."

She could easily call for Ariadne through the bond, but she abstains to give herself time to calm before facing her. She tries to remember when she last saw her, but it only causes more pain.

"I'll stay with her," Salvador says, and Crescentia gives her thanks before she leaves.

Groaning, Iona puts her head in her hands, breathing heavily, her heart racing in her chest.

"Here," Salvador offers her a cup of amber liquid.

"What… is it?" Iona pants.

"Orujo," Salvador says. "Spanish brandy."

She takes it and tries to drink it in one gulp, but it burns her throat terribly, and she coughs into her hand.

"Easy there," Salvador chuckles.

"That's poisonous," Iona sputters, then takes another swig.

"That's it," Salvador says, giving her a moment to catch her breath. "Now, I am no longer your professor so you've no obligation to tell me, but I must ask what happened out there."

Iona sighs, the shards of ice clinking against the glass as she swirls it around.

"It's nothing, I…" Iona sighs. "The blood bond got the better of me again, but it is just… I shouldn't let it upset me but… it's driving me insane. I cannot take this anymore. I cannot stand it, the figments and… the visceral memories, and I…"

The confession is as much a comfort as it is mortifying to admit to Salvador of all people. When Iona dares to look at her, Salvador's brown eyes are cast down on her shoes as she fiddles with the button of her jacket cuff.

"Ariadne told me of your disapproval when you learned of our bond, after we escaped from the tunnels in the forest," Iona says.

"Did she?" Salvador still doesn't look up.

"I suppose we must've seemed rather foolish in your eyes." Iona bites her lip to keep it from trembling.

"No, it wasn't that," Salvador says, then sighs and comes to sit beside Iona, taking the glass from her and drinking deeply. "I was once bonded to my life's great love, Dayana. We were only a year or two older than you and Ariadne are now. So, you see, I would be a terrible hypocrite to criticize your choices."

The same thinly veiled pain crosses Salvador's expression, that which Iona had noticed when she'd asked about her family earlier.

"We grew apart," Salvador says in answer to Iona's unspoken question. "Time had its effect and as we changed, we found we had less and less in common. We were constantly aware of it, of the ways we vexed each other and disappointed each other, unable to escape our mutual discontentment for nearly a decade. It was… hell."

Iona worries at her bottom lip, mustering the courage to ask what is really on her mind. "How does it feel… after the bond is severed?"

Salvador's expression darkens. "It was a different sort of torture. I couldn't see beyond the emptiness, the loss of her, but much like the illusions I cast in class, when I learned how to see what's true, beyond the veneer of romanticization, I saw that I had only fallen in love with my perception of her, then became melded into her. We'd ceased to be individuals and when we separated, it took time to reform my worth, redefine my life's purpose, and heal… Anyhow, I have come a long way since that time."

"Indeed," Iona says. "If I may say so, you were my favorite professor at college. Apart from Samuel, of course, but he has a familial advantage."

"That's very kind." She smiles. "I trust you've been practicing your illusions then? You've a talent for casting them, but you never did master the art of seeing beyond them. It isn't a skill that can be perfected in only one year."

"I… I have practiced a bit, but my studies have been focused elsewhere for a while," Iona says.

"Do not forget," Salvador says. "Some never master it but for those who do, it can be quite liberating. It can happen in an instant, a sudden revelation that renders them practically transparent to the-"

The sound of yelling in the distance makes them tense with alarm, until Iona recognizes one of the voices.

"Oh no…" She sprints from the atrium and into the hall, with Salvador following close behind.

"What's happened?" Salvador asks.

The moment they turn a corner and find a red-faced Ariadne and unperturbed Rebekka, Salvador hesitates.

"Uh... I should return to the festivities," Salvador says, wisely removing herself from their presence. "Unless you'd prefer me to-"

"I have it well in hand," Iona assures her, gesturing for her to go, for Ariadne might combust at the very sight of Salvador in her current state of mind.

"She is mine alone. Do you understand?" Ariadne yells.

"What a fuss you're making," Rebekka chuckles incredulously. "There's no need for hysterics."

"Do not act so cavalier," Ariadne persists. "I know well how you seduce women."

"Only those who want me, as you well know," Rebekka says, then a sensual smile curves her lips. "Is that why you are so incensed? You've seen her lust for me in her mind?"

Blushing furiously, Iona runs up and braces herself before grasping Ariadne's arm to hold her back, unfettered rage radiating from her, and their magic hitting Iona like a storm wind, but she fights to keep her expression neutral.

"Please," Iona begs, her voice shaking. "Do not make a scene."

"Listen to her, Ari," Rebekka says.

"Don't call me that," Ariadne spits, then in a marginally gentler tone she says, "Iona, please go."

"No." Iona's grip tightens around her arm. "Not without you."

Sighing, Ariadne glares at Rebekka, and Iona watches her face, taken aback when she looks to be on the verge of tears.

"You swore to me," Ariadne whispers.

Rebekka furrows her brow ever so slightly, her expression otherwise unreadable.

But before Iona can ask what she means, Samaira runs down the hall, eyes wide with terror as she cries, "Blood. There's so much blood..."

## 26 - Ariadne

The Satos' absence from the equinox ritual had been thought to be a mere abstention, but Samaira's vision alludes to something far more sinister. She advises them to dress warmly, as her vision was of ice, blood, and Kokuro's desolate cries. They journey to the Satos' estate just outside the great city of Edo, and hope they aren't too late.

"Time to redeem yourself," Moira whispers in Iona's ear before slinking off with a mocking grin.

"Leave her be," Ariadne snarls as she closes her portal.

"Ladies, please!" Aunt Xiomara sighs. "Iona and I will brave this alone if you insist on bickering."

"Make yourself useful and keep us hidden," Moira says, gesturing to the staff. "We mustn't draw any unwanted attention."

"Your silence would accomplish that just as well," Iona says.

"No, dearest. You misunderstand." Moira's smile turns condescending. "Foreigners have not been permitted on Japanese soil for nearly two centuries. If anyone were to see us, we could have samurai hunting us, too, and I am in no mood to duel with them when we have more pressing matters to attend to."

"Oh…" Iona reaches for Ariadne's hand, then hesitates and pretends to fuss with her trousers.

Ariadne despises the uncertainty in her eyes, and all it implies of their growing rift, but she cannot focus on it while Kokuro's life hangs in the balance.

"The Satos' estate is over that hill, past the village." Aunt Xiomara points to the northeast.

"Let's go then." Ariadne's staff glows as she casts an illusion to obscure them from view and takes Iona's hand firmly in hers.

Iona holds on so tightly that she loses feeling in her fingers, and it bolsters her resolve. There is no denying what they face, the weaknesses the Crone will almost certainly exploit, and the crushing urgency of their quest, Iona's quest. Ariadne's hatred for the malefician was always assured, but after their most recent encounter, killing the Crone turned from an obligation to a vendetta.

She will never hold Iona's lifeless body in her arms again.

Never. She will burn entire cities to the ground, lay waste to forests, brave any storm, whatever it takes. If she must fight against fate herself, Ariadne will never live without Iona, regardless of their current strife, which they will also overcome, somehow. Iona will live many countless years, a full and happy life, and Ariadne will love her for every second of it, and into eternity. No other future will satisfy her.

"Wait here," Moira says, motioning for them to stay, when they reach the threshold of the Satos' residence, a five-tiered structure of black and white stone with curved shingled roofs marking each level, and surrounded by a moat.

Instead of taking the singular road into the courtyard of the castle, Moira withdraws her wand and crafts a wooden bridge across the water, walking over it with casual grace, though there is slight tension in her shoulders.

Moira disappears inside, and they wait with bated breath until she exits and runs across the bridge.

"They are in their beds, asleep like the dead," Moira says. "All except Kokuro."

"And no sign of the Crone?" Aunt Xiomara asks.

"Obviously not," Moira says, earning a smack upside her head from her mother.

"We must search the grounds with great care," Aunt Xiomara says. "Death is in our midst, claiming many souls. I can sense his presence…"

Iona goes pale as a sheet, then gestures to her fox to lead the way. Wisp puts her nose down to the grass and sniffs, searching for Kokuro's scent, while Aster stays close by, guarding Iona as Ariadne asked him to.

"Is that…" Moira points straight ahead of them and sure enough, Kokuro walks along the bank of a winding stream, through a patch of red spider lilies, their thin petals fluttering in the light breeze.

"Should we call to her?" Iona asks.

"No," Xiomara says. "We should watch over her and see when the malefician will strike. For once, we may have the element of surprise."

"Oh, my word…" Moira says, her jaw dropping.

Ariadne searches for what upsets her but finds nothing amiss. Aster raises his nose to the sky and sniffs, whining faintly. There is a small village not far from them with modest townspeople going about their business as the sun sinks lower on the horizon.

"What is it?" Iona asks.

"You cannot see?" Moira's red eyes are wide.

Ariadne squints, willing her eyes to permeate any illusion that might obscure her vision, then gasps in horror as the mirage fades and reveals the town as it truly is. The houses are all aflame, burning to cinders in an uncontrollable blaze. The scent of smoke hits her soon after, tainting the sweet air and darkening the orange sky.

Any townsfolk visible to them are long dead, their bodies deflated and grey as their blood seeps from their eyes, their ears, their mouths, and trickles downhill into the stream, turning the water a sickening shade of pink.

When Ariadne's gaze returns to Kokuro standing by the stream, there is an eerie smile on the woman's face, as tears of blood drip down, tarnishing her pale cheeks. Then she turns and walks along the edge of the stream to the west.

"She's an illusion, too," Iona whispers. "When I concentrate, she fades into nothing."

"We should follow her," Moira says.

"Are you certain?" Ariadne asks, scarcely able to fill her lungs enough to speak the words. "It could be leading us into a trap."

"The malefician already knows we're here," Moira says. "That smile was meant to frighten us and she left this massacre for us to find. Don't let her disarm you."

"I won't, I…" Ariadne's words fade.

Hecate walks barefoot through the grass just outside the small village, the bottoms of her feet and the hem of her white gown stained red with blood. She takes in the carnage with a solemn expression.

"Do not disturb her," Aunt Xiomara warns.

"She is not here to slay your enemy for you, if that is what you hope," Moira whispers, and Ariadne glares at her.

"We shall follow the river," Aunt Xiomara says firmly, with a final despondent look at the fallen village.

The babbling of the stream sets Ariadne's teeth on edge. It's far too peaceful a sound when the blood of innocents saturates the water, growing darker in color the farther they walk until it matches the spindly petals of the blooming spider lilies that sway in the gentle breeze. A distinct, revolting metallic scent turns Ariadne's stomach.

Iona busies herself with conjuring a breastplate and imbuing it with protection spells, and offers to do the same for Ariadne, who reluctantly acquiesces. She cannot deny that the weight of the metal encapsulating her torso is a small comfort, knowing that Iona's magic is trapped inside, protecting her from harm.

The farther they trek, the more destruction they encounter, entire villages decimated along the path of the stream, the homes and businesses burned to ash, and blood seeping into the water. Ariadne wonders grimly if they might be too late, and they're merely here to recover Kokuro's corpse as they did with Sara.

"Wait." Aunt Xiomara puts out a hand to halt their grim procession.

She points ahead where the water strays from its path downstream and rushes through the grass toward another open field. Following the direction of the diverted flow, they come upon a tower of impressive height with stairs running along the outside leading to the top, which is obscured by dense, looming clouds. The structure glistens in the evening sun, a menacing edifice made entirely of blood turned to ice.

"One witch made this?" Iona's voice trembles.

A piercing scream cuts through the silence, coming from the sky.

"We should take flight," Moira suggests, but just then the clouds open up, creating a deluge of sleet and tempestuous winds. She tries throwing fire at the base of the tower, but the blood merely reforms the moment she relents. She yells over the wind, "Make a portal!"

"I cannot see the top!" Ariadne points to the clouds covering the tower's peak.

"Halfway then!" Moira yells. "We'll climb the rest!"

Ariadne squints, trying to make out the highest point she could safely transport them to, then makes a portal. A violent gust of wind bursts from the doorway the moment it's opened, making it quite difficult to step through, but in time they've all made it onto the icy stairs beneath the cloud cover.

"Come, Wisp," Iona yells, but the fox stays behind with her ears pressed against her skull.

"Aster?" Ariadne calls, but she knows the wolf won't come.

It unnerves her, just how terrified the familiars are. They hadn't reacted this way to Elise, but as they are becoming increasingly aware, the Crone is altogether different.

*I'll send them back to Rome.* Ariadne forges another portal and snaps at the familiars, who jump through without looking back.

*Is that normal?* Iona asks.

*None of this is normal, Iona.* Ariadne sighs, not from frustration, but out of complete overwhelm.

When they've all crossed over to the frozen steps, Ariadne pulls Iona close and takes what little comfort she can from her proximity.

"Stay close to the wall!" Aunt Xiomara beckons them onward, putting up a hand to shield against the ice and wind cutting her face.

Taking her first step, Iona nearly slips and falls on the icy surface, but Ariadne catches her and holds her up. They continue to struggle to keep their footing as the howling wind tries to push them over the edge. One wrong step, and they'd need to conjure wings to prevent their swift descent.

"At this rate we'll make it to the top by Yule!" Moira complains.

"Keep going!" Aunt Xiomara says, then slips and nearly falls on her side against the sharp edges of the stairs before Moira catches her.

The wind only worsens within the clouds, the unrelenting sleet blinding them.

"Something's out there!" Moira yells, pointing into the gray expanse.

Ariadne tries to look, and at first all she sees is endless mist, until a black wing cuts through the haze.

"Pyrkagiá!" Aunt Xiomara propels an impressive burst of fire, illuminating shadows within the clouds, but the monsters do not attack. They linger, gliding against the wind, as the fire dims and shrouds them again.

"We cannot-" Aunt Xiomara screams as a demon lurches from the clouds and catapults them out into the open sky.

"Mother!" Moira screams, reaching out for her.

Fire explodes from within the clouds, illuminating a battle between Aunt Xiomara and the lurking demons circling her, biting and clawing, two of them catching fire and writhing as they fall to their deaths. Three more take their place.

Moira hesitates, then beckons them forward. "We mustn't stop!"

"But should we not help?" Iona hesitates.

A barrage of wings, teeth, and claws descends upon them, arms reaching and groping to try and rip them away from the stairs. Ariadne shoves Iona against the wall and shields them with her magic. The demons try to rip their way through, but their claws have no effect. Their awful chorus of outraged screams are deafening, until suddenly it stops. Iona sighs with relief, then goes on her toes to look over Ariadne's shoulder.

"Moira?" Iona calls. "Oh no..."

Ariadne searches frantically, but her cousin is nowhere to be seen, nor can they hear Aunt Xiomara's battle in the clouds. Either she fell or was drawn deeper into the storm. Another strangled cry from the top of the tower has them looking up. It sounds much closer, maybe only a few flights of stairs above them.

"We must press on," Ariadne says, stepping away to give Iona room to climb. "Find a higher vantage point and-"

Moira bursts from the clouds and tumbles down the stairs in front of them, covered in jagged cuts and awful bruises. Her trail of blood is absorbed by the ice before the rain can dilute it. She tries to rise, then goes limp, so Iona runs to her side, reaching out to heal her.

Ariadne tries to follow but slips and falls hard. In her haste, Iona does not realize it, and ascends to where Moira has fallen, just outside the protective barrier of the shield.

"Iona!" Ariadne calls.

Another demon lurches from the darkness to drag Moira away, digging its claws into the flesh of her thigh. Iona makes it just in time to grasp one of Moira's hands to hold her back, nearly being pulled out in the storm along with her.

"Azkura!" Iona incants at the demon, making it writhe from the prickly irritation just long enough for her to cut off one of its dark wings.

The creature screams in agony as it plummets to its death, while Iona pulls Moira back to safety. Ariadne hastens her steps up the stairs to help, but their reprieve is short-lived as another two demons appear and tackle them, wrenching them apart.

Three searing lines of pain slice down Ariadne's back as a demon comes up behind her, pulling her hair loose from its bun and using it to drag her away, but she points the labradorite stone directly in its eyes, making it glow so brightly, it lights up the sky.

The demon cringes away, screaming as it tries to cover its eyes, now clouded white from blindness. It flies aimlessly until a demon bathed in fire falls onto him, dragging them both down to their deaths. It was Iona's fire, the pendant still glowing from her spell, but Moira is nowhere in sight.

"Ari!" Iona cries, pointing to Moira being carried off beyond their reach.

Ariadne's feet slip and slide over the ice, only making it up two steps. Iona holds out her hand to her, their fingertips almost touching.

The very moment she takes Iona's hand, a lance of clear ice whips through the air, piercing through the iron of Iona's breastplate as if it were made of gauze, plunging itself deep into her stomach and out the other side.

The force of it has her falling backwards and tumbling down the steps, screaming in agony. She looks down in horror at the ice protruding from her abdomen, while Ariadne doubles over from the force of Iona's maddening pain, making it impossible to think. Her grip on her staff loosens as her consciousness wavers.

"Pyrkagiá," Iona whimpers the spell, using fire to melt the ice away.

"No," Ariadne tries to reach for her. If she removes the ice, she may bleed out in seconds.

"Ph…" Iona swallows, then coughs up blood. Her gaping wound gushes red all down her white shirt. "Philisa."

Placing her hand over Iona's, both of them will the spell to work. It takes what feels like forever for the organs to regenerate, the spine to reattach, and skin to wrap itself over the carnage, but finally, it heals, leaving them both winded.

"Oh, thank goodness," Iona wipes the blood from her chin with a trembling hand.

"No…" Ariadne whispers, her heartbeat thundering in her ears.

It had almost been too much for her in Ashland, bringing Iona back from the brink of death. Together they are able to heal wounds that devastating, but the staff alone barely managed it. She might not be able to save Iona again if her mind and body were destroyed.

As her mother so cruelly told her, the staff is not the pendant. Not as strong… not possessing the same threshold of magic. It is another painful reminder of just how fallible, how vulnerable they are. Still flesh and bone, still capable of destruction. She isn't invincible, and neither is Iona.

Her thoughts become cyclical. She cannot lose her. Would not survive without her. She cannot lose her… She won't.

Ariadne creates a portal back to the front steps of the Villa Mitriora, the bright light of the midday sun like something from a distant memory.

"What are…" Iona's eyes go wide. "Wait… Ariadne, wait!"

She shoves Iona through the portal where she falls onto her back against the cobblestones. Scrambling to her feet, Iona calls out for her to stop, the betrayal in her eyes more than Ariadne can bear. After a final moment's hesitation, she closes the portal just before Iona can jump back through and sighs with short-lived relief.

*Ariadne Zerynthos! You bring me back right now!* Iona screams through the bond.

Ariadne ignores her, using the staff to push herself back onto her feet and continue the trek to the top of the tower.

*You cannot fight the malefician alone! What are you thinking?* Iona cries. *You'll be killed and Kokuro along with you!*

Perhaps, but better her than Iona. She is the fighter, the soldier, the fated guardian. This is her lot in life, what she was bred to do. Hecate may have tasked Iona with this quest, but she is not made for it. She has far too gentle a soul to cause any substantial harm to another witch. Ariadne won't let her own unforgivable lapse in judgement, her weakness and cowardice in giving away the pendant, destroy the one person she loves most in this world.

*I'll make a portal,* Iona threatens. *I'll come right back and bring you to your senses!*

But Iona doesn't know that spell. She never needed to learn it. It's far too advanced to be taught at Lysander College, too advanced for some witches to master over an entire lifetime. With the pendant it may be possible to learn quicker than most, but it would still take time.

*I'll never forgive you if you die this way,* Iona warns. *Eternity will be a punishment when I join you in the afterlife, of that I swear.*

Ariadne doesn't respond and she senses Iona's frustration at being ignored.

*All that talk of my supposed strength… It was all lies. You think I'm weak just like all the others do.*

Ariadne's steps pause a moment, her eyes closing as she fights to maintain her composure, then she surges ahead. She expects Iona to continue, but the bond goes silent. She doesn't know if she feels relieved or bereft without Iona's anger, but she hasn't the time to dwell.

Round and round she goes, the freezing wind numbing her fingers, her toes, her legs, making every step a challenge. The wind dies down only slightly when she makes it above the clouds to an arched doorway cut into the ice. Carefully she glances over the edge of the stairs to see if there is any sign of Moira or Aunt Xiomara flying within the storm clouds, but there is only the whistle of thin air and the boom of distant thunder.

She shivers, rain dripping from her clothes and hair. She tries to make a flame, a hot coal, anything that could provide even the smallest bit of heat, but whenever she tries, there is no warmth to be found. Fire gets smothered by some unseen force, coals go cold within seconds, and even the sun hides beneath the horizon, abandoning her in gelid darkness. She's glad Aster was left behind, so he won't have to suffer along with her.

She steps through the archway and into a rounded empty chamber, the walls so slick that she can see herself in the reflection. On the opposite side is another arch leading to a new set of stairs, and above her is a flat ceiling of red ice.

A scream comes from above, the closest it's ever sounded, and confirming what Ariadne suspects. This is not quite the peak, but she's nearly there. She resolves herself to fighting the malefician alone.

Her footsteps echo through the cavernous chamber as she runs to the other end. Then she cries out when she collides straight into a wall of pristine ice, the surface so clear that she hadn't seen it. She rubs her nose and looks around, suddenly wary of other panes of ice.

Stepping with more care, and her arms outstretched, she only walks a few paces to her left before her fingers touch the wet surface of another piece of ice. She follows it to a corner, then walks along another panel.

In her periphery, a motionless, dark figure appears. Ariadne aims her staff in the direction of the stranger, but when she turns, there's no one there.

"Show yourself!" Ariadne yells.

"I see your fear," a gravelly voice whispers directly into her left ear.

Ariadne flinches and turns to face the Crone, but she is still alone. Spinning slowly, her staff hits a pane of ice that hadn't been there before. When she finds a fourth pane, her heartbeat quickens when she realizes the ice has boxed her in. She tries to find an opening but the more she moves, the more the ice converges until she is trapped within a cramped square of space.

"No…" Ariadne's breath comes in short gasps as she spins around in frantic circles.

She goes rigid when she turns to find her mother staring at her from the other side of the ice, her eyes filled with rage.

"No…" Ariadne shakes her head manically. "You're not here."

"I smell your fear, rotting you from the inside out," the

gravelly voice says, from far too close.

Ariadne turns away and Tatiana is there where her mother once stood, watching her with the same simmering anger in her gaze. Ariadne blinks, and a massive black snake takes Tatiana's place, its mouth opening wide, flashing its sharp fangs, as it moves to strike.

Ariadne screams and ducks down, until she hears laughter. She looks up to behold Elise, appearing as she had under the blood moon, with black bile staining her chin and teeth. She's doubled over in hysterics at Ariadne's expense, pointing at her where she cowers on the floor.

Ariadne screams, "Pyrkagiá!"

The fire does nothing against the ice and it's then she notices the nearly imperceptible tinge of red, revealing the glassy ice to be part of the tower, impervious to fire.

Turning away from the illusion of Elise, Ariadne searches for an opening in the ice, trying to think of any spell that could break through. The cruel laughter has tears forming in her eyes, making it harder to see and impossible to think.

"So afraid."

Ariadne squeezes her eyes shut, pressing her forehead against the cool surface of her frozen cage.

"So… weak," Iona continues, the replica of her voice so perfect, it's uncanny.

"Izrezati!" Ariadne cuts the ice, but it barely makes a scratch.

Beyond it, the illusion of Iona regards her with smug satisfaction.

"How disappointing," the illusion says, "I'd have thought Hecate's soldiers would prove a more formidable challenge, but it seems her standards have lapsed."

Even while knowing it is only an apparition, the words spoken in Iona's soft voice still lacerate Ariadne all the same. She shifts, looking away from the illusion, refusing to react or cower while she works toward escape. She'll chisel her way out with a hammer if she must.

But her attention is drawn back when Iona's skin putrefies until it's tinged blue, barely clinging to the bones beneath. Her hazel eyes become clouded, her nails long and jagged, her hair tangled and stringy, having lost its vibrant orange hue. When the illusion smiles, Iona's teeth are rotten, the muscles in her face straining against the movement. Ariadne cringes and looks away.

"You cannot save her from this fate," the illusion of Iona says.

"I saw how you defended her, fending off my attacks, keeping her from the fight. So noble. So futile."

"You won't," Ariadne's breath stutters. "You shan't harm her."

"But it seems her death is not all you fear," the illusion muses, squinting as she peers into Ariadne's aura unbidden. "You dread her betrayal. My… it consumes your every waking thought."

"Get out of my head!" Ariadne screams.

"She's better off without you anyhow," the illusion says. "Isn't that right, Ariadne?"

She cannot resist looking and regrets it immediately. Salvador stands behind a revitalized Iona, her dark eyes gloating as she presses her lips to Iona's neck again and again. Ariadne cannot feel it, but if anything, that hurts her more, seeing of version of Iona unbound to her, leaving her behind.

Frantically, Ariadne makes another cut in the ice, but the spell still doesn't break through. When she blinks, Salvador becomes Euphemia, her sapphire eyes twinkling with mischief.

"You'll have to do better than that." Iona grins as she takes Euphemia's hands and wraps them tighter around her waist.

"Diminuir," Ariadne casts, trying to shrink the ice down, but it has no effect.

"Not quite." Iona lifts her chin to give Rebekka better access to her neck.

Ariadne sucks in a gasp as Rebekka's hands roam over Iona's body, caressing every curve with eager appreciation and alarming familiarity. Iona moans softly at her caresses, making Ariadne's skin crawl. Rebekka's hand drifts lower, down Iona's stomach…

"Démolir!" Ariadne's spell explodes, sending her hurtling back into the unyielding wall of ice behind her. She coughs and recoils, groaning in pain when she tries to move, and when she looks up, Iona stands inches away from the ice, peering down at her, while Rebekka makes a trail of kisses from her hand to her wrist, her elbow, all the way up her arm.

"Don't fret. I'll kill her long before she has the chance to leave you," Iona says with an evil grin, "and I'll enjoy every second of it."

"No," Ariadne rasps. "You will never set eyes on her again, Crone."

Iona's hazel eyes sparkle with glee. "We shall see."

Ariadne trembles as she takes her staff and struggles to stand.

With a lazy wave of her hand, the Crone makes Rebekka disappear, having grown tired of the masquerade.

"Or rather, I shall," the Crone corrects herself, "You will be long dead by that time, and maybe then that sniveling dilettante will prove a true challenge for me, when grief putrefies her soul and makes her a bit more... interesting."

The Crone steps through the ice as if it were nothing, but Ariadne creates a shield around herself.

Still using Iona's face, the Crone rolls her eyes. "That won't work here."

"Your spells cannot permeate it," Ariadne says.

"Most cannot," the Crone agrees, "though I've found some still work quite well, indeed, when you're caught unaware, and left vulnerable to my superior powers."

"What are you..."

A hand slaps hard across her cheek, the sting bringing new tears to Ariadne's eyes as she blinks and sees beyond the illusion.

"Wake up!" Moira screams, raising her hand to strike her again.

"I'm awake!" Ariadne puts out her arms to stop her.

Moira slumps with relief, then pulls Ariadne onto her feet. "Where is Iona?"

Ariadne lowers her gaze, but Moira shakes her roughly.

"Is she dead?" Moira asks.

"No!" Ariadne keeps her eyes down. "She's safe."

Upon realizing her meaning, Moira's brow furrows with resentment. "Well, how grand for her."

"Where is Aunt Xiomara?" Ariadne shrugs her hands away.

The tower quakes with the force of a spell cast directly above them, as if in answer to her question.

"Prepare yourself," Moira says. "The Crone is stronger still and you are shaking like a leaf."

"I'm ready," Ariadne says, willing it to be so.

"You'd better be," Moira says.

They run across the empty chamber where another set of stairs takes them one flight up to the peak of the tower, where the roof is held aloft by thick columns of red ice. At the other side of the platform, Kokuro lays on her side within a circle of runes, struggling to free herself from the malefician's chains. Her brown eyes widen when she sees Ariadne, and nearly cries out her name, but Ariadne puts a finger to her lips to silence her.

Aunt Xiomara is splayed across the ice, her nose broken and

the fingers of her wand hand contorted at unnatural angles. With her other hand she reaches for her wand where it's rolled away across the floor.

The malefician floats above her, a mocking, gravelly laugh muffled by the black wrappings covering her face. Ariadne imagines the Crone's face is covered in warts, her sunken eyes jaundiced and black teeth rotting from the bile spewed with each spell. It's high time Ariadne beheld it, and she cares not whether it will be before or after the infernal witch is slain.

Holding out a hand, the Crone sends a wave of sharp spikes rising up from the floor, fast approaching where Aunt Xiomara lays.

"Kuelea!" Ariadne lifts her aunt above the spikes just as she manages to grasp her wand.

"Philisa." Aunt Xiomara heals her dominant hand. "Halat!"

A net of rope encircles the Crone, constricting tightly around her and rendering her immobile. Clutching a longer string connected to the net, Aunt Xiomara hurls her up, over, and down into the spikes of ice on the floor, puncturing the Crone's legs, abdomen, and neck, and just barely missing her skull.

Ariadne's blood chills when the malefician doesn't utter a single groan of pain, or the guttural scream she would have uttered had their positions been reversed. Instead, the ice sinks back into the floor and the Crone's wounds heal before their eyes as she stands again, hunched and haggard, but alive.

"How many maleficians did you say you've killed?" Ariadne asks in a low voice.

"Enough," Moira says. "Why?"

"No one else will die today," Ariadne decides. "Keep the Crone distracted."

Moira frowns. "The victim is as much a diversion as she is a sacrifice, a way to use our compassion against us. Iona made the same mistake."

"I am not Iona," Ariadne says. "Can you manage it?"

Moira studies her, then nods.

"Stand back." Her eyes narrow to slits as she incants. "Hraunkvika."

Magma erupts from beneath the malefician's feet before she can fly above it and spreads across the platform with alarming swiftness. Ariadne stumbles backwards and quickly conjures wings to fly through the columns and into the sky.

She glides in a circle around the tower as the magma overflows, spilling through the spaces between the columns, but even boiling lava isn't enough to melt the Crone's ice. Ariadne dives down to where Kokuro lays. Fortunately, the magma does not permeate the runes, instead parting around the circle that imprisons her. Ariadne chooses to believe Moira knew this would happen but isn't altogether sure.

"Ariadne, please!" Kokuro cries. "Don't let her kill me! Please… Oh, please help me, I beg you!"

"I am helping, if you could please stop screaming!" Ariadne snaps, her patience hanging by a thread.

Kokuro sniffles, trying to pull her arms free, while Ariadne racks her brain for any spell that could break the chains. Her back begins to ache as she flaps her wings to keep herself hovering above the magma.

Moira and Aunt Xiomara do their best to distract the malefician, but the moment she sees Ariadne hovering over Kokuro, the Crone lunges for her with her hand outstretched. Ariadne concentrates, holding her staff so tightly her hand cramps, and time slows, and slows, and slows, until it stops.

"What do I do," Ariadne mutters to herself. "What do I do… Damn it all, there must be a way!"

Her wings scream at her to rest, but she has nowhere to land and making herself float would require more magic to sustain. She treads air and wills her time spell to last just a little while longer.

She knows she cannot touch the chains, she cannot conjure them away, there is no lock that she can see, no gap in the fetters that could be used to unravel them, and cutting through them might cut Kokuro's skin, too. But perhaps…

"Izrezati!" Ariadne unleashes a cutting spell that slices through the metal of the chain but also leaves an ugly gash across Kokuro's chest. Ariadne winces but persists. She cuts and cuts, sweat dripping down her neck from the exertion, until she breaks through one link. Then she heals the wounds away, before Kokuro can even perceive of them.

She does this to as many links as she can before her strength fades and she cannot fly one second longer. She hasn't the time to be proud of how long she'd stopped time. She casts a water spell on the magma to cool it beneath her feet, turning it to rock, and collapses onto her knees. Time starts again the moment she touches the steaming ground.

The Crone stops in midair, looking around in confusion, just as Kokuro breaks through the chains and gasps in surprise. Screaming in outrage, the Crone spews her awful spell that has them all writhing in pain. The magma flows away from the sound, dripping off the edges of the platform and down to the earth below, as if escaping the spell just as Ariadne wishes to.

"Skáse!" Ariadne incants, and to her delight, the Crone's mouth seems to meld shut, though it's impossible to see through her wrappings.

But her triumph is short-lived. The Crone unleashes another spear of ice that embeds itself into Ariadne's shoulder, and within that time, the Crone manages to tear her lips apart and continue her screeching spell.

No sooner does Ariadne deafen her hearing than the malefician reaches for Kokuro's throat, wrenching her up into the air, unsheathing her golden dagger, and cutting open her abdomen, sending blood and sinew splashing onto the ice below them. Ariadne screams, trying to unfurl her wings to fly up to them, but her exhausted muscles won't allow her.

Kokuro sobs, struggling against the malefician's grip, steadily losing strength as she bleeds out. The Crone delves her hand inside Kokuro's chest cavity, searching around through the assortment of exposed organs until she rips out the stomach and clutches it close to her chest, then tosses Kokuro away like a broken doll.

A portal opens and the malefician is moments away from escaping before Aunt Xiomara tackles her, throwing them both through. Moira tries to follow but isn't fast enough to make it before the entrance closes. She spews what is almost certainly a string of curses that Ariadne cannot decipher. Numbly, she renews her hearing, then goes rigid at the sound of Kokuro sputtering, still clinging to life.

She throws herself onto the ground beside Kokuro, putting a hand over her gaping stomach and using what little strength she has left to heal her. She moans in pain as the last of her magic is siphoned from her and into Kokuro's moribund body.

"Please, please, please, please." Ariadne says it over and over again, until the word loses its meaning.

"Ariadne," Kokuro weeps.

She pushes herself farther than she ever has, refusing to give in. The labradorite flickers like a candle nearly snuffed, but she won't accept limitations. She won't relent, not now.

"Hold on," Ariadne says through gritted teeth.

Moira kneels on Kokuro's other side and puts her hand over Ariadne's. It's a smaller contribution, not half as strong as when Iona aids her, but it's enough. Kokuro's chest slowly mends, the stomach she'd lost reforming and attaching itself to her bowels, her deathly pale cheeks turning pink with renewed blood.

It's not enough to fully heal her, a hideous bruise blooming along her fractured ribs, but it's enough to save her. Ariadne slumps, her wheezing breaths coming slow and labored.

"Thank you," Kokuro embraces her, her cheeks wet with tears.

Ariadne can barely keep her head up as Moira pulls her to her feet, but the floor is not as solid as it had been. The blood is melting and when Ariadne musters the strength to look up, her hope dwindles.

The roof looks moments away from caving in, icy drops raining down on them and staining their clothes with red dots. There is no possible likelihood that they could climb down the icy stairs in their current state, not before the structure loses its integrity.

"Make a portal!" Moira cries.

Ariadne tries, holding out her staff in front of her, then she goes limp and would have fallen on her face if it weren't for Moira holding her up.

"Oh… no," Moira sighs. "Perfect. Just perfect."

Kokuro takes Ariadne's other arm. "We must fly down!"

"She cannot walk, let alone fly," Moira says.

"Heal her-"

"Not my forte, I'm afraid."

"Nor mine… We shall carry her then," Kokuro says, frustrated, "I've healing potions in my room that will revive her."

The ice cracks ominously beneath their feet as the tower sways to and fro.

"When your mother called you delicate, this is what she was referring to," Moira mumbles as she readjusts Ariadne's arm, so it's wrapped tightly around her neck.

They drag her to the edge of the platform, and with her eyes cast down, she admires the beauty of the white clouds as the storm recedes. She wonders if it might be the last time she sees the sky.

"On three!" Moira says. "One-"

The floor gives way beneath their feet, and they lose hold of each other. The columns melt and crumble, the tower's roof caves in, and a boulder sized piece of ice hits Ariadne square in the back, throwing her onto her stomach. She screams as her bones crack under the weight, until Moira hurls it away and manages to pull her up just as Kokuro pushes them all over the edge. They hurtle through the air, and all Ariadne can think of is the certainty that Iona will never forgive her... She'll never...

"Stay awake," Moira smacks her cheek, hard.

Ariadne's eyes pop open and the pain in her ribs returns in full force. She groans as Kokuro and Moira make an uneven flight back to the ground, very, very slowly. Ariadne's stomach drops when they suddenly plummet until Moira catches her in mid-air, the collision bringing stars to her eyes. Her only solace is knowing the pain means she's still alive.

Her consciousness fades and when she opens her eyes, she's lying in the grass only a little way away from the melting tower. Blood saturates the ground, rushing over her ears, into her hair, and all over her clothes. She squirms with discomfort, close to losing consciousness from the pain. The pain... Iona will feel... everything...

Ariadne opens her eyes again and Aunt Xiomara cradles her in her arms while screaming unintelligibly at Moira, the blinding rage in her aunt's eyes frightening even when it isn't directed at her. Aunt Xiomara's face is covered in cuts and bruises, making her nearly unrecognizable when Ariadne gazes up at her, then at Moira, who frowns petulantly.

The Satos emerge from their home in the distance, both of them enveloping their daughter in a fierce embrace, and Kokuro speaks urgently while pointing at Ariadne where she lays. She tries to speak, but she can barely move her lips. Then she remembers that Kokuro won't remember any of this for much longer anyhow, so whatever she might say doesn't matter. She closes her eyes.

When she opens them again, she's staring up at the ceiling of the Villa Mitriora's atrium, floating on her back within the pool of shallow water beneath Hecate's statue.

"What are you waiting for?" Aunt Xiomara yells.

With great effort, Ariadne turns her neck to look to her right, and there in the water stands Iona, her expression beyond sadness, anger, or pain. She stares back without a tear or a harsh word. Just stares with her arms crossed.

"Uncle Petro can brew a potion," Moira says.

Before she can fetch him, Iona steps closer and reaches out both her hands to delicately cup Ariadne's face between them. Her touch is so gentle, barely there at all. Magic seeps through her fingertips and fills Ariadne with vitality. She sighs heavily as her wounds heal, wincing as her bones snap back into place, leaving her fatigued but alive.

"…I tried but she kept jumping through to another portal," Aunt Xiomara says in hushed tones. "I couldn't keep her in one place for long. She was uninterested in fighting me, only in escape."

"She cannot evade us forever," Moira says with frustration. "At least no one died this time. Or well… only humans."

Iona climbs out of the pool, wiping Ariadne's blood onto her skirts, then leans down to pick up Wisp and hold her close to her chest.

"Where were you?" Moira asks bitterly.

Iona doesn't speak, simply walks out the front door, leaving it open behind her. Ariadne sits up in the pool and watches with sickening dread as Iona descends the front steps, climbs into a carriage, and rides off alone.

# 27 - Iona

The darkness is warm and inviting. It cradles her, pacifying her until she's numb to anything but her screaming thoughts. She fights against its tranquilizing effects, pushing herself up onto her feet and running wildly into the abyss until her foot gets caught and she crumples to the ground. Pulling at her leg, she manages to dislodge it, only to run straight into another tangle of strings that cling to her skin.

Writhing and bucking, she tries to free herself, but her movements only further entoil her until she's unable to move. Then she squeals at the alarming prickle of tiny legs running across her back, to her shoulder. The spider perches there, and when Iona tries to shake it off of her, it only seems to startle the creature into running aimlessly over her captive form, until she's utterly repulsed.

She cries out for help, but her only answer is the echo of her own sobs, until she hears the distant sound of footsteps. She abruptly swallows her cries, pulling at her arms and legs in a vain effort at escape. The spider creeps away, and Iona envies its freedom.

A bright, blinding light permeates the darkness, making Iona flinch away, until she sees who holds the glowing beacon in their palm. The Crone stares up at her where she's strung up in a tangle of threads, and though the old varlet's face is still concealed by bandages, they shift distinctly to indicate her menacing smile.

Iona screams, tries to cast any spell she can remember, but she looks down at her chest, it is bare. The pendant is gone.

To her greater horror, the malefician approaches her, reaching out a mangled hand to run a cracked nail against her cheek, taunting her, making her squirm away in disgust. The wheezing, gloating laugh of the malefician only fuels her outrage.

"Let me go!" Iona cries. "Let me go! Let me go…"

The light extinguishes, cloaking the malefician in darkness again, though her horrible laugh persists.

"Let me go!" Iona cries, startling herself awake.

A fluttering of wings comes from overhead as a group of startled birds soar to more peaceful branches. Petrichor fills

Iona's lungs with every gasping breath, mixed with the faint odor of smoke from the campfire.

"Nightmare?" Jacira asks.

Iona glances at her where she stands ankle deep in the Rio Paraná.

"Of sorts," Iona says glumly, sitting up and rubbing her face. Wisp's nose pokes at her hands until she lets them fall away. The fox licks at her face, sniffing at her intently.

She mistakenly thought her dreams wouldn't scare her any longer now that she knows where they come from, but her subconscious mind is not so rational as all that. She trembles with fevered perturbation, the pinpricks of the spider's tiny legs still ghosting over her skin, making her itch.

"Come." Jacira beckons her closer.

Iona eyes the water warily. "Is that wise?"

"Do not concern yourself with wisdom. You've decades yet to amass it," Jacira says.

"Was it not you who said to beware of the river-"

"Without me," Jacira finishes for her.

"Very well." She stands and twists her back to stretch her spine, until it lets out a satisfying crack.

Then she approaches the very edge of the water and gathers up the skirt of her chemise. Very carefully, she dips one foot into the cool water. She waits, but nothing happens.

"All the way," Jacira says impatiently.

Iona puts her other foot in, then wades through the water to where Jacira stands.

"That's it," she says, closing her eyes.

Iona follows suit and takes a deep cleansing breath. She waits, but Jacira doesn't give further instructions.

"What now?" Iona asks.

"Hmm?" Jacira asks.

Iona cracks open an eye. "Should I... incant something? Or-"

"There is no spell or incantation," Jacira says. "Simply enjoy the water. Let it renew you."

"Oh," Iona says, slightly disappointed.

"Magic cannot solve every one of your problems," Jacira says. "You must find peace within yourself."

They stand there in meditative silence for an unknowable amount of time. Iona's thoughts drift to the limitations of magic, the potential of it, the temptation to numb herself with it. She could have another witch take her memories away, as Moira did to the Satos. She is accumulating yet more friends whom she cannot bear to face. At the next ritual she will be surrounded by those she's forsaken, and she cannot even beg their forgiveness.

Worst of all the haunting anamneses is the memory of Ariadne's battered form when she'd returned from Japan. She'd been covered head to toe in blood, cuts, and bruises, a near corpse. Iona's heart had raced at the sight of her beloved so completely broken, barely conscious enough to notice her presence beside her. It was all she could do to heal her as well as she was able before she departed.

Those hours alone in the villa had been torturous. She'd removed herself from Ariadne's mind, not wanting to see her felled or afflicted. It had never once occurred to her until then that she had no knowledge of how to create a portal, as Ariadne always makes them for her. Mere manifestation hadn't worked, even when she'd tried to quell her tumultuous thoughts enough to focus on where she wished to go, nor did she know the incantation to compel the magic forth.

It was in search of that incantation that Iona had flown to the villa's library. She'd poured over the many tomes and scrolls, tossing them aside in a pile on the floor in her haste, but she could scarcely concentrate enough to read the words, to comprehend their meaning. They may as well have been in a foreign tongue. Many of the books were indeed written in Italian, Greek, Arabic, Latin, rarely ever English.

Even so, it was shocking to her that in that sprawling library, not one single book could aid her. She could have sworn there were once many more books crowding the shelves and wondered if perhaps Xiomara had taken a choice few for her own research, then she decided it did not matter.

Her efforts, it seemed, were futile and she'd collapsed on the library floor, relenting her utter impuissance. She'd tried to cry, but no tears would come, which allowed her to think instead. In that time, she'd determined that Ariadne's lack of belief in her is well founded, though she still greatly resents Ariadne's choice to cast her aside as she had.

Moira's criticism of her is not misled, either. She cannot take a life, but the Crone has no such qualms. She cannot possibly hope to oppose such a formidable foe without the use of force, and the very thought of it sickens her.

When Moira had looked her over with utter repugnance and asked, *"Where were you?"* Iona had been overcome with shame, as she had no answer.

She now reckons with the possibility that Hecate has indeed

placed her trust in the wrong witch. She is not strong in the way Zerynthos witches are. Perhaps in time she may come to adopt their strengths and virtues, but the Crone is growing too strong.

She cannot help feeling a sense of inequity in her plight. Ariadne had been right in saying she cannot possibly learn a lifetime of spells, technique, and instinct in mere weeks or even months. Ariadne always praises her for her natural proclivity for magic, but that is not enough when faced with a brutal maven like the Crone.

It is as Xiomara feared. Maleficians are depending on Iona's inexperience to wreak their havoc while they can. She's failed to inspire fear in their hearts, the way Katrin had. She is not Katrin. She could never be. Morgan hadn't expected her to be, when she'd sought her out on Samhain.

She's been going against her own nature for so long, she's almost forgotten who she is anymore.

And so, she left for Brazil, borrowing one of the Zerynthos' carriages to make the journey, so that she might continue to improve her healing magic with Jacira. Perhaps in that she can be of some use.

"Arrange these in their proper order," Jacira instructs, conjuring a full set of human bones.

Iona sighs inwardly but leans forward to sort the bones in piles.

"Now tell me what is troubling you," Jacira says.

"I do not wish to burden-"

"Enough of that pitying drivel," Jacira snaps. "We are all of us burdens at one time or other. That is the very purpose of community. It is no sin to rely on the good will of others, but crumbling in silence is pernicious indeed."

Iona frowns, thinking on the many times Ariadne has done just that, withdrew from others to suffer in silence.

"I miss my mother," Iona says.

Jacira's eyes soften. "Samhain is fast approaching."

"It would be just my luck that some other renowned figure of historical significance should visit me instead," Iona says, then sighs, "inundating me with their cryptic demands."

"Then refuse them," Jacira says.

Iona's brow furrows. "I cannot, when I have the power to protect the innocent."

"You don't owe your power to anyone," Jacira says.

"But I do."

"No, you don't."

"I cannot sit idly by while others suffer," Iona says stubbornly.

"No one is asking you to," Jacira says, "but do not wail and whimper at your misfortunes when you decided to involve yourself. Do not offer your assistance only to let resentment fester in you. No one forced that pendant around your neck."

Tossing a femur into the dirt, Iona looks down at her pendant and considers her great aunt's words.

"I should like to take a walk," she says, beckoning Wisp to follow her.

"The bones," Jacira starts to say.

With a frustrated wave of Iona's hand, the bones scatter in all directions. "I'll fix them upon my return."

"You needn't bother," Jacira says.

Iona goes to ask why, then her mouth falls open at seeing the assemblage of the bones in the shape of a full skeleton laid out on the ground. She hadn't intended it, which somehow makes it all the more infuriating.

"Don't wander too far," Jacira says, "and stay out of the water."

The river's ever constant gurgling is a comfort to her, until she is reminded of a similar refrain. All of that blood… it had taken so much sacrifice to construct the tower. She imagines Moira and Xiomara have taken painstaking measures to ensure the carnage was seen as some awful plague or battlefield, so the humans will not suspect magic was the true cause of the devastation.

A prickle of awareness goes down Iona's spine. She stops short, scanning the trees for any sign of movement, then looks out across the river and gasps. There floating above the water is a woman draped in white. She is nearly translucent, as if she were made of the finest mist. The sun shines brightly on her and creates a thin rainbow that arches out and into the water below her.

"Iona?"

She flinches, spinning around to find Ariadne standing there, clad in a simple black gown, a portal closing behind her, and Aster sitting at her feet. When Iona looks back at the river, her great grandmother has gone.

"I know you do not wish to see me," Ariadne says, a slight edge to her voice, "but I felt your distress this morning and wished to ensure you were unharmed. Did you have another nightmare?"

"Yes," Iona says, "but I am well now."

Ariadne studies her. "Good."

"And I am glad to see you," Iona says, truthfully. Their mere proximity is an immediate balm to her afflicted nerves.

Ariadne's eyes glimmer with hope, and she goes to speak, then thinks better of it.

"Ari," Iona sighs, but a hand brushes down her spine. She blinks.

"When are you coming back?" Ariadne asks brusquely.

"Pardon?" Iona asks, then winces and brings a hand to her forehead when a sharp pain radiates in her skull. Wisp jumps up against her and licks at her other hand, chirping with distress.

"I know you claimed to need time apart, but it's been nearly a month," Ariadne clenches her jaw. "How much longer do you intend to stay?"

Iona stares at her with wide eyes. "But..."

"Tell me because I cannot... I cannot sleep without you and..." Ariadne's voice breaks. "Just tell me so I might have hope-"

"But I've not been gone that long." Iona struggles to comprehend her.

Ariadne scoffs and angrily holds out a package wrapped in blue paper. Iona looks down at it, entirely disoriented, then reaches out and takes it.

"Since you wouldn't return for your birthday." Ariadne looks anywhere but at her. "It's a book."

Cold dread seeps into her despite the heavy warmth of the jungle. She rips open the paper to reveal a leather-bound copy of Shakespeare's sonnets, the title embossed in gold leaf. There is a lavender ribbon dangling from within its pages, and when she pulls at it, the pages open to Sonnet 29, a poem describing the joy that comes when thinking of your beloved.

Her hands tremble as she beholds it, still struggling to understand where she is, when she is. All she does know is that her birthday is the twenty-fourth of September, but Ariadne claims it's been a month since...

"You don't like it," Ariadne says.

"No," Iona says. "No, I love it. Truly, I do, but... What day is it?"

Ariadne regards her quizzically. "October the twentieth."

Iona's mouth falls open in horror, and her head pounds with

a pulsing ache, her chest constricting. She puts a hand over her rapidly beating heart and would have sunk to her knees if Ariadne were not there to catch her.

"Iona?" Ariadne cups her chin when her head droops down.

Her heartbeat races as sweat coats her brow and her breaths come in syncopated gasps, until she thinks she might faint.

"Something is… very wrong with me," Iona gasps. "I am not remembering…"

"Did you lose track of the days?" Ariadne asks.

"I'm losing time…" Iona says. "What is happening to me?"

"Losing time?" Ariadne's eyes widen with her realization. "This must be the Crone's doing."

Iona trembles as she mourns all that time lost. Who could say what had happened to her in all those weeks, what had been done to her when she was mindless and vulnerable. Wordlessly, Ariadne pulls her back onto her feet, pressing a steadying hand against her back while creating a new portal.

"Where is that?" Iona asks, as Ariadne pulls her through.

"Andorra," she says, then explains. "Aunt Xiomara told me in her letter that she would be here at Uncle Raul's house."

They approach a manor of grey stone with mullioned windows; the walls covered in ivy. Iona vaguely recalls Raul mentioning Andorra, a small country between Spain and France where he was born. There is a cool breeze that makes Iona shiver, but soon they are inside, and hasten down a long corridor.

It is Ariadne's tense reticence that unnerves her the most, so uncharacteristic for one so prone to outbursts in moments of stress. She would almost prefer it to this awful void of silence between them. Ariadne takes her to a room with a high ceiling and equally tall windows left open to invite the chilled air. Xiomara sits at a desk of cypress wood reading a grimoire that looks older than time itself.

"Aunt Xiomara," Ariadne says.

She looks up and smiles, "Oh, Iona, how good it is to see you again. I trust your travels have been rejuvenating."

"I'm afraid not," Iona says.

"We need your help. The Crone has done something to her," Ariadne says with impatience.

Xiomara frowns and sets her book aside. "Tell me everything."

They explain it all as best they can. Iona tells what she can remember, the odd moments on the solstice and equinox, and the last memory she had before waking up after weeks of unawareness. Ariadne has a great deal more to say, having been cognizant of the time Iona had lost.

"She wouldn't look at me or hardly speak to me when I visited," Ariadne says, her voice thick with stifled emotions. "I'd assumed it was anger that compelled her aversion, and thought nothing more of it except to give her the time she required to pardon me, but the days turned to weeks and..." She clears her throat. "This morning, I sought Jacira for guidance, but she claims not to have seen Iona in weeks."

Iona is taken aback by this revelation, as is Xiomara. The skirts of her white gown brush against the stone floor as she approaches and takes Iona's face in her hands to inspect her.

"Are your memories distant like a fading dream? Or can you not remember a thing?" Xiomara asks.

"Not a thing," Iona says.

Xiomara drifts tender fingers along her brow, pressing them into her temples, and captures Iona's gaze with a penetrating stare. The tension in her shoulders slackens, her vision blurs, and her thoughts scramble until her mind goes blank.

"I cannot sense anything out of the ordinary," Xiomara muses, removing her hands. "Whatever it is must be deeply obscured."

Iona blinks rapidly and wavers on her feet.

"It must be a memory spell," Ariadne says.

"To take weeks of memory at once..." Xiomara's expression is grave. "I suppose it's possible. Are there any recurring signs that preface the lapse of memory? Or perhaps a sensation afterwards that indicates the spell's effects?"

"My head aches afterward." Iona strains to remember. "I cannot recall anything before..."

"Here is what I can best intuit from all of this," Xiomara says, "As a newly appointed champion of Morgan, the Crone must have anticipated your interference in her affairs, and rightly feared your knowledge of her activities, and so she is harassing you in particular. It makes me wonder if my mother once fought her as well, before she'd gone into hiding, and so she recognizes the pendant bearer's potential to vanquish darkness. This is precisely why we choose to keep our work a secret, or otherwise these devils would be our constant tormenters."

"What can be done?" Iona asks, hoping it will not require a drastic solution.

"We should perform a cleansing ritual," Xiomara decides,

giving her a reassuring look. "We shall remedy this somehow."

"Breathe in," Xiomara says, her voice lulling Iona into a sense of calm.

She inhales deeply the smoke from a bundle of smoldering juniper branches, coughing at the burn in her lungs. Xiomara rubs her back until the coughs subside, then moves the branches so the smoke touches her arms, her torso, her legs.

"Védeni," Xiomara murmurs over and over, ghosting a hand over the crown of her head.

"Will it work?" Iona whispers.

"Only time will tell," she says.

It is oddly comforting to hear. Iona has no use for placating lies. She takes another deep breath and admires the peaceful waters of Lake Avernus. They'd traveled here at Xiomara's behest because the waters are considered sacred, pooled within the crater of an extinct volcano, which can augment a Zerynthos witch's magic, as they garner power from magma, the earth's blood.

Xiomara cups Iona's face in her palms and closes her eyes. "Védeni."

The back of Iona's neck prickles with goosebumps from the distinctive warmth emanating from Xiomara's palms.

"Now, bathe in the water and cleanse yourself," Xiomara says.

Iona eyes the lake, its waters frigid from the autumn chill, endlessly dark without a moon to light its surface.

"Go on," Xiomara says with an encouraging smile.

Steeling herself, Iona strips down to her chemise and approaches the lake with careful steps, not wanting to cut her feet on the sharp rocks. Placing one foot into the water, she flinches at the cold. Her every muscle tenses as she inches her way deeper and deeper until she submerges herself.

Unable to escape the sting of the freezing water enveloping her, she centers herself and finds that the cold forces her into a state of calm. She cannot worry, cannot even think beyond its icy grip. She lingers there longer than she thought she would, until she thinks her lungs might burst.

She opens her eyes. No longer floating beneath the surface of the water, instead she is lying on her back in a very comfortable bed. The ceiling above her is strikingly familiar and when she looks to her right, she can make out the dim design of symmetrically patterned blue flowers with green leaves adorning the white wallpaper.

A heavy sigh makes her tense and look to her left to find Ariadne lying on her back beside her, her dark curls fanned out across her pillow, her eyes closed in peaceful sleep, the bedsheet pooled at her waist, and the glossy selenite dream talisman resting between her breasts.

It seems not only moonstone can elicit a praephora vision, to Iona's great disappointment and slight fascination. She looks down to find the pendant in its place around her own neck, indicating that she must have traveled to a time after the trials. She doesn't give herself much more than a brief moment to marvel at her unexpected journey through time, as she doesn't know how long she can expect to stay.

Gingerly, she slides out of bed, takes her wand from the bedside table, and strains her eyes to search for her discarded chemise, a pile of white fabric on the Turkish rug. She pulls it on over her head, takes her robe hanging on the back of the bathroom door, and pulls that on, too. Wisp trots up to her, yawning, and Iona scratches the top of her head, then beckons her to follow. Aster's head lifts up at the sound of her lacing up her boots, but she motions for him to stay. He obeys with a heavy sigh, resting his head against his paws.

Once outside, when the cool mountain air fills her lungs, a peace fills her unlike any she's felt in months. The moon is not quite full, but its light is enough to bathe the grass and trees with a white glow.

Lysander Forest calls to her as it always does, and she runs into the thicket to behold a dense array of blackthorn trees, their crooked branches sharp and angular, with tiny sprouts of green leaves. The ground is littered with blooming snowdrops, their white petals stark against the otherwise barren dirt.

Part of her wonders if Elise is hidden away nearby, performing some ritual or other to prepare for her imminent attack, then Iona decides she doesn't care. She's grown so exceedingly weary of fear that she's beginning to become desensitized to it.

"Iona."

The gentle whisper has her heart racing, until she recognizes the voice.

"What on earth are you doing wandering about on your own?" Morgan asks, her form materializing in a haze of mist. "The malefician is still out there."

A litany of emotions rushes over her until she settles on

anger, for it's all she has left.

"Why did you do this to me?" Iona asks.

"I beg your pardon?" Morgan asks, her green eyes narrowing.

"I am not from this time," Iona says for her benefit. "Months from now, the world is in utter turmoil because of your inability to properly choose a worthy champion. What were you thinking giving your pendant to me?"

Morgan's shock is a satisfying sight. Iona hopes her words incite an inescapable regret.

"What has happened to make you say such awful things?" Morgan asks.

"Do not feign ignorance of the future," Iona says. "How is it that you knew of Elise and not-"

"I am not omniscient, whatever your assumptions may be," Morgan snaps. "You shall need to explain yourself, or otherwise I shan't decipher the brazen accusations you lay at my feet."

With great impatience, Iona recounts the events of the past several months, explains her praephora powers, and the breadth of the devastation the Crone has already wrought on the innocent. She even tells her of the Zerynthos coven's true calling, thinking that the rules shouldn't apply to a centuries old ghost. By the end, Morgan's indignance turns to utter astonishment.

"Why did you give me the pendant?" Iona asks again.

"I did not," Morgan says. "Ariadne did."

Iona scoffs, "Then why did you let her?"

Morgan's eyes shift away. "I shall not force my pendant upon someone. She could have taken it and chose not to."

"Neither would I have accepted it if you hadn't planted the notion in my head," Iona says. "I never would have considered it possible if not for your intervention on Samhain, with your inscrutable warnings of Elise's schemes. Why is it that you came to me and not Ariadne?"

Morgan sighs, and for the first time, Iona can perceive her humanity beyond her guise of divinity. She is no more than a witch, capable of fallibility and doubt.

"Younger maleficians are far less disciplined in their efforts at concealment. They wreak of dark magic, leave traces of it everywhere. I knew there was one somewhere on this campus but did not know precisely who it would be. That was your mystery to solve," Morgan says. "I've already expressed my admiration for you, my hopes for your future as my champion, so I can only assume your original question is more so an inquiry regarding my view of Ariadne, rather than yourself. "

Iona nods, her ire receding in the face of Morgan's calm.

"Ariadne is a prolific witch, it is true, but in her I saw a soldier, an avenging angel, with the capacity to become a tyrant as Katrin had been. That is not the future I sought, as I told you in the orchard. I desire a peaceful diplomat to craft a future where violence is no longer necessary and the disparity between bloodlines could be a thing of the past. Perhaps it was an idealistic hope," Morgan says, then shakes her head. "If I'd known what Katrin had done…"

"You didn't know?" Iona asks.

"No," Morgan says. "I knew of her empire, her sovereignty, and her bloodline's alliance with Hecate, but I had no knowledge of this secret order of malefician slayers. Perhaps Hecate shrouded her coven's true purpose beyond what clairvoyance or prophecy could perceive, if what you say is true. Even I cannot defy the will of a Goddess."

"Then we are all of us truly powerless in this," Iona says bitterly.

"I am just as much a pawn in fate's game as you are," Morgan says, "even in death."

Before Iona can respond, Morgan reaches out a hand and lightly taps her finger against her forehead, and all goes dark.

Her lungs burn when she jerks awake, the movement making her muscles ache terribly. Still, she pushes herself up onto her elbows and reorients herself. She's no longer floating in the lake but rather lying in Ariadne's bed in the Villa Mitriora.

"I trust your vision was worth the effort?" Ariadne's voice is lifeless.

She sits in a chair across the room by the small fireplace with her head turned away, so Iona cannot see her expression, but she can feel Ariadne's distress.

Iona clears her dry throat. "What happened?"

"You drowned," she says, "Or you nearly did, but Xiomara revived you, then drew her runes upon you again, and that seemed to help."

Iona reaches for her throat. When she attempts a deep breath, the air gets caught and she coughs. The slightest taste of a healing potion still lingers on her taste buds.

"Where did you go?" Ariadne asks.

"Lysander College," Iona rasps. "In May, I think."

"Fascinating," Ariadne says, her voice still devoid of warmth.

"I did not know it would happen… Or even could happen," Iona says.

"Yet another method for you to die," Ariadne murmurs. "Can I leave you alone to bathe without worrying you'll drown in your own bath water? Can you go anywhere at all without slipping through time at an inopportune moment?"

The thought makes a shiver run down Iona's spine. "But I thought moonstone was all that could cause it."

"Apparently it's your own mental state that sets it off," Ariadne says. "The moonstone actuated the ability, but Aunt Xiomara claims it can be entirely random, and so some consider it more of an ailment than a skill. She said it is why you've lost time. It was not the Crone at all. I suppose I should have guessed it… Stupid of me."

"But I have not traveled to the past since Pari's class," Iona argues.

"Your future self traveled into their past," Ariadne says, "inhabiting your current body."

Iona stiffens, then shakes her head, unwilling to accept it. "But… why would my future self ignore you all those weeks? Why would I not explain what was happening?"

Ariadne shrugs. "Perhaps we are at odds sometime in our future, and you could not bear to converse with me."

"No," Iona says. "Of course not."

"You cannot know for certain," Ariadne says. "Who can say what I may have done to deserve it."

"There is nothing you could do that would…" Iona says, then trails off when a realization dawns on her. She slips out of bed and approaches Ariadne where she sits. By the firelight, her heart sinks when she finds Ariadne's reddened face abused with tears. She dreads to ask, "Did you feel me drowning?"

Ariadne's face contorts with pain as she breaks down in awful sobs.

"Oh, Ari," Iona kneeling before her and reaches for her hands, but Ariadne wrenches them away.

"I shouldn't have forced you through the portal! I did not know you would hate me for it! I only knew I could not live without you, even if… I did not know what to do!" Ariadne's every word is punctuated by a gasping breath.

"I do not hate you," Iona cups her cheeks, and doesn't let her pull away. "Ari, look at me."

She wipes Ariadne's tears with her thumbs and pushes her errant curls from her eyes.

"You saved Kokuro's life. If I'd have been there, you would have only been distracted and the Crone would have used that against both of us," Iona says, though it pains her to admit her shortcomings, her weakness.

"You left me," Ariadne says with such dejection that Iona's heart breaks.

"I know," she whispers. "It was wretched of me. I shouldn't have done it."

"I thought you may never come back," Ariadne whispers.

"That's not possible," Iona says. "I love you too much."

Ariadne besieges her with bruising kisses, her hands everywhere at once. The salt of her tears is like poison on Iona's tongue; every kiss wet with them until it's all she tastes. They're soon ripping at each other's clothes, wanting nothing but their skin between them as they fall into bed.

Ariadne's embrace becomes a desperate, covetous rapture, as if she's afraid Iona might disappear and clinging to her will keep her tangible, or otherwise she'll turn to smoke and slip through her fingers. As if every wave of pleasure she coaxes from Iona's writhing form will convince her to stay just a while longer.

"Ari," Iona gasps, stroking her flushed cheek. "I am here. I-"

Ariadne silences her with another all-consuming kiss, and Iona lets her do whatever she wants in the hope that it might console her in this unnerving state. Ariadne worships her, every loving touch tainted by unrelenting fear.

She keeps repeating her love, whispering it, moaning it, demonstrating it with her hands, her mouth, without teasing even once, until Iona swoons and begs her to stop, too sensitive to bear it any longer. Only then is Ariadne's trance broken, and she seems to remember herself.

"I..." Ariadne pants. "I love you."

Iona sighs with slight exasperation. "I know it well enough by now."

The jest is lost on Ariadne in her naked fragility, her emotions entirely exposed in a way she rarely allows. Iona caresses her neck and runs her hands over the smooth planes of her back, until Ariadne's breathing slows and the crazed look in her eye fades as her muscles go slack and she slumps atop Iona in a languorous heap.

"You are the one who taught me love, in all its many forms," Iona reminds her. "Please, my darling, hold me and know that my devotion to you is not capricious, no matter our quarrels, or the dangers we may face."

Through their bond, Ariadne's panic is lessened by her words but even then, even still, her worries persist. Iona doesn't know how to pacify such a monstrous incertitude. She does not know if she can.

Her concern persists when Samhain is upon them and she grips her golden token, the metal branded with a skull. She hopes beyond hope for a moment she's longed for more than anything. Four steps into the brush of a nearby forest, and she's transported to the other side once again.

The grove turns from moss-covered beech trees to drooping willows. The sweet air is perfectly cool, and the sky above is brilliant with clusters of luminescent stars that shine almost like daylight.

"Mother?" Iona calls and even speaking the word aloud is enough to bring her close to tears. "Father?"

"Iona?" Ariadne calls, and to their mutual surprise, they meet in a small clearing. "I thought-"

"We did cross over," Iona says, without doubt. "I suppose we are meeting our ghost together."

Ariadne lets out a heavy sigh of relief, then explains, "I thought… I dreaded seeing Grandmother again. I do not know if I could stomach it."

"Oh," Iona says softly, then takes Ariadne's free hand. "You needn't worry about that any longer. I imagine she won't wish to speak with you ever again, for a woman like her would find you repulsive."

Ariadne's eyes widen, her face falling.

"And that is a very good thing," Iona says, a small smile lifting her lips, and to her great pleasure, Ariadne smiles wryly, too.

They make their way through the thicket until there is a break in the trees. There hidden is a blue roofed cottage with a stone chimney and a flourishing herb garden in the yard. When they reach the front door, Iona knocks.

Less than a second later the door is wrenched open, and her mother stands there with wide hazel eyes, her long crimson hair weaved into a single braid, and her lips stretching into a smile. She looks how Iona prefers to remember her, untouched by sickness, with blood in her cheeks and strength in her limbs.

"Meu querida," She opens her arms and Iona runs to her, finding incomparable solace in her mother's warm embrace.

"I've dreamt of this day for so very long," Iona says, smiling wide.

"Let me look at you." Her mother places her hands on Iona's shoulders. "Que beleza."

Iona flushes and says, "I missed you terribly. Are you well?"

"My renewal is everlasting," her mother says. "All I miss these days is you."

"Iona?" Her father comes barreling into the house wearing a paint-stained apron. "When did you get in?"

"Just now," Iona says, and is surprised to find herself shy.

"I've lost all track of time," he says apologetically as he removes the apron and drapes it on a kitchen chair.

Iona grins at his dishevelment. "Easy to do, I expect."

"You've no idea," he winks, then embraces her.

"Don't blame time for your tardiness," her mother chides. "He was like this in life, too."

"Now, now, let us not relent on my many faults," he says, then looks over Iona's shoulder. "And who might this be?"

Ariadne stands awkwardly in the doorway, uncertainty written all over her face, and Iona admonishes herself for her thoughtlessness.

"Father, Mother, I'd like you to meet Ariadne Zerynthos," Iona says, beckoning her inside.

She steps in, closing the door behind her, then curtsies, "Good evening."

"Much prettier than Tamsyn," her mother whispers.

"Mother," Iona hisses, flushing scarlet at the mention of the girl she'd pined over in her youth. She did not realize her mother had noticed.

"I suppose you'll do," her father says, giving Ariadne a once over, "though I would have preferred if you'd asked for my blessing before taking up with my only beloved daughter."

"Oh," Ariadne's own cheeks redden. "Uh…"

"Father," Iona groans. "Please, be polite."

He grins unapologetically, but acquiesces, "I'll consider us square if you assist me in the garden. I have it on good authority that you are rather skilled with plants."

"Yes, sir. I'd say that I am," Ariadne says with a small smile, before glancing at Iona for reassurance.

*If he gives you trouble-*

*I'd more than deserve it,* Ariadne jests, but her humor is hollow.

The two of them step out the back door into a botanical garden worthy of a king.

"How are you, my darling?" her mother asks.

Iona averts her eyes. "I… I thought ancestors kept watch over their descendants."

"Some do," her mother says, "but we trust you to live well and wouldn't wish to impede on your liberty. Do tell, how is your life? Tell me more of Ariadne and the pendant."

When once she would've had countless stories to tell, Iona finds herself at a loss for words.

"Are you well?" her mother asks with a trace of concern.

She feels the prick of tears but refuses to let them fall and waste precious time.

"Perhaps you should sit." Her mother takes her arm and ushers her to a chair by the hearth.

In a sudden deluge, Iona tells her all that's happened; Hecate's quest, the relentless attacks, the wretched dreams, and the strain it's all taken on her bond with Ariadne.

"How could you stand it for all those years?" Iona asks. "How did it not poison the love you shared? There must be something I've done wrong."

"Oh darling…" Her mother's brow furrows, conveying her conflicted thoughts, before she says, "We were never bonded."

"What?" Iona asks. "But… I assumed you would be. You love each other."

"Hopelessly," she agrees with a small smile, "but we never saw the need."

Iona leans back in her chair. "How then did you find each other in death?"

"I traversed this plane of existence until I found him," her mother says. "It took time, but we were reunited in the end. You see, a blood bond tethers you to Ariadne inexplicably, instantaneously, but that is not the only way to be bound. I spent a life with your father, over weeks, months, years, until our souls did entwine of their own accord. Some are afraid theirs will not do so in the natural way, if their time runs short or their connection should fade for any number of reasons, so they form a blood bond to ensure nothing will impede them in the afterlife. I worried when I spent so many years without your father, until my time came, but when I reawakened here, I heard him calling me home."

Iona smiles at the resilience of her parents' idyllic love, until her own doubts resurface. She wonders now more than ever why Ariadne is so vehemently against breaking the bond. There's no questioning her knowledge of this, after years of diligent study, and yet she chose not to mention it. Iona can only surmise that Ariadne fears their love's decay, should it prevent them from finding each other in the afterlife, but that would never happen. She must know it would never happen.

"You've not done wrong by bonding with her," her mother says, observing Iona's disheartened expression. "I've heard it can be absolutely wonderful in good times, and difficult in dark ones. Relationships of any kind can become strained in times of strife, and with all you've told me, I would be astonished if all was perfectly well between you two. You will endure this adversity together and become all the stronger for it. You must only be patient and compassionate, as I've always taught you."

"Yes, mother," Iona says.

"And if all else fails, you must be honest with her," she advises. "If her love is true, she will understand."

Then her father and Ariadne return to the house carrying a bounty of produce to cook a goulash. Iona directs Ariadne to a chair in the kitchen, for anytime she attempts to cook, she burns everything, despite being so prolific at brewing potions.

Iona takes her place at her father's side, helping to prepare the ingredients and follow his rather flexible instructions. He refuses to measure anything, using only his eyes and his instincts, until the food is declared perfect.

They sit at a wrought iron table in the garden where they eat, tell jokes, and trade stories to their heart's content. Iona doesn't remember when last she laughed so hard, or felt so completely safe, and though Ariadne is a more reserved version of herself, as she tends to be upon meeting new people, her smile is bright as the stars above them, and it warms Iona's heart.

It is bittersweet when Iona opens her eyes, waking on the forest floor, back in the land of the living. She knows she will see her family again, and treasures the time she's spent with them, but it was all too fleeting. Ariadne lays beside her, sighing and stretching her limbs before she sits up.

"They like you," Iona says, for she knows Ariadne will need that assurance.

Her responding smile is weary, and there is something else hidden behind her eyes, but she turns her face away before Iona can identify it. Ariadne needn't have bothered, for the emotion becomes so heightened that she unwittingly disseminates it across the bond. A fierce, overwhelming manifestation of envy.

"They were lovely," Ariadne says, a melancholic tinge to her tone that Iona has never heard before. She stands and walks away, leaving Iona to ponder her words, and all that they imply.

# PART THREE

## OBLIVION

## 28 - Iona

"On this day, the twenty-third of November in the year eighteen hundred and two, I call to order the trial of Élise Lysander of Vienna, who stands accused of the use of maleficium to commit the following crimes: The attempt of a wraith spell, the attempt to force consumption of a love potion, blood magic, leeching spells, and multiple counts of attempted murder through the use of sirens, illusion magic, shrinking spells, and other varied methods," Xiomara says. "Do you understand the charges brought against you, Ms. Lysander?"

Elise lets out an exasperated sigh. Her head rests against her arms, her greasy reddish-brown hair dragging across the table in front of her where her wrists are bound with iron chains. Her raggedy white dress is soaked with her sweat as she trembles uncontrollably, like an opium addict suffering from withdrawals.

The council members shift uneasily in the seats on a stone bench that curves in a semi-circle high above where Elise now sits, while the crowd of angry witches and warlocks watch on with disgust from their seats in the limestone amphitheater. There are about as many in attendance as there would be at one of the solstice rituals, all of them filled with anticipation at watching such an unprecedented proceeding.

From the front row, seated between Ariadne and Crescentia, Iona wrings her hands and tries not to let the sight of Elise's withered form unnerve her.

"I will have an answer, Ms. Lysander," Xiomara says cooly.

"I understand," Elise says as she lifts her head, "that you are a self-righteous band of sycophantic hypocrites and I would have gladly watched you rot if given the chance!"

The onlookers explode with angry cries and calls for Elise's head, or for her to be burned at the stake for her evil deeds. Xiomara bangs her gavel many a time before the crowd calms enough to continue, their vitriol reverberating across the amphitheater and into the night.

"I invite to the stand Crescentia Léandre of Lyon," Xiomara

433

announces.

The crowd murmurs as she approaches the witness' seat and addresses the council, all of whom Iona is now acquainted. Xiomara sits at the center of the stone bench with Aurelia Serrano of Spain, Lady Monton of England, Eleanor Kimball of the United States, her eyes red from recent tears shed for her son, Aron Magnusson of Iceland, Hina Sato of Japan, Ife Nassry of Egypt, her grief over her youngest daughter's death nearly imperceptible in her countenance, Lilavati Verma of India, Olesya Ulanova of Russia, Delara Amani of Persia, Cháo Tian of China, Rayowa Salum of Abyssinia, and Samuel, who cannot stand to look his daughter in the eye, though she seems keen to stare him down.

"I had finished washing and dressing for the ritual that night when I heard a knock upon my door, though I had not been expecting company," Crescentia says. "It was Elise who knocked, but she seemed... out of sorts."

"Out of sorts?" Delara Amani asks.

"Her hair was all tangled, her clothes rumpled and stained, and she was trembling," Crescentia says. "She surely hadn't slept in days, though earlier that afternoon she appeared altogether normal, with a smile on her face. Now I know that to be artifice."

Crescentia spares a glance at Elise, who watches her, expressionless.

"I asked after her health, and she told me she would be well enough by night's end. Then she held out her hand and I was strewn across the room and into the far wall," Crescentia says.

The crowd murmurs in response and she swallows her fear to continue.

"She cut me across the chest, twice, until I stayed prone. Then she cast a leeching spell and took almost all of my magic away." Crescentia's voice grows thick with emotion. "It was the worst pain I've ever known. Worse than breaking my spine, worse than..."

"Not half of what you deserved, common scum," Elise mutters under her breath.

"Skáse!" Xiomara waves her hand and Elise's lips disappear, leaving her mute beyond muffled noises of outrage. Xiomara gives Crescentia an encouraging smile. "Continue, Ms. Léandre."

"With the last of my magic, I made myself like mist to slip through the floor to the drawing room below me, before Elise could steal all of it away," Crescentia says. "Rather fortunately, I landed on a chaise, which broke my fall, but I was stunned for quite a while, and bleeding from cuts I had no magic left to heal. When I did manage to rise from the chaise to seek help, the other witches had all left for the forest. I ran until I found Iona and Ariadne conversing with an imposter. Elise had tried using my face to trick them. We fought her but... she was too strong. She took what remained of my power and... broke my spine. Next, I remember, Professor Lysander found me, I told him what had happened, and I was carried back to campus where Professor Yun inspected my injuries and attempted a healing potion. If not for Iona and Ariadne's intervention, I may have lost my legs and would have certainly never cast another spell for the remainder of my life."

Iona does not have long to comfort Crescentia when she returns to her seat before she herself is called to testify. She refuses to look at Elise, not once, or risk losing her nerve. She tells of how she'd first met Elise, how their friendship had flourished after learning of their relation, or so Iona had thought. They'd practiced their spells together on many occasions, and Elise had never once given her any indication of duplicity or malice. She'd been a consummate actress, enough to fool her, Ariadne, even her own father.

Iona provides brief accounts of the many times Elise attacked her, at least the ones she can remember. She tells of Ariadne's disappearance in the night, and finding her dangling from a cliffside, moments away from letting go. She tells of the tunnels beneath Lysander Forest, of her power being leeched while she'd been trapped in total darkness.

She has no memory of her duel with Elise in the snow after she had first used Crescentia's face to trick her, or of the blood magic that had nearly been successful in compelling her to kill Ariadne, but she can tell of their subsequent decision to establish a blood bond, which elicits a muffled chuckle from Elise that Iona pointedly ignores. Finally, she reaches the night of the blood moon.

"She confessed to every crime when her disguise was shed away," Iona says. "She was so arrogant... So sure that she would triumph. She nearly did."

Despite the overwhelming emotions brewing in her gut, she still does not cry. She pauses in her story, willing her eyes to brim with water, to purge the wretched passions trapped inside her, but she cannot muster even a single tear.

"When we happened upon the meadow, Elise cast an illusion spell on Ariadne to incapacitate her, then tackled me to the ground," Iona says. "I tried to fight her but... it was futile. I could hardly take in breaths from running, and my spells had hardly any effect. She cast a wraith spell so she might control me and the pendant. That is the last I remember, until Ariadne saved me."

Iona looks to Ariadne where she sits, her fists clenched in her lap, her red eyes softening when their gazes meet.

"She saved us all," Iona says.

When Ariadne takes the stand, the whole of the amphitheater goes deathly silent, hanging on her every word as she recounts her own experience fighting Elise, until she reaches the illusory meadow and its horrors.

"Within her illusion, she told me of the love potion she'd brewed, how her living skeletons procured my hair, my tears..." Ariadne says. "When I escaped, that is when the staff presented itself to me from within the roots of the great oak tree. I deflected Elise's leeching spell, which then was cast upon her."

"Is that when you stole her magic?" Olesya Ulanova asks.

Ariadne's jaw tightens. "Elise's own spell accomplished that. It was not my magic that caused it."

"Have you experienced any effects of the maleficium since that day?" Olesya asks.

The crowd murmurs for the first time since Ariadne began speaking, and Iona tenses with unease at the suspicion in many of the council members' eyes.

"No," Ariadne says, her voice strong and clear. "I did not take Elise's magic willingly. It was an effect of the rebounded spell, one that I did not anticipate or desire."

Elise scoffs from where she sits, drawing Ariadne's glare to her.

"Any part of you that may linger in my soul only fills me with disgust," Ariadne seethes. "I am  delighted in knowing you will live the remainder of your pathetic life without an ounce of magic to comfort you in your disgrace."

"Ariadne." Xiomara's tone is a warning. "That will be all."

She nods, then goes to sit beside Iona again, her eyes cast down to the floor. Iona startles slightly when Ariadne reaches out to take her hand, clenching it tightly. At first, she thinks it's to comfort her, but when Iona looks to Ariadne's face, she is only barely maintaining her composure.

*She cannot hurt us anymore,* Iona thinks.

Ariadne nods nearly imperceptibly, but her fear and shame seeps through the bond. If it weren't for the hundreds of onlookers behind them, Iona would have coaxed Ariadne closer, let her find comfort in her arms, if only to erase the thinly veiled sorrow from Ariadne's downtrodden face.

The final two witnesses are Samuel and Violet. Fortunately, their testimonies are brief, but they may as well have been hours long for the toll it takes on them both. They explain the influence Elise's grandmother evidently had, the beliefs the woman harbored about supremacy and power, and the vehemence they both held for those backwards ideals.

"Such hatred can often be generational," Samuel says softly. "It is not inherent. Not natural. Something to be left behind far in our pasts so that we might look to a more tolerant and benevolent future. I wished to end that cycle and… I see now that I was unsuccessful, where my daughter is concerned. I apologize for my failure."

Iona's heart breaks for a man she so greatly admires and grows to hate Elise all the more for the pain he suffers. Then the council adjourns for nearly an hour to deliberate. The time passes at a painful creep.

*And to think… we once thought her terrifying,* Ariadne muses.

Elise is slumped against the table again, seemingly oblivious to the scornful glares targeting her from all angles.

*She was,* Iona thinks.

Ariadne's fists clench until her muscles cramp and Iona winces at the residual pain creeping into her own joints. She goes to reach for Ariadne's hand again to soothe her, when another visceral image accosts her, overtaking her vision.

All Iona can make out are shimmering shards of glass amid furious waves, a mixture of salt water and blood.

She gasps, flinching away at the pure rage emanating from Ariadne, until she seems to remember herself, and her expression shifts to regret.

*What was that?* Iona asks.

*I…* Ariadne's eyes are wide with astonishment, grasping for some sort of response.

But then the council returns to their seats and calls the court to order. Ariadne faces forward and refuses to look Iona in the eye. Crestfallen, Iona follows suit, for she doesn't know if she truly wishes to understand what she unwittingly saw in Ariadne's mind.

"With all the evidence and testimony thus provided, in a

nearly unanimous decision with one noted abstention, we find you, Elise Lysander, to be guilty of all charges and have hereby agreed upon the following sentence," Xiomara says. "Your soul shall be expelled from this world and banished to purgatory for all time, where you shall never find rest, even in death. Your body shall be destroyed to leave you no method of escape or end to your punishment. This is our decision. May any god you follow have mercy on you, for we have none to give."

Iona shivers at the prospect of an eternal punishment, while Elise seems entirely unsurprised to hear of her fate. From then, the crowd disperses, and Iona finds herself in a daze. Ariadne goes off to speak with Xiomara in hushed tones.

Though Iona knows it to be wrong, she finds herself browsing the auras of the other witches and warlocks as they leave, hoping for any indication that one may be the Crone she seeks, but of course it could never be so simple as that.

"Who do you spy on?"

Iona grimaces, her fists clenching. "You'd best leave before Ariadne returns."

"Ariadne is my friend. Why would I flee from her?" Rebekka asks. She wears a red orchid pinned to her lapel of her black suit jacket, her short flaxen hair slicked back against her scalp.

"You are brave to confront her so casually," Iona observes. "Or you are fool."

"Are those the only options I'm afforded?" Rebekka asks.

"What could possibly compel you to risk the ruin of your friendship?" Iona asks, aghast.

"Your beauty drives all those around you mad with avarice," Rebekka whispers back. "Or is that not how you brought a Zerynthos witch to her knees?"

Iona flushes, though she tries not to. "Your flattery is wasted on me and is most unwelcome on this horrid occasion."

It's then she notices Ariadne watching them from across the way, her expression guarded, her jaw set tight.

"Tis an unweeded garden that grows to seed; things rank and gross in nature possess it merely," Rebekka recites from Hamlet.

Iona raises an eyebrow. "Is that meant to impress me?"

"Not at all," Rebekka grins. "I tend to impress women with far more... tactile pursuits."

"What utter nonsense." Iona rolls her eyes. "Leave me be, or I shall set Ariadne on you."

Rebekka's chuckles follow her as she walks away aimlessly until, fortuitous or not, she happens upon a staircase that takes her beneath the amphitheater, where she finds Elise in her holding cell. Numbly, she approaches the metal bars and observes Elise sitting at a dingey wooden table with a deck in her hands. She takes a card and places it faced down upon the wood.

"I knew you would come," Elise says.

Iona's brow furrows at the declaration. Even she had not known she would.

"Come and sit with me," Elise says. "That is what you want, isn't it, Iona? Sweet, boring Iona."

Her cousin's humorless grin reveals her blackened teeth, now left in their grim state without magic to heal them.

"And why would I do that?" Iona asks.

"Because you are attempting to defeat the malefician running amok out there," Elise says.

Standing up straighter, Iona asks, "How do you know of that?"

"Whispers reach me even here," Elise says. "I also happen to be the only one who knows the mind of your adversary, and you are far too curious a creature to resist interrogating me, or otherwise you would not have wandered your way down here."

"You do not know me so well as you might think," Iona grumbles, resenting how accurate her assessment truly is.

"I know you," Elise jeers, "I've spent days, weeks in that mind of yours, sifting through your thoughts, your emotions, to determine the very best ways to strip you apart piece by piece. I know your fears, your hopes, your desires, and every single flaw, as well as Ariadne's. If fate hadn't been so against me, I would have made quick work of you both… A pity the cosmos is so obscenely biased."

Elise sets another card faced down on the table, seemingly ignorant to Iona's look of horror at her admission, at the thought of being violated so completely. Ariadne would detest learning of her innermost thoughts left so exposed to another's scrutiny. She wonders if she should mention it at all, or spare Ariadne the added torment.

"Just keep that pet of yours outside the cell." Elise's lip pulls back in a snarl. "I don't want it anywhere near me."

Glancing down at Wisp, Iona grins haughtily. "I'm glad she made an impression."

"Nearly took my arm off…" Elise mumbles, setting a third card down on the table, flinching only slightly when Wisp snarls with her teeth bared, taunting her.

Biting her lip, Iona looks over her shoulder, but they are entirely alone, apart from the faint clamor of voices heard through the stairwell.

"What was the spell Crescentia used to escape you the night of the blood moon?" Iona asks.

"Incorporelle," Elise says.

Iona incants the spell and becomes like mist, just as Crescentia described. She doesn't recall finding this spell listed in any of the grimoires she's poured over these past months, but Ariadne once mentioned some unique incantations are passed down within families as a sort of heirloom.

Once she's stepped through the bars and made herself tangible again, she conjures a chair and sits across from Elise.

"Is there a way to defeat a malefician that does not result in death?" Iona asks.

"I am still here, aren't I?" Elise asks glumly.

"We cannot expect every malefician to be as idiotic as you," Iona retorts. "Any who now know of Ariadne's shielding will not risk inflicting the same demise upon themself."

"Fair enough." Elise's words are clipped.

"Then what exactly do you suggest?" Iona asks.

"Outsmart them," she says. "Abandon your morals. Cut them to pieces. Turn their blood to air and liquify their bones."

"I cannot..." Iona cringes at the thought.

"How predictable."

"I am not so immune to the horrors of violence as you."

"And that shall be your downfall."

Iona frowns, slumping back in her chair. "This was a fool's errand... I never should have come here."

"You are free to leave whenever you wish," Elise mumbles.

Iona knows the futility of her question before even asking it. "Is there no way to defeat a malefician without the use of violence? Is that truly the only way?"

Elise pauses in her shuffling of cards to truly consider her question. Her brow furrows slightly, then she says, "All that occupied my mind in that time were my insatiable cravings, feeding on maleficium and growing ever stronger. The hunger was... unbearable. It consumed my every waking thought. Maleficium drove me to take increasingly desperate measures in my quest for dominance and victory, so I might..." She trails off, shaking her head. "My mind is clearer now. I see how the maleficium affected me, and though I regret nothing, I cannot reconcile the impending ramifications if I would have continued down that path. It would have ruined me regardless…"

In that moment, Iona sees but a glimpse of the Elise she once knew, the young woman who was once so unsure of herself.

"Do not think of any malefician as rational or motivated by anything but avarice. She will not stop. She will not waver. Neither should you," Elise says.

A rush of dread sends a shiver down Iona's spine. "But… I fear that she is too strong-"

"Would you like a tarot reading?" Elise asks.

Iona reels at the sudden shift in topic. "Why would I-"

"If you don't, you may leave," Elise says. "I tire of your whinging."

Iona glares at her, but Elise keeps her eyes on her deck of cards, shuffling them one more time, before setting three upside down on the table between them.

"Past, present, and future." She points to each card. "Or perhaps you'd prefer the comfort of ignorance."

"No," Iona says, deciding to play along. "Will it work without magic?"

"Tarot is not magic," Elise says. "Fate determines your reading, as well as the events the cards foretell."

She turns over the first card, revealing this deck to be quite simplistic in its art style compared with the one she'd used at college, with tattered edges and faded colors. The first card depicts a sun shedding light onto a prosperous valley.

"The Sun," Elise says. "An indication of victory, joy, love, and all that. You were contented in your past, having everything you could want in a time of peaceful bliss."

Elise flips the card in the middle, revealing a tower set ablaze and people falling from it to their deaths. Iona's heartbeat quickens at the sight, reminded of the blood tower in Japan.

"The Tower," Elise says. "It seems your victory was short-lived. You've been thrown into sudden chaos, forcing you to change and grow through often painful and difficult means. Your strife shall be plentiful, but it can lead to necessary acceptance of inconvenient truths. If you allow these revelations to occur, your suffering will not be in vain."

Elise flips the final card, depicting a man on the ground with ten swords piercing his corpse.

"The ten of swords," Elise says, blinking in surprise. "My word… this is grim."

"What does it mean?" Iona asks, the fervency in her tone drawing Elise's blue eyes up to hers.

"This card indicates a painful, abrupt, inevitable end. A time of anguish and loss. It can allude to a betrayal in your future, made by someone dear to you. It will leave you at your lowest point," Elise says.

Iona stares at the card, trying to ignore the sinking feeling in her gut. The only person whose betrayal would leave her at her lowest point would be Ariadne, but that could not be so. It must indicate something else.

"I suppose I shall not take it too much to heart. When last you read my cards, you claimed I would die," Iona says, willing her words to be flippant.

"You will die," Elise says. "Eventually."

Iona rolls her eyes. "You claimed it would happen soon."

"Did I claim that?" Elise asks.

"You seemed so sure of it," Iona muses. "You said I was always meant to die. It seems you were wrong."

Elise shrugs, gathering the three cards to reshuffle her deck. "The cards and my grandmother's scrying bones showed death in your future. Evidently it will not be immediate, and perhaps it is not your death specifically. With the bones… the future is not always straightforward."

Death has indeed been an ever-present force orbiting Iona of late, so perhaps Elise's reading had been accurate after all. She doesn't know how many more times she can hope to escape it, even with Ariadne's protection.

"What would you have done," Iona asks, "if you'd turned me into a wraith as you planned?"

"Burned the world down city by city until there was nothing left," Elise says. "Rebuild in a way that suited me."

Iona stares at her incredulously. "Who would have been left to inhabit this new world of yours, if all was burned to ash?"

"Only the strongest," Elise says. "The weak would have been weeded out, at long last. We have no need of them anyhow."

"You were once weak."

"Only until I embraced the darkness and found true power."

"It took two of us to defeat you at your very strongest," Iona says, then Elise raises an eyebrow, and she amends. "One of us. Even more pitiful."

"She cheated," Elise says. "I am far more impressed by your prowess. It was quite the unexpected surprise."

"What are you on about?" Iona fumes. "You rendered me unconscious in the meadow."

"Not the meadow," Elise says. "That day in the snow."

442

"You know well I cannot remember it. Anyhow, I am not a natural fighter. Not like Ariadne." When Elise gives her a dubious look, Iona asks, "Do you not agree?"

Ariadne rushes down the stairs, and when she finds Iona in the cell with Elise, she exclaims, "What are you doing in there?"

Elise's lips stretch into a humorless smile. "Ah, how nice of you to grace us with-"

Ariadne makes a portal through the bars, goes right up to Elise, and spits in her face. Iona watches with acute satisfaction as the spittle drips down Elise's cheek, but the fiend only smirks as she wipes it away on her dirty sleeve.

"How is the blood bond treating you?" Elise glares up at her from beneath her lashes.

"Exceedingly well," Ariadne says without a moment's pause, then offers her hand to Iona.

"Wait," she says, than narrows her eyes at Elise. "Why do you ask?"

Elise's wheezing chuckle turns into a visceral hacking cough that steals the breath from her lungs. They watch, unconcerned, until Elise spits on the ground, a tiny puddle of black sludge expelling from her lips, the same bile that she had once spewed when she'd cast maleficium spells.

"I hope that tastes like the most bitter of poisons," Iona says in a low voice.

Elise grimaces and clears her throat, then says, "Do you wish to remember our duel? I cannot recover your memory, but I can tell you what happened."

"It would be worthless lies," Ariadne says.

"Cast a truth spell," Elise says, leaning back in her chair, entirely undaunted by the prospect.

"Verita," Iona casts, sparing only one glance Ariadne's way to mark her disapproval. "Tell me."

"By then, I had become quite desperate, I must admit. I knew my time was running short and wondered if I might fail after all. I thought I would have killed you by then… so I lured you away and attacked." Elise winces. "That was a mistake."

"All of your attacks were mistakes," Ariadne murmurs.

"It's a pity you will never remember, but…" Elise loses her words. "I've never beheld such unmitigated rage, except in myself. Perhaps it is a familial trait. Our Lysander madness…"

A far-off look fills Elise's eyes, as if in a trance. Curiosity getting the better of her yet again, Iona peers into Elise's unprotected aura to behold the memory at the very forefront of her mind, an unsettling image of her own face through Elise's eyes.

There, in plain view, is the rage Elise had described, Iona's tears cutting through the dirt and grime splattered across her cheeks. She's never seen herself this way, not in a mirror, or a portrait, or even in Ariadne's memories of her.

It's like looking at an alternate version of herself, one that doesn't often store her anger away in favor of more practical, palatable emotions. Another glance in Ariadne's direction indicates her appraisal of the same images, having peered into Elise's mind as well.

"I made the mistake of boasting what I planned to do to Ariadne when I was victorious," Elise says, then mutters, "I did not anticipate-"

"That I would defend her to my last breath?" Iona asks. "That was quite stupid of you."

Ariadne's heightened emotions slip through the bond, that of gratitude, pride, and that persisting, maddening, overwhelming fear that never seems to leave her, no matter the circumstance. Iona tries to block it out, to ignore it, but it's proved impossible these many months.

Within Elise's memory, the forest burns where they spar in the freezing floodwater. Iona had thrown fire without thought or care, many of the balls of flame hitting their mark and leaving Elise so badly burned that she could barely move her limbs. She did not have as much power then, before her subsequent rituals in the forest, and her leeching of Iona's power in the tunnels.

"Anyhow, I'd managed to put you to sleep before you could overpower me," Elise says. "I took your blood while I was at it, and left you for Ariadne to discover, so she would know I can always find you."

That had led to many a restless night for them both, but especially Ariadne, who had fought against sleep for days until Iona insisted she take a sleeping potion before she went mad from the deprivation.

"I never did determine how you resisted my blood spell… I choked as Ariadne did, as if your hands were crushing my throat instead of hers, even after I relented and left your mind. It wasn't until I cast a counter spell that I could breathe again. So strange…" Elise muses, until her grin returns. "It was just as well, because I knew then that I'd truly terrified you. The looks on your faces in class… You hardly spoke to any of our classmates before, too afraid of their potential involvement in my supposed crimes, but from then on you were perpetually swept up by your paranoia, only further isolating yourself from others to my advantage."

"This does not matter anymore," Ariadne interrupts. "You lost in the end. Whether it had been by my hand or Iona's, your demise was fated."

"Perhaps," Elise allows, "but if I faced my demise, then so would you."

*She's talking in riddles now*, Ariadne grumbles.

"Speak plainly," Iona says with a glare.

"I wondered how you two might attempt to combat my blood magic," Elise says. "You see, Ariadne has always been quite vocal about her abhorrence for blood bonds, claimed she would never under any circumstances enter into one."

"Yes, I already know of that," Iona says, her impatience growing.

"It would seem she exaggerated her disgust." Elise stares Ariadne down until she shifts uncomfortably. "Or perhaps not. I knew precisely when you bonded, could see it in your exchanges, in your eyes, and I was admittedly shocked, but not discouraged, because I knew it would be its own revenge. It would never work. Not in any lasting way. It would tear your love apart."

"You're wrong," Ariadne says. "It has only brought us closer."

Elise scrutinizes Iona's carefully composed expression, then grins. "Too close. More of a curse than a bond, if you ask me."

"No one did ask you," Ariadne spits, practically vibrating with irritation.

"She did it to save me," Iona says softly.

"At what cost?" Elise asks. "You've turned yourselves into twin parasites, eating each other alive, and with one so broken as Ariadne it is only a matter of time before-"

"She is not broken!" Iona recoils in disgust. "How dare you say such a thing!"

"Iona, please," Ariadne says. *If I stay here much longer, I might hurt her.*

"You know as well as I how damaged, insecure, pathetic she truly is," Elise spits, watching Ariadne intently, delighting in the effect of her cruel words. "Her beauty only compensates for part of it. If only she'd allowed me to cure her flaws as I'd intended, she would have-"

It happens so fast, Iona isn't sure at first if it is her magic or

Ariadne's that hurls the wooden table across the room where it shatters to splinters against the stone wall. Elise rises off the floor, suspended in air, grasping for her neck, her face turning bright red.

"Iona," Ariadne reaches for her hesitantly.

She doesn't take Ariadne's outstretched hand. Not yet. Instead, she stands and takes measured steps closer to Elise to watch her struggle.

"I once thought there was good in all of us," Iona says in a level voice. "That we are all like… clay. Those who we encounter, the trials we face, the adversity of our world molds us in ways we cannot fully anticipate or prevent. I've tried… Truly tried to employ empathy when I can, to afford people grace, and reserve judgement, because fate is kinder to some than others. I see now how foolish that was in your case. How truly wasted my sympathy was."

Elise's color turns from red to cyanotic blue, her legs kicking through the air beneath her.

"You are a monster. You will die a monster. The world will be all the better for it," Iona says.

Elise scratches at her throat, her nails cutting thin lines of blood, and her eyes bugling from their sockets. A moment longer…

*You'll regret it*, Ariadne warns.

It takes great effort for Iona to drag her eyes away from Elise's face to Ariadne's, and she is surprised to see a lack of judgement conveyed in her expression. There is only wary concern.

When she regards Elise again, nearly unconscious from the lack of air, Iona wonders whether she truly would regret it, or if she should heed Moira's advice and take her first life to make the others easier to commit.

"You are the broken one," Iona says. "You are."

Elise falls to the floor, coughing violently and taking horrible, heaving gasps, but Iona does not give her a second glance. She takes Ariadne's hand, utter relief in her red eyes as she leads Iona through a portal back to Rome.

*You did not recant the truth spell*, Ariadne reminds her.

"I know," Iona says.

An incredulous chuckle escapes her before she shrugs and closes the portal. "I forgot how ruthless you can be."

Lowering her eyes, Iona's anger fades and leaves her feeling numb again. She decides that yes, she would have regretted killing Elise, but for the first time she can admit to herself that she is capable of it, despite what she may have claimed to Moira or Ariadne.

"She did not speak truth anyhow. Only her twisted version of it," Ariadne says, her eyes searching for reassurance.

"She only meant to hurt us," Iona says. "We should put it out of our minds."

Ariadne's gaze remains locked with hers, still waiting for a reprieve of her doubts. "And the bond is not a curse, as she claimed."

Averting her gaze, Iona moderates her expression and says, "No."

Ariadne will sense her lie, but there's no helping that. She stares at the front steps of the villa and recalls the moment she'd first considered breaking the blood bond, and Ariadne's fervent plea to keep it. She doesn't know how to broach the subject again without inciting Ariadne's panic, her deeply rooted fear of abandonment, her chronic wound of betrayal. Iona's love for her has never, could never change, but Elise is right. The bond is a poison, and if they keep it much longer, it will ruin them.

Despite finally admitting this to herself, she cannot do anything about it now. The Crone would only benefit from the separation of their minds. So long as their connection protects them, Iona will hold her tongue, but the very moment the Crone is defeated and they find some semblance of normalcy again, she will speak to Ariadne with total honesty, come what may.

## 29 - Ariadne

The lie haunts her day and night. She recognizes it the moment it passes Iona's lips, and it takes everything in her to keep from seeking answers, from searching Iona's mind for the truth, until she cannot bear it anymore.

By the time she musters the courage to look, Iona's thoughts have shifted to other things. Ariadne could delve deeper, sift through her psyche like a woman possessed, but she'd be the foulest of hypocrites to do so after she'd expressly asked for the privacy of her own mind, which Iona has respected without fail.

For days, she cannot stop obsessing over the lie, and Elise's cruel words in the prison cell. She cannot decide what part of it would be worse for Iona to agree with, Elise's description of her many flaws, the disadvantages of the bond, or perhaps both.

She would never dream of attempting to force Iona to keep the bond should she ask to be rid of it but breaking it would undoubtedly exacerbate the rift between them that is already growing into a canyon of unspoken words and resentments. What if her mother is right, and Iona's love will inevitably fade as all good things do… She should have known it would never last forever.

*Why would magic tie me to someone like you?* Iona once whispered.

Ariadne had no answer then, and even now, after all her many failures to protect Iona from pain, from fear, from all that threatens them, she still cannot understand why fate would do this. Why Arachne would do this. Ariadne prevailed once against Elise, but even that, it seems, was no true victory. They'd escaped with their lives, but what is life without Iona?

Her catastrophizing thoughts leave her incurably restless, wandering the halls of the Villa Mitriora like a phantom. They both wish to leave this place but cannot agree on where best to go. Iona has expressed her reluctance to return to Brazil after the many weeks she'd unknowingly lost there.

Nor does she wish to visit Samuel again, only to be constantly reminded of Elise's impending demise. They decide not to impose on Crescentia either, to Ariadne's relief, for she is so wrapped up in her romance with Frankie and neither of them wish to put a damper on their bliss, especially since they cannot fully express what torments them.

Nonna's inevitable interrogation is not worth the sanctuary of her veritable eden. Her keen perceptiveness would have her sensing the tension between them in seconds and demanding answers that Ariadne is unwilling to divulge. Likewise, even Samaira's quiet observation would only grate on her and make her unbearably self-conscious. They are running out of havens, without a true home to speak of, but the thought of putting down roots now is a revolting prospect, though she cannot quite explain why.

Her thoughts drift to Euphemia, though she wouldn't wish to impose upon her either. Her perfect life should not be sullied by this disharmony. And yet, Ariadne waxes nostalgic for those awful parties when Euphemia had made a game of cheering her with any method at her disposal and convinced her friends to accept Ariadne despite her sullen nature and unsociable disposition. In hindsight, those months were some of her happiest, until she'd met Iona.

The November chill raises goosebumps on Ariadne's arms as she leans against the balcony rail and looks out at a spectacular view of Rome, dark and silent in the early hours of morning. Sleep still evades her and Iona's proximity in her bed only serves to disorient her with constant worries and yearnings. She left Aster behind to guard over Iona while she slumbers.

"What are you brooding about?"

Ariadne flinches at the sound but refuses to look. "Go back to Thessaly. You're not wanted here."

"You are still my daughter. You will speak to me with the respect I deserve," her mother's voice harbors a warning, but not the usual vitriol Ariadne has come to expect.

"I'm only your daughter when it suits you," she says.

"Oh, poor Ariadne," her mother says with mocking melodrama. "Kept in splendorous luxury without want of anything, born with more magic than any could dream of, instructed by the very best on how to wield it. Such an awful tragedy indeed."

"Enough," Ariadne snaps. "Iona does not want you here and-"

"And what? She'll send her guard dog to chase me away? Or perhaps she'll break another one of my bones for good measure?" her mother sneers.

Ariadne sighs and pushes away from the balcony to haunt another part of the villa.

"Ariadne Zerynthos, you shan't turn your back on me!" her mother roars.

She goes still, her heartbeat quickening, then turns to glare with as much defiance as she can muster in her exhausted state.

"You think yourself above me now? Is that it?" her mother asks. "You would be nothing without me."

"Whatever you say," Ariadne mumbles. "I tire of quarreling. Take Moira as your progeny and disown me as you threatened. It would be best if we never spoke to each other again."

Her mother's eyes flare. "And what of your father? You shan't pick and choose your parents at your whim."

"Keep him," Ariadne says. "He constantly chose you over me anyhow. I'm more of a tiresome pet to you both, and I won't stand for it any longer."

"You are so ungrateful," her mother seethes.

"Aunt Xiomara was more of a mother to me than you ever were," she says, unable to resist the barb.

"My sister was always the pitying sort," Cintia retorts. "Do not mistake her compassion for anything but charity. She was the fortunate one to sire two devoted daughters worthy of their name."

"They are devoted to her because she loves them dearly," Ariadne says.

Her mother rolls her eyes. "You knew what was required to earn my love and respect, but it seems your lewd infatuation was worth more-"

"Please," Ariadne says. "Go and leave us be. I won't... I cannot endure this anymore."

"I was right about her," she gloats, her smirk returning. "Admit it."

"I will not." Ariadne stands taller.

"She is not the leader you or Morgan thought her to be. The trail of dead bodies in her wake are proof of that," she says. "As per usual, Ariadne, you did not think this through. This mess is entirely your fault."

Clenching her fists, Ariadne storms up to her mother until they are nose to nose. "I am not the one who lied for years on end! If you wished for me to make an informed decision, then you should have told me the damned truth!" she shrieks, her voice echoing into the night. "Never would I have given her the wretched pendant if I knew what was at stake, that the obligations would be more than just parties and politics and rituals. In that Iona would surely thrive, if that's all it had been.

Never would I have knowingly subjected her to this hell! I would have gladly taken it and let it drain the life from me before I'd let harm befall her, but because of *your* incompetence, we are the both of us endangered!" Cintia tries to interject but Ariadne speaks over her. "If you think Iona is so poorly suited to this, then go and fight the Crone yourself, and die for all I care!"

Her mother's look of shock is at least a small satisfaction to be had, but as Ariadne's rage abates, all she feels is emptiness.

"Do not shame me for what I chose. Don't you dare..." She blinks as her fatigue sets in. "Just because you were too old and weak to claim the pendant yourself."

Ariadne does leave then, running down the northward stairs and out the side door into the peristylum. She shivers, then uses the staff to conjure a cloak lined with fur and wraps it tightly around herself.

"Inauspicious stars," Marina whispers.

Ariadne startles, tripping on her feet as she whirls around. "Must you always sneak about like that?"

"I wasn't." Marina's eyebrows lift above her dreamy red eyes. "You weren't paying attention."

"Leave me be," Ariadne mutters. "Go and pester Moira."

"She's away. Another council meeting... the covens grow restless. Moira did not wish for Mother to travel alone when their assembly will likely be a detestable contretemps," Marina says, then looks up and any peace in her countenance fades. Her jaw slackens, her neck craning into an unnatural angle, and her red eyes go so wide, it's a wonder they don't pop from her skull.

Ariadne looks up too, a creeping unease sobering her. "What do you see?"

"A star has died," Marina whispers. "It's brilliant death is a most gruesome omen. I fear we will be met with the very worst of hostilities this night, and not all will survive it."

She points up and just as she'd described, a new light much larger than an ordinary star glitters in the dark sky.

"Where will she strike?" Ariadne asks.

Marina squints, "North..."

"Where north?" Ariadne asks with impatience.

Marina goes silent and still. Ariadne waits, having been taught to leave Marina be in those moments of consummate perception.

"I see clouds and fire," Marina whispers, "and wings... clipped."

"What do you mean by-" Ariadne chokes on her words, then grasps Marina's shoulders and shakes her, willing her to look down. "Where? Where north?"

When Marina takes too long to answer, Ariadne sprints back inside, running to the atrium where, on a table beside the front door, sits a letter. Ariadne grasps for it blindly, nearly ripping it in half in her haste, and reads Samaira's hurried scrawl with voracity. *Go at once to Sweden! It may be too late, but...*

"No," she gasps, the letter slipping from her fingers. "Not her."

Marina runs up behind her. "Ariadne, wait. We must find-"

She conjures a portal and jumps through only to flinch away from the burning wind, ash, and embers. Every breath she takes is suffocating, the smoke so black it blocks out the moon.

*Iona!* Ariadne screams through the bond, putting up a hand to shield against the wind and behold, with bone-chilling dread, the monstrous blaze that has overtaken the Drakenström's woodlands. Flames stretch high and bright, like claws reaching up to the stars that betrayed their awful intentions.

"Ariadne," Leonid runs up to her, then falls to his knees in a fit of violent coughs.

*What is it?* Iona calls back. *What's happened?*

"Where is she?" Ariadne asks, already knowing the answer.

Leonid points to the blazing forest.

"She just..." He coughs and gasps. "I tried to stop her but... she walked into the flames. They parted for her-"

Leaving the portal to Rome open behind her, Ariadne runs towards the forest. *The Crone has Euphemia.*

"Neró," she incants, but the water does nothing against the flames except to create a cloud of steam.

She hasn't much time to relent its ineffectiveness before she sprints into the trees anyway and despite the shield emanating from her staff, the flames lick at her skin and spread across her cloak. She grits her teeth to keep from screaming as she rips apart the tie at her neck and tosses the cloak aside. Bringing the neckline of her chemise over her nose, she squints to try and see through the smoke to discern a path between the burning trees.

"Euphemia!" Ariadne cries, again and again, but there is no answer.

*You should have awaited my arrival!* Iona's indignation is overshadowed by concern. *You will burn yourself!*

*I couldn't wait.* She winces, unwilling to retrace her steps all over again. *I left the portal open.*

*Yes, I've already gone through,* Iona thinks. There is a long pause before she speaks again. *The flames are parting for me.*

Ariadne stops short in her frantic dash through the burning trees to look back where she'd come. *They are?*

*There's a path made for me but...* Iona's emotions are riddled with doubt. *The Crone would not make it this easy without awful consequences. Perhaps I should not enter-*

*But if you wait, she may die.* Ariadne clenches and unclenches her fists.

*I'll go then,* Iona decides, *but you must find us. I cannot fight her alone.*

*Where is Marina?* Ariadne asks and looks around in all directions for any sign of movement.

*She's here, but whenever she attempts to follow me, the flames converge again,* Iona relents. *Why did you go without me?*

Ariadne huffs angrily, *I... I wasn't thinking. I just-*

*I know.* Iona's enduring compassion seeps through the bond. *Try to make another portal.*

Just like when she followed Moira and Iona to Denmark, Ariadne closes her eyes and wills herself to glimpse Iona's sight and distinguish where the portal's exit should be, but all Iona can see are swaths of white flames and blackened trees without any discernible landmarks. The fire does indeed part for her, and though Iona sweats from the unbearable heat, she is not burned. She takes careful steps through the smoke, holding a damp cloth over her mouth.

Ariadne's staff glows and a portal emerges, showing flames on the other side, but when she jumps through, she is alone in another empty part of the forest. Black plumes of smoke billow about, burning her lungs with every inhalation.

*Ari?* Iona calls.

*I'm coming.* Ariadne closes her eyes again but still finds the trees and flickering flames indistinguishable from anything else, obscured by waves of embers cascading down upon Iona, so that she can hardly perceive anything while her eyes water from the oppressive fumes.

She makes another portal anyway, but she only goes to another empty part of the forest, and another, and another.

*I think I see the end.* Iona coughs from deep in her chest, and Ariadne brings a hand to her own throat.

*I'm... I'll find you. Just don't panic.*

*Please hurry!*

Ariadne conjures a small wave of water to drench herself in

an effort to stave off the fire, then picks a direction and runs, uncaring of the searing pain against her arms and ankles where her chemise doesn't cover her and her shield doesn't seem to reach.

Relenting her grave misjudgment, she crafts a portal back to Euphemia's manor, hoping to reenter the forest from a different angle or seek help from Aunt Xiomara or Marina, or any of her family members, but the portal opens, and there is nothing but flames on the other side. Her heartbeat stuttering in her chest, she tries again, but still her magic does not listen.

"Arachne, please," Ariadne mutters. "I'll never forgive you. Never..."

A guttural cough brings her to her knees. The distant echo of the Crone's laugh on the wind makes Ariadne scream with all consuming rage. She cranes her neck to look up into the sky where the haze of smoke turns the moon red, a familiar sight that horrifies her to her core.

*I've found her!* Iona calls. *Where are you?*

Ariadne sobs with relief. *My portals are sending me in useless circles. It's the Crone, I'm sure of it.*

*She's in chains like the others.* Iona is careful not to touch them and reassures Euphemia that she's not alone, that Ariadne isn't far behind. Euphemia looks up at her, stricken with terror, her sobs unintelligible as she strains against her bindings.

*Is there any sign of the Crone?* Ariadne asks.

*No.* Iona looks about to be sure, but there is only fire.

*You must cut Euphemia free before she returns,* Ariadne instructs.

*But how... How am I meant to cut through without causing her pain?* Iona asks.

She squeezes her eyes shut, ridden with regret. Iona cannot stop time, and Ariadne doesn't know if her unpredictable ability can span the length of the entire forest. Even if she could, there's no saying whether she could stop it for Iona as well as her, or how long the spell would last, and it consumes too much magic to test it thoughtlessly. She weaves a hand through her hair, ripping strands from her scalp with the gesture, and sighs in resignation.

*You must numb her to pain as you did for Phoebe's father,* Ariadne hesitates. *Then you must cut through however you can and heal her as you work, or she will bleed out.*

Iona's thoughts revolt at the idea.

"There is no other way!" Ariadne yells aloud. "You must do it! Do it now!"

Iona startles at her harsh demand, then jumps into action. She explains to Euphemia what she plans to do, casts the spell to take away her pain, then stands above Euphemia and hesitantly holds out her hand.

"Forgive me," Iona says, then chokes out, "Izrezati."

A shallow cut slices across Euphemia's back, and their only comfort is a lack of a scream in response to the wound, but the blood seeping through Euphemia's white chemise remains a sickening sight. Iona's hand trembles, her eyes blinking rapidly.

Only the slightest divot can be seen in the metal link, and Iona is struck by the horrific realization that this will take countless strikes before she can break through.

*Good. Keep going.* Ariadne encourages.

Iona casts the spell again, then again, each time drawing more blood, until Euphemia's back is coated with red. Iona's stomach turns, but she doesn't relent.

All the while, Ariadne sprints through the smoldering wilderness in search of them, or the Crone. At times she tries again to use a portal with no success. She considers flying above the flames, but the dense smoke would only blind her, and her feathers would surely burn away.

Ariadne looks back through Iona's eyes and grimaces at the mess of bloody cuts across Euphemia's back, as if she's been lashed by a cat o' nine tails. Iona heals the lacerations, only to make them all over again.

"Hold on," Iona's voice trembles. "I… I'm nearly done."

It's an outright lie. Her cuts have only made the slightest notch through one metal link. Just as it had been for Ariadne when she'd worked to free Kokuro, the spell is only marginally, infinitesimally effective.

*Keep aware of your surroundings,* Ariadne warns. *She's out there somewhere and likely watching you right now.*

Iona goes rigid, searching the trees again for any sign of black robes or the glint of a dagger.

*I don't see-*

She screams as she's propelled through the air and away from Euphemia, falling hard onto her back and knocking the air from her lungs.

The Crone descends from a plume of angry smoke and floats above Euphemia's bleeding body to shriek her awful spell, so thunderous it reaches Ariadne as a distinctive echo due north. The Crone hurls a barrage of jagged silver knives that slice through the air between them, but Iona holds up a hand to turn them from metal to wood. They instantly catch fire and whither to ash by the time they reach her.

Using the grey cloud of ash as cover, Iona ducks down and darts to the right only to nearly be swallowed up by a wave of fire. She conjures a metal shield to cover her, but her arms and legs are terribly scorched by the intense heat. She grits her teeth through the pain.

Ariadne runs toward the pealing sound of the Crone's screams. She tries to make a portal again, but it only takes her farther from the sound. Dangerously close to tossing her useless staff into the flames in her anger, she reigns in her aggravation and runs, runs until she thinks her lungs might give out, until her muscles nearly succumb to her crippling exhaustion.

There's fire in her lungs, singeing her hair, blistering her skin. She tries to keep watch over Iona through the bond and almost collides into a tree in her distraction, but there is a tug against her back, diverting her just enough to avoid it.

Fragmented images of Iona's vision flit over Ariadne's eyes, showing the truly spectacular display of opposing might. Iona throws every spell in her arsenal without hesitation and without faltering. She cannot shield herself from maleficium as Ariadne can but instead uses the spells in her favor and evades the ones she cannot withstand.

Breaking through the trunk of a nearby tree, Iona wills it to expand, growing in size exponentially, so the Crone is forced to weave away from it, and Euphemia. While she's distracted, Iona makes the earth shift, so Euphemia rolls down an incline and lands by Iona's feet. Then she channels all her will into conjuring an avalanche of stone that falls from the sky, relentlessly pelting the Crone until she's buried beneath a mountain of rock.

Ariadne's chest swells with pride when for a brief moment she wonders if Iona prevailed, until the Crone explodes from beneath the stones and retaliates with a leeching curse.

The splitting pain, like blades puncturing Iona's skull and dragging across her brain, is more than either of them can bear. Ariadne falls to her knees and screams with her.

While the Crone isn't likely capable of stealing all of Iona's power when the pendant regenerates it so quickly, it also means there's no reprieve from the misery of the spell's effects.

*Help me! Please!* Iona begs. *I cannot best her!*

*Hold on!* Ariadne staggers to her feet and takes haphazard steps forward, but she cannot manage to run when her head feels like it's being cloven in two.

"Leave her be! Just take me and let her go!" Euphemia cries.

Ariadne forces her way through the flames into the clearing right as the Crone hurls Euphemia back towards her, away from where Iona lies crumpled on the charred ground.

"Euphemia!" Ariadne calls.

"Ari!" She cries, her sapphire eyes filling with hope.

The Crone laughs as she unsheathes her golden dagger.

"Incorporelle!" Iona screams, a split second before the Crone plunges the dagger into Euphemia's stomach, but the blade doesn't puncture her, instead going straight through into the dirt beneath.

The Crone screeches in outrage and tries twice more to cut Euphemia open, but she's completely intangible, and in the Crone's distraction her leeching spell finally abates. All that still clings to Euphemia are those terrible chains, though she attempts to break through them.

*Hold the spell!* Ariadne encourages as she helps Iona back onto her feet.

The Crone turns her attention back on them, her fist clenched around the hilt of her jagged blade, when all at once gravity shifts and eludes them altogether as they float off the ground toward the smoldering canopy above. The rocks Iona had conjured float with them, one of them striking Ariadne across her back. Iona's grip on her arm slips, and they're pulled apart.

The Crone hovers, unhindered by the shift in gravity, and reaches for Iona, but Ariadne takes one of the floating rocks, imbues it with a spell and hurls it at the infernal witch. When it collides with her, it ignites, the explosion throwing the Crone flailing away and into the burning trees.

*I've lost concentration,* Iona relents, indicating the spell on Euphemia has waned. "I must return to her."

Reaching out, Ariadne grasps Iona's arm and pulls her in close. *We should anchor ourselves to-*

The Crone bursts through the branches, scoops Euphemia up into her arms, and hurtles them up towards the sky.

Iona screams, and her pendant glows, the blinding light swirling and condensing into the shape of wings, glistening scales, and jagged teeth.

Morgan's dragon roars, the sound compelling the Crone to look back and though they cannot see her face, there is no mistaking her fear.

*Climb on!* Iona reaches for her, and Ariadne takes her hand, settling behind her and gripping the ridges of the dragon's back as he unfurls his wings and propels them up past the burning forest, through the suffocating smoke, and into the silver clouds.

*Do you see her?* Iona asks then coughs violently, the poisonous air taking its toll.

Ariadne goes to say no, but a small bit of movement from the corner of her eye has her pause. Frida strains her delicate white wings to fly much higher than she ought.

"Follow the dove!" Ariadne orders, pointing it out for Iona to see.

The dragon obeys. Freezing wind whips across their faces as he flies after Frida through the darkening clouds limned with moonlight, until even he strains against the blustering weather. Iona conjures warm cloaks for the both of them, but it does little to stave off their shivers.

"Are we sure-" Ariadne clenches her jaw to keep her teeth from chattering. "-that she is still in the air?"

Iona shakes her head, then ducks down when a jagged line of lightning stretches through the sky as if reaching out for them, followed by a frightening crack of thunder. Frida and the dragon pull in their wings and dive out of the way. They scream as their stomachs drop, and Ariadne clutches Iona's waist to keep them both from falling off, when finally, the dragon unfurls his wings again and they glide.

Another strike of lightning cracks with a thunderous boom, and the dragon weaves this way and that, evading the flashing white currents, until one strikes his wing and he roars in pain.

"Philisa." Iona reaches out to heal the wound, but the dragon becomes restless.

He flies higher, higher, permeating a swirling cloud. It's there they finally find the Crone floating in a sphere of rain, fog, and glittering lightning, with Euphemia still chained and thrown over the Crone's shoulder.

The dragon holds back his fire, wisely cautious of burning Euphemia by mistake, but Frida does not hesitate. As she flies, her feathers grow, her body transforming until she is more than double her normal size. Her sharpened talons reach for Euphemia.

"Frida, stay back!" she cries.

To Ariadne's amazement, the Crone does nothing to prevent the transformed dove from latching her talons around one of Euphemia's chains in an effort to lift her away, then sees why when the dove lets out a cry of pain and releases the chain.

"Frida don't" Iona cries, but before they can react, the Crone reaches out and takes one of Frida's wings, snapping it in two as if it were nothing, and tosses the bird away.

"Frida!" Euphemia weeps. "No… No…"

Ariadne crafts a portal to the ground beneath the dove before she falls too far for her to see, hoping someone on the ground can find her and heal her wing.

*Cast Crescentia's spell again,* Ariadne instructs. *I shall separate the two of them somehow and catch Euphemia when she falls.*

*But how? The chains-*

*I'll withstand the pain until she's safely on the ground.*

*But you may drop her-*

*Iona, please, we haven't the time!* Ariadne sprouts wings and without another word, she propels herself up and though every part of her wants to cower, she dives toward the Crone.

"Nun-eul humchida!" Ariadne incants, taking the Crone's sight.

She screams in outrage, her grip slipping just enough for Ariadne to glide down and wrench Euphemia away. The moment she's far enough, the dragon unleashes its fiery breath onto the Crone, but she falls out of the way right before the flames can touch her.

Just as Iona warned, the moment Ariadne's fingers touch the chains, an excruciating pain radiates through her, the metal like a burning ice against her skin. She nearly drops Euphemia right then but manages to lift her staff and create a portal to the ground outside Drakenström Manor. She flaps her wings erratically, seconds away from tossing Euphemia through, but the Crone tackles her, pulling her away from the portal, and holding out a hand to close the doorway against Ariadne's will. She squirms and kicks, her grip on the chains slipping.

Leaping from the dragon's back, Iona latches herself onto the Crone's back instead, wrapping one arm around her neck and putting a hand against her forehead over top of the black wrappings.

Her incantation is a desperate plea. "Sove!"

The Crone wavers, her arms dropping limply at her sides, and for a moment it appears as if she might sleep. Ariadne wrenches herself free, keeping her hold on Euphemia, and opens her mouth to speak, but the Crone reaches behind herself, lacing her fingers in Iona's wet hair and pulling Iona around to face her.

"Save Euphemia!" Iona cries, then screams when the Crone's hands turn to claws and slash across her from her cheek, down her neck, her torso, to her hip, then pulls back to strike another blow.

"Take her!" Ariadne throws Euphemia up, and the dragon bites down on the chain and carries her out of the swirling sphere of clouds.

Ariadne plunges on the wind, curving her wings to dive down where the Crone hovers, and collides into Iona, scooping her up and out of the Crone's clawed grip, finding brief solace in Iona's warmth, her face burrowing into her neck.

"She's too strong," Iona cries. "She's too strong… How are we meant…"

Then Iona gasps, and Ariadne searches the skies for what alarms her. The dragon's dark wings struggle to keep him and Euphemia aloft, and at first Ariadne wonders if the Crone has attacked, but when she squints, she can see the wretched chains have broken straight through his teeth. Thick blood spills from his mouth and falls in large red drops.

Ariadne cries out when a curse strikes her back, leeching away her power. Iona screams too, from both the residual pain and the sight of the Crone hurtling towards them. Any power she has left is stripped away, just as her wings catch fire and burn until they are reduced to smoldering feathers.

"I'll carry us!" Iona tries to reposition herself as they plummet down to Earth. "Keep hold of me!"

Ariadne's grip slackens on both Iona and her staff, and from the corner of her eye she sees a cloud of lightning enveloping the dragon, striking him again and again, and though he still tries to keep hold of Euphemia, the chains slip from his mouth, and she falls, too. The dragon shimmers, then disappears back to his plane of existence.

"Ari! Can you hear me?" Iona screams over the wind, trying to gather her up so she can make her own wings.

But the Crone grabs Iona by her hair again, making her cry out and lose her hold, reaching up to try and break free, until the Crone puts a hand against her forehead, screaming another spell that pierces the air. Iona convulses, her eyes sliding back into her head.

"No!" Ariadne's scream rivals the Crone's and an explosion of yellow and orange spectral light detonates in the space between Iona and the Crone, separating them in a brilliant flash.

Iona is flung out into the dark sky to Ariadne's right. Then they fall through a cloud, the algid crystalline water drenching them, and when they make it to the other side, Ariadne hears

Euphemia's screams to her left, still helplessly bound in chains. She glances to her right, and finds Iona is unconscious. Whatever spell the Crone had cast was a reckoning.

"Iona!" Ariadne screams, but she does not wake.

"Ariadne!" Euphemia calls.

She tries to conjure wings, a broom, anything that might save them, but her magic wanes. Her vision blurs, distorted by the thin air rushing past her, so loud and so very cold.

The Crone hovers above them, waiting, watching, anticipating their next move. She wants Euphemia, but Ariadne supposes the sacrifice would be satisfied by Iona's murder just as well. Again, Ariadne looks to Euphemia, who screams something to her, but she cannot hear over the wind.

Exerting well beyond her limits, Ariadne stops time. She's shocked when the magic works, and doesn't know how long it will last, then realizes she still doesn't know what to do. Again, she tries to make wings so she might gather both women in her arms and make a portal, if she can, but when she looks over her shoulder, the ground is much closer than she anticipated. She knows the very moment she goes for one of them, the Crone will go for the other.

Then time starts again, her stomach lurching as she drops, and Ariadne sobs, at a complete loss for what to do. She tries making a portal beneath Euphemia, but to her great despair, it closes with a slight wave of the Crone's hand.

"No…" Ariadne weeps, struggling to keep her eyes open.

She tries to stop time again, and it works but only for a few seconds before it slips back into its normal tempo. She looks to Euphemia; her blue eyes filled with terror as she shakes her head.

Ariadne lets out a wretched bellow, all her self-hatred and regret unleashed in the sound, then lunges for Iona and tumbles them through a portal that doesn't close, because the Crone goes for Euphemia, taking her up in her arms and unsheathing her dagger.

Ariadne hasn't the strength to watch, closing the portal mere moments before the jagged edge meets Euphemia's skin. Ariadne screams, screams until her voice gives out and her lungs burn. She rocks Iona against her, clinging to her where they lay in the grass just outside the blazing forest.

"Where is she?" Leonid yells as he approaches.

Ariadne turns away, unable to face him, but his scream makes her go rigid, thinking the Crone has followed them. She looks up and watches as Euphemia's body falls, her stomach drenched with blood. She disappears within the burning trees, taken by the flames.

Leonid's cries are too much to bear, filled with the sort of grief Ariadne knows she would never survive. She holds Iona close, their clothes partially burned off their bodies, the remaining scraps drenched with freezing cloud water, their skin beneath covered in burns and blisters.

She jerks at the feeling of hands against her back, healing hands that take the pain away, and she looks up into Xiomara's solemn face, her compassionate eyes enough to break what's left of Ariadne's composure.

Embers float through the air like snowflakes, until the flames diminish, and an awful silence grows, broken only by the anguished lamentations of Euphemia's loved ones mourning her demise.

# 30 - Ariadne

Draped in the most exquisite white satin, adorned with all her best jewels, and with white daisies braided into her golden hair, Euphemia is as much an ethereal beauty in death as she was in life. Her familiar's broken body lies just beside her head, her pale feathers having been thoroughly washed to rid them of ash, cushioned by a white pillow bordered with intricate lace.

Ariadne cannot repel the disturbing image of the bloody laceration ripped across Euphemia's stomach, now hidden beneath her funeral dress. The stench of smoke still lingers in the air within the manor's walls despite the many lilies, gladiolus, and orchids she'd conjured for the service, which have already begun to wilt.

She never thought she'd see her friend's face again, and beholding it now, her eyes closed in what could be mistaken for serene sleep, Ariadne almost wishes she hadn't. It was a surprise to them all that Euphemia's body was found within the steaming wreckage of the blackened trees. She wasn't burnt to cinders, swept away by the wind, as everyone had expected. The Crone left her there.

And upon the recovery of Euphemia's body the night before, a healer preparing her for burial discovered her uterus had been stolen. Leonid had choked out the news that morning, barely able to speak the words, terrible as they are.

The funeral's reception is held in Moscow, within familiar walls that Ariadne half-hoped never to walk through again. The Ulanova's castle is a dark, inhospitable tomb of black stone. Despite the fires burning in every hearth, the rooms are always freezing, the floors and walls persistently damp.

The Morozovas, Ulanovas, Drakenströms, and other mourners gather in a saturnine assembly, holding their goblets of untouched wine and speaking in hushed tones. Candles flicker within the crystal chandeliers hanging from the ballroom ceiling and Ariadne finds herself gazing up at them, ignoring the persisting stares that creep across her skin.

A shoulder brushes against hers, and her heart nearly stops at the sight of Tatiana Nicolo glancing at her, her face unreadable, before turning to walk away. Clenching her jaw, Ariadne follows her out into the hallway.

"What is it you wish to say to me?" Ariadne asks.

Tatiana turns to look back at her, her eyebrows raising in surprise.

"Spit it out!" Ariadne attempts malice, but she sounds pitiful even to her own ears. "Tell me so we might get on with our lives."

Tatiana shakes her head with revulsion. "I never wished to speak to you again after what you did. Neither do I relish the sight of you, but I haven't a quarrel to pick. Perhaps it is your own guilt that's left you paranoid."

Ariadne blinks at her, recalling every time Tatiana had stared pointedly at her, her gaze penetrating and accusatory.

"My, you have unraveled," Tatiana observes, her voice shrill. "I suppose for your true friends, you are capable of remorse."

Ariadne flinches. "I was a wreck after... I couldn't eat... I hadn't the strength to leave my bed-"

"Neither did my sister," Tatiana hisses. "She lost years."

"When she woke, all she did was beg for my forgiveness for what your family compelled her to do. You should reserve your resentful stares for them, not I," Ariadne says, then forces out. "All I did was to defend myself."

At that, Tatiana looks away, showing the first trace of shame, that then turns back into resentment. "It was a gross retaliation. Your power was thrice what my sister had at her disposal and the moment you had the chance to unleash it; you did not hesitate."

"I was a child," Ariadne says, as Iona constantly reminds her.

"You think healing her absolves you of your crime?" Tatiana asks. "I am only glad you are not Morgan's champion, as everyone wrongfully assumed you'd be. You're not a killer, but worse. A torturer. Not worthy of power. Not worthy of anything. My sister, childlike as she still remains, should not be the metric by which you measure your redemption. The illusions you must have crafted... to shatter a child's mind..."

Tatiana turns her head away in disgust, and Ariadne clenches her fists until her nails cut into the skin of her palms.

"You will forever be a monster," Tatiana spits. "Any pain you've endured is deserved many times over for what you've done."

With that Tatiana does not spare her a second glance as she leaves, pulling out a handkerchief to wipe away her silent tears. Ariadne envies her the luxury of weeping and of leaving, for she can do neither. She must return to the ballroom, to the ever-present stares, and pretend, as she always does, that she is fine.

Making herself numb, she does just that. She plays her part, for the sake of Euphemia's family most of all, and barely remembers how she makes it from the hallway to the banquet table where an array of untouched fruit, cheeses, meats, and cakes have been laid out.

"Ari," Iona whispers.

Her posture straightens as her vision refocuses. "Hmm?"

"I… I could make you a plate," Iona says softly. "If you'd like, I could-"

"No," Ariadne shakes her head.

Iona bites her lip, then says, "But you've not eaten in days."

Ariadne's brow furrows. She intends to contradict her but cannot recall her last meal. She's been too distracted by her grief and doubts she could keep down much more than water.

"You needn't trouble yourself," Ariadne says instead, not wishing to burden her or explain her state of mind. Such attentiveness, such kindness is offensive to her when she could never deserve it. Not after all she's done and all she's failed to do. She could never deserve anything good or decent or gentle or-

"It is no trouble," Iona says softly. "I could conjure you something instead, if you'd prefer-"

"Iona." Her restraint snaps like a taut rope put under too much strain. "I do not need you telling me when to eat. You are not my mother, as I recall. Stop acting like it."

Iona pulls away, stung on the quick, her bloodshot hazel eyes widening.

Ariadne's regret is immediate. "I didn't-"

"Very well. Forget I asked." Iona steps away and as she goes, she takes a glass of wine from one of the banquet tables, downing its contents in one gulp.

*Iona,* Ariadne calls, trying to follow her, but she disappears into the crowd without looking back.

Not wanting to leave things as they are without properly apologizing, Ariadne follows, weaving through the dense crowd of mournful faces.

A hand brushes down her spine, and she flinches away, any warmth left within her turning to ice. She shivers but refuses to be distracted. Pressing forward, she searches for any glimpse of red hair, but there is only an endless sea of black silk.

Another hand touches her shoulder, and she grows faint, almost collapsing onto the marble floor. She swears she can hear

the whisper of a mocking laugh and turns in the direction of the sound, only to trip on her feet when someone shoves her quite hard. She loses her balance and would have fallen on her face if she hadn't been clinging to her staff, but when she looks back, no one is there. Aster looks about too, trying to identify their attacker.

"Iona?" Ariadne calls, then flinches when another ghostly hand traces a line across her shoulders.

She stumbles, her thoughts all scattered, then makes it through the crowd only to find Iona slumped in a chair by the fire with a half empty bottle of wine cradled in one arm, the other propping up her head against the tufted arm of the chair. She is positively foxed, though Ariadne has no notion of how she could have managed such a feat within mere seconds. Rebekka sits directly across from her, tankard in hand, and similarly inebriated.

Out of the corner of her eye, she notes Ksenia brooding in the corner, her exhaustion somehow even more pronounced than when Ariadne had last seen her. Before she can think too much of it, Rebekka's booming voice breaks the silence.

"To Euphemia." Rebekka lifts her tankard high. "A truer friend could never be found. A gentler soul has never before walked this earth. May she find peace in the next realm."

"To Euphemia," Iona mumbles, and struggles to lift her bottle and bring it to her lips. She drinks deeply, a stray drop of red dripping down her chin.

Approaching them, Ariadne says, "I called for you."

Iona lowers her bottle and squints up from beneath her long red lashes. "No."

"Yes, I did." Ariadne strains to keep her voice level. "Did you not hear me?"

"Clearly not." Iona frowns.

"Neither did I," Rebekka says.

"I did not ask you," Ariadne snaps.

Rebekka's eyebrows shoot up. "Come now, Ari. There's no need for animosity. Let us celebrate Euphemia's life together. It's what she would have wanted."

For a moment, she truly considers it, until the back of her neck prickles with the distinct feeling of eyes trained on her. She dares to look and finds her mother watching with a sour expression. She hasn't said a word since their argument on the balcony, and Ariadne is most grateful for it, though her silence is as much a cry for Ariadne's attention as any of her screams.

Cintia stands beside Olesya Ulanova and leans in to whisper something into her ear, which compels Olesya to laugh.

It's a most offensive sound, entirely unwelcome on such an occasion as this, and it serves to break what is left of Ariadne's spirit. Her vision blurs with unwanted tears that she tries to blink away.

Numb to everything again, she quietly makes her way to a pianoforte nestled in a dark corner by a tall window and props her staff against the wall. As she takes her seat and rests her fingers lightly over the keys, Olesya crosses the room to where Iona and Rebekka are drinking their troubles away.

"Might I join you?" Olesya asks. "I thought-"

Ariadne slams her hands down against the ivory keys, the opening notes inciting a startled gasp or two and drawing all eyes to her. She plays the third movement of Beethoven's Moonlight Sonata, the part that she cannot seem to master, despite her many, many attempts. Euphemia had expressed her hope to hear the full sonata performed when she finished learning it, but that's impossible now.

"As I was saying," Olesya says, annoyed, "I thought I might inquire upon a rumor I overheard."

"Rumors are a cancer." Iona's speech is slurred.

"Indeed." Olesya chuckles almost nervously. "However, I must insist. Is it true you intend on bequeathing marks to the common folk you've taken to inviting to your rituals? I cannot help wondering how you plan to determine which should deserve-"

"I suppose you are also of the opinion that your mark is a divine right?" Iona wipes a hand down her face with exasperation.

The agitated tempo of the song only grows increasingly erratic as Ariadne attempts to drown out the conversation, but even if the sound doesn't reach her, the bond will compensate for her hearing.

"I wouldn't say divine," Olesya says, half-heartedly.

"Yes, I imagine you'd avoid saying that sort of thing aloud," Iona grumbles.

"I merely wish to raise concerns of the potential ramifications," Olesya says. "If they were to misuse their newfound abilities, it could lead to unmitigated chaos."

"As opposed to the tranquility we now find ourselves in?" Iona asks.

"It could always be worse," Olesya says.

The arpeggiated passages become simple as scales when Ariadne's unrest grows, her gaze locked on her hands.

"I've recently found myself questioning the necessity of marks at all," Iona continues. "I've come to detest the worthless things... No one should possess so much power within themselves."

"Apart from you, I suppose," Olesya says dryly.

"Least of all me." Iona hiccups.

Sighing heavily, Ariadne claws at the keys like a madwoman, the chords swirling like a brewing storm.

"Why should I be owed power? What, because of a mark that can only be observed whilst I'm practically naked?" Iona rambles on, and Rebekka fails to suppress a laugh.

"Perhaps you've had enough." Rebekka reaches for the bottle, but Iona wrenches it away.

"And another thing," Iona says, far too loud. "It's a miracle that any of us should reach adulthood at all! These poor children... You treat them so abominably. Your daughter is awful!"

"I beg your pardon?" Olesya stutters.

Ariadne ignores the cramp in her right hand, forcing her fingers to crawl up the key block in a rapid burst of notes.

"She is an awful contemptuous shrew. She cut my hand!" Iona lifts up her palm, but of course there is no scar to prove it. "And it's your fault! Or... I suppose she's responsible for her actions now, but she did not become so terrible on her own, I assure you."

Olesya gasps, "Well I never-"

"You should be ashamed. You all should," Iona yells, then lifts her bottle in Cintia's direction. "You most of all. Did you truly procreate only to torment your own child?"

"Iona..." Rebekka winces.

"Children should not be put under such undue pressure, should not be bestowed power they cannot possibly comprehend," Iona insists. "Why, Ariadne is proof enough of this."

She tries to ignore it but finds it impossible to do so when Iona speaks again.

"She was nearly killed by her own friend for her part to play in your pointless war over magic," Iona yells. "Then nearly killed that friend in defense of herself! Why would I subject others to that same fate, so their children will only be used as pawns for their parents' selfish connivances?"

Ariadne's jaw drops, her song ending abruptly. She jumps up, taking her staff and storming to Iona, stopping time mid-stride before letting loose her fury.

"How dare you!" Ariadne screams.

Iona flinches, her eyes widening as her drunkenness fades almost entirely. "What-"

"How dare you speak of Vivien! How could you?" Her throat aches from the force of her cry. "When you know well my shame? My regret?"

Iona's face falls as she seems to recognize her failing. "I only meant…Indeed, I do know how deeply hurt you were. It should never, never have happened, and I do not wish for another witch or warlock to fall victim to the same fate."

"I am not a victim," Ariadne seethes. "Nor am I a cautionary anecdote. I should never have told you-"

"Please forgive me," Iona implores, stumbling to her feet. "I am not thinking clearly."

"I'm surprised you can stand, let alone think." Ariadne looks her over. "This is perhaps the worst possible time for you to take up drinking. We are meant to be mourning Euphemia."

"I am mourning her." Iona's face contorts with pain.

"By dulling your grief with wine?" Ariadne asks, scoffing in exasperation. "Another Lysander meltdown."

She regrets her words again as they make their mark, the hurt in Iona's eyes nearly enough for Ariadne to set aside her anger and run to her, begging for forgiveness.

"It is your coldness towards me that drove me to it," Iona says, blinking to stave off her tears. "I would have hoped to find solace from my partner in such dark times. Instead, you withdraw into yourself and leave me to suffer alone."

Huffing with annoyance, Ariadne paces back and forth, trying to temper her anger before she might say something else she truly regrets. Or perhaps she should take her leave and calm herself elsewhere away from prying eyes.

"Yes, you may as well," Iona says bitterly. "Disappear again, for I am clearly no comfort to you anymore."

"You left me for weeks!" Ariadne reminds her.

"Not intentionally!"

"I suppose that remedies it, then."

"It is not remotely the same! You constantly choose to isolate yourself, regardless of my steadfast desire to lend an ear to your troubles. I cannot force you to let me in."

"You can let yourself in whenever you wish."

"And if you truly think me capable of betraying your trust in that way, then you do not know me at all." Iona's lip trembles. "Why then did you agree to the bond if you only planned to resent me for it? I offered to break it-"

"I do not wish the break it," Ariadne says immediately.

Iona stares at her for a long while, then says, "I do."

She is almost relieved to hear Iona finally say it, admit it aloud, after days of silence. A myriad of emotions cross Iona's face, guilt that settles into fortitude.

"You did lie, then," Ariadne says. "Elise's plot to ruin us proved quite effective."

"We need not be ruined." Iona closes the distance between them, grasping one of Ariadne's hands. "You think this means my love has lessened-"

"It has," Ariadne relents.

"No," Iona insists, imploring with her eyes. "That anyone would willingly subject themselves to this bond and call it love is ludicrous. I could love you far better without it." She hesitantly lifts a hand to cup Ariadne's cheek. "You came to my aid when I most needed it, crafted this bond despite the semi-permanence of it, despite the danger of it going wrong, and I shall never forget your loyalty in doing so, but Elise is right. This bond is a curse."

Ariadne lowers her gaze and steps away, leaving Iona's warmth, pulling her hand back to her side.

"You do not need it either," Iona says.

"Do not presume to tell me what I need," Ariadne says, hugging her stomach.

"Please, Ari, speak to me." Iona weaves her fingers together to keep from reaching for her again. "Tell me what you need from me, and I shall do it."

"I want to keep the bond," Ariadne says.

Iona looks away, entirely at a loss.

"Perhaps I should have let Elise have you then," Ariadne says.

Iona flinches, stepping back as if the words were a physical blow.

"Or let Samuel find some way of saving you," Ariadne says.

"But there was no other way," Iona whispers.

"None that were pleasant. Do you think I did not consider every possible, awful alternative?" Ariadne asks. "I could have placed you in a prolonged slumber and locked you in your room until Elise was discovered. I could have stolen your blood and usurped your mind instead so Elise could not control it, even if it corrupted my soul beyond redemption. I could have stolen your wand, taken your memories of magic and hid you away until Elise was dead, and put your mind back to rights when it was over."

A trace of fear fills Iona's eyes, yet more of it trickling through the bond unbidden.

"There were other options, but none that I would ever take. None that you would have forgiven me for. None that Samuel would have the heart to suggest," Ariadne says.

"Nor did he suggest the bond," Iona points out.

"Because we were fools to enter into this nightmare! I told you this would happen," Ariadne says with still greater heat. "I knew you would regret tying yourself to me."

"That is not why-"

"I've felt you pulling away for weeks, if not months," Ariadne says. "Your love is fading-"

"No, it certainly is not," Iona insists, her patience waning. "If you've not noticed, the past months have been rather strenuous upon my health and wellbeing. My melancholy is for those we've lost. You are not the cause of my every adverse emotion, and I cannot reassure you every single time I frown or neglect to speak."

"You resent me for our current circumstances," Ariadne rambles. "You blame me for your pain."

"No," Iona tries to say.

"You only confessed your love to me after I saved your life, time and again. You didn't love me before," Ariadne says.

"You were awful before," Iona says.

Ariadne flushes. "That's not the point. You only loved me when I saved you and now that I've failed in protecting you-"

"No, that's not true!" Iona cries. "Why do you say such things?"

"You'll leave," Ariadne says, her voice small. "You wish to break the bond to leave, and I cannot live without you."

"Ari," Iona sighs. "You are using this bond as a substitute for trust in me, but it shall never work. You do not decide how I feel about you. I tell you my feelings and you discard them as lies unless they reinforce your own insecurities. These delusions of my betrayal, your malignant habit of deception and omission, and your crippling doubts of my devotion… Even with our souls connected you still cannot believe that my love is as true as yours, no matter what vows I promise to keep. This anticipatory grief is tearing you apart, poisoning our love, and the bond only worsens it."

Iona's stare is like looking into the sun, but Ariadne refuses to let a single tear fall.

"I will love you eternally, but it seems that is not enough for you. You still doubt it even now," Iona observes. "That's the difference, isn't it? I bonded with you because I trust you with every part of me. You bonded with me because you are afraid. You do not trust me-"

"But I do-"

"No! Stop lying to me! I hate your lies. I cannot bear to hear them a moment longer! Do you think I cannot feel your fear? I live with it day and night! Your paranoia, your forgeries of jealousy, are my constant companions. I shall go mad from them... I don't..." Iona chokes on a sob. "I cannot take away your pain. There is nothing more in this world I wish I could do..."

"Stop," Ariadne whispers, hating the pity in Iona's voice. She would rather it be hatred, disgust, anything else.

"I won't. I cannot live with these words unspoken. No longer."

"I do not need your pity."

"There is a difference between pity and sympathy."

"A subtlety you've yet to master."

"I've grown immune to your malice." Iona straightens her spine. "Your mistrust has naught to do with me. I've done nothing to deserve it. It is of your own construction, and so long as you refuse to believe me, we can never be content."

Despite her very best efforts, despite knowing it will do no good for either of them, Ariadne's heart is entombed in stone, fortifying it from harm, rendering her cold and numb.

"How could I possibly depend on you?" Ariadne asks, and Iona's face falls. "I cannot rely on you to protect me. I can depend on no one but myself! You and everyone else expect me to fix... everything! I cannot be the only one... I cannot keep you alive in a manner that is palatable to you. Not when there is a monster out there threatening to hurt you! Who's nearly killed you thrice now!" Her voice echoes across the desolate hall. "The bond is necessary, or otherwise you could be dead within days. I may hate it more even than you, but we cannot break it, even if it has... less than desirable effects."

"You've not given me a chance to protect you! Always casting me aside and pushing me away whenever danger comes for us.

What use were all those lessons? Was it merely to preoccupy my time and humor me in my ambitions?" Iona asks.

Ariadne scowls. "I told you that first day, it was all in an overabundance of caution and-"

"I'd say that our circumstances have vastly changed since that first day," Iona says. "Others are relying on me to defend them, as well as myself. I must stand on my own two feet! I have the pendant-"

"You would not possess it if it weren't for me. You had hardly any magic after Elise's leeching curse. I fended off the wolves and healed the dragon's wing. I taught you spells and kept you alive long enough to enter the trials at all. Without my guidance and protection, you would not have succeeded," Ariadne says.

"And now you've come to regret giving it to me. Is that it?" Iona asks. "What of the things you said to me in your dream? When you held me and told me that the pendant would never come between us? I told you to take it-"

"I did not want it!" Ariadne shouts.

"Yes, you did!" Iona yells, "but I see now why you abstained. It was not an abstention at all! It was an abdication. I now shoulder obligations to your Goddess, to covens who look to me and Xiomara and others for protection from darkness. You were not forthcoming about any of it! I entered this world for you, endure your family for you, stayed at college for you! Why are you now punishing me for it?"

Ariadne turns away, her mother's words repeating in her head, making her rethink her every motivation, her every choice and action.

"You blame me for Euphemia's death," Iona whispers.

"No," Ariadne says immediately.

"I fought all I could-"

"I know," Ariadne says. "I shouldn't have entered the woods alone. It was… It was my fault."

Iona stays silent.

"If I hadn't sent you back to Rome, Kokuro would be dead, too," Ariadne says, hating the words even as she says them, but unable to stop.

"You do not know that for certain. I am not so helpless as you claim. I rescued Nenet in the desert, I healed you after you so recklessly decided to face the Crone without me, saved you from Elise when you nearly flung yourself off a cliff!"

Ariadne's anger reforms as she's inundated by memories of aster flowers.

"And I more than illustrated my improvement when I fought the Crone alone and lived to tell of it. I was so close... I nearly..." Iona lets out a frustrated sigh. "I would rather die than let anyone harm you."

Ariadne rolls her eyes. "You say you would die for me? Well, I would in turn. That is easily done. But I would fight for you, kill for you, if need be, and that is the difference between us."

Iona's jaw drops. "I do not want you to... kill for me. I never asked-"

"And you would never need to. You never.... You gave in. When Elise was near to overtaking us, you relented, were willing to die and leave me to live without you. I cannot live without you! You didn't fight for me like I do for you, and so I must fight for the both of us," Ariadne says bitterly. *I love her more than she loves me.*

"That's not true," Iona says, her face falling.

"Stay out of my head!" Ariadne screams, and Iona flinches away.

"Do not raise your voice at me!" she cries. "I could never harm Elise. How could I face Samuel again if I cut down his only daughter, regardless of her crimes? Her betrayal left me wretched... I could hardly think! How could you possibly compare that to this? It is not the same."

"You will kill the Crone then, when the time comes?" Ariadne challenges.

Iona hesitates, her brow furrowing to betray her conflicted emotions as she falls silent.

Ariadne sighs angrily and puts a hand against her brow, then runs it across her face and lets it fall in a gesture of utter abandon and loss of hope, only to behold Iona's big hazel eyes appraising her.

"You said you were not a killer," she whispers.

"I did not wish to be," Ariadne says, "but after what the Crone has done... A quick death will be a mercy compared to what I truly wish to unleash upon her."

Another trace of fear crosses Iona's face, and hatred blooms within Ariadne, resenting the constant battle between who she was born to be and who Iona wishes for her to become.

She sets her jaw. "What point is there to any of this if you will only grow to hate me later?"

"What?" Iona asks.

"Your future self ignored me all those times I came to find you in Brazil," Ariadne says. "You would not... You would not even set your eyes upon me."

Iona throws her hands up in exasperation. "I cannot account for what may or may not happen in the future. If I ever did turn away from you, I swear it would be some sort of self-fulfilling prophecy, if you insist upon ignoring my words and actions in favor of your rampant paranoia."

"This is not all in my head, and I resent your saying so," Ariadne says.

"I knew from the start that you were insecure," Iona says, recalling her first aura reading a year ago, "but this is ridiculous, Ariadne. I cannot go on this way."

Ariadne winces slightly as the beginnings of a migraine brews behind Iona's eyes. She brings a hand to her forehead and lightly runs her fingertips across her freckled brow.

"Why do you try so hard to maintain a bond you know is hurting us?" Iona asks. "Why do you cling to a bond you frequently ask me not to use? What are you so afraid I might see?"

Ariadne's thoughts flit erratically, until she stifles them, hiding them away. Iona's scowl deepens.

"I've decided… that my mind has changed," she says, and Ariadne's stomach turns. "I do not believe I'm owed your every secret, but so long as they lie between us, I see now that we cannot move forward. Do with that what you will."

Ariadne stares at her. "If you knew what I did… you would not love me."

"So long as you refuse to show me, you will never know," Iona says.

"I know."

"No, you merely think that you do."

Jaw clenching, Ariadne stares at her, appraising her stubborn frown and glistening eyes, her arms crossed, and feet planted firmly on the ground, and the very slight waver of her balance betraying her persisting inebriation.

"You wish to gaze upon my greatest shame, and believe that will somehow fix this?" Ariadne asks.

"I want what you are willing to give me," Iona says. "Do not speak a single word if you mean to hurl them back at me later. You decide if I am worthy of your candor, if I've proven by now that my love for you," her voice breaks, "is everlasting. Or otherwise, do not speak at all."

Hanging her head, Ariadne closes her eyes, indecision rendering her speechless. The fear of losing Iona makes her tremble, until warm hands reach up to cup her cheeks. For a moment, all she wants is to pull away, but Iona's gentle fingers push her stray curls behind her ears, running her thumbs along Ariadne's cheekbones, and it's all she can do to keep from collapsing in Iona's arms and begging her to let this go.

"We will trust each other. We will protect each other. We will be loyal," Iona whispers.

"Those are words easily spoken," Ariadne says.

Opening her eyes, the sight of Iona's imploring ones is enough to make her resolve crumble. She reaches out to touch Iona's fire touched hair, which still has specks of ash within its strands despite her washing it thoroughly that morning.

Inhaling sharply, Ariadne takes Iona's hand and lets her defenses down, letting Iona slip inside her mind, delving into the very depths of her consciousness where her darkest memories lay dormant, unwanted and inescapable.

For a moment her thoughts flit here and there, showing the moment she'd found her obsidian wand on the volcanic island of Nisyros with her mother watching nearby, to the time she'd dove into the freezing water to save Samaira from drowning, and a time her father had sat with her at the pianoforte in Thessaly and taught her how to practice chords.

Until all other thoughts and memories fade, and she recalls the moonless sky that had stretched above her. She was bit shorter all those years ago, at the age of four and ten, and her limbs were far more lithe than they've since become. The enormity of her life's misfortune had yet to weigh her down. Vivien ran ahead, leading the way through the trees, her blonde hair turned grey in the near darkness.

"It's just ahead!" Vivien had called to her, her voice sweet and unassuming.

"It's far too dark to swim," Ariadne called back.

"Nonsense," Vivien said. "What, are you frightened? A Zerynthos witch afraid of the dark? Or is it the water that intimidates you?"

"Neither." Ariadne had frowned and quickened her steps to keep pace with her friend.

"Come on then!" Vivien hastened as they reached a break in the trees and beheld the river Pineiós.

She'd pulled impatiently at her buttons, practically tearing off her dress, before she waded into the dark water. Ariadne had done the same, still a touch hesitant but refusing to be upstaged. She'd taken a step and flinched at the cold, but forced herself to step further and further in, until the water reached her waist.

It was then she noticed Vivien's eyes, which did not reflect the strained smile spread across her lips. There was an odd emotion there, something Ariadne could not quite place, but that put her on edge.

"Are you well, Vivien?" Ariadne had asked her.

"Quite well," she had responded, too quickly and forcefully.

"It's much too cold," Ariadne decided, making her way back to shore. "Perhaps we can return later when the sun is out and-"

Arms had wrapped around her neck and pulled her back. At first, she'd thought Vivien was only roughhousing, and she'd laughed, played along, trying halfheartedly to break free, until Vivien's grip had tightened.

"Vivien," Ariadne had tried to say, but her friend had flung her out into deeper water.

That's when Vivien had drawn her wand and whispered an incantation, conjuring a cage of wood around Ariadne. Through the gaps in the wooden boards, water seeped through in steady torrents as the box steadily sank into the water.

"This is not amusing," Ariadne had called, her smile fading. "I'd like to return home now."

Vivien did not listen. The water quickly rose until it reached Ariadne's waist.

"Vivien!" she had cried, "Let me out!"

But her pleas fell on deaf ears. She'd drawn her own wand, grateful to have kept it within a pocket of her chemise and tried to break through the wood to free herself, but Vivien would only repair it, keeping her imprisoned until the water reached her chin.

"Please!" Ariadne implored. "Why are you doing this!"

"Forgive me!" Vivien sobbed. "I'm so sorry, I..."

It was that apology that had broken her, as if it would be any consolation to her at all. The admission that Vivien knew well what she did was evil, and yet she did it anyhow.

She has since agonized over the memory time and again, whenever her thoughts drift in idle moments, or whenever her nightmares return, and she believes this must have been what drove her to frenzy, to exhibit an anger she'd never before felt, and hopes never to feel again.

When the water rose over her head, and her screams were reduced to bubbles expelling from her unhinged jaw, her lungs screaming for air, she did not even need to speak the incantation, such was the fervor of her intention.

Delving into Vivien's mind, the first illusion was formed, placing her in a pelagic landscape of pristine white sand with dark clouds above and an angry green sea stretched out before her. Ariadne could see it all from a distance, unseen and silent.

Embedded within the sand were jagged shards of broken glass. In her distress, Vivien tried to run, and the shards cut at the soles of her feet until she'd bled and cried out. Then the sky had opened up, showering her with glistening fragments of glass that lacerated every inch of her skin until she was covered with deep gashes, her blood coating her as she screamed.

Monstrous waves overtook her, the salt of the water burning the opened wounds, floating glass lodging into her back, her arms, and legs, making her writhe in utter agony. The waves would almost drown her, giving her just enough air to survive, only to drag her under again. She'd swallowed small pieces of glass that cut up her mouth and throat. An endless cycle of pain.

The illusion continued in a fluctuating, never-ending nightmare of carnage. Soon the procellous water turned acidic, burning Vivien's skin until it had blistered, disintegrating her hair, burning her insides until she'd vomited blood, and she became unrecognizable. Then it shifted again so she was falling endlessly through a black sky with barely enough light to see the fast-approaching ground. On and on it went.

Ariadne had watched in a trancelike state, observing the pain she caused but not taking any measures to stop it. She had no way of knowing how long it had lasted. The only indications were Vivien's screams, which started strong and horrific, but over time became weak and hopeless, until she went silent.

Then all at once, it ended. Ariadne left Vivien's mind as quickly as she'd entered it, returning to the reality of cold water and a moonless sky. The broken boards of wood that had nearly been her grave gently drifted downstream. Beside her, Vivien had floated on her back, her eyes open but unseeing, her arms swaying limply at her sides.

Ariadne had remained frozen in place a moment longer until the current almost took Vivien downstream, too. She had forced her limbs to move and reached out to take Vivien's arm, finding her skin freezing cold. She shook Vivien's shoulder, but she didn't speak or cower away. Her chest still moved with her inhales and exhales.

"Vivien?" Ariadne's voice had been foreign to her own ears.

Her friend did not answer, did not even blink.

Ariadne's memory fractures, moving past the hours it took for her to carry her friend back to the Nicolos' manor without magic left to conjure a single thing, or even make Vivien float to ease the burden of her limp weight. The illusions had consumed every last bit of power she'd had, leaving her empty and exposed.

She recalls Tatiana's keening lamentations as she had stood there silent and helpless to undo what she'd done. Mrs. Nicolo had dragged her into the sitting room and cast a truth spell on her, forcing Ariadne to relive the horrible event all over again. She had hardly been able to speak through her tears, until her mother had arrived and put an abrupt end to the interrogation.

Mrs. Nicolo had cursed the Zerynthos name, screaming until she had no words left, and wept over her youngest daughter's comatose body.

*Ari.*

Ariadne blinks and the memory fades. She looks up into Iona's cautious gaze, searching for any signs of terror or disgust, then peers into Iona's mind, searching frantically through her thoughts. There she finds what she expects; fear, disbelief, shock, but also compassion and confusion.

"I was…" Ariadne searches for the best word, and finds none that are appropriate, "angry."

Iona gives a shallow nod, averting her eyes, processing what she's just seen.

"It's a miracle that Vivien does not remember it," Ariadne says. "All that time, I thought…"

Iona still does not speak.

"If she had remembered," Ariadne shivers, "I very much doubt she would have forgiven me."

"She tried to kill you," Iona whispers, as if she were reminding herself of that fact.

"Yes, she did," Ariadne nods, her throat growing thick. "Even so… it came to me so naturally. It terrified me, that I was capable of such evil. To call it defensive magic would be absurd. It was… merciless retribution."

Iona meets her gaze again, and it demolishes what's left of her restraint.

"If you wish to break the bond, I shan't defy you. You shouldn't be shackled to someone like me. I never should have agreed to it in the first place. I love you, but… I know that is not enough." Ariadne swipes angrily at her cheeks to wipe away her tears. "All I know is that you are the greatest part of my life and… I feel you slipping away from me and…"

In an instant, time falls back into its normal rhythm, with both of them still weeping openly.

"What…" Olesya looks from the chair Iona had once sat in to where she now stands by Ariadne. "How did you manage that?"

Iona opens her mouth to answer but all that comes out is a violent cough. She doubles over, one hand against her chest and the other outstretched to break her fall.

"Iona?" Ariadne reaches for her, catching her before she collapses.

"The smoke," Olesya says, just as Iona spits a clump of black mucus, only to cough even harder.

"Philisa," Ariadne incants, pressing a hand to Iona's back, and it seems to help, but her breathing remains labored and rasped.

"Perhaps she should rest," Rebekka suggests.

Ariadne nods, creating a portal to Triora, and carries Iona through.

"Nonna!" she calls. "Help!"

Her grandmother comes running with Frankie at her heels and they help her carry Iona inside. While Nonna brews a potion to relieve her ailing lungs, Ariadne tucks her into bed, keeps a tight hold of her hand, whispering healing spells over her, but the magic doesn't seem to help in a lasting way.

Nonna administers her potion, but even she seems unnerved by the amount of effort Iona exerts just to breathe in and out. Within an hour, Iona's breath is perilously shallow and weak, her eyes closed in fitful sleep.

"Summon Xiomara," Nonna says. "We need her guidance."

Ariadne crafts a portal and sends Frankie to fetch her, unwilling to leave Iona's side for even a moment.

"She's white as a sheet," Nonna murmurs.

"Iona," Ariadne says softly, running a gentle hand through her hair. "Can you hear me?"

# 31 - *Iona*

To move is to suffer. Her every muscle aches at rest, and if she dares to shift even the smallest amount, shooting pain accosts her entire body and steals away what little energy she has, until sleep takes her again, fraught with perturbing nightmares of gore, and desolate screams.

Lifting her eyelids is a feat she cannot muster for long, though she tries anyway so she might gaze upon Ariadne's worry-stricken face, wishing she could speak so she might lessen her concern. Ariadne never leaves, takes every meal at her bedside, and frequently drifts off in a chair with her head braced against her arms, leaning against the mattress, as close as she can be without touching.

Xiomara demands the separation in an abundance of caution, for they do not know the nature of Iona's ailments, or how they might be transferred. It pains them both, for Iona is certain her pain would be marginally more endurable if only she could lay with Ariadne at her back, curled up against her, whispering in her ear that it will all be over soon.

Healing potions, brewed with meticulous care by Ariadne's father, are administered by having the cup hover by Iona's lips for her to drink. Sometimes at night, when they are alone, Ariadne takes to brushing her hair, careful not to touch her skin, and it seems as much a comfort to Ariadne as it is a respite for Iona.

In her brief moments of lucidity, she watches Ariadne while she dreams and listens to her mumble in her sleep, "Not her… not her, too… not her… not her…"

Worst of all, she cannot respond to Ariadne's revelatory confession at Euphemia's funeral, not even through the bond. She tries many a time to form a coherent thought and send it to her and doesn't know if it is her state of enervation that prevents her, or her total lack of clarity.

She cannot make sense of what she's seen, cannot reconcile the woman she loves being capable of inflicting torture on another girl. She knows Ariadne to be capable of aggression in her worst moments, but Iona never thought it possible for her to do those things. It makes her sick just thinking of it, but in her state of incapacitation, she finds herself fixating on the dreadful memories, Vivien's screams haunting her as they have Ariadne.

And so, the seconds, minutes, hours, days tick by, a chasm of unspoken words inhabiting the space between them, filled with wretched uncertainty, longing, and guilt.

"She's nearly died thrice now on your Goddess' errand!" Ariadne screams, "And where then were you when the Crone nearly burned us alive and slaughtered my friend?"

Her slumber interrupted, Iona tries to open her eyes, but her lids are heavy as lead.

"I was with Mother while she defended your incompetence!" Moira yells. "The council is in an absolute uproar! All this death in so short a time-"

"We are doing all we can, but I shan't sacrifice her-"

"Enough," Xiomara yells, with a tone of finality. "We cannot lose our heads."

Moira huffs, followed by loud footsteps and the slam of a door.

Silence follows until Xiomara asks, in a much softer tone, "Are you well, Ariadne?"

"I..." She sighs with frustration. "Can I not just hold her hand?"

"We do not know what affliction has made her-"

"I do not care if I fall sick."

"We cannot lose you, too," Xiomara says firmly. "You are too important."

"She needs me," Ariadne says, her voice small. "She looks so much like..."

She cannot finish the thought, but Iona knows of whom she speaks. There is a swish of skirts as Xiomara crosses the room to comfort Ariadne, but a divot in the mattress indicates her shrinking away from Xiomara's touch, leaning against her elbows to hover over Iona as close as she dares.

"Others need us now," Xiomara says. "She will not even notice your absence-"

"I shan't leave her," Ariadne says.

"You are the only one of us capable of shielding against maleficium-"

"A lot of good it's done me," Ariadne says, bleak and hopeless.

"You've saved many lives already, including hers," Xiomara says. "We require your help and-"

"I will not leave her," Ariadne says cooly.

"We cannot afford to be selfish when there are countless

innocents whose loved ones will be taken from them permanently without our intervention."

"Let them fight for themselves as I have."

"We possess greater magic, and even we struggle to-"

"Where is Hecate?"

The question stops Xiomara short so abruptly, it makes Iona tense with apprehension, the small movement sending shockwaves of pain through her every nerve ending.

"Is she a Goddess, or isn't she?" Ariadne asks. "She should heal Iona-"

"Ariadne," Xiomara chuckles nervously.

"Let her come and strike me down for saying so!" Ariadne cries. "First Morgan, now her! I tire of their cryptic excuses to justify their lack of intervention. At least Morgan is dead, excuse enough I suppose, but Hecate simply watches and does nothing! All because of a damned spider!"

"Fate is absolute," Xiomara says.

"I tire of that, too," her voice breaks. "I am... I am so tired. Sleep gives me no rest..."

"I'll have your father brew a potion."

"Just leave me with her," Ariadne whispers.

Another silence draws out, and for a moment Iona thinks Xiomara did leave as Ariadne asked, until she finally says, "I will call upon Hecate."

Ariadne shifts, her surge of hope palpable.

"I cannot guarantee she will respond, but I shall call to her," Xiomara says. "You must go."

"What?" Ariadne asks, "But why-"

"She does not wish to see you," Xiomara says. "She may not wish to see Iona either, after all that's happened..."

Another silence, the air thick with tension.

"How can she possibly blame either one of us for this?" Ariadne says, her voice so soft, Iona strains to hear. "We've broken ourselves many times over-"

"If you wish for her aid, it would be wise not to challenge her judgement," Xiomara says, not unkindly, as if she hates being put in the middle of their quarrel. "This is how it must be."

Sighing heavily, with great regret, Ariadne stands. "Very well. Fetch me when it's done, the very second she's gone."

"Of course," Xiomara says. "I suggest you take the time to rest."

"I'll rest when she's well again," Ariadne says, opening the door and closing it gently behind her.

"Goddess help me," Xiomara murmurs to herself.

More than ever, Iona wishes to open her eyes, to call Ariadne back to her, but listening to their tense conversation is enough to bring on another wave of fatigue. She faintly perceives the press of Xiomara's hand against her forehead as she drifts away into another amorphous dream.

Something soft and light touches her skin, and her eyelids flutter open as she reaches for it, plucking a purple petal from her cheek and holding it up to her eyes. Blinking, she realizes the movement causes no pain, her vision is clearer, and her breaths take less effort.

Above her, wisteria blossoms hang from the ceiling, and all around her, growing from the floor and the walls, are so many flowers, she can hardly comprehend them. She's only seen such a marvel once before in Ariadne's dream, a projected depiction of her childhood bedroom while she wore the dream talisman.

"You are safe," Xiomara says. She sits in a chair in the corner with her hands folded in her lap. "We brought you to Thessaly for your convalescence."

Sitting up, she winces at how sore her muscles have become, bringing a hand to her forehead. "How long... Where is Ariadne?"

"She is not far. She took a walk in the forest to clear her head," Xiomara says. "You've been quite ill for weeks. As I'd hoped, the Winter Solstice provided magic enough to heal you."

Reeling, Iona tries to do the math in her head. Last she remembers, it was the very end of November. Yet again, weeks of time have been stolen from her.

Wisp trills and jumps up to lick at her face, and she scoops the fox into her arms, kissing her head and whispering soothing words. Then Aster approaches, his ears flat and his eyes cautious. Iona beckons him closer, understanding the significance of his presence here. Ariadne must have left him to watch over her. The wolf's yellow eyes shimmer when she scratches his head, but it only reminds her that her beloved is somewhere on the grounds, praying for her recovery.

"I must go to her." Iona swings her legs over the edge of the bed and tries to stand, but her head pounds, her limbs prickling, and she nearly faints as she falls back into bed.

Xiomara jumps up and rushes across the room, crushing flowers underfoot in her haste. "For goodness sake, Iona, take caution! You've only just awoken. Please, allow yourself time to adjust."

Nodding reluctantly, she takes deep steadying breaths, pressing a hand to her chest until her pulse slows beneath her palm.

"I must impart a message to you before your departure," Xiomara says, an edge to her tone.

Iona glances at her, and any relief she harbors swiftly fades.

"Hecate was the one who healed you," Xiomara says, "and she bid me tell you it shall be her final blessing."

Her heart sinks. "What… What does that mean? Why?"

"Iona." Xiomara takes her hand and looks her in the eye with great sympathy. "I regret the position you've been forced into. I am certainly not the first to tell you that this was never meant to be your-"

"What did she say?"

When Xiomara averts her eyes, Iona braces herself for the worst.

"The death toll has risen too high," Xiomara says. "You made a valiant effort despite your disadvantages, but the time has come to accept that you are not ready to face so formidable an adversary."

Iona cannot even muster a plea for another chance when she knows in her heart that Hecate is right.

"Ariadne might still help," is all Iona can think to say.

"Yes, of course, but you know as well as I, the staff is not the pendant. It can only protect those in the Crone's path, but has not the potency to defeat her," Xiomara says. "My mother prevailed against darkness in part due to the pendant, but most importantly due to her many years of diligent study. I have no doubt, none at all, that you shall reach, and perhaps even surpass that distinction someday but-"

"You needn't comfort me in my disgrace," Iona says numbly.

"No, it is not disgraceful," Xiomara insists. "Please do not despair. It seems Morgan wished for you to use her magic in other pursuits. You should continue your work with Marcel and his comrades. That is your true calling."

"I suppose," Iona says, entirely unsure of her purpose anymore.

"With that settled, I'm afraid I must be going," Aunt Xiomara says as she stands. "The covens are gathered for the solstice ritual, and I've agreed to preside over it in your stead. You should rest and regain your strength. You are welcome to stay as long as you need."

A bundle of flowers with the smallest of purple blossoms, tied together with a red ribbon, sits on the bedside table.

"Heliotropes," Xiomara says with fondness. "Such a lovely token."

Iona recalls the meaning from her studies, that of devotion and eternal love. Her heart swells as she takes the arrangement of blossoms and brings them to her nose, breathing in their sweet fragrance.

"Ariadne has a resilient heart," Xiomara says. "Go to her, tell her of what I've told you, and know that the Zerynthos Coven shall continue our work until our last breath. Whatever you choose to do instead, I'm sure, shall be a credit to you and Morgan, and in time, we will see fate's design and know it was all meant to be."

Before Iona can say another word, Xiomara steps out of the room, leaving her painfully alone with her roiling thoughts and conflicting loyalties, unable to reconcile them.

She finds herself unable to deny what she's feared to be true all along. Morgan was wrong. She was so terribly, completely wrong. If a Goddess of such power and insight as Hecate can make this determination, then perhaps Iona should finally accept the harsh reality of her flaws, for the greater good.

She reaches behind her neck to unclasp the pendant's chain, cupping the opal in her palm for the briefest moment, before setting it on the bedside table beside the heliotropes.

She senses the loss of power and feels somehow bolstered by it, and by the knowledge that Arachne allowed her to take it off.

"Aster." Iona beckons him over, then points at a spot in front of the bedside table. "Sit. Stay."

Aster obeys, and though Iona knows the pendant cannot be moved by anyone else, she is comforted by the thought of it being guarded.

Then she runs from the room, across the hall, down the stairs, trailed by Wisp. She flings open the front door and is about to call for Ariadne through the bond.

"Iona?" Ariadne asks.

"Oh!" Iona jumps, not having seen her standing a little way away between two barren cypress trees. "There you are."

Her red eyes appraise Iona's elation, no doubt sensing it, too. "You are well again."

"Yes," Iona says, wringing her hands, "Hecate healed me."

A flurry of snowflakes silently falls between them and get trapped within Ariadne's mass of dark curls, the candlelight in a nearby window dimly illuminating the darkness.

"I've decided something," Iona says. "Or rather, Hecate did."

"Oh…" Ariadne says. "And what would that be?"

"I've been such a fool," Iona sighs, stepping closer to her, and hushing Wisp when she barks.

Ariadne's brow furrows. "What are you-"

"Please, let me speak," Iona implores.

Ariadne studies her, then nods her ascent.

"Your family is right," Iona says. "You should have claimed the pendant."

"What?" Ariadne recoils, unable to believe her words.

Iona finds herself out of breath, putting a hand over her rapidly beating heart.

"Even Morgan could not ignore your obvious claim to it. She was well meaning, but I think she was wrong to let you give it away, so long as this darkness exists and the pendant is all that may vanquish it." Iona says. "You must take it back, for I don't believe it was ever truly mine. You were the one who claimed it first, and only gave it away to protect me, but we must protect others now. They should not suffer on my account. You are so convinced that power in your hands would be a mistake, but it is not so. Very few could have endured all you have and survived with their capacity for empathy still intact. You've never been weak. Quite the opposite."

Iona takes another step closer, but hesitates, cognizant of the enduring wariness in Ariadne's countenance.

"You've studied for years on end until you were nearly sick of something so wondrous as magic. I could never measure up to that. It was foolish of me to think it possible, even with Hecate's encouragement. It was always you she wanted, and I understand why. I am not bitter. I swear to you, I'm not. I am so in awe of you, your strength, your wisdom, your courage. I always have been, though you never let me say it enough, but you'd best get used to it."

Iona can barely articulate past her gasping breaths, and rushes through her words before she loses the ability to speak.

"You can no longer claim I haven't seen the darkest parts of you, that I know not who I love, that I would run or abandon you if I did. No longer can you say it of me, and I am glad for it," Iona says. "I've seen it all and still, I love you. I will always love you. That will *never* change. We could argue whether it be fate's intervention that makes it so, but I find that pointless now when my heart beats for you all the same. You who have risked everything, sacrificed everything for me, and yet are still somehow convinced you could never deserve me. I am telling you now, once and for all, that you do, Ariadne. I will remind you every day if I must, if that is what will give you peace. I won't let you leave or push me away because you're frightened. You need not be afraid. Don't you know, my love, that I would fight for you, too?"

Hot tears stream down Iona's cheeks, but she smiles through them.

"I would, to my last breath," Iona vows. "You don't need a blood bond to keep me at your side, and in fact, I insist we break it, for we do not need such compulsory truth to preserve our love. I do not need to read your thoughts to know you live for me as I do for you, that you would never betray me, or forsake me. I trust you with everything, with my life, with my heart, all that I am. You must accept that my love is not fickle or thoughtless or conditional. No other woman could satisfy me, understand me as you do. You must know, forevermore, that I am yours and you are mine, and it shall always be so... if you'll still have me."

Iona's sobs overtake her then, and she wipes away her tears with frustration.

"I was not slipping away..." she gasps, "I was frightened... confused... but I could never slip away from you. I am yours."

She's run out of words to say without speaking in circles and making a bigger fool of herself than she already feels she is. Ariadne stares deeply into her very soul, then glances down the road for only a moment. Iona nearly looks, too, until Ariadne's eyes return to hers, burning with startling determination.

When Ariadne closes the distance between them, cupping her face, and kissing her with urgency, Iona weeps. She sinks into the kiss, placing her hand over Ariadne's, and lets out a sigh of happiness, until she overhears Wisp's menacing growl, and she's overcome with the creeping sense of something... wrong.

# 32 - Ariadne

She has no earthly idea what compels her to say such terrible things and not mean a single word of them. She doesn't know what's wrong with her, or if Iona will wait long enough for her to make sense of her feeble, perfidious mind.

Her exchange with Iona at the funeral is all she's thought of while guarding her body and sending her thoughts through the bond that do not seem to reach her. Myriad apologies have been stuck in Ariadne's throat for weeks, near to bursting from her lips, but Iona cannot hear her.

Her hazel eyes are clouded, her face grimacing at the pain that besieges her, rendering her immobile. The echo of the pain seeps through the bond, and Ariadne lingers within it, seeks it out, so she might suffer with her. It should be her in that bed, not Iona.

The fresh air does little to comfort her, the cutting chill of winter making her tremble, but she refuses to conjure a cloak. She'd decided to leave Aster behind to watch over Iona in her stead, despite the wolf's many protests. And so, she walks aimlessly through the Thessalian wilderness, the ground covered in a layer of virgin snow, waiting, hoping, praying that Hecate will heal her beloved and Arachne will not cut her thread.

Eventually she comes upon the meadow, bereft of its many aster flowers. Deciding she may as well entertain herself while she waits or at least distract herself from her dread-ridden thoughts, she conjures a pianoforte right there in the snow, taking a seat on the bench and lifting the lid to reveal the keys, and plays the first song that comes to mind, from Clementi's Piano Sonata in F-Sharp Minor, Piú tosto allegro con esperessione.

"Ariadne."

Her breath catches in her throat as she turns in her seat. Aunt Xiomara trudges through the snow to reach her.

"Did Hecate answer?" she asks.

"Yes," Aunt Xiomara says with an exhausted smile. "Iona is awake. She is well again."

A sob bursts from deep in Ariadne's chest at hearing weeks of tortuous waiting are finally at an end, but before she can make a portal to her bedroom, Aunt Xiomara puts up a hand in caution.

"She is well, but..." Aunt Xiomara hesitates.

"But what?"

"She's relinquished Hecate's quest. She will battle the Crone no longer."

Ariadne blinks at her, unable to comprehend her words, until she realizes the full implications of them.

"The loss of Iona's magic is a significant one," Aunt Xiomara says. "We will be at a great disadvantage. In truth... we have been all this time. You are our only advantage now."

"Me?" Ariadne breathes.

"Do you mean to abandon us, too?" Aunt Xiomara asks, her eyes flitting to the staff with trepidation.

"No," Ariadne says compulsively, her hands clenching into fists. "Euphemia's death must be avenged."

"Indeed," Aunt Xiomara murmurs, scrutinizing her with care.

Though as she thinks of it, Ariadne is unsure of how Iona will feel about her continued involvement in their crusade without her. Then she shakes her head, unable to accept it. "But Iona would never leave innocents to die. Perhaps this is only a momentary lapse of courage."

"She nearly died," Aunt Xiomara says softly. "She wasted away in that bed for weeks. I cannot say I'm surprised by her choice to abstain, as bitterly inconvenient as it may be for us. You said it yourself. She almost suffered the same fate as Vivien."

The comparison makes her hands tremble as she stands and paces about in agitation. "I would never allow that to happen."

"You cannot always control such things, dearest. It was Hecate who healed her, and next time," Aunt Xiomara lowers her gaze, "we may not be so fortunate. I spoke with Hecate on her behalf, and we are all agreed, it is for the best. The family shall convene in the sitting room within the hour to strategize, for we must determine the best way to divide our efforts prudently. There is an alarming barrage of attacks littering the countryside. It's becoming like it was before Mother came to power."

"I could try to convince Iona to persevere," Ariadne says, with slight reluctance. "I imagine the Crone will not simply let us go. She knows our faces."

"Quite right... However, I must respectfully decline," Aunt Xiomara says.

"But you just said-"

"I agree with Iona's decision, as does Hecate. I regret to say it has become abundantly clear that she was never meant for this life, and clearer still that you were made for it." Aunt Xiomara reaches for her and takes her face in her hands, looking down on her with adoration. "Your mother tried to stifle your fire. Wrought with jealousy that woman is, but she could not hide who you truly are. My successor."

Ariadne's mouth falls open. "But… I didn't…"

"You never needed the pendant, dearest," Aunt Xiomara says. "It certainly wouldn't have hurt if you'd claimed it, but you are a Zerynthos witch all the same. Your staff aided in your heroism, but the artifact is not what makes a witch exceptional. That depends only upon the witch herself."

Beyond words, Ariadne closes her eyes when Aunt Xiomara presses her lips to her forehead before pulling away.

"But…" she stutters, still unable to accept it. "What of Moira or Marina or-"

"A skilled soldier and seer," Aunt Xiomara says. "Neither of them are leaders."

"I do not know if I…"

"Fortify your confidence. You've more than proven your worth in battle. I would not make this determination thoughtlessly," Aunt Xiomara says. "For now, I ask that you take a moment to clear your mind, bolster your strength, and return to the manor when you are ready." She turns to leave then stops short to mention. "But please do not take too long. The ritual is set for midnight, and the other covens will be arriving any moment-"

"Of course," Ariadne says. "I shan't be long."

"Very good," Aunt Xiomara smiles, then turns to walk back up the path to the manor, leaving Ariadne to her musings.

For a moment, she considers using a portal to return to Iona's bedside, but she forces herself to heed her aunt's advice. It would not do for her to be overwhelmed by her emotions when she joins her family.

She looks up, disappointed to find another moonless sky. She has no way of knowing how close to midnight it might be, but she imagines the covens will arrive soon. She should like to find Iona before they impose upon their solitude.

There is a place hidden among the towering rocks where the ritual will almost certainly be conducted. In times past, Aunt Xiomara would preside over the ritual, then lead the crowd back to the manor for the reception in the ballroom.

As a child, Ariadne would often sit on her balcony and watch the arcing lights from afar, then sneak out of her room to sit by the stairs and listen to the music and laughter.

On very rare occasions, her father would allow her to sneak in amongst the crowd for as long as it took for her mother to discover her and send her back to bed. She'd longed to be a part of the festivities, before she knew how tiresome they can truly be.

Iona will certainly resume her rituals once she's recovered fully from her illness. That is what had appealed to her in the first place, sharing magic with those who have very little. She can dedicate herself to noble causes, reshape the world into a kinder, more tolerant place, while Ariadne keeps the monsters at bay, and comes home to her when evil is vanquished once more. In time all this darkness will fade, and they will finally be able to rest. Ariadne will do all she can to make it so.

She's been such a fool to let her fears cloud her judgement. She will grovel. She will beg for Iona's forgiveness on her knees if she must. Despite all her worst intrusive thoughts, she somehow knows in her heart that Iona will forgive her, that their love is not so fragile that it would shatter in adversity. That if anything, with no secrets left between them, they may flourish now more than they had before. Her shame has been brought to light, and if Iona can still love her despite it, then there is no greater love she could ever find. She allows herself to hope, to believe that Iona won't forsake her.

As she makes her way up toward her family's manor, her feet crunching through the snow, her excitement grows at the thought of seeing Iona well again, her cheeks rosy and her eyes bright. She barely notices Rebekka's carriage stationed by the roadside as she trudges down the front path to the manor. She must be the first to arrive for the ritual, one that Ariadne will gladly abstain from so she might embrace Iona again and never let her go. She only thinks of Iona and what she means to say when-

Ariadne's heart stops. Her breath stops. Everything... stops.

Iona stands under the cover of barren cypress trees, likely thinking herself obscured from view, while she kisses Rebekka within a flurry of snow. At first, Ariadne cannot believe it. It must be some awful trick. The Crone must have found them here and aimed to use Ariadne's worst fears against her again to distract her before attempting a killing blow.

But Ariadne dares to reach through the bond, only barely delving in, like dipping a toe into water to check its temperature for fear of its freezing embrace. Though Iona's eyes are closed, Ariadne can sense her feelings of lips against her own, of relief mixed with guilt and passion. She rips herself away from Iona's mind before she can see anymore and only intensify her agony. It is her… It is Iona before her very eyes.

Overwrought with a stifling wave of fury that shatters her to her core, she remains frozen in place. She's only ever felt such anguish one other time in her life and had not been able to control herself then. She can take it no longer, cannot stand the sight of her love in another's arms. She must go, or she might…

She conjures a portal and practically dives through the doorway, tripping over her feet before closing it behind her with finality. Her breath comes in awful, heaving gasps. If she'd eaten at all that day, surely, she'd have purged it all over her bedroom floor, covering the clusters of flowers that wilt beneath her feet.

Then she goes rigid in surprise as she regards her surroundings, momentarily disturbed. She hadn't realized she'd meant to go here, had intended to go someplace far away, but her mind was all asunder, fractured by shock.

Aster, who had been sitting by the bed, jumps up and goes to her, sniffing at her hand, trying to determine what has harmed her. With shaking legs, she goes to her bed and slumps onto it, pressing a hand to her thrumming heart.

Iona swore. She'd sworn it was nothing more than shallow attraction, had looked Ariadne in the eyes as she said it, had made her feel foolish to even think it, had even jested about it, to make her feel wrong for even suggesting it. She knew it was not only paranoia. She'd seen Iona's appreciation for Rebekka's beauty, her charm, her confidence. Ariadne had known it, and yet still she was made blind by her infatuation, her lust, her delusional hopes.

Perhaps Iona had meant it then, but her mind had changed after all the awful things they'd said at Euphemia's funeral, seeing what had happened to Vivien, and lying in that bed tormented by pain. Iona did not even wait a day before seeking comfort in another's arms. It seems she's not just turning her back on Hecate. Iona is leaving this entire life behind, leaving her behind, because she's failed one too many times, and never deserved her to begin with.

Ariadne's jaw clenches until the bone clicks painfully. That is true no longer. Not after what she has done. Iona knows well how this will break her, and yet she did it anyhow. Ariadne must be rid of this bond immediately and not a moment too soon. She blocks out every semblance, every trace of a feeling or thought stemming from Iona's mind, finding them revolting. Ariadne could never forgive this betrayal, not even for her. Especially for her.

She should have known love could never be so true. It never had been before. Everyone always hurts her in the end. She should have known better, but she never does. She always hopes, always risks her heart for it to be battered and bruised by those who claim to care for her.

Rebekka had sworn never to hurt her, but those were only pretty words to seduce her, to lure her into complacency. She never should have believed it. She is nothing more than a conquest, a hollow ornament, a warm body.

She recalls Morgan's words at the end of the trials, telling them they would be the most powerful coupling in centuries, their bond unbreakable. What a sickening joke. Morgan was just as wrong about that as she'd been when she allowed the pendant to go to Iona, or to Katrin for that matter. Her supposed wisdom has been all but folly, and Ariadne was stupid enough to believe it.

She will never love again. Nor will she ever believe it when someone claims to love her. How could they? How could anyone love her, in all her ugliness and inferiority? Her infirmity runs through her very veins. She will always be her mother's unwanted daughter, her father's regret, her family's disappointment. Her friends only pity her. Her lovers only ever want her for her beauty. Morgan did not want her. Hecate resents her. Everyone only tolerates her. She is nothing... nothing... nothing...

"Nothing like young love to set one's heart aflame."

Ariadne startles at the sound, her mouth falling open. Hecate stands in the corner of the bedroom admiring a trellis of pink rambling roses. Jumping to her feet, Ariadne performs something between a curtsy and a bow, unsure how best to address the Goddess.

Hecate's responding chuckle is as endearing as it is patronizing. "You needn't bow, child."

Flushing with embarrassment, Ariadne straightens and lowers her head, picking at her nails in agitation. Then, when she remembers her sorrow, her reverence turns to hatred as she levels Hecate with an accusatory stare.

"You are the reason this happened in the first place," Ariadne says bitterly. "We were happy before you imposed upon us and now…"

"I am the reason?" Hecate asks, her eyebrows raising in astonishment. "What a monstrous claim! That is not so at all."

"Who then should I blame?" Ariadne asks.

"Perhaps the woman who ripped your heart open the moment loving you proved too difficult," Hecate says. "Or the weaver who tied you to a woman destined to betray you."

Ariadne's breath stutters as she turns her back to her and blinks away tears, then gasps, unable to believe her eyes. There on the bedside table, next to her conjured heliotropes, sits the pendant, glittering in the candlelight.

"Ah, yes," Hecate says. "Iona relinquished it."

"What?" Ariadne gapes at her. "But… No, she would never-"

"Oh, but she did," Hecate says with a sigh. "I imagine she no longer wishes to be burdened by it. It's truly a shame… I'd hoped for another era of renewed peace. So many will suffer because of this, but I suppose there's no helping that."

"But… it should go to the next bearer," Ariadne says, but Hecate shakes her head.

"So long as Iona is alive, it shall be fallow and squandered."

"Well… Perhaps if you had not been so hard on her-"

"I gave her so many chances to prove her mettle," Hecate says. "I'm afraid this is the end of my reliance on her. My coven will continue their work alone or risk the death toll rising beyond what we can stomach. In truth, it already has…"

With great regret, Ariadne gazes upon the shimmering opal. "Why did Arachne doom us to failure?"

"Only she would know." Hecate's brow furrows with frustration. "Sometimes I wonder… if she is not on our side after all."

Ariadne takes slow steps towards the pendant, reaches out, but hesitates. Behind her, Hecate approaches, her proximity exuding an icy chill that makes Ariadne shiver.

"It seems you may have given your heart to the wrong person," Hecate says. She gently pushes a lock of Ariadne's hair over her shoulder. "Perhaps that applies to the pendant as well."

Ariadne looks to her, losing herself in the depths of Hecate's red eyes. "Perhaps you're right."

Hecate smiles as she cups Ariadne's cheek. "Then take it back, my daughter. Claim what should have always been yours and take your rightful place at my side."

Ariadne turns her gaze back to the pendant, marveling at its glittering stones so perfectly cut and overflowing with pure magic. She sets her staff against the wall, and, with shaking hands, she takes the pendant, holds it delicately, her fingers trembling as she clasps it around her neck. Power unlike anything she's ever felt before surges through her in waves until she almost falls to her knees from the intensity of it.

When she looks to Hecate again, she stands beside an opened portal with her hand outstretched. "No one will ever hurt you again."

Ariadne would have never believed such a promise if it hadn't come from a Goddess' lips, but indeed it has. She beckons Aster to follow, then takes Hecate's hand and lets herself be guided through the portal to the Underworld.

# 33 - Iona

For a moment, she isn't quite sure what disturbs her, finding it difficult to concentrate with Ariadne's lips against hers, their bodies pressing together in a warm embrace, as she loses herself in the kiss. Then she breathes in and marks a distinct, alarming abnormality.

Ariadne does not smell of gardenias, nor of cloves. She always does, in the mornings when they wake in each other's arms, every day they sat beside each other in their classes at college, and especially after she bathes in a tub filled with white gardenia petals, as she tends to do.

Then a sharp, unfamiliar pain shoots through Iona's chest, making her go rigid in Ariadne's arms.

"Wait," Iona says against Ariadne's lips, but she won't release her, even when she struggles. "I said wait!"

She wrenches herself out of Ariadne's grasp, unable to fathom her behavior. Ariadne never ignores her when she expresses her wish to stop. She reaches out through the bond, but there is a barrier there that she has never before experienced, something so potent and unyielding, that she cannot see beyond it. Wisp snarls angrily, stepping in front of Iona with her fangs bared.

Without snowflakes obscuring her vision as it had moments ago, Iona squints against the dimness so that she might regard the woman standing before her, her mannerisms, her appearance, and the more Iona looks, the more she knows. It's a masterful likeness, it's true, but not Ariadne. Not her love, who she has memorized just as Ariadne had bid her to do more than a year ago on Samhain.

And just as Salvador told her it would, the illusion melts away into nothing, an effortless revelatory unveiling, even without the pendant augmenting her magic, revealing Rebekka's face instead.

"Rebekka?" Iona raises her fingers to her lips. "How could you? How…"

Her eyes are white voids, her stormy green irises missing, her white shirt soiled and tattered from the many cuts littering her arms and hands, and a newly made gash across her neck that seeps blood onto her collar.

"What has she done to you?" Iona whispers, though she

already knows the answer. This is blood magic, just as she'd read about in her grimoires, and just as Ariadne had described to her at college after she herself was subjected to Elise's infernal spell.

Rebekka stares at her with a vacant expression, as if she's been left without a puppet master to pull her strings. Iona admonishes herself for her speech, hating that the Crone will have heard it when it was only meant for Ariadne's ears.

"Rebekka?" Iona backs away, wondering if she might attack, but Rebekka only turns and runs in the direction of the forest. "Wait!"

Iona goes to run after her, then hesitates when she remembers the pendant is still upstairs and the Crone is now aware of that fact. She must retrieve it, she must find Ariadne wherever she's wandered off to, and they must fight the Crone together, or risk Rebekka meeting the same fate as poor Euphemia.

*Ari?* Iona calls, but there is no answer.

She searches for the architect of the illusion along the border of trees below the mountaintop upon which the manor sits, but there is no one in sight. Her heart pounds in her chest as she crosses the snow dusted courtyard and climbs up the stairs to the second floor, meaning to go to Ariadne's room when another door opens and Moira steps out.

"Moira," Iona gasps. "I think… I don't know…"

"Whatever is wrong?" Moira asks, as Marina comes up behind her.

"The Crone. She's here in Thessaly," Iona says. "She's inflicted blood magic on Rebekka."

Marina's face goes pale as she reaches for Iona's hand, and glances at Moira with dismay, "Where is Mother?"

"She's left already, but we should send word to her at once," Moira says. "The covens may well be in danger, too."

"What do you mean?" Iona asks, then remembers Xiomara mentioning the Winter Solstice. They will all gather here for the Yule ritual.

Moira draws her wand. "We must warn them."

"I must find Ariadne first," Iona says. "Keep your wits. The Crone has resorted to illusions. Strong ones."

"Of course, I will help you search," Marina says, her hand drifting to Iona's shoulder.

Then Moira's gaze lowers to Iona's neck, her eyes widening in disbelief. "For goodness sake, put on the pendant! What are you doing wandering the grounds without it?"

"I…" Iona doesn't know how to explain, and merely says, "I'll fetch it."

She hastens down the hall, throws open Ariadne's bedroom door, going straight for the bedside table, but… the pendant isn't there and neither is Aster. She searches frantically, throwing back the bed sheets, scouring the floor, knowing without a shred of doubt that she'd left it there, but there is no sign of it. An impossibility, given that no one alive is capable of even touching the stones, except…

*Ariadne, please answer me!* Iona calls, but the empty silence remains unbroken.

She cannot feel Ariadne's essence as she usually can, as if the bond has been severed, but somehow, she knows that isn't so. There is something else warding her off. She wonders if it might be one of Ariadne's shields, until she notices the staff left leaning against the wall. She takes it, hugging it close to her chest, as she examines the room for any clue as to where Ariadne has gone. She must have been here recently and without the staff's portals, she can't have made it very far, unless she used a carriage.

Not knowing what else to do, Iona keeps the staff and draws her wand, running down the hall to where Marina and Moira were, but the sitting room is empty. She checks every room in the manor, but all are empty and dark, the candles snuffed out.

Unwilling to waste another second, she runs outside and into the cold. Wisp leaps through the thickening blanket of snow, sniffing the ground and trilling nervously as Iona trudges after her, using the staff to steady herself.

"Ariadne!" she calls, her voice echoing against the towering monoliths of stone.

Her breath is too loud in her ears as she waits, but still there is no response. She knows well that she could be overheard by Rebekka, or the Crone herself, but she doesn't know how else to find Ariadne within the vast wilderness. Perhaps the Crone already has her, and that is why she can no longer feel her. The thought has Iona running ever faster, stumbling farther down the mountainside, until she reaches a clearing.

There sits a pianoforte of dark wood, the bench pulled back and the keys exposed. Iona goes to it, searching frantically for any footprints in the snow, but the flurries of snowflakes fall around her, already covering her own steps down the mountain.

"Ariadne!" she calls again.

"Where are we meant to go?"

Iona shrieks in fright, then sighs angrily when it's only Ksenia in a simple black dress shivering with her arms wrapped tightly around herself. She must have just arrived for the solstice ritual.

"I've no time for you. Go find the others on your own." Iona turns on her heels and trudges onward.

"I beg your pardon?" Ksenia huffs. "Oh, I see. This is about the dragon."

Iona stops short, her brow furrowing when she looks back at her. "What dragon?"

"I did what I must to incapacitate it. You'd have done the same," Ksenia says.

"What are you on about?" Iona asks, observing her shivering. "Conjure a cloak before you freeze to death."

"Don't you think I tried that the moment I stepped through?" Ksenia snaps. "It seems my wand has disappeared. I cannot imagine what Morgan expects us to learn without the use of magic. This entire ordeal has become rather tedious."

Iona blinks at the mention of Morgan, then her mouth falls open. "Stepped through? The moonstone arches, you mean?"

"Yes, of course! What else would I be referring to?" Ksenia throws up her hands in frustration. "I swear, Ariadne must have rationed every ounce of patience to court the likes of you."

"But Ksenia, I am not..." Iona shakes her head, unsure if she should divulge the future, then deciding she hasn't the patience to consider the potential ramifications. "It's been many months since the trials. The pendant has already been claimed."

Ksenia's ice blue eyes widen, then narrow with mistrust. "You're tricking me."

"I swear it," Iona insists. "The arches are portals through time. I claimed the pendant. It's done."

Ksenia studies her with shrewd suspicion but seems to believe her. She looks away in a rare show of uncertainty. "But why would Morgan send me here, then? Is she mocking my efforts?"

"She doesn't seem like the sort of witch to bother with that," Iona says, recollecting her own journeys within the arches. The magic always sent her to a witch in need. "I must find Ariadne. She may be in grave danger."

"Call to her through your bond," Ksenia says.

"She's blocked our connection somehow," Iona mutters. "I must track her down on foot. She must have been here."

She gestures to the pianoforte, but Ksenia only stares with indifference.

"Off you go, then," she says, and when Iona glares at her, she sneers. "Who am I to interfere in a lover's quarrel?"

"She was once your friend," Iona says. "Did those years mean nothing to you?"

"She's more than capable of protecting herself, and if you were adept enough to usurp her, then I see no reason for my involvement, even if I did have my wand." Ksenia's gaze drifts to Iona's bare neck, prompting her to frown. "If you claimed the pendant, then why are you not wearing it?"

Iona bites her lip. "I haven't time to waste on explanations. Either walk with me or-"

"Fine," She huffs, though it is difficult to comprehend past her chattering teeth.

Iona conjures a wool cloak and offers it. Ksenia eyes it with contempt, until a frigid gust of wind blows through the trees, showering them in snow that had collected on the boughs overhead, and she wisely decides that her pride is not worth her suffering. Once she has fastened the cloak around herself, Wisp leads the way with a renewed urgency.

"Thank you," Ksenia says.

Iona nods absentmindedly, too concerned with Ariadne's safety.

"Why then do you not have the pendant?" Ksenia asks again.

"I… finally admitted to myself that Ariadne is better suited to bear it than I," she says. "It's rather complicated but in the end, Morgan allowed us to choose who should have it, and Ariadne gave it to me."

"Then… Ariadne spoke true when she renounced her claim. I never would have thought a Zerynthos witch capable of resisting power," Ksenia muses. "I imagine her family was not pleased."

"They took it rather well, actually," Iona says. "Well… all accept Cintia. The others shifted their ambitions to me, as it were."

Ksenia snorts. "What a terrible misjudgment."

Iona's cheeks burn, but she cannot contradict her. "They'll surely be relieved when they learn Ariadne has the pendant instead, as they'd always hoped."

Ksenia walks in silence a moment, then says, "I always found it odd they chose Ariadne. You'd have thought Moira would be the one they forced to train all those years, sequestered from the world."

Their eyes drift up in the direction of the manor on the

mountaintop, an ominous presence amid the white trees and overcast sky.

"Moira attempted the trials, too, did she not?" Iona asks.

"Yes," Ksenia nods contemplatively. "My elder sister was in her year, but she claimed Moira hardly studied at all and did not seem the least bit nervous on the day of the trials, as if she didn't care what happened."

"That is in her nature," Iona shrugs. "She takes very little seriously."

Ksenia nods again but seems deep in thought. Iona waits for her to speak.

"What possessed you to think the pendant wasn't meant for you if Morgan herself told you it was?" Ksenia finally asks.

Iona hesitates, unsure if she should mention her dealings with Hecate. Then she supposes it wouldn't hurt, if she does not mention maleficians, or the Crone specifically.

"Hecate told me as much, in her way," Iona says.

"You spoke with Hecate? You?" Ksenia asks incredulously.

"Yes, me." Iona cuts her a glare. "If a Goddess of magic tells me I'm not worthy, who am I to disagree?"

"Why should she care? A Goddess of her caliber could craft any number of artifacts at her leisure if one was required. It is only a feat for mere mortals like us, or lesser immortals, I suppose."

Iona's brow furrows. "I... I couldn't say. Perhaps Xiomara might know."

"That silver tongued harpy?" Ksenia asks. "Do not believe a word she says."

Taken aback, Iona stops mid-stride. "Xiomara? She's only ever been kind to me."

"Oh, I'm sure she has, while you possessed something she wanted," Ksenia says. "I have a clairvoyant gift for detecting lies, annoying but useful. I don't recall ever hearing a true word come from that woman's mouth."

"You're sorely mistaken," Iona says. "She's been like a mother to Ariadne, and a mentor to me."

"If you say so," Ksenia says. "I wager her kindness will dwindle away the moment she sees your neck is bare."

"Not everyone deals in fickle loyalty as you do, Ksenia," Iona retorts.

Ksenia grows silent again, but not out of offense. When Iona peers over at her, she is consumed by her musings.

"What are you thinking of?" Iona finally asks as she trudges on ahead.

"Something isn't right about this whole affair," Ksenia murmurs.

"Can you not think and walk at once?"

"Do you want my help or don't you?"

Reluctantly, Iona crosses her arms and waits.

"What do you have that Hecate would want?" Ksenia asks.

"Nothing," Iona says. "I doubt a Goddess wants for anything, especially one of her caliber, as you said."

"Yes… Yes…" Ksenia says. "Then what does Xiomara want that you possess?"

"The pendant," Iona says, "but no longer."

"Because Xiomara's Goddess convinced you to take it off," Ksenia says.

"For good reason," Iona argues.

"And you just allowed their sophistry to convince you to discard your only means of protection?" Ksenia asks. "So that their golden child could take it in your stead? Do you not see how that could potentially benefit them at your expense?"

"They aren't what they seem," Iona says. "They protect… I cannot say exactly, but you must believe me-"

Ksenia brings her fingers to her temples and lets out a heavy sigh. "You are an idiot."

"That's uncalled for!" Iona cries. "There is much you don't know, that I cannot tell you."

"We must find Ariadne so I might converse with one of marginally higher intelligence," Ksenia says. "You'd best hope we find her first. I cannot think of many forces strong enough to ward against a blood bond, except perhaps a Goddess's power."

That gives Iona pause. She shifts restlessly on her feet, unable to ignore the sinking feeling in her gut. "But… why would Hecate do such a thing?"

Iona waits for an answer, but when she looks, Ksenia is gone.

"Ksenia?" Iona calls, then sighs angrily, "Everyone must stop disappearing!"

"Iona!"

She ducks down at the sound, until she spies Samaira's worry-stricken face from afar and runs through the snow to meet her.

"You're a sight for sore eyes," Iona says.

"Something is wrong," Samaira says. "Very, very wrong."

"What did you see?" Iona's heart sinks. "Another attack?"

"I saw Hecate," Samaira says. "At least, I believe it to be her."

"Iona!" Ksenia calls.

"Oh, for goodness sake!" Iona yells. "What? What is it?"

She barely has a chance to turn in the direction of Ksenia's voice before she collides into her, nearly toppling them both. She grips Iona's arms and shakes her.

"Did you just see me?" Ksenia asks.

Iona looks down at her rumpled green dress and brown cloak, not the black gown and cloak she had just been wearing. The shadows under her blue eyes are enough for Iona to know she's speaking with the version of her from present day. "Yes, but-"

"We must leave," Ksenia says. "Now!"

"Why?" Samaira asks.

"I cannot explain until..." Ksenia scans the trees. "We cannot speak here."

"I am not leaving without Ariadne," Iona says.

"She isn't here," Ksenia says.

"How could you possibly know that?" Iona narrows her eyes.

"I've searched the entire forest all day," she says. "There's been no sign of her."

"What?" Samaira and Iona ask in unison.

"Though my eyes may deceive me... They wouldn't let her roam unaccompanied," Ksenia trails off, distracted. "They've shrouded her... left nothing to chance."

"She was here; I know it. There was a pianoforte in the clearing back there." Iona points behind her. "She must be at the manor somewhere. Perhaps the library or-"

"You mustn't go back there," Ksenia says fervently.

"But Ariadne-"

"Iona, listen to me," Ksenia begs. "This is beyond petty grudges, beyond country or family, or anything at all. It is life and death."

Iona stares at her, at the unhinged panic in her eyes.

"Where?" she finally asks.

"Somewhere far and warm," Ksenia says, "Please tell me you know how to work that staff."

"I'm not... I have never used it before," Iona stutters.

"You'd best learn," Ksenia says, "and quickly."

Iona's doubt creeps up as it always does, but she mustn't let it.

"Iona?"

She stiffens at the call of Marina, her dreamy, anodyne voice drifting across the frozen forest like a summer breeze.

"Hurry," Ksenia hisses.

Ariadne had only ever thought the portals into existence, but when Iona tries to envision a location in her mind, nothing happens. She squeezes her eyes shut, manifests as best she can, but still nothing.

"Take me to São Paolo," Iona whispers.

Slowly, a portal shimmers before them, showing the Rio Tamanduateí on the outskirts of the city.

"Good, good," Ksenia takes her arm and drags her through with urgency.

"What of Marina?" Samaira asks.

"Leave her." Ksenia reaches through and yanks Samaira to the other side. "Close it now."

Iona does so and is about to ask what has Ksenia so frightened, when she grasps her arm again and drags her down to the river.

"What are you doing?" Iona asks.

"Take off your dress," Ksenia says, pulling them into the river.

"What are you playing at?" Iona shrinks away from her.

Ksenia rolls her eyes. "Do not flatter yourself. I've seen more of you than I'd care to at rituals."

"If you would only explain your intentions," Samaira takes Iona's other hand.

"You must cleanse yourself." Ksenia looks over her shoulder, her eyes just as manic as they'd been in Thessaly. "They can see us so long as you're marked by them."

"By whom?" Iona asks.

"If you love Ariadne at all, you'll listen to me," Ksenia says, going behind Iona's back to unfasten her buttons, gesturing to Samaira. "Help me. Then, and only then, may we speak frankly."

Samaira looks to Iona for permission, and she reluctantly nods. Once they've removed her clothes, Ksenia pulls Iona into the river and withdraws her marble wand to conjure a bowl of salt, taking handfuls of it and scrubbing all over Iona's body with frantic thoroughness until her skin turns pink.

"Védeni," Ksenia incants in hushed tones. "Védeni."

"You needn't scrub so hard," Iona winces, curling into herself for want of modesty.

"Sit still," Ksenia snaps.

"If this is some sort of foolish capriccio, I shall be very cross with you," Iona warns.

"We're well past that now," Ksenia mutters, and after

scrubbing Iona's arms and legs as well, she steps back and regards her warily. "I'm not sure… It should be enough, but I can't be sure."

"If cleansing is what you're after," Samaira says, "perhaps lavender oil to ward against evil."

Ksenia bites her lip and nods. "That could help."

"For heaven's sake, do it quickly!" Iona's teeth chatter.

"I told you someplace warm," Ksenia reminds her.

"Not many places would be at night in mid-winter," Iona retorts. "I can only craft portals to places I've been to before."

Ksenia conjures a bottle of lavender oil, tipping it over and dousing Iona with it until she's covered.

"I can manage it myself," Iona says when they reach for her.

She rubs the oil into her salt-covered skin, only allowing Samaira to help rub her back, while Ksenia incants her protections spells, until Iona notices a distinct shift. Her limbs were once heavy as lead, though she hadn't perceived it until they are suddenly light and easily moved. The colors in her vision grow in vibrance and clarity, her thoughts forming quicker, her movements more blithe. It's as if an imperceivable fog has been lifted.

"How do you feel?" Ksenia asks.

"Much better," Iona says in amazement. "But why-"

"Not here." Ksenia wraps a warm towel around her.

Taking back the staff, Iona conjures new clothes and a blue cotton shawl that she wraps around her shoulders.

Ksenia leans in close and whispers in her ear. "Moscow."

Iona nods and creates a portal, finding it much easier to manage the second time. They step through and only once the doorway is shut does Ksenia visibly relax only slightly. They now inhabit a dark stone hallway of the Ulanova's castle, the bitter cold turning Iona's lips blue.

She conjures a flame and holds it close to her chest to warm herself, her wet hair like ice against her scalp and neck.

"Come." Ksenia beckons them to follow her.

She takes them up two flights of stairs and throws open the door to a bedroom. Iona's jaw drops at beholding the total disarray. Books, scrolls, and loose papers are strewn about on Ksenia's bed, her desk, and all over the floor. The only beauty to be found in the derelict space is a pot of flourishing red poppies by the lancet window.

"Is your family here?" Iona asks.

"They left for the ritual…" Ksenia murmurs. "Tried to take

me, but obviously I couldn't go with them."

In the corner is a well-worn cauldron filled with what looks distinctly of energy potion, with dirty cups littering the floor. A cockroach scurries from inside one of the cups to a crack between two stones in the wall. Iona grimaces, then regards Ksenia with rising unease.

"When did you last sleep?" she asks.

"There wasn't time!" Ksenia's impatience persists. "Close the door behind you."

Samaira does so, then comes up to Iona and whispers, "Has she gone mad?"

"I couldn't confront you until the loop was completed," Ksenia says, shuffling through a mountain of papers on her desk, "or it would-"

"Tangle the threads of time," Iona says. "I know all too well."

"Good, one less thing to explain," Ksenia sighs, then leans her hands against the desk. "I know not where to start."

"Do sit down and I'll make tea," Samaira suggests.

"No time," Ksenia mutters.

She goes to the chairs by the fire, frantically tossing papers and books this way and that in her haste. When she still hasn't found what she's looking for, she weaves her fingers through her matted blonde tresses.

"Do you know where Ariadne is?" Iona asks. "That is of the most importance to me at present."

"No, I don't know where she is," Ksenia says, slumping in a chair.

"Then I must go and find her, and we may speak later," Iona says, but Ksenia leaps up and grasps her wrist so tightly it smarts.

"No!" she pleads. "Please, you must let me speak!"

"Alright!" Iona wrenches her wrist away. "Be swift or-"

"I've been observing you for months. You and Ariadne," Ksenia says.

"For what purpose?" Iona asks.

"What you told me during the trials… I knew it wasn't right," Ksenia says. "I would have spoken sooner… I couldn't. It was torture."

Ksenia spots a paper on the floor and reaches down to take it and shove it in Iona's hands. She looks at it, then realizes it's upside down. Turning it to rights, she reviews a map marked red with what were once Katrin Zerynthos' territories, underlaid by the humans' borders. The red stretches over most of Europe, part of Asia, Africa, and the Americas.

"I felt something was very wrong and took it upon myself to find out what. That proved more difficult than I'd anticipated." Ksenia rubs her face with her hands.

"What do you mean?" Iona asks, setting the map aside. "What have you been doing all this time?"

"Waiting. Watching. Studying," Ksenia murmurs. "I cannot tell you why one so honorable as Hecate would allow this... It strains credulity... My only doubt..." She looks about the room, her eyes darting wildly to inspect every corner. "She hasn't noticed me thus far, but it's only a matter of time."

"She is a benevolent Goddess," Iona says. "She would not-"

"You are too easily beguiled," Ksenia scoffs.

"Even when I failed her, she healed me from the brink of death," Iona insists, struggling to make sense of her abstruse ramblings.

"Of course, she would be beguiling..." Ksenia mutters. "But the manner in which... Why the secrecy? Perhaps a false god... But who?"

She flies to the other end of the room to comb through a bookshelf so filled with heavy tomes; it slants lopsided under the weight. She takes a book and tosses it to Iona, who catches it awkwardly, creasing the pages before she can arrange it properly in her hands. The cover is titled A History of the Greek Pantheon.

Iona cuts the book in half, flipping through the pages from Eris, Goddess of Discord, to Hemera, Goddess of the Day, then Thanatos, God of Peaceful Death-

"Xiomara must have adored you... So acquiescent. A walking, bleeding heart," Ksenia says. "You let them mark you... You bird-witted fool."

"Insult me once more, and I shan't stay another moment," Iona warns, tossing the book aside in her frustration.

"So easily affronted," Ksenia continues, "and so heavily guarded."

Iona looks to Samaira, but her brow is furrowed in deep concentration, her eyes remaining fixed on Ksenia as she erratically flits about the room. Iona reaches out to capture one of Ksenia's wrists to hold her in place.

"What has any of this got to do with Ariadne?" Iona asks.

"I underestimated her true importance... Never quite understood the significance of her power... I was a fool. We all were," Ksenia laments, then levels Iona with a sobering look.

"You must understand that I wouldn't care about you or any of this if it wasn't of dire significance. I have no reason to fabricate my findings."

"Of your indifference to me, I'm altogether sure," Iona says.

Ksenia returns to her desk where she rifles through the many drawers.

"Forgive me," Samaira says with contrition.

"Of what?" Iona asks, having almost forgotten her where she stands quietly observing.

"I… perused your aura," Samaira says. "I couldn't stand my apparent ignorance of all these developments and thought it would save time."

Iona bristles at the invasion of her private thoughts, then sighs. "You've seen it all, then?"

"As have I," Ksenia says. "Your mind is barely protected. You've grown complacent with the pendant doing all the work for you."

"Has everyone read my mind?" Iona throws up her hands in frustration.

"You should assume so," Ksenia says. "Even with the pendant, a Goddess could see all of what you are."

Deciding there's no point in lying if they already know the truth, Iona says, "The Crone is still out there. She could have Ariadne bound in chains as we speak. I must search for her!"

"I cannot fathom why Ariadne would let you anywhere near a Crone. You were more often a hinderance than an asset, but that's to be expected from one so inexperienced as you," Ksenia says.

Iona's cheeks burn. "That is why I relinquished the pendant. Ariadne is better equipped to wield it. It seems she agreed, since she is the only one who could have taken it. I'm not… I'm not strong enough."

"You could be," Ksenia says. "That is what confounded me the most, and what birthed my suspicion. The very same women who once trained Ariadne could just as easily have done the same to you, with all the potential you possess and the raw power you once bore. It's all that separates you from Ariadne, after all. Instruction, practice, time. Ariadne knows it well. It's why she was once so threatened by you when you arrived at Lysander College unannounced. Xiomara Zerynthos would surely see it, too, but it seems as though she deliberately sent you out into combat to fall on your face, failing time and again until you conceded."

"That's not…" Iona stutters. "Why would they do something so counterintuitive when the Crone terrorizes our people? Why would they go to such lengths to trick me when I was so obliging to them all this time?"

"Haven't you guessed by now?" Ksenia asks. "There is no crone."

Iona's heart stops, and Samaira sucks in a breath behind her.

"But… that's not true at all." Iona shakes her head vigorously. "I've seen her with my own eyes! I've fought her with Ariadne and her family alongside me."

"You fought a malefician, to be sure," Ksenia says, "but not a crone."

"Who then?" Iona asks.

"All of them at once," Ksenia says. "I can only guess which one of them attacked when, but-"

"All of whom?" Iona asks.

"The Zerynthos witches, of course!" Ksenia exclaims, "and Sebastian, I suppose."

Iona laughs, her unbearable anxiety pouring out of her as unhinged hysteria. She doubles over, hugging her aching chest with her arms.

"Are you actually insinuating that the Zerynthos witches are maleficians?" Samaira asks, the notion so outlandish that Iona laughs harder. "Every single one?"

"Every single one," Ksenia gives a resolute nod.

Iona cannot stop laughing no matter how hard she tries, until Ksenia walks up to her and slaps her hard across the face.

"Pull yourself together!" Ksenia snaps. "There's no time. There's simply no time!"

"You truly are mad!" Iona brings a hand to her stinging cheek. "We would have sensed… We would have known if this were true."

"Like you did with Elise?" Ksenia asks.

Iona frowns and looks away, reeling against the absurdity of her ravings.

"It's not possible," Samaira agrees. "What you are implying… it could never be. Maleficians cannot form covens."

"None have thought it possible," Ksenia agrees. "Maleficians are far too volatile, too destructive. They would only turn on each other, cannibalizing on their magic until one remained. Or so we've always believed. This is unlike any instance of maleficium ever recorded. The sheer power they've cultivated for all those years, siphoning magic from sacred sites on every continent without restriction, it is beyond imagining…"

Iona paces the floor, her hands trembling. "But the other covens would have noticed. Someone would have seen… something. Someone must have…"

"When Katrin lived, the other covens were kept blissfully content, gorging themselves on magic while others were deprived. Why would they disrupt an arrangement that exclusively benefited them?" Ksenia asks. "An arrangement you perpetuated at Xiomara's behest."

"This is an outrageous claim to bring to me without tangible proof," Iona insists, "I have months of evidence to the contrary. Marina, Moira, Xiomara, every one of them put their lives in the gravest danger to protect those who the Crone abducted. How am I meant to believe you at all, in anything, when I know you were sneaking letters to Ariadne's mother during your mockery of a friendship? For all we know, you're in league with them and this is all just a distraction to keep me from Ariadne. It was not long ago that she and I thought you were a malefician."

Ksenia grimaces. "Fools, the both of you. I would never defile myself with dark magic."

"So you say." Iona crosses her arms.

Samaira puts a comforting hand on her shoulder and frowns. "Ksenia, you'd better have proof of this."

"Strong, undeniable proof," Iona agrees.

Ksenia returns to her papers and books with renewed vigor, and out of impatience, Iona shifts through the papers, too.

"What is it you're searching for?" Iona asks.

"This!" Ksenia says triumphantly when she spots an old book with a cracked spine and a familiar cover.

It is the conjuration book Iona had skimmed through when she'd gone to the library with Ariadne and Xiomara the night before the summer solstice. Ksenia slams it upon her desk and beckons them closer.

"It wasn't easy sneaking into their library, but I managed somehow, with invisibility potions and a bit of luck," Ksenia says, rubbing her eyes. "I searched every tome for any indication of their plans, any notes in the margins…"

She opens to a page she'd marked and points at an ancient illustration of a coven cloaked in black, their arms raised upwards towards the black sky. Between them lies a screaming child upon a burning pyre.

"A sacrifice?" Iona asks.

Ksenia shakes her head. "A birth."

When Iona looks closer, there are thin tendrils of magic emanating from each of the witches and into the baby.

"The conjuration of a child," Ksenia says.

"Ariadne once told me of this sort of magic," Iona says with a small smile. "That one day we might... That it is possible to use magic to create life."

"Yes, she once mentioned this spell to me, too, when we were children, and I always found it quite odd for her to speak of it as if it were commonplace," Ksenia says.

"Why?" Iona asks.

"Why?" she scoffs incredulously. "Creating a soul from nothing? What could possibly be complicated about that sort of magic?"

Iona shrinks at her cutting sarcasm. "I... I suppose I thought it would be like conjuring a bird or a kitten."

"We are much more complex. A ritual like this is very rare and takes an astronomical amount of power to perform successfully. Most cannot even attempt it," Ksenia says. "And yet Ariadne spoke of it with such a casual air, as if it were only a trifle. I tried telling her how complicated the ritual could be, but she insisted it was not so rare as I claimed, that her mother told her otherwise in their lessons. She'd dragged me to her library to prove it, showed me this very illustration, and insisted that I was merely uneducated."

Iona sighs. "I'm still confused."

"As am I," Samaira says.

Ksenia grunts with frustration, then lifts another book and places it on top of the conjuration one. The title reads Possession and Death Magic. She turns it to a page that lists ingredients for a spell that calls a soul back from the other side.

"But this is an unnatural spell," Samaira says, and though she seems to know the answer, still she asks, "You found this grimoire in the Villa Mitriora's library?"

"I could not understand why they would want Ariadne as their leader, to be Hecate's voice here on Earth, when they harbor such brazen disdain for her. They kept her apart from society, treated her differently from her cousins, for what possible reason? They did not expect her to be here for long." Ksenia gestures to the grimoire. "What has the crone been stealing from her victims?"

Iona drags a trembling finger down the page. "A heart, a liver, lungs, a stomach, and a uterus."

Ksenia brings back the conjuration grimoire and points to the page beside the illustration of the birthing ritual. "This can only be performed during the Spring equinox, taking an entire day to complete, and only manifesting on-"

"Ariadne's birthday…" Tears well in Iona's eyes as she looks to Samaira, her only lifeline in this awful exchange, but she, too, is at a loss for words. Iona swallows hard, then whispers, "Do you mean to say… that they intend to bring a soul back-"

"Into a new body, cultivated with care," Ksenia says, "and missing only one final attribute, until recently."

Iona's hand lifts to her neck, grasping for stones that are no longer there.

"Well? What are you doing just standing there?" Ksenia grips Iona's shoulders and shakes her, staring with wide, bloodshot eyes. "Don't you see! We must find Ariadne, before it's too late!"

## 34 - Ariadne

"I cannot feel her," Ariadne murmurs.

"I've obstructed that pesky bond for you," Hecate says with a sympathetic smile. "We'll remedy it all soon."

Ariadne's stomach turns, wondering what it will feel like to rip their souls apart. Perhaps Hecate will remove the pain, or at least the physical manifestation of it, but she will never recover from Iona's betrayal. The agony shall live in her heart forever.

"Come along." Hecate takes her hand and guides her onward.

"Where... Where are we going?" She regards their dark surroundings with disdain, wishing they had gone to the asphodel fields instead. "Why are we here?"

"To right a wrong," Hecate says.

She takes Ariadne down the dark tunnel to the iridescent web.

"There lies the weaver of your fate." Hecate gestures above them to where Arachne perches on a thread. "The reason for your suffering."

"Iona is the reason for my suffering." Ariadne tries to turn away, but Hecate places an arm around her shoulders and fixes her in place.

"It's as you said," Hecate insists. "The Crone, Iona, your family, all of them are beholden to Arachne's directive. Every wound, every disappointment, every awful thing is her doing. She gave you Iona only to rip her away. She gave you a family who only served to torment you, a friend who nearly killed you, others who only used you. She crafted every nightmare, cut every scar, ingrained in you every flaw you possess."

Ariadne glares at the spider with burning contempt until, for the first time, the spider stops her weaving and looks up, all eight black eyes trained on her.

"I could not blame you for hating her. Fate is cruel indeed." Hecate gently strokes her hair. "Even after millennia of observing the toil of mortals, I still cannot comprehend the need for such recurrent suffering. What right does she have to do this to you? What right does anyone have to cause you harm? You, who have only tried to survive, to love... to be worthy of love."

Ariadne tries to blink her tears away, but her emotions are so raw, so exposed. She can no longer muster the strength to bury her feelings away anymore.

"If not for her, would you have been subjected to such mistreatment by your scornful mother, while your father looked on and did nothing?" Hecate asks.

"You did not intervene either," Ariadne murmurs, "even when I called for your aid."

"I couldn't," Hecate says, pointing with a long sharp finger, "because of her."

Blood roars in Ariadne's ears, her hands shaking, her entire form trembling.

"You wish never to be hurt again?" Hecate asks, still stroking her hair. "To possess the peace you've always longed for? To be freed of all your pain?"

"Yes," Ariadne rasps.

"What price would you pay for your freedom?" Hecate asks.

Hot tears drip down her cheeks. "Anything."

"Then take her, my daughter." Hecate's breath tickles her ear. "Rid the world of her tyranny, once and for all."

Ariadne looks up at her, struck with a cold realization of what she implies, but Hecate only stares solemnly back at her.

"Take her," Hecate says again, "before the Crone succeeds in usurping Arachne's will. Protect your world from catastrophe and ruin."

When Ariadne looks back at the spider, she expects her to run, to scurry away into a crevice in the rock never to be seen again, but Arachne remains still, balancing on a single shimmering thread.

"She will keep you tethered to Iona even if your blood bond is broken," Hecate reminds her. "You cannot resist Arachne's decree. You will worship at the feet of a woman who only desires you due to unseen forces contriving your attachment. Iona never truly loved you. Never."

A pathetic sob racks Ariadne's body, and Hecate hushes her, caressing her cheeks and wiping away her tears.

"There, there," Hecate says. "Heed my words and all shall be well again."

Ariadne takes one step toward the creature, then another, and another, until she's close enough to reach out and scoop her up into her palm. The spider doesn't squirm, or bite, or try to escape. Arachne only looks up at her, so seemingly fragile and meek, and yet capable of such devastation.

"She took Euphemia," Hecate whispers in her ear.

Ariadne flinches away, but Hecate keeps her in a firm embrace.

"An innocent baby boy is left motherless. A kind young man widowed," Hecate continues.

Her fingers twitch as she's wracked with violent sobs that echo within the vast cave.

"She is why the one you love has left you for another." Hecate gently pushes one of her curls behind her shoulder.

"She's alive," Ariadne mouths.

"She's a monster," Hecate says.

"If I did this…"

"You would be a hero."

"A killer."

"She is the killer," Hecate says softly, wiping away another of Ariadne's tears. "The harbinger of death to countless millions. Those whose lives were tragically cut short. Those whose dreams are never realized, whose potential is squandered by mere circumstance. Should our fate not lie in our own hands?"

Ariadne's vision is obscured by her vengeful tears. She can barely see the spider as she wraps her fingers around its body, then closes her fist, clenching it shut.

"Pyrkagiá," she chokes out, channeling all the magic now afforded her, and a flame bursts between her fingers, burning the creature inside.

When Ariadne opens her hand again, all that's left are specks of ash. She blinks, unable to believe what she's done. Around them, the threads glow, then turn to ash, too, and scatter across the damp floor of the cave, until there are none left, turning the cavern into a dark void.

All felt suddenly very strange, as if nothing were real, or suddenly everything is.

"What does that mean?" I ask, looking up at Hecate, and my heart stops.

Her mouth is upturned into a sharp toothed smile, her eyes the darkest I have ever seen them.

"Finally," she says, as she places her palm over my forehead, and all goes black.

# 35 - Iona

"But there is one flaw in your logic." I pull myself from Ksenia's grip and turn my back to her to pace about the room. "Hecate would never, never preside over maleficians. She is an honorable Goddess of magic with power enough to sustain herself without resorting to such nefarious tactics. She would never-"

A loud clanging startles me into silence and has me whirling about to find Samaira with her hand over her mouth, and Ksenia lying prone on the stone floor fast asleep, her limbs splayed out around her.

"Oh, you must be joking." I rush to Ksenia's side. "Wake up! Damn you! Wake up!"

No matter how vigorously I shake her, Ksenia's eyes won't open, having reached the limit of an energy potion's potency. Sleep cannot be prevented indefinitely and given how many empty cups litter the dirty floor, it's a miracle she hasn't fainted sooner. I sigh with frustration at the many questions I can no longer ask her.

"Iona." Samaira's voice is enough to cut through my anger.

Looking over my shoulder, I behold her astonished expression as she looks around in horrified wonder.

"What is it?" I ask.

"The threads," Samaira whispers. "They've gone."

"Gone?" I glance about, wishing I could see what she can. "What do you mean, gone?"

"They've disappeared." Samaira meets my gaze. "I don't... I do not know what that means."

"Neither do I." I push myself back up to standing. "And quite frankly, I cannot care about it now. We must find Ariadne."

"But Iona... I feel so strange." Samaira puts a hand to her forehead. "Something's happened. Can you not feel it?"

"It can wait until we've found Ariadne." I take her hand and craft a portal. "We've waited longer than I would have chosen, if Ksenia hadn't been so insistent-"

"We cannot go there!" Samaira points through the portal at the Villa Mitriora on the other side. "They will be there. If Ksenia's theory is true..."

"Then they will have Ariadne and so that is where I must go."
Samaira's face goes deathly pale, and I huff with impatience.

"You needn't follow me. Stay here with Ksenia until she
wakes. We'll need elaboration on her many claims." I try to step
through, but Samaira keeps hold of my hand.

"I wouldn't let you go alone," she says, "but we must be
careful."

"Of course." Though caution is not at the forefront of my
mind. All I can think of is Ariadne, the pain she might be in, the
thoughts I can no longer read.

Wisp sprints up the front steps, pushing her nose against the
front door until I manage to run up and blast it open, so it hangs
off its hinges. The fox runs past the atrium and down the long,
winding hallway so swiftly Samaira and I struggle to keep pace
with her.

I should have known she would take me to the purple door,
to the room where Hecate had first appeared to us. Bracing
myself, I push open the door and poke my head inside, half
expecting Xiomara or Moira to be there waiting for me, but the
room is empty and dark, the air still smelling faintly of incense.

"Perhaps we shouldn't linger," Samaira says, wringing her
hands.

"Wisp." I reach down to pet my fox's head. "Is Ariadne
here?"

Wisp scurries across the dusty floor and scratches at a
wooden panel on the Eastern wall.

"What is this room?" Samaira asks.

"They perform rituals here." I approach the panel, knocking
on it with my knuckles and finding it hollow.

Samaira stays at the threshold, too unsettled to enter. I cannot
fault her, for I too can sense the heaviness of the air, almost like
humidity, that makes it difficult to breathe. A prickle of
awareness runs down my neck.

"Meydana çıkarmak," I incant, and all at once my vision goes
dark from the sheer volume of maleficium floating like smoke in
the small space.

"Stars above," Samaira whispers.

I step back and point the labradorite stone at the wall.
"Démolir."

The wood explodes into a cloud of splinters, revealing a
hidden compartment holding shelves of maleficium grimoires,
their leather spines carved with the same acicular symbols that
I've grown to hate, and that hatred makes my skin hot with

outrage and burning regret.

"No…" Samaira says from the doorway.

"Why would she…" My knees threatened to buckle. "Why would Hecate allow this?"

"Perhaps she is unaware," Samaira says halfheartedly.

I slam the staff against the floor, envisioning the field of endless asphodels, and a portal bursts to life in the center of the room.

"What do you intend to do?" Samaira asks, but I've already stepped across and run through the stalks of white blossoms.

"Hecate!" I call, my voice echoing across the abyss.

Samaira follows and takes my wrist in her firm grip.

"Take care in how you confront her," Samaira cautions. "She is still a Goddess."

I pull my arm back. "I fought and nearly died in her name. Now she must answer for her coven's misdeeds. She must tell me where Ariadne is. She must. She will!"

Samaira purses her lips. "If Ariadne is here, you know there is nothing to be done to-"

"No." I turn away, refusing to consider it for even a moment. "Hecate!"

Again, no one responds, and the silence does nothing to remit my untempered emotions threatening to explode.

Then a crackle of flame in the distance makes me hold my breath, straining to hear it, wondering if it might have been my imagination. Again, there is a faint snap and the very distant sound of music, and I run towards it with Wisp just ahead of me and Samaira not far behind.

I reach a crossroads, a connection of paths within the endless asphodels where Hecate, draped in a simple robe the color of saffron, sits on the ground within a collection of plush cushions.

Her torch is like a fallen star suspended in air, casting such brilliant light across the abyss, that it's almost possible to see the limits of the emptiness. It's far, far brighter than ever been before, the flames so entrancing, it takes my breath away for a moment, before I remember my purpose.

Hecate lounges beneath the blazing torch with her eyes closed, a golden bowl filled with grapes and pieces of cheese nestled in her lap, and a ring of golden keys strapped to her waist. A lyre plays a delicate melody that floats across the otherwise silent void.

"Where is Ariadne?" I ask, not bothering with pleasantries.

Hecate's eyes pop open, beholding her red irises, but the color and emotion within them are softer than I remember, not scrutinizing me to the point of discomfiture.

"Tell me where she is!" I yell. "If you've hurt her-"

"Iona," Samaira takes my arm and whispers, "do not make brazen accusations."

Hecate sets her bowl aside and stands in one graceful motion, her eyes never leaving mine as she approaches.

"Are we acquainted, child?" she asks, her brow furrowing with concern and her voice deeper in pitch than I remember.

My heart sinks, but I refuse to accept the lack of recognition in her gaze, with eyes so starkly different from the ones that dissected me and made me feel woefully small and insignificant.

"Are you the one who altered fate?" Hecate asks. "I felt it but a moment ago, an undeniable shift. It's been so very long since existence was so permanently transformed into something new."

"New?" Samaira asks. "But is fate not an eternal principle? Surely it cannot... cease to exist."

"Nothing is truly eternal," Hecate says, her gaze becoming unfocused. "Fate is malleable now. No longer fixed in time and space, no longer locked by predestination. There were once multiple forces in the universe with power over fate, working in tandem, but Arachne was the final anchor keeping it as it always was. Now she is gone-"

"Gone?" I gape at her. "But she is an immortal."

"A lesser immortal. She is dead," Hecate says, "and so there was an irrevocable shift. Now fate is... indeterminate. A fleeting, oscillating uncertainty."

"We can determine our own fates?" Samaira breathes, likely wondering how this will affect the magic of her artifact.

"Indeed. Destiny is no longer set, no longer inevitable," Hecate says. "It is truly remarkable."

"I know nothing of that," I say, though the reworking of the universe is admittedly distracting. "Tell me where Ariadne is. I must find her."

"Perhaps the two are related somehow," she says. "Regardless, I've only ever heard of one notable Ariadne in my existence, and I'm afraid she's not here. Dionysus has her."

Hecate looks up, peering through the darkness above, seeking a soul I have no use for.

"Not that Ariadne." I keep my voice steady. "Ariadne Zerynthos."

Hecate appears truly perplexed then, and I can no longer

ignore her lack of recognition.

"Don't you know me?" I ask, imploring her to have a sudden realization and tell me she'd only forgotten somehow.

"I'm afraid not," Hecate says, looking me over, "but I will always welcome the presence of fellow witches. I can see you are clearly in distress, so I will ignore your insolence."

Heat fills my cheeks, but I cannot spare too much thought on my impropriety. My mind is reeling at the thought of another imposter. A truly blasphemous subterfuge, but I suppose if the coven could construct a false crone, they could possibly do the same to Hecate.

"Can you still not see through the bond?" Samaira asks.

"No." I shake my head. "I haven't felt her for hours."

"But that's impossible," Samaira says. "Blood bonds are impervious to another witch's interference. Even a coven… I suppose we do not know the full extent of a malefician coven's power."

"A coven of maleficians?" Hecate repeats, outraged.

Samaira lowers her head. "It would seem so."

"Who are you?" Hecate narrows her eyes at me.

"Iona Evora Lysander," I say, shrinking beneath her gaze.

"Are you in league with this coven?" she asks.

"No," I say, then wince. "Or… I was until I learned of their true nature. I am in search of my beloved to free her from their clutches and…"

Hecate looks away, and nothing could have prepared me for the singular dread that befalls me at witnessing a Goddess betray true fear in their countenance, for what could possibly frighten her that would not be a reckoning for me and mine?

"Your friend speaks true," Hecate says softly. "A witch, malefician or otherwise, could not interfere with a blood bond. Only a God could perform such a feat."

Hecate meets my gaze again and wordlessly we come to the same conclusion. Not an illusion, but another Goddess using Hecate's name and likeness.

"Please," I beg. "I cannot live without her."

Hecate beckons me closer and eagerly I approach, putting my hands in hers, immediately sensing the power locked within her grip.

"Can you find her?" I ask.

"You can," Hecate says, a cabinet appearing beside her, and from it she takes a bottle of purple oil and unstoppers it.

I close my eyes when Hecate draws a line of oil across my

forehead, the concoction smelling distinctly of mint. I recoil unconsciously, reminded of Xiomara doing the same, and what it had cost me to trust her, but I would give anything to find Ariadne. I cannot wait anymore.

When I open my eyes, a small wooden table stands between Hecate and I, upon which sits a circular mirror of black stone. I recognize it as obsidian, the same material as Ariadne's wand.

"What is it?" I ask.

"A scrying mirror," Hecate says. "I may be able to connect you to your beloved, so you might hear her and see through her eyes. She may even be able to hear you, too, in which case you must both determine where she is so you may rescue her."

I nod in acknowledgment, my vision blurring as I peer into the mirror, unable to look away.

"Think of her. Reach out to her," Hecate says, "and pray that she is doing the same."

I center myself, thinking only of Ariadne's laugh, her smile, her eyes that hold so many regrets and longings, her hands that hold the diametric potential to be gentle or brutal, and her mind, which is at once a familiar haven and an indecipherable mystery.

"Invenio," Hecate incants, and I cry out as magic, potent and pure, burns my hands as it seeps from Hecate into me, calling upon Ariadne's blood saturated with mine, until my vision goes black.

At first, I wonder if I may have fainted, but my consciousness persists. It takes a moment more for me to realize I'm seeing what Ariadne can, which is nothing at all.

*Ari?*

There is no response, but I can perceive the light brush of wind against her arms and legs, the smell of the ocean on the breeze, the hard surface of rock beneath her, and the cold metal of chains cutting into the skin of her wrists and ankles.

Then her emotions become clearer to me, a mixture of bitter resentment and fear. I frown, unsure where her animosity comes from, until I look into her mind and see her recollection of Rebekka kissing me, and Ariadne's eventual assumption that her eyes did not deceive her.

And it's as if a flood of repressed enmity forces its way through to the forefront of my mind, and though I know there's limited time, I let loose only a fraction of my indignation.

*You should have known I would never betray you!* I feel her tense at my words. *You are more a fool in love than you ever were in hatred. I mean, honestly. What is wrong with you?*

*Iona?* Ariadne calls back.

It takes considerable effort to transmit every syllable, different from the effortlessness of our usual bond, but my outrage compensates for half the exertion. *How many countless times must I tell you of my absolute disinterest in Rebekka? If you had bothered to confront me before prematurely casting me out of your heart, you would have seen-*

*No…* Ariadne's remorse is immediate when she peers into my mind in turn and sees the full account of my unwanted kiss from Rebekka, my horror when her true identity had been revealed, and the many scars riddling Rebekka's arms and neck, indicating just how long the ruse has lasted.

*Utter, inexpiable fool! You feather-headed, miserable excuse for a-*

*I didn't know*, Ariadne tries to interject, but she winces at my unbridled anger.

*Your doubt in me has been made abundantly clear*, I seethe. *And how precisely has that served you?*

I take shameless pleasure from her mortification and the heat that fills her cheeks from her embarrassment. I let her stew in it for a moment or two.

*Where are you?* I finally ask, but I am met with silence. *Where, Ariadne?! Tell me before-*

*It's too late*, Ariadne relents.

*No, I can find you and-*

*Everything has changed now.*

*Why? What's happened?* I ask.

Ariadne makes an impressive effort to try and hide her thoughts, but by now I'm beyond politeness or restraint. I delve into the darkest recesses of her consciousness until I find what it is she's attempting to hide, and I gasp, unable to believe what I've seen.

*What have you done?*

"Ariadne?"

We both tense at the sound of Xiomara's voice, and all it implies of her involvement in this plot against us. A part of me had hoped beyond reason that she of all of them was ignorant as we were, but it is not so. Ariadne tries to respond, but to her horror, her voice does not obey her.

"Do not try to speak, dearest," Xiomara says, her voice closer now.

Bucking and writhing against the chains, Ariadne tries to break free, but it only causes her pain.

"Now, now, none of that." Xiomara places a hand upon Ariadne's shoulder and in an instant, her muscles go slack as paralysis takes hold. "There. All better."

*Don't panic*, I say, panicking. *We must determine where you are-*
*How?* Ariadne asks. *I cannot see! I cannot move!*
*You must convince her to... Or perhaps she might let slip-*
*They mean to kill me.* Ariadne begins to weep silently.
*No.* I try to send her calming thoughts. *I won't allow it, I-*

"I thought it only fair to explain our position to you," Xiomara says. "They all think me mad for it, but... consider this the last vestige of decency in me. After all, you were my niece, in a way."

There's a shuffling of feet and fabric as Xiomara comes to sit beside Ariadne on the slab of rock she's chained to.

"What a mess," Xiomara sighs. "It will all be over soon, at long last, but that is little comfort to either of us now. I suppose... I'll start at the beginning, shall I? With Mother. She inherited a coven that had fallen from grace, when new empires rose to prominence, but she would not accept less than the life her name promised. She studied and trained, became the very best of witches in her generation, and claimed Morgan's pendant as her own, but that was only the beginning. She strived for more and went in search of it.

Many Gods have withdrawn from our world in favor of others, and their reasons are their own. I shan't speculate on them... Regardless, we now find ourselves incredibly alone. I'm sure you've felt that loneliness, the silence, when Hecate ignored your pleas to intervene on your behalf. All your prayers were left unanswered, as was the case for our recent ancestors. I know not when or why the connection with Hecate was severed, only that our family chose not to disclose the separation and risk losing the distinguished status of our coven, which proved convenient for Mother.

She sought enlightenment and found a new Goddess, our savior. Guided by Her hand, Mother learned the true potential of maleficium, honed and mastered it, so the magic would not surmount her, poison her, as it does the others. She became the first of her kind, a malefician unhindered by madness, her mind clear, her vision pure.

But of course, there are still those who fear maleficians, who would kill us on sight. Mother knew there was no hope of convincing all the covens of her superiority over other lesser maleficians. Those primitive hags who bathe in blood and cast their crude hexes in the cover of night were a scourge upon our world, one that meant little to our mother, but she could see it would not do to let them wreak havoc at her detriment. Instead, she exterminated them one by one, leeching away their magic, and in so doing rid the world of any who would challenge us.

All the while, our Goddess showed Mother the secrets of the universe, of fate and time. Despite Mother's enlightenment, Arachne proved a constant nuisance, always preventing Mother's greatest plans from coming to fruition. The spider's supposed 'interpretation' of fate was never in our favor.

Every step forward was followed by another setback, another disappointment, an eternal struggle, but whenever Mother used her power to cut down another malefician, Arachne never saw fit to intervene. It suited her well enough for innocents to be spared, and it suited Mother for the covens to believe the lie, that she vanquished evil out of charity, not survival. She used the pendant as a medal of honor to credit her, should any doubts arise as to her character. Morgan was none the wiser, dead and oblivious, though near the end I wondered if she might have suspected… In any case, there was nothing she could do to us from beyond the grave.

All was well until an unexpected peace took hold, an unintentional byproduct of Mother's intervention, which also meant there was no maleficium left to pillage. By then, Zephyra, Cintia, and I were coming of age. We knew Mother's secret and practiced maleficium by her side, but she could see the world we would inherit, the obstacles we would face.

Our Goddess had become exceedingly fond of Mother and did not wish for Death to take her. Even with maleficium, and the pendant's magic, she could not delay the inevitable forever, and though our Goddess has a fearsome, spectacular might, she regrettably does not possess the ability to create immortals.

We could alter Mother's face, her skin, to maintain the appearance of youth, but the tissue beneath would still age as any other's, the decay only preventable for so long, until the body dies. Casting a necromantic spell on Mother's body would have reanimated her, but not in a lasting way. She would have come back changed, infirm, and the pendant would have been lost to another.

When the time came that the pendant's magic began to fade, marking the end of Mother's reign, we knew we'd run out of time. We scoured the earth for any recourse, any spell, potion, or incantation that could keep my mother alive. In the end, we found one, singular solution.

By conjuring a vessel, we could transfer our mother's soul to a younger body so she might live on. The pendant is tied to the soul and so our theory was that it would not be lost in the process, though we couldn't be sure until we attempted it. And so, that night, on the eve of your birth-"

Ariadne jerks with sudden revelatory shock, and my heart sinks.

"-our coven performed a ritual to craft the vessel. It was... 1782, I believe, within this crater on the day of the spring equinox. We incanted for hours, starting in the early morning, used all the plentiful magic at our disposal, and still nearly lost our lives before the night was through. I hope to never again endure that dreadful emptiness. The strain it took... it was agony. Then, that vermin-" Xiomara pauses a moment to reign in her disgust. "Arachne did what we had all been led to believe was impossible. She more than intervened. In that we could have possibly tried again another day, searched for a different avenue, but no. At the stroke of midnight, when the equinox waned, Arachne deviated our spell, corrupted its true purpose, so that instead of the vessel we'd intended, we were left with you. A baby with its own soul, its own thread of life, and altogether useless to us and our cause."

Hot tears pool in Ariadne's sightless eyes, and I am left speechless. Ksenia had been right after all.

"At once, our plans were foiled. The spell took such a devastating toll on Mother and, whether it was due to Arachne's further interference or not, the pendant's magic faded in earnest. She had mere years left and, with her power greatly enervated, there was no hope of her attempting the spell again. Without her, we could not craft a vessel perfect enough. Mother couldn't very well inhabit your body, forced to live as a baby, and then a child for years on end, and unable to bear the pendant.

Even so, we did all we could to fix you. Zephyra even tried brewing a growth potion to accelerate your age, but it was not to be. None have mastered that sort of complicated transformation yet, and it likely would not have been permanent either. Zephyra's potions only sickened you and left us to nurse you back to health. All our efforts were in vain. We had no other option but to wait, but Mother has always been patient, as am I.

Mother passed on, as Arachne and Morgan intended, and the pendant went to Lysander College to await the next bearer. It was our undertaking, as our mother's true daughters, to raise you to achieve only one goal, taking back the pendant for your family."

I realize then that if Katrin had unwittingly bore Ariadne through the ritual, using the pendant's magic, then she was not Cintia's daughter at all, but her sister. I'm not given much time to process the new development before Xiomara continues with her tale.

"I could not take you in. Not with Moira and Marina to look after. They wouldn't have let you live long enough to use you," Xiomara says, with a sickeningly adoring chuckle. "Zephyra had Sebastian, who would have done far worse, I assure you. We had very much to teach them and couldn't have you in our way, with the constant threat of you learning the truth too soon.

Cintia never wanted children, which made her the only one able to raise you away from us and the rest of society until you came of age. She taught you magic, kept you in line, ingrained in you the importance of our sovereignty, so that when the time came, you would do your duty.

It had been our plan anyhow, if the vessel had been a success, to pretend Cintia had a daughter without anyone's knowledge. I'd say she was the one most frustrated by all this, as I'm sure you've noticed. Cintia detests waiting… but I saw it as an opportunity.

Initially, we'd intended to raise you as a prodigy, preparing you for the trials, ensuring your power was undeniable, orchestrating occasional, brief appearances in society while under our watchful eye, so that when Mother claimed your body, she could live as you and no one would suspect a thing. However, after Mother's many years of waiting, she's become increasingly uninterested in that plan and unsatisfied by assimilation… That time has passed, it seems.

While our elevated status has empowered us to gain complete control over the world's magic, feasting on it, growing ever stronger, still we are forced to hide. No longer does Mother wish to live in the shadows. No longer will she suffer this world to obstruct us.

Anyhow, all was going according to plan until your encounter with the Nicolo girl," Xiomara says, and Ariadne cringes. "Even Marina did not foresee it, but we suspect the girl's parents placed protective charms over her before sending her off to kill you. They knew nothing of the hex we'd placed on you."

Ariadne goes rigid.

"A powerful defensive hex that could only be awakened if you came to the brink of death at the hand of an enemy. We could not simply allow you to roam about freely without one," Xiomara says. "It's a shame the girl's parents sent her to commit their crime for them, but these are the consequences. You only thought the illusions were of your own making, and we never deemed it necessary to contradict your assumption."

*Oh Ari...* I know not what to say, cannot fathom how anyone could be so cruel as to torture a child, only to blame another child for it. Ariadne doesn't respond, made speechless by her devastating shock.

"Then that damned blood bond nullified our hex... Yet another annoyance," Xiomara sighs. "We never dreamed that you would subject yourself to that sort of magic in only a year, that you could find someone you would willingly surrender yourself to so entirely."

Ariadne recalls her mother's rage when she'd told her of the bond in the greenhouse. Then she remembers her small fights with me, overwhelming relief filling her that the hex hadn't seen fit to attack me unnecessarily. Possibly because Ariadne had wanted to fight, had almost enjoyed it, and I was never any real threat to her.

If only Elise had dueled her earlier, rather than implementing indirect, cowardly attacks. Then perhaps the hex could have defeated her without Ariadne needing to lift a finger.

*The hex impeded Elise's blood magic,* I realize. *She would have choked you using me if it hadn't-*

"Again, Arachne interfered." Xiomara huffs in annoyance. "I'd always assumed she would simply orchestrate the pendant's bequeathal to another witch as swiftly as possible, in which case we would have been forced to kill the young pendant bearers as many times as was necessary to ensure it was available when you were of age to attempt the trials.

Instead, Arachne tied you to that common scum, distracted you from your Goddess-given role, shedding away years of careful grooming in mere months. Even a visit from Mother wasn't enough to set you to rights. Cintia had no luck, either. I am admittedly impressed by Iona's influence. I wouldn't have thought it possible if I hadn't seen it with my own eyes.

Yet again, we were left to make sense of this new obstacle, to find some way of salvaging our plans. At first, our objective was clear. Iona must die so you'd be given another chance to claim the pendant."

Ariadne jerks despite the spell of paralysis weighing down her limbs. Xiomara's speech pauses nearly imperceptibly, then she continues as if she'd not noticed.

"Inadvertently, due to your confession at dinner, we learned of an alternate option. If you could still bear the pendant, then all was not yet lost. We simply needed to determine a way to convince you to take it back or convince Iona to relinquish it. We cared not how it would be accomplished, only that it was done, once and for all.

We took on different approaches. It was almost like a game to see who could destroy one or both of you the most, tear down your confidence, turn you against each other." Xiomara chuckles. "Zephyra still preferred the notion of killing Iona so you might take the pendant from her corpse, but you are far too protective of her, as I predicted. Marina suggested we inundate Iona with the worst of our magic, compelling you to doubt your giving the pendant away. You see, we couldn't harm you too terribly or risk marring Mother's vessel, Moira's lapse of judgement in Japan aside, so Iona took the brunt of everything, the poor dear."

Ariadne's thoughts are suddenly deafening, a flurry of rage-filled admonishments, berating herself for her damned foolish pride in considering herself so much better, stronger than me, when I'd simply had it worse in comparison, an entire coven's power working in tandem to crush me, discourage me, humiliate me.

"Cintia has grown to know you the best, and sure enough her methods proved the most effective. She killed Euphemia-"

Again, Ariadne jerks, trying with all her might to break free of the spell, but it's no use.

"-leaving her for last, knowing how it would destroy you. And Moira, my darling, devious, girl, bet on your fears, your mistrust, your jealousy driving you to self-destruction. I believe it was Rebekka Magnúsdóttir she chose to seduce Iona. To her credit, your beloved did not waver, but she did not need to. You were convinced of it all the same," Xiomara says, almost ruefully. "In truth, I've never seen a love so restorative as yours. It was beautiful. Take solace in that. Some live their entire lives never experiencing anything like it."

Tears drip down Ariadne's cheeks, and I try to speak through the bond, but the strain proves too much for me, and my own cries fall on deaf ears.

"With a bit of theater, we used the 'Crone' to terrify and

overwhelm you, along with Sebastian's gift at corrupting dreams and his hex on Samaira's ring. We couldn't have her visions getting in our way, or she would have warned you of your impending death. I hear she still managed to see aspects of it, but never enough to impede us." Xiomara runs a finger lightly over the inside of Ariadne's wrist. "We drew our runes upon your skin, manipulated your bond to bring forth ruinous memories, take away time without your noticing, make you fall ill without cure. Our combined efforts seemed to be enough. You cannot say no labor was given on our part. We've earned this victory," Xiomara chuckles darkly. "All of it contrived by either us or her, the spider, though it seems she longed for the escape of death more than she wished to save you. "

*Ari, you must think hard,* I plead, my head pounding. *Where could they have taken you?*

*I don't know.* Ariadne's thoughts are devoid of hope.

*We cannot give in,* I insist. *There must be a way!*

"I tell you all of this not to boast." Xiomara lets out a low chuckle. "Though I am admittedly quite proud of our achievements. I say this so you know without a shred of doubt that there was nothing you could have done to prevent it. You needn't torture yourself over it, truly, though you will have an eternity to do so, if you insist upon it. I hope the knowledge of your insignificance may be a comfort. When you surrender yourself to chaos, it can be quite liberating, I find."

She takes a deep, cleansing breath as she basks in her blood-soaked triumph.

"Our Goddess aided us all this time, using her power to cripple Arachne's influence just enough to allow our victory on those days of our sacrificial rituals." Xiomara's voice conveys her reverence. "I wondered... I worried that it wouldn't be enough, but I needn't have. A new dawn is breaking where divine chaos will reign anew. Mother will rule again with our Goddess at her side as we preside over humans and witches alike, for a time. Oh, the humans..." Xiomara's voice loses its dreamy cadence, becoming low and sinister. "They will regret their transgressions against our kind... The hangings... the burnings... the drownings. They will suffer tenfold for what they've done."

Ariadne jerks again, her muscles screaming at her to stop. A finger drifts across her forehead, and all at once her sobs ring out as her voice is returned to her.

*Make her tell you where you are!* I scream through the bond.

Ariadne's voice wavers. "You knew I blamed myself for Vivien. You let me suffer with the guilt-"

"We couldn't very well tell you of the hex," Xiomara says, as if she were dimwitted to even suggest such a thing. "You survived the attack, did you not?"

Ariadne gasps for air, entirely at a loss, as all her memories reform to take on new meaning.

"I won't let them torture you, like they planned, for making this so difficult for them," Xiomara assures her. "It will still hurt, but it will be as brief as possible. Of that, I swear."

Ariadne laughs despite herself, laughs through her tears that flow freely now.

"You loved me at least?" Ariadne asks, surprising me and herself with the question.

"I do not know," Xiomara muses. "I would say yes, but not nearly as much as my beloved daughters."

"And not enough to save me," Ariadne says with bitterness.

"No, dearest. You were never meant to exist but worry not. Eris swore she would find a place for your soul to rest," Xiomara says.

*Eris.* My heart nearly stops at hearing her name, remembering it from the book Ksenia had tossed to me in her room. It was the first page I'd opened to, detailing the many attributes of The Goddess of Discord, the harbinger of chaos.

*You must keep her distracted. Ask more questions,* I encourage, but Ariadne is overtaken by a chilling sense of calm, her terror leaving her exhausted.

"I could never find true rest without Iona," Ariadne finally says.

There is a brief silence, until Xiomara says, "Then I shall bring her to you soon."

Ariadne shakes her head violently. "No, that is not- No, don't hurt her! Please!"

"She will die. We only healed her so she might deal the final crushing blow. With that purpose fulfilled, she remains the only one left alive who could wield the pendant. We cannot allow her to live and interfere with our plans. And in that endeavor, I regret I cannot protect her. Moira has… rather gruesome plans for her," Xiomara says, with something like sympathy. "Marina lost her, but I expect it to be quite simple to recapture her. Iona is too prim, too weak to be any real threat, especially without you or Arachne protecting her. Soon she will be freed of life. Your souls can live out eternity together and none of this need be your concern anymore."

I can hardly hear Xiomara's words over Ariadne's unintelligible screams.

"No! No!" She cries, trying in vain to move. "You cannot do this!"

"Shhh," Xiomara hushes her, running a hand through Ariadne's hair. "It will all be over soon."

"Stop coddling her."

Ariadne's cries are cut short at the sound of her mother's foul voice. Or rather, Cintia's.

"You weren't wanted. A dispensable soul. A parasite to be excised. Nothing more." Cintia's sneer is audible in her tone. "Now be quiet and die with dignity. I've waited long, insufferable decades for this day. Let's get on with it."

"I suppose it is time," Xiomara says, and rises from her seat on the rock.

*Do not let her walk away!* I urge.

"What does the ritual entail?" Ariadne asks, struggling to speak through her staggered breathing.

"I wonder if telling you would only add to your suffering," Xiomara muses.

"I wish to know," Ariadne says.

"...Very well," Xiomara says, with reluctance. "It will be taxing for us both, as I must pierce your consciousness to excavate your soul and send it on its way. You will doubtless try to resist the spell, so it could take hours."

Ariadne trembles, her mind reeling. "You said it would be brief."

"Far more so than the weeks of torture they devised for you," Xiomara says, and a shiver runs down Ariadne's spine.

*Beg for your sight! Keep them speaking for any hint they let slip could be our salvation,* I insist. *Perhaps there's some spell that could... I won't stop-*

"What if I didn't fight it?" Ariadne asks.

Cintia snorts. "That would be the day."

"If I did not try to outlast you, if I made it easy for you, would you still kill Iona?" Ariadne asks.

*Ari, don't! Please!*

"Of course, we must kill her," Moira says, making her presence known. "You've no say in the matter, mongrel."

"She will die regardless," Xiomara agrees.

Ariadne hesitates, then says, "Would you swear not to torture her then, at least."

"She's stalling," Moira says. "I will do as I wish to that sniveling little-"

"If I swear Iona will feel no pain, you will go willingly?" Xiomara asks, with slight incredulity.

"Yes," Ariadne says.

*Don't you dare do this, Ariadne! You must resist them until the very end!* I protest.

*I won't let them hurt you,* Ariadne vows.

*What use are their promises when all they do is lie?* I try to reason with her, but her stubbornness prevails.

"I grow tired of this," Sebastian says with a yawn. "If it will expedite the ritual, then I see no harm in such an agreement, so long as the Lysander witch is slain. Moira can have her fun elsewhere."

"I'm never allowed to have any fun," Moira whines, then sighs. "Very well."

Xiomara places a hand on Ariadne's shoulder, and she wishes she could squirm away from it. "I swear on Eris' name-"

"No," Ariadne interrupts. "That means nothing to me. Swear by the river Styx."

There is a prolonged silence.

*What difference does it make what they swear by?* I ask. *It will be a lie.*

*Not if they swear on Styx. It is a binding oath beyond even a God's ability to break or risk the destruction of their entire bloodline,* Ariadne explains.

Finally, Xiomara speaks. "I swear by the river Styx, Iona will not suffer by our hand. Her death shall be swift."

"Then I won't fight it," Ariadne's voice breaks.

*Please,* I weep. *Don't leave me. Don't let them-*

*I will find you in the afterlife,* Ariadne promises.

*What of those we would leave behind?* I ask, and Ariadne doesn't respond.

"Heavens above, if I knew a pretty face would sway her this easily, I would have raised her in a brothel and saved myself the trouble," Cintia cackles and Moira joins in.

*You must fight back! You must call out for help!* I beg. *Someone may hear you and-*

*Listen to me, Iona.*

*No, I shan't. You're giving in! You're a damned coward!*

*Hate me if you must but listen. You cannot trust anyone. If they stole Rebekka's blood, they could very well have anyone else's. No one is safe, do you understand? You must hide as your parents did, hide until this is all resolved somehow… I know not how. I only know that you are no match for them all. Neither of us were.*

A pitiful whine makes Ariadne pause in her beseeching, then grit her teeth at a subsequent yelp as someone kicks at the metal bars of a cage.

"Can't we kill the mutt now?" Moira asks. "I tire of his incessant whimpers."

"If you'd like, dearest," Xiomara says distractedly.

"Let him go!" Ariadne screams, flinching at the sound of Aster's cries as Moira opens the cage and drags him out.

"Consider this a preview of your imminent demise," Moira says with deranged glee.

But her laughter is cut short when she cries out in agony, Aster growls, and all the witches make appalled noises as the wolf releases Moira and flees. His heavy breaths grow louder as he approaches.

"No!" Ariadne yells. "Go! Run! Get away!"

Aster hesitates, making a small whine, but Ariadne screams at him to go, and to our collective shock, he obeys.

"Don't let him escape!" Zephyra cries.

There are terribly loud noises that Ariadne cannot decipher, implying the use of all kinds of magic to trap or kill the wolf, until at once there's silence again, and Moira sighs.

"It matters not," she says petulantly. "We'll hunt him down later…"

"Let me see your hand," Xiomara says.

"I am fine, Mother," Moira snaps.

"The stars are silent," Marina says with a mourning lilt to her dulcet voice.

"Who cares about the bloody stars?" Moira rages. "We've more important business."

"Indeed," Sebastian agrees. "Shall we begin?"

Xiomara clears her throat, then goes to stand at the top of the slab of rock, placing a hand on either side of Ariadne's head. "Remain calm."

But Ariadne's heartbeat races, her breathing coming in short, staccato gasps.

"Take up your spoils, and may our voices ring," Xiomara says.

The awful wet sounds of fleshy organs being handled makes Ariadne's stomach turn, imagining them dripping with clotted blood and bile. Footsteps tap on the rock as the coven takes their places around them, readying themselves for the ritual.

*There's still time.* I know it's a lie. *We… We can find a way.*

I'm frozen in place, unsure if I should stay with Ariadne a moment longer in the vain hope of determining where she could be or leaving her so I might turn the earth over in search of her, but I do not know where to begin, except to traverse every coastline, but there is no time.

*I never feared death until I knew you… Isn't that worst of all? They should have done this before… before I loved you. I may have welcomed it.*

*Please don't speak this way.* I become conscious of my body again for a moment, the strain of my every muscle, as I sob with her. *You must fight! You must-*

*I killed her…* Ariadne's thought is but a whisper. *I… I am just like them. I am a killer. This is what I deserve.*

*Ari, no! You're not-*

The awful earsplitting cries of the Zerynthos witches makes Ariadne flinch, unable to cover her ears against it, unable to run. Visceral, head splitting pain emanates from the tips of Xiomara's fingers where she gently holds Ariadne's head in place.

*Forgive me,* Ariadne pleads. *I… wasn't strong enough.*

I tremble as she screams from the blinding pain that eviscerates her. *I will find you… I will…*

Then the pain reaches me, and all the words I wish to say are forgotten. I scream as molten fire runs up my veins, permeating my organs, radiating through my skull.

"Iona!" Samaira shakes me. "Iona, what's happening?"

"This is worse than I feared…" Hecate whispers.

"Why?" Samaira asks, holding me close as I shudder in the throes of unimaginable torment.

I try to speak, but I cannot form words beyond my screams.

"Oh no," Samaira whispers, with grave recognition. "Help her! Bring her back!"

But Hecate leaves me to suffer, for she must know that I wish to stay within Ariadne's mind and could never abandon her to die alone.

It is like sinking into a pool of boiling water, scalding my skin, searing my insides, until the pain becomes so heightened that my screams, and Ariadne's, grow silent, the agony too acute to process. All I can do is wallow in it.

A memory resurfaces of Ariadne lying on the beach with me beside her, during our Yule holiday, when she'd turned to look at me and I'd smiled at her, my eyes sparkling in the sunlight. I'd long forgotten it, hadn't thought much of it at the time, but

Ariadne cherishes the memory beyond what I'd ever realized, a crystallized moment in time. It is how she sees me, how she will remember me while she awaits our reunion.

Ariadne's thoughts drift as she slowly fades, slipping away. *I love you.* I vow.

Her heartbeat slows, a decelerating tempo, each beat taking longer than the last, until she releases her final breath. *You are my love.*

The most primal, vital part of me shatters as her soul is torn away, leaving me all alone.

"No!" I scream. "No... no... no..."

I collapse into the soft grass with Samaira holding me, questioning me, but I cannot speak. I cannot move. I cannot do anything at all, now that my love is gone.

# 36 - Iona

Every labored inhale is a torturous offense, knowing Ariadne no longer breathes with me. To feel the life leave her body…

"Iona, breathe," Samaira says, still finding it in herself to comfort me despite her own sorrow.

"I couldn't see," I sob. "She couldn't…"

Wisp trembles in my arms, pressing her head against my chin, burrowing close to me, so that I cannot tell which of us is comforting the other. I weep into her soft fur.

"Ksenia's accusations were true?" Samaira asks, though she knows the answer.

I can only nod, the heavy scent of sulphur accosting my senses.

"What can we do?" Samaira asks Hecate, but the Goddess has sunk into her own thoughts.

"Did you hear?" I ask.

"Yes. Forgive my intrusion." Hecate appraises me with compassion.

"Do you know where she is?" I ask, moments away from rage, but Hecate shakes her head no.

"Eris has always been a meddling fool," Hecate murmurs. "She's concealed their location well."

"Are you not meant to protect us?" I ask. "How could you let them do this in your name?"

Hecate's brow furrows. "I ceased being the patron of the Zerynthos family generations ago, when I could clearly see they were headed down a dark path, one I could not absolve and-"

"You did not think to intervene?" I ask, appalled. "You've abandoned us."

A trace of guilt crosses Hecate's face as she admits, "Very few remain invested in the wellbeing of Earth when so often we've watched your kind repeat the same unending mistakes again and again despite our intervention. Other Gods have long been diverted by other planes of existence, but there are those still compelled to interfere as Eris has done. Neither have I abandoned all witches entirely."

I blink once, then glare up at her. "Ariadne prayed to you ceaselessly and you neglected to answer."

"I swear to you, on my honor as a Goddess, I did not hear her prayers," Hecate says, confusion crossing her expression, as if she is trying to recall every prayer made to her. "It may be possible that her prayers were intercepted, prevented from reaching me."

"It no longer matters..." I decide, my head swimming with endless possibilities, my sorrow turning to rage at how little I know for sure. "If you cannot help us, then please leave us be."

Hecate's eyebrows raise, surprised at my boldness. I turn away from her to face Samaira, who has been lost to tears.

"I am so terribly sorry." I embrace her, allowing us both a moment to grieve our beloved Ariadne before I pull away and reach for her hand. I pull the sapphire ring from her finger and toss it away, uncaring of the burning sensation that pales in comparison to the pain I'd just endured.

"Sebastian cursed it," I explain. "You mustn't wear it."

Samaira stares at the ring where it rests in the grass, likely remembering every vision she'd suffered through, all for nothing. She pulls out a handkerchief and places it over the ring, picking it up through the barrier of the fabric, and converting it into a little pouch, which she stows away in her pocket.

"We must stop them," I say.

"How?" Samaira asks. "We know not where they are or what they plan to do."

"They would need to perform this sort of ritual in a place of great power, and likely somewhere significant to Ariadne, or the coven, or Katrin..." Hecate muses.

"Thessaly?" Samaira asks.

"No." My brow furrows in concentration. "Ariadne is... was very cold but not freezing from snow and ice. She smelled the ocean, and there was wind..."

"Constantinople is surrounded by water," Samaira says. "They have a manor there on the coast of the Sea of Marmara, where Zephyra and her son reside."

"I've never visited it." I say.

"I have," Samaira says, hesitantly reaching for the staff, but the magic burns her before her fingertips can even graze the wood, and she quickly pulls her hand back.

"Let me see in your aura," I suggest.

Samaira nods and unveils it, the color of a sunrise, and I peer in to find an image of Constantinople, a city of vibrant colors and Byzantine castles with domed roofs and tall towers.

A portal emerges, and without a second glance at Hecate, I

jump through, running straight down the gravel road.

Samaira follows fast behind me, and we behold what looks like a monastery, a tall building on a foundation of stone with arched corridors, a plaza at the entrance, and not a single candle lit. The angry sea waves crash against the rock, splashing water onto us as we run.

"Xiomara!" I bellow, making Samaira jump. "Moira!"

"Do not provoke them!" Samaira cautions.

"I mean to do more than provoke," I say, my voice low as I approach the manor and hold out a hand, sending a gust of wind to blow in all the doors, shatter every window, and ensure that our presence cannot be ignored.

"Marina!" I yell. "Zephyra! Show yourselves!"

But there is no response, only the clinking of broken glass, creaking of swinging doors, and crashing of waves.

Samaira approaches with caution. "I do not think-"

"Where else could they be?" I ask. "I will search every shoreline until we find them."

"Perhaps we should-"

"Iceland," I say, making a portal and jumping through.

"Hecate said it must be a place significant to the coven," Samaira reminds me.

"This could… It might be significant to Ariadne," I say, looking about for any signs of light or magic, but there are only endless stretches of green and dark stone, with the calming scent of the ocean on the air.

"Iona."

I whirl around to find Rebekka, bloodied and disheveled, ambling toward me.

"What's happened?" she asks. "I remember waking in a snowstorm, then someone forced me through a portal, and I found myself here. I thought it might be Ariadne, but she wouldn't… I am ever so confused."

I keep a firm hold on the staff, but my ire recedes as pity takes its place. "You've been cursed."

Rebekka looks down at her arms, the cuts and terrible bruises marking every time her blood had been stolen away. "Blood magic, I expect?"

"Yes." I swallow down my emotions. "I… Forgive me, Rebekka, but we must go. Ariadne is…"

"What?" Rebekka asks. "Is she in trouble?"

I cannot say the words, so Samaira speaks for me. "She is dead."

"What?" Rebekka exclaims. "No... No, that cannot be!"

She sinks to her knees, and I wish I could join her in mourning and cry until I haven't tears left, but I cannot stop.

"Stay here and regain your strength. I will return, but for now I must go." I hesitate, then say to Samaira, "Stay with her."

"But you should not be alone-"

"Neither should she." I gesture to Rebekka who has succumbed to her tears.

Samaira looks at me, then Rebekka, torn between two lost souls, but I shake my head. "Stay. I will return."

"What do you mean to do?" Samaira asks, seemingly reluctant to inquire for fear of how I may respond.

"I do not know," I reply honestly, "but this cannot go unpunished. And if I should die... then I will be reunited with Ariadne."

"Iona." Samaira's tears return. "She would not want that for you."

I turn away and harken back on every memory, every precious story Ariadne told, every morsel of information I've learned, but still, I'm at a loss of where to go.

Self-hatred burgeons within me. If our roles had been reversed, Ariadne would have turned over half the globe by now. She would have burned every manor to the ground to smoke out her enemies and bring them to their knees. She always protected me, protected everyone, even while others scorned her, even before she had full use of her magic, she was an ardent protector and-

It strikes me then. Ariadne's wand. She told me of the volcanic island in the southern Aegean Sea where she'd found it. Nisyros.

My breath quickening, I recall a glimpse of her memory when she'd allowed me to see Vivien's attack; Ariadne as a girl sitting within the crater of a dormant volcano when her wand had rolled up to her. She had set aside her doll to pick it up, admiring the perfect piece of obsidian glistening in the sunlight, while Cintia had watched on with a knowing smile.

"Take me to Nisyros," I whisper, and a portal opens.

I jump through, but rather than finding an empty crater under a dark sky, I'm greeted by the low hum of voices. Hundreds of them.

"Iona?" Frankie calls.

I look around in confusion at the covens, every single one, all gathered together in their finest clothes. Off to the side, Marcel converses with his colleagues, a diverse group which has tripled since the equinox, a couple hundred at least.

"Whatever are you doing down here?" Frankie asks when he runs over to greet me.

"I could ask you the same question." I find it difficult to keep eye contact with him. "Should you not be in Thessaly for the ritual? I thought you were all waiting… there…"

An abrupt sense of foreboding makes me tense with dread when I notice not one of the Zerynthos witches are present within the crowd, and nor would they be. They are all still constellated for their own secret ritual somewhere on this island. I know it somehow, can feel it in my bones. They are here.

"I thought you would be preparing with Ariadne," Frankie says. "The letter said you wouldn't be ready until midnight."

"Letter? What letter?" I ask.

Frankie gives me an odd look. "The letter that you and Ariadne sent telling us it was imperative that we attend and-"

I yelp when Crescentia barrels into me, embracing me fiercely. "Oh, how I've missed you! We must find time to speak during the party, for I have so much to tell you and-"

"Ariadne has… died." I choke out the last word.

Frankie's umber eyes go wide. "I beg your pardon?"

I look to Crescentia, who only stares back at me, confused. "But… No, that can't be. She sent us a letter-"

"That wasn't sent by her or me," I say.

"Who sent it then?" Frankie asks, all manner of geniality gone from his countenance.

A gasp from the crowd makes me jump, searching for any sign of the Zerynthos coven, until I find Phoebe across the crowd of faces, pointing upwards to the flank of the volcanic crater where Ariadne now stands wearing only her chemise.

I see her there, her unparalleled beauty unmarred, everything about her seemingly unaltered, except for her devious red eyes. They reflect nothing of the woman I have come to know, to love. They hold resentment and the promise of violence. Not Ariadne, but Katrin.

"We must go now," I say, just as a mournful howl resounds from the west, an awful, sorrowful sound.

"Why would you tell such a terrible falsehood?" Frankie asks. "Ariadne is there. She is not dead!"

"She is," I insist. "That is not her."

"Why is she wearing the pendant?" Crescentia whispers.

Katrin surveys the crater, the many covens converged like

lambs to slaughter, until her eyes rest on Marcel and his friends, and her eyes darken with distaste as the pendant's opal emanates an ominous red glow.

"Marcel!" I scream, and he immediately turns to look my way, a friendly smile forming on his lips when he sees me.

At the sound of my cry, Katrin's gaze shifts to me, a menacing smile forming on her lips as she incants, "Hirudovis."

The effect is immediate. Every single witch and warlock falls to their knees from the harrowing force of the leeching spell. I flinch away, bracing myself for the familiar agony, but pain doesn't come. When I open my eyes, a protective shield is emitted from the staff's labradorite stone, protecting me, Crescentia, and Frankie from harm. The others left outside the shield scream with anguish as their power is ripped away.

"What is she doing?" Crescentia screams and clings to me with fright.

"It's not her," I insist. "It's Katrin."

Crescentia and Frankie's stricken expressions are nearly enough to fracture what's left of my composure, but I haven't time to mourn with them. I make a portal to the very first place I can think of; the sea cliff in Cornwall where my first home once stood.

"Run! Run to the portal now!" I cry.

Some try to struggle to their feet, but the pain of the spell keeps them prostrate. All except Marcel and his friends whose magic is stolen away in too short a time, releasing them from the spell only to weep over their great loss.

"Run!" I scream at them, and many obey, jumping through the portal and away from the awful scene.

Marcel stays back to ensure everyone makes it across, helping those still recovering from the pain, and directing them to the portal.

A low rumbling growl is the only warning given before molten fire rains down upon us. Morgan's dragon emerges, perching on the edge of the crater, and when Katrin points to the sky, he unfurls his wings and launches himself into the air.

His flames engulf the few of Marcel's friends still left behind. They shriek, tossing and turning to try and escape the fire that blisters their flesh, until they collapse to the ground dead. Marcel saves who he can, then sprints across the dirt, ducking and weaving to evade the torrents of flame, making his way to the portal.

"Keep hold of me!" I yell, then run with Crescentia and

Frankie flanking me, careful not to leave the bounds of my protective magic. "Run Marcel!"

Mere moments before my magic can cloak him, the dragon lets loose another alluvion of fire that swallows him whole.

"No…" I stop short, but I haven't a moment to process the loss before the dragon redirects his destructive path, targeting the covens instead, and I scream, "NO!"

My shield shimmers, then blasts apart, it's glistening bounds stretching out far and wide to cover almost the entirety of the crater's circumference, releasing the covens from the curse that plagues them, and keeping the dragon's flames at bay.

"Get up!" I scream. "Run!"

They all make a mad scramble to the opened doorway as I fight to maintain the shield. The dragon spews fire and slashes at the boundary with his claws, while Katrin frowns at the new obstacle.

Frankie douses Marcel with water, his skin burned and blistered, but the softest of wheezes expels from his mouth as he clings to life.

Professor Yun separates from the crowd to take Marcel's arm, pulling him through the portal and immediately administering healing magic on him the moment they're through.

Then the ground trembles again, this time much worse than before, until it cracks open, pieces of earth floating upwards as lava rises from beneath them, pooling in a steady stream within the bounds of the shield, the volcano dormant no longer.

Along the edge of the crater, the Zerynthos Coven reveal themselves, looking down at them with emotions ranging from glee to triumph to apathy.

I try conjuring water to stave off the lava, as Ariadne had done in Lysander Forest, but to my great dismay, I feel my power waning. I haven't a clue how Ariadne managed to conserve it as she must have, and I've grown so accustomed to the pendant's abundant magic that I'd almost forgotten the limitations of others.

The shield falters, letting in tendrils of flame. I employ every bit of strength I have to keep the doorway open as witches and warlocks trample over themselves to push their way through. Wisp attempts to corral them and aid those who've fallen, without being trampled underfoot.

"I can't…" I wince. "I cannot hold it-"

"You must!" Crescentia begs, looking in horror at how many people remain.

"Go!" Frankie screams, directing people as Marcel had, lifting those who have fallen back to their feet, while Crescentia stays by my side to hold me up.

I lock eyes with Katrin, who smiles at my apparent weakness.

"We must go!" I don't give Crescentia any recourse, gripping her arm and dragging her towards the portal.

Crescentia tries to pull away. "But Frankie-"

"We must get through!" I scream at him, and he doesn't delay in following us and taking Crescentia's hand.

When Wisp returns to me, I use what little magic I can spare to craft another portal so small we almost don't fit but just manage to squeeze through moments before it closes behind us.

Then we run to the mouth of the original portal and grasp at outstretched hands to pull people through. Kokuro, Phoebe, Nenet, and Lady Monton all make it out, with many already on the other side, more than half of the crowd. I try to widen the doorway while still maintaining the shield, but my power fades, the shield giving way almost entirely.

My heart stops when I see him, and I scramble forward, trying to jump back to Nisyros, but Crescentia grabs my waist to hold me back.

"What are you doing?" Crescentia exclaims.

"Samuel!" I point through the doorway.

Still on the other side, he helps Phoebe's grandmother, Eleanor, whose old bones no longer allow her to run. I'd almost forgotten my invitation, my hope that Samuel might witness one of my rituals and find some solace in knowing that our family name will not be forever stained by Elise's crimes. I struggle against Crescentia's hold, trying to make it through, but there is too vast a distance for them still to tread.

The shield collapses above them as the lava cages them in. Samuel withdraws his wand, positioning Eleanor behind him, then glances through the portal to meet my gaze, his eyes conveying something like gratitude, though for what I cannot imagine.

An eruption explodes, sending me and everyone close to the portal hurtling backwards from the blast of smoke and fire. The portal closes, and I collapse onto the frozen ground.

"Wake her up!"

"She must answer for this-"

"She would not have saved us if she were in league with the Zerynthos Coven."

"How could you know? All is uncertain now."

I groan, my head pounding, my muscles protesting, and I squint to behold a mob of witches and warlocks circling around me like a pack of hungry lions, regarding me with fear, disgust, anger, disappointment.

"She's awake!" Someone yells.

"Stay back!" Crescentia screams.

She cradles my torso in her lap, her arms wrapped protectively around me, while Wisp snarls before me with her ears pinned back in distress. I tighten my hold on the staff and try to make a shield, but I've no magic left.

"Iona!" Crescentia's arms pull me closer. "Are you alright?"

I nod, but when I try to move, I wince in pain.

"Give her room, for pity's sake!" Frankie yells, waving the crowd back.

They roar with impatient cries, having little sympathy for my indisposition. They yell pleas for help from those whose family members were left behind, cries of anguish for those whose loved ones were killed by fire and lava, and roars of anger from those whose magic is permanently stolen. Magic that I can no longer recover for them. Not without the pendant.

The next hour is a blur of accusations and incomprehensible jeers as the crowd tries to make sense of what happened, all while I sit and stare out at the ocean in a state of frozen panic. My heart pounds in my ears, making it difficult to decipher the pandemonium brewing behind me. Crescentia's hand rubs my back as she tries to bring me back to reality with soothing, insistent whispers.

Until Olesya Ulanova's voice rings out. "How Ariadne Zerynthos stole the pendant, I cannot say, but we all know her sensibilities! Her temper! Her past! We've all dreaded her impending reign, and now it seems our fears are realized!"

"It is not her." My throat is so dry, my voice comes out as a soft rasp.

"She's gone mad, it seems," Olesya ignores me. "It was only a matter of time. We all know what she did to Vivien Nicolo all those years ago. We know of Elise Lysander's recent demise, which was achieved through the use of a malefician spell."

"No, it's not true," I say, frustrated by my weakened voice.

"And you." Olesya turns to glare at me. "For all we know, you are in league with these devils, too."

"Of course not," Lady Monton objects. "Why would she risk her own life to save ours if she were a malefician?"

"To trick us into trusting her," Olesya says bitterly. "And even if she is not one of them, she was in their company for months. We've no assurance that her blood isn't in their possession, that she isn't cursed or controlled to be a spy in our midst."

The thought makes my stomach turn. "I am no spy."

"So you claim," Olesya says. "You are only a failure, then. A pitiful excuse for a pendant bearer."

"Leave her be," Crescentia snaps. "If not for her, we would all be dead."

"Half our council is either captive or slain! Many of our kin have been taken from us," Olesya says, and it's then I notice her husband is not by her side.

"Please, you must hear me." I push myself up to standing and with effort I project my voice. "Ariadne Zerynthos is dead!"

The crowd murmurs with confusion and skepticism.

"I swear it. I felt her death through our bond. Her family are indeed the devils you describe. They took her and cast out her soul to implant Katrin's instead-"

"A likely story" Olesya scoffs. "She would say anything to defend her lover's honor."

"She has stolen Ariadne's body," I insist. "Please, you must believe me!"

"We will do nothing of the sort!" Olesya spits. "You are not the leader Morgan promised. Whatever virtue she saw in you was spurious if you could not protect us from this calamity. The council, whomever of us remain, must convene so we might retaliate before it's too late."

"Perhaps casting a truth spell would alleviate any doubt," Josephine Salvador suggests.

"Her mind could be altered in any number of ways," Olesya protests with a glare. "She would only regurgitate her skewed version of reality. Her own cousin was seduced by dark magic, and now her lover as well! Far too blatant a coincidence to be ignored. Her word cannot be trusted, and we mustn't waste time arguing. We must find refuge someplace remote and form a plan."

I scrutinize the crowd, searching for any allies, but find none. Only wary, disillusioned faces stare back at me, and some, like Gisela, pointedly avoid my gaze.

The earth trembles gently, enough to elicit cries of distress. We turn to the east where a plume of dense black smoke shrouds the sky, obscuring the moon and the stars, until total darkness falls and volcanic ash rains like snow.

"Is that…" Crescentia holds out her hand, catching pieces of soot in her palm. "But surely it couldn't reach this far…"

"We must away," Olesya cries, sparing a brief glance at me. "You are not welcome."

"You cannot cast us out," Crescentia protests, and my heart swells at her immediate loyalty, not implying for even a second that she would join them and leave me behind.

"If you are devoted to her, then you are no friend to me," Olesya says to Crescentia, then addresses the crowd. "Any who wish to survive this doom, follow me!"

The crowd murmurs amongst themselves, but eventually every one of them either follows Olesya or goes off on their own to hide and wait out this storm. Josephine gives me a pitying glance before conjuring a broom and flying off into the black night. Only Crescentia and Frankie remain by my side.

I drag my heavy feet to the edge of the cliff where the oak and yew trees stand entwined. Ariadne had conjured them for me over the ground where my childhood home once stood, their trunks twisting together, their branches bereft of leaves. The winter wind stirs the ocean below, and I breathe in the briny air, falling to my knees before the twin trees, entirely unsure of where to go or what to do. I long to cry, to succumb to the crushing weight of my despair, but I have nothing left.

# 37 - Iona

They call for Ariadne's head. They want her to burn, to die. They do not know that she already has. I beseech them to listen, but my pleas remain unheeded by those I can manage to locate. The rest have gone into hiding.

Three days have passed since the eruption that blackened the sky and sent the world into a volcanic winter that may never end. There is no sun, no warmth, and our magic wanes. Whatever maleficium stagnates within the ever-present umbra has suppressed our spells, leaving us vulnerable to attacks that have already begun.

The Zerynthos Coven has unleashed themselves upon the world, burning and terrorizing those with magic and those without. I've grown numb to the news of their exploits, though Crescentia insists upon keeping me informed as I regain my strength.

I do not know what she expects when I recover. I've failed. Ariadne told me plainly. I'm no match for them. They'd been toying with us all along. Olesya is right. I am no leader. I am no savior. I am nothing without Ariadne.

I've found sanctuary in the Nepalese mountains with Samaira, who is kind enough to care for me in my despondent state. Crescentia visits daily with Frankie, who have both decided to stay with Nonna to safeguard her should any of the Zerynthos witches come knocking on her door, since she has apparently refused to vacate her home despite the present danger, stubborn as ever even in the midst of her mourning.

My own grief extends to those almost certainly killed by the volcanic eruption, including my dear Uncle Samuel, and at least two and ninety other souls. No bodies have been recovered, but the blast was far too violent to have much hope that they survived, or Aster, who was not far off when he'd escaped Moira's clutches. Wisp often whines and trills in a forlorn manner, lamenting her companion.

I was once accustomed to a solitary existence in Cornwall. It was not until I'd reached adulthood that I grew restless and forlorn, but as a child, I was quite content, finding peace in silence. Now my isolation brings me loneliness, a constant reminder of what I have lost. It is a distinctly different feeling, an emptiness, a bereavement that I hoped never to endure, for I saw it in my mother's face every day.

I've taken to cradling Samaira's orange cat in my arms, the one Ariadne had conjured on our first day at college, whose name is Sanu. He is a piece of Ariadne, a piece of her magic still living and breathing, and his gentle purrs give me comfort.

"You must eat," Samaira says, setting a bowl of steaming rice in front of me.

The concern reflected in her eyes is all that motivates me to set Sanu down and take the bowl. She motions for me to raise the spoon to my lips, so I force my limbs to move, taking a mouthful of rice, chewing, and swallowing, each action a great effort.

"Thank you," Samaira says, sitting beside me.

I grunt softly in response, forcing subsequent spoonfuls into my mouth one by one. A silence grows, but I am not inclined to speak.

"I never did finish my story," Samaira says.

I look to her in question, but she is staring out into the darkness, despite it being midday.

"I didn't wish to make her uncomfortable. However, I cannot seem to think of anything else since…" Samaira cannot speak the words, but I understand her meaning. "I feel compelled to tell you now."

I take a final bite of rice, setting the empty bowl down by my feet, pulling my wool blanket tighter around myself as I shift to face her.

"When Ariadne and I were bundled up together by the fire, after she'd saved me from drowning, Moira and Sebastian converged upon her like… rabid dogs," Samaira grimaces. "Threatening to tell Cintia what she'd done, nearly throwing away her life for mine. Apparently, they'd attempted to restrain her, to keep her from running to my aid, but she eluded them."

"Did they tell her mother?" I ask, and Samaira nods solemnly.

"I woke the next morning to Ariadne's cries coming from my window. Cintia had dragged her out into the rain and beat her with a leather strap, beat her with such vigor. I was appalled." Samaira's gaze lowers where her hands are firmly clasped in her lap. "I threw myself between them. Cintia was so blinded by her rage, it took her a moment to realize I was taking the blows instead of Ariadne. She demanded that I step aside, but I refused."

"That was very brave," I murmur, recalling that Samaira was only seven years old at the time.

"Ariadne was the brave one. She saved me despite knowing the abuse she would face," Samaira says, still retaining her incredulity despite the time that's passed. "I never saw her the same afterward."

I nod my understanding. It is what made me fall in love with Ariadne after all, her chivalry, her amity, her strong sense of justice.

"Cintia hated me from that day forward, but I cared not. I welcome hatred when it comes from one so blackhearted as her, who hates with such ease and ardor," Samaira says. "It made my friendship with Ariadne exceedingly difficult to cultivate, but I was quite persistent. In the time before Vivien's attack, they did not keep her so rigidly sequestered. Whenever our paths did cross, we were inseparable." She smiles briefly, but it doesn't reach her eyes. "In the time after Vivien's attack, I visited Thessaly every day for a week until they permitted me to enter. She was positively wretched... and her parents did hardly anything to console her."

"Not even her father?" I ask.

"He does as he's bid by his wife. Nothing more," Samaira says. "I took on the task of restoring her. Otherwise, I now fear they would have let her rot away in her room for years and done nothing to aid her so long as she eventually resumed her lessons. Their only concern was the pendant and..."

"Killing her," I say with great bitterness.

Samaira nods, tears brimming in her brown eyes. "All I ever wished was to help a girl I knew was more than her pain. I did not wish to see her goodness snuffed out. My grandmother once told me of familial curses, generations of anguish passed down endlessly, until someone transcends it. I hoped she might break away from her family and free herself from inherited misery."

"She did," I say. "For a brief time... she did free herself, but Arachne did not see fit to protect her. I cannot decipher why she would allow this..."

"Neither can I," Samaira says. "I suppose I may never know if those visions... if they came from Arachne or Sebastian."

"It does not matter anymore," I say. "She is gone."

Another silence stretches on, broken only by wind chimes jingling in the wind.

"The future has changed..." Samaira murmurs.

"You see it still?" I ask.

She instinctively reaches for her ring, but it is no longer in its proper place on her finger. "Before you took the ring from my finger, I saw something. A cave filled with darkness."

"Arachne's cave," I murmur, wondering what it could mean.

"I'm not sure it's hers…" Samaira muses. "At least, it certainly isn't hers any longer."

I wonder at her meaning, squinting in the darkness to scrutinize her face.

"That woman, Cintia." Samaira's voice is tinged with uncharacteristic menace. "She is abhorrent… She and her ilk are irredeemable scourges upon this earth."

"Indeed," I agree.

She meets my gaze, her eyes imploring. "I have always been a pacifist by nature, but there comes a time when such sensibilities become a vice. One that our enemies will not share." She takes my hand, grasping it tightly. "We must avenge her."

"They will just kill me, too." I pull my hand away. "Ariadne told me to run. To hide as my mother did."

Samaira lowers her head, then asks, "Is that what you want?"

I stare at her, my brow furrowing as I try to form an answer, but Samaira only takes the empty bowl, and pats Wisps' head before disappearing inside the house.

All these months, despite our wanderings, we never did find a place to call home. The timing always seemed wrong, nor did we ever find a place that suited us both. Consequently, I still possess Ariadne's eternal gardenia flowers that have yet to be planted. She'd warned me not to let them take root for that is where they will stay forever, unaffected by weather or drought.

I hold the clipping of pristine white flowers gingerly in my hands as I step through a portal to Nisyros, far from the active volcano where the crater once was. Plumes of toxic smoke and ash billow in a cloud that stretches up and outwards in all directions, overtaking the sky.

I find a place that overlooks the Aegean Sea, where flowers may have bloomed if it weren't for the bitter cold of December. Digging with my hands, I make a hole in the ground and I'm moments away from placing the clipping in the dirt. A floral gravestone.

"Iona."

I tense, reaching for my staff where it rests at my feet, until Ksenia approaches with a lantern, looking more like her normal self. The circles under her eyes are far less pronounced and the hem of her black linen dress is covered in sand. Gingerly, I put the gardenia clipping back in its box, covering it with the lid, then stand to address her.

"You look well," I observe, hugging the small box to my chest.

"I slept for two days straight," Ksenia says dryly. "I could have slept longer but-"

"What are you doing here?" I interrupt.

"I wasn't finished speaking when I..." Her cheeks splotch with red at her memory of fainting. "It's good that you are here."

A howl interrupts us and makes Wisp's ears pin back against her skull.

"Aster?" I run in the direction of the sound, making my way down to the beach where the grey wolf is chained to a massive boulder. He jerks his head against his leash, trying to break free and bolt.

"Aster," I put up my hand, slowing my steps so as not to frighten him further.

Foaming at the mouth, his eyes wide and bloodshot, he fights against his apparent exhaustion. He must have been running aimlessly about the island for days after miraculously surviving the volcano's eruption. He glances at me, his gaze feral and unfriendly. He doesn't seem to know me, and I hesitate rather than approach him.

"How did he survive the eruption?" I ask incredulously, in awe of the resilience of familiars.

"I know not, but I found him wandering the island," Ksenia says. "He bit me, so I chained him. I would have thought one of the Zerynthos wretches would have killed him after they were through with Ariadne."

"He escaped, and she told him to run," I say over Aster's snarls.

"That would explain his agitation," Ksenia says, "but not his existence."

"Whatever do you..." My face goes slack upon my realization.

I recall Euphemia's funeral, when Frida the dove had been placed on the pillow by her head where she lay in her coffin.

"When a witch dies, so does their familiar," Ksenia says, then lets out an exasperated sigh. "You truly must study more, for I cannot explain everything to you-"

"Ksenia, please, not now," I snap. "Tell me what this means."

She hesitates and I refuse to hope until she speaks.

"I felt her die," I choke out. "Surely that must have been what it was."

"You felt her soul leave this world," Ksenia says, "but it seems she is not dead. At least not entirely, or Aster would be dead, too."

"But... if she is neither dead nor alive, where is she?" I ask, fearing that my suspicions are correct.

"If she hasn't reached her heaven, and nor is she here on Earth, then there is only one plane of existence she could inhabit," Ksenia says softly. "The place in-between. Purgatory."

A chill goes through me at remembering Ariadne's description of purgatory. A fate worse than death.

"But... where-"

"She could be anywhere. Some hidden place on the other side where Katrin saw fit to imprison her and keep her from passing on into Death. With the help of Eris, it would be a place she'd have no hope of escape or reprieve of her eternal suffering. She'll go mad in there..."

I shut my eyes. "No... Why could they not let her soul rest, at the very least?"

"I can only guess." Ksenia turns her gaze to Aster with a contemplative frown. "Ariadne's body was conjured to be a vessel for Katrin's soul to inhabit."

"No," I shake my head. "You were correct in all but that. They intended to craft an empty vessel, but Ariadne was conjured instead."

"How on earth did that happen?" Ksenia asks, her brow furrowing.

"Arachne altered the spell," I declare, knowing she would only sense my lie if I claimed anything different.

"The weaver?" Ksenia asks. "Why would she-"

"I'll explain later," I say, still unsure if I should tell anyone of Ariadne's crime, still unsure of its significance, or its merit. If Arachne allowed her own death to occur, was it something she wanted? Does that absolve Ariadne of her reprehensible lapse in judgement? I still cannot decide, and until I do, I shall keep it to myself. I've asked Samaira to do the same.

"All you need know is that Arachne was once the weaver of fate, but no longer," I say. "We are alone now. Our future is ours to determine."

Ksenia's eyes glint with curiosity, but she continues in her own explanation. "Once Ariadne's soul came into being, the body became intrinsically tied to her as is the case for all of us. One soul for one body. Once that soul has left, the body will decay. Katrin cannot allow Ariadne's soul to pass on. She's keeping her suspended between life and death so long as she chooses to inhabit the body she's stolen. Possession is truly what this is, not death."

Bile rises in my throat. Her words resurrect the memory of Elise cursing me, nearly subjecting me to a similar fate. Ariadne had defeated her before she could succeed in transforming me into a wraith. I failed to do the same for her, and the thought makes me tremble with barely tempered rage.

Ksenia is too lost in thought to notice. "At least... that is the best I can intuit. I am not altogether sure. If I'm correct, so long as Ariadne's soul still has the faintest tether to her body, Katrin can inhabit it and use Ariadne's face to enact her terror on the world."

"I could still wield the pendant," I say. "I could... I could try to take it back, though I know not how. There are too many of them." A stab of fear takes all the air from my lungs. "Moira wishes to kill me, though her mother swore it will not be painful. I still doubt."

Ksenia grimaces. "That's particularly dire."

I clench my jaw. "I thought her enduring interest in me was purely out of concern for my ignorance."

"Knowing her disposition, she was likely only advising you so your inevitable duel would prove a more entertaining challenge for her," Ksenia says offhandedly, but her words ring so true, it sickens me, that Moira would go to such lengths to corrupt me simply for her own amusement.

Aster, who still bucks and pulls against his chain, throws back his head and howls again, a mournful, wretched cry that obliterates what's left of my reticence.

Sebastian, his dark clothes rumpled and covered in sand, traipses down the beach with an unhurried gait. Wisp growls beside me but I silence her with a look.

Ksenia tenses, but I refuse to show fear as he approaches. He barely spares us a glance; his eyes trained on Aster. As I'd anticipated, his expectations of me are far too low for him to be on his guard.

"How kind of you to trap him for me," he sneers. "I've been dredging this forsaken island for days and-"

The weight of time crushes me as I will it to slow, then stop. The sensation is nearly unbearable, and I cannot fathom how Ariadne endured it with comparable ease, though her tolerance for pain was always much higher than mine. It's made slightly easier due to my hours of ceaseless practice in Nepal. With nothing else to do, it was a welcome distraction.

I craft a portal directly beneath Sebastian's feet that opens up above the Nisyros volcano. Red lava bubbles and glows beneath him, emanating immense heat in an instant.

With heavy, dragging steps, I approach him, and push him down into the portal, so that first his feet, his ankles, and his knees are submerged before the heaviness of time proves too great, and all at once it starts again.

His screams are immediate as a gruesome scene unfolds, his body sinking fully into the lava as he claws at the air, trying to escape, but in his panicked agony he's unable to think, unable to do anything more than writhe. I know the feeling well.

His skin melts off his bones and he roars, but it's too late. He's beyond magic's ability to heal. I revel in his desolate cries when he seems to realize the sudden inevitability of his death, and I memorize his expression as his anger turns to fear, helplessness, regret.

It's far less than he deserves, and I wish the agony could be prolonged, as Ariadne's death had been, so he can fully comprehend the pain he'd caused her, and me, but I suppose his final requiem of excruciation will have to do. For Ariadne. For Samaira. For William Kimball, and his grieving family.

Once Sebastian has sunk beneath the surface, never to be seen again, I take a deep, cleansing breath and close the portal.

Ksenia's expression is one of utter shock. When she notices my stare, she quickly closes her mouth and feigns nonchalance.

"Sove," I incant, and Aster slumps against the sand in peaceful sleep. "He is wild now. He will need to be caged. I cannot leave him here for Moira to find, once they realize Sebastian will not return."

"I expect it won't be so simple to kill them from now on," Ksenia murmurs.

"So be it," I say.

Wisp trots over to sniff at Aster's face, willing him to wake, while I quickly draft a letter to Samaira and another to Crescentia, the ink forming words I cannot decipher as my amethyst ring interprets my thoughts into their respective languages. The papers vanish into thin air.

"What shall we do now?" Ksenia asks, still surreptitiously reeling from the death she's just witnessed.

"You should return home," I say.

Taken aback, she protests, "If you truly believe I will sit by and watch as the world is destroyed-"

"You've never shown any semblance of compassion for anyone," I scoff.

"You need my help," she insists, lifting her chin. "As you said, the Zerynthos Coven shall be damn near impossible to defeat, and the council of witches has turned their back on you."

"Your mother made sure of that, and I trust you only marginally more than her."

"I know what you mean to do, and it cannot be done alone," Ksenia insists. "You're of no use to anyone dead. Without you, we'd be left to defeat these devils alone with no hope of succeeding!"

"I never requested your help-"

"My every waking hour has been spent poring over every book and scroll in existence to unearth heavily guarded secrets at great risk to my own safety! You know nothing of my toil, and we shall never know why Arachne subjected me to this..." Ksenia lets out a shuddering sigh and I'm admittedly shocked when tears form in her icy blue eyes, but it means little to me now.

"You kept a malefician informed of their prisoner's behaviors, divulging secrets told to you in the strictest confidence," I say with great resentment. "You betrayed her."

"Do you think I'm unaware of that?" she yells. "I did wrong! I know that now. I do not need you throwing my every offense back in my face! I tried to save her. I... I've thought of nothing else."

I stare at her, conflicting emotions at war within me, until I decide I no longer care. In light of what she has told me, only one thing matters now.

"Do as you will," I say, my voice devoid of emotion. "But hinder me in any way-"

"I shan't," Ksenia swears.

With a terse nod, I craft a portal to Rome, and the sight of the Villa Mitriora has Ksenia gasping and gripping my arm to hold me back.

"Are you mad?" she cries. "Surely you cannot mean to..."

Calmly, I glance down at her hands, then up into her panic-stricken eyes, and she recoils at the apparent menace in my gaze.

Once she's released my arm, I step through the portal. "Bring Aster."

The windows are dark, the street empty in all directions, and it's as I suspected. They've abandoned the villa. They've no further use for it. It was merely their chosen stage.

Behind me, Ksenia conjures a gilded cage around Aster's sleeping form and casts a spell to have it float through the opened portal. When she's stepped through, I close it and bring my eyes back to the manor, with its pristine marble steps, smooth white columns, and the wooden door left ajar, hanging off its hinges and swaying back and forth on the wind.

"They've gone," Ksenia says.

"Neither are they in Constantinople, and I'd venture to guess they've left Thessaly as well," I say. "We will need to find them, eventually. Or perhaps they will find us."

"Why then are we here?" Ksenia asks.

"You are right," I say. "I cannot do this alone, nor do I particularly want to."

I take a seat on the marble stairs and Wisp jumps onto my lap, pressing her head up against my chin. I pet her idly while I wait.

"Isolation cannot be abided. Not anymore," I say. "I am done trying to keep others in ignorance at my own detriment. We all have reason to fight, and I shan't stand in anyone's way. No more secrets. No more lies. No more hiding."

I craft a portal to Nepal, and Samaira stands there waiting with someone I do not expect.

"Rebekka." I stand and Ksenia flanks me with her wand drawn.

"She is not a threat," Samaira assures us. "She merely wishes to speak."

Once they've both stepped through, Rebekka shifts nervously on her feet. She's changed clothes but her hair is mussed and the scars on her neck are still visible.

"Please forgive me, Iona," Rebekka says as she chokes back tears. "I promised her… I swore I would never hurt her… She must hate me…"

I reach out to take Rebekka's hand, which is alarmingly cold and makes me worry for her loss of blood.

"There is nothing to forgive. It was not you." I heal her scars and renew her stolen blood, feeling her palm heat against mine. "Ariadne learned of your innocence before she passed on."

"She did?" Rebekka's eyes glisten with tears. "Oh… Oh thank goodness."

"What Moira did to you was shameful and she shall suffer greatly for it," I promise.

Rebekka's eyes widen for a moment, until her expression

reflects her gratitude. "She could still use me to harm you. By rights, I should not be here."

I know this, of course, and yet I cannot find it within myself to turn her away. I remember what it was like to be vulnerable to blood magic, the awful guilt and paranoia.

"Ariadne was your friend, too." I look up into her sea green eyes. "I won't prevent you from fighting for her."

"Is that wise?" Ksenia asks, still eyeing Rebekka with mistrust.

"It shall be your responsibility to watch over her," I decide. "If she shows any signs of blood magic, you will stop her before she can cause any harm to herself or others."

"Why must I do it?" Ksenia gripes.

"Because I told you to," I say with a glare.

She glares back, and for a moment I think she might protest, until she looks away. "Very well."

The sound of wheels draws our attention down the road where a white carriage approaches. Before it can come to a full stop, Crescentia jumps out and runs to me, enveloping me in a fierce embrace.

She pulls away and asks, "Are you sure?"

"Are you?" I ask.

There's a moment's hesitation as a healthy amount of fear shadows her expression, but in the end, Crescentia nods with resounding fortitude. "She saved me once. I should like to return the favor."

The smallest of smiles reaches my lips, but it is short lived when Nonna exits the carriage dressed in black with a veil obscuring her tear-streaked face. Frankie helps her step down onto the cobblestoned street, his jovial smile missing, making him almost a stranger. I go to speak, but Nonna puts up a hand to stop me.

"Apologies are pointless now, especially from you. They did this to her," she says, her voice rough as gravel. "They betrayed their own kind and killed… they killed her…"

Frankie keeps a firm hold on Nonna's arm to keep her from collapsing, her inconsolable sobs nearly inciting my own.

"She is not dead," Frankie consoles her.

"Her soul is lost to us," Nonna relents. "We can never see her on Samhain. We can never reach her when our time on Earth is ended. How could we ever hope to find her?"

"We shall," I say with absolute certainty. "Wherever she may be, I will find her."

Nonna grips my forearm and pulls me in close, leveling me with her stare through the gauze of her dark veil, and says, "I would follow you if my old bones would allow it, but it's not to be. I can only impart you with this; Eris is daughter to a primordial goddess with power as old as the universe. We do not aim to oppose mere chaos in its purest form, but Night itself. Katrin chose her patron well. Eris's protection, and that of Nyx, will bolster Katrin's claim to power. You must know what it is you are up against. You mustn't descend into the Underworld whilst blind to the danger you face, or Ariadne shall be truly lost forever and you with her."

"There is nothing…" I take a steadying breath. "Nothing that could keep me from her."

I kneel on the dirty cobblestones with Wisp's head resting in my lap, running my fingers through her dark fur, as I contemplate my chosen destiny. I'm calm, entirely sure of what I must do, even if the way may be obscured.

Far too often I've been confused, manipulated, disadvantaged, underestimated. I was so preoccupied with keeping up appearances, acquiescing to others' agendas and expectations, betraying myself for the sake of witches, or Gods, or fate. I was so blind, but I've got nothing left to lose anymore, and knowing so liberates me.

Ariadne, my love. My everything. I shan't forsake her as she's always feared, for it would be like abandoning my own heart. There is no life without her in it. Even if the journey kills me, even if it destroys all that's left of me, I shall find her, and if I can, I shall bring her back. She wished to be together in the light of day, and so we shall.

I admire the inferno of glass, wood, and stone, the sparks that twirl and flicker up towards the black sky devoid of stars. With Nonna's resounding consent, my fire turns the Villa Mitriora to smoldering rubble, and it is a small satisfaction to me. A message to those who once inhabited its unhallowed halls. Burning to ash all the malefician grimoires, the ritual room, and any other hidden atrocities secreted away.

An omen of what's to come, though fate has no sway. Not anymore.

"Iona," Samaira says.

Reluctantly, I turn away from the blaze to survey the faces of those who've decided to join me, despite my warnings. Samaira, Crescentia, and Frankie are likely allies, their magic still preserved, not stolen away during the ritual massacre. They're huddled together a few paces away, watching me with increasing concern.

Samaira points down the street, her eyes wide. Almost entirely obscured by darkness, Hecate stands there with otherworldly stillness, her red eyes gleaming, so familiar that it pains me to behold them. Though I know a Goddess should not be kept waiting, I remain where I am. I'm perhaps a bit too close to the gnawing fire, but I know this will likely be the last semblance of warmth I'll encounter in the coming days, weeks, or months. I let the heat envelop me; let it turn my freckled skin pink.

Rebekka stands apart in the cool shadows, her physical wounds healed, her haunted expression implying deeper scars made by Moira's blood magic. I relent the pain she's endured, the guilt she harbors at knowing the harm she's unwillingly caused. May her remorse be alleviated by our impending retribution.

Ksenia paces to and fro, her impatience surpassing even mine. She knows what lies before us. A descent into the deepest depths of the Underworld, an endless hellscape holding any number of unspeakable horrors, and should we succeed, we'll only return here to defeat yet more devils that nip at our heels. She shows no fear, and neither do I.

The Zerynthos Coven will lament their schemes. They will regret what they've done to my beloved. I will not rest until every single one of them takes her place in the grave. If I cannot have peace, then I shall have justice. If I cannot have justice, then my vengeance will be won with blood.

*Acknowledgements*

First and foremost, I'd like to thank the readers who have supported my writing and encouraged me to think of myself as an author with the right to take up space and be proud of what I've accomplished. I wouldn't have had the courage to write this book without all of you cheering me on!

In particular, I'd like to thank Kathryn for her enthusiastic support over the course of this writing process, especially near the end. Thank you for answering all my many questions and I'm sorry you cried when you read the ending. I still feel guilty about it but what can you do.

I'd like to thank my best friend who shall remain nameless, but she knows who she is. When I told her about all this, and how I write under a pseudonym, she said I was like Hannah Montana, and now I can't get that image out of my head. Thanks for giving me the idea to become an author in the first place. Here's to the next fifteen years of friendship.

I'd also like to thank my dad, who has always believed in me and gave me a love of storytelling. He taught me that introverted people can still make their way in this world, and that strength comes in many forms. Everything good about me is because of my dad.

I'm excited to get started on book 3, which will be about healing and revenge. Until then!

www.ingramcontent.com/pod-product-compliance
Lightning Source LLC
Chambersburg PA
CBHW060809120726
47909CB00006B/1839